THE BEST

# American Short Stories

OF THE CENTURY

# The
# BEST
# AMERICAN
# SHORT
# STORIES
## *of the Century*

John Updike · EDITOR
Katrina Kenison · COEDITOR

WITH AN INTRODUCTION
BY JOHN UPDIKE

HOUGHTON MIFFLIN COMPANY
BOSTON · NEW YORK 1999

ISSN 0067-6233
ISBN 0-395-84368-5

Book design by Robert Overholtzer

Printed in the United States of America

QUM 10 9 8 7 6 5 4 3 2 1

"Zelig" by Benjamin Rosenblatt. Copyright © 1915 by the Bellman Co. Copyright © 1916 by Benjamin Rosenblatt. "Little Selves" by Mary Lerner. Copyright © 1916 by The Atlantic Monthly Co. Copyright © 1917 by Mary Lerner. "A Jury of Her Peers" by Susan Glaspell. Copyright © 1917 by the Crowell Publishing Co. Copyright © 1918 by Susan Glaspell Cook. "The Other Woman" by Sherwood Anderson. Copyright © 1920 by Margaret C. Anderson. Copyright © 1921 by Sherwood Anderson. "The Golden Honeymoon" by Ring Lardner. Copyright © 1922 by The International Magazine Company (Cosmopolitan). Copyright © 1923 by Ring Lardner. Renewal copyright © 1950. "Blood-Burning Moon" by Jean Toomer. Copyright © 1923 by Prairie. Copyright © 1923 by Boni and Liveright, Inc. "The Killers" by Ernest Hemingway. Reprinted with permission of Scribner, a division of Simon & Schuster, from *Men Without Women* by Ernest Hemingway. Copyright © 1927 Charles Scribner's Sons. Copyright renewed 1955 by Ernest Hemingway. "Double Birthday" by Willa Cather. Copyright © 1929 by Willa Cather. Reprinted with permission of the estate of Willa Cather. "Wild Plums" by Grace Stone Coates. Copyright © 1928 by H. G. Merriam. "Theft" by Katherine Anne Porter. Copyright © 1930 by Katherine Anne Porter. Reprinted with permission of the trustees for the literary estate of Katherine Anne Porter. "That Evening Sun Go Down" by William Faulkner. From *Collected Stories of William Faulkner* by William Faulkner. Copyright © 1931 and renewed 1959 by William Faulkner. Reprinted by permission of Random House, Inc. "Here We Are" by Dorothy Parker. Copyright © 1931, renewed copyright © 1959 by Dorothy Parker, from *The Portable Dorothy Parker* by Dorothy Parker. Used by permission of Viking Penguin, a division of Penguin Putnam Inc. "Crazy Sunday" by F. Scott Fitzgerald. Reprinted with permission of Scribner, a division of Simon & Schuster, from *The Short Stories of F. Scott Fitzgerald*, edited by Matthew J. Bruccoli. Copyright © 1932 by American Mercury Inc. Copyright renewed © 1960 by Frances Scott Fitzgerald Lanahan. "My Dead Brother Comes to America" by Alexander Godin. Copyright © 1933 by Frederick B. Maxham. "Resurrection of a Life" by William Saroyan. Copyright © 1934, 1936, 1959 by William Saroyan. Reprinted by permission of Leland Stanford Junior University. "Christmas Gift" by Robert Penn Warren. Copyright © 1938, renewed 1966 by Robert Penn Warren. Reprinted by permission of William Morris Agency, Inc. on behalf of the author. "Bright and Morning Star" by Richard Wright. Copyright © 1938 by Richard Wright. Copyright © renewed 1966 by Ellen Wright. Reprinted by permission of HarperCollins Publishers, Inc. "The Hitch-Hikers" by Eudora Welty. From *A Curtain of Green and Other Stories* by Eudora Welty. Copyright © 1939 and renewed 1967 by Eudora Welty, reprinted by permission of Harcourt Brace & Company. "The Peach Stone" by Paul Horgan. From *The Peach Stone* by Paul Horgan. Copyright © 1967 by Paul Horgan. Copyright renewed © 1995 by Thomas B. Catron, III. "That in Aleppo Once . . ." by Vladimir Nabokov. From *The Stories of Vladimir Nabokov* by Vladimir Nabokov. Copyright © 1995 by Dimitri Nabokov. Reprinted by permission of Alfred A. Knopf Inc. "The Interior Castle" by Jean Stafford. From *The Collected Stories* by Jean Stafford. Copyright © 1969 by Jean Stafford. "Miami–New York" by Martha Gellhorn. Copyright 1948 by Martha Gellhorn. Reprinted with permission of the Estate of Martha Gellhorn. "The Second Tree from the Corner" (continues on page 776)

# Contents

# Foreword

EDWARD J. O'BRIEN was twenty-three years old, already a published poet and playwright, when he began work on the first volume of *The Best American Short Stories*. He sold the idea to the Boston house of Small, Maynard & Company, which launched the series in 1915. "Because an American publisher has been found who shares my faith in the democratic future of the American short story as something by no means ephemeral," he wrote in his first introduction, "this yearbook of American fiction is assured of annual publication for several years."

Nearly eight-five years and eighty-five volumes later, the annual anthology that a young Harvard graduate envisioned on the eve of World War I has become not only an institution but an invaluable record of our century. Although the series was briefly published by Dodd, Mead & Company before it became an integral part of the Houghton Mifflin list in 1933, it has been published without interruption every year since its inception.

In almost all respects, the world we now inhabit is vastly different from the world that is reflected in the earliest volumes. In the first years of the century, America was receiving tides of immigrants; indeed, immigration was perhaps the greatest human story of the time, and its themes reverberated in the stories O'Brien found. The orderly evolution of a national literature, as could be traced in a more homogeneous European culture, was nearly impossible to discern in the United States. But O'Brien saw virtue in our diversity, and while other critics of the time dismissed American fiction for its lack of sophistication and technique, he detected stirrings of something altogether new — a distinctly American literature worth recognizing and encouraging on its own terms.

O'Brien sensed that the short story was about to come into its own as a particularly American genre, and he presciently set out, as he explained, "to trace its development and changing standards from year to year as the field of its interest widens and its technique becomes more and more assured."

If anything, O'Brien's ability to spot and crusade for quality fiction seems all the more remarkable from our vantage point. Upon Sherwood Anderson's first appearance in print, in 1916, O'Brien recognized both a new talent of the first rank and the real emergence of the modern short story. "Out of Chicago have come a band of writers, including Anderson, Ben Hecht, Lindsay, Masters, and Sandburg," he announced, "with an altogether new substance, saturated with the truth of the life they are experiencing."

Suddenly, it seemed, fiction was being written that was worthy of the devotion O'Brien was ready to bring to it. "This fight for sincerity in the short story is a fight that is worth making," he wrote in 1920. "It is at the heart of all that for which I am striving. The quiet sincere man who has something to tell you should not be talked down by the noisemakers. He should have his hearing. He is real. And we need him. That is why I have set myself the annual task of reading so many short stories."

The results of O'Brien's labors over the next twenty years are revealed in the roster of authors who found early recognition and support in his anthology, including Ring Lardner, Willa Cather, William Faulkner, J. P. Marquand, Dorothy Parker, Erskine Caldwell, F. Scott Fitzgerald, Thomas Wolfe, William Saroyan, John Steinbeck, Irwin Shaw, Kay Boyle, and Richard Wright.

In 1923, O'Brien broke his own cardinal rule — that only previously published short stories are eligible for consideration — in order to publish a short story by a struggling young writer he had just met in Switzerland. All of Ernest Hemingway's short stories to date had been rejected by editors; when he met O'Brien, he poured out a tragic tale of a lost suitcase full of manuscripts and admitted that he was so discouraged he was ready to give up writing. O'Brien asked to see the two stories he had left, and decided to publish one of them, "My Old Man." He not only gave Hemingway his first publication, he dedicated that year's volume to Hemingway, then a twenty-four-year-old reporter for the *Toronto Star*, thereby launching one of the most celebrated literary careers of our century.

Typically, O'Brien would spend the entire weekend ensconced in his upstairs study, emerging only for meals. By Monday morning, he would have read through the week's worth of periodicals from both America and Great Britain (he also edited an annual anthology of the best British short stories), and he would have filed and graded every short story published during the previous week. Some years, he estimated that he read as many as 8,000 short stories.

If he hadn't been a literary editor, O'Brien might well have found fulfill-ment as a statistician. Indeed, he brought nearly as much zeal to the tables and charts at the back of the books as he did to selecting the stories themselves. First he divided all of the stories he read into four groups, according to their merit. In addition, he provided his readers with a fully annotated index of all short stories published during the year; a separate index of critical articles on the short story and noteworthy reviews publish-ed on both sides of the Atlantic; addresses of American magazines publish-ing short stories; author biographies for all the writers included on his Roll of Honor (as well as those whose work appeared in the book); a Roll of Honor of foreign short stories in American magazines; a critical summary of the best books of short stories published during the year; an index of foreign short stories translated into English; an elaborate chart of magazine averages based on the number of "distinguished" stories he found in each; an index of all the short stories published in books; and, finally, a bibliog-raphy of all of the British and American short story collections published in the course of the year. In the 1918 volume, O'Brien's "Yearbook of the American Short Story" ran for 108 pages — fully one third of the book.

To a modern sensibility, O'Brien's sundry lists and grading systems seem excessive at best, fussy and arbitrary at worst. But O'Brien was blessed with a confidence — and perhaps a naive optimism as well — that no contem-porary editor could match. He knew that he could stake out his territory and cover it all, that nothing would slip through the cracks, and that at year's end, he could survey America's short story landscape and feel certain that he had left no rock unturned. Today we offer these annual volumes accompanied by caveats — that we do the best we can; that we try to lay eyes on everything, but to do so is simply impossible; and that "best" is a purely subjective adjective, reflecting no more than a particular reader's sensibility at a particular moment in time. The publishing world has grown too large, and we readers too exhausted by sheer volume, for it to be any other way. I read through the hundreds of issues of the three hundred–plus periodicals to which I subscribe with the uneasy awareness that I can never keep up, that the 'zines, electronic media, desktop publications, college journals, and literary magazines are all part of a landscape that I will never fully excavate, no matter how many hours I spend mining it. There was no doubt in O'Brien's mind that the stories he published were in fact "the best," at least according to his criteria. One can't help but envy both the clarity of his task and the confidence with which he executed it.

An ardent Anglophile, O'Brien spent most of his adult life in England. When war broke out, he chose not to return to the safety of America. He was killed in London amid falling bombs on February 24, 1941, at age fifty-one. In the midst of all the blitzkrieg coverage, newspapers all over Europe paid extensive homage to this man who was considered a vital representative of American literature.

O'Brien's death coincided with the end of Martha Foley's marriage to the writer and publisher Whit Burnett. Together they had founded the influential literary magazine *Story* and had presided over its publication for ten years. In fact, Edward O'Brien had called the years from 1931 to 1941 "the *Story* decade," so influential had the magazine become as a proving ground for new writers.

Once, while visiting O'Brien in London, Martha Foley had asked him what would ever become of *The Best American Short Stories* if something should happen to him. O'Brien had casually replied, "Oh, you'll take care of it." As it turned out, Houghton Mifflin turned immediately to the editors of *Story* after O'Brien's sudden death and offered them both the job. According to Foley, "Whit said he didn't want to read all those damn magazines." And so, in 1941, Foley left both Burnett and *Story* behind to "take care of" *The Best American Short Stories*. It was a job she would perform tenaciously for the next thirty-seven years.

By the time she stepped into her new role, Martha Foley was already famous among writers as a passionate advocate for serious literature. As coeditor of *Story*, she had, as Irwin Shaw wrote, "kept the flag, tattered but brave, flying, and held out glimmers of hope for all of us." Now, as the most powerful and most visible arbiter of taste in short fiction in America, she set out to find stories of literary value that might otherwise remain unknown and forgotten, and to give them permanence in book form. Like her predecessor, she believed that our literature was a reflection of our national soul, and that as such it was worth defending. "Against the tragic backdrop of world events today a collection of short stories may appear very unimportant," she wrote in her first introduction, in 1942. "Nevertheless, since the short story always has been America's own typical form of literary expression, from Washington Irving and Edgar Allan Poe onward, and since America is defending today what is her own, the short story has a right to be considered as among the cultural institutions the country now is fighting to save. . . . In its short stories, America can hear something being said that can be heard even above the crashing of bombs and the march of Panzer divisions. That is the fact that America is aware of human values as never before, posed as they are against a Nazi conception of a world dead to such values."

Foley continued to make, as she had at *Story*, a distinction between established writers and the new ones just finding their way, observing that "while their writing is often uncertain, it always is fresh and stimulating." Similarly, she paid particular attention to the small and regional magazines that nurtured these emerging voices. Her efforts were well rewarded. During her reign as series editor, she was among the first to recognize the talents of dozens of writers who would go on to receive wide acclaim, including Saul Bellow, Bernard Malamud, Philip Roth, Stanley Elkin, Delmore Schwartz, Flannery O'Connor, W. H. Gass, Vladimir Nabokov, Peter Taylor, Eudora Welty, Joyce Carol Oates, J. F. Powers, Ray Bradbury, Lionel Trilling, Shirley Jackson, Jack Kerouac, James Agee, John Updike, Robert Coover, and Jean Stafford.

All through the forties, the fifties, and the sixties, Martha Foley was solely responsible for reading and judging the two thousand or so American stories being published in any given year. She never lacked for good works from which to choose, but she couldn't bear to see the magazine editors, or their contributors, become complacent. Each year she commented, often with brutal frankness, on the stories that had disappointed her, on the writers who seemed to her to be selling out, and on the magazines that were failing to live up to their reputations.

By the late 1950s, she could see the conservatism of the time creeping into fiction, and she protested: "In a land where in the realm of thinking nearly everyone crosses on the green, it would be good to have a few more jaywalkers." She was opinionated and outspoken, and there was never any question about where her loyalties lay — with serious literature and the committed men and women who wrote and published it. Commercialism — fiction as product — was to be fought at all costs. "There used to be a place called Hell," she railed in one introduction, "but the name seems to have been changed to Madison Avenue." She took particular umbrage over magazine editors — "fiction-blind men," as she called them — who tried to foist inferior goods onto the reading public.

Foley spent a lifetime reading and publishing short stories, and she deserved her reputation as "the best friend the short story ever had." But as she advanced in age, her tastes narrowed rather than broadened. Not surprisingly, some readers and critics felt that the volumes were becoming increasingly predictable. In her seventies, and increasingly out of touch with the shifting currents in contemporary fiction, Foley was no longer able to bring the kind of vitality to the series that had once made it the bellwether of new literary trends.

She spent the last years of her life living alone in a furnished two-room apartment in Northampton, Massachusetts. Although she was in desperate financial straits and plagued by constant back pain, she never considered stepping down from her job. Instead, she put a brave face on her situation, worked each day on her memoirs, and read short stories as she always had. Martha Foley died, at the age of eighty, on September 5, 1977. She had been a major force in American literature for half a century.

For only the second time in the series' sixty-two-year history, Houghton Mifflin had to find someone willing to carry it on. The publishers turned first to Ted Solotaroff, a distinguished editor and critic. Solotaroff declined the position but countered with an idea of his own. Rather than try to replace Martha Foley, he suggested, why not invite a different writer or critic to edit each volume? Houghton Mifflin wisely agreed, noting that "a variety of fresh points of view should add liveliness to the series and provide a new dimension to the title, with 'best' thereby becoming a sequence of informed opinions that gains reliability from its very diversity." With Solotaroff's agreement to serve as the first guest editor, a new editorial direction was established.

Shannon Ravenel, a bright young literary editor at Houghton Mifflin, had tried to bolster Martha Foley's work during her last years, even offering to scout stories for her. Although most of her assistance was rebuffed, Ravenel had nevertheless become a supporter of the series within the house. She seemed an obvious choice for the role of series editor; it was up to her to preside over the anthology's rebirth. Now, with a different well-known literary figure selecting the stories each year, it seemed that some of the suspense would return to the annual publication of *The Best American Short Stories*. By 1990, when Ravenel left her post, *The Best American Short Stories* had once again claimed its place as America's preeminent annual anthology.

In her own first volume, Martha Foley had offered this simple, open-ended definition of a successful short story: "A good short story is a story which is not too long and which gives the reader the feeling he has undergone a memorable experience." In the process of reading 120 or more stories and selecting those that will appear in the book, all guest editors must, at some point, articulate their own criteria — if not by defining what a short story is, then at least by grappling with the questions raised by their own choices. What do they expect from a good short story? How do they judge elements of style, subject, and characterization? Reading through the introductions contributed over the past two decades by some of our foremost writers, one is struck not only by their passionate support for the form but also by their willingness to read, reread, and attempt to quantify a human endeavor that is, in the end, so subjective. If the guest editors as a group lack Edward O'Brien's supreme self-assurance when it comes to choosing the "best," they bring to their task an abundance of experience, a wide range of viewpoints, and a vitality that could not possibly be contained in or sustained by a single annual editor. What's more, the introductions — all twenty of them now — offer a veritable education in what makes for a successful short story, at least according to some of our most highly regarded practitioners of the art.

"Abjure carelessness in writing, just as you would in life," Raymond Carver advised in 1986.

"I want stories in which the author shows frank concern, not self-protective, 'sensible' detachment," John Gardner wrote in 1982.

"The more you respect and focus on the singular and the strange," mused Gail Godwin in 1985, "the more you become aware of the universal and the infinite."

In her 1983 introduction, Anne Tyler advocated generosity: "The most appealing short story writer is the one who's a wastrel. He neither hoards his best ideas for something more 'important' (a novel) nor skimps on his material because this is 'only' a short story."

Ten years later, Louise Erdrich backed her up: "The best short stories contain novels. Either they are densely plotted, with each line an insight, or they distill emotions that could easily have spread on for pages, chapters."

Since 1988, when Mark Helprin elected to read the stories with the authors' names blacked out, so that he would not be prejudiced by names or reputations, most of the guest editors of this series have followed suit. As Tobias Wolff wrote in 1994, reading "blind" ensures that one chooses "stories, not writers." As a result, in recent years the collections have featured an extraordinarily rich variety of stories by new writers, as well as works by established writers in the fullness of their powers.

When I took the job of series editor in 1990, I was conscious, above all, of the dedication with which my three predecessors had presided over this anthology. Edward O'Brien and Martha Foley were, to my mind, almost mythical figures who had died with their boots on, reading stories to the very end. Shannon Ravenel, whose discerning judgment and unerring taste brought her to national prominence in this field, had been largely responsible for bringing the series to a new level of popularity and critical success. The shoes I was about to step into seemed very large indeed.

Ravenel, echoing Foley, passed on these words of wisdom: "Read everything," she said, "without regard for who wrote it or how you've felt about that author's work in the past." It was good advice. In the course of an average year, I may read three thousand stories published in American and

Canadian periodicals. From these, I cull about 120 to pass on to the guest editor, who then makes the final selection. As we discuss stories and compare notes, a collection begins to come together. I am invariably grateful for the process, which ensures that *The Best American Short Stories* will never be simply a collection of "the stories I myself like best," as it was for Foley. During my tenure as series editor, this anthology has been shaped by the tastes and predilections of such varied talents as Robert Stone, Alice Adams, Louise Erdrich, Tobias Wolff, Jane Smiley, John Edgar Wideman, Annie Proulx, and Garrison Keillor. The collections they've assembled are reflections both of who they are and of the healthy vigor of the American short story at the end of this century.

In his introduction to the first volume of *The Best American Short Stories,* Edward O'Brien wrote, "During the past year, I have read over twenty-two hundred short stories in a critical spirit, and they have made me lastingly hopeful of our literary future." During the past year I have read every one of the two thousand stories that have been collected in these volumes since 1915. It is an experience I would not have missed, and it has made me deeply proud of our literary past.

O'Brien often said that "a year which produced one great story would be an exceptional one." Sometimes, of course, a great story is not recognized as such until later; and sometimes a story that garners much praise when first published fails to withstand the test of time. John Updike, who bears the distinction of being the only living writer whose work has appeared in these volumes in each consecutive decade since the 1950s, generously agreed to take on the daunting challenge of determining which of our century's "best" stories merited inclusion in this volume. When it came to whether or not to include his own work, Mr. Updike deferred to me, although he would not agree to the long story that would have been my choice and insisted on a much shorter piece instead. As witness to Mr. Updike's scrupulous, and at times agonizing, process of selection and rejection, I can only attest to the painstaking deliberation behind each and every story that appears in this collection. He made it a point to take up these stories decade by decade and to consider each one of them both on its own terms and in the context of our times. Suffice it to say that there is no other writer, editor, or critic alive today who could have performed this task with such acumen and devotion to his fellow writers. He has done us all, readers and writers alike, a great service.

KATRINA KENISON

# Introduction

THESE STORIES have been four times selected. First, they were selected for publication, against steep odds. *Story* reports twenty thousand submissions a year, *Ploughshares* seven hundred fifty a month, *The New Yorker* five hundred a week. Next, published stories — now amounting annually, Katrina Kenison tells us in her foreword, to three thousand, from over three hundred American journals — were sifted for the annual volumes of the *Best American Short Stories of the Year.* The eighty-four volumes since 1915 held a total of two thousand stories; Ms. Kenison read all these and gave me more than two hundred, and I asked to read several dozen more. Of this third selection I have selected, with her gracious advice and counsel, these fifty-five — less than one in four. A fathomless ocean of rejection and exclusion surrounds this brave little flotilla, the best of the best.

Certain authors had to be included, that was clear from the outset. An anthology of this century's short fiction that lacked a story by Hemingway, Faulkner, or Fitzgerald would be perversely deficient. Almost as compulsory, I felt, was the female trio of Katherine Anne Porter, Flannery O'Connor, and Eudora Welty. Of postwar writers, there had to be Bellow, Roth, and Malamud, even though only Malamud could be said to have devoted a major portion of his energy to the short story. If John O'Hara and Mary McCarthy — two Irish-Americans with a sociological bent — had been available, I might have included them, but neither ever made a *Best.* Traditionally, in the compilation of this annual short-story collection, excerpts from a larger work are excluded, though some do creep in; among my choices were a pair, by Jack Kerouac and William Goyen, that turned out to be pieces of novels.

Two personal principles, invented for the occasion, guided me. First, I wanted this selection to reflect the century, with each decade given roughly equal weight — what amounted to between six and eight stories per decade. As it turned out, the 1950s, with the last-minute elimination of Peter Taylor's "A Wife of Nashville" and James Baldwin's "Sonny's Blues," were shortchanged, even though it was a healthy decade for short fiction, just before television's fabulations took center stage.

My second rule, enforcing the reflection of an American reality, was to exclude any story that did not take place on this continent or deal with characters from the United States or Anglophone Canada. This would seem to exclude little, and yet in Ms. Kenison's selection I encountered a story about Russian soldiery in World War I ("Chautonville," by Will Levington Comfort), another taking place in a polygamous Chinese household ("The Kitchen Gods," by Guliema Fell Alsop), one involving Gypsies near the Black Sea ("The Death of Murdo," by Konrad Bercovici), a supernatural tale of a woodchopper in New Spain ("The Third Guest," by B. Traven), another of a Czech concert violinist ("The Listener," by John Berry), one set in an African village ("The Hill People," by Elizabeth Marshall), one concerning a magician from nineteenth-century Bratislava ("Eisenheim the Illusionist," by Steven Millhauser), a linked set of Elizabethan epistles dealing with the death of Christopher Marlowe ("A Great Reckoning in a Little Room," by Geoffrey Bush), an astringent account of a Danish semi-orphan ("The Forest," by Ella Leffland), a story beginning "In Munich are many men who look like weasels" ("The Schreuderspitze," by Mark Helprin), several stories of Irish life by Maeve Brennan and Mary Lavin, a lyrical tale of arranged marriage among the Parisian bourgeoisie ("Across the Bridge," by Mavis Gallant), and a deeply feminist, humorously epic account of how a few Latin American women inhabited Antarctica and reached the South Pole some years before Amundsen did ("Sur," by Ursula K. Le Guin). All these are not here. "'That in Aleppo Once . . .,'" by Vladimir Nabokov, and "The Shawl," by Cynthia Ozick, *are* here, on the weak excuse that some of their characters are on the way (unknowingly, in Ozick's case) to America.

Immigration is a central strand in America's collective story, and the first two stories in my selection deal with the immigrant experience — Jewish in the first case, Irish in the second. The third portrays the rural life, one of drudgery and isolation, that was once the common lot and is presently experienced by a mere one percent of the population, who feed the rest of us — one of the more remarkable shifts the century has witnessed.

The 1920s, which open here with Sherwood Anderson, are a decade with a distinct personality, fixed between the onset of Prohibition in 1920 and the stock market crash of 1929 and marked by a new sharpness and vivacity, a jazzy American note, in style and in the arts. The urban minority of Americans that produced most of the writing felt superior if not hostile to what H. L. Mencken called the "booboisie," whose votes had brought on Prohibition, puritanical censorship, the Scopes trial, and Calvin Coolidge. Members of the prospering middle class figure as objects of satire in the fiction of Sinclair Lewis and Ring Lardner, though since both men were sons of the booster-driven Midwest, the satire is more affectionate than it first seemed. Lardner's "Golden Honeymoon" is almost surreal in the circumstantiality of its monologue, a veritable lode of data as to how a certain class of Easterner managed a Florida vacation. The device of the self-incriminating narrator — used here more subtly and gently than in Lardner's better-known "Haircut" — generates a characteriology of American types not to be confused with the author, who may well be sitting at a Paris café table in happy expatriation. Except in stories based on his boyhood, Hemingway couldn't bear to dwell on life in America. It was, for many, a drab, workaday life. The small town or city surrounded by farmland, adrift in a post-Calvinist dreaminess, with the local doctor the closest thing to a hero, is a venue ubiquitous in this period's fiction, not only in Anderson and Lewis but in the "Summit" of Hemingway's chilling yet (with its boy narrator) faintly Penrodian "The Killers," and in the Pittsburgh named in Willa Cather's "Double Birthday," a great city as cozy and inturned as a Southern hamlet.

Provincial smugness and bewilderment cease to be quite so urgent a theme in the Depression-darkened thirties. Dorothy Parker's "Here We Are" hovers above its honeymooning couple as if not knowing whether to smile or weep. The heroine of Katherine Anne Porter's "Theft" faces without self-pity the waste of her life amid the passing, predatory contacts of the city. This is a boom period for the short story, a heyday of *Story* and *The American Mercury.* With an exuberant, cocky sweep William Saroyan sums up in a few headlong paragraphs a life and the religious mystery, "somehow deathless," of being alive; William Faulkner and Robert Penn Warren impart to their Southern microcosms the scope and accumulated intensity of a novelist's vision. Faulkner had previously tucked the denouement of "That Evening Sun Go Down" into his 1929 novel, *The Sound and the Fury.* Though he was a staple of *Best American Short Story* collections, represented almost annually in the 1930s, there seemed no avoiding this particular masterpiece, his most anthologized tale, a minimally rhetorical conjuration of impending doom. Fitzgerald's knowing, disheveled tale of Hollywood took preference, narrowly, over his more familiar "Babylon Revisited," a rueful reprise of the twenties' expatriate culture. Alexander

Godin's "My Dead Brother Comes to America" revisits the experience of immigration in a tone of amplifying remembrance that anticipates magic realism. The longest story in these pages, and perhaps the most melodramatic, is Richard Wright's "Bright and Morning Star," a painful relic of a time when American blacks could see their lone friend and best hope in the Communist party. The African-American has inhabited, and to a lamentable degree still inhabits, another country within the United States, where most white signposts of security and stability are absent. I have tried to give this country representation, from Jean Toomer's "Blood-Burning Moon" of 1923 to Carolyn Ferrell's "Proper Library" of 1994. Had space permitted, stories by James Baldwin and Ann Petry would have added to the picture's many tints of violence and despair. Even the amiable, detached Ivy Leaguer of James Alan McPherson's "Gold Coast" finds himself, in the end, on the losing side of a racial divide.

I tried not to select stories because they illustrated a theme or portion of the national experience but because they struck me as lively, beautiful, believable, and, in the human news they brought, important. The temptations of the illustrative pulled strongest in the early decades, which were basically historical for me — the times of my fathers. With the 1940s, the times become my own, and the short story takes an inward turn, away from states of society toward states of mind. To an elusive but felt extent, facts become more enigmatic. It is no longer always clear what the author wants us to feel. The short-story writer has gone into competition with the poet, asking the same charged economy of his images as the narrator of *The Waste Land*, whose narrative lay in shards.

Small-town coziness, with its rules and repressions, is absent from the seething but listless town visited by Eudora Welty's traveling salesman in "The Hitch-Hikers." He thinks of himself: "He is free: helpless." Welty, though habitually linked with her fellow Mississippian Faulkner, here appears more a disciple of Hemingway, and a sister of Flannery O'Connor, the queen of redneck Gothic. Free equals helpless: our American freedom — to thrive, to fail, to hit the road — has a bleak and bitter underside, a *noir* awareness of ultimate pointlessness that haunts as well the big-city protagonists of Jean Stafford's "The Interior Castle" and E. B. White's "The Second Tree from the Corner." White's story, incidentally, marks the earliest appearance in my selection of *The New Yorker*, which was founded in 1925. Its editors, White's wife Katharine foremost, sought for its fiction a light, quick, unforced, casual quality that was slow to catch on with *Best American Short Stories* and that, however telling in its magazine setting, stacks up as slight against earthier, more strenuous stories. *The New Yorker* might have run, but didn't, Elizabeth Bishop's crystalline "The Farmer's Children," an almost unbearably brilliant fable in which farm machinery and Canadian cold become emissaries of an infernal universe; only a poet of genius and a child of misery could have coined this set of wounding, glittering images.

All was not *noir:* from the bleakest of bases, the burial of a child, Paul Horgan's "The Peach Stone" builds to a redemptive affirmation, and Vladimir Nabokov, portraying the refugee chaos and panic on the edge of Hitler's war, imports into English an early sample of his unique legerdemain. It surprised me that World War II, that all-consuming paroxysm, left so meager a trace in the fiction of this decade, as selected by others. Perhaps it takes time for great events to sift into art; however, I remember the magazines of the forties as being full of stories from the camps and the fronts — many of them no doubt too sentimental and jocular for our taste, but functioning as bulletins to the home front. On request, Ms. Kenison came up with several, including Edward Fenton's harrowing "Burial in the Desert," which depicts the North African campaign's harvest of corpses. In the end only Martha Gellhorn's account of an unsatisfactory flirtation, "Miami–New York," conveyed to me the feel of wartime America — the pervasive dislocation that included erotic opportunity, constant weariness, and contagious recklessness.

The fifties, though underrepresented, are represented handsomely, with two of the century's supreme masters of the short story, John Cheever and Flannery O'Connor. They occupied different parts of the country, of the society, and of the literary world, yet were similar in the authority with which they swiftly built their fictional castles right on the edge of the absurd. They wrote with an inspired compression and heightened clarity; their prose brooked no contradiction or timid withholding of belief. Both were religious — O'Connor, fated to die young, fiercely so — and transcendent currents, perhaps, enabled them to light up their characters like paper lanterns, to impart an electric momentum to their narratives, and to situate human misadventure in a crackling moral context. Both "Greenleaf" and "The Country Husband" display animals — a bull, a dog — as spiritual presences; J. F. Powers's "Death of a Favorite" is told by a cat. The effect is not frivolous. For Powers, like O'Connor a Catholic, the mundane, heavily politicized celibate life of male priests was a serious and all but exclusive obsession. Few story writers of high merit have staked so narrow a territory. And why, the reader may ask, with so many thoroughly crafted works to choose from, have I included a thinly fictionalized piece that drifts off into ellipses and appeared in the ephemeral, chichi *Flair?* Well, there are some grave turnings caught in the courtly diffidence of Tennessee Williams's "The Resemblance Between a Violin Case and a Coffin." The narrator, though fearing "that this story will seem to be losing itself like a path that has climbed a hill and then lost itself in an overgrowth of brambles," comes to the double realization that his sister is mentally ill and that he is gay. Overall, there were fewer stories of gay experience than I had expected — not many were written, I think, before 1970 or so — but more about music and its performance; Phillip Lopate's "The Chamber Music Evening" and Charles Baxter's "Harmony of the World" were especially fine and heartfelt, and it pained me to lack space for them.

The sixties, at least until President Kennedy was assassinated in 1963 and perhaps until President Johnson deepened our Vietnam commitment in 1965, were a scarcely distinguishable extension of the fifties. In any case, while looking to fiction to mirror its time, we must remember that writers generally write through a number of decades and gather their formative impressions in decades earlier still. Saul Bellow's world, for example, remains essentially a thirties world of scramble and survival. "The Ledge," by Lawrence Sargent Hall, is timeless — a naturalistic anecdote terrible in its tidal simplicity and inexorability, fatally weighted in every detail. Philip Roth's "Defender of the Faith" looks back to the time of World War II, as does Bernard Malamud's "The German Refugee." Roth's story, written by a man too young to have served, has the authentic khaki texture and unfolds with a layered irony that would have been hard to muster in 1945. The Malamud was chosen, after some dithering, over his famous "The Magic Barrel"; less fantastic, beginning like a small anecdote, "The German Refugee" ends surprisingly and powerfully, with Malamud's sense of Jewishness as a mystical force founded on suffering. Jewishness! What would postwar American fiction be without it — its color, its sharp eye, its colloquial verve, its comic passions, its exuberant plaintiveness? Stanley Elkin rarely knew when to stop, and "Criers and Kibitzers, Kibitzers and Criers" could be shorter, beginning with its title. But it gives us what seldom gets into fiction, the taste and texture of doing business, the daily mercenary pressures that compete with even the deepest personal grief for a man's attention. No one could strike the Hebraic ethnic note more purely, with a more silvery touch, than the Yiddish writer Isaac Bashevis Singer. "The Key" fashions a religious epiphany, adorned with heavenly omens, from a distrustful old lady's inadvertent night on the town. We are reminded of Chagall and Bruno Schultz and the midnight ordeals of the Old Testament.

Scanning the sixties stories for signs of revolution, we wonder if the grotesque hero of Joyce Carol Oates's "Where Are You Going, Where Have

You Been?" — a misshapen yet irresistible troll out of a youth culture that won't quit — might be taken as the call of the counterculture, luring the fifties' restless Connies out from their cramping domestic security and onto the road. The story is dedicated to Bob Dylan. Fifteen years of civil rights agitation and selective advancement lie behind the educated, self-pampered narrator of McPherson's "Gold Coast," who for a time moves smoothly — "I only had to be myself, which pleased me" — through a multiracial world. And could Mary Ladd Gavell's airy, melancholy pastiche, "The Rotifer," leaping so gracefully from the microscopic to the historic to the contemporarily romantic, have been composed ten years earlier, without the examples of Barthelme's pastiches or Salinger's interloping authorial voice? This gem was Gavell's only published story; the managing editor of the magazine *Psychiatry,* she died in 1967 at the age of forty-eight, and the magazine ran the story as a memorial.

Something of Gavell's mulling, quizzical approach can be heard in the next decade's "How to Win," by Rosellen Brown, and "Roses, Rhododendron," by Alice Adams. There are the facts — a dysfunctional child, a girlhood friendship — and there is the female mind that views the facts with a certain philosophical élan. This is feminism in literary action, the contemplative end of a continuum that includes this era's angry confessional memoirs. When Lardner or Parker deployed the first person, it was apt to be an exercise in dramatic irony: we knew more than the crass and innocent narrator. Now the first person is deployed in earnest, for lack of a trustworthy other; the writer and reader are partners in a therapeutic search that will be, we know, inconclusive. Harold Brodkey's "Verona: A Young Woman Speaks" is an exercise of quite another kind: an attempt to plumb the depths, to portray a bliss at life's root, to express the never hitherto quite expressed, at a point where family complication and shining white Alps and "miraculously deep" blue shadows converge. If Brodkey sought, through the laborious dissection of sensations, depths, Donald Barthelme and Ann Beattie and Raymond Carver offer surfaces — uninflected dialogue, a bluntly notational (if not, as with Barthelme, hilariously absurdist) manner of description. No writer ever gratefully claimed the title of "minimalist," yet the term "minimalism," borrowed from the art world, did identify something new, or new since the thirties' rampant imitation of Hemingway — a withdrawal of authorial guidance, an existential determination to let things speak out of their own silence. Such writing expressed post-Vietnam burnout much as Hemingway spoke for the disillusioned mood after World War I. The reader's hunger for meaning and *gloire* is put on starvation rations; the nullity of quiddity is matched by the banality of normal conversation. Beattie was the first to put forth the no-frills, somewhat faux-naive style (Martha Foley shunned her early efforts, leaving us with only the later, not entirely typical but still dispassionate "Janus"); Carver became the darling of the college crowd and Barthelme of the New York intelligentsia. English style needs a periodic chastening, and minimalism gave college instructors in the proliferating writing courses a teachable ideal: keep it clean, keep it concrete. As William Carlos Williams immortally put it, "No ideas but in things." The dictum is congenial, bespeaking no-nonsense American pragmatism.

But ideas exist in human heads, and the more baroque possibilities of language, conceptualization, and a companionable authorial voice will not go away. Who would deny "A Silver Dish" its tumbling richness, as with the usual Bellovian superabundance of characterization, a kind of urban hurry and crowding, the master pursues his usual theme, the vagaries of human vitality? "That was how he was" — the story's last sentence shrugs in plain wonder at life, its barbarities and family feeling. "Do they still have such winter storms in Chicago as they used to have?" An epic trolley-car ride in a blizzard serves as an image of our brave human pertinacity. Cynthia Ozick is a baroque artist of the next generation: her brief, desolating "The Shawl," which comes as close to the reality of the death camps as imagination can take us, should be read in conjunction with its expansive American sequel, "Rosa," set in a surreal Florida of Jewish retirees. My own story seemed of the several available to offer the most graceful weave, mingling the image of a defenestrating skyscraper with those from a somewhat gaily collapsing marriage. Marriages and relationships, as the century progresses, are on ever shakier ground, with fewer and fewer communal alternates like the band of farm wives in "A Jury of Her Peers" or the Communist brotherhood of "Bright and Morning Star." Domestic life, with piped-in entertainment and takeout meals, is our scarcely escapable mode of living, though the urge to escape is widely chronicled.

The health of the short story? Its champions claim that as many short stories are published as ever. But there is a difference, in a consumer society, between something we have to have and something that is nice to have around. Few magazines still pay the kind of fees that kept Scott Fitzgerald in champagne. If *The New Yorker* published eleven of my last twenty selections, one reason may be that it had less and less competition as a market. Whatever statistics show, my firm impression is that in my lifetime the importance of short fiction as a news-bearing medium — bringing Americans news of how they live, and why — has diminished. In reaction to this diminishment, short-story writers, called upon less often, seem to be trying to get more and more into each opportunity to perform. Alice Munro, ever more a panoramist, gets into "Meneseteung" an entire late-Victorian Ontario town, and a woman's entire life with it. Susan Sontag gets an entire microcosm of New York's artistic crowd into "The Way We Live Now," as a circle of friends reacts with gales of gossip, like a hive of stirred-up bees, to the blighting of one of their number by a mysterious disease that, though unnamed, must be AIDS. Tim O'Brien gets the Vietnam War, its soldiers and their materiel, into "The Things They Carried"; O'Brien's plain, itemizing style bears a trace of minimalism, but the scope of his topic, as First Lieutenant Jimmy Cross learns to "dispense with love," moves him into maximal territory.

In a short-story world that has lost many potential practitioners to the rewards of television sitcoms and the gambler's odds of the novel, Lorrie Moore and Thom Jones have emerged as strong voices, at home in a medium length that gives them space to express (not without some gaudy gallows humor) the smoldering rage of the radically discontented female and of the barely tamed, battle-loving male, respectively. The image that ends "You're Ugly, Too" — the heroine's nearly consummated desire to push off the edge of a skyscraper a man dressed, in a marked-up body stocking, as a naked woman — holds worlds of conflicted contemporary female feeling. Jones, a celebrant of pugilists, soldiers, and men on pills, in "I Want to Live!" tells in clairvoyant, appalling detail of a woman's descent, medicine by medicine, through the last stages of cancer. In Alice Elliott Dark's "In the Gloaming," a mother tends her son as he dies of AIDS, and in doing so reclaims the maternal bond; few of these stories are more quietly modulated and more moving than this one.

A quality of meltdown pervades the last selections here, which may reflect a fin-de-siècle desperation — a fear that our options are exhausted — or may reflect my own difficulties in choosing them. "Proper Library," by Carolyn Ferrell, gives us one of those shifting, precarious black households of such concern to legislators and social workers and moralists, and from the viewpoint of an especially unpromising member of it, a none too sharp-witted boy coping with homosexual desires. Yet a sense of human connection and striving comes through: "Please give me a chance." The hero of Gish Jen's "Birthmates" belongs to a group, Asian-Americans, that has lately found its English voice. He is near the end of his rope, and being in the thick of the computer revolution doesn't help him make a connection where it counts. "Soon," by Pam Durban, takes us back to the turn of the century and a botched operation on a little girl's eyes, and beyond that deep into the previous century, when one of those propertied Protestant lines established its stake in the New World; now that stake is mostly memory in an old woman's mind. And Annie Proulx's "The Half-Skinned Steer," taken from the 1998 *Best American Short Stories,* revisits the West, the West that has seemed to this country the essence of itself. An elderly former rancher finds it empty and murderous. I would have liked to finish this volume with a choice less dark, with an image less cruel and baleful than that of a half-skinned steer, but the American experience, story after story insisted, has been brutal and hard. The continent has demanded a price from its takers, let alone from those who surrendered it. I regret that no story about Native Americans could be worked into the table of contents; the closest was James Ferry's "Dancing Ducks and Talking Anus," updating a cult of pain that was here before the white man.

As I picked my way through the selecting, I was always alert for stories that showed what William Dean Howells called "the more smiling aspects of life, which are the more American." A number of lighter stories I had thought of including — "The Girl with Flaxen Hair," by Manuel Komroff; "Your Place Is Empty," by Anne Tyler — had to yield to the pressure of weightier or more aggressive competitors. But one story that did survive — and the only one of my final selection not yet mentioned — is the delicious trifle "Wild Plums," by Grace Stone Coates, published in *The Frontier* in 1929. In it, a child tugs against her parents' puritanical injunctions, hardened by immigrant caution and rural class-consciousness. The obedient child, it seems, is being barred from the experience of life itself. A veteran short-story reader dreads the worst, rendered with some dying fall and bitter moral. But the outcome is in fact like "wild honey, holding the warmth of sand that sun had fingered, and the mystery of water under leaning boughs." A story exceedingly simple, and unexpectedly benign, but not false for that, nor less American than the rest.

JOHN UPDIKE

## Benjamin Rosenblatt

......................................................................................................

# Zelig

FROM *The Bellman*

OLD ZELIG was eyed askance by his brethren. No one deigned to call him "Reb" Zelig, nor to prefix to his name the American equivalent — "Mr." "The old one is a barrel with a stave missing," knowingly declared his neighbors. "He never spends a cent; and he belongs nowheres." For "to belong," on New York's East Side, is of no slight importance. It means being a member in one of the numberless congregations. Every decent Jew must join "A Society for Burying Its Members," to be provided at least with a narrow cell at the end of the long road. Zelig was not even a member of one of these. "Alone, like a stone," his wife often sighed.

In the cloakshop where Zelig worked he stood daily, brandishing his heavy iron on the sizzling cloth, hardly ever glancing about him. The workmen despised him, for during a strike he returned to work after two days' absence. He could not be idle, and thought with dread of the Saturday that would bring him no pay envelope.

His very appearance seemed alien to his brethren. His figure was tall, and of cast-iron mold. When he stared stupidly at something, he looked like a blind Samson. His gray hair was long, and it fell in disheveled curls on gigantic shoulders somewhat inclined to stoop. His shabby clothes hung loosely on him; and, both summer and winter, the same old cap covered his massive head.

He had spent most of his life in a sequestered village in Little Russia, where he tilled the soil and even wore the national peasant costume. When his son and only child, a poor widower with a boy of twelve on his hands, emigrated to America, the father's heart bled. Yet he chose to stay in his native village at all hazards, and to die there. One day, however, a letter arrived from the son that he was sick; this sad news was

followed by words of a more cheerful nature — "and your grandson
Moses goes to public school. He is almost an American; and he is not
forced to forget the God of Israel. He will soon be confirmed. His Bar
Mitsva is near." Zelig's wife wept three days and nights upon the receipt
of this letter. The old man said little; but he began to sell his few possessions.

To face the world outside his village spelled agony to the poor rustic.
Still he thought he would get used to the new home which his son
had chosen. But the strange journey with locomotive and steamship
bewildered him dreadfully; and the clamor of the metropolis, into
which he was flung pell-mell, altogether stupefied him. With a vacant
air he regarded the Pandemonium, and a petrifaction of his inner being
seemed to take place. He became "a barrel with a stave missing." No
spark of animation visited his eye. Only one thought survived in his
brain, and one desire pulsed in his heart: to save money enough for
himself and family to hurry back to his native village. Blind and dead to
everything, he moved about with a dumb, lacerating pain in his heart,
— he longed for home. Before he found steady employment, he walked
daily with titanic strides through the entire length of Manhattan, while
children and even adults often slunk into byways to let him pass. Like a
huge monster he seemed, with an arrow in his vitals.

In the shop where he found a job at last, the workmen feared him at
first; but, ultimately finding him a harmless giant, they more than once
hurled their sarcasms at his head. Of the many men and women employed there, only one person had the distinction of getting fellowship
from old Zelig. That person was the Gentile watchman or janitor of the
shop, a little blond Pole with an open mouth and frightened eyes. And
many were the witticisms aimed at this uncouth pair. "The big one
looks like an elephant," the joker of the shop would say; "only he likes to
be fed on pennies instead of peanuts."

"Oi, oi, his nose would betray him," the "philosopher" of the shop
chimed in; and during the dinner hour he would expatiate thus: "You
see, money is his blood. He starves himself to have enough dollars to go
back to his home; the Pole told me all about it. And why should he stay
here? Freedom of religion means nothing to him, he never goes to synagogue; and freedom of the press? Bah — he never even reads the conservative Tageblatt!"

Old Zelig met such gibes with stoicism. Only rarely would he turn up
the whites of his eyes, as if in the act of ejaculation; but he would soon

contract his heavy brows into a scowl and emphasize the last with a heavy thump of his sizzling iron.

When the frightful cry of the massacred Jews in Russia rang across the Atlantic, and the Ghetto of Manhattan paraded one day through the narrow streets draped in black, through the erstwhile clamorous thoroughfares steeped in silence, stores and shops bolted, a wail of anguish issuing from every door and window — the only one remaining in his shop that day was old Zelig. His fellow-workmen did not call upon him to join the procession. They felt the incongruity of "this brute" in line with mourners in muffled tread. And the Gentile watchman reported the next day that the moment the funeral dirge of the music echoed from a distant street, Zelig snatched off the greasy cap he always wore, and in confusion instantly put it on again. "All the rest of the day," the Pole related with awe, "he looked wilder than ever, and so thumped with his iron on the cloth that I feared the building would come down."

But Zelig paid little heed to what was said about him. He dedicated his existence to the saving of his earnings, and only feared that he might be compelled to spend some of them. More than once his wife would be appalled in the dark of night by the silhouette of old Zelig in nightdress, sitting up in bed and counting a bundle of bank notes which he always replaced under his pillow. She frequently upbraided him for his niggardly nature, for his warding off all requests outside the pittance for household expense. She pleaded, exhorted, wailed. He invariably answered: "I haven't a cent by my soul." She pointed to the bare walls, the broken furniture, their beggarly attire.

"Our son is ill," she moaned. "He needs special food and rest; and our grandson is no more a baby; he'll soon need money for his studies. Dark is my world; you are killing both of them."

Zelig's color vanished; his old hands shook with emotion. The poor woman thought herself successful, but the next moment he would gasp: "Not a cent by my soul."

One day old Zelig was called from his shop, because his son had a sudden severe attack; and, as he ascended the stairs of his home, a neighbor shouted: "Run for a doctor; the patient cannot be revived." A voice as if from a tomb suddenly sounded in reply, "I haven't a cent by my soul."

The hallway was crowded with the ragged tenants of the house, mostly women and children; from far off were heard the rhythmic cries of the mother. The old man stood for a moment as if chilled from the roots of his hair to the tips of his fingers. Then the neighbors heard his sepulchral mumble: "I'll have to borrow somewheres, beg some one," as he retreated down the stairs. He brought a physician; and when the grandson asked for money to go for the medicine, Zelig snatched the prescription and hurried away, still murmuring: "I'll have to borrow, I'll have to beg."

Late that night, the neighbors heard a wail issuing from old Zelig's apartment; and they understood that the son was no more.

Zelig's purse was considerably thinned. He drew from it with palsied fingers for all burial expenses, looking about him in a dazed way. Mechanically he performed the Hebrew rites for the dead, which his neighbors taught him. He took a knife and made a deep gash in his shabby coat; then he removed his shoes, seated himself on the floor, and bowed his poor old head, tearless, benumbed.

The shop stared when the old man appeared after the prescribed three days' absence. Even the Pole dared not come near him. A film seemed to coat his glaring eye; deep wrinkles contracted his features, and his muscular frame appeared to shrink even as one looked. From that day on, he began to starve himself more than ever. The passion for sailing back to Russia, "to die at home at last," lost but little of its original intensity. Yet there was something now which by a feeble thread bound him to the New World.

In a little mound on the Base Achaim, the "House of Life," under a tombstone engraved with old Hebrew script, a part of himself lay buried. But he kept his thoughts away from that mound. How long and untiringly he kept on saving! Age gained on him with rapid strides. He had little strength left for work, but his dream of home seemed nearing its realization. Only a few more weeks, a few more months! And the thought sent a glow of warmth to his frozen frame. He would even condescend now to speak to his wife concerning the plans he had formed for their future welfare, more especially when she revived her pecuniary complaints.

"See what you have made of us, of the poor child," she often argued, pointing to the almost grown grandson. "Since he left school, he works for you, and what will be the end?"

At this, Zelig's heart would suddenly clutch, as if conscious of some indistinct, remote fear. His answers touching the grandson were abrupt, incoherent, as of one who replies to a question unintelligible to him, and is in constant dread lest his interlocutor should detect it.

Bitter misgivings concerning the boy began to mingle with the reveries of the old man. At first, he hardly gave a thought to him. The boy grew noiselessly. The ever-surging tide of secular studies that runs so high on the East Side caught this boy in its wave. He was quietly preparing himself for college. In his eagerness to accumulate the required sum, Zelig paid little heed to what was going on around him; and now, on the point of victory, he became aware with growing dread of something abrewing out of the common. He sniffed suspiciously; and one evening he overheard the boy talking to grandma about his hatred of Russian despotism, about his determination to remain in the States. He ended by entreating her to plead with grandpa to promise him the money necessary for a college education.

Old Zelig swooped down upon them with wild eyes. "Much you need it, you stupid," he thundered at the youngster in unrestrained fury. "You will continue your studies in Russia, durak, stupid." His timid wife, however, seemed suddenly to gather courage and she exploded: "Yes, you should give your savings for the child's education here. Woe is me, in the Russian universities no Jewish children are taken."

Old Zelig's face grew purple. He rose, and abruptly seated himself again. Then he rushed madly, with a raised, menacing arm, at the boy in whom he saw the formidable foe — the foe he had so long been dreading.

But the old woman was quick to interpose with a piercing shriek: "You madman, look at the sick child; you forget from what our son died, going out like a flickering candle."

That night Zelig tossed feverishly on his bed. He could not sleep. For the first time, it dawned upon him what his wife meant by pointing to the sickly appearance of the child. When the boy's father died, the physician declared that the cause was tuberculosis.

He rose to his feet. Beads of cold sweat glistened on his forehead, trickled down his cheeks, his beard. He stood pale and panting. Like a startling sound, the thought entered his mind — the boy, what should be done with the boy?

The dim, blue night gleamed in through the windows. All was shrouded in the city silence, which yet has a peculiar, monotonous ring in it. Somewhere, an infant awoke with a sickly cry which ended in a suffocating cough. The grizzled old man bestirred himself, and with hasty steps he tiptoed to the place where the boy lay. For a time he stood gazing on the pinched features, the under-sized body of the lad; then he raised one hand, passed it lightly over the boy's hair, stroking his cheeks and chin. The boy opened his eyes, looked for a moment at the shriveled form bending over him, then he petulantly closed them again.

"You hate to look at granpa, he is your enemy, he?" The aged man's voice shook, and sounded like that of the child's awaking in the night. The boy made no answer; but the old man noticed how the frail body shook, how the tears rolled, washing the sunken cheeks.

For some moments he stood mute, then his form literally shrank to that of a child's as he bent over the ear of the boy and whispered hoarsely: "You are weeping, eh? Granpa is your enemy, you stupid! To-morrow I will give you the money for the college. You hate to look at granpa; he is your enemy, eh?"

## Mary Lerner

..................................................................................................................

# Little Selves

FROM *The Atlantic Monthly*

MARGARET O'BRIEN, a great-aunt and seventy-five, knew she was near the end. She did not repine, for she had had a long, hard life and she was tired. The young priest who brought her communion had adminis-tered the last rites — holy oils on her eyelids (Lord, forgive her the sins of seeing!); holy oils on her lips (Lord, forgive her the sins of speaking!), on her ears, on her knotted hands, on her weary feet. Now she was ready, though she knew the approach of the dread presence would mean greater suffering. So she folded quiet hands beneath her heart, there where no child had ever lain, yet where now something grew and fat-tened on her strength. And she seemed given over to pleasant revery.

Neighbors came in to see her, and she roused herself and received them graciously, with a personal touch for each. — "And has your Julia gone to New York, Mrs. Carty? Nothing would do her but she must be going, I suppose. 'T was the selfsame way with me, when I was coming out here from the old country. Full of money the streets were, I used to be thinking. Well, well; the hills far away are green."

Or to Mrs. Devlin: "Terence is at it again, I see by the look of you. Poor man! There's no holding him? Eh, woman dear! Thirst is the end of drinking and sorrow is the end of love."

If her visitors stayed longer than a few minutes, however, her atten-tion wandered; her replies became cryptic. She would murmur some-thing about "all the seven parishes," or the Wicklow hills, or "the fair cove of Cork tippytoe into the ocean;" then fall into silence, smiling, eyes closed, yet with a singular look of attention. At such times her callers would whisper: "Glory b' t' God! she's so near it there's no fun in it," and slip out soberly into the kitchen.

Her niece, Anna Lennan, mother of a fine brood of children, would stop work for the space of a breath and enjoy a bit of conversation.

"Ain't she failing, though, the poor afflicted creature?" Mrs. Hanley cried one day. "Her mind is going back on her already."

"Are you of that opinion? I'm thinking she's mind enough yet, when she wants to attend; but mostly she's just drawn into herself, as busy as a bee about something, whatever it is that she's turning over in her head day-in, day-out. She sleeps scarce a wink for all she lies there so quiet, and, in the night, my man and I hear her talking to herself. 'No, no,' she'll say. 'I've gone past. I must be getting back to the start.' Or, another time, 'This is it, now. If I could be stopping!'"

"And what do you think she is colloguing about?"

"There's no telling. Himself does be saying it's in an elevator she is, but that's because he puts in the day churning up and down in one of the same. What else can you expect? 'T is nothing but 'Going up! going down!' with him all night as it is. Betune the two of them they have me fair destroyed with their traveling. 'Are you lacking anything, Aunt Margaret?' I call out to her. 'I am not,' she answers, impatient-like. 'Don't be ever fussing and too-ing, will you?'"

"Tch! tch!"

"And do you suppose the children are a comfort to her? Sorra bit. Just a look at them and she wants to be alone. 'Take them away, let you,' says she, shutting her eyes. 'The others is realer.'"

"And you think she's in her right mind all the same?"

"I do. 'T is just something she likes to be thinking over, — something she's fair dotty about. Why, it's the same when Father Flint is here. Polite and riverintial at the first, then impatient, and, if the poor man doesn't be taking the hint, she just closes up shop and off again into her whimsies. You'd swear she was in fear of missing something."

The visitor, being a young wife, had an explanation to hazard. "If she was a widow woman, now, or married — perhaps she had a liking for somebody once. Perhaps she might be trying to imagine them young days over again. Do you think could it be that?"

Anna shook her head. "My mother used to say she was a born old maid. All *she* wanted was work and saving her bit of money, and to church every minute she could be sparing."

"Still, you can't be telling. 'T is often that kind weeps sorest when 't is too late. My own old aunt used to cry, 'If I could be twenty-five again, wouldn't I do different!'"

"Maybe, maybe, though I doubt could it be so."

Nor was it so. The old woman, lying back so quietly among her pillows with closed eyes, yet with that look of singular intentness and concentration, was seeking no lover of her youth; though, indeed, she had had one once, and from time to time he did enter her revery, try as she would to prevent him. At that point, she always made the singular comment, "Gone past! I must be getting back to the beginning," and, pressing back into her earliest consciousness, she would remount the flooding current of the years. Each time, she hoped to get further, — though remoter shapes were illusive, and, if approached too closely, vanished, — for, once embarked on her river of memories, the descent was relentlessly swift. How tantalizing that swiftness! However she yearned to linger, she was rushed along till, all too soon, she sailed into the common light of day. At that point, she always put about, and laboriously recommenced the ascent.

To-day, something her niece had said about Donnybrook Fair — for Anna, too, was a child of the old sod — seemed to swell out with a fair wind the sails of her visionary bark. She closed her mind to all familiar shapes and strained back — way, way back, concentrating all her powers in an effort of will. For a bit she seemed to hover in populous space. This did not disturb her; she had experienced the same thing before. It simply meant she had mounted pretty well up to the fountainhead. The figures, when they did come, would be the ones she most desired.

At last, they began to take shape, tenuously at first, then of fuller body, each bringing its own setting, its own atmospheric suggestion — whether of dove-feathered Irish cloud and fresh greensward, of sudden downpour, or equally sudden clearing, with continual leafy drip, drip, drip, in the midst of brilliant sunshine.

For Margaret O'Brien, ardent summer sunlight seemed suddenly to pervade the cool, orderly little bedchamber. Then, "Here she is!" and a wee girl of four danced into view, wearing a dress of pink print, very tight at the top and very full at the bottom. She led the way to a tiny new house whence issued the cheery voice of hammers. Lumber and tools were lying round; from within came men's voices. The small girl stamped up the steps and looked in. Then she made for the narrow stair.

"Where's Margaret gone to?" said one of the men. "The upper floor's not finished. It's falling through the young one will be."

"Peggy!" called the older man. "Come down here with you."

There was a delighted squeal. The pink dress appeared at the head of the stairs. "Oh, the funny little man, daddy! Such a funny little old man with a high hat! Come quick, let you, and see him."

The two men ran to the stairs.

"Where is he?"

She turned back and pointed. Then her face fell.

"Gone! the little man is gone!"

Her father laughed and picked her up in his arms. "How big was he, Peg? As big as yourself, I wonder?"

"No, no! Small."

"As big as the baby?"

She considered a moment. "Yes, just as big as that. But a man, da."

"Well, why aren't you after catching him and holding him for ransom? 'T is pots and pots o' gold they've hidden away, the little people, and will be paying a body what he asks to let them go."

She pouted, on the verge of tears. "I want him to come back."

"I mistrust he won't be doing that, the leprechaun. Once you take your eye away, it's off with him for good and all."

Margaret O'Brien hugged herself with delight. *That* was a new one; she had never got back that far before. Yet how well she remembered it all! She seemed to smell the woody pungency of the lumber, the limy odor of whitewash from the field-stone cellar.

The old woman's dream went on. Out of the inexhaustible storehouse of the past, she summoned, one by one, her much-loved memories. There was a pigtailed Margaret in bonnet and shawl, trudging to school one wintry day. She had seen many wintry school-days, but this one stood out by reason of the tears she had shed by the way. She saw the long benches, the slates, the charts, the tall teacher at his desk. With a swelling of the throat, she saw the little girl sob out her declaration: "I'm not for coming no more, Mr. Wilde."

"What's that, Margaret? And why not? Haven't I been good to you?"

Tears choked the child. "Oh, Mr. Wilde, it's just because you're so terrible good to me. They say you are trying to make a Protestant out of me. So I'll not be coming no more."

The tall man drew the little girl to his knee and reassured her. Margaret O'Brien could review that scene with tender delight now. She had not been forced to give up her beloved school. Mr. Wilde had explained to her that her brothers were merely teasing her because she was so quick and such a favorite.

A little Margaret knelt on the cold stone floor at church and stared at the pictured saints or heard the budding branches rustle in the orchard outside. Another Margaret, a little taller, begged for a new sheet of ballads every time her father went to the fair. — There were the long flimsy sheets, with closely printed verses. These you must adapt to familiar tunes. This Margaret, then, swept the hearth and stacked the turf and sang from her bench in the chimney-corner. Sometimes it was something about "the little old red coat me father wore," which was "All buttons, buttons, buttons, buttons; all buttons down before"; or another beginning "Oh, dear, what can the matter be? Johnny's so long at the fair! He promised to buy me a knot of blue ribbon to tie up my bonnie brown hair."

Then there was a picture of the time the fairies actually bewitched the churn, and, labor as you might, no butter would form, not the least tiny speck. Margaret and her mother took the churn apart and examined every part of it. Nothing out of the way. "'T is the fairies is in it," her mother said. "All Souls' Day a-Friday. Put out a saucer of cream the night for the little people, let you." A well-grown girl in a blue cotton frock, the long braids of her black hair whipping about her in the windy evening, set out the cream on the stone flags before the low doorway, wasting no time in getting in again. The next day, how the butter "came!" Hardly started they were, when they could feel it forming. When Margaret washed the dasher, she "kept an eye out" for the dark corners of the room, for the air seemed thronged and murmurous.

After this picture, came always the same tall girl still in the same blue frock, this time with a shawl on her head. She brought in potatoes from the sheltered heaps that wintered out in the open. From one pailful she picked out a little flat stone, rectangular and smoother and more evenly proportional than any stone she had ever seen.

"What a funny stone!" she said to her mother.

Her mother left carding her wool to look. "You may well say so. 'T is one of the fairies' tables. Look close and you'll be turning up their little chairs as well."

It was as her mother said. Margaret found four smaller stones of like appearance, which one might well imagine to be stools for tiny dolls.

"Shall I be giving them to little Bee for playthings?"

"You will not. You'll be putting them outside. In the morning, though you may be searching the countryside, no trace of them will you find, for the fairies will be taking them again."

So Margaret stacked the fairy table and chairs outside. Next morning, she ran out half reluctantly, for she was afraid she would find them and that would spoil the story. But, no! they were gone. She never saw them again, though she searched in all imaginable places. Nor was that the last potato heap to yield these mysterious stones.

Margaret, growing from scene to scene, appeared again in a group of laughing boys and girls.

"What'll we play now?"

"Let's write the ivy test."

"Here's leaves."

Each wrote a name on a leaf and dropped it into a jar of water. Next morning, Margaret, who had misgivings, stole down early and searched for her leaf. Yes, the die was cast! At the sight of its bruised surface, ready tears flooded her eyes. She had written the name of her little grandmother, and the condition of the leaf foretold death within the year. The other leaves were unmarred. She quickly destroyed the ill-omened bit of ivy and said nothing about it, though the children clamored. "There's one leaf short. Whose is gone?" "Mine is there!" "Is it yours, John?" "Is it yours, Esther?" But Margaret kept her counsel, and, within the year, the little grandmother was dead. Of course, she was old, though vigorous; yet Margaret would never play that game again. It was like gambling with fate.

And still the girls kept swinging past. Steadily, all too swiftly, Margaret shot up to a woman's stature; her skirts crept down, her braids ought to have been bobbed up behind. She let them hang, however, and still ran with the boys, questing the bogs, climbing the apple trees, storming the wind-swept hills. Her mother would point to her sister Mary, who, though younger, sat now by the fire with her "spriggin'" [embroidery] for "the quality." Mary could crochet, too, and had a fine range of "shamrogue" patterns. So the mother would chide Margaret.

"What kind of a girl are you, at all, to be ever leping and tearing like a redshanks [deer]? 'T is high time for you to be getting sensible and learning something. Whistles and scouting-guns is all you're good for, and there's no silver in them things as far as I can see."

What fine whistles she contrived out of the pithy willow shoots in the spring! And the scouting-guns hollowed out of elder-stalks, which they charged with water from the brook by means of wadded sticks, working piston-wise! They would hide behind a hedge and bespatter enemies and friends alike. Many's the time they got their ears warmed in consequence or went supperless to bed, pretending not to see the table spread with baked potatoes, — "laughing potatoes," they called them, because they were ever splitting their sides, — besides delicious buttermilk, new-laid eggs, oat-cakes and fresh butter. "A child without supper is two to breakfast," their mother would say, smiling, when she saw them "tackle" their stirabout the next day.

How full of verve and life were all these figures! That glancing creature grow old? How could such things be! The sober pace of maturity
even seemed out of her star. Yet here she was, growing up, for all her
reluctance. An awkward gossoon leaned over the gate in the moonlight,
though she was indoors, ready to hide. But nobody noticed her alarm.

"There's that long-legged McMurray lad again; scouting after Mary,
I'll be bound," said her mother, all unawares.

But it was not Mary that he came for, though she married him just
the same, and came out to America with their children some years after
her sister's lone pilgrimage.

The intrusion of Jerry McMurray signaled the grounding of her
dream bark on the shoals of reality. Who cared about the cut-and-dried
life of a grown woman? Enchantment now lay behind her, and, if the
intervals between periods of pain permitted, she again turned an expectant face toward the old childish visions. Sometimes she could make the
trip twice over without being overtaken by suffering. But her intervals
of comfort grew steadily shorter; frequently she was interrupted before
she could get rightly launched on her delight. And always there seemed
to be one vision more illusive than the rest which she particularly
longed to recapture. At last, chance words of Anna's put her on its trail
in this wise.

When she was not, as her niece said, "in her trance, wool-gathering,"
Anna did her best to distract her, sending the children in to ask "would
she have a sup of tea now," or a taste of wine jelly. One day, after the
invalid had spent a bad night, she brought in her new long silk coat for
her aunt's inspection, for the old woman had always been "tasty" and
"dressy," and had made many a fine gown in her day. The sharp old eyes
lingered on the rich and truly striking braid ornament that secured the
loose front of the garment.

"What's that plaster?" she demanded, disparagingly.

Anna, inclined to be wroth, retorted: "I suppose you'd be preferring
one o' them tight ganzy [sweater] things that fit the figger like a jersey,
all buttoned down before."

A sudden light flamed in the old face. "I have it!" she cried. "'T is
what I've been seeking this good while. 'T will come now — the red
coat! I must be getting back to the beginning."

With that, she was off, relaxing and composing herself, as if surren-
dering to the spell of a hypnotist.

To reach any desired picture in her gallery, she must start at the
outset. Then they followed on, in due order — all that procession of

little girls: pink clad, blue-print clad, bare-legged or brogan-shod; flirt-
ing their short skirts, plaiting their heavy braids. About half way along,
a new figure asserted itself — a girl of nine or ten, who twisted this way
and that before a blurred bit of mirror and frowned at the red coat that
flapped about her heels, — bought oversize, you may be sure, so that
she should n't grow out of it too soon. The sleeves swallowed her little
brown hands, the shoulders and back were grotesquely sack-like, the
front had a puss [pout] on it.

"'T is the very fetch of Paddy the gander I am in it. I'll not be wearing
it so." She frowned with sudden intentness. "Could I be fitting it a bit, I
wonder, the way mother does cut down John's coats for Martin?"

With needle, scissors and thread, she crept up to her little chamber
under the eaves. It was early in the forenoon when she set to work
ripping. The morning passed, and the dinner hour.

"Peggy! Where's the girl gone to, I wonder?"

"To Aunt Theresa's, I'm thinking."

"Well, it's glad I am she's out o' my sight, for my hands itched to be
shaking her. Stand and twist herself inside out she did, fussing over the
fit of the good coat I'm after buying her. The little fustherer!"

For the small tailoress under the roof, the afternoon sped on winged
feet: pinning, basting, and stitching; trying on, ripping out again, and
re-fitting. "I'll be taking it in a wee bit more." She had to crowd up to
the window to catch the last of the daylight. At dusk, she swept her dark
hair from her flushed cheeks and forced her sturdy body into the red
coat. It was a "fit," believe you me! Modeled on the lines of the riding-
habit of a full-figured lady she had seen hunting about the countryside,
it buttoned up tight over her flat, boyish chest and bottled up her
squarish little waist. About her narrow hips, it rippled out in a short
"frisk." Beneath, her calico skirt, and bramble-scratched brown legs.

Warmed with triumph, she flew downstairs. Her mother and a neighbor were sitting in the glow of the peat fire. She tried to meet them with
assurance, but, at sight of their amazed faces, misgiving clutched her.
She pivoted before the mirror.

"Holy hour!" cried her mother. "What sausage-skin is that you've got
into?" Then, as comprehension grew: "Glory b' t' God, Ellen! 't is the
remains of the fine new coat I'm after buying her, large enough to last
her the next five years!"

"'T was too large!" the child whimpered. "A gander I looked in
it!" Then, cajolingly, "I'm but after taking it in a bit, ma. 'T will do grand

now, and maybe I'll not be getting much fatter. Look at the fit of it, just!"

"Fit! God save the mark!" cried her mother.

"Is the child after making that jacket herself?" asked the neighbor.

"I am," Margaret spoke up, defiantly. "I cut it and shaped it and put it together. It has even a frisk to the tail."

"Maggie," said the neighbor to Margaret's mother. "'T is as good a piece o' work for a child of her years as ever I see. You ought not to be faulting her, she's done that well. And," bursting into irrepressible laughter, "it's herself will have to be wearing it, woman dear! All she needs now is a horse and a side-saddle to be an equeestrieen!"

So the wanton destruction of the good red coat — in that house where good coats were sadly infrequent — ended with a laugh after all. How long she wore that tight jacket, and how grand she felt in it, let the other children laugh as they would!

What joy the old woman took in this incident! With its fullness of detail, it achieved a delicious suggestion of permanence, in contrast to the illusiveness of other isolated moments. Margaret O'Brien *saw* all these other figures, but she really *was* the child with the red coat. In the long years between, she had fashioned many fine dresses — gowned gay girls for their conquests and robed fair brides for the altar. Of all these, nothing now remained; but she could feel the good stuff of the red kersey under her little needle-scratched fingers, and see the glow of its rich color against her wind-kissed brown cheek.

"To the life!" she exclaimed aloud, exultantly. "To the very life!"

"What life, Aunt Margaret?" asked Anna, with gentle solicitude. "Is it afraid of the end you are, darling?"

"No, no, asthore. I've resigned myself long since, though 't was bitter knowledge at the outset. Well, well, God is good and we can't live forever."

Her eyes, opening to the two flaring patent gas-burners, winked as if she had dwelt long in a milder light. "What's all this glare about?" she asked playfully. "I guess the chandler's wife is dead. Snuff out the whole of them staring candles, let you. 'T is daylight yet; just the time o' day I always did like the best."

Anna obeyed and sat down beside the bed in the soft spring dusk. A little wind crept in under the floating white curtains, bringing with it the sweetness of new grass and pear-blossoms from the trim yard. It seemed an interval set apart from the hurrying hours of the busy day for rest and thought and confidences — an open moment. The old woman must have felt its invitation, for she turned her head and held out a shy hand to her niece.

"Anna, my girl, you imagine 't is the full o' the moon with me, I'm thinking. But, no, never woman was more in her right mind than I. Do you want I should be telling you what I've been hatching these many long days and nights? 'T will be a good laugh for you, I'll go bail."

And, as best she could, she gave the trend of her imaginings. Anna did not laugh, however. Instead, with the ever-ready sympathy and comprehension of the Celt, she showed brimming eyes. "'T is a thought I've often myself, let me tell you," she admitted. "Of all the little girls that were me, and now can be living no longer."

"You've said it!" cried the old woman, delighted at her unexpected responsiveness. "Only with me, 't is fair pit'yus. There's all those poor dear lasses there's nobody but me left to remember, and soon there'll not be even that. Sometimes they seem to be pleading just not to be forgotten, so I have to be keeping them alive in my head. I'm succeed-ing, too, and, if you'll believe me, 't is them little whips seem to be the real ones, and the live children here the shadders." Her voice choked with sudden tears. "They're all the children ever I had. My grief! that I'll have to be leaving them! They'll die now, for no man lives who can remember them any more."

Anna's beauty, already fading with the cares of house and children, seemed to put on all its former fresh charm. She leaned forward with girlish eagerness. "Auntie Margaret," she breathed, with new tenderness, "there's many a day left you yet. I'll be sitting here aside of you every evening at twilight just, and you can be showing me the lasses you have in mind. Many's the time my mother told me of the old place, and I can remember it well enough myself, though I was the youngest of the lot. So you can be filling it with all of our people — Mary and Margaret, John, Martin and Esther, Uncle Sheamus and the rest. I'll see them just as clear as yourself, for I've a place in my head where pictures come as thick and sharp as stars on a frosty night, when I get thinking. Then, with me ever calling them up, they'll be dancing and stravaging about till doomsday."

So the old woman had her heart's desire. She recreated her earlier selves and passed them on, happy in the thought that she was saving them from oblivion. "Do you mind that bold lass clouting her pet bull, now?" she would ask, with delight, speaking more and more as if of a third person. "And that other hussy that's after making a ganzy out of her good coat? I'd admire to have the leathering of that one."

Still the old woman lingered, a good month beyond her allotted time. As spring ripened, the days grew long. In the slow-fading twilights, the two women set their stage, gave cues for entrances and exits. Over the white counterpane danced the joyous figures, so radiant, so incredibly young, the whole cycle of a woman's girlhood. Grown familiar now, they came of their own accord, soothing her hours of pain with their laughing beauty, or, suddenly contemplative, assisting with seemly decorum at her devotional ecstasies.

"A saintly woman," the young priest told Anna on one of the last days. "She will make a holy end. Her meditations must be beautiful, for she has the true light of Heaven on her face. She looks as if she heard already the choiring of the angels."

And Anna, respectfully agreeing, kept her counsel. He was a good and sympathetic man and a priest of God, but, American-born, he was, like her stolid, kindly husband, outside the magic circle of comprehension. "He sees nothing, poor man," she thought, indulgently. "But he does mean well." So she set her husband to "mind" the young ones, and, easily doffing the sordid preoccupations of every day, slipped back into the enchanted ring.

1917

*Susan Glaspell*

..................................................................................................................

# A Jury of Her Peers

<small>FROM</small> *Every Week*

WHEN MARTHA HALE opened the storm-door and got a cut of the
north wind, she ran back for her big woolen scarf. As she hurriedly
wound that round her head her eye made a scandalized sweep of her
kitchen. It was no ordinary thing that called her away — it was probably
farther from ordinary than anything that had ever happened in Dickson
County. But what her eye took in was that her kitchen was in no shape
for leaving: her bread all ready for mixing, half the flour sifted and half
unsifted.

She hated to see things half done; but she had been at that when the
team from town stopped to get Mr. Hale, and then the sheriff came
running in to say his wife wished Mrs. Hale would come too — adding,
with a grin, that he guessed she was getting scarey and wanted another
woman along. So she had dropped everything right where it was.

"Martha!" now came her husband's impatient voice. "Don't keep
folks waiting out here in the cold."

She again opened the storm-door, and this time joined the three men
and the one woman waiting for her in the big two-seated buggy.

After she had the robes tucked around her she took another look at
the woman who sat beside her on the back seat. She had met Mrs. Peters
the year before at the county fair, and the thing she remembered about
her was that she didn't seem like a sheriff's wife. She was small and thin
and didn't have a strong voice. Mrs. Gorman, sheriff's wife before Gorman went out and Peters came in, had a voice that somehow seemed
to be backing up the law with every word. But if Mrs. Peters didn't
look like a sheriff's wife, Peters made it up in looking like a sheriff. He
was to a dot the kind of man who could get himself elected sheriff — a
heavy man with a big voice, who was particularly genial with the law-

abiding, as if to make it plain that he knew the difference between criminals and non-criminals. And right there it came into Mrs. Hale's mind, with a stab, that this man who was so pleasant and lively with all of them was going to the Wrights' now as a sheriff.

"The country's not very pleasant this time of year," Mrs. Peters at last ventured, as if she felt they ought to be talking as well as the men.

Mrs. Hale scarcely finished her reply, for they had gone up a little hill and could see the Wright place now, and seeing it did not make her feel like talking. It looked very lonesome this cold March morning. It had always been a lonesome-looking place. It was down in a hollow, and the poplar trees around it were lonesome-looking trees. The men were looking at it and talking about what had happened. The county attorney was bending to one side of the buggy, and kept looking steadily at the place as they drew up to it.

"I'm glad you came with me," Mrs. Peters said nervously, as the two women were about to follow the men in through the kitchen door.

Even after she had her foot on the door-step, her hand on the knob, Martha Hale had a moment of feeling she could not cross that threshold. And the reason it seemed she couldn't cross it now was simply because she hadn't crossed it before. Time and time again it had been in her mind, "I ought to go over and see Minnie Foster" — she still thought of her as Minnie Foster, though for twenty years she had been Mrs. Wright. And then there was always something to do and Minnie Foster would go from her mind. But *now* she could come.

The men went over to the stove. The women stood close together by the door. Young Henderson, the county attorney, turned around and said, "Come up to the fire, ladies."

Mrs. Peters took a step forward, then stopped. "I'm not — cold," she said.

And so the two women stood by the door, at first not even so much as looking around the kitchen.

The men talked for a minute about what a good thing it was the sheriff had sent his deputy out that morning to make a fire for them, and then Sheriff Peters stepped back from the stove, unbuttoned his outer coat, and leaned his hands on the kitchen table in a way that seemed to mark the beginning of official business. "Now, Mr. Hale," he said in a sort of semi-official voice, "before we move things about, you tell Mr. Henderson just what it was you saw when you came here yesterday morning."

The county attorney was looking around the kitchen.

"By the way," he said, "has anything been moved?" He turned to the sheriff. "Are things just as you left them yesterday?"

Peters looked from cupboard to sink; from that to a small worn rocker a little to one side of the kitchen table.

"It's just the same."

"Somebody should have been left here yesterday," said the county attorney.

"Oh — yesterday," returned the sheriff, with a little gesture as of yesterday having been more than he could bear to think of. "When I had to send Frank to Morris Center for that man who went crazy — let me tell you, I had my hands full *yesterday*. I knew you could get back from Omaha by to-day, George, and as long as I went over everything here myself — "

"Well, Mr. Hale," said the county attorney, in a way of letting what was past and gone go, "tell just what happened when you came here yesterday morning."

Mrs. Hale, still leaning against the door, had that sinking feeling of the mother whose child is about to speak a piece. Lewis often wandered along and got things mixed up in a story. She hoped he would tell this straight and plain, and not say unnecessary things that would just make things harder for Minnie Foster. He didn't begin at once, and she noticed that he looked queer — as if standing in that kitchen and having to tell what he had seen there yesterday made him almost sick.

"Yes, Mr. Hale?" the county attorney reminded.

"Harry and I had started to town with a load of potatoes," Mrs. Hale's husband began.

Harry was Mrs. Hale's oldest boy. He wasn't with them now, for the very good reason that those potatoes never got to town yesterday and he was taking them this morning, so he hadn't been home when the sheriff stopped to say he wanted Mr. Hale to come over to the Wright place and tell the county attorney his story there, where he could point it all out. With all Mrs. Hale's other emotions came the fear now that maybe Harry wasn't dressed warm enough — they hadn't any of them realized how that north wind did bite.

"We come along this road," Hale was going on, with a motion of his hand to the road over which they had just come, "and as we got in sight of the house I says to Harry, 'I'm goin' to see if I can't get John Wright to take a telephone.' You see," he explained to Henderson, "unless I can get somebody to go in with me they won't come out this branch road except for a price *I* can't pay. I'd spoke to Wright about it once before; but he put me off, saying folks talked too much anyway, and all he asked was peace and quiet — guess you know about how much he talked himself. But I thought maybe if I went to the house and talked about it before his wife, and said all the women-folks liked the telephones, and that in this lonesome stretch of road it would be a good thing — well, I said to Harry that that was what I was going to say — though I said at the same time that I didn't know as what his wife wanted made much difference to John — "

Now, there he was! — saying things he didn't need to say. Mrs. Hale tried to catch her husband's eye, but fortunately the county attorney interrupted with:

"Let's talk about that a little later, Mr. Hale. I do want to talk about that, but I'm anxious now to get along to just what happened when you got here."

When he began this time, it was very deliberately and carefully:

"I didn't see or hear anything. I knocked at the door. And still it was all quiet inside. I knew they must be up — it was past eight o'clock. So I knocked again, louder, and I thought I heard somebody say, 'Come in.' I wasn't sure — I'm not sure yet. But I opened the door — this door," jerking a hand toward the door by which the two women stood, "and there, in that rocker" — pointing to it — "sat Mrs. Wright."

Every one in the kitchen looked at the rocker. It came into Mrs. Hale's mind that that rocker didn't look in the least like Minnie Foster — the Minnie Foster of twenty years before. It was a dingy red, with wooden rungs up the back, and the middle rung was gone, and the chair sagged to one side.

"How did she — look?" the county attorney was inquiring.

"Well," said Hale, "she looked — queer."

"How do you mean — queer?"

As he asked it he took out a note-book and pencil. Mrs. Hale did not like the sight of that pencil. She kept her eye fixed on her husband, as if to keep him from saying unnecessary things that would go into that note-book and make trouble.

Hale did speak guardedly, as if the pencil had affected him too.

"Well, as if she didn't know what she was going to do next. And kind of — done up."

"How did she seem to feel about your coming?"

"Why, I don't think she minded — one way or other. She didn't pay much attention. I said, 'Ho' do, Mrs. Wright? It's cold, ain't it?' And she said, 'Is it?' — and went on pleatin' at her apron.

"Well, I was surprised. She didn't ask me to come up to the stove, or to sit down, but just set there, not even lookin' at me. And so I said: 'I want to see John.'

"And then she — laughed. I guess you would call it a laugh.

"I thought of Harry and the team outside, so I said, a little sharp, 'Can I see John?' 'No,' says she — kind of dull like. 'Ain't he home?' says I. Then she looked at me. 'Yes,' says she, 'he's home.' 'Then why can't I see him?' I asked her, out of patience with her now. ''Cause he's dead,' says she, just as quiet and dull — and fell to pleatin' her apron. 'Dead?' says I, like you do when you can't take in what you've heard.

"She just nodded her head, not getting a bit excited, but rockin' back and forth.

"'Why — where is he?' says I, not knowing *what* to say.

"She just pointed upstairs — like this" — pointing to the room above.

"I got up, with the idea of going up there myself. By this time I — didn't know what to do. I walked from there to here; then I says: 'Why, what did he die of?'

"'He died of a rope round his neck,' says she; and just went on pleatin' at her apron."

Hale stopped speaking, and stood staring at the rocker, as if he were still seeing the woman who had sat there the morning before. Nobody spoke; it was as if every one were seeing the woman who had sat there the morning before.

"And what did you do then?" The county attorney at last broke the silence.

"I went out and called Harry. I thought I might — need help. I got Harry in, and we went upstairs." His voice fell almost to a whisper. "There he was — lying over the — "

"I think I'd rather have you go into that upstairs," the county attorney interrupted, "where you can point it all out. Just go on now with the rest of the story."

"Well, my first thought was to get that rope off. It looked — "

He stopped, his face twitching.

"But Harry, he went up to him, and he said, 'No, he's dead all right, and we'd better not touch anything.' So we went downstairs.

"She was still sitting that same way. 'Has anybody been notified?' I asked. 'No,' says she, unconcerned.

"'Who did this, Mrs. Wright?' said Harry. He said it businesslike, and she stopped pleatin' at her apron. 'I don't know,' she says. 'You don't *know?*' says Harry. 'Weren't you sleepin' in the bed with him?' 'Yes,' says she, 'but I was on the inside.' 'Somebody slipped a rope round his neck and strangled him, and you didn't wake up?' says Harry. 'I didn't wake up,' she said after him.

"We may have looked as if we didn't see how that could be, for after a minute she said, 'I sleep sound.'

"Harry was going to ask her more questions, but I said maybe that weren't our business; maybe we ought to let her tell her story first to the coroner or the sheriff. So Harry went fast as he could over to High Road — the Rivers' place, where there's a telephone."

"And what did she do when she knew you had gone for the coroner?" The attorney got his pencil in his hand all ready for writing.

"She moved from that chair to this one over here" — Hale pointed to a small chair in the corner — "and just sat there with her hands held together and looking down. I got a feeling that I ought to make some conversation, so I said I had come in to see if John wanted to put in a telephone; and at that she started to laugh, and then she stopped and looked at me — scared."

At sound of a moving pencil the man who was telling the story looked up.

"I dunno — maybe it wasn't scared," he hastened; "I wouldn't like to say it was. Soon Harry got back, and then Dr. Lloyd came, and you, Mr. Peters, and so I guess that's all I know that you don't."

He said that last with relief, and moved a little, as if relaxing. Every one moved a little. The county attorney walked toward the stair door.

"I guess we'll go upstairs first — then out to the barn and around there."

He paused and looked around the kitchen.

"You're convinced there was nothing important here?" he asked the sheriff. "Nothing that would — point to any motive?"

The sheriff too looked all around, as if to re-convince himself.

"Nothing here but kitchen things," he said, with a little laugh for the insignificance of kitchen things.

The county attorney was looking at the cupboard — a peculiar, ungainly structure, half closet and half cupboard, the upper part of it being built in the wall, and the lower part just the old-fashioned kitchen cupboard. As if its queerness attracted him, he got a chair and opened the upper part and looked in. After a moment he drew his hand away sticky.

"Here's a nice mess," he said resentfully.

The two women had drawn nearer, and now the sheriff's wife spoke.

"Oh — her fruit," she said, looking to Mrs. Hale for sympathetic understanding. She turned back to the county attorney and explained: "She worried about that when it turned so cold last night. She said the fire would go out and her jars might burst."

Mrs. Peters' husband broke into a laugh.

"Well, can you beat the woman! Held for murder, and worrying about her preserves!"

The young attorney set his lips.

"I guess before we're through with her she may have something more serious than preserves to worry about."

"Oh, well," said Mrs. Hale's husband, with good-natured superiority, "women are used to worrying over trifles."

The two women moved a little closer together. Neither of them spoke. The county attorney seemed suddenly to remember his manners — and think of his future.

"And yet," said he, with the gallantry of a young politician, "for all their worries, what would we do without the ladies?"

The women did not speak, did not unbend. He went to the sink and began washing his hands. He turned to wipe them on the roller towel — whirled it for a cleaner place.

"Dirty towels! Not much of a housekeeper, would you say, ladies?"

He kicked his foot against some dirty pans under the sink.

"There's a great deal of work to be done on a farm," said Mrs. Hale stiffly.

"To be sure. And yet" — with a little bow to her — "I know there are some Dickson County farm-houses that do not have such roller towels." He gave it a pull to expose its full length again.

"Those towels get dirty awful quick. Men's hands aren't always as clean as they might be."

"Ah, loyal to your sex, I see," he laughed. He stopped and gave her a keen look. "But you and Mrs. Wright were neighbors. I suppose you were friends, too."

Martha Hale shook her head.

"I've seen little enough of her of late years. I've not been in this house — it's more than a year."

"And why was that? You didn't like her?"

"I liked her well enough," she replied with spirit. "Farmers' wives have their hands full, Mr. Henderson. And then — " She looked around the kitchen.

"Yes?" he encouraged.

"It never seemed a very cheerful place," said she, more to herself than to him.

"No," he agreed; "I don't think any one would call it cheerful. I shouldn't say she had the home-making instinct."

"Well, I don't know as Wright had, either," she muttered.

"You mean they didn't get on very well?" he was quick to ask.

"No; I don't mean anything," she answered, with decision. As she turned a little away from him, she added: "But I don't think a place would be any the cheerfuler for John Wright's bein' in it."

"I'd like to talk to you about that a little later, Mrs. Hale," he said. "I'm anxious to get the lay of things upstairs now."

He moved toward the stair door, followed by the two men.

"I suppose anything Mrs. Peters does'll be all right?" the sheriff inquired. "She was to take in some clothes for her, you know — and a few little things. We left in such a hurry yesterday."

The county attorney looked at the two women whom they were leaving alone there among the kitchen things.

"Yes — Mrs. Peters," he said, his glance resting on the woman who was not Mrs. Peters, the big farmer woman who stood behind the sheriff's wife. "Of course Mrs. Peters is one of us," he said, in a manner of entrusting responsibility. "And keep your eye out, Mrs. Peters, for anything that might be of use. No telling; you women might come upon a clue to the motive — and that's the thing we need."

Mr. Hale rubbed his face after the fashion of a show man getting ready for a pleasantry.

"But would the women know a clue if they did come upon it?" he said; and, having delivered himself of this, he followed the others through the stair door.

The women stood motionless and silent, listening to the footsteps, first upon the stairs, then in the room above them.

Then, as if releasing herself from something strange, Mrs. Hale began to arrange the dirty pans under the sink, which the county attorney's disdainful push of the foot had deranged.

"I'd hate to have men comin' into my kitchen," she said testily — "snoopin' round and criticizin.'"

"Of course it's no more than their duty," said the sheriff's wife, in her manner of timid acquiescence.

"Duty's all right," replied Mrs. Hale bluffly; "but I guess that deputy sheriff that come out to make the fire might have got a little of this on." She gave the roller towel a pull. "Wish I'd thought of that sooner! Seems mean to talk about her for not having things slicked up, when she had to come away in such a hurry."

She looked around the kitchen. Certainly it was not "slicked up." Her eye was held by a bucket of sugar on a low shelf. The cover was off the wooden bucket, and beside it was a paper bag — half full.

Mrs. Hale moved toward it.

"She was putting this in there," she said to herself — slowly.

She thought of the flour in her kitchen at home — half sifted, half not sifted. She had been interrupted, and had left things half done. What had interrupted Minnie Foster? Why had that work been left half done? She made a move as if to finish it, — unfinished things always bothered her, — and then she glanced around and saw that Mrs. Peters was watching her — and she didn't want Mrs. Peters to get that feeling she had got of work begun and then — for some reason — not finished.

"It's a shame about her fruit," she said, and walked toward the cupboard that the county attorney had opened, and got on the chair, murmuring: "I wonder if it's all gone."

It was a sorry enough looking sight, but "Here's one that's all right," she said at last. She held it toward the light. "This is cherries, too." She looked again. "I declare I believe that's the only one."

With a sigh, she got down from the chair, went to the sink, and wiped off the bottle.

"She'll feel awful bad, after all her hard work in the hot weather. I remember the afternoon I put up my cherries last summer."

She set the bottle on the table, and, with another sigh, started to sit down in the rocker. But she did not sit down. Something kept her from sitting down in that chair. She straightened — stepped back, and, half turned away, stood looking at it; seeing the woman who had sat there "pleatin' at her apron."

The thin voice of the sheriff's wife broke in upon her: "I must be getting those things from the front room closet." She opened the door into the other room, started in, stepped back. "You coming with me, Mrs. Hale?" she asked nervously. "You — you could help me get them."

They were soon back — the stark coldness of that shut-up room was not a thing to linger in.

"My!" said Mrs. Peters, dropping the things on the table and hurrying to the stove.

Mrs. Hale stood examining the clothes the woman who was being detained in town had said she wanted.

"Wright was close!" she exclaimed, holding up a shabby black shirt that bore the marks of much making over. "I think maybe that's why she kept so much to herself. I s'pose she felt she couldn't do her part; and then, you don't enjoy things when you feel shabby. She used to wear pretty clothes and be lively — when she was Minnie Foster, one of the town girls, singing in the choir. But that — oh, that was twenty years ago."

With a carefulness in which there was something tender, she folded the shabby clothes and piled them at one corner of the table. She looked up at Mrs. Peters, and there was something in the other woman's look that irritated her.

"She don't care," she said to herself. "Much difference it makes to her whether Minnie Foster had pretty clothes when she was a girl."

Then she looked again, and she wasn't so sure; in fact, she hadn't at any time been perfectly sure about Mrs. Peters. She had that shrinking manner, and yet her eyes looked as if they could see a long way into things.

"This all you was to take in?" asked Mrs. Hale.

"No," said the sheriff's wife; "she said she wanted an apron. Funny thing to want," she ventured in her nervous little way, "for there's not much to get you dirty in jail, goodness knows. But I suppose just to make her feel more natural. If you're used to wearing an apron — . She said they were in the bottom drawer of this cupboard. Yes — here they are. And then her little shawl that always hung on the stair door."

She took the small gray shawl from behind the door leading upstairs, and stood a minute looking at it.

Suddenly Mrs. Hale took a quick step toward the other woman.

"Mrs. Peters!"

"Yes, Mrs. Hale?"

"Do you think she — did it?"

A frightened look blurred the other thing in Mrs. Peters' eyes.

"Oh, I don't know," she said, in a voice that seemed to shrink away from the subject.

"Well, I don't think she did," affirmed Mrs. Hale stoutly. "Asking for an apron, and her little shawl. Worryin' about her fruit."

"Mr. Peters says — ." Footsteps were heard in the room above; she stopped, looked up, then went on in a lowered voice: "Mr. Peters says — it looks bad for her. Mr. Henderson is awful sarcastic in a speech, and he's going to make fun of her saying she didn't — wake up."

For a moment Mrs. Hale had no answer. Then, "Well, I guess John Wright didn't wake up — when they was slippin' that rope under his neck," she muttered.

"No, it's *strange*," breathed Mrs. Peters. "They think it was such a — funny way to kill a man."

She began to laugh; at sound of the laugh, abruptly stopped.

"That's just what Mr. Hale said," said Mrs. Hale, in a resolutely natural voice. "There was a gun in the house. He says that's what he can't understand."

"Mr. Henderson said, coming out, that what was needed for the case was a motive. Something to show anger — or sudden feeling."

"Well, I don't see any signs of anger around here," said Mrs. Hale. "I don't — "

She stopped. It was as if her mind tripped on something. Her eye was caught by a dish-towel in the middle of the kitchen table. Slowly she moved toward the table. One half of it was wiped clean, the other half messy. Her eyes made a slow, almost unwilling turn to the bucket of sugar and the half empty bag beside it. Things begun — and not finished.

After a moment she stepped back, and said, in that manner of releasing herself:

"Wonder how they're finding things upstairs? I hope she had it a little more red up up there. You know," — she paused, and feeling gathered, — "it seems kind of *sneaking*: locking her up in town and coming out here to get her own house to turn against her!"

"But, Mrs. Hale," said the sheriff's wife, "the law is the law."

"I s'pose 'tis," answered Mrs. Hale shortly.

She turned to the stove, saying something about that fire not being much to brag of. She worked with it a minute, and when she straightened up she said aggressively:

"The law is the law — and a bad stove is a bad stove. How'd you like to cook on this?" — pointing with the poker to the broken lining. She opened the oven door and started to express her opinion of the oven; but she was swept into her own thoughts, thinking of what it would mean, year after year, to have that stove to wrestle with. The thought of Minnie Foster trying to bake in that oven — and the thought of her never going over to see Minnie Foster — .

She was startled by hearing Mrs. Peters say: "A person gets discouraged — and loses heart."

The sheriff's wife had looked from the stove to the sink — to the pail of water which had been carried in from outside. The two women stood there silent, above them the footsteps of the men who were looking for evidence against the woman who had worked in that kitchen. That look of seeing into things, of seeing through a thing to something else, was in the eyes of the sheriff's wife now. When Mrs. Hale next spoke to her, it was gently:

"Better loosen up your things, Mrs. Peters. We'll not feel them when we go out."

Mrs. Peters went to the back of the room to hang up the fur tippet she was wearing. A moment later she exclaimed, "Why, she was piecing a quilt," and held up a large sewing basket piled high with quilt pieces.

Mrs. Hale spread some of the blocks out on the table.

"It's log-cabin pattern," she said, putting several of them together. "Pretty, isn't it?"

They were so engaged with the quilt that they did not hear the footsteps on the stairs. Just as the stair door opened Mrs. Hale was saying:

"Do you suppose she was going to quilt it or just knot it?"

The sheriff threw up his hands.

"They wonder whether she was going to quilt it or just knot it!"

There was a laugh for the ways of women, a warming of hands over the stove, and then the county attorney said briskly:

"Well, let's go right out to the barn and get that cleared up."

"I don't see as there's anything so strange," Mrs. Hale said resentfully, after the outside door had closed on the three men — "our taking up our time with little things while we're waiting for them to get the evidence. I don't see as it's anything to laugh about."

"Of course they've got awful important things on their minds," said the sheriff's wife apologetically.

They returned to an inspection of the block for the quilt. Mrs. Hale was looking at the fine, even sewing, and preoccupied with thoughts of the woman who had done that sewing, when she heard the sheriff's wife say, in a queer tone:

"Why, look at this one."

She turned to take the block held out to her.

"The sewing," said Mrs. Peters, in a troubled way. "All the rest of them have been so nice and even — but — this one. Why, it looks as if she didn't know what she was about!"

Their eyes met — something flashed to life, passed between them; then, as if with an effort, they seemed to pull away from each other. A moment Mrs. Hale sat there, her hands folded over that sewing which was so unlike all the rest of the sewing. Then she had pulled a knot and drawn the threads.

"Oh, what are you doing, Mrs. Hale?" asked the sheriff's wife, startled.

"Just pulling out a stitch or two that's not sewed very good," said Mrs. Hale mildly.

"I don't think we ought to touch things," Mrs. Peters said, a little helplessly.

"I'll just finish up this end," answered Mrs. Hale, still in that mild, matter-of-fact fashion.

She threaded a needle and started to replace bad sewing with good. For a little while she sewed in silence. Then, in that thin, timid voice, she heard:

"Mrs. Hale!"

"Yes, Mrs. Peters?"

"What do you suppose she was so — nervous about?"

"Oh, I don't know," said Mrs. Hale, as if dismissing a thing not important enough to spend much time on. "I don't know as she was — nervous. I sew awful queer sometimes when I'm just tired."

She cut a thread, and out of the corner of her eye looked up at Mrs. Peters. The small, lean face of the sheriff's wife seemed to have tightened up. Her eyes had that look of peering into something. But next moment she moved, and said in her thin, indecisive way:

"Well, I must get those clothes wrapped. They may be through sooner than we think. I wonder where I could find a piece of paper — and string."

"In that cupboard, maybe," suggested Mrs. Hale, after a glance around.

One piece of the crazy sewing remained unripped. Mrs. Peters' back turned, Martha Hale now scrutinized that piece, compared it with the dainty, accurate sewing of the other blocks. The difference was startling.

Holding this block made her feel queer, as if the distracted thoughts of the woman who had perhaps turned to it to try and quiet herself were communicating themselves to her.

Mrs. Peters' voice roused her.

"Here's a bird-cage," she said. "Did she have a bird, Mrs. Hale?"

"Why, I don't know whether she did or not." She turned to look at the cage Mrs. Peters was holding up. "I've not been here in so long." She sighed. "There was a man round last year selling canaries cheap — but I don't know as she took one. Maybe she did. She used to sing real pretty herself."

Mrs. Peters looked around the kitchen.

"Seems kind of funny to think of a bird here." She half laughed — an attempt to put up a barrier. "But she must have had one — or why would she have a cage? I wonder what happened to it."

"I suppose maybe the cat got it," suggested Mrs. Hale, resuming her sewing.

"No; she didn't have a cat. She's got that feeling some people have about cats — being afraid of them. When they brought her to our house yesterday, my cat got in the room, and she was real upset and asked me to take it out."

"My sister Bessie was like that," laughed Mrs. Hale.

The sheriff's wife did not reply. The silence made Mrs. Hale turn round. Mrs. Peters was examining the bird-cage.

"Look at this door," she said slowly. "It's broke. One hinge has been pulled apart."

Mrs. Hale came nearer.

"Looks as if some one must have been — rough with it."

Again their eyes met — startled, questioning, apprehensive. For a moment neither spoke nor stirred. Then Mrs. Hale, turning away, said brusquely:

"If they're going to find any evidence, I wish they'd be about it. I don't like this place."

"But I'm awful glad you came with me, Mrs. Hale." Mrs. Peters put the bird-cage on the table and sat down. "It would be lonesome for me — sitting here alone."

"Yes, it would, wouldn't it?" agreed Mrs. Hale, a certain determined naturalness in her voice. She had picked up the sewing, but now it dropped in her lap, and she murmured in a different voice: "But I tell you what I *do* wish, Mrs. Peters. I wish I had come over sometimes when she was here. I wish — I had."

"But of course you were awful busy, Mrs. Hale. Your house — and your children."

"I could've come," retorted Mrs. Hale shortly. "I stayed away because it weren't cheerful — and that's why I ought to have come. I" — she looked around — "I've never liked this place. Maybe because it's down in a hollow and you don't see the road. I don't know what it is, but it's a lonesome place, and always was. I wish I had come over to see Minnie Foster sometimes. I can see now — " She did not put it into words.

"Well, you mustn't reproach yourself," counseled Mrs. Peters. "Somehow, we just don't see how it is with other folks till — something comes up."

"Not having children makes less work," mused Mrs. Hale, after a silence, "but it makes a quiet house — and Wright out to work all day — and no company when he did come in. Did you know John Wright, Mrs. Peters?"

"Not to know him. I've seen him in town. They say he was a good man."

"Yes — good," conceded John Wright's neighbor grimly. "He didn't drink, and kept his word as well as most, I guess, and paid his debts. But he was a hard man, Mrs. Peters. Just to pass the time of day with him — ." She stopped, shivered a little. "Like a raw wind that gets to the bone." Her eye fell upon the cage on the table before her, and she added, almost bitterly: "I should think she would've wanted a bird!"

Suddenly she leaned forward, looking intently at the cage. "But what do you s'pose went wrong with it?"

"I don't know," returned Mrs. Peters; "unless it got sick and died."

But after she said it she reached over and swung the broken door. Both women watched it as if somehow held by it.

"You didn't know — her?" Mrs. Hale asked, a gentler note in her voice.

"Not till they brought her yesterday," said the sheriff's wife.

"She — come to think of it, she was kind of like a bird herself. Real sweet and pretty, but kind of timid and — fluttery. How — she — did — change."

That held her for a long time. Finally, as if struck with a happy thought and relieved to get back to everyday things, she exclaimed:

"Tell you what, Mrs. Peters, why don't you take the quilt in with you? It might take up her mind."

"Why, I think that's a real nice idea, Mrs. Hale," agreed the sheriff's wife, as if she too were glad to come into the atmosphere of a simple kindness. "There couldn't possibly be any objection to that, could there? Now, just what will I take? I wonder if her patches are in here — and her things."

They turned to the sewing basket.

"Here's some red," said Mrs. Hale, bringing out a roll of cloth. Underneath that was a box. "Here, maybe her scissors are in here — and her things." She held it up. "What a pretty box! I'll warrant that was something she had a long time ago — when she was a girl."

She held it in her hand a moment; then, with a little sigh, opened it.

Instantly her hand went to her nose.

"Why — !"

Mrs. Peters drew nearer — then turned away.

"There's something wrapped up in this piece of silk," faltered Mrs. Hale.

"This isn't her scissors," said Mrs. Peters, in a shrinking voice.

Her hand not steady, Mrs. Hale raised the piece of silk. "Oh, Mrs. Peters!" she cried. "It's — "

Mrs. Peters bent closer.

"It's the bird," she whispered.

"But, Mrs. Peters!" cried Mrs. Hale. "*Look* at it! Its *neck* — look at its neck! It's all — other side *to*."

She held the box away from her.

The sheriff's wife again bent closer.

"Somebody wrung its neck," said she, in a voice that was slow and deep.

And then again the eyes of the two women met — this time clung together in a look of dawning comprehension, of growing horror. Mrs. Peters looked from the dead bird to the broken door of the cage. Again their eyes met. And just then there was a sound at the outside door.

Mrs. Hale slipped the box under the quilt pieces in the basket, and sank into the chair before it. Mrs. Peters stood holding to the table. The county attorney and the sheriff came in from outside.

"Well, ladies," said the county attorney, as one turning from serious things to little pleasantries, "have you decided whether she was going to quilt it or knot it?"

"We think," began the sheriff's wife in a flurried voice, "that she was going to — knot it."

He was too preoccupied to notice the change that came in her voice on that last.

"Well, that's very interesting, I'm sure," he said tolerantly. He caught sight of the bird-cage. "Has the bird flown?"

"We think the cat got it," said Mrs. Hale in a voice curiously even.

He was walking up and down, as if thinking something out.

"Is there a cat?" he asked absently.

Mrs. Hale shot a look up at the sheriff's wife.

"Well, not *now*," said Mrs. Peters. "They're superstitious, you know; they leave."

She sank into her chair.

The county attorney did not heed her. "No sign at all of any one having come in from the outside," he said to Peters, in the manner of continuing an interrupted conversation. "Their own rope. Now let's go upstairs again and go over it, piece by piece. It would have to have been some one who knew just the — "

The stair door closed behind them and their voices were lost.

The two women sat motionless, not looking at each other, but as if peering into something and at the same time holding back. When they spoke now it was as if they were afraid of what they were saying, but as if they could not help saying it.

"She liked the bird," said Martha Hale, low and slowly. "She was going to bury it in that pretty box."

"When I was a girl," said Mrs. Peters, under her breath, "my kitten — there was a boy who took a hatchet, and before my eyes — before I could get there — " She covered her face an instant. "If they hadn't held me back I would have" — she caught herself, looked upstairs where footsteps were heard, and finished weakly — "hurt him."

Then they sat without speaking or moving.

"I wonder how it would seem," Mrs. Hale at last began, as if feeling her way over strange ground — "never to have had any children around?" Her eyes made a slow sweep of the kitchen, as if seeing what that kitchen had meant through all the years. "No, Wright wouldn't like the bird," she said after that — "a thing that sang. She used to sing. He killed that too." Her voice tightened.

Mrs. Peters moved uneasily.

"Of course we don't know who killed the bird."

"I knew John Wright," was Mrs. Hale's answer.

"It was an awful thing was done in this house that night, Mrs. Hale," said the sheriff's wife. "Killing a man while he slept — slipping a thing round his neck that choked the life out of him."

Mrs. Hale's hand went out to the bird-cage.

"His neck. Choked the life out of him."

"We don't *know* who killed him," whispered Mrs. Peters wildly. "We don't *know*."

Mrs. Hale had not moved. "If there had been years and years of — nothing, then a bird to sing to you, it would be awful — still — after the bird was still."

It was as if something within her not herself had spoken, and it found in Mrs. Peters something she did not know as herself.

"I know what stillness is," she said, in a queer, monotonous voice. "When we homesteaded in Dakota, and my first baby died — after he was two years old — and me with no other then — "

Mrs. Hale stirred.

"How soon do you suppose they'll be through looking for the evidence?"

"I know what stillness is," repeated Mrs. Peters, in just that same way. Then she too pulled back. "The law has got to punish crime, Mrs. Hale," she said in her tight little way.

"I wish you'd seen Minnie Foster," was the answer, "when she wore a white dress with blue ribbons, and stood up there in the choir and sang."

The picture of that girl, the fact that she had lived neighbor to that girl for twenty years, and had let her die for lack of life, was suddenly more than she could bear.

"Oh, I *wish* I'd come over here once in a while!" she cried. "That was a crime! That was a crime! Who's going to punish that?"

"We mustn't take on," said Mrs. Peters, with a frightened look toward the stairs.

"I might 'a' *known* she needed help! I tell you, it's *queer*, Mrs. Peters. We live close together, and we live far apart. We all go through the same things — it's all just a different kind of the same thing! If it weren't — why do you and I *understand?* Why do we *know* — what we know this minute?"

She dashed her hand across her eyes. Then, seeing the jar of fruit on the table, she reached for it and choked out:

"If I was you I wouldn't *tell* her her fruit was gone! Tell her it *ain't*. Tell her it's all right — all of it. Here — take this in to prove it to her! She — she may never know whether it was broke or not."

She turned away.

Mrs. Peters reached out for the bottle of fruit as if she were glad to take it — as if touching a familiar thing, having something to do, could

keep her from something else. She got up, looked about for something to wrap the fruit in, took a petticoat from the pile of clothes she
had brought from the front room, and nervously started winding that
round the bottle.

"My!" she began, in a high, false voice, "it's a good thing the men
couldn't hear us! Getting all stirred up over a little thing like a — dead
canary." She hurried over that. "As if that could have anything to do
with — with — My, wouldn't they *laugh?*"

Footsteps were heard on the stairs.

"Maybe they would," muttered Mrs. Hale — "maybe they wouldn't."

"No, Peters," said the county attorney incisively; "it's all perfectly
clear, except the reason for doing it. But you know juries when it comes
to women. If there was some definite thing — something to show.
Something to make a story about. A thing that would connect up with
this clumsy way of doing it."

In a covert way Mrs. Hale looked at Mrs. Peters. Mrs. Peters was
looking at her. Quickly they looked away from each other. The outer
door opened and Mr. Hale came in.

"I've got the team round now," he said. "Pretty cold out there."

"I'm going to stay here awhile by myself," the county attorney suddenly announced. "You can send Frank out for me, can't you?" he asked
the sheriff. "I want to go over everything. I'm not satisfied we can't do
better."

Again, for one brief moment, the two women's eyes found one another.

The sheriff came up to the table.

"Did you want to see what Mrs. Peters was going to take in?"

The county attorney picked up the apron. He laughed.

"Oh, I guess they're not very dangerous things the ladies have picked
out."

Mrs. Hale's hand was on the sewing basket in which the box was
concealed. She felt that she ought to take her hand off the basket. She
did not seem able to. He picked up one of the quilt blocks which she
had piled on to cover the box. Her eyes felt like fire. She had a feeling
that if he took up the basket she would snatch it from him.

But he did not take it up. With another little laugh, he turned away,
saying:

"No; Mrs. Peters doesn't need supervising. For that matter, a sheriff's
wife is married to the law. Ever think of it that way, Mrs. Peters?"

Mrs. Peters was standing beside the table. Mrs. Hale shot a look up at her; but she could not see her face. Mrs. Peters had turned away. When she spoke, her voice was muffled.

"Not — just that way," she said.

"Married to the law!" chuckled Mrs. Peters' husband. He moved toward the door into the front room, and said to the county attorney:

"I just want you to come in here a minute, George. We ought to take a look at these windows."

"Oh — windows," said the county attorney scoffingly.

"We'll be right out, Mr. Hale," said the sheriff to the farmer, who was still waiting by the door.

Hale went to look after the horses. The sheriff followed the county attorney into the other room. Again — for one final moment — the two women were alone in that kitchen.

Martha Hale sprang up, her hands tight together, looking at that other woman, with whom it rested. At first she could not see her eyes, for the sheriff's wife had not turned back since she turned away at that suggestion of being married to the law. But now Mrs. Hale made her turn back. Her eyes made her turn back. Slowly, unwillingly, Mrs. Peters turned her head until her eyes met the eyes of the other woman. There was a moment when they held each other in a steady, burning look in which there was no evasion nor flinching. Then Martha Hale's eyes pointed the way to the basket in which was hidden the thing that would make certain the conviction of the other woman — that woman who was not there and yet who had been there with them all through that hour.

For a moment, Mrs. Peters did not move. And then she did it. With a rush forward, she threw back the quilt pieces, got the box, tried to put it in her handbag. It was too big. Desperately she opened it, started to take the bird out. But there she broke — she could not touch the bird. She stood there helpless, foolish.

There was the sound of a knob turning in the inner door. Martha Hale snatched the box from the sheriff's wife, and got it in the pocket of her big coat just as the sheriff and the county attorney came back into the kitchen.

"Well, Henry," said the county attorney facetiously, "at least we found out that she was not going to quilt it. She was going to — what is it you call it, ladies?"

Mrs. Hale's hand was against the pocket of her coat.

"We call it — knot it, Mr. Henderson."

1920

*Sherwood Anderson*

# The Other Woman

FROM *The Little Review*

"I AM IN LOVE with my wife," he said — a superfluous remark, as I had not questioned his attachment to the woman he had married. We walked for ten minutes and then he said it again. I turned to look at him. He began to talk and told me the tale I am now about to set down.

The thing he had on his mind happened during what must have been the most eventful week of his life. He was to be married on Friday afternoon. On Friday of the week before he got a telegram announcing his appointment to a government position. Something else happened that made him very proud and glad. In secret he was in the habit of writing verses and during the year before several of them had been printed in poetry magazines. One of the societies that give prizes for what they think the best poems published during the year put his name at the head of their list. The story of his triumph was printed in the newspapers of his home city, and one of them also printed his picture.

As might have been expected, he was excited and in a rather highly strung nervous state all during that week. Almost every evening he went to call on his fiancée, the daughter of a judge. When he got there the house was filled with people and many letters, telegrams and packages were being received. He stood a little to one side and men and women kept coming to speak with him. They congratulated him upon his success in getting the government position and on his achievement as a poet. Everyone seemed to be praising him, and when he went home to bed he could not sleep. On Wednesday evening he went to the theatre and it seemed to him that people all over the house recognized him. Everyone nodded and smiled. After the first act five or six men and two women left their seats to gather about him. A little group was formed. Strangers sitting along the same row of seats stretched their necks and looked. He had never received so much attention before, and now a fever of expectancy took possession of him.

As he explained when he told me of his experience, it was for him an altogether abnormal time. He felt like one floating in air. When he got into bed after seeing so many people and hearing so many words of praise his head whirled round and round. When he closed his eyes a crowd of people invaded his room. It seemed as though the minds of all the people of his city were centered on himself. The most absurd fancies took possession of him. He imagined himself riding in a carriage through the streets of a city. Windows were thrown open and people ran out at the doors of houses. "There he is. That's him," they shouted, and at the words a glad cry arose. The carriage drove into a street blocked with people. A hundred thousand pairs of eyes looked up at him. "There you are! What a fellow you have managed to make of yourself!" the eyes seemed to be saying.

My friend could not explain whether the excitement of the people was due to the fact that he had written a new poem or whether, in his new government position, he had performed some notable act. The apartment where he lived at that time was on a street perched along the top of a cliff far out at the edge of the city and from his bedroom window he could look down over trees and factory roofs to a river. As he could not sleep and as the fancies that kept crowding in upon him only made him more excited, he got out of bed and tried to think.

As would be natural under such circumstances, he tried to control his thoughts, but when he sat by the window and was wide awake a most unexpected and humiliating thing happened. The night was clear and fine. There was a moon. He wanted to dream of the woman who was to be his wife, think out lines for noble poems or make plans that would affect his career. Much to his surprise his mind refused to do anything of the sort.

At a corner of the street where he lived there was a small cigar store and newspaper stand run by a fat man of forty and his wife, a small active woman with bright grey eyes. In the morning he stopped there to buy a paper before going down to the city. Sometimes he saw only the fat man, but often the man had disappeared and the woman waited on him. She was, as he assured me at least twenty times in telling me his tale, a very ordinary person with nothing special or notable about her, but for some reason he could not explain being in her presence stirred him profoundly. During that week in the midst of his distraction she was the only person he knew who stood out clear and distinct in his mind. When he wanted so much to think noble thoughts, he could think only of her. Before he knew what was happening his imagination had taken hold of the notion of having a love affair with the woman.

"I could not understand myself," he declared, in telling me the story. "At night, when the city was quiet and when I should have been asleep, I thought about her all the time. After two or three days of that sort of thing the consciousness of her got into my daytime thoughts. I was terribly muddled. When I went to see the woman who is now my wife I found that my love for her was in no way affected by my vagrant thoughts. There was but one woman in the world I wanted to live with me and to be my comrade in undertaking to improve my own character and my position in the world, but for the moment, you see, I wanted this other woman to be in my arms. She had worked her way into my being. On all sides people were saying I was a big man who would do big things, and there I was. That evening when I went to the theatre I walked home because I knew I would be unable to sleep, and to satisfy the annoying impulse in myself I went and stood on the sidewalk before the tobacco shop. It was a two story building, and I knew the woman lived upstairs with her husband. For a long time I stood in the darkness with my body pressed against the wall of the building and then I thought of the two of them up there, no doubt in bed together. That made me furious.

"Then I grew more furious at myself. I went home and got into bed shaken with anger. There are certain books of verse and some prose writings that have always moved me deeply, and so I put several books on a table by my bed.

"The voices in the books were like the voices of the dead. I did not hear them. The words printed on the lines would not penetrate into my consciousness. I tried to think of the woman I loved, but her figure had also become something far away, something with which I for the moment seemed to have nothing to do. I rolled and tumbled about in the bed. It was a miserable experience.

"On Thursday morning I went into the store. There stood the woman alone. I think she knew how I felt. Perhaps she had been thinking of me as I had been thinking of her. A doubtful hesitating smile played about the corners of her mouth. She had on a dress made of cheap cloth, and there was a tear on the shoulder. She must have been ten years older than myself. When I tried to put my pennies on the glass counter behind which she stood my hand trembled so that the pennies made a sharp rattling noise. When I spoke the voice that came out of my throat did not sound like anything that had ever belonged to me. It barely arose above a thick whisper. 'I want you,' I said. 'I want you very much. Can't you run away from your husband? Come to me at my apartment at seven tonight.'

"The woman did come to my apartment at seven. That morning she did not say anything at all. For a minute perhaps we stood looking at each other. I had forgotten everything in the world but just her. Then she nodded her head and I went away. Now that I think of it I cannot remember a word I ever heard her say. She came to my apartment at seven and it was dark. You must understand this was in the month of October. I had not lighted a light and I had sent my servant away.

"During that day I was no good at all. Several men came to see me at my office, but I got all muddled up in trying to talk with them. They attributed my rattle-headedness to my approaching marriage and went away laughing.

"It was on that morning, just the day before my marriage, that I got a long and very beautiful letter from my fiancée. During the night before she also had been unable to sleep and had got out of bed to write the letter. Everything she said in it was very sharp and real, but she herself, as a living thing, seemed to have receded into the distance. It seemed to me that she was like a bird, flying far away in distant skies, and I was like a perplexed bare-footed boy standing in the dusty road before a farm house and looking at her receding figure. I wonder if you will understand what I mean?

"In regard to the letter. In it she, the awakening woman, poured out her heart. She of course knew nothing of life, but she was a woman. She lay, I suppose, in her bed feeling nervous and wrought up as I had been doing. She realized that a great change was about to take place in her life and was glad and afraid too. There she lay thinking of it all. Then she got out of bed and began talking to me on the bit of paper. She told me how afraid she was and how glad too. Like most young women she had heard things whispered. In the letter she was very sweet and fine. 'For a long time, after we are married, we will forget we are a man and woman,' she wrote. 'We will be human beings. You must remember that I am ignorant and often I will be very stupid. You must love me and be very patient and kind. When I know more, when after a long time you have taught me the way of life, I will try to repay you. I will love you tenderly and passionately. The possibility of that is in me, or I would not want to marry at all. I am afraid but I am also happy. O, I am so glad our marriage time is near at hand.'

"Now you see clearly enough into what a mess I had got. In my office, after I read my fiancée's letter, I became at once very resolute and strong. I remember that I got out of my chair and walked about, proud of the fact that I was to be the husband of so noble a woman. Right away I felt concerning her as I had been feeling about myself before I found out what a weak thing I was. To be sure I took a strong resolution that I would not be weak. At nine that evening I had planned to run in to see my fiancée. 'I'm all right now,' I said to myself. 'The beauty of her character has saved me from myself. I will go home now and send the other woman away.' In the morning I had telephoned to my servant and told him that I did not want him to be at the apartment that evening and I now picked up the telephone to tell him to stay at home.

"Then a thought came to me. 'I will not want him there in any event,' I told myself. 'What will he think when he sees a woman coming to my place on the evening before the day I am to be married?' I put the telephone down and prepared to go home. 'If I want my servant out of the apartment it is because I do not want him to hear me talk with the woman. I cannot be rude to her. I will have to make some kind of an explanation,' I said to myself.

"The woman came at seven o'clock, and, as you may have guessed, I let her in and forgot the resolution I had made. It is likely I never had any intention of doing anything else. There was a bell on my door, but she did not ring, but knocked very softly. It seems to me that everything she did that evening was soft and quiet but very determined and quick. Do I make myself clear? When she came I was standing just within the door, where I had been standing and waiting for a half hour. My hands were trembling as they had trembled in the morning when her eyes looked at me and when I tried to put the pennies on the counter in the store. When I opened the door she stepped quickly in and I took her into my arms. We stood together in the darkness. My hands no longer trembled. I felt very happy and strong.

"Although I have tried to make everything clear I have not told you what the woman I married is like. I have emphasized, you see, the other woman. I make the blind statement that I love my wife, and to a man of your shrewdness that means nothing at all. To tell the truth, had I not started to speak of this matter I would feel more comfortable. It is inevitable that I give you the impression that I am in love with the tobacconist's wife. That's not true. To be sure I was very conscious of her all during the week before my marriage, but after she had come to me at my apartment she went entirely out of my mind.

"Am I telling the truth? I am trying very hard to tell what happened to me. I am saying that I have not since that evening thought of the woman who came to my apartment. Now, to tell the facts of the case, that is not true. On that evening I went to my fiancée at nine, as she had asked me to do in her letter. In a kind of way I cannot explain the other woman went with me. This is what I mean — you see I had been thinking that if anything happened between me and the tobacconist's wife I would not be able to go through with my marriage. 'It is one thing or the other with me,' I had said to myself.

"As a matter of fact I went to see my beloved on that evening filled with a new faith in the outcome of our life together. I am afraid I muddle this matter in trying to tell it. A moment ago I said the other woman, the tobacconist's wife, went with me. I do not mean she went in fact. What I am trying to say is that something of her faith in her own desires and her courage in seeing things through went with me. Is that clear to you? When I got to my fiancée's house there was a crowd of people standing about. Some were relatives from distant places I had not seen before. She looked up quickly when I came into the room. My face must have been radiant. I never saw her so moved. She thought her letter had affected me deeply, and of course it had. Up she jumped and ran to meet me. She was like a glad child. Right before the people who turned and looked inquiringly at us, she said the thing that was in her mind. 'O, I am so happy,' she cried. 'You have understood. We will be two human beings. We will not have to be husband and wife.'

"As you may suppose, everyone laughed, but I did not laugh. The tears came into my eyes. I was so happy I wanted to shout. Perhaps you understand what I mean. In the office that day when I read the letter my fiancée had written I had said to myself, 'I will take care of the dear little woman.' There was something smug, you see, about that. In her house when she cried out in that way, and when everyone laughed, what I said to myself was something like this: 'We will take care of ourselves.' I whispered something of the sort into her ears. To tell you the truth I had come down off my perch. The spirit of the other woman did that to me. Before all the people gathered about I held my fiancée close and we kissed. They thought it very sweet of us to be so affected at the sight of each other. What they would have thought had they known the truth about me God only knows!

"Twice now I have said that after that evening I never thought of the other woman at all. That is partially true but sometimes in the evening when I am walking alone in the street or in the park as we are walking now, and when evening comes softly and quickly as it has come tonight, the feeling of her comes sharply into my body and mind. After that one meeting I never saw her again. On the next day I was married and I have never gone back into her street. Often however as I am walking along as I am doing now, a quick sharp earthy feeling takes possession of me. It is as though I were a seed in the ground and the warm rains of the spring had come. It is as though I were not a man but a tree.

"And now you see I am married and everything is all right. My marriage is to me a very beautiful fact. If you were to say that my marriage is not a happy one I could call you a liar and be speaking the absolute truth. I have tried to tell you about this other woman. There is a kind of relief in speaking of her. I have never done it before. I wonder why I was so silly as to be afraid that I would give you the impression I am not in love with my wife. If I did not instinctively trust your understanding I would not have spoken. As the matter stands I have a little stirred myself up. To-night I shall think of the other woman. That sometimes occurs. It will happen after I have gone to bed. My wife sleeps in the next room to mine and the door is always left open. There will be a moon to-night, and when there is a moon long streaks of light fall on her bed. I shall awake at midnight to-night. She will be lying asleep with one arm thrown over her head.

"What is that I am talking about? A man does not speak of his wife lying in bed. What I am trying to say is that, because of this talk, I shall think of the other woman to-night. My thoughts will not take the form they did the week before I was married. I will wonder what has become of the woman. For a moment I will again feel myself holding her close. I will think that for an hour I was closer to her than I have ever been to anyone else. Then I will think of the time when I will be as close as that to my wife. She is still, you see, an awakening woman. For a moment I will close my eyes and the quick, shrewd, determined eyes of that other woman will look into mine. My head will swim and then I will quickly open my eyes and see again the dear woman with whom I have undertaken to live out my life. Then I will sleep and when I awake in the morning it will be as it was that evening when I walked out of my dark apartment after having had the most notable experience of my life. What I mean to say, you understand, is that, for me, when I awake, the other woman will be utterly gone."

1922

*Ring Lardner*

....................................................................................................................

# The Golden Honeymoon

FROM *The Cosmopolitan*

MOTHER SAYS that when I start talking I never know when to stop. But I tell her the only time I get a chance is when she ain't around, so I have to make the most of it. I guess the fact is neither one of us would be welcome in a Quaker meeting, but as I tell Mother, what did God give us tongues for if He didn't want we should use them? Only she says He didn't give them to us to say the same thing over and over again, like I do, and repeat myself. But I say:

"Well, Mother," I say, "when people is like you and I and been married fifty years, do you expect everything I say will be something you ain't heard me say before? But it may be new to others, as they ain't nobody else lived with me as long as you have."

So she says:

"You can bet they ain't, as they couldn't nobody else stand you that long."

"Well," I tell her, "you look pretty healthy."

"Maybe I do," she will say, "but I looked even healthier before I married you."

You can't get ahead of Mother.

Yes, sir, we was married just fifty years ago the seventeenth day of last December and my daughter and son-in-law was over from Trenton to help us celebrate the Golden Wedding. My son-in-law is John H. Kramer, the real estate man. He made $12,000 one year and is pretty well thought of around Trenton; a good, steady, hard worker. The Rotarians was after him a long time to join, but he kept telling them his home was his club. But Edie finally made him join. That's my daughter.

Well, anyway, they come over to help us celebrate the Golden Wedding and it was pretty crimpy weather and the furnace don't seem to heat up no more like it used to and Mother made the remark that she hoped this winter wouldn't be as cold as the last, referring to the winter previous. So Edie said if she was us, and nothing to keep us home, she certainly wouldn't spend no more winters up here and why didn't we just shut off the water and close up the house and go down to Tampa, Florida? You know we was there four winters ago and staid five weeks, but it cost us over three hundred and fifty dollars for hotel bill alone. So Mother said we wasn't going no place to be robbed. So my son-in-law spoke up and said that Tampa wasn't the only place in the South, and besides we didn't have to stop at no high price hotel but could rent us a couple rooms and board out somewheres, and he had heard that St. Petersburg, Florida, was *the* spot and if we said the word he would write down there and make inquiries.

Well, to make a long story short, we decided to do it and Edie said it would be our Golden Honeymoon and for a present my son-in-law paid the difference between a section and a compartment so as we could have a compartment and have more privatecy. In a compartment you have an upper and lower berth just like the regular sleeper, but it is a shut in room by itself and got a wash bowl. The car we went in was all compartments and no regular berths at all. It was all compartments.

We went to Trenton the night before and staid at my daughter and son-in-law and we left Trenton the next afternoon at 3.23 P.M.

This was the twelfth day of January. Mother set facing the front of the train, as it makes her giddy to ride backwards. I set facing her, which does not affect me. We reached North Philadelphia at 4.03 P.M. and we reached West Philadelphia at 4.14, but did not go into Broad Street. We reached Baltimore at 6.30 and Washington, D.C., at 7.25. Our train laid over in Washington two hours till another train come along to pick us up and I got out and strolled up the platform and into the Union Station. When I come back, our car had been switched on to another track, but I remembered the name of it, the La Belle, as I had once visited my aunt out in Oconomowoc, Wisconsin, where there was a lake of that name, so I had no difficulty in getting located. But Mother had nearly fretted herself sick for fear I would be left.

"Well," I said, "I would of followed you on the next train."

"You couldn't of," said Mother, and she pointed out that she had the money.

"Well," I said, "we are in Washington and I could of borrowed from the United States Treasury. I would of pretended I was an Englishman."

Mother caught the point and laughed heartily.

Our train pulled out of Washington at 9.40 P.M. and Mother and I turned in early, I taking the upper. During the night we passed through the green fields of old Virginia, though it was too dark to tell if they was green or what color. When we got up in the morning, we was at Fayetteville, North Carolina. We had breakfast in the dining car and after breakfast I got in conversation with the man in the next compartment to ours. He was from Lebanon, New Hampshire, and a man about eighty years of age. His wife was with him and two unmarried daughters and I made the remark that I should think the four of them would be crowded in one compartment, but he said they had made the trip every winter for fifteen years and knowed how to keep out of each other's way. He said they was bound for Tarpon Springs.

We reached Charleston, South Carolina, at 12.50 P.M. and arrived at Savannah, Georgia, at 4.20. We reached Jacksonville, Florida, at 8.45 P.M. and had an hour and a quarter to lay over there, but Mother made a fuss about me getting off the train, so we had the darkey make up our berths and retired before we left Jacksonville. I didn't sleep good as the train done a lot of hemming and hawing, and Mother never sleeps good on a train as she says she is always worrying that I will fall out. She says she would rather have the upper herself, as then she would not have to worry about me, but I tell her I can't take the risk of having it get out that I allowed my wife to sleep in an upper berth. It would make talk.

We was up in the morning in time to see our friends from New Hampshire get off at Tarpon Springs, which we reached at 6.53 A.M.

Several of our fellow passengers got off at Clearwater and some at Belleair, where the train backs right up to the door of the mammoth hotel. Belleair is the winter headquarters for the golf dudes and everybody that got off there had their bag of sticks, as many as ten and twelve in a bag. Women and all. When I was a young man we called it shinny and only needed one club to play with and about one game of it would of been a-plenty for some of these dudes, the way we played it.

The train pulled into St. Petersburg at 8.20 and when we got off the train you would think they was a riot, what with all the darkeys barking for the different hotels.

I said to Mother, I said:

"It is a good thing we have got a place picked out to go to and don't have to choose a hotel, as it would be hard to choose amongst them if every one of them is the best."

She laughed.

We found a jitney and I give him the address of the room my son-in-law had got for us and soon we was there and introduced ourselves to the lady that owns the house, a young widow about forty-eight years of age. She showed us our room, which was light and airy with a comfortable bed and bureau and washstand. It was twelve dollars a week, but the location was good, only three blocks from Williams Park.

St. Pete is what folks calls the town, though they also call it the Sunshine City, as they claim they's no other place in the country where they's fewer days when Old Sol don't smile down on Mother Earth, and one of the newspapers gives away all their copies free every day when the sun don't shine. They claim to of only give them away some sixty-odd times in the last eleven years. Another nickname they have got for the town is "the Poor Man's Palm Beach," but I guess they's men that comes there that could borrow as much from the bank as some of the Willie boys over to the other Palm Beach.

During our stay we paid a visit to the Lewis Tent City, which is the headquarters for the Tin Can Tourists. But maybe you ain't heard about them. Well, they are an organization that takes their vacation trips by auto and carries everything with them. That is, they bring along their tents to sleep in and cook in and they don't patronize no hotels or cafeterias, but they have got to be bona fide auto campers or they can't belong to the organization.

They tell me they's over 200,000 members to it and they call themselves the Tin Canners on account of most of their food being put up in tin cans. One couple we seen in the Tent City was a couple from Brady, Texas, named Mr. and Mrs. Pence, which the old man is over eighty years of age and they had came in their auto all the way from home, a distance of 1,641 miles. They took five weeks for the trip, Mr. Pence driving the entire distance.

The Tin Canners hails from every State in the Union and in the summer time they visit places like New England and the Great Lakes region, but in the winter the most of them comes to Florida and scatters all over the State. While we was down there, they was a national convention of them at Gainesville, Florida, and they elected a Fredonia, New York man as their president. His title is Royal Tin Can Opener of the World. They have got a song wrote up which everybody has got to learn it before they are a member:

> The tin can forever! Hurrah, boys! Hurrah!
> Up with the tin can! Down with the foe!

> We will rally round the campfire, we'll rally once again,
> Shouting, "We auto camp forever!"

That is something like it. And the members has also got to have a tin can fastened on to the front of their machine.

I asked Mother how she would like to travel around that way and she said:

"Fine, but not with an old rattle brain like you driving."

"Well," I said, "I am eight years younger than this Mr. Pence who drove here from Texas."

"Yes," she said, "but he is old enough to not be skittish."

You can't get ahead of Mother.

Well, one of the first things we done in St. Petersburg was to go to the Chamber of Commerce and register our names and where we was from as they's great rivalry amongst the different States in regards to the number of their citizens visiting in town and of course our little State don't stand much of a show, but still every little bit helps, as the fella says. All and all, the man told us, they was eleven thousand names registered, Ohio leading with some fifteen hundred-odd and New York State next with twelve hundred. Then come Michigan, Pennsylvania and so on down, with one man each from Cuba and Nevada.

The first night we was there, they was a meeting of the New York–New Jersey Society at the Congregational Church and a man from Ogdensburg, New York State, made the talk. His subject was Rainbow Chasing. He is a Rotarian and a very convicting speaker, though I forget his name.

Our first business, of course, was to find a place to eat and after trying several places we run on to a cafeteria on Central Avenue that suited us up and down. We eat pretty near all our meals there and it averaged about two dollars per day for the two of us, but the food was well cooked and everything nice and clean. A man don't mind paying the price if things is clean and well cooked.

On the third day of February, which is Mother's birthday, we spread ourselves and eat supper at the Poinsettia Hotel and they charged us seventy-five cents for a sirloin steak that wasn't hardly big enough for one.

I said to Mother: "Well," I said, "I guess it's a good thing every day ain't your birthday or we would be in the poorhouse."

"No," says Mother, "because if every day was my birthday, I would be old enough by this time to of been in my grave long ago."

You can't get ahead of Mother.

In the hotel they had a cardroom where they was several men and ladies playing five hundred and this new fangled whist bridge. We also seen a place where they was dancing, so I asked Mother would she like to trip the light fantastic toe and she said no, she was too old to squirm like you have got to do now days. We watched some of the young folks at it awhile till Mother got disgusted and said we would have to see a good movie to take the taste out of our mouth. Mother is a great movie heroyne and we go twice a week here at home.

But I want to tell you about the Park. The second day we was there we visited the Park, which is a good deal like the one in Tampa, only bigger, and they's more fun goes on here every day than you could shake a stick at. In the middle they's a big bandstand and chairs for the folks to set and listen to the concerts, which they give you music for all tastes, from Dixie up to classical pieces like Hearts and Flowers.

Then all around they's places marked off for different sports and games — chess and checkers and dominoes for folks that enjoys those kind of games, and roque and horseshoes for the nimbler ones. I used to pitch a pretty fair shoe myself, but ain't done much of it in the last twenty years.

Well, anyway, we bought a membership ticket in the club which costs one dollar for the season, and they tell me that up to a couple years ago it was fifty cents, but they had to raise it to keep out the riffraff.

Well, Mother and I put in a great day watching the pitchers and she wanted I should get in the game, but I told her I was all out of practice and would make a fool of myself, though I seen several men pitching who I guess I could take their measure without no practice. However, they was some good pitchers, too, and one boy from Akron, Ohio, who could certainly throw a pretty shoe. They told me it looked like he would win the championship of the United States in the February tournament. We come away a few days before they held that and I never did hear if he win. I forget his name, but he was a clean cut young fella and he has got a brother in Cleveland that's a Rotarian.

Well, we just stood around and watched the different games for two or three days and finally I set down in a checker game with a man named Weaver from Danville, Illinois. He was a pretty fair checker player, but he wasn't no match for me, and I hope that don't sound like bragging. But I always could hold my own on a checkerboard and the folks around here will tell you the same thing. I played with this Weaver pretty near all morning for two or three mornings and he beat me one game and the only other time it looked like he had a chance, the noon whistle blowed and we had to quit and go to dinner.

While I was playing checkers, Mother would set and listen to the band, as she loves music, classical or no matter what kind, but anyway she was setting there one day and between selections the woman next to her opened up a conversation. She was a woman about Mother's own age, seventy or seventy-one, and finally she asked Mother's name and Mother told her her name and where she was from and Mother asked her the same question, and who do you think the woman was?

Well, sir, it was the wife of Frank M. Hartsell, the man who was engaged to Mother till I stepped in and cut him out, fifty-two years ago!

Yes, sir!

You can imagine Mother's surprise! And Mrs. Hartsell was surprised, too, when Mother told her she had once been friends with her husband, though Mother didn't say how close friends they had been, or that Mother and I was the cause of Hartsell going out West. But that's what we was. Hartsell left his town a month after the engagement was broke off and ain't never been back since. He had went out to Michigan and become a veterinary, and that is where he had settled down, in Hillsdale, Michigan, and finally married his wife.

Well, Mother screwed up her courage to ask if Frank was still living and Mrs. Hartsell took her over to where they was pitching horseshoes and there was old Frank, waiting his turn. And he knowed Mother as soon as he seen her, though it was over fifty years. He said he knowed her by her eyes.

"Why, it's Lucy Frost!" he says, and he throwed down his shoes and quit the game.

Then they come over and hunted me up and I will confess I wouldn't of knowed him. Him and I is the same age to the month, but he seems to show it more, some way. He is balder for one thing. And his beard is all white, where mine has still got a streak of brown in it. The very first thing I said to him, I said:

"Well, Frank, that beard of yours makes me feel like I was back north. It looks like a regular blizzard."

"Well," he said, "I guess yourn would be just as white if you had it dry cleaned."

But Mother wouldn't stand that.

"Is that so!" she said to Frank. "Well, Charley ain't had no tobacco in his mouth for over ten years!"

And I ain't!

Well, I excused myself from the checker game and it was pretty close to noon, so we decided to all have dinner together and they was nothing for it only we must try their cafeteria on Third Avenue. It was a little more expensive than ours and not near as good, I thought. I and Mother had about the same dinner we had been having every day and our bill was $1.10. Frank's check was $1.20 for he and his wife. The same meal wouldn't of cost them more than a dollar at our place.

After dinner we made them come up to our house and we all set in the parlor, which the young woman had give us the use of to entertain company. We begun talking over old times and Mother said she was a-scared Mrs. Hartsell would find it tiresome listening to we three talk over old times, but as it turned out they wasn't much chance for nobody else to talk with Mrs. Hartsell in the company. I have heard lots of women that could go it, but Hartsell's wife takes the cake of all the women I ever seen. She told us the family history of everybody in the State of Michigan and bragged for a half hour about her son, who she said is in the drug business in Grand Rapids, and a Rotarian.

When I and Hartsell could get a word in edgeways we joked one another back and forth and I chafed him about being a horse doctor.

"Well, Frank," I said, "you look pretty prosperous, so I suppose they's been plenty of glanders around Hillsdale."

"Well," he said, "I've managed to make more than a fair living. But I've worked pretty hard."

"Yes," I said, "and I suppose you get called out all hours of the night to attend births and so on."

Mother made me shut up.

Well, I thought they wouldn't never go home and I and Mother was in misery trying to keep awake, as the both of us generally always takes a nap after dinner. Finally they went, after we had made an engagement to meet them in the Park the next morning, and Mrs. Hartsell also invited us to come to their place the next night and play five hundred. But she had forgot that they was a meeting of the Michigan Society that evening, so it was not till two evenings later that we had our first card game.

Hartsell and his wife lived in a house on Third Avenue North and had a private setting room besides their bedroom. Mrs. Hartsell couldn't quit talking about their private setting room like it was something wonderful. We played cards with them, with Mother and Hartsell partners against his wife and I. Mrs. Hartsell is a miserable card player and we certainly got the worst of it.

After the game she brought out a dish of oranges and we had to pretend it was just what we wanted, though oranges down there is like a young man's whiskers; you enjoy them at first, but they get to be a pesky nuisance.

We played cards again the next night at our place with the same partners and I and Mrs. Hartsell was beat again. Mother and Hartsell was full of compliments for each other on what a good team they made, but the both of them knowed well enough where the secret of their success laid. I guess all and all we must of played ten different evenings and they was only one night when Mrs. Hartsell and I come out ahead. And that one night wasn't no fault of hern.

When we had been down there about two weeks, we spent one evening as their guest in the Congregational Church, at a social give by the Michigan Society. A talk was made by a man named Bitting of Detroit, Michigan, on How I was Cured of Story Telling. He is a big man in the Rotarians and give a witty talk.

A woman named Mrs. Oxford rendered some selections which Mrs. Hartsell said was grand opera music, but whatever they was my daughter Edie could of give her cards and spades and not made such a hullaballoo about it neither.

Then they was a ventriloquist from Grand Rapids and a young woman about forty-five years of age that mimicked different kinds of birds. I whispered to Mother that they all sounded like a chicken, but she nudged me to shut up.

After the show we stopped in a drug store and I set up the refreshments and it was pretty close to ten o'clock before we finally turned in. Mother and I would of preferred tending the movies, but Mother said we mustn't offend Mrs. Hartsell, though I asked her had we came to Florida to enjoy ourselves or to just not offend an old chatterbox from Michigan.

I felt sorry for Hartsell one morning. The women folks both had an engagement down to the chiropodist's and I run across Hartsell in the Park and he foolishly offered to play me checkers.

It was him that suggested it, not me, and I guess he repented himself before we had played one game. But he was too stubborn to give up and set there while I beat him game after game and the worst part of it was that a crowd of folks had got in the habit of watching me play and there they all was, looking on, and finally they seen what a fool Frank was making of himself, and they began to chafe him and pass remarks. Like one of them said:

"Who ever told you you was a checker player!"

And:

"You might maybe be good for tiddle-de-winks, but not checkers!"

I almost felt like letting him beat me a couple games. But the crowd would of knowed it was a put up job.

Well, the women folks joined us in the Park and I wasn't going to mention our little game, but Hartsell told about it himself and admitted he wasn't no match for me.

"Well," said Mrs. Hartsell, "checkers ain't much of a game anyway, is it?" She said: "It's more of a children's game, ain't it? At least, I know my boy's children used to play it a good deal."

"Yes, ma'am," I said. "It's a children's game the way your husband plays it, too."

Mother wanted to smooth things over, so she said:

"Maybe they's other games where Frank can beat you."

"Yes," said Mrs. Hartsell, "and I bet he could beat you pitching horse-shoes."

"Well," I said, "I would give him a chance to try, only I ain't pitched a shoe in over sixteen years."

"Well," said Hartsell, "I ain't played checkers in twenty years."

"You ain't never played it," I said.

"Anyway," says Frank, "Lucy and I is your master at five hundred."

Well, I could of told him why that was, but had decency enough to hold my tongue.

It had got so now that he wanted to play cards every night and when I or Mother wanted to go to a movie, why one of us would have to pretend we had a headache and then trust to goodness that they wouldn't see us sneak into the theater. I don't mind playing cards when my partner keeps their mind on the game, but you take a woman like Hartsell's wife and how can they play cards when they have got to stop every couple seconds and brag about their son in Grand Rapids?

Well, the New York–New Jersey Society announced that they was going to give a social evening too and I said to Mother, I said:

"Well, that is one evening when we will have an excuse not to play five hundred."

"Yes," she said, "but we will have to ask Frank and his wife to go to the social with us as they asked us to go to the Michigan social."

"Well," I said, "I had rather stay home than drag that chatterbox everywheres we go."

So Mother said:

"You are getting too cranky. Maybe she does talk a little too much but she is good hearted. And Frank is always good company."

So I said:

"I suppose if he is such good company you wished you had of married him."

Mother laughed and said I sounded like I was jealous. Jealous of a cow doctor!

Anyway we had to drag them along to the social and I will say that we give them a much better entertainment than they had given us.

Judge Lane of Paterson made a fine talk on business conditions and a Mrs. Newell of Westfield imitated birds, only you could really tell what they was the way she done it. Two young women from Red Bank sung a choral selection and we clapped them back and they gave us Home to Our Mountains and Mother and Mrs. Hartsell both had tears in their eyes. And Hartsell, too.

Well, some way or another the chairman got wind that I was there and asked me to make a talk and I wasn't even going to get up, but Mother made me, so I got up and said:

"Ladies and gentlemen," I said. "I didn't expect to be called on for a speech on an occasion like this or no other occasion as I do not set myself up as a speech maker, so will have to do the best I can, which I often say is the best anybody can do."

Then I told them the story about Pat and the motorcycle, using the brogue, and it seemed to tickle them and I told them one or two other stories, but altogether I wasn't on my feet more than twenty or twenty-five minutes and you ought to of heard the clapping and hollering when I set down. Even Mrs. Hartsell admitted that I am quite a speechifier and said if I ever went to Grand Rapids, Michigan, her son would make me talk to the Rotarians.

When it was over, Hartsell wanted we should go to their place and play cards, but his wife reminded him that it was after 9.30 P.M., rather a late hour to start a card game, but he had went crazy on the subject of cards, probably because he didn't have to play partners with his wife. Anyway, we got rid of them and went home to bed.

It was the next morning, when we met over to the Park, that Mrs. Hartsell made the remark that she wasn't getting no exercise so I suggested that why didn't she take part in the roque game.

She said she had not played a game of roque in twenty years, but if Mother would play she would play. Well, at first Mother wouldn't hear of it, but finally consented, more to please Mrs. Hartsell than anything else.

Well, they had a game with a Mrs. Ryan from Eagle, Nebraska, and a young Mrs. Morse from Rutland, Vermont, who Mother had met down to the chiropodist's. Well, Mother couldn't hit a flea and they all laughted at her and I couldn't help from laughing at her myself and finally she quit and said her back was too lame to stoop over. So they got another lady and kept on playing and soon Mrs. Hartsell was the one everybody was laughing at, as she had a long shot to hit the black ball, and as she made the effort her teeth fell out on to the court. I never seen a woman so flustered in my life. And I never heard so much laughing, only Mrs. Hartsell didn't join in and she was madder than a hornet and wouldn't play no more, so the game broke up.

Mrs. Hartsell went home without speaking to nobody, but Hartsell staid around and finally he said to me, he said:

"Well, I played you checkers the other day and you beat me bad and now what do you say if you and me play a game of horseshoes?"

I told him I hadn't pitched a shoe in sixteen years, but Mother said:

"Go ahead and play. You used to be good at it and maybe it will come back to you."

Well, to make a long story short, I give in. I oughtn't to of never tried it, as I hadn't pitched a shoe in sixteen years, and I only done it to humor Hartsell.

Before we started, Mother patted me on the back and told me to do my best, so we started in and I seen right off that I was in for it, as I hadn't pitched a shoe in sixteen years and didn't have my distance. And besides, the plating had wore off the shoes so that they was points right where they stuck into my thumb and I hadn't throwed more than two or three times when my thumb was raw and it pretty near killed me to hang on to the shoe, let alone pitch it.

Well, Hartsell throws the awkwardest shoe I ever seen pitched and to see him pitch you wouldn't think he would ever come nowheres near, but he is also the luckiest pitcher I ever seen and he made some pitches where the shoe lit five and six feet short and then schoonered up and was a ringer. They's no use trying to beat that kind of luck.

They was a pretty fair size crowd watching us and four or five other ladies besides Mother, and it seems like, when Hartsell pitches, he has got to chew and it kept the ladies on the anxious seat as he don't seem to care which way he is facing when he leaves go.

You would think a man as old as him would of learnt more manners.

Well, to make a long story short, I was just beginning to get my distance when I had to give up on account of my thumb, which I showed it to Hartsell and he seen I couldn't go on, as it was raw and bleeding. Even if I could of stood it to go on myself, Mother wouldn't of allowed it after she seen my thumb. So anyway I quit and Hartsell said the score was nineteen to six, but I don't know what it was. Or don't care, neither.

Well, Mother and I went home and I said I hoped we was through with the Hartsells as I was sick and tired of them, but it seemed like she had promised we would go over to their house that evening for another game of their everlasting cards.

Well, my thumb was giving me considerable pain and I felt kind of out of sorts and I guess maybe I forgot myself, but anyway, when we was about through playing Hartsell made the remark that he wouldn't never lose a game of cards if he could always have Mother for a partner.

So I said:

"Well, you had a chance fifty years ago to always have her for a partner, but you wasn't man enough to keep her."

I was sorry the minute I had said it and Hartsell didn't know what to say and for once his wife couldn't say nothing. Mother tried to smooth things over by making the remark that I must of had something stronger than tea or I wouldn't talk so silly. But Mrs. Hartsell had froze up like an iceberg and hardly said good night to us and I bet her and Frank put in a pleasant hour after we was gone.

As we was leaving, Mother said to him: "Never mind Charley's nonsense, Frank. He is just mad because you beat him all hollow pitching horseshoes and playing cards."

She said that to make up for my slip, but at the same time she certainly riled me. I tried to keep ahold of myself, but as soon as we was out of the house she had to open up the subject and begun to scold me for the break I had made.

Well, I wasn't in no mood to be scolded. So I said:

"I guess he is such a wonderful pitcher and card player that you wished you had married him."

"Well," she said, "at least he ain't a baby to give up pitching because his thumb has got a few scratches."

"And how about you," I said, "making a fool of yourself on the roque court and then pretending your back is lame and you can't play no more!"

"Yes," she said, "but when you hurt your thumb I didn't laugh at you, and why did you laugh at me when I sprained my back?"

"Who could help from laughing!" I said.

"Well," she said, "Frank Hartsell didn't laugh."

"Well," I said, "why didn't you marry him?"

"Well," said Mother, "I almost wished I had!"

"And I wished so, too!" I said.

"I'll remember that!" said Mother, and that's the last word she said to me for two days.

We seen the Hartsells the next day in the Park and I was willing to apologize, but they just nodded to us. And a couple days later we heard they had left for Orlando, where they have got relatives.

I wished they had went there in the first place.

Mother and I made it up setting on a bench.

"Listen, Charley," she said. "This is our Golden Honeymoon and we don't want the whole thing spoilt with a silly old quarrel."

"Well," I said, "did you mean that about wishing you had married Hartsell?"

"Of course not," she said, "that is, if you didn't mean that you wished I had, too."

So I said:

"I was just tired and all wrought up. I thank God you chose me instead of him as they's no other woman in the world who I could of lived with all these years."

"How about Mrs. Hartsell?" says Mother.

"Good gracious!" I said. "Imagine being married to a woman that plays five hundred like she does and drops her teeth on the roque court!"

"Well," said Mother, "it wouldn't be no worse than being married to a man that expectorates towards ladies and is such a fool in a checker game."

So I put my arm around her shoulder and she stroked my hand and I guess we got kind of spooney.

They was two days left of our stay in St. Petersburg and the next to the last day Mother introduced me to a Mrs. Kendall from Kingston, Rhode Island, who she had met at the chiropodist's.

Mrs. Kendall made us acquainted with her husband, who is in the grocery business. They have got two sons and five grandchildren and one great-grandchild. One of their sons lives in Providence and is way up in the Elks as well as a Rotarian.

We found them very congenial people and we played cards with them the last two nights we was there. They was both experts and I only wished we had met them sooner instead of running into the Hartsells. But the Kendalls will be there again next winter and we will see more of them, that is, if we decide to make the trip again.

We left the Sunshine City on the eleventh day of February, at 11 A.M. This give us a day trip through Florida and we seen all the country we had passed through at night on the way down.

We reached Jacksonville at 7 P.M. and pulled out of there at 8.10 P.M. We reached Fayetteville, North Carolina, at nine o'clock the following morning, and reached Washington, D.C., at 6.30 P.M., laying over there half an hour.

We reached Trenton at 11.01 P.M. and had wired ahead to my daughter and son-in-law and they met us at the train and we went to their house and they put us up for the night. John would of made us stay up all night, telling about our trip, but Edie said we must be tired and made us go to bed. That's my daughter.

The next day we took our train for home and arrived safe and sound, having been gone just one month and a day.

Here comes Mother, so I guess I better shut up.

## Jean Toomer

........................................................................................................................

# Blood-Burning Moon

FROM *Prairie*

1

UP FROM THE SKELETON stone walls, up from the rotting floor boards
and the solid hand-hewn beams of oak of the pre-war cotton factory,
dusk came. Up from the dusk the full moon came. Glowing like a fired
pine-knot it illumined the great door and soft showered the Negro
shanties aligned along the single street of factory town. The full moon
in the great door was an omen. Negro women improvised songs against
its spell.

Louisa sang as she came over the crest of the hill from the white folk's
kitchen. Her skin was the color of oak leaves on young trees in fall. Her
breasts, firm and up-pointed like ripe acorns. And her singing had the
low murmur of winds in fig trees. Bob Stone, younger son of the people
she worked for, loved her. By the way the world reckons things he had
won her. By measure of that warm glow which came into her mind at
thought of him, he had won her. Tom Burwell, whom the whole town
called Big Boy, also loved her. But working in the fields all day, and far
away from her, gave him no chance to show it. Though often enough of
evenings he had tried to. Somehow, he never got along. Strong as he was
with hands upon the axe or plow, he found it difficult to hold her. Or so
he thought. But the fact was that he held her to factory town more
firmly than he thought for. His black balanced, and pulled against the
white of Stone, when she thought of them. And her mind was vaguely
upon them as she came over the crest of the hill, coming from the white
folk's kitchen. As she sang softly at the veil face of the full moon.

A strange stir was in her. Indolently she tried to fix upon Bob or Tom
as the cause of it. To meet Bob in the canebrake as she was going to do
an hour or so later, was nothing new. And Tom's proposal which she felt

on its way to her could be indefinitely put off. Separately, there was no unusual significance to either one. But for some reason they jumbled when her eyes gazed vacantly at the rising moon. And from the jumble came the stir that was strangely within her. Her lips trembled. The slow rhythm of her song grew agitant and restless. Rusty black and tan spotted hounds, lying in the dark corners of porches or prowling around back yards, put their noses in the air and caught its tremor. They began to plaintively yelp and howl. Chickens woke up, and cackled. Intermittently, all over the country-side dogs barked and roosters crowed as if heralding a weird dawn or some ungodly awakening. The women sang lustily. Their songs were cottonwads to stop their ears. Louisa came down into factory town and sank wearily upon the step before her home. The moon was rising towards a thick cloud-bank which soon would hide it.

> *Red nigger moon. Sinner!*
> *Blood-burning moon. Sinner!*
> *Come out that fact'ry door.*

2

Up from the deep dusk of a cleared spot on the edge of the forest a mellow glow arose and spread fan-wise into the low-hanging heavens. And all around the air was heavy with the scent of boiling cane. A large pile of cane-stalks lay like ribboned shadows upon the ground. A mule, harnessed to a pole, trudged lazily round and round the pivot of the grinder. Beneath a swaying oil lamp, a Negro alternately whipped out at the mule, and fed cane-stalks to the grinder. A fat boy waddled pails of fresh ground juice between the grinder and the boiling stove. Steam came from the copper boiling pan. The scent of cane came from the copper pan and drenched the forest and the hill that sloped to factory town, beneath its fragrance. It drenched the men in circle seated round the stove. Some of them chewed at the white pulp of stalks, but there was no need for them to, if all they wanted was to taste the cane. One tasted it in factory town. And from factory town one could see the soft haze thrown by the glowing stove upon the low-hanging heavens.

Old David Georgia stirred the thickening syrup with a long ladle, and ever so often drew it off. Old David Georgia tended his stove and told tales about the white folks, about moonshining and cotton picking and about sweet nigger gals, to the men who sat there about his stove to listen to him. Tom Burwell chewed cane-stalk and laughed with the others till someone mentioned Louisa. Till someone said something about Louisa and Bob Stone, about the silk stockings she must have gotten from him. Blood ran up Tom's neck hotter than the glow that flooded from the stove. He sprang up. Glared at the men and said, "She's my gal." Will Manning laughed. Tom strode over to him. Yanked him up, and knocked him to the ground. Several of Manning's friends got up to fight for him. Tom whipped out a long knife and would have cut them to shreds if they hadn't ducked into the woods. Tom had had enough. He nodded to old David Georgia and swung down the path to factory town. Just then, the dogs started barking and the roosters began to crow. Tom felt funny. Away from the fight, away from the stove, chill got to him. He shivered. He shuddered when he saw the full moon rising towards the cloud-bank. He who didn't give a godam for the fears of old women. He forced his mind to fasten on Louisa. Bob Stone. Better not be. He turned into the street and saw Louisa sitting before her home. He went towards her, ambling, touched the brim of a marvelously shaped, spotted, felt hat, said he wanted to say something to her, and then found that he didn't know what he had to say, or if he did, that he couldn't say it. He shoved his big fists in his overalls, grinned, and started to move off.

"Youall want me, Tom?"

"That's what us wants sho, Louisa."

"Well, here I am — "

"An' here I is, but that ain't ahelpin' none, all th' same."

"You wanted to say something . . . ?"

"I did that, sho. But words is like th' spots on dice; no matter how y' fumbles 'em there's times when they jes won't come. I dunno why. Seems like th' love I feels fo' yo' done stole m' tongue. I got it now. Whee! Louisa, honey, I oughtn't tell y', I feel I oughtn't cause yo' is young an' goes t' church an' I has had other gals, but Louisa I sho do love y'. Lil' gal I'se watched y' from them first days wen youall sat right here befo' yo' door befo' th' well an' sang sometimes in a way that like t' broke m' heart. I'se carried y' with me into th' fields, day after day, an' after that, an' I sho can plow when yo' is ther, an' I can pick cotton. Yassur! Come near beatin' Barlo yesterday. I sho did. Yassur! An' next year if ol'e Stone'll trust me, I'll have a farm. My own. My bales will buy yo' what y' gets from white folks now. Silk stockings, an' purple dresses — course I don't believe what some folks been whisperin' as t'how y' gets them things now. White folks always did do for niggers what they likes. An' they jes can't help alikin' yo, Louisa. Bob Stone like y'. Course he does. But not th' way folks is awhisperin'. Does he, hon?"

"I don't know what you mean, Tom."

"Course y' don't. I'se already cut two niggers. Had t' hon, t' tell 'em so. Niggers always tryin' t' make somethin' out a'nothin'. An' then besides, white folks ain't up t' them tricks so much nowadays. Godam better not be. Leastwise not with yo'. Cause I wouldn't stand f' it. Nassur."

"What would you do, Tom?"

"Cut him jes like I cut a nigger."

"No, Tom — "

"I said I would an' there ain't no mo' to it. But that ain't th' talk f' now. Sing, honey Louisa, an' while I'm listenin' t' y' I'll be makin' love."

Tom took her hand in his. Against the tough thickness of his own, hers felt soft and small. His huge body slipped down to the step beside her. The full moon sank upward into the deep purple of the cloud-bank. An old woman brought a lighted lamp and hung it on the common well whose bulky shadow squatted in the middle of the road, opposite Tom and Louisa. The old woman lifted the well-lid, took hold of the chain, and began drawing up the heavy bucket. As she did so, she sang. Figures shifted, restless-like, between lamp and window in the front rooms of the shanties. Shadows of the figures fought each other on the grey dust of the road. Figures raised the windows and joined the old woman in song. Louisa and Tom, the whole street, singing:

> *Red nigger moon. Sinner!*
> *Blood-burning moon. Sinner!*
> *Come out that fact'ry door.*

Bob Stone sauntered from his veranda out into the gloom of fir trees and magnolias. The clear white of his skin paled, and the flush of his cheeks turned purple. As if to balance this outer change, his mind became consciously a white man's. He passed the house with its huge open hearth which in the days of slavery was the plantation cookery. He saw Louisa bent over that hearth. He went in as a master should, and took her. Direct, honest, bold. None of this sneaking that he had to go through now. The contrast was repulsive to him. His family had lost ground. Hell no, his family still owned the niggers, practically. Damned if they did, or he wouldn't have to duck around so. What would they think if they knew? His mother? His sister? He shouldn't mention them, shouldn't think of them in this connection. There in the dusk he blushed at doing so. Fellows about town were all right, but how about

his friends up north? He could see them incredible, repulsed. They
didn't know. The thought first made him laugh. Then, with their eyes
still upon him, he began to feel embarrassed. He felt the need of explaining things to them. Explain hell. They wouldn't understand, and
moreover who ever heard of a Southerner getting on his knees to any
Yankee, or anyone. No sir. He was going to see Louisa tonight, and love
her. She was lovely — in her way. Nigger way. What way was that?
Damned if he knew. Must know. He'd known her long enough to know.
Was there something about niggers that you couldn't know? Listening
to them at church didn't tell you anything. Looking at them didn't tell
you anything. Talking to them didn't tell you anything, — unless it was
gossip, unless they wanted to talk. Of course about farming, and licker,
and craps, — but those weren't niggers. Nigger was something more.
How much more? Something to be afraid of, more? Hell no. Who ever
heard of being afraid of a nigger? Tom Burwell, Cartwell had told him
that Tom went with Louisa after she reached home. No sir. No nigger
had ever been with his girl. He'd like to see one try. Some position for
him to be in. Him, Bob Stone, of the old Stone family, in a scrap with a
nigger over a nigger girl. In the good old days . . . Ha! Those were the
days. His family had lost ground. Not so much, though. Enough for him
to have to cut through old Lemon's canefield by way of the woods, that
he might meet her. She was worth it. Beautiful nigger gal. Why nigger?
Why not, just gal? No, it was because she was nigger that he went to her.
Sweet . . . The scent of boiling cane came to him. Then he saw the rich
glow of the stove. He heard the voices of the men circled round it. He
was about to skirt the clearing when he heard his own name mentioned.
He stopped. Quivering. Leaning against a tree, he listened.

"Bad nigger. Yassur he sho' is one bad nigger when he gets started."

"Tom Burwell's been on th' gang three times fo' cuttin' men."

"What y' think he's agwine t' do t' Bob Stone?"

"Dunno yet. He ain't found out. When he does — Baby!"

"Ain't no tellin'."

"Young Stone ain't no quitter an' I ken tell y' that. Blood of th' old uns
in his veins."

"That's right. He'll scrap sho'."

"Be gettin' too hot f' niggers 'round this away."

"Shut up nigger. Y' don't know what y' talking 'bout."

Bob Stone's ears burnt like he had been holding them over the stove.
Sizzling heat welled up within him. His feet felt as if they rested on red
hot coals. They stung him to quick movement. He circled the fringe of

the glowing. Not a twig cracked beneath his feet. He reached the path that led to factory town. Plunged furiously down it. Half way along, a blindness within him veered him aside. He crashed into the bordering canebrake. Cane leaves cut his face and lips. He tasted blood. He threw himself down and dug his fingers in the ground. The earth was cool. Cane-roots took the fever from his hands. After a long while, or so it seemed to him, the thought came to him that it must be time to see Louisa. He got to his feet, and walked calmly to their meeting place. No Louisa. Tom Burwell had her. Veins in his forehead bulged and distended. Saliva moistened the dried blood on his lips. He bit down on his lips. He tasted blood. Not his own blood; Tom Burwell's blood. Bob drove through the cane, and out again upon the road. A hound swung down the path before him towards factory town. Bob couldn't see it. The dog loped aside to let him pass. Bob's blind rushing made him stumble over it. He fell with a thud that dazed him. The hound yelped. Answering yelps came from all over the country-side. Chickens cackled. Roosters crowed, heralding the blood-shot eyes of southern awakening. Singers in the town were silenced. They shut their windows down. Palpitant between the rooster crows, a chill hush settled upon the huddled forms of Tom and Louisa. A figure rushed from the shadow and stood before them. Tom popped to his feet.

"What's y' want?"

"I'm Bob Stone."

"Yassur — an' I'm Tom Burwell. What's y' want?"

Bob lunged at him. Tom side stepped, caught him by the shoulder, and flung him to the ground. Straddled him.

"Let me up."

"Yassur — but watch yo' doin's Bob Stone."

A few dark figures, drawn by the sound of scuffle, stood about them. Bob sprang to his feet.

"Fight like a man Tom Burwell an' I'll lick y'."

Again he lunged. Tom side stepped and flung him to the ground. Straddled him.

"Get off me you godam nigger you."

"Yo' sho has started somethin' now. Get up."

Tom yanked him up and began hammering at him. Each blow sounded as if it smashed into a precious, irreplaceable soft something. Beneath them, Bob staggered back. He reached in his pocket and whipped out a knife.

"That's my game, sho."

Blue flashed, a steel blade slashed across Bob Stone's throat. He had a sweetish sick feeling. Blood began to flow. Then he felt a sharp twitch of pain. He let his knife drop. He slapped one hand against his neck. He pressed the other on top of his head as if to hold it down. He groaned. He turned, and staggered toward the crest of the hill in the direction of white town. Negroes who had seen the fight slunk into their homes and blew the lamps out. Louisa, dazed, hysterical, refused to go indoors. She slipped, crumbled, her body loosely propped against the wood-work of the well. Tom Burwell leaned against it. He seemed rooted there.

Bob reached Broad Street. White men rushed up to him. He collapsed in their arms.

"Tom Burwell . . ."

White men like ants upon a forage rushed about. Except for the taut hum of their moving, all was silent. Shotguns, revolvers, rope, kerosene, torches. Two high powered cars with glaring search lights. They came together. The taut hum rose to a low roar. Then nothing could be heard but the flop of their feet in the thick dust of the road. The moving body of their silence preceded them over the crest of the hill into factory town. It flattened the Negroes beneath it. It rolled to the wall of the factory, where it stopped. Tom knew that they were coming. He couldn't move. And then he saw the search lights of the two cars glaring down on him. A quick stock went through him. He stiffened. He started to run. A yell went up from the mob. Tom wheeled about and faced them. They poured on him. They swarmed. A large man with dead white face and flabby cheeks came to him and almost jabbed a gun-barrel through his guts.

"Hands behind y' nigger."

Tom's wrists were bound. The big man shoved him to the well. Burn him over it, and when the wood-work caved in, his body would drop to the bottom. Two deaths for a godam nigger. Louisa was driven back. The mob pushed in. Its pressure, its momentum was too great. Drag him to the factory. Tom moved in the direction indicated. But they had to drag him. They reached the great door. Too many to get in there. The mob divided, and flowed around the walls to either side. The big man shoved him through the door. The mob pressed in from the sides. Taut humming. No words. A stake was sunk into the ground. Rotting floor boards piled around it. Kerosene poured on the rotting floor boards. Tom bound to the stake. His breast was bare. Nail scratches let little lines of blood trickle down, and mat into the hair. His face, his eyes were set and stony. Except for irregular breathing, one would have thought him already dead. Torches were flung onto the pile. A great flare muffled in black smoke shot upward. The mob yelled. The mob was silent. Now Tom could be seen within the flames. Only his head, erect, like a blackened stone. Stench of burning flesh soaked the air. Tom's eyes popped. His head settled downward. The mob yelled. Its yell echoed against the skeleton stone walls and sounded like a hundred yells. Like a hundred mobs yelling. Its yell thudded against the thick front wall, and fell back. Ghost of a yell slipped through the flames, and out the great door of the factory. It fluttered like a dying thing down the single street of factory town. Louisa, upon the step before her home, did not hear it, but her eyes opened slowly. They saw the full moon glowing in the great door. The full moon, an evil thing, an omen, soft showering the homes of folks she knew. Where were they, these people? She'd sing, and perhaps they'd come out and join her. Perhaps Tom Burwell would come. At any rate, the full moon in the great door was an omen which she must sing to:

> *Red nigger moon. Sinner!*
> *Blood-burning moon. Sinner!*
> *Come out that fact'ry door.*

1927

*Ernest Hemingway*

......................................................................................................

# The Killers

FROM *Scribner's Magazine*

THE DOOR of Henry's lunch-room opened and two men came in. They sat down at the counter.

"What's yours?" George asked them.

"I don't know," one of the men said. "What do you want to eat, Al?"

"I don't know," said Al. "I don't know what I want to eat."

Outside it was getting dark. The street-light came on outside the window. The two men at the counter read the menu. From the other end of the counter Nick Adams watched them. He had been talking to George when they came in.

"I'll have a roast pork tenderloin with apple sauce and mashed potato," the first man said.

"It isn't ready yet."

"What the hell do you put it on the card for?"

"That's the dinner," George explained. "You can get that at six o'clock."

George looked at the clock on the wall behind the counter.

"It's five o'clock."

"The clock says twenty minutes past five," the second man said.

"It's twenty minutes fast."

"Oh, to hell with the clock," the first man said. "What have you got to eat?"

"I can give you any kind of sandwiches," George said. "You can have ham and eggs, bacon and eggs, liver and bacon; or a steak."

"Give me chicken croquettes with green peas and cream sauce and mashed potatoes."

"That's the dinner."

"Everything we want's the dinner, eh? That's the way you work it."

"I can give you ham and eggs, bacon and eggs, liver — "

"I'll take ham and eggs," the man called Al said. He wore a derby hat and a black overcoat buttoned across the chest. His face was small and white and he had tight lips. He wore a silk muffler and gloves.

"Give me bacon and eggs," said the other man. He was about the same size as Al. Their faces were different, but they were dressed like twins. Both wore overcoats too tight for them. They sat leaning forward, their elbows on the counter.

"Got anything to drink?" Al asked.

"Silver beer, Bevo, ginger ale," George said.

"I mean you got anything to drink?"

"Just those I said."

"This is a hot town," said the other. "What do they call it?"

"Summit."

"Ever hear of it?" Al asked his friend.

"No," said the friend.

"What do you do here nights?" Al asked.

"They eat the dinner," his friend said. "They all come here and eat the big dinner."

"That's right," George said.

"So you think that's right?" Al asked George.

"Sure."

"You're a pretty bright boy, aren't you?"

"Sure," said George.

"Well, you're not," said the other little man. "Is he, Al?"

"He's dumb," said Al. He turned to Nick. "What's your name?"

"Adams."

"Another bright boy," Al said. "Ain't he a bright boy, Max?"

"The town's full of bright boys," Max said.

George put the two platters, one of ham and eggs, the other of bacon and eggs, on the counter. He set down two side-dishes of fried potatoes and closed the wicket into the kitchen.

"Which is yours?" he asked Al.

"Don't you remember?"

"Ham and eggs."

"Just a bright boy," Max said. He leaned forward and took the ham and eggs. Both men ate with their gloves on. George watched them eat.

"What are *you* looking at?" Max looked at George.

"Nothing."

"The hell you were. You were looking at me."

"Maybe the boy meant it for a joke, Max," Al said.

George laughed.

"*You* don't have to laugh," Max said to him. "*You* don't have to laugh at all, see?"

"All right," said George.

"So he thinks it's all right." Max turned to Al. "He thinks it's all right. That's a good one."

"Oh, he's a thinker," Al said. They went on eating.

"What's the bright boy's name down the counter?" Al asked Max.

"Hey, bright boy," Max said to Nick. "You go around on the other side of the counter with your boy friend."

"What's the idea?" Nick asked.

"There isn't any idea."

"You better go around, bright boy," Al said. Nick went around behind the counter.

"What's the idea?" George asked.

"None of your damn business," Al said. "Who's out in the kitchen?"

"The nigger."

"What do you mean the nigger?"

"The nigger that cooks."

"Tell him to come in."

"What's the idea?"

"Tell him to come in."

"Where do you think you are?"

"We know damn well where we are," the man called Max said. "Do we look silly?"

"You talk silly," Al said to him. "What the hell do you argue with this kid for? Listen," he said to George, "tell the nigger to come out here."

"What are you going to do to him?"

"Nothing. Use your head, bright boy. What would we do to a nigger?"

George opened the slit that opened back into the kitchen. "Sam," he called. "Come in here a minute."

The door to the kitchen opened and the nigger came in. "What was it?" he asked. The two men at the counter took a look at him.

"All right, nigger. You stand right there," Al said.

Sam, the nigger, standing in his apron, looked at the two men sitting at the counter. "Yes, sir," he said. Al got down from his stool.

"I'm going back to the kitchen with the nigger and bright boy," he said. "Go on back to the kitchen, nigger. You go with him, bright boy." The little man walked after Nick and Sam, the cook, back into the kitchen. The door shut after them. The man called Max sat at the counter opposite George. He didn't look at George but looked in the mirror that ran along back of the counter. Henry's had been made over from a saloon into a lunch-counter.

"Well, bright boy," Max said, looking into the mirror, "why don't you say something?"

"What's it all about?"

"Hey, Al," Max called, "bright boy wants to know what it's all about."

"Why don't you tell him?" Al's voice came from the kitchen.

"What do you think it's all about?"

"I don't know."

"What do you think?"

Max looked into the mirror all the time he was talking.

"I wouldn't say."

"Hey, Al, bright boy says he wouldn't say what he thinks it's all about."

"I can hear you, all right," Al said from the kitchen. He had propped open the slit that dishes passed through into the kitchen with a catsup bottle. "Listen, bright boy," he said from the kitchen to George. "Stand a little further along the bar. You move a little to the left, Max." He was like a photographer arranging for a group picture.

"Talk to me, bright boy," Max said. "What do you think's going to happen?"

George did not say anything.

"I'll tell you," Max said. "We're going to kill a Swede. Do you know a big Swede named Ole Andreson?"

"Yes."

"He comes here to eat every night, don't he?"

"Sometimes he comes here."

"He comes here at six o'clock, don't he?"

"If he comes."

"We know all that, bright boy," Max said. "Talk about something else. Ever go to the movies?"

"Once in a while."

"You ought to go to the movies more. The movies are fine for a bright boy like you."

"What are you going to kill Old Andreson for? What did he ever do to you?"

"He never had a chance to do anything to us. He never even seen us."

"And he's only going to see us once," Al said from the kitchen.

"What are you going to kill him for, then?" George asked.

"We're killing him for a friend. Just to oblige a friend, bright boy."

"Shut up," said Al from the kitchen. "You talk too goddam much."

"Well, I got to keep bright boy amused. Don't I, bright boy?"

"You talk too damn much," Al said. "The nigger and my bright boy are amused by themselves. I got them tied up like a couple of girl friends in the convent."

"I suppose you were in a convent."

"You never know."

"You were in a kosher convent. That's where you were."

George looked up at the clock.

"If anybody comes in you tell them the cook is off, and if they keep after it, you tell them you'll go back and cook yourself. Do you get that bright boy?"

"All right," George said. "What you going to do with us afterward?"

"That'll depend," Max said. "That's one of those things you never know at the time."

George looked up at the clock. It was a quarter past six. The door from the street opened. A street-car motorman came in.

"Hello, George," he said. "Can I get supper?"

"Sam's gone out," George said. "He'll be back in about half an hour."

"I'd better go up the street," the motorman said. George looked at the clock. It was twenty minutes past six.

"That was nice, bright boy," Max said. "You're a regular little gentleman."

"He knew I'd blow his head off," Al said from the kitchen.

"No," said Max. "It ain't that. Bright boy is nice. He's a nice boy. I like him."

At six-fifty-five George said: "He's not coming."

Two other people had been in the lunch-room. Once George had gone out to the kitchen and make a ham-and-egg sandwich "to go" that a man wanted to take with him. Inside the kitchen he saw Al, his derby hat tipped back, sitting on a stool beside the wicket with the muzzle of a sawed-off shotgun resting on the ledge. Nick and the cook were back to back in the corner, a towel tied in each of their mouths. George had cooked the sandwich, wrapped it up in oiled paper, put it in a bag, brought it in, and the man had paid for it and gone out.

"Bright boy can do everything," Max said. "He can cook and everything. You'd make some girl a nice wife, bright boy."

"Yes?" George said. "Your friend, Ole Andreson, isn't going to come."

"We'll give him ten minutes," Max said.

Max watched the mirror and the clock. The hands of the clock marked seven o'clock, and then five minutes past seven.

"Come on, Al," said Max. "We better go. He's not coming."

"Better give him five minutes," Al said from the kitchen.

In the five minutes a man came in, and George explained that the cook was sick. "Why the hell don't you get another cook?" the man asked. "Aren't you running a lunch-counter?" He went out.

"Come on, Al," Max said.

"What about the two bright boys and the nigger?"

"They're all right."

"You think so?"

"Sure. We're through with it."

"I don't like it," said Al. "It's sloppy. You talk too much."

"Oh, what the hell," said Max. "We got to keep amused, haven't we?"

"You talk too much, all the same," Al said. He came out from the kitchen. The cut-off barrels of the shotgun made a slight bulge under the waist of his too tight-fitting overcoat. He straightened his coat with his gloved hands.

"So long, bright boy," he said to George. "You got a lot of luck."

"That's the truth," Max said. "You ought to play the races, bright boy."

The two of them went out the door. George watched them through the window pass under the arc-light and cross the street. In their tight overcoats and derby hats they looked like a vaudeville team. George went back through the swinging door into the kitchen and untied Nick and the cook.

"I don't want any more of that," said Sam, the cook. "I don't want any more of that."

Nick stood up. He had never had a towel in his mouth before.

"Say," he said. "What the hell?" He was trying to swagger it off.

"They were going to kill Ole Andreson," George said. "They were going to shoot him when he came in to eat."

"Ole Andreson?"

"Sure."

The cook felt the corners of his mouth with his thumbs.

"They all gone?" he asked.

"Yeah," said George. "They're gone now."

"I don't like it," said the cook. "I don't like any of it at all."

"Listen," George said to Nick. "You'd better go see Ole Andreson."

"All right."

"You better not have anything to do with it at all," Sam, the cook, said. "You better stay way out of it."

"Don't go if you don't want to," George said.

"Mixing up in this ain't going to get you anywhere," the cook said. "You stay out of it."

"I'll go see him," Nick said to George. "Where does he live?"

The cook turned away.

"Little boys always know what they want to do," he said.

"He lives up at Hirsch's rooming-house," George said to Nick.

"I'll go up there."

Outside the arc-light shone through the bare branches of a tree. Nick walked up the street beside the car-tracks and turned at the next arc-light down a side street. Three houses up the street was Hirsch's rooming-house. Nick walked up the two steps and pushed the bell. A woman came to the door.

"Is Ole Andreson here?"

"Do you want to see him?"

"Yes, if he's in."

Nick followed the woman up a flight of stairs and back to the end of a corridor. She knocked on the door.

"Who is it?"

"It's somebody to see you, Mr. Andreson," the woman said.

"It's Nick Adams."

"Come in."

Nick opened the door and went into the room. Ole Andreson was lying on the bed with all his clothes on. He had been a heavyweight prizefighter and he was too long for the bed. He lay with his head on two pillows. He did not look at Nick.

"What was it?" he asked.

"I was up at Henry's," Nick said, "and two fellows came in and tied up me and the cook, and they said they were going to kill you."

It sounded silly when he said it. Ole Andreson said nothing.

"They put us out in the kitchen," Nick went on. "They were going to shoot you when you came in to supper."

Ole Andreson looked at the wall and did not say anything.

"George thought I better come and tell you about it."

"There isn't anything I can do about it," Ole Andreson said.

"I'll tell you what they were like."

"I don't want to know what they were like," Ole Andreson said. He looked at the wall. "Thanks for coming to tell me about it."

"That's all right."

Nick looked at the big man lying on the bed.

"Don't you want me to go and see the police?"

"No," Ole Andreson said. "That wouldn't do any good."

"Isn't there something I could do?"

"No. There ain't anything to do."

"Maybe it was just a bluff."

"No. It ain't just a bluff."

Ole Andreson rolled over toward the wall.

"The only thing is," he said, talking toward the wall, "I just can't make up my mind to go out. I been in here all day."

"Couldn't you get out of town?"

"No," Ole Andreson said. "I'm through with all that running around."

He looked at the wall.

"There ain't anything to do now."

"Couldn't you fix it up some way?"

"No. I got in wrong." He talked in the same flat voice. "There ain't anything to do. After a while I'll make up my mind to go out."

"I better go back and see George," Nick said.

"So long," said Ole Andreson. He did not look toward Nick. "Thanks for coming around."

Nick went out. As he shut the door he saw Ole Andreson with all his clothes on, lying on the bed looking at the wall.

"He's been in his room all day," the landlady said downstairs. "I guess he don't feel well. I said to him: 'Mr. Andreson, you ought to go out and take a walk on a nice fall day like this,' but he didn't feel like it."

"He doesn't want to go out."

"I'm sorry he don't feel well," the woman said. "He's an awfully nice man. He was in the ring, you know."

"I know it."

"You'd never know it except from the way his face is," the woman said. They stood talking just inside the street door. "He's just as gentle."

"Well, good night, Mrs. Hirsch," Nick said.

"I'm not Mrs. Hirsch," the woman said. "She owns the place. I just look after it for her. I'm Mrs. Bell."

"Well, good night, Mrs. Bell," Nick said.

"Good night," the woman said.

Nick walked up the dark street to the corner under the arc-light, and then along the car-tracks to Henry's eating-house. George was inside, back of the counter.

"Did you see Ole?"

"Yes," said Nick. "He's in his room and he won't go out."

The cook opened the door from the kitchen when he heard Nick's voice.

"I don't even listen to it," he said, and shut the door.

"Did you tell him about it?" George asked.

"Sure. I told him but he knows what it's all about."

"What's he going to do?"

"Nothing."

"They'll kill him."

"I guess they will."

"He must have got mixed up in something in Chicago."

"I guess so," said Nick.

"It's a hell of a thing."

"It's an awful thing," Nick said.

They did not say anything. George reached down for a towel and wiped the counter.

"I wonder what he did?" Nick said.

"Double-crossed somebody. That's what they kill them for."

"I'm going to get out of this town," Nick said.

"Yes," said George. "That's a good thing to do."

"I can't stand to think about him waiting in the room and knowing he's going to get it. It's too damned awful."

"Well," said George, "you better not think about it."

1929

*Willa Cather*

# Double Birthday

FROM *The Forum*

I

EVEN IN American cities, which seem so much alike, where people seem all to be living the same lives, striving for the same things, thinking the same thoughts, there are still individuals a little out of tune with the times — there are still survivals of a past more loosely woven, there are disconcerting beginnings of a future yet unforeseen.

Coming out of the gray stone Court House in Pittsburgh on a dark November afternoon, Judge Hammersley encountered one of these men whom one does not readily place, whom one is, indeed, a little embarrassed to meet, because they have not got on as they should. The Judge saw him mounting the steps outside, leaning against the wind, holding his soft felt hat on with his hand, his head thrust forward — hurrying with a light, quick step, and so intent upon his own purposes that the Judge could have gone out by a side door and avoided the meeting. But that was against his principles.

"Good day, Albert," he muttered, seeming to feel, himself, all the embarrassment of the encounter, for the other snatched off his hat with a smile of very evident pleasure, and something like pride. His gesture bared an attractive head — small, well-set, definite and smooth, one of those heads that look as if they had been turned out of some hard, rich wood by a workman deft with the lathe. His smooth-shaven face was dark — a warm coffee color — and his hazel eyes were warm and lively. He was not young, but his features had a kind of quick-silver mobility. His manner toward the stiff, frowning Judge was respectful and admiring — not in the least self-conscious.

The Judge inquired after his health and that of his uncle.

"Uncle Albert is splendidly preserved for his age. Frail, and can't

stand any strain, but perfectly all right if he keeps to his routine. He's
going to have a birthday soon. He will be eighty on the first day of
December, and I shall be fifty-five on the same day. I was named after
him because I was born on his twenty-fifth birthday."

"Umph." The Judge glanced from left to right as if this announcement were in bad taste, but he put a good face on it and said with a
kind of testy heartiness, "That will be an — occasion. I'd like to remember it in some way. Is there anything your uncle would like, any —
recognition?" He stammered and coughed.

Young Albert Engelhardt, as he was called, laughed apologetically,
but with confidence. "I think there is, Judge Hammersley. Indeed, I'd
thought of coming to you to ask a favor. I am going to have a little
supper for him, and you know he likes good wine. In these dirty boot-
legging times, it's hard to get."

"Certainly, certainly." The Judge spoke up quickly and for the first
time looked Albert squarely in the eye. "Don't give him any of that
bootleg stuff. I can find something in my cellar. Come out to-morrow
night after eight, with a gripsack of some sort. Very glad to help you out,
Albert. Glad the old fellow holds up so well. Thank'ee, Albert," as Engelhardt swung the heavy door open and held it for him to pass.

Judge Hammersley's car was waiting for him, and on the ride home
to Squirrel Hill he thought with vexation about the Engelhardts. He was
really a sympathetic man, and though so stern of manner, he had deep
affections; was fiercely loyal to old friends, old families, and old ideals.
He didn't think highly of what is called success in the world to-day, but
such as it was he wanted his friends to have it, and was vexed with them
when they missed it. He was vexed with Albert for unblushingly, almost
proudly, declaring that he was fifty-five years old, when he had nothing
whatever to show for it. He was the last of the Engelhardt boys, and they
had none of them had anything to show. They all died much worse off
in the world than they began. They began with a flourishing glass factory up the river, a comfortable fortune, a fine old house on the park
in Allegheny, a good standing in the community; and it was all gone,
melted away.

Old August Engelhardt was a thrifty, energetic man, though pig-
headed — Judge Hammersley's friend and one of his first clients. August's five sons had sold the factory and wasted the money in fantastic
individual enterprises, lost the big house, and now they were all dead
except Albert. They ought all to be alive, with estates and factories and
families. To be sure, they had that queer German streak in them; but so

had old August, and it hadn't prevented his amounting to something. Their bringing-up was wrong; August had too free a hand, he was too proud of his five handsome boys, and too conceited. Too much tennis, Rhine wine punch, music, and silliness. They were always running over to New York, like this Albert. Somebody, when asked what in the world young Albert had ever done with his inheritance, had laughingly replied that he had spent it on the Pennsylvania Railroad.

Judge Hammersley didn't see how Albert could hold his head up. He had some small job in the County Clerk's office, was dependent upon it, had nothing else but the poor little house on the South Side where he lived with his old uncle. The county took care of him for the sake of his father, who had been a gallant officer in the Civil War, and afterward a public-spirited citizen and a generous employer of labor. But, as Judge Hammersley had bitterly remarked to Judge Merriman when Albert's name happened to come up, "If it weren't for his father's old friends seeing that he got something, that fellow wouldn't be able to make a living." Next to a charge of dishonesty, this was the worst that could be said of any man.

Judge Hammersley's house out on Squirrel Hill sat under a grove of very old oak trees. He lived alone, with his daughter, Margaret Parmenter, who was a widow. She had a great many engagements, but she usually managed to dine at home with her father, and that was about as much society as he cared for. His house was comfortable in an old-fashioned way, well appointed — especially the library, the room in which he lived when he was not in bed or at the Court House. To-night, when he came down to dinner, Mrs. Parmenter was already at the table, dressed for an evening party. She was tall, handsome, with a fine, easy carriage, and her face was both hard and sympathetic, like her father's. She had not, however, his stiffness of manner, that contraction of the muscles which was his unconscious protest at any irregularity in the machinery of life. She accepted blunders and accidents smoothly if not indifferently.

As the old colored man pulled back the Judge's chair for him, he glanced at his daughter from under his eyebrows.

"I saw that son of old Gus Engelhardt's this afternoon," he said in an angry, challenging tone.

As a young girl his daughter had used to take up the challenge and hotly defend the person who had displeased or disappointed her father. But as she grew older she was conscious of that same feeling in herself when people fell short of what she expected; and she understood now that when her father spoke as if he were savagely attacking someone, it merely meant that he was disappointed or sorry for them; he never spoke thus of persons for whom he had no feeling. So she said calmly:

"Oh, did you really? I haven't seen him for years, not since the war. How was he looking? Shabby?"

"Not so shabby as he ought to. That fellow's likely to be in want one of these days."

"I'm afraid so," Mrs. Parmenter sighed. "But I believe he would be rather plucky about it."

The Judge shrugged. "He's coming out here to-morrow night, on some business for his uncle."

"Then I'll have a chance to see for myself. He must look much older. I can't imagine his ever looking really old and settled, though."

"See that you don't ask him to stay. I don't want the fellow hanging around. He'll transact his business and get it over. He had the face to admit to me that he'll be fifty-five years old on the first of December. He's giving some sort of birthday party for old Albert, a-hem." The Judge coughed formally but was unable to check a smile; his lips sarcastic, but his eyes full of sly humor.

"Can he be as old as that? Yes, I suppose so. When we were both at Mrs. Sterrett's, in Rome, I was fifteen, and he must have been about thirty."

Her father coughed. "He'd better have been in Homestead!"

Mrs. Parmenter looked up; that was rather commonplace, for her father. "Oh, I don't know. Albert would never have been much use in Homestead, and he was very useful to Mrs. Sterrett in Rome."

"What did she want the fellow hanging round for? All the men of her family amounted to something."

"To too much! There must be some butterflies if one is going to give house parties, and the Sterretts and Dents were all heavyweights. He was in Rome a long while; three years, I think. He had a gorgeous time. Anyway, he learned to speak Italian very well, and that helps him out now, doesn't it? You still send for him at the Court House when you need an interpreter?"

"That's not often. He picks up a few dollars. Nice business for his father's son."

After dinner the Judge retired to his library, where the gas fire was lit, and his book at hand, with a paper-knife inserted to mark the place where he had left off reading last night at exactly ten-thirty. On his way he went to the front door, opened it, turned on the porch light, and looked at the thermometer, making an entry in a little notebook. In a few moments his daughter, in an evening cloak, stopped at the library door to wish him good night and went down the hall. He listened for the closing of the front door; it was a reassuring sound to him. He liked the feeling of an orderly house, empty for himself and his books all evening. He was deeply read in divinity, philosophy, and in the early history of North America.


II

While Judge Hammersley was settling down to his book, Albert Engelhardt was sitting at home in a garnet velvet smoking-jacket, at an upright piano, playing Schumann's *Kreisleriana* for his old uncle. They lived, certainly, in a queer part of the city, on one of the dingy streets that run uphill off noisy Carson Street, in a little two-story brick house, a workingman's house, that Albert's father had taken over long ago in satisfaction of a bad debt. When his father had acquired this building, it was a mere nothing — the Engelhardts were then living in their big, many-gabled, so-German house on the Park, in Allegheny; and they owned many other buildings, besides the glass factory up the river. After the father's death, when the sons converted houses and lands into cash, this forgotten little house on the South Side had somehow never been sold or mortgaged. A day came when Albert, the last surviving son, found this piece of property the only thing he owned in the world besides his personal effects. His uncle, having had a crushing disappointment, wanted at that time to retire from the practice of medicine, so Albert settled in the South Side house and took his uncle with him.

He had not gone there in any mood of despair. His impoverishment had come about gradually, and before he took possession of these quarters he had been living in a boarding house; the change seemed going up instead of going down in the world. He was delighted to have a home again, to unpack his own furniture and his books and pictures — the most valuable in the world to him, because they were full of his own history and that of his family, were like part of his own personality. All the years and the youth which had slipped away from him still clung to these things.

At his piano, under his Degas drawing in black and red — three ballet girls at the bar — or seated at his beautiful inlaid writing table, he was still the elegant young man who sat there long ago. His rugs were fine ones, his collection of books was large and very personal. It was full of works which, though so recent, were already immensely far away and diminished. The glad, rebellious excitement they had once caused in the world he could recapture only in memory. Their power to seduce and stimulate the young, the living, was utterly gone. There was a complete file of the *Yellow Book*, for instance; who could extract sweet poison from those volumes now? A portfolio of the drawings of Aubrey Beardsley — decadent, had they been called? A slender, padded volume — the complete works of a great new poet, Ernest Dowson. Oscar Wilde, whose wickedness was now so outdone that he looked like the poor old hat of some Victorian belle, wired and feathered and garlanded and faded.

Albert and his uncle occupied only the upper floor of their house. The ground floor was let to an old German glass engraver who had once been a workman in August Engelhardt's factory. His wife was a good cook, and every night sent their dinner up hot on the dumb-waiter. The house opened directly upon the street, and to reach Albert's apartment one went down a narrow paved alley at the side of the building and mounted an outside flight of wooden stairs at the back. They had only four rooms — two bedrooms, a snug sitting room in which they dined, and a small kitchen where Albert got breakfast every morning. After he had gone to work, Mrs. Rudder came up from downstairs to wash the dishes and do the cleaning, and to cheer up old Doctor Engelhardt.

At dinner this evening Albert had told his uncle about meeting Judge Hammersley, and of his particular inquiries after his health. The old man was very proud and received this intelligence as his due, but could not conceal a certain gratification.

"The daughter, she still lives with him? A damned fine-looking woman!" he muttered between his teeth. Uncle Albert, a bachelor, had been a professed connoisseur of ladies in his day.

Immediately after dinner, unless he were going somewhere, Albert always played for his uncle for an hour. He played extremely well. Doctor Albert sat by the fire smoking his cigar. While he listened, the look of wisdom and professional authority faded, and many changes went over his face, as if he were playing a little drama to himself; moods of scorn and contempt, of rakish vanity, sentimental melancholy . . . and something remote and lonely. The Doctor had always flattered himself that he resembled a satyr, because the tops of his ears were slightly pointed; and he used to hint to his nephews that his large pendulous nose was the index of an excessively amorous disposition. His mouth was full of long, yellowish teeth, all crowded irregularly, which he snapped and ground together when he uttered denunciations of modern art or the Eighteenth Amendment. He wore his mustache short and twisted up at the corners. His thick gray hair was cut close and upright, in the bristling French fashion. His hands were small and fastidious, high-knuckled, quite elegant in shape.

Across the doctor's throat ran a long, jagged scar. He used to mutter to his young nephews that it had been justly inflicted by an outraged husband — a pistol shot in the dark. But his brother August always said that he had been cut by glass, when, wandering about in the garden one night after drinking too much punch, he had fallen into the cold-frames.

After playing Schumann for some time, Albert, without stopping, went into Stravinsky.

Doctor Engelhardt by the gas fire stirred uneasily, turned his important head toward his nephew, and snapped his teeth. "Br-r-r, that stuff! Poverty of imagination, poverty of musical invention; *fin-de-siècle!*"

Albert laughed. "I thought you were asleep. Why will you use that phrase? It shows your vintage. Like this any better?" He began the second act of *Pélleas et Mélisande.*

The Doctor nodded. "Yes, that is better, though I'm not fooled by it." He wrinkled his nose as if he were smelling out something, and squinted with superior discernment. "To this *canaille* that is all very new; but to me it goes back to Bach."

"Yes, if you like."

Albert, like Judge Hammersley, was jealous of his solitude — liked a few hours with his books. It was time for Uncle Doctor to be turning in. He ended the music by playing half a dozen old German songs which the old fellow always wanted but never asked for. The Doctor's chin sank into his shirt front. His face took on a look of deep, resigned sadness; his features, losing their conscious importance, seemed to shrink a good deal. His nephew knew that this was the mood in which he would most patiently turn to rest and darkness. Doctor Engelhardt had had a heavy loss late in life. Indeed, he had suffered the same loss twice.

As Albert left the piano, the Doctor rose and walked a little stiffly across the room. At the door of his chamber he paused, brought his hand up in a kind of military salute and gravely bowed, so low that one saw only the square up-standing gray brush on the top of his head and the long pear-shaped nose. After this he closed the door behind him. Albert sat down to his book. Very soon he heard the bath water running.

Having taken his bath, the Doctor would get into bed immediately to avoid catching cold. Luckily, he usually slept well. Perhaps he dreamed of that unfortunate young singer whom he sometimes called, to his nephew and himself, "the lost Lenore."

III

Long years ago, when the Engelhardt boys were still living in the old house in Allegheny with their mother, after their father's death, Doctor Engelhardt was practising medicine, and had an office on the Park, five minutes' walk from his sister-in-law. He usually lunched with the family, after his morning office hours were over. They always had a good cook, and the Allegheny market was one of the best in the world. Mrs. Engelhardt went to market every morning of her life; such vegetables and poultry, such cheeses and sausages and smoked and pickled fish as one could buy there! Soon after she had made her rounds, boys in white aprons would come running across the Park with her purchases. Every one knew the Engelhardt house, built of many-colored bricks, with gables and turrets, and on the west a large stained-glass window representing a scene on the Grand Canal in Venice, the Church of Santa Maria della Salute in the background, in the foreground a gondola with a slender gondolier. People said August and Mrs. Engelhardt should be solidly seated in the prow to make the picture complete.

Doctor Engelhardt's especial interest was the throat, preferably the singing throat. He had studied every scrap of manuscript that Manuel Garcia had left behind him, every reported conversation with him. He had doctored many singers, and imagined he had saved many voices. Pittsburgh air is not good for the throat, and traveling artists often had need of medical assistance. Conductors of orchestras and singing societies recommended Doctor Engelhardt because he was very lax about collecting fees from professionals, especially if they sent him a photograph floridly inscribed. He had been a medical student in New York while Patti was still singing; his biography fell into chapters of great voices as a turfman's falls into chapters of fast horses. This passion for the voice had given him the feeling of distinction, of being unique in his profession, which had made him all his life a well-satisfied and happy man, and had left him a poor one.

One morning when the Doctor was taking his customary walk about the Park before office hours, he stopped in front of the Allegheny High School building because he heard singing — a chorus of young voices.

It was June, and the chapel windows were open. The Doctor listened for a few moments, then tilted his head on one side and laid his forefinger on his pear-shaped nose with an anxious, inquiring squint. Among the voices he certainly heard one Voice. The final bang of the piano was followed by laughter and buzzing. A boy ran down the steps. The Doctor stopped him and learned that this was a rehearsal for Class Day exercises. Just then the piano began again, and in a moment he heard the same voice, alone:

*"Still wie die Nacht, tief wie das Meer."*

No, he was not mistaken; a full, rich soprano voice, so easy, so sure; a golden warmth, even in the high notes. Before the second verse was over he went softly into the building, into the chapel, and for the first time laid eyes on Marguerite Thiesinger. He saw a sturdy, blooming German girl standing beside the piano; good-natured, one knew at a glance, glowing with health. She looked like a big peony just burst into bloom and full of sunshine — sunshine in her auburn hair, in her rather small hazel eyes. When she finished the song, she began waltzing on the platform with one of the boys.

Doctor Albert waited by the door, and accosted her as she came out carrying her coat and schoolbooks. He introduced himself and asked her if she would go over to Mrs. Engelhardt's for lunch and sing for him.

Oh, yes! she knew one of the Engelhardt boys, and she'd always wanted to see that beautiful window from the inside.

She went over at noon and sang for them before lunch, and the family took stock of her. She spoke a very ordinary German and her English was still worse; her people were very ordinary. Her flat, slangy speech was somehow not vulgar because it was naïve — she knew no other way. The boys were delighted with her because she was jolly and interested in everything. She told them about the glorious good times she had going to dances in suburban Turner halls, and to picnics in the damp, smoke-smeared woods up the Allegheny. The boys roared with laughter at the unpromising places she mentioned. But she had the warm bubble in her blood that makes everything fair; even being a junior in the Allegheny High School was "glorious," she told them!

She came to lunch with them again and again, because she liked the boys, and she thought the house magnificent. The Doctor observed her narrowly all the while. Clearly she had no ambition, no purpose; she sang to be agreeable. She was not very intelligent, but she had a kind of personal warmth that, to his way of thinking, was much better than brains. He took her over to his office and poked and pounded her. When he had finished his examination, he stood before the foolish, happy young thing and inclined his head in his peculiar fashion.

"Miss Thiesinger, I have the honor to announce to you that you are on the threshold of a brilliant, possibly a great career."

She laughed her fresh, ringing laugh. "Aren't you nice, though, to take so much trouble about me!"

The Doctor lifted a forefinger. "But for that you must turn your back on this childishness, these sniveling sapheads you play marbles with. You must uproot this triviality." He made a gesture as if he were wringing a chicken's neck, and Marguerite was thankful she was able to keep back a giggle.

Doctor Engelhardt wanted her to go to New York with him at once, and begin her studies. He was quite ready to finance her. He had made up his mind to stake everything upon this voice.

But not at all. She thought it was lovely of him, but she was very fond of her classmates, and she wanted to graduate with her class next year. Moreover, she had just been given a choir position in one of the biggest churches in Pittsburgh, though she was still a schoolgirl; she was going to have money and pretty clothes for the first time in her life and wouldn't miss it all for anything.

All through the next school year Doctor Albert went regularly to the church where she sang, watched and cherished her, expostulated and lectured, trying to awaken fierce ambition in his big peony flower. She was very much interested in other things just then, but she was patient with him; accepted his devotion with good nature, respected his wisdom, and bore with his "stagey" manners as she called them. She graduated in June, and immediately after Commencement, when she was not quite nineteen, she eloped with an insurance agent and went to Chicago to live. She wrote Doctor Albert: "I do appreciate all your kindness to me, but I guess I will let my voice rest for the present."

He took it hard. He burned her photographs and the foolish little scrawls she had written to thank him for presents. His life would have been dull and empty if he hadn't had so many reproaches to heap upon her in his solitude. How often and how bitterly he arraigned her for the betrayal of so beautiful a gift. Where did she keep it hidden now, that jewel, in the sordid life she had chosen?

Three years after her elopement, suddenly, without warning, Marguerite Thiesinger walked into his office on Arch Street one morning and told him she had come back to study! Her husband's "affairs were involved"; he was now quite willing that she should make as much as possible of her voice — and out of it.

"My voice is better than it was," she said, looking at him out of her rather small eyes — greenish yellow, with a glint of gold in them. He believed her. He suddenly realized how uncommonly truthful she had always been. Rather stupid, unimaginative, but carried joyously along on a flood of warm vitality, and truthful to a degree he had hardly known in any woman or in any man. And now she was a woman.

He took her over to his sister-in-law's. Albert, who chanced to be at home, was sent to the piano. She was not mistaken. The Doctor kept averting his head to conceal his delight, to conceal, once or twice, a tear — the moisture that excitement and pleasure brought to his eyes. The voice, after all, he told himself, is a physical thing. She had been growing and ripening like fruit in the sun, and the voice with the body. Doctor Engelhardt stepped softly out of the music room into the conservatory and addressed a potted palm, his lips curling back from his teeth: "So we get that out of you, *Monsieur le commis voyageur,* and now we throw you away like a squeezed lemon."

When he returned to his singer, she addressed him very earnestly from under her spring hat covered with lilacs: "Before my marriage, Doctor Engelhardt, you offered to take me to New York to a teacher, and lend me money to start on. If you still feel like doing it, I'm sure I could repay you before very long. I'll follow your instructions. What was it you used to tell me I must have — application and ambition?"

He glared at her; "Take note, Gretchen, that I change the prescription. There is something vulgar about ambition. Now we will play for higher stakes; for ambition read aspiration!" His index finger shot upward.

In New York he had no trouble in awakening the interest of his friends and acquaintances. Within a week he had got his protégée to a very fine artist, just then retiring from the Opera, a woman who had been a pupil of Pauline Garcia Viardot. In short, Doctor Engelhardt had realized the dream of a lifetime: he had discovered a glorious voice, backed by a rich vitality. Within a year Marguerite had one of the best church positions in New York; she insisted upon repaying her benefactor before she went abroad to complete her studies. Doctor Engelhardt went often to New York to counsel and advise, to gloat over his treasure. He often shivered as he crossed the Jersey ferry; he was afraid of Fate. He would tell over her assets on his fingers to reassure himself. You might have seen a small, self-important man of about fifty, standing by the rail of the ferry boat, his head impressively inclined as if he were addressing an amphitheatre full of students, gravely counting upon his fingers.

But Fate struck, and from the quarter least under suspicion — through that blooming, rounded, generously molded young body, from that abundant, glowing health which the Doctor proudly called peasant vigor. Marguerite's success had brought to his office many mothers of singing daughters. He was not insensible to the compliment, but he usually dismissed them by dusting his fingers delicately in the air and growling; "Yes, she can sing a little, she has a voice; *aber kleine, kleine!*" He exulted in the opulence of his cabbage rose. To his nephews he used to match her possibilities with the singers of that period. Emma Eames he called *die Puritan,* Geraldine Ferrar *la voix blanche,* another was *trop raffinée.*

Marguerite had been in New York two years, her path one of uninterrupted progress, when she wrote the Doctor about a swelling of some sort; the surgeons wanted to operate. Doctor Albert took the next train for New York. An operation revealed that things were very bad indeed; a malignant growth, so far advanced that the knife could not check it. Her mother and grandmother had died of the same disease.

Poor Marguerite lived a year in a hospital for incurables. Every weekend when Doctor Albert went over to see her he found great changes — it was rapid and terrible. That winter and spring he lived like a man lost in a dark morass, the Slave in the Dismal Swamp. He suffered more than his Gretchen, for she was singularly calm and hopeful to the very end, never doubting that she would get well.

The last time he saw her she had given up. But she was noble and sweet in mood, and so piteously apologetic for disappointing him — like a child who has broken something precious and is sorry. She was wasted, indeed, until she was scarcely larger than a child, her beautiful hair cut short, her hands like shadows, but still a stain of color in her cheeks.

"I'm so sorry I didn't do as you wanted instead of running off with Phil," she said. "I see now how little he cared about me — and you've just done everything. If I had my twenty-six years to live over, I'd live them very differently."

Doctor Albert dropped her hand and walked to the window, the tears running down his face. *"Pourquoi, pourquoi?"* he muttered, staring blindly at that brutal square of glass. When he could control himself and came back to the chair at her bedside, she put her poor little sheared head out on his knee and lay smiling and breathing softly.

"I expect you don't believe in the hereafter," she murmured. "Scientific people hardly ever do. But if there is one, I'll not forget you. I'll love to remember you."

When the nurse came to give her her hypodermic, Doctor Albert went out into Central Park and wandered about without knowing where or why, until he smelled something sweet which suddenly stopped his breath, and he sat down under a flowering linden tree. He dropped his face in his hands and cried like a woman. Youth, art, love, dreams, true-heartedness — why must they go out of the summer world into darkness? *Warum, warum?* He thought he had already suffered all that man could, but never had it come down on him like this. He sat on that bench like a drunken man or like a dying man, muttering Heine's words, "God is a grimmer humorist than I. Nobody but God could have perpetrated anything so cruel." She was ashamed, he remembered it afresh and struck his bony head with his clenched fist — ashamed at having been used like this; she was apologetic for the power, whatever it was, that had tricked her. "Yes, by God, she apologized for God!"

The tortured man looked up through the linden branches at the blue arch that never answers. As he looked, his face relaxed, his breathing grew regular. His eyes were caught by puffy white clouds like the cherub-heads in Raphael's pictures, and something within him seemed to rise and travel with those clouds. The moment had come when he could bear no more. . . . When he went back to the hospital that evening, he learned that she had died very quietly between eleven and twelve, the hour when he was sitting on the bench in the park.

Uncle Doctor now sometimes spoke to Albert out of a long silence: "Anyway, I died for her; that was given to me. She never knew a death-struggle — she went to sleep. That struggle took place in my body. Her dissolution occurred within me."


IV


Old Doctor Engelhardt walked abroad very little now. Sometimes on a fine Sunday, his nephew would put him aboard a street car that climbs the hills beyond Mount Oliver and take him to visit an old German graveyard and a monastery. Every afternoon, in good weather, he walked along the pavement which ran past the front door, as far as the first corner, where he bought his paper and cigarettes. If Elsa, the pretty little granddaughter of his housekeeper, ran out to join him and see him over the crossings, he would go a little farther. In the morning, while Mrs. Rudder did the sweeping and dusting, the Doctor took the air on an upstairs back porch, overhanging the court.

The court was bricked, and had an old-fashioned cistern and hydrant, and three ailanthus trees — the last growing things left to the Engelhardts, whose flowering shrubs and greenhouses had once been so well known in Allegheny. In these trees, which he called *les Chinoises,* the Doctor took a great interest. The clothes line ran about their trunks in a triangle, and on Mondays he looked down upon the washing. He was too near-sighted to be distressed by the sooty flakes descending from neighboring chimneys upon the white sheets. He enjoyed the dull green leaves of his *Chinoises* in summer, scarcely moving on breathless, sticky nights, when the moon came up red over roofs and smoke-stacks. In autumn he watched the yellow fronds drop down upon the brick pavement like great ferns. Now, when his birthday was approaching, the trees were bare; and he thought he liked them best so, especially when all the knotty, curly twigs were outlined by a scurf of snow.

As he sat there, wrapped up in rugs, a stiff felt hat on his head — he would never hear to a cap — and woolen gloves on his hands, Elsa, the granddaughter, would bring her cross-stitch and chatter to him. Of late she had been sewing on her trousseau, and that amused the Doctor highly — though it meant she would soon go to live in lower Allegheny, and he would lose her. Her young man, Carl Abberbock, had now a half-interest in a butcher stall in the Allegheny market, and was in a hurry to marry.

When Mrs. Rudder had quite finished her work and made the place neat, she would come and lift the rug from his knees and say, "Time to go in, Herr Doctor."

v

The next evening after dinner Albert left the house with a suitcase, the bag that used to make so many trips to New York in the opera season. He stopped downstairs to ask Elsa to carry her sewing up and sit with his uncle for a while, then he took the street car across the Twenty-second Street Bridge by the blazing steel mills. As he waited on Soho Hill to catch a Fifth Avenue car, the heavy, frosty air suddenly began to descend in snow flakes. He wished he had worn his old overcoat; didn't like to get this one wet. He had to consider such things now. He was hesitating about a taxi when his car came, bound for the East End.

He got off at the foot of one of the streets running up Squirrel Hill, and slowly mounted. Everything was white with the softly-falling snow. Albert knew all the places; old school friends lived in many of them. Big, turreted stone houses, set in ample grounds with fine trees and shrubbery and driveways. He stepped aside now and then to avoid a car, rolling from the gravel drives on to the stone-block pavement. If the occupants had recognized Albert, they would have felt sorry for him. But he did not feel sorry for himself. He looked up at the lighted windows, the red gleam on the snowy rhododendron bushes, and shrugged. His old schoolfellows went to New York now as often as he had done in his youth; but they went to consult doctors, to put children in school, or to pay the bills of incorrigible sons.

He thought he had had the best of it; he had gone a-Maying while it was May. This solid comfort, this iron-bound security, didn't appeal to him much. These massive houses, after all, held nothing but the heavy domestic routine; all the frictions and jealousies and discontents of family life. Albert felt light and free, going up the hill in his thin overcoat. He believed he had had a more interesting life than most of his friends who owned real estate. He could still amuse himself, and he had lived to the full all the revolutions in art and music that his period covered. He wouldn't at this moment exchange his life and his memories — his memories of his teacher, Rafael Joseffy, for instance — for any one of these massive houses and the life of the man who paid the upkeep. If Mephistopheles were to emerge from the rhododendrons and stand behind his shoulder with such an offer, he wouldn't hesitate. Money? Oh, yes, he would like to have some, but not what went with it.

He turned in under Judge Hammersley's fine oak trees. A car was waiting in the driveway, near the steps by which he mounted to the door. The colored man admitted him, and just as he entered the hall Mrs. Parmenter came down the stairs.

"Ah, it's you, Albert! Father said you were coming in this evening, and I've kept the car waiting, to have a glimpse of you."

Albert had dropped his hat and bag, and stood holding her hand with the special grace and appreciation she remembered in him.

"What a pleasure to see you!" he exclaimed, and she knew from his eyes it was. "It doesn't happen often, but it's always such a surprise and pleasure." He held her hand as if he wanted to keep her there. "It's a long while since the Villa Scipione, isn't it?"

They stood for a moment in the shrouded hall light. Mrs. Parmenter was looking very handsome, and Albert was thinking that she had all her father's authority, with much more sweep and freedom. She was impulsive and careless, where he was strong and shrinking — a powerful man terribly afraid of little annoyances. His daughter, Albert believed, was not afraid of anything. She had proved more than once that if you aren't afraid of gossip, it is harmless. She did as she pleased. People took it. Even Parmenter had taken it, and he was rather a stiff sort.

Mrs. Parmenter laughed at his allusion to their summer at Mrs. Sterrett's, in Rome, and gave him her coat to hold.

"You remember, Albert, how you and I used to get up early on fête days, and go down to the garden gate to see the young king come riding in from the country at the head of the horse guards? How the sun flashed on his helmet! Heavens, I saw him last summer! So grizzled and battered."

"And we were always going to run away to Russia together, and now there is no Russia. Everything has changed but you, Mrs. Parmenter."

"Wish I could think so. But you don't know any Mrs. Parmenter. I'm Marjorie, please. How often I think of those gay afternoons I had with you and your brothers in the garden behind your old Allegheny house. There's such a lot I want to talk to you about. And this birthday — when is it? May I send your uncle some flowers? I always remember his goodness to poor Marguerite Thiesinger. He never got over that, did he? But I'm late, and father is waiting. Good night, you'll have a message from me."

Albert bent and kissed her hand in the old-fashioned way, keeping it a moment and breathing in softly the fragrance of her clothes, her furs, her person, the fragrance of that other world to which he had once belonged and out of which he had slipped so gradually that he scarcely realized it, unless suddenly brought face to face with something in it that was charming. Releasing her, he caught up his hat and opened the door to follow her, but she pushed him back with her arm and smiled over her shoulder. "No, no, father is waiting for you in the library. Good night."

Judge Hammersley stood in the doorway, fingering a bunch of keys and blinking with impatience to render his service and have done with it. The library opened directly into the hall; he couldn't help overhearing his daughter, and he disliked her free and unreproachful tone with this man who was young when he should be old, single when he should be married, and penniless when he should be well fixed.

Later, as Albert came down the hill with two bottles of the Judge's best champagne in his bag, he was thinking that the greatest disadvantage of being poor and dropping out of the world was that he didn't meet attractive women any more. The men he could do without, Heaven knew! But the women, the ones like Marjorie Hammersley, were always grouped where the big fires burned — money and success and big houses and fast boats and French cars; it was natural.

Mrs. Parmenter, as she drove off, resolved that she would see more of Albert and his uncle — wondered why she had let an old friendship lapse for so long. When she was a little girl, she used often to spend a week with her aunt in Allegheny. She was fond of the aunt, but not of her cousins, and she used to escape whenever she could to the Engelhardts' garden only a few doors away. No grass in that garden — in Allegheny grass was always dirty — but glittering gravel, and lilac hedges beautiful in spring, and barberry hedges red in the fall, and flowers and bird cages and striped awnings, boys lying about in tennis clothes, making mint juleps before lunch, having coffee under the sycamore trees after dinner. The Engelhardt boys were different, like people in a book or a play. All the young men in her set were scornful of girls until they wanted one; then they grabbed her rather brutally, and it was over. She had felt that the Engelhardt boys admired her without in the least wanting to grab her, that they enjoyed her æsthetically, so to speak, and it pleased her to be liked in that way.

VI

On the afternoon of the first of December, Albert left his desk in the County Clerk's office at four o'clock, feeling very much as he used to when school was dismissed in the middle of the afternoon just before the Christmas holidays. It was his uncle's birthday that was in his mind; his own, of course, gave him no particular pleasure. If one stopped to think of that, there was a shiver waiting round the corner. He walked over the Smithfield Street Bridge. A thick brown fog made everything dark, and there was a feeling of snow in the air. The lights along the sheer cliffs of Mount Washington, high above the river, were already lighted. When Albert was a boy, those cliffs, with the row of lights far up against the sky, always made him think of some far-away, cloud-set city in Asia; the forbidden city, he used to call it. Well, that was a long time ago; a lot of water had run under this bridge since then, and kingdoms and empires had fallen. Meanwhile, Uncle Doctor was still hanging on, and things were not so bad with them as they might be. Better not reflect too much. He hopped on board a street car, and old women with market baskets shifted to make room for him.

When he reached home, the table was already set in the living room. Beautiful table linen had been one of his mother's extravagances (he had boxes of it, meant to give some to Elsa on her marriage), and Mrs. Rudder laundered it with pious care. She had put out the best silver. He had forgotten to order flowers, but the old woman had brought up one of her blooming geraniums for a centerpiece. Uncle Albert was dozing by the fire in his old smoking jacket, a volume of Schiller on his knees.

"I'll put the studs in your shirt for you. Time to dress, Uncle Doctor."

The old man blinked and smiled drolly. "So? *Die* claw-hammer?"

"Of course *die* claw-hammer! Elsa is going to a masquerade with Carl, and they are coming up to see us before they go. I promised her you would dress."

"Albert," the Doctor called him back, beckoned with a mysterious smile; "where did you get that wine now?"

"Oh, you found it when she put it on ice, did you? That's Judge Hammersley's, the best he had. He insisted on sending it to you, with his compliments and good wishes."

Uncle Albert rose and drew up his shoulders somewhat pompously. "From my own kind I still command recognition." Then dropping into homely vulgarity he added, with a sidelong squint at his nephew, "By God, some of that will feel good, running down the gullet."

"You'll have all you want for once. It's a great occasion. Did you shave carefully? I'll take my bath, and then you must be ready for me."

In half an hour Albert came out in his dress clothes and found his uncle still reading his favorite poet. "The trousers are too big," the Doctor complained. "Why not *die* claw-hammer and my old trousers? Elsa wouldn't notice."

"Oh, yes, she would! She's seen these every day for five years. Quick change!"

Doctor Engelhardt submitted, and when he was dressed, surveyed himself in his mirror with satisfaction, though he slyly slipped a cotton handkerchief into his pocket instead of the linen one Albert had laid out. When they came back to the sitting room, Mrs. Rudder had been up again and had put on the wine glasses. There was still half an hour before dinner, and Albert sat down to play for his uncle. He was beginning to feel that it was all much ado about nothing, after all.

A gentle tap at the door, and Elsa came in with her young man. She was dressed as a Polish maiden, and Carl Abberbock was in a Highlander's kilt.

"Congratulations on your birthday, Herr Doctor, and I've brought you some flowers." She went to his chair and bent down to be kissed, putting a bunch of violets in his hand.

The Doctor rose and stood looking down at the violets. "Hey, you take me for a Bonapartist? What is Mussolini's flower, Albert? Advise your friends in Rome that a Supreme Dictator should always have a flower." He turned the young girl around in the light and teased her about her thin arms — such an old joke, but she laughed for him.

"But that's the style now, Herr Doctor. Everybody wants to be as thin as possible."

"Bah, there are no styles in such things! A man will always want something to take hold of, till Hell freezes over! Is dat so, Carl?"

Carl, a very broad-faced, smiling young man with outstanding ears, was suddenly frightened into silence by the entrance of a fine lady, and made for the door to get his knotty knees into the shadow. Elsa, too, caught her breath and shrank away.

Without knocking, Mrs. Parmenter, her arms full of roses, appeared in the doorway, and just behind her was her chauffeur, carrying a package. "Put it down there and wait for me," she said to him, then swept into the room and lightly embraced Doctor Engelhardt without waiting to drop the flowers or take off her furs. "I wanted to congratulate you in person. They told me below that you were receiving. Please take these flowers, Albert. I want a moment's chat with Doctor Engelhardt."

The Doctor stood with singular gravity, like some one in a play, the violets still in his hand. "To what," he muttered with his best bow, "to what am I indebted for such distinguished consideration?"

"To your own distinction, my dear sir — always one of the most distinguished men I ever knew."

The Doctor, to whom flattery was thrice dearer than to ordinary men, flushed deeply. But he was not so exalted that he did not notice his little friend of many lonely hours slipping out of the entry-way — the bare-kneed Highland chief had already got down the wooden stairs. "Elsa," he called commandingly, "come here and kiss me good night." He pulled her forward. "This is Elsa Rudder, Mrs. Parmenter, and my very particular friend. You should have seen her beautiful hair before she cut it off." Elsa reddened and glanced up to see whether the lady understood. Uncle Doctor kissed her on the forehead and ran his hand over her shingled head. "Nineteen years," he said softly. "If the next nineteen are as happy, we won't bother about the rest. *Behüt' dich, Gott!*"

"Thank you, Uncle Doctor. Good night."

After she fluttered out, he turned to Mrs. Parmenter. "That little girl," he said impressively, "is the rose in winter. She is my heir. Everything I have, I leave to her."

"Everything but my birthday present, please! You must drink that. I've brought you a bottle of champagne."

Both Alberts began to laugh. "But your father has already given us two!"

Mrs. Parmenter looked from one to the other. "My father? Well, that is a compliment! It's unheard of. Of course he and I have different lockers. We could never agree when to open them. I don't think he's opened his since the Chief Justice dined with him. Now I must leave you. Be as jolly as the night is long; with three bottles you ought to do very well! The good woman downstairs said your dinner would be served in half an hour."

Both men started toward her. "Don't go. Please, please, stay and dine with us! It's the one thing we needed." Albert began to entreat her in Italian, a language his uncle did not understand. He confessed that he had been freezing up for the last hour, couldn't go on with it alone. "One can't do such things without a woman — a beautiful woman."

"Thank you, Albert. But I've a dinner engagement; I ought to be at the far end of Ellsworth Avenue this minute."

"But this is once in a lifetime — for him! Still, if your friends are waiting for you, you can't. Certainly not." He took up her coat and held it for her. But how the light had gone out of his face; he looked so different, so worn, as he stood holding her coat at just the right height. She slipped her arms into it, then pulled them out. "I can't, but I just will! Let me write a note, please. I'll send Henry on with it and tell them I'll drop in after dinner." Albert pressed her hand gratefully and took her to his desk. "Oh, Albert, your Italian writing table, and all the lovely things on it, just as it stood in your room at the Villa Scipione! You used to let me write letters at it. You had the nicest way with young girls. If I had a daughter, I'd want you to do it all over again."

She scratched a note, and Albert put a third place at the table. He noticed Uncle Doctor slip away, and come back with his necktie set straight, attended by a wave of *eau de cologne*. While he was lighting the candles and bringing in the wine cooler, Mrs. Parmenter sat down beside the Doctor, accepted one of his cigarettes, and began to talk to him simply and naturally about Marguerite Theisinger. Nothing could have been more tactful, Albert knew; nothing could give the old man more pleasure on his birthday. Albert himself couldn't do it any more; he had worn out his power of going over that sad story. He tried to make up for it by playing the songs she had sung.

"Albert," said Mrs. Parmenter when they sat down to dinner, "this is the only spot I know in the world that is before-the-war. You've got a period shut up in here; the last ten years of one century, and the first ten of another. Sitting here, I don't believe in aëroplanes, or jazz, or Cubists. My father is nearly as old as Doctor Engelhardt, and we never buy anything new; yet we haven't kept it out. How do you manage?"

Albert smiled a little ruefully. "I suppose it's because we never have any young people about. They bring it in."

"Elsa," murmured the Doctor. "But I see; she is only a child."

"I'm sorry for the young people now," Mrs. Parmenter went on. "They seem to me coarse and bitter. There's nothing wonderful left for them, poor things; the war destroyed it all. Where could any girl find such a place to escape to as your mother's house, full of chests of linen like this? All houses now are like hotels; nothing left to cherish. Your house was wonderful! And what music we used to have. Do you remember the time you took me to hear Joseffy play the second Brahms, with Gericke? It was the last time I ever heard him. What did happen to him, Albert? Went to pieces in some way, didn't he?"

Albert sighed and shook his head; wine was apt to plunge him into pleasant, poetic melancholy. "I don't know if any one knows. I stayed in Rome too long to know, myself. Before I went abroad, I'd been taking lessons with him right along — I saw no change in him, though he gave fewer and fewer concerts. When I got back, I wrote him the day I landed in New York — he was living up the Hudson then. I got a reply from his house-keeper, saying that he was not giving lessons, was ill and was seeing nobody. I went out to his place at once. I wasn't asked to come into the house. I was told to wait in the garden. I waited a long while. At last he came out, wearing white clothes, as he often did, a panama hat, carrying a little cane. He shook hands with me, asked me about Mrs. Sterrett — but he was another man, that's all. He was gone; he wasn't there. I was talking to his picture."

"Drugs!" muttered the Doctor out of one corner of his mouth.

"Nonsense!" Albert shrugged in derision. "Or if he did, that was secondary; a result, not a cause. He'd seen the other side of things; he'd let go. Something had happened in his brain that was not paresis."

Mrs. Parmenter leaned forward. "Did he *look* the same? Surely, he had the handsomest head in the world. Remember his forehead? Was he gray? His hair was a reddish chestnut, as I remember."

"A little gray; not much. There was no change in his face, except his eyes. The bright spark had gone out, and his body had a sort of trailing languor when he moved."

"Would he give you a lesson?"

"No. Said he wasn't giving any. Said he was sorry, but he wasn't seeing people at all any more. I remember he sat making patterns in the gravel with his cane. He frowned and said he simply couldn't see people; said the human face had become hateful to him — and the human voice! 'I am sorry,' he said, 'but that is the truth.' I looked at his left hand, lying on his knee. I wonder, Marjorie, that I had the strength to get up and go away. I felt as if everything had been drawn out of me. He got up and took my hand. I understood that I must leave. In desperation I asked him whether music didn't mean anything to him still. 'Music,' he said slowly, with just a ghost of his old smile, 'yes — some music.' He went back into the house. Those were the last words I ever heard him speak."

"Oh, dear! And he had everything that is beautiful — and the name of an angel! But we're making the Doctor melancholy. Open another bottle, Albert — father did very well by you. We've not drunk a single toast. Many returns, we take for granted. Why not each drink a toast of our own, to something we care for." She glanced at Doctor Engelhardt, who lifted the bunch of violets by his plate and smelled them absently. "Now, Doctor Engelhardt, a toast!"

The Doctor put down his flowers, delicately took up his glass and held it directly in front of him; everything he did with his hands was deft and sure. A beautiful, a wonderful look came over his face as she watched him.

"I drink," he said slowly, "to a memory; to the lost Lenore."

"And I," said young Albert softly, "to my youth, to my beautiful youth!"

Tears flashed into Mrs. Parmenter's eyes. "Ah," she thought, "that's what liking people amounts to; it's liking their silliness and absurdities. That's what it really is."

"And I," she said aloud, "will drink to the future; to our renewed friendship, and many dinners together. I like you two better than anyone I know."

When Albert came back from seeing Mrs. Parmenter down to her car, he found his uncle standing by the fire, his elbow on the mantel, thoughtfully rolling a cigarette. "Albert," he said in a deeply confidential tone, "good wine, good music, beautiful women; that is all there is worth turning over the hand for."

Albert began to laugh. The old man wasn't often banal. "Why, Uncle, you and Martin Luther — "

The Doctor lifted a hand imperiously to stop him, and flushed darkly. He evidently hadn't been aware that he was quoting — it came from the heart. "Martin Luther," he snapped, "was a vulgarian of the first water; cabbage soup!" He paused a moment to light his cigarette. "But don't fool yourself; one like her always knows when a man has had success with women!"

Albert poured a last glass from the bottle and sipped it critically. "Well, you had success to-night, certainly. I could see that Marjorie was impressed. She's coming to take you for a ride to-morrow, after your nap, so you must be ready."

The Doctor passed his flexible, nervous hand lightly over the thick bristles of his French hair-cut. *"Even in our ashes,"* he muttered haughtily.

1929

*Grace Stone Coates*

......................................................................................................................

# Wild Plums

FROM *The Frontier*

I KNEW about wild plums twice before I tasted any.

The first time was when the Sunday school women were going plum-ming; Father hunched his shoulders and laughed without making any sound. He said wild plums were small and inferior, and told us of fruits he had eaten in Italy.

Mother and father were surprised that Mrs. Guare and the school teacher would go with Mrs. Slump to gather plums. I knew it was not nice to go plumming, but I didn't know why. I wanted to go once, so that I would understand. The women stopped at the house to invite mother. She explained that we did not care for wild plums; but father said we feared to taste the sacred seed lest we be constrained to dwell forever in the nether regions.

Mrs. Slump said, "Huh? You don't eat the pits. You spit 'em out," and father hunched his shoulders and laughed the noiseless laugh that bothered mother.

When father talked to people he didn't like he sorted his words, and used only the smooth, best ones. Mother explained to me it was because he had spoken only German when he was little.

After the women had gone mother and father quarreled. They spoke low so I would not hear them. Just before mother sent me out to play she said that even wild plums might give savor to the dry bread of monotony.

The second time I knew about plums was at Mrs. Slump's house when she was making plum butter. She said she couldn't ask us in because the floor was dirty from stirring jam. The Slumps didn't use chairs. They had boxes to sit on, and the children sat on the floor with the dogs. They were the only people I knew who had hounds. I wanted to go in. We never had visited them. We were at their house now because father needed to take home a plow they had borrowed. Father didn't like to have his machinery stand outdoors. He had a shed where he kept plows when he was not using them, but the Slumps left theirs where they unhitched.

Mrs. Slump was standing in the door with her back toward us when we drove up. She was fat, and wore wrappers. Her wrapper was torn down the back.

Mr. Slump came out, and father talked to him. He was tall and lean. Mrs. Slump came and stood by the buggy, too. Mother and father sat on the front seat of the buggy, and Teressa and I on the back seat. Teressa was older than I, and had longer legs. When she stretched her feet straight out she could touch the front seat with her toes, and I couldn't. She bumped the seat behind mother, and mother turned around and told her to stop. My feet didn't touch father's seat, so I wasn't doing anything and didn't have to stop it. Teressa pinched me.

I climbed out of the buggy without asking if I might. Teressa started to tell mother I was getting out, but waited to see what I intended to do. I was going to walk around behind Mrs. Slump. She had no stockings on, and the Sunday school women said she didn't wear underclothes. I wanted to see if this was so.

Mother called me back. Sometimes mother knew what I was thinking about without asking me. She took hold of my arm, hard, as I climbed onto the buggy step, and said under her breath, "I'd be ashamed! I'd be ashamed!" Her face was twisted because she tried not to stop smiling at Mrs. Slump while she shook my arm. I kept trying to explain, but she wouldn't let me. Her stopping me made me want to say the thing she thought I was going to, but I didn't dare.

Mr. Slump said he would bring the plow back in the morning. Father wanted to take it home himself, then; but Mr. Slump said he wouldn't hear to it, being as how he had borrowed it and all. He would bring it behind the lumber wagon the next day, and leave it in the road. They were going after more plums and would be passing the house anyway.

The next morning after breakfast, father, mother, and I were in the kitchen. Teressa had scraped the plates and gone to feed the chickens. She did not like to sit still while people talked. She liked to do things that made her move around. Mother and father were talking, and I was looking out of the window. If I looked at the sun and then away, it made enormous morning-glories float over the yard. Father had told me they were in my eyes and not in the air, so I didn't call him to look at them.

While I was watching them, Clubby Slump came up the lane in the middle of a lavender one. Clubby was bigger than I, and stupider. When any one spoke to him, he stood with his mouth open and didn't answer. His hair needed combing, and he didn't use a handkerchief. Mother said good morning to him. He pointed to a wagon at the end of the lane. He said, "Plums!" and ran back down the path.

Mother and father started toward the road, and I went ahead of them. The wagon had stopped at the foot of the cottonwood lane. Mr. Slump sat on the high board seat, holding the reins. Mrs. Slump was beside him, with the baby on her lap. Liney Slump was between them. On the seat behind were Mrs. Guare and two women I didn't know. The rest of the wagon was full of children. Mr. Slump had forgotten the plow.

"All you'uns pile in," Mrs. Slump called to us. "We're goin' plummin' on the Niniscaw and stay all night. The younguns can go wadin'. There ain't no work drivin' you this time a' year, so just pile in. We got beddin' for everybody."

Mr. Slump sat looking at the horses' ears. Whenever Mrs. Slump stopped talking he would say, "I *tole* you they'all wouldn't go, but you *would* stop," and Mrs. Slump would answer, "There now, Paw, you hush!"

I had not known one could live so long without breathing as I lived while Mrs. Slump was asking us to go. I could see my heart-beats shaking my collar — a lace collar that was hanging by one end down my chest; I had forgotten to put it on right.

I waited for mother to lift her foot and plant it on the wagon hub, ready for "pilin' in"; for father to take her elbow, and lift. Every one would laugh a little, and talk loud. They always did when women got into wagons. I had never seen mother climb into a wagon, but I knew how it would be. I wondered if father would jump in without tossing me up first. Father got into wagons quick, without laughing or joking. I wondered if he would forget me. The children would see me, and lean over the end-board, and dangle me up by one arm. I thought frantically of Teressa.

Then father was speaking, and my breath came back.

He was saying, "If you happen on a plum thicket, an outcome highly unlikely, you still face the uncertainty of finding plums. The season has been too dry. And should you find them, they will prove acrid and unfit for human consumption."

My collar hung limp and motionless. My heart was dead. Father was spoiling things again.

Mrs. Slump said, "They make fine jell," and Mr. Slump repeated, "I *tole* you they-all wouldn't go, but you *would* stop." He was gathering up the lines.

I hated to see mother's face, feeling the stricken look it would have. But I knew I must smile at her not to care. Strangely enough, she had a polite look on her face. It was the look that made my fingers think of glass. My mind slipped off from it without knowing what it meant. She was smiling.

"Really, it isn't possible for us to go with you to-day," she said. "It was kind of you to ask us. I hope you will have a lovely outing, and find lots of plums."

As she spoke she glanced at me. She moved closer, and took my hand. Mrs. Slump looked down at me, too, and said, "Can't the kid go? Kids like bein' out."

Mother's hand closed firmly on mine. "I'm afraid not, without me. Besides," with a severe look at my collar, "she isn't properly dressed."

"Oh, we kin wait while she takes off that purty dress," Mrs. Slump suggested comfortably; but mother flushed and shook her head.

Mr. Slump was twitching at the lines and clucking to the horses. His last "I tole you" was drowned in shouted good-bys, and the wagon clattered down the road.

Mother walked back to the house still holding my hand. Once inside, she turned to me. "Would you really have gone with those —" She hesitated, and finished, "with those persons?"

"They were going to sleep outdoors all night," I said.

Mother shuddered. "Would you have gone with them?"

"Mrs. Guare was with them," I parried, knowing all she did not say.

"Would you have gone?"

"Yes."

She stood for a long time looking out of the window at the prairie horizon, then searched my face curiously. "It might have been as well," she said. "It might be as well," and turning, she began to clear the breakfast table.

The next day I played in the road. Usually I spent the afternoons under the box-elder trees, or by the ditch behind the machine-sheds, where dragon-flies and pale blue moths circled just out of reach. But this day I spent beside the road. Mother called me to the house to bring cobs, and called me again to gather eggs in the middle of the afternoon. She called me a third time. Her face looked uncomfortable.

She said, "If the Slumps go by, do not ask them for any plums."

Mother knew I would not ask.

"If they offer any, do not take them."

"What shall I say?"

"Say we do not care for them."

"If they make me take them?"

"Refuse them."

When the Slumps came in sight the horses were walking. The Niniscaw was fifteen miles away, and the team was tired. I thought I could talk to the children as the wagon passed, but just before it reached me, Mr. Slump hit the horses twice with a willow branch. They trotted, and the wagon rattled by.

The children on the last seat were facing toward me. They laughed and waved their arms. Clubby leaned backward and caught up a handful of plums. The wagon bed must have been half filled. He flung them toward me; and then another handful. They fell, scattering, in the thick dust, which curled around them in little eddies, almost hiding them before I could catch them up.

The plums were small and red. They felt warm to my fingers. I wiped them on the front of my dress, and dropped them in my apron. I waited only for one secret rite, before I ran, heart pounding, to tell my mother what I had discovered.

She interrupted me, "Did they see you picking them up?"

I thought of myself standing like Clubby Slump, mouth open, without moving. I laughed till two plums rolled out of my apron. "Oh, yes! I had them picked up almost before the dust stopped wriggling. I called, 'Thank you.'"

Still mother was not pleased. "Throw them away," she said. "Surely you would not care to eat something flung to you in the road."

It was hard to speak. I moved close to her and whispered, "Can't I keep them?"

Mother left the room. It seemed long before she came back. She put her arm around me and said, "Take them to the pump and wash them thoroughly. Eat them slowly, and do not swallow the skins. You will not want many of them, for you will find them bitter and not fit to eat."

I went out quietly, knowing I would never tell her that they were strange on my tongue as wild honey, holding the warmth of sand that sun had fingered, and the mystery of water under leaning boughs.

For I had eaten one at the road.

## Katherine Anne Porter

# Theft

FROM *The Gyroscope*

SHE HAD the purse in her hand when she came in. Standing in the middle of the floor, holding her bathrobe around her and trailing a damp towel in one hand, she surveyed the immediate past and remembered everything clearly. Yes, she had opened the flap and spread it out on the bench after she had dried the purse with her handkerchief.

She had intended to take the Elevated, and naturally she looked in her purse to make certain she had the fare, and was pleased to find forty cents in the coin envelope. She was going to pay her own fare, too, even if Camilo did have the habit of seeing her up the steps and dropping a nickel in the machine before he gave the turnstile a little push and sent her through it with a bow. Camilo by a series of compromises had managed to make effective a fairly complete set of the smaller courtesies, ignoring the larger and more troublesome ones. She had walked with him to the station in a pouring rain, because she knew he was almost as poor as she was, and when he insisted on a taxi, she was firm and said, "You know it simply will not do." He was wearing a new hat of a pretty biscuit shade, for it never occurred to him to buy anything of a practical colour; he had put it on for the first time and the rain was spoiling it. She kept thinking, "But this is dreadful, where will he get another?" and compared it with Eddie's hats that always seemed to be precisely seven years old and as if they had been quite purposely left out in the rain, and they sat with a careless and incidental rightness on Eddie. But Camilo was far different, if he wore a shabby hat it would be merely shabby on him, and he would lose his spirits over it. If she had not feared Camilo would take it badly, for he insisted on the practise of his little ceremonies up to the point he had fixed for them, she would have said to him as they left Thora's house, "Do go home. I can surely reach the station by myself."

"It is written that we must be rained upon to-night," said Camilo, "so let it be together."

At the foot of the platform stairway she staggered slightly — they were both nicely set up on Thora's cocktails — and said: "At least, Camilo, do me the favor not to climb these stairs in your present state, since for you it is only a matter of coming down again at once, and you'll certainly break your neck."

He made three quick bows, he was Spanish, and leaped off through the rainy darkness. She stood watching him, for he was a very graceful young man, thinking that to-morrow morning he would gaze soberly at his spoiled hat and soggy shoes and possibly associate her with his misery. And as she watched, he stopped at the far corner and took off his hat and hid it under his overcoat. She felt she had betrayed him by seeing, because he would have been humiliated if he thought she even suspected him of trying to save his hat.

Roger's voice sounded over her shoulder above the clang of the rain falling on the stairway shed, wanting to know what she was doing out in the rain at this time of night, and did she take herself for a duck? His long, imperturbable face was streaming with water, and he tapped a bulging spot on the breast of his buttoned-up overcoat: "Hat," he said. "Come on, let's take a taxi."

She settled back against Roger's arm which he laid around her shoulders, and with the gesture they exchanged a glance full of long amiable associations, then she looked through the window at the rain changing the shapes of everything, and the colours. The taxi dodged in and out between the pillars of the Elevated, skidding slightly on every curve, and she said: "The more it skids the calmer I feel, so I really must be drunk."

"You must be," said Roger. "This bird is a homicidal maniac, and I could do with a cocktail myself this minute."

They waited on the traffic at Fortieth Street and Sixth Avenue, and three boys walked before the nose of the taxi. Under the globes of light they were cheerful scarecrows, all very thin and wearing very seedy snappy-cut suits and gay neckties. They were not very sober either, and they stood for a moment wobbling in front of the car, and there was an argument going on among them. They leaned toward each other as if they were getting ready to sing, and the first one said: "When I get married it won't be jus' for getting married, I'm gonna marry for *love*, see?" and the second one said, "Aw, gwan and tell that stuff to *her*, why'nt yuh?" and the third one gave a kind of hoot, and said, "Hell, dis guy? Wot the hell's he got?" and the first one said: "Aaah, shurrup yuh mush, I got plenty." Then they all squealed and scrambled across the street beating the third one on the back and pushing him around.

"Nuts," commented Roger, "pure nuts."

Two girls went skittering by in short transparent raincoats, one green, one red, their heads tucked against the drive of the rain. One of them was saying to the other, "Yes, I know all about *that*. But what about me? You're always so sorry for *him* . . ." and they ran on with their little pelican legs flashing back and forth.

The taxi backed up suddenly and leaped forward again, and after a while Roger said: "I had a letter from Stella to-day, and she'll be home on the 26th, so I suppose she's made up her mind and it's all settled."

"I had a sort of letter to-day too," she said. "I think it is time for you and Stella to do something definite."

When the taxi stopped on the corner of West Fifty-third Street, Roger said, "I've just enough if you'll add ten cents," so she opened her purse and gave him a dime, and he said, "That's beautiful, that purse."

"It's a birthday present," she told him, "and I like it. How's your show coming?"

"Oh, still hanging on, I guess. I don't go near the place. Nothing sold yet. I mean to keep right on the way I'm going and they can take it or leave it. I'm through with the argument."

"It's absolutely a matter of holding out, isn't it?"

"Holding out's the tough part."

"Good-night, Roger."

"Good-night, you should take aspirin and push yourself into a tub of hot water, you look as though you're catching cold."

"I will."

With the purse under her arm she went upstairs, and on the first landing Bill heard her step and poked his head out with his hair tumbled and his eyes red, and he said: "For Christ's sake come in and have a drink with me. I've had some bad news.

"You're perfectly sopping," said Bill. They had two drinks, and Bill told how the director had thrown his play out after the cast had been picked over twice, and had gone through three rehearsals. "I said to him, 'I didn't say it was a masterpiece, I said it was a good show.' And he said, 'It just doesn't *play*, do you see? It needs a doctor.' So I'm stuck, absolutely stuck," said Bill, on the edge of weeping again. "I've been crying," he told her, "in my cups." And he went on to ask her if she realized that his wife was ruining him with her extravagance. "I send her ten dollars every week of my unhappy life, and I don't really have to. She threatens to jail me if I don't, but she can't do it. God, let her try it after the way she treated me! She's no right to alimony, and she knows it. But I send it because I can't bear to see anybody suffer. And I'm way behind on the piano and the victrola, both — "

"Well, this is a pretty rug, anyhow," she said.

Bill stared at it and blew his nose. "I got it at Ricci's for ninety-five dollars," he said. "Ricci said it once belonged to Marie Dressler and cost fifteen hundred dollars, but there's a burnt place on it. Can you beat that?"

"No," she said.

They had another drink and she went to her apartment on the floor above, and there, she now remembered distinctly, she had taken the letter out of the purse before she spread the purse out to dry.

She had sat down and read the letter over again: but there were phrases that insisted on being read many times, they had a life of their own separate from the others, and when she tried to read past and around them, they moved with the movement of her eyes, and she could not escape them . . . "thinking about you more than I mean to . . . yes, I even talk about you . . . why were you so anxious to destroy . . . even if I could see you now I would not . . . not worth all this abomina-ble . . . the end . . ."

Carefully she tore the letter into narrow strips and touched a lighted match to them in the coal grate.

Early the next morning she was in the bath tub when the janitress knocked and then came in, calling out that she wished to examine the radiators before she started the furnace going for the winter. After moving about the room for a few minutes, the janitress went out closing the door very sharply.

She came out of the bathroom to get a cigarette from the package in the purse. The purse was gone. She dressed and made coffee, and sat by the window while she drank it. Certainly the janitress had taken the purse, and certainly it would be impossible to get it back without a great deal of ridiculous excitement. Then let it go. With this decision of her mind, there rose coincidentally in her blood a deep almost murderous anger. She set the cup carefully in the centre of the table, and walked unsteadily downstairs, three long flights and a short hall and a steep short flight into the basement, where the janitress, her face streaked with coal dust, was shaking up the furnace. "Will you please give me back my purse? There isn't any money in it. It was a present, and I don't want to lose it."

The janitress turned without straightening up and peered at her with hot flickering eyes, a red light reflected from the furnace in them. "What do you mean, your purse?"

"The gold cloth purse you took from the wooden bench in my room," she said. "I must have it back."

"Before God I never laid eyes on your purse, and that's the holy truth," said the janitress.

"Oh, well then, keep it," she said, but in a very bitter voice, "keep it if you want it so much." And she walked away.

She remembered how she had never locked a door in her life, on some principle of rejection in her that made her uncomfortable in the ownership of things, and her paradoxical boast before the warnings of her friends, that she had never lost a penny by theft; and she had been pleased with the bleak humility of this concrete example designed to illustrate and justify a certain fixed, otherwise baseless and general faith which ordered the movements of her life without regard to her will in the matter.

In this moment she felt that she had been robbed of an enormous number of valuable things, whether material or intangible: things lost or broken by her own fault, things she had forgotten and left in houses when she moved: books borrowed and not returned, journeys she had planned and had not made, words she had waited to hear spoken to her and had not heard, and the words she had meant to answer with bitter alternatives and intolerable substitutes worse than nothing, and yet inescapable: the long patient suffering of dying friendships and the dark inexplicable death of love — all that she had had, and all that she had missed, were lost together, and were twice lost in this landslide of remembered losses.

The janitress was following her upstairs with her purse in her hand and the same deep red fire flickering in her eyes. The janitress thrust the purse towards her while they were still a half dozen steps apart, and said: "Don't never tell on me. I musta been crazy. I get crazy in the head sometimes, I swear I do. My son can tell you."

She took the purse after a moment, and the janitress went on: "I got a niece who is going on seventeen, and she's a nice girl and I thought I'd give it to her. She needs a pretty purse. I musta been crazy, I thought maybe you wouldn't mind, you leave things around and don't seem to notice much."

She said: "I missed this because it was a present to me from some one . . ."

The janitress said: "He'd get you another if you lost this one. My niece is young and needs pretty things, we oughta give the young ones a chance. She's got young men after her maybe will want to marry her. She oughta have nice things. She needs them bad right now. You're a grown woman, you've had your chance, you ought to know how it is!"

She held the purse out to the janitress saying: "You don't know what you're talking about. Here, take it, I've changed my mind. I really don't want it."

The janitress looked up at her with hatred and said: "I don't want it either now. My niece is young and pretty, she don't need fixin' up to be pretty, she's young and pretty anyhow! I guess you need it worse than she does!"

"It wasn't really yours in the first place," she said, turning away. "You mustn't talk as if I had stolen it from you."

"It's not from me, it's from her you're stealing it," said the janitress, and went back downstairs.

She laid the purse on the table and sat down with the cup of chilled coffee, and thought. I was right not to be afraid of any thief but myself, who will end by leaving me nothing.

1931

*William Faulkner*

# That Evening Sun Go Down

FROM *The American Mercury*

I

MONDAY IS no different from any other week day in Jefferson now. The streets are paved now, and the telephone and the electric companies are cutting down more and more of the shade trees — the water oaks, the maples and locusts and elms — to make room for iron poles bearing clusters of bloated and ghostly and bloodless grapes, and we have a city laundry which makes the rounds on Monday morning, gathering the bundles of clothes into bright-colored, specially made motor-cars: the soiled wearing of a whole week now flees apparition-like behind alert and irritable electric horns, with a long diminishing noise of rubber and asphalt like a tearing of silk, and even the Negro women who still take in white people's washing after the old custom, fetch and deliver it in automobiles.

But fifteen years ago, on Monday morning the quiet, dusty, shady streets would be full of Negro women with, balanced on their steady turbaned heads, bundles of clothes tied up in sheets, almost as large as cotton bales, carried so without touch of hand between the kitchen door of the white house and the blackened wash-pot beside a cabin door in Negro Hollow.

Nancy would set her bundle on the top of her head, then upon the bundle in turn she would set the black straw sailor hat which she wore Winter and Summer. She was tall, with a high, sad face sunken a little where her teeth were missing. Sometimes we would go a part of the way down the lane and across the pasture with her, to watch the balanced bundle and the hat that never bobbed nor wavered, even when she walked down into the ditch and climbed out again and stooped through the fence. She would go down on her hands and knees and crawl through the gap, her head rigid, up-tilted, the bundle steady as a rock or a balloon, and rise to her feet and go on.

Sometimes the husbands of the washing women would fetch and deliver the clothes, but Jubah never did that for Nancy, even before father told him to stay away from our house, even when Dilsey was sick and Nancy would come to cook for us.

And then about half the time we'd have to go down the lane to Nancy's house and tell her to come on and get breakfast. We would stop at the ditch, because father told us to not have anything to do with Jubah — he was a short black man, with a razor scar down his face — and we would throw rocks at Nancy's house until she came to the door, leaning her head around it without any clothes on.

"What you all mean, chunking my house?" Nancy said. "What you little devils mean?"

"Father says for you to come and get breakfast," Caddy said. "Father says it's over a half an hour now, and you've got to come this minute."

"I ain't studying no breakfast," Nancy said. "I going to get my sleep out."

"I bet you're drunk," Jason said. "Father says you're drunk. Are you drunk, Nancy?"

"Who says I is?" Nancy said. "I got to get my sleep out. I ain't studying no breakfast."

So after a while we quit chunking the house and went back home. When she finally came, it was too late for me to go to school. So we thought it was whiskey until that day when they arrested her again and they were taking her to jail and they passed Mr. Stovall. He was the cashier in the bank and a deacon in the Baptist church, and Nancy began to say:

"When you going to pay me, white man? When you going to pay me, white man? It's been three times now since you paid me a cent — " Mr. Stovall knocked her down, but she kept on saying, "When you going to pay me, white man? It's been three times now since — " until Mr. Stovall kicked her in the mouth with his heel and the marshal caught Mr. Stovall back, and Nancy lying in the street, laughing. She turned her head and spat out some blood and teeth and said, "It's been three times now since he paid me a cent."

That was how she lost her teeth, and all that day they told about Nancy and Mr. Stovall, and all that night the ones that passed the jail could hear Nancy singing and yelling. They could see her hands holding to the window bars, and a lot of them stopped along the fence, listening to her and to the jailer trying to make her shut up. She didn't shut up until just before daylight, when the jailer began to hear a bumping and scraping upstairs and he went up there and found Nancy hanging from the window bar. He said that it was cocaine and not whiskey, because no nigger would try to commit suicide unless he was full of cocaine, because a nigger full of cocaine was not a nigger any longer.

The jailer cut her down and revived her; then he beat her, whipped her. She had hung herself with her dress. She had fixed it all right, but when they arrested her she didn't have on anything except a dress and so she didn't have anything to tie her hands with and she couldn't make her hands let go of the window ledge. So the jailer heard the noise and ran up there and found Nancy hanging from the window, stark naked.

When Dilsey was sick in her cabin and Nancy was cooking for us, we could see her apron swelling out; that was before father told Jubah to stay away from the house. Jubah was in the kitchen, sitting behind the stove, with his razor scar on his black face like a piece of dirty string. He said it was a watermelon that Nancy had under her dress. And it was Winter, too.

"Where did you get a watermelon in the Winter?" Caddy said.

"I didn't," Jubah said. "It wasn't me that give it to her. But I can cut it down, same as if it was."

"What makes you want to talk that way before these chillen?" Nancy said. "Whyn't you go on to work? You done et. You want Mr. Jason to catch you hanging around his kitchen, talking that way before these chillen?"

"Talking what way, Nancy?" Caddy said.

"I can't hang around white man's kitchen," Jubah said. "But white man can hang around mine. White man can come in my house, but I can't stop him. When white man want to come in my house, I ain't got no house. I can't stop him, but he can't kick me outen it. He can't do that."

Dilsey was still sick in her cabin. Father told Jubah to stay off our place. Dilsey was still sick. It was a long time. We were in the library after supper.

"Isn't Nancy through yet?" mother said. "It seems to me that she has had plenty of time to have finished the dishes."

"Let Quentin go and see," father said. "Go and see if Nancy is through, Quentin. Tell her she can go on home."

I went to the kitchen. Nancy was through. The dishes were put away and the fire was out. Nancy was sitting in a chair, close to the cold stove. She looked at me.

"Mother wants to know if you are through," I said.

"Yes," Nancy said. She looked at me. "I done finished." She looked at me.

"What is it?" I said. "What is it?"

"I ain't nothing but a nigger," Nancy said. "It ain't none of my fault."

She looked at me, sitting in the chair before the cold stove, the sailor hat on her head. I went back to the library. It was the cold stove and all, when you think of a kitchen being warm and busy and cheerful. And with a cold stove and the dishes all put away, and nobody wanting to eat at that hour.

"Is she through?" mother said.

"Yessum," I said.

"What is she doing?" mother said.

"She's not doing anything. She's through."

"I'll go and see," father said.

"Maybe she's waiting for Jubah to come and take her home," Caddy said.

"Jubah is gone," I said. Nancy told us how one morning she woke up and Jubah was gone.

"He quit me," Nancy said. "Done gone to Memphis, I reckon. Dodging them city po-lice for a while, I reckon."

"And a good riddance," father said. "I hope he stays there."

"Nancy's scaired of the dark," Jason said.

"So are you," Caddy said.

"I'm not," Jason said.

"Scairy cat," Caddy said.

"I'm not," Jason said.

"You, Candace!" mother said. Father came back.

"I am going to walk down the lane with Nancy," he said. "She says Jubah is back."

"Has she seen him?" mother said.

"No. Some Negro sent her word that he was back in town. I won't be long."

"You'll leave me alone, to take Nancy home?" mother said. "Is her safety more precious to you than mine?"

"I won't be long," father said.

"You'll leave these children unprotected, with that Negro about?"

"I'm going too," Caddy said. "Let me go, father."

"What would he do with them, if he were unfortunate enough to have them?" father said.

"I want to go, too," Jason said.

"Jason!" mother said. She was speaking to father. You could tell that by the way she said it. Like she believed that all day father had been trying to think of doing the thing that she wouldn't like the most, and that she knew all the time that after a while he would think of it. I stayed quiet, because father and I both knew that mother would want him to make me stay with her, if she just thought of it in time. So father didn't even look at me. I was the oldest. I was nine and Caddy was seven and Jason was five.

"Nonsense," father said. "We won't be long."

Nancy had her hat on. We came to the lane. "Jubah always been good to me," Nancy said. "Whenever he had two dollars, one of them was mine." We walked in the lane. "If I can just get through the lane," Nancy said, "I be all right then."

The lane was always dark. "This is where Jason got scared on Hallowe'en," Caddy said.

"I didn't," Jason said.

"Can't Aunt Rachel do anything with him?" father said. Aunt Rachel was old. She lived in a cabin beyond Nancy's, by herself. She had white hair and she smoked a pipe in the door, all day long; she didn't work any more. They said she was Jubah's mother. Sometimes she said she was and sometimes she said she wasn't any kin to Jubah.

"Yes you did," Caddy said. "You were scairder than Frony. You were scairder than T.P. even. Scairder than niggers."

"Can't nobody do nothing with him," Nancy said. "He say I done woke up the devil in him, and ain't but one thing going to lay it again."

"Well, he's gone now," father said. "There's nothing for you to be afraid of now. And if you'd just let white men alone."

"Let what white men alone?" Caddy said. "How let them alone?"

"He ain't gone nowhere," Nancy said. "I can feel him. I can feel him now, in this lane. He hearing us talk, every word, hid somewhere, waiting. I ain't seen him, and I ain't going to see him again but once more, with that razor. That razor on that string down his back, inside his shirt. And then I ain't going to be even surprised."

"I wasn't scaired," Jason said.

"If you'd behave yourself, you'd have kept out of this," father said. "But it's all right now. He's probably in St. Louis now. Probably got another wife by now and forgot all about you."

"If he has, I better not find out about it," Nancy said. "I'd stand there and every time he wropped her, I'd cut that arm off. I'd cut his head off and I'd slit her belly and I'd shove —"

"Hush," father said.

"Slit whose belly, Nancy?" Caddy said.

"I wasn't scaired," Jason said. "I'd walk right down this lane by myself."

"Yah," Caddy said. "You wouldn't dare to put your foot in it if we were not with you."

## II

Dilsey was still sick, and so we took Nancy home every night until mother said, "How much longer is this going to go on? I to be left alone in this big house while you take home a frightened Negro?"

We fixed a pallet in the kitchen for Nancy. One night we waked up, hearing the sound. It was not singing and it was not crying, coming up the dark stairs. There was a light in mother's room and we heard father going down the hall, down the back stairs, and Caddy and I went into the hall. The floor was cold. Our toes curled away from the floor while we listened to the sound. It was like singing and it wasn't like singing, like the sounds that Negroes make.

Then it stopped and we heard father going down the back stairs, and we went to the head of the stairs. Then the sound began again, in the stairway, not loud, and we could see Nancy's eyes half way up the stairs, against the wall. They looked like cat's eyes do, like a big cat against the wall, watching us. When we came down the steps to where she was she quit making the sound again, and we stood there until father came back up from the kitchen, with his pistol in his hand. He went back down with Nancy and they came back with Nancy's pallet.

We spread the pallet in our room. After the light in mother's room went off, we could see Nancy's eyes again. "Nancy," Caddy whispered, "are you asleep, Nancy?"

Nancy whispered something. It was oh or no, I don't know which. Like nobody had made it, like it came from nowhere and went nowhere, until it was like Nancy was not there at all; that I had looked so hard at her eyes on the stair that they had got printed on my eyelids, like the sun does when you have closed your eyes and there is no sun. "Jesus," Nancy whispered. "Jesus."

"Was it Jubah?" Caddy whispered. "Did he try to come into the kitchen?"

"Jesus," Nancy said. Like this: Jeeeeeeeeeeeeeeeeesus, until the sound went out like a match or a candle does.

"Can you see us, Nancy?" Caddy whispered. "Can you see our eyes too?"

"I ain't nothing but a nigger," Nancy said. "God knows. God knows."

"What did you see down there in the kitchen?" Caddy whispered. "What tried to get in?"

"God knows," Nancy said. We could see her eyes. "God knows."

Dilsey got well. She cooked dinner. "You'd better stay in bed a day or two longer," father said.

"What for?" Dilsey said. "If I had been a day later, this place would be to rack and ruin. Get on out of here, now, and let me get my kitchen straight again."

Dilsey cooked supper, too. And that night, just before dark, Nancy came into the kitchen.

"How do you know he's back?" Dilsey said. "You ain't seen him."

"Jubah is a nigger," Jason said.

"I can feel him," Nancy said. "I can feel him laying yonder in the ditch."

"To-night?" Dilsey said. "Is he there to-night?"

"Dilsey's a nigger too," Jason said.

"You try to eat something," Dilsey said.

"I don't want nothing," Nancy said.

"I ain't a nigger," Jason said.

"Drink some coffee," Dilsey said. She poured a cup of coffee for Nancy. "Do you know he's out there to-night? How come you know it's to-night?"

"I know," Nancy said. "He's there, waiting. I know. I done lived with him too long. I know what he fixing to do 'fore he knows it him-self."

"Drink some coffee," Dilsey said. Nancy held the cup to her mouth and blew into the cup. Her mouth pursed out like a spreading adder's, like a rubber mouth, like she had blown all the color out of her lips with blowing the coffee.

"I ain't a nigger," Jason said. "Are you a nigger, Nancy?"

"I hell-born, child," Nancy said. "I won't be nothing soon. I going back where I come from soon."

### III

She began to drink the coffee. While she was drinking, holding the cup in both hands, she began to make the sound again. She made the sound into the cup and the coffee sploshed out on to her hands and her dress. Her eyes looked at us and she sat there, her elbows on her knees, holding the cup in both hands, looking at us across the wet cup, making the sound.

"Look at Nancy," Jason said. "Nancy can't cook for us now. Dilsey's got well now."

"You hush up," Dilsey said. Nancy held the cup in both hands, looking at us, making the sound, like there were two of them: one looking at us and the other making the sound. "Whyn't you let Mr. Jason telefoam the marshal?" Dilsey said. Nancy stopped then, holding the cup in her long brown hands. She tried to drink some coffee again, but it sploshed out of the cup, on to her hands and her dress, and she put the cup down. Jason watched her.

"I can't swallow it," Nancy said. "I swallows but it won't go down me."

"You go down to the cabin," Dilsey said. "Frony will fix you a pallet and I'll be there soon."

"Won't no nigger stop him," Nancy said.

"I ain't a nigger," Jason said. "Am I, Dilsey?"

"I reckon not," Dilsey said. She looked at Nancy. "I don't reckon so. What you going to do, then?"

Nancy looked at us. Her eyes went fast, like she was afraid there wasn't time to look, without hardly moving at all. She looked at us, at all three of us at one time. "You 'member that night I stayed in you all's room?" she said. She told about how we waked up early the next morning, and played. We had to play quiet, on her pallet, until father woke and it was time for her to go down and get breakfast. "Go and ask you maw to let me stay here to-night," Nancy said. "I won't need no pallet. We can play some more," she said.

"addy asked mother. Jason went too. "I can't have Negroes sleeping
ouse," mother said. Jason cried. He cried until mother said he
have any dessert for three days if he didn't stop. Then Jason

said he would stop if Dilsey would make a chocolate cake. Father was there.

"Why don't you do something about it?" mother said. "What do we have officers for?"

"Why is Nancy afraid of Jubah?" Caddy said. "Are you afraid of father, mother?"

"What could they do?" father said. "If Nancy hasn't seen him, how could the officers find him?"

"Then why is she afraid?" mother said.

"She says he is there. She says she knows he is there to-night."

"Yet we pay taxes," mother said. "I must wait here alone in this big house while you take a Negro woman home."

"You know that I am not lying outside with a razor," father said.

"I'll stop if Dilsey will make a chocolate cake," Jason said. Mother told us to go out and father said he didn't know if Jason would get a chocolate cake or not, but he knew what Jason was going to get in about a minute. We went back to the kitchen and told Nancy.

"Father said for you to go home and lock the door, and you'll be all right," Caddy said. "All right from what, Nancy? Is Jubah mad at you?" Nancy was holding the coffee cup in her hands, her elbows on her knees and her hands holding the cup between her knees. She was looking into the cup. "What have you done that made Jubah mad?" Caddy said. Nancy let the cup go. It didn't break on the floor, but the coffee spilled out, and Nancy sat there with her hands making the shape of the cup. She began to make the sound again, not loud. Not singing and not un-singing. We watched her.

"Here," Dilsey said. "You quit that, now. You get a-holt of yourself. You wait here. I going to get Versh to walk home with you." Dilsey went out.

We looked at Nancy. Her shoulders kept shaking, but she had quit making the sound. We watched her. "What's Jubah going to do to you?" Caddy said. "He went away."

Nancy looked at us. "We had fun that night I stayed in you all's room, didn't we?"

"I didn't," Jason said. "I didn't have any fun."

"You were asleep," Caddy said. "You were not there."

"Let's go down to my house and have some more fun," Nancy said.

"Mother won't let us," I said. "It's too late now."

"Don't bother her," Nancy said. "We can tell her in the morning. She won't mind."

"She wouldn't let us," I said.

"Don't ask her now," Nancy said. "Don't bother her now."

"They didn't say we couldn't go," Caddy said.

"We didn't ask," I said.

"If you go, I'll tell," Jason said.

"We'll have fun," Nancy said. "They won't mind, just to my house. I been working for you all a long time. They won't mind."

"I'm not afraid to go," Caddy said. "Jason is the one that's afraid. He'll tell."

"I'm not," Jason said.

"Yes, you are," Caddy said. "You'll tell."

"I won't tell," Jason said. "I'm not afraid."

"Jason ain't afraid to go with me," Nancy said. "Is you, Jason?"

"Jason is going to tell," Caddy said. The lane was dark. We passed the pasture gate. "I bet if something was to jump out from behind that gate, Jason would holler."

"I wouldn't," Jason said. We walked down the lane. Nancy was talking loud.

"What are you talking so loud for Nancy?" Caddy said.

"Who; me?" Nancy said. "Listen at Quentin and Caddy and Jason saying I'm talking loud."

"You talk like there was four of us here," Caddy said. "You talk like father was here too."

"Who; me talking loud, Mr. Jason?" Nancy said.

"Nancy called Jason 'Mister,'" Caddy said.

"Listen how Caddy and Quentin and Jason talk," Nancy said.

"We're not talking loud," Caddy said. "You're the one that's talking like father — "

"Hush," Nancy said; "hush, Mr. Jason."

"Nancy called Jason 'Mister' aguh — "

"Hush," Nancy said. She was talking loud when we crossed the ditch and stooped through the fence where she used to stoop through with the clothes on her head. Then we came to her house. We were going fast then. She opened the door. The smell of the house was like the lamp and the smell of Nancy was like the wick, like they were waiting for one another to smell. She lit the lamp and closed the door and put the bar up. Then she quit talking loud, looking at us.

"What're we going to do?" Caddy said.

"What you all want to do?" Nancy said.

"You said we would have some fun," Caddy said.

There was something about Nancy's house; something you could smell. Jason smelled it, even. "I don't want to stay here," he said. "I want to go home."

"Go home, then," Caddy said.

"I don't want to go by myself," Jason said.

"We're going to have some fun," Nancy said.

"How?" Caddy said.

Nancy stood by the door. She was looking at us, only it was like she had emptied her eyes, like she had quit using them.

"What do you want to do?" she said.

"Tell us a story," Caddy said. "Can you tell a story?"

"Yes," Nancy said.

"Tell it," Caddy said. We looked at Nancy. "You don't know any stories," Caddy said.

"Yes," Nancy said. "Yes, I do."

She came and sat down in a chair before the hearth. There was some fire there; she built it up; it was already hot. You didn't need a fire. She built a good blaze. She told a story. She talked like her eyes looked, like her eyes watching us and her voice talking to us did not belong to her. Like she was living somewhere else, waiting somewhere else. She was outside the house. Her voice was there and the shape of her, the Nancy that could stoop under the fence with the bundle of clothes balanced as though without weight, like a balloon, on her head, was there. But that was all. "And so this here queen come walking up to the ditch, where that bad man was hiding. She was walking up the ditch, and she say, 'If I can just get past this here ditch,' was what she say. . . ."

"What ditch?" Caddy said. "A ditch like that one out there? Why did the queen go into the ditch?"

"To get to her house," Nancy said. She looked at us. "She had to cross that ditch to get home."

"Why did she want to go home?" Caddy said.

IV

Nancy looked at us. She quit talking. She looked at us. Jason's legs stuck straight out of his pants, because he was little. "I don't think that's a good story," he said. "I want to go home."

"Maybe we had better," Caddy said. She got up from the floor. "I bet they are looking for us right now." She went toward the door.

"No," Nancy said. "Don't open it." She got up quick and passed Caddy. She didn't touch the door, the wooden bar.

"Why not?" Caddy said.

"Come back to the lamp," Nancy said. "We'll have fun. You don't have to go."

"We ought to go," Caddy said. "Unless we have a lot of fun." She and Nancy came back to the fire, the lamp.

"I want to go home," Jason said. "I'm going to tell."

"I know another story," Nancy said. She stood close to the lamp. She looked at Caddy, like when your eyes look up at a stick balanced on your nose. She had to look down to see Caddy, but her eyes looked like that, like when you are balancing a stick.

"I won't listen to it," Jason said. "I'll bang on the floor."

"It's a good one," Nancy said. "It's better than the other one."

"What's it about?" Caddy said. Nancy was standing by the lamp. Her hand was on the lamp, against the light, long and brown.

"Your hand is on that hot globe," Caddy said. "Don't it feel hot to your hand?"

Nancy looked at her hand on the lamp chimney. She took her hand away, slow. She stood there, looking at Caddy, wringing her long hand as though it were tied to her wrist with a string.

"Let's do something else," Caddy said.

"I want to go home," Jason said.

"I got some popcorn," Nancy said. She looked at Caddy and then at Jason and then at me and then at Caddy again. "I got some popcorn."

"I don't like popcorn," Jason said. "I'd rather have candy."

Nancy looked at Jason. "You can hold the popper." She was still wringing her hand; it was long and limp and brown.

"All right," Jason said. "I'll stay a while if I can do that. Caddy can't hold it. I'll want to go home, if Caddy holds the popper."

Nancy built up the fire. "Look at Nancy putting her hands in the fire," Caddy said. "What's the matter with you, Nancy?"

"I got popcorn," Nancy said. "I got some." She took the popper from under the bed. It was broken. Jason began to cry.

"We can't have any popcorn," he said.

"We ought to go home, anyway," Caddy said. "Come on, Quentin."

"Wait," Nancy said; "wait. I can fix it. Don't you want to help me fix it?"

"I don't think I want any," Caddy said. "It's too late now."

"You help me, Jason," Nancy said. "Don't you want to help me?"

"No," Jason said. "I want to go home."

"Hush," Nancy said; "hush. Watch. Watch me. I can fix it so Jason can hold it and pop the corn." She got a piece of wire and fixed the popper.

"It won't hold good," Caddy said.

"Yes, it will," Nancy said. "You all watch. You all help me shell the corn."

The corn was under the bed too. We shelled it into the popper and Nancy helped Jason hold the popper over the fire.

"It's not popping," Jason said. "I want to go home."

"You wait," Nancy said. "It'll begin to pop. We'll have fun then." She was sitting close to the fire. The lamp was turned up so high it was beginning to smoke.

"Why don't you turn it down some?" I said.

"It's all right," Nancy said. "I'll clean it. You all wait. The popcorn will start in a minute."

"I don't believe it's going to start," Caddy said. "We ought to go home, anyway. They'll be worried."

"No," Nancy said. "It's going to pop. Dilsey will tell um you all with me. I been working for you all long time. They won't mind if you at my house. You wait, now. It'll start popping in a minute."

Then Jason got some smoke in his eyes and he began to cry. He dropped the popper into the fire. Nancy got a wet rag and wiped Jason's face, but he didn't stop crying.

"Hush," she said. "Hush." He didn't hush. Caddy took the popper out of the fire.

"It's burned up," she said. "You'll have to get some more popcorn, Nancy."

"Did you put all of it in?" Nancy said.

"Yes," Caddy said. Nancy looked at Caddy. Then she took the popper and opened it and poured the blackened popcorn into her apron and began to sort the grains, her hands long and brown, and we watching her.

"Haven't you got any more?" Caddy said.

"Yes," Nancy said; "yes. Look. This here ain't burnt. All we need to do is — "

"I want to go home," Jason said. "I'm going to tell."

"Hush," Caddy said. We all listened. Nancy's head was already turned toward the barred door, her eyes filled with red lamplight. "Somebody is coming," Caddy said.

Then Nancy began to make that sound again, not loud, sitting there above the fire, her long hands dangling between her knees; all of a sudden water began to come out on her face in big drops, running down her face, carrying in each one a little turning ball of firelight until it dropped off her chin.

"She's not crying," I said.

"I ain't crying," Nancy said. Her eyes were closed. "I ain't crying. Who is it?"

"I don't know," Caddy said. She went to the door and looked out. "We've got to go home now," she said. "Here comes father."

"I'm going to tell," Jason said. "You all made me come."

The water still ran down Nancy's face. She turned in her chair. "Listen. Tell him. Tell him we going to have fun. Tell him I take good care of you all until in the morning. Tell him to let me come home with you all and sleep on the floor. Tell him I won't need no pallet. We'll have fun. You remember last time how we had so much fun?"

"I didn't have any fun," Jason said. "You hurt me. You put smoke in my eyes."


                    v

Father came in. He looked at us. Nancy did not get up.

"Tell him," she said.

"Caddy made us come down here," Jason said. "I didn't want to."

Father came to the fire. Nancy looked up at him. "Can't you go to Aunt Rachel's and stay?" he said. Nancy looked up at father, her hands between her knees. "He's not here," father said. "I would have seen. There wasn't a soul in sight."

"He in the ditch," Nancy said. "He waiting in the ditch yonder."

"Nonsense," father said. He looked at Nancy. "Do you know he's there?"

"I got the sign," Nancy said.

"What sign?"

"I got it. It was on the table when I come in. It was a hog bone, with blood meat still on it, laying by the lamp. He's out there. When you all walk out that door, I gone."

"Who's gone, Nancy?" Caddy said.

"I'm not a tattletale," Jason said.

"Nonsense," father said.

"He out there," Nancy said. "He looking through that window this minute, waiting for you all to go. Then I gone."

"Nonsense," father said. "Lock up your house and we'll take you on to Aunt Rachel's."

"'Twon't do no good," Nancy said. She didn't look at father now, but he looked down at her, at her long, limp, moving hands.

"Putting it off won't do no good."

"Then what do you want to do?" father said.

"I don't know," Nancy said. "I can't do nothing. Just put it off. And that don't do no good. I reckon it belong to me. I reckon what I going to get ain't no more than mine."

"Get what?" Caddy said. "What's yours?"

"Nothing," father said. "You all must get to bed."

"Caddy made me come," Jason said.

"Go on to Aunt Rachel's," father said.

"It won't do no good," Nancy said. She sat before the fire, her elbows on her knees, her long hands between her knees. "When even your own kitchen wouldn't do no good. When even if I was sleeping on the floor in the room with your own children, and the next morning there I am, and blood all — "

"Hush," father said. "Lock the door and put the lamp out and go to bed."

"I scared of the dark," Nancy said. "I scared for it to happen in the dark."

"You mean you're going to sit right here, with the lamp lighted?" father said. Then Nancy began to make the sound again, sitting before the fire, her long hands between her knees. "Ah, damnation," father said. "Come along, chillen. It's bedtime."

"When you all go, I gone," Nancy said. "I be dead to-morrow. I done had saved up the coffin money with Mr. Lovelady — "

Mr. Lovelady was a short, dirty man who collected the Negro insurance, coming around to the cabins and the kitchens every Saturday morning, to collect fifteen cents. He and his wife lived in the hotel. One morning his wife committed suicide. They had a child, a little girl. After his wife committed suicide Mr. Lovelady and the child went away. After a while Mr. Lovelady came back. We would see him going down the lanes on Saturday morning. He went to the Baptist church.

Father carried Jason on his back. We went out Nancy's door; she was sitting before the fire. "Come and put the bar up," father said. Nancy didn't move. She didn't look at us again. We left her there, sitting before the fire with the door opened, so that it wouldn't happen in the dark.

"What, father?" Caddy said. "Why is Nancy scared of Jubah? What is Jubah going to do to her?"

"Jubah wasn't there," Jason said.

"No," father said. "He's not there. He's gone away."

"Who is it that's waiting in the ditch?" Caddy said. We looked at the ditch. We came to it, where the path went down into the thick vines and went up again.

"Nobody," father said.

There was just enough moon to see by. The ditch was vague, thick, quiet. "If he's there, he can see us, can't he?" Caddy said.

"You made me come," Jason said on father's back. "I didn't want to."

The ditch was quite still, quite empty, massed with honeysuckle. We couldn't see Jubah, any more than we could see Nancy sitting there in her house, with the door open and the lamp burning, because she didn't want it to happen in the dark. "I just done got tired," Nancy said. "I just a nigger. It ain't no fault of mine."

But we could still hear her. She began as soon as we were out of the house, sitting there above the fire, her long brown hands between her knees. We could still hear her when we had crossed the ditch, Jason high and close and little about father's head.

Then we had crossed the ditch, walking out of Nancy's life. Then her life was sitting there with the door open and the lamp lit, waiting, and the ditch between us and us going on, the white people going on, dividing the impinged lives of us and Nancy.

"Who will do our washing now, father?" I said.

"I'm not a nigger," Jason said on father's shoulders.

"You're worse," Caddy said, "you are a tattletale. If something was to jump out, you'd be scairder than a nigger."

"I wouldn't," Jason said.

"You'd cry," Caddy said.

"Caddy!" father said.

"I wouldn't," Jason said.

"Scairy cat," Caddy said.

"Candace!" father said.

1931

## Dorothy Parker

# Here We Are

FROM *Cosmopolitan*

THE YOUNG MAN in the new blue suit finished arranging the glistening luggage in tight corners of the Pullman compartment. The train had leaped at curves and bounced along straightaways, rendering balance a praiseworthy achievement and a sporadic one; and the young man had pushed and hoisted and tucked and shifted the bags with concentrated care.

Nevertheless, eight minutes for the settling of two suitcases and a hat-box is a long time.

He sat down, leaning back against bristled green plush, in the seat opposite the girl in beige. She looked as new as a peeled egg. Her hat, her fur, her frock, her gloves were glossy and stiff with novelty. On the arc of the thin, slippery sole of one beige shoe was gummed a tiny oblong of white paper, printed with the price set and paid for that slipper and its fellow, and the name of the shop that had dispensed them.

She had been staring raptly out of the window, drinking in the big weathered signboards that extolled the phenomena of codfish without bones and screens no rust could corrupt. As the young man sat down, she turned politely from the pane, met his eyes, started a smile and got it about half done, and rested her gaze just above his right shoulder.

"Well!" the young man said.

"Well!" she said.

"Well, here we are," he said.

"Here we are," she said. "Aren't we?"

"I should say we were," he said. "Eeyop. Here we are."

"Well!" she said.

"Well!" he said. "Well. How does it feel to be an old married lady?"

"Oh, it's too soon to ask me that," she said. "At least — I mean. Well,

I mean, goodness, we've only been married about three hours, haven't we?"

The young man studied his wrist watch as if he were just acquiring the knack of reading time.

"We have been married," he said, "exactly two hours and twenty-six minutes."

"My," she said. "It seems like longer."

"No," he said. "It isn't hardly half past six yet."

"It seems like later," she said. "I guess it's because it starts getting dark so early."

"It does, at that," he said. "The nights are going to be pretty long from now on. I mean. I mean — well, it starts getting dark early."

"I didn't have any idea what time it was," she said. "Everything was so mixed up, I sort of don't know where I am, or what it's all about. Getting back from the church, and then all those people, and then changing all my clothes, and then everybody throwing things and all. Goodness, I don't see how people do it every day."

"Do what?" he said.

"Get married," she said. "When you think of all the people, all over the world, getting married just as if it was nothing. Chinese people and everybody. Just as if it wasn't anything."

"Well, let's not worry about people all over the world," he said. "Let's don't think about a lot of Chinese. We've got something better to think about. I mean. I mean — well, what do we care about them?"

"I know," she said. "But I just sort of got to thinking of them, all of them, all over everywhere, doing it all the time. At least, I mean — getting married, you know. And it's — well, it's sort of such a big thing to do, it makes you feel queer. You think of them, all of them, all doing it just like it wasn't anything. And how does anybody know what's going to happen next?"

"Let them worry," he said. "We don't have to. We know darn well what's going to happen next. I mean. I mean — well, we know it's going to be great. Well, we know we're going to be happy. Don't we?"

"Oh, of course," she said. "Only you think of all the people, and you have to sort of keep thinking. It makes you feel funny. An awful lot of people that get married, it doesn't turn out so well. And I guess they all must have thought it was going to be great."

"Come on, now," he said. "This is no way to start a honeymoon, with all this thinking going on. Look at us — all married and everything done. I mean. The wedding all done and all."

"Ah, it was nice, wasn't it?" she said. "Did you really like my veil?"

"You looked great," he said. "Just great."

"Oh, I'm terribly glad," she said. "Ellie and Louise looked lovely, didn't they? I'm terribly glad they did finally decide on pink. They looked perfectly lovely."

"Listen," he said. "I want to tell you something. When I was standing up there in that old church waiting for you to come up, and I saw those two bridesmaids, I thought to myself, I thought, 'Well, I never knew Louise could look like that!' Why, she'd have knocked anybody's eye out."

"Oh, really?" she said. "Funny. Of course, everybody thought her dress and hat were lovely, but a lot of people seemed to think she looked sort of tired. People have been saying that a lot, lately. I tell them I think it's awfully mean of them to go around saying that about her. I tell them they've got to remember that Louise isn't so terribly young any more, and they've got to expect her to look like that. Louise can say she's twenty-three all she wants to, but she's a good deal nearer twenty-seven."

"Well, she was certainly a knock-out at the wedding," he said. "Boy!"

"I'm terribly glad you thought so," she said. "I'm glad some one did. How did you think Ellie looked?"

"Why, I honestly didn't get a look at her," he said.

"Oh, really?" she said. "Well, I certainly think that's too bad. I don't suppose I ought to say it about my own sister, but I never saw anybody look as beautiful as Ellie looked to-day. And always so sweet and unselfish, too. And you didn't even notice her. But you never pay attention to Ellie, anyway. Don't think I haven't noticed it. It makes me feel just terrible. It makes me feel just awful, that you don't like my own sister."

"I do so like her!" he said. "I'm crazy for Ellie. I think she's a great kid."

"Don't think it makes any difference to Ellie!" she said. "Ellie's got enough people crazy about her. It isn't anything to her whether you like her or not. Don't flatter yourself she cares! Only, the only thing is, it makes it awfully hard for me you don't like her, that's the only thing. I keep thinking, when we come back and get in the apartment and everything, it's going to be awfully hard for me that you won't want my own sister to come and see me. It's going to make it awfully hard for me that you won't ever want my family around. I know how you feel about my family. Don't think I haven't seen it. Only, if you don't ever want to see them, that's your loss. Not theirs. Don't flatter yourself!"

"Oh, now, come on!" he said. "What's all this talk about not wanting your family around? Why, you know how I feel about your family. I think your old woman — I think your mother's swell. And Ellie. And your father. What's all this talk?"

"Well, I've seen it," she said. "Don't think I haven't. Lots of people they get married, and they think it's going to be great and everything, and then it all goes to pieces because people don't like people's families, or something like that. Don't tell me! I've seen it happen."

"Honey," he said, "what is all this? What are you getting all angry about? Hey, look, this is our honeymoon. What are you trying to start a fight for? Ah, I guess you're just feeling sort of nervous."

"Me?" she said. "What have I got to be nervous about? I mean. I mean, goodness, I'm not nervous."

"You know, lots of times," he said, "they say that girls get kind of nervous and yippy on account of thinking about — I mean. I mean — well, it's like you said, things are all so sort of mixed up and everything, right now. But afterwards, it'll be all right. I mean. I mean — well, look, honey, you don't look any too comfortable. Don't you want to take your hat off? And let's don't ever fight, ever. Will we?"

"Ah, I'm sorry I was cross," she said. "I guess I did feel a little bit funny. All mixed up, and then thinking of all those people all over everywhere, and then being sort of 'way off here, all alone with you. It's so sort of different. It's sort of such a big thing. You can't blame a person for thinking, can you? Yes, don't let's ever, ever fight. We won't be like a whole lot of them. We won't fight or be nasty or anything. Will we?"

"You bet your life we won't," he said.

"I guess I will take this darned old hat off," she said. "It kind of presses. Just put it up on the rack, will you, dear? Do you like it, sweetheart?"

"Looks good on you," he said.

"No, but I mean," she said, "do you really like it?"

"Well, I'll tell you," he said. "I know this is the new style and everything like that and it's probably great. I don't know anything about things like that. Only I like the kind of a hat like that blue hat you had. Gee, I liked that hat."

"Oh, really?" she said. "Well, that's nice. That's lovely. The first thing you say to me, as soon as you get me off on a train away from my family and everything, is that you don't like my hat. The first thing you say to your wife is you think she has terrible taste in hats. That's nice, isn't it?"

"Now, honey," he said, "I never said anything like that. I only said —"

"What you don't seem to realize," she said, "is this hat cost twenty-two dollars. Twenty-two dollars. And that horrible old blue thing you think you're so crazy about, that cost three ninety-five."

"I don't give a darn what they cost," he said. "I only said — I said I liked that blue hat. I don't know anything about hats. I'll be crazy about this one as soon as I get used to it. Only it's kind of not like your other hats. I don't know about the new styles. What do I know about women's hats?"

"It's too bad," she said, "you didn't marry somebody that would get the kind of hats you'd like. Hats that cost three ninety-five. Why didn't you marry Louise? You always think she looks so beautiful. You'd love her taste in hats. Why didn't you marry her?"

"Oh, now, honey," he said. "For heaven's sakes!"

"Why didn't you marry her?" she said. "All you've done, ever since we got on this train, is talk about her. Here I've sat and sat, and just listened to you saying how wonderful Louise is. I suppose that's nice, getting me all off here alone with you, and then raving about Louise right in front of my face. Why didn't you ask her to marry you? I'm sure she would have jumped at the chance. There aren't so many people asking her to marry them. It's too bad you didn't marry her. I'm sure you'd have been much happier."

"Listen, baby," he said, "while you're talking about things like that, why didn't you marry Joe Brooks? I suppose he could have given you all the twenty-two-dollar hats you wanted, I suppose!"

"Well, I'm not so sure I'm not sorry I didn't," she said. "There! Joe Brooks wouldn't have waited until he got me all off alone and then sneered at my taste in clothes. Joe Brooks wouldn't ever hurt my feelings. Joe Brooks has always been fond of me. There!"

"Yeah," he said. "He's fond of you. He was so fond of you he didn't even send a wedding present. That's how fond of you he was."

"I happen to know for a fact," she said, "that he was away on business, and as soon as he comes back he's going to give me anything I want, for the apartment."

"Listen," he said. "I don't want anything he gives you in our apartment. Anything he gives you, I'll throw right out the window. That's what I think of your friend Joe Brooks. And how do you know where he is and what he's going to do, anyway? Has he been writing to you?"

"I suppose my friends can correspond with me," she said. "I didn't hear there was any law against that."

"Well, I suppose they can't!" he said. "And what do you think of that?

I'm not going to have my wife getting a lot of letters from cheap traveling salesmen!"

"Joe Brooks is not a cheap traveling salesman!" she said. "He is not!
He gets a wonderful salary."

"Oh, yeah!" he said. "Where did you hear that?"

"He told me so himself," she said.

"Oh, he told you so himself," he said. "I see. He told you so himself."

"You've got a lot of right to talk about Joe Brooks," she said. "You and
your friend Louise. All you ever talk about is Louise."

"Oh, for heaven's sakes!" he said. "What do I care about Louise? I just
thought she was a friend of yours, that's all. That's why I ever even
noticed her."

"Well, you certainly took an awful lot of notice of her to-day," she
said. "On our wedding day! You said yourself when you were standing
there in the church you just kept thinking of her. Right up at the altar.
Oh, right in the presence of God! And all you thought about was
Louise."

"Listen, honey," he said, "I never should have said that. How does
anybody know what kind of crazy things come into their heads when
they're standing there waiting to get married? I was just telling you that
because it was so kind of crazy. I thought it would make you laugh."

"I know," she said. "I've been all sort of mixed up to-day, too. I told
you that. Everything so strange and everything. And me all the time
thinking about all those people all over the world, and now us here all
alone, and everything. I know you get all mixed up. Only I did think,
when you kept talking about how beautiful Louise looked, you did it
with malice and forethought."

"I never did anything with malice and forethought!" he said. "I
just told you that about Louise because I thought it would make you
laugh."

"Well, it didn't," she said.

"No, I know it didn't," he said. "It certainly did not. Ah, baby, and we
ought to be laughing, too. Hell, honey lamb, this is our honeymoon.
What's the matter?"

"I don't know," she said. "We used to squabble a lot when we were
going together and then engaged and everything, but I thought everything would be so different as soon as you were married. And now I feel
so sort of strange and everything. I feel so sort of alone."

"Well, you see, sweetheart," he said, "we're not really married yet. I mean. I mean — well, things will be different afterwards. Oh, hell. I mean, we haven't been married very long."

"No," she said.

"Well, we haven't got much longer to wait now," he said. "I mean — well, we'll be in New York in about twenty minutes.Then we can have dinner, and sort of see what we feel like doing. Or I mean. Is there anything special you want to do to-night?"

"What?" she said.

"What I mean to say," he said, "would you like to go to a show or something?"

"Why, whatever you like," she said. "I sort of didn't think people went to theaters and things on their — I mean, I've got a couple of letters I simply must write. Don't let me forget."

"Oh," he said. "You're going to write letters to-night?"

"Well, you see," she said, "I've been perfectly terrible. What with all the excitement and everything, I never did thank poor old Mrs. Sprague for her berry spoon, and I never did a thing about those book ends the McMasters sent. It's just too awful of me. I've got to write them this very night."

"And when you've finished writing your letters," he said, "maybe I could get you a magazine or a bag of peanuts."

"What?" she said.

"I mean," he said, "I wouldn't want you to be bored."

"As if I could be bored with you!" she said. "Silly! Aren't we married? Bored!"

"What I thought," he said, "I thought when we got in, we could go right up to the Biltmore and anyway leave our bags, and maybe have a little dinner in the room, kind of quiet, and then do whatever we wanted. I mean. I mean — well, let's go right up there from the station."

"Oh, yes, let's," she said. "I'm so glad we're going to the Biltmore. I just love it. The twice I've stayed in New York we've always stayed there, Papa and Mamma and Ellie and I, and I was crazy about it. I always sleep so well there. I go right off to sleep the minute I put my head on the pillow."

"Oh, you do?" he said.

"At least, I mean," she said. "'Way up high it's so quiet."

"We might go to some show or other to-morrow night instead of to-night," he said. "Don't you think that would be better?"

"Yes, I think it might," she said.

He rose, balanced a moment, crossed over and sat down beside her.

"Do you really have to write those letters to-night?" he said.

"Well," she said, "I don't suppose they'd get there any quicker than if I wrote them to-morrow."

There was a silence with things going on in it.

"And we won't ever fight any more, will we?" he said.

"Oh, no," she said. "Not ever! I don't know what made me do like that. It all got so sort of funny, sort of like a nightmare, the way I got thinking of all those people getting married all the time; and so many of them, it goes to pieces on account of fighting and everything. I got all mixed up thinking about them. Oh, I don't want to be like them. But we won't be, will we?"

"Sure we won't," he said.

"We won't go all to pieces," she said. "We won't fight. It'll all be different, now we're married. It'll all be lovely. Reach me down my hat, will you, sweetheart? It's time I was putting it on. Thanks. Ah, I'm so sorry you don't like it."

"I do so like it!" he said.

"You said you didn't," she said. "You said you thought it was perfectly terrible."

"I never said any such thing," he said. "You're crazy."

"All right, I may be crazy," she said. "Thank you very much. But that's what you said. Not that it matters — it's just a little thing. But it makes you feel pretty funny to think you've gone and married somebody that says you have perfectly terrible taste in hats. And then goes and says you're crazy, beside."

"Now, listen here," he said. "Nobody said any such thing. Why, I love that hat. The more I look at it the better I like it. I think it's great."

"That isn't what you said before," she said.

"Honey," he said. "Stop it, will you? What do you want to start all this for? I love the damned hat, I mean, I love your hat. I love anything you wear. What more do you want me to say?"

"Well, I don't want you to say it like that," she said.

"I said I think it's great," he said. "That's all I said."

"Do you really?" she said. "Do you honestly? Ah, I'm so glad. I'd hate you not to like my hat. It would be — I don't know, it would be sort of such a bad start."

"Well, I'm crazy for it," he said. "Now we've got that settled, for heaven's sakes. Ah, baby. Baby lamb. We're not going to have any bad starts. Look at us — we're on our honeymoon. Pretty soon we'll be regular old married people. I mean. I mean, in a few minutes we'll be getting in to New York, and then we'll be going to the hotel, and then everything will be all right. I mean — well, look at us! Here we are, married! Here we are!"

"Yes, here we are," she said. "Aren't we?"

1933

F. Scott Fitzgerald

........................................................................................................

# Crazy Sunday

FROM *The American Mercury*

I

IT WAS SUNDAY — not a day, but rather a gap between two other days.
Behind, for all of them, lay sets and sequences, the struggles of rival
ingenuities in the conference rooms, the interminable waits under the
crane that swung the microphone, the hundred miles a day by automobiles to and fro across Hollywood county, the ceaseless compromise, the
clash and strain of many personalities fighting for their lives. And now
Sunday, with individual life starting up again, with a glow kindling in
eyes that had been glazed with monotony the afternoon before. Slowly
as the hours waned they came awake like *Puppenfeen* in a toy shop: an
intense colloquy in a corner, lovers disappearing to kiss in a hall. And
the feeling of "Hurry, it's not too late, but for God's sake hurry before
the blessed forty hours of leisure are over."

Joel Coles was writing continuity. He was twenty-eight and not yet
broken by Hollywood. He had had what were considered nice assign-
ments since his arrival six months before and he submitted his scenes
and sequences with enthusiasm. He referred to himself modestly as a
hack but really did not think of it that way. His mother had been a
successful actress; Joel had spent his childhood between London and
New York trying to separate the real from the unreal, or at least to keep
one guess ahead. He was a handsome man with the pleasant cow-
brown eyes that in 1913 had gazed out at Broadway audiences from his
mother's face.

When the invitation came it made him sure that he was getting
somewhere. Ordinarily he did not go out on Sundays but stayed sober
and took work home with him. Recently they had given him a Eugene
O'Neill play destined for a very important lady indeed. Everything he

had done so far had pleased Miles Calman, and Miles Calman was the only director on the lot who refused to work under a supervisor and was responsible to the money men alone. Everything was clicking into place in Joel's career. ("This is Mr. Calman's secretary. Will you come to tea from four to six Sunday — he lived in Beverly Hills, number ———.")

Joel was flattered. It would be a party out of the top-drawer. It was a tribute to himself as a young man of promise. The Marion Davies crowd, the high-hats, the big currency numbers, perhaps even Dietrich and Garbo and the Marquise, people who were not seen everywhere, would probably be at Calman's.

"I won't take anything to drink," he assured himself. Calman was audibly tired of rummies, and thought it was a pity the industry could not get along without them.

Joel agreed that writers drank too much — he did himself, but he wouldn't this afternoon. He wished Miles would be within hearing when the cocktails were passed to hear his succinct, unobtrusive, No, thank you.

Miles Calman's house was built for great emotional moments — there was an air of listening, as if the far silences of its vistas hid an audience, but this afternoon it was thronged, as though people had been bidden rather than asked. Joel noted with pride that only two other writers from the studio were in the crowd, an ennobled limey and, somewhat to his surprise, Nat Keogh, who had evoked Calman's impatient comment on drunks.

Stella Calman (Stella Walker, of course) did not move on to her other guests after she spoke to Joel. She lingered — she looked at him with the sort of beautiful look that demands some sort of acknowledgment and Joel drew quickly on the dramatic adequacy inherited from his mother:

"Well, you look about sixteen! Where's your kiddy car?"

She was visibly pleased; she lingered. He felt that he should say something more, something confident and easy — he had first met her when she was struggling for bits in New York. At the moment a tray slid up and Stella put a cocktail glass into his hand.

"Everybody's afraid, aren't they?" he said, looking at it absently. "Everybody watches for everybody else's blunders, or tries to make sure they're with people that'll do them credit. Of course that's not true in your house," he covered himself hastily. "I just meant generally in Hollywood."

Stella agreed. She presented several people to Joel as if he were very important. Reassuring himself that Miles was at the other side of the room, Joel drank the cocktail.

"So you have a baby?" he said. "That's the time to look out. After a pretty woman has had her first child, she's very vulnerable, because she wants to be reassured about her own charm. She's got to have some new man's unqualified devotion to prove to herself she hasn't lost anything."

"I never get anybody's unqualified devotion," Stella said rather resentfully.

"They're afraid of your husband."

"You think that's it?" She wrinkled her brow over the idea; then the conversation was interrupted at the exact moment Joel would have chosen.

Her attentions had given him confidence. Not for him to join safe groups, to slink to refuge under the wings of such acquaintances as he saw about the room. He walked to the window and looked out toward the Pacific, colorless under its sluggish sunset. It was good here — the American Riviera and all that, if there were ever time to enjoy it. The handsome, well-dressed people in the room, the lovely girls, and the — well, the lovely girls. You couldn't have everything.

He saw Stella's fresh boyish face, with the tired eyelid that always drooped a little over one eye, moving about among her guests and he wanted to sit with her and talk a long time as if she were a girl instead of a name; he followed her to see if she paid anyone as much attention as she had paid him. He took another cocktail — not because he needed confidence but because she had given him so much of it. Then he sat down beside the director's mother.

"Your son's gotten to be a legend, Mrs. Calman — Oracle and a Man of Destiny and all that. Personally, I'm against him but I'm in a minority. What do you think of him? Are you impressed? Are you surprised how far he's gone?"

"No, I'm not surprised," she said calmly. "We always expected a lot from Miles."

"Well now, that's unusual," remarked Joel. "I always think all mothers are like Napoleon's mother. My mother didn't want me to have anything to do with the entertainment business. She wanted me to go to West Point and be safe."

"We always had every confidence in Miles." . . .

He stood by the built-in bar of the dining room with the good-humored, heavy-drinking, highly-paid Nat Keogh.

" — I made a hundred grand during the year and lost forty grand gambling, so now I've hired a manager."

"You mean an agent," suggested Joel.

"No, I've got that too. I mean a manager. I make over everything to my wife and then he and my wife get together and hand me out the money. I pay him five thousand a year to hand me out my money."

"You mean your agent."

"No, I mean my manager, and I'm not the only one — a lot of other irresponsible people have him."

"Well, if you're irresponsible why are you responsible enough to hire a manager?"

"I'm just irresponsible about gambling. Look here — "

A singer performed; Joel and Nat went forward with the others to listen.

II

The singing reached Joel vaguely; he felt happy and friendly toward all the people gathered there, people of bravery and industry, superior to a *bourgeoisie* that outdid them in ignorance and loose living, risen to a position of the highest prominence in a nation that for a decade had wanted only to be entertained. He liked them — he loved them. Great waves of good feeling flowed through him.

As the singer finished his number and there was a drift toward the hostess to say good-bye, Joel had an idea. He would give them "Building It Up," his own composition. It was his only parlor trick, it had amused several parties and it might please Stella Walker. Possessed by the hunch, his blood throbbing with the scarlet corpuscles of exhibitionism, he sought her.

"Of course," she cried. "Please! Do you need anything?"

"Someone has to be the secretary that I'm supposed to be dictating to."

"I'll be her."

As the word spread the guests in the hall, already putting on their coats to leave, drifted back and Joel faced the eyes of many strangers. He had a dim foreboding, realizing that the man who had just performed was a famous radio entertainer. Then someone said "Sh!" and he was alone with Stella, the center of a sinister Indian-like half-circle. Stella smiled up at him expectantly — he began.

His burlesque was based upon the cultural limitations of Mr. Dave Silverstein, an independent producer; Silverstein was presumed to be dictating a letter outlining a treatment of a story he had bought.

" — a story of divorce, the younger generators and the Foreign Legion," he heard his voice saying, with the intonations of Mr. Silverstein. "But we got to build it up, see?"

A sharp pang of doubt struck through him. The faces surrounding him in the gently molded light were intent and curious, but there was no ghost of a smile anywhere; directly in front the Great Lover of the screen glared at him with an eye as keen as the eye of a potato. Only Stella Walker looked up at him with a radiant, never faltering smile.

"If we make him a Menjou type, then we get a sort of Michael Arlen only with a Honolulu atmosphere."

Still not a ripple in front, but in the rear a rustling, a perceptible shift toward the left, toward the front door.

" — then she says she feels this sex appil for him and he burns out and says 'Oh go on destroy yourself' — "

At some point he heard Nat Keogh snicker and here and there were a few encouraging faces, but as he finished he had the sickening realization that he had made a fool of himself in view of an important section of the picture world, upon whose favor depended his career.

For a moment he existed in the midst of a confused silence, broken by a general trek for the door. He felt the undercurrent of derision that rolled through the gossip; then — all this was in the space of ten seconds — the Great Lover, his eye hard and empty as the eye of a needle, shouted "Boo! Boo!" voicing in an overtone what he felt was the mood of the crowd. It was the resentment of the professional toward the amateur, of the community toward the stranger, the thumbs-down of the clan.

Only Stella Walker was still standing near and thanking him as if he had been an unparalleled success, as if it hadn't occurred to her that anyone hadn't liked it. As Nat Keogh helped him into his overcoat, a great wave of self-disgust swept over him and he swung desperately to his rule of never betraying an inferior emotion until he no longer felt it.

"I was a flop," he said lightly, to Stella. "Never mind, it's a good number when appreciated. Thanks for your cooperation."

The smile did not leave her face — he bowed rather drunkenly and Nat drew him toward the door . . .

The arrival of his breakfast awakened him into a broken and ruined world. Yesterday he was himself, a point of fire against an industry, today he felt that he was pitted under an enormous disadvantage, against those faces, against individual contempt and collective sneer. Worse than that, to Miles Calman he was become one of those rummies, stripped of dignity, whom Calman regretted he was compelled to use. To Stella Walker, on whom he had forced a martyrdom to preserve the courtesy of her house — her opinion he did not dare to guess. His gastric juices ceased to flow and he set his poached eggs back on the telephone table. He wrote:

Dear Miles
     You can imagine my profound self-disgust. I confess to a taint of exhibitionism, but at six o'clock in the afternoon, in broad daylight! Good God! My apologies to your wife.

Yours ever,

JOEL COLES

Joel emerged from his office on the lot only to slink like a malefactor to the tobacco store. So suspicious was his manner that one of the studio police asked to see his admission card. He had decided to eat lunch outside when Nat Keogh, confident and cheerful, overtook him.

"What do you mean you're in permanent retirement? What if that Three Piece Suit did boo you?

"Why listen," he continued, drawing Joel into the studio restaurant. "The night of one of his premiers at Grauman's, Joe Squires kicked his tail while he was bowing to the crowd. The ham said Joe'd hear from him later but when Joe called him up at eight o'clock next day and said, 'I thought I was going to hear from you,' he hung up the phone."

The preposterous story cheered Joel, and he found a gloomy consolation in staring at the group at the next table, the sad, lovely Siamese twins, the mean dwarfs, the proud giant from the circus picture. But looking beyond at the yellow-stained faces of pretty women, their eyes all melancholy and startling with mascara, their ball gowns garish in full day, he saw a group who had been at Calman's and winced.

"Never again," he exclaimed aloud, "absolutely my last social appearance in Hollywood!"

The following morning a telegram was waiting for him at his office:

You were one of the most agreeable people at our party. Expect you at my sister June's buffet supper next Sunday.

STELLA WALKER CALMAN

The blood rushed fast through his veins for a feverish minute. Incredulously he read the telegram over.

"Well, that's the sweetest thing I ever heard of in my life!"

III

Crazy Sunday again. Joel slept until eleven, then he read a newspaper to catch up with the past week. He lunched in his room on trout, avocado salad and a pint of California wine. Dressing for the tea, he selected the nuances of a pin-check suit, a blue shirt, a burnt orange tie. There were dark circles of fatigue under his eyes. In his second-hand car he drove to the Riviera apartments. As he was introducing himself to Stella's sister, Miles and Stella arrived in riding clothes — they had been quarreling fiercely most of the afternoon on all the dirt roads back of Beverly Hills.

Miles Calman, tall, nervous, with a desperate humor and the unhappiest eyes Joel ever saw, was an artist from the top of his curiously shaped head to his niggerish feet. Upon these last he stood firmly — he had never made a cheap picture though he had sometimes paid heavily for the luxury of making experimental flops. In spite of his excellent company, one could not be with him long without realizing that he was not a well man.

From the moment of their entrance Joel's day bound itself up inextricably with theirs. As he joined the group around them Stella turned away from it with an impatient little tongue click — and Miles Calman said to the man who happened to be next to him:

"Go easy on Eva Goebel. There's hell to pay about her at home." Miles turned to Joel, "I'm sorry I missed you at the office yesterday. I spent the afternoon at the analyst's."

"You being psychoanalyzed?"

"I have been for months. First I went for claustrophobia, now I'm trying to get my whole life cleared up. They say it'll take over a year."

"There's nothing the matter with your life," Joel assured him.

"Oh, no? Well, Stella seems to think so. Ask anybody — they can all tell you about it," he said bitterly.

A girl perched herself on the arm of Miles' chair; Joel crossed to Stella, who stood disconsolately by the fire.

"Thank you for your telegram," he said. "It was darn sweet. I can't imagine anybody as good looking as you are being so good-humored."

She was a little lovelier than he had ever seen her and perhaps the unstinted admiration in his eyes prompted her to unload on him — it did not take long, for she was obviously at the emotional bursting point.

" — and Miles has been carrying on this thing for *two years,* and I never knew. Why, she was one of my best friends, always in the house. Finally when people began to come to me, Miles had to admit it."

She sat down vehemently on the arm of Joel's chair. Her riding breeches were the color of the chair and Joel saw that the mass of her hair was made up of some strands of red gold and some of pale gold, so that it could not be dyed, and that she had on no make-up. She was that good looking —

Still quivering with the shock of her discovery, Stella found unbearable the spectacle of a new girl hovering over Miles; she led Joel into a bedroom, and seated at either end of a big bed they went on talking. People on their way to the washroom glanced in and made wisecracks, but Stella, emptying out her story, paid no attention. After a while Miles stuck his head in the door and said, "There's no use trying to explain something to Joel in half an hour that I don't understand myself and the psychoanalyst says will take a whole year to understand."

She talked on as if Miles were not there. She loved Miles, she said — under considerable difficulties she had always been faithful to him.

"The psychoanalyst told Miles that he had a mother complex. In his first marriage he transferred his mother complex to his wife, you see — and then his sex turned to me. But when we married the thing repeated itself — he transferred his mother complex to me and all his libido turned toward this other woman."

Joel knew that this probably wasn't gibberish — yet it sounded like gibberish. He knew Eva Goebel; she was a motherly person, older and probably wiser than Stella, who was a golden child.

Miles now suggested impatiently that Joel come back with them since Stella had so much to say, so they drove out to the mansion in Beverly Hills. Under the high ceilings the situation seemed more dignified and tragic. It was an eerie bright night with the dark very clear outside of all the windows and Stella all rose-gold raging and crying around the room. Joel did not quite believe in picture actresses' grief. They have other preoccupations — they are beautiful rose-gold figures blown full of life by writers and directors, and after hours they sit around and talk in whispers and giggled innuendoes, and the ends of many adventures flow through them.

Sometimes he pretended to listen and instead thought how well she was got up — sleek breeches with a matched set of legs in them, an

Italian-colored sweater with a little high neck, and a short brown chamois coat. He couldn't decide whether she was an imitation of an English lady or an English lady was an imitation of her. She hovered somewhere between the realest of realities and the most blatant of impersonations.

"Miles is so jealous of me that he questions everything I do," she cried scornfully. "When I was in New York I wrote him that I'd been to the theatre with Eddie Baker. Miles was so jealous he phoned me ten times in one day."

"I was wild," Miles snuffled sharply, a habit he had in times of stress. "The analyst couldn't get any results for a week."

Stella shook her head despairingly. "Did you expect me just to sit in the hotel for three weeks?"

"I don't expect anything. I admit that I'm jealous. I try not to be. I worked on that with Dr. Bridgebane, but it didn't do any good. I was jealous of Joel this afternoon when you sat on the arm of his chair."

"You were?" She started up. "You *were!* Wasn't there somebody on the arm of your chair? And did you speak to me for two hours?"

"You were telling your troubles to Joel in the bedroom."

"When I think that that woman" — she seemed to believe that to omit Eva Goebel's name would be to lessen her reality — "used to come here — "

"All right — all right," said Miles wearily. "I've admitted everything and I feel as bad about it as you do." Turning to Joel he began talking about pictures, while Stella moved restlessly along the far walls, her hands in her breeches pockets.

"They've treated Miles terribly," she said, coming suddenly back into the conversation as if they'd never discussed her personal affairs. "Dear, tell him about old Beltzer trying to change your picture."

As she stood hovering protectively over Miles, her eyes flashing with indignation in his behalf, Joel realized that he was in love with her. Stifled with excitement he got up to say good-night.

With Monday the week resumed its workaday rhythm, in sharp contrast to the theoretical discussions, the gossip and scandal of Sunday; there was the endless detail of script revision — "Instead of a lousy dissolve, we can leave her voice on the sound track and cut to a medium shot of the taxi from Bell's angle or we can simply pull the camera back to include the station, hold it a minute and then pan to the row of taxis" — by Monday afternoon Joel had again forgotten that people whose business was to provide entertainment were ever privileged to be entertained. In the evening he phoned Miles' house. He asked for Miles but Stella came to the phone.

"Do things seem better?"

"Not particularly. What are you doing next Saturday evening?"

"Nothing."

"The Perrys are giving a dinner and theatre party and Miles won't be here — he's flying to South Bend to see the Notre Dame–California game, I thought you might go with me in his place."

After a long moment Joel said, "Why — surely. If there's a conference I can't make dinner but I can get to the theatre."

"Then I'll say we can come."

Joel walked his office. In view of the strained relations of the Calmans, would Miles be pleased, or did she intend that Miles shouldn't know of it? That would be out of the question — if Miles didn't mention it Joel would. But it was an hour or more before he could get down to work again.

Wednesday there was a four-hour wrangle in a conference room crowded with planets and nebulae of cigarette smoke. Three men and a woman paced the carpet in turn, suggesting or condemning, speaking sharply or persuasively, confidently or despairingly. At the end Joel lingered to talk to Miles.

The man was tired — not with the exaltation of fatigue but life-tired, with his lids sagging and his beard prominent over the blue shadows near his mouth.

"I hear you're flying to the Notre Dame game."

Miles looked beyond him and shook his head.

"I've given up the idea."

"Why?"

"On account of you." Still he did not look at Joel.

"What the hell, Miles?"

"That's why I've given it up." He broke into a perfunctory laugh at himself. "I can't tell what Stella might do just out of spite — she's invited you to take her to the Perrys', hasn't she? I wouldn't enjoy the game."

The fine instinct that moved swiftly and confidently on the set, muddled so weakly and helplessly through his personal life.

"Look, Miles," Joel said frowning. "I've never made any passes *whatsoever* at Stella. If you're really seriously cancelling your trip on account of me, I won't go to the Perrys' with her. I won't see her. You can trust me absolutely."

Miles looked at him, carefully now.

"Maybe." He shrugged his shoulders. "Anyhow there'd just be somebody else. I wouldn't have any fun."

"You don't seem to have much confidence in Stella. She told me she'd always been true to you."

"Maybe she has." In the last few minutes several more muscles had sagged around Miles' mouth. "But how can I ask anything of her after what's happened? How can I expect her — " He broke off and his face grew harder as he said, "I'll tell you one thing, right or wrong and no matter what I've done, if I ever had anything on her I'd divorce her. I can't have my pride hurt — that would be the last straw."

His tone annoyed Joel, but he said:

"Hasn't she calmed down about the Eva Goebel thing?"

"No." Miles snuffled pessimistically. "I can't get over it either."

"I thought it was finished."

"I'm trying not to see Eva again, but you know it isn't easy just to drop something like that — it isn't some girl I kissed last night in a taxi! The psychoanalyst says — "

"I know," Joel interrupted. "Stella told me." This was depressing. "Well, as far as I'm concerned if you go to the game I won't see Stella. And I'm sure Stella has nothing on her conscience about anybody."

"Maybe not," Miles repeated listlessly. "Anyhow I'll stay and take her to the party. Say," he said suddenly, "I wish you'd come too. I've got to have somebody sympathetic to talk to. That's the trouble — I've influenced Stella in everything. Especially I've influenced her so that she likes all the men I like — it's very difficult."

"It must be," Joel agreed.

IV

Joel could not get to the dinner. Self-conscious in his silk hat against the unemployment, he waited for the others in front of the Hollywood Theatre and watched the evening parade: obscure replicas of bright, particular picture stars, spavined men in polo coats, a stomping dervish with the beard and staff of an apostle, a pair of chic Filipinos in collegiate clothes, reminder that this corner of the Republic opened to the seven seas, a long fantastic carnival of young shouts which proved to be a fraternity initiation. The line split to pass two smart limousines that stopped at the curb.

There she was, in a dress like ice-water, made in a thousand pale blue pieces, with icicles trickling at the throat. He started forward.

"So you like my dress?"

"Where's Miles?"

"He flew to the game after all. He left yesterday morning — at least I think — " She broke off. "I just got a telegram from South Bend saying that he's starting back. I forgot — you know all these people?"

The party of eight moved into the theatre.

Miles had gone after all and Joel wondered if he should have come. But during the performance, with Stella a profile under the pure grain of light hair, he thought no more about Miles. Once he turned and looked at her and she looked back at him, smiling and meeting his eyes for as long as he wanted. Between the acts they smoked in the lobby and she whispered:

"They're all going to the opening of Jack Johnson's night club — I don't want to go, do you?"

"Do we have to?"

"I suppose not." She hesitated. "I'd like to talk to you. I suppose we could go to our house — if I were only sure — "

Again she hesitated and Joel asked:

"Sure of what?"

"Sure that — oh, I'm haywire I know, but how can I be sure Miles went to the game?"

"You mean you think he's with Eva Goebel?"

"No, not so much that — but supposing he was here watching everything I do. You know Miles does odd things sometimes. Once he wanted a man with a long beard to drink tea with him and he sent down to the casting agency for one, and drank tea with him all afternoon."

"That's different. He sent you a wire from South Bend — that proves he's at the game."

After the play they said good night to the others at the curb and were answered by looks of amusement. They slid off along the golden garish thoroughfare through the crowd that had gathered around Stella.

"You see he could arrange the telegrams," Stella said, "very easily."

That was true. And with the idea that perhaps her uneasiness was justified, Joel grew angry: if Miles had trained a camera on them he felt no obligations toward Miles. Aloud he said:

"That's nonsense."

There were Christmas trees already in the shop windows and the full moon over the boulevard was only a prop, as scenic as the giant boudoir lamps of the corners. On into the dark foliage of Beverly Hills that flamed as eucalyptus by day, Joel saw only the flash of a white face under his own, the arc of her shoulder. She pulled away suddenly and looked up at him.

"Your eyes are like your mother's," she said. "I used to have a scrap book full of pictures of her."

"Your eyes are like your own and not a bit like any other eyes," he answered.

Something made Joel look out into the grounds as they went into the house, as if Miles were lurking in the shrubbery. A telegram waited on the hall table. She read aloud:

> Chicago
>
> Home tomorrow night. Thinking of you. Love.
>
> MILES

"You see," she said, throwing the slip back on the table, "he could easily have faked that." She asked the butler for drinks and sandwiches and ran upstairs, while Joel walked into the empty reception rooms. Strolling about he wandered to the piano where he had stood in disgrace two Sundays before.

"Then we could put over," he said aloud, "a story of divorce, the younger generators and the Foreign Legion."

His thoughts jumped to another telegram.

*"You were one of the most agreeable people at our party —* "

An idea occurred to him. If Stella's telegram had been purely a gesture of courtesy then it was likely that Miles had inspired it, for it was Miles who had invited him. Probably Miles had said:

"Send him a wire — he's miserable — he thinks he's queered himself."

It fitted in with "I've influenced Stella in everything. Especially I've influenced her so that she likes all the men I like." A woman would do a thing like that because she felt sympathetic — only a man would do it because he felt responsible.

When Stella came back into the room he took both her hands.

"I have a strange feeling that I'm a sort of pawn in a spite game you're playing against Miles," he said.

"Help yourself to a drink."

"And the odd thing is that I'm in love with you anyhow."

The telephone rang and she freed herself to answer it.

"Another wire from Miles," she announced. "He dropped it, or it says he dropped it, from the airplane at Kansas City."

"I suppose he asked to be remembered to me."

"No, he just said he loved me. I believe he does. He's so very weak."

"Come sit beside me," Joel urged her.

It was early. And it was still a few minutes short of midnight a half hour later, when Joel walked to the cold hearth, and said tersely:

"Meaning that you haven't any curiosity about me?"

"Not at all. You attract me a lot and you know it. The point is that I suppose I really do love Miles."

"Obviously."

"And tonight I feel uneasy about everything."

He wasn't angry — he was even faintly relieved that a possible entanglement was avoided. Still as he looked at her, the warmth and softness of her body thawing her cold blue costume, he knew she was one of the things he would always regret.

"I've got to go," he said. "I'll phone a taxi."

"Nonsense — there's a chauffeur on duty."

He winced at her readiness to have him go, and seeing this she kissed him lightly and said, "You're sweet, Joel." Then suddenly three things happened: he took down his drink at a gulp, the phone rang loud through the house and a clock in the hall struck twelve in triumphant trumpet notes.

*Nine — ten — eleven — twelve —*

v

It was Sunday again. Joel realized that he had come to the theatre this evening with the work of the week still hanging about him like cerements. He had made love to Stella as he might attack some matter to be cleaned up hurriedly before the day's end. But this was Sunday — the lovely, lazy perspective of the next twenty-four hours unrolled before him — every minute was something to be approached with lulling indirection, every moment held the germ of innumerable possibilities. Nothing was impossible — everything was just beginning. He poured himself another drink.

"What kind of wise-crack do you think that is?" said Stella into the phone. Then still hanging on to the phone she slid softly to the floor, moaning. Joel picked her up and laid her on the sofa. He squirted soda-water on a handkerchief and slapped it over her face. The receiver was still grinding and he put it to his ear.

" — the plane fell just this side of Kansas City. The body of Miles Calman has been identified and — "

He hung up the receiver.

"Lie still," he said, stalling, as Stella opened her eyes.

"Oh, what's happened?" she whispered. "Call them back. Oh, what's happened?"

"I'll call them right away. What's your doctor's name?"

"Did they say Miles was dead?"

"Lie quiet — is there a servant still up?"

"Hold me — I'm frightened."

He put his arm around her.

"I want the name of your doctor," he said sternly. "It may be a mis-take but I want someone here."

"It's Doctor — Oh, God, is Miles dead?"

Joel ran upstairs and searched through strange medicine cabinets for spirits of ammonia. When he came down Stella cried:

"He isn't dead — I know he isn't. This is part of his scheme. He's torturing me. I know he's alive. I can feel he's alive."

"I want to get hold of some close friends of yours, Stella. You can't stay here alone tonight."

"Oh, no," she cried. "I can't see anybody. You stay. I haven't got any friend." She got up, tears streaming down her face. "Oh, Miles is my only friend. He's not dead — he can't be dead. I'm going there right away and see. Get a train. You'll have to come with me."

"You can't. There's nothing to do tonight. I want you to tell me the name of some woman I can call: Lois? Joan? Carmel? Isn't there some-body?"

Stella stared at him blindly.

"Eva Goebel was my best friend," she said.

Joel thought of Miles, his sad and desperate face in the office two days before. In the awful silence of his death all was clear about him. He was the only American-born director with both an interesting temperament and an artistic conscience. Meshed in an industry, he had paid with his ruined nerves for having no resilience, no healthy cynicism, no refuge — only a pitiful and precarious escape.

There was a sound at the outer door — it opened suddenly, and there were footsteps in the hall.

"Miles!" Stella screamed. "Is it you, Miles? Oh, it's Miles."

A telegraph boy appeared in the doorway.

"I couldn't find the bell. I heard you talking inside."

The telegram was a duplicate of the one that had been phoned. While Stella read it over and over, as though it were a black lie, Joel telephoned. It was still early and he had difficulty getting anyone; when finally he succeeded in finding some friends he made Stella take a stiff drink.

"You'll stay here, Joel," she whispered, as though she were half asleep. "You won't go away. Miles liked you — he said you — " She shivered violently, "Oh, my God, you don't know how alone I feel." Her eyes closed, "Put your arms around me. Miles had a suit like that." She started bolt upright. "Think of what he must have felt. He was afraid of almost everything, anyhow."

She shook her head dazedly. Suddenly she seized Joel's face and held it close to hers.

"You won't go. You like me — you love me, don't you? Don't call up anybody. Tomorrow's time enough. You stay here with me tonight."

He stared at her, at first incredulously, and then with shocked understanding. In her dark groping Stella was trying to keep Miles alive by sustaining a situation in which he had figured — as if Miles' mind could not die so long as the possibilities that had worried him still existed. It was a distraught and tortured effort to stave off the realization that he was dead.

Resolutely Joel went to the phone and called a doctor.

"Don't, oh, don't call anybody!" Stella cried. "Come back here and put your arms around me."

"Is Doctor Bales in?"

"Joel," Stella cried. "I thought I could count on you. Miles liked you. He was jealous of you — Joel, come here."

Ah then — if he betrayed Miles she would be keeping him alive — for if he were really dead how could he be betrayed?

" — has just had a very severe shock. Can you come at once, and get hold of a nurse?"

"Joel!"

Now the doorbell and the telephone began to ring intermittently, and automobiles were stopping in front of the door.

"But you're not going," Stella begged him. "You're going to stay, aren't you?"

"No," he answered. "But I'll be back, if you need me."

Standing on the steps of the house which now hummed and palpitated with the life that flutters around death like protective leaves, he began to sob a little in his throat.

"Everything he touched he did something magical to," he thought. "He even brought that little gamin alive and made her a sort of masterpiece."

And then:

"What a hell of a hole he leaves in this damn wilderness — already!"

And then with a certain bitterness, "Oh, yes, I'll be back — I'll be back!"

1934

*Alexander Godin*

........................................................................................................

# My Dead Brother Comes to America

FROM *The Windsor Quarterly*

WHEN WE ARRIVED in New York Bay it was already winter, and the ground was covered with a hard brittle coat of snow. The whole harbor, as far as our eyes could reach, seemed to have been enameled with one vigorous sweep of the brush: standing on the deck, the sun high over-head, it hurt our eyes to look upon so much whiteness.

Near us the water was green and transparent, and farther away it was very blue and seemed dirty. The tugboats maneuvered noisily about our ship, belched smoke from their chimneys, and sent soot flying up the deck and into our faces. It was foggy in the bay, and other boats roared distractingly.

As the city came to meet us, as the greyness of its aspect became greyer still, and its skyscrapers towered all the time higher and higher above us, we felt small, frightened, cowed. The New World breathed a chill upon us and this chill, we felt, was not due entirely to the season.

When the ship came as near to the shore as it could, the tugboats disengaged themselves and steamed quickly out of the way; afterwards there was a rattling of rusty chains, the huge anchor hit the water with a booming sound, sending spray in all directions.

There were shouts from the water below: small boats drew up along-side the ship, and their occupants tried to attract the attention of the immigrants on board. These shouts were followed by frantic yells of recognition on both sides, and a package containing oranges was hurled up from below; the paper tore and the oranges went rolling over the deck, pursued by screaming women and children. Other packages were aimed too low and fell back into the water with a splash, and the occupants of the small boats instinctively covered their faces with their hands.

A shout, followed by another, calling mother's name. It was shrill and seemed to come from far off. We all crowded to the railing of the ship, but mother was the only one who could look over it and into the water below. My oldest sister was fourteen, I was thirteen, and the youngest girl was nine; but our hard life had left us too short and thin for our ages.

We climbed the railing till our knees touched the topmost beam, and we could see the skyscrapers and all the rest of the harbor hanging head downward in the water. But mother was too moved, too agitated to take care we should not fall overboard. She waved, and we followed the sweep of her hand; we strained our eyes.

It was father.

I was the first of the children to recognize him and, with an unhappy instinct, tried to gauge my feelings towards him. He had left me a five year old child, and now I was a growing boy. But this moment did not have the same meaning for me that it had for the others.

My oldest sister was wild with joy, and cried freely; she remembered the good side of father because he had been kinder to her than to all the rest. I remembered nothing but a child's bitterness and frustration and pain. The youngest child was still in the cradle when he had sailed, and now she tugged mother by the sleeve and said:

"Which one is *my* father, mother?"

While the remains of my dead brother were rotting somewhere beneath a low mound across the sea. The earth which covered the mound was hard and cold and the young aspens shook in the wind, helplessly.

He had died so suddenly, and his very old and wise eyes had looked up to us at the moment of death and had seemed to say: "I know I am going to die; you need not trouble. It is useless to cry over such a trifle as death!"

Eight years had passed since father sailed to America. My brother, who came after me, had died during the War. But either through negligence or fear, mother had all the time kept father in the dark about my brother's death.

We had lived through a heroic period of history without having anything of the heroic in our natures, and many things had happened to us during that time. Our lives had been broken into many shards and, standing there, I felt we should never be able to piece those shards together again. And the uselessness of it all could not break my indifferent heart: nothing, I felt, could ever break my heart again as the death of my only brother had left it broken, the first and most terrible death I had ever witnessed.

They told me afterwards that I had wept as if my whole world had collapsed; and I believed them. They told me, too, that I had torn my clothes and had beaten my head against the walls of the house; and I believed them. But when they said that the grief of this loss would pass, and my heart would become clean like the vast fields of the Ukraine after the grain and the rest of the harvest had been stored, I was silent.

Standing upon the deck with the others, I felt thankful that the ship was so high and father could not see that one was missing. I felt, at that moment, that mother had done well in not writing him about the death of his younger son. It was not out of charity to the feelings of my father that I thought these thoughts and felt as I did. I did not like my father; he meant less than a stranger to me.

But I envied him his suffering, if he should learn, and I was fiercely jealous of his pain. Rightly perhaps, I felt I was more entitled to grieve for my brother than he.

That night we slept aboard the ship, symbol of all the suffering we endured in crossing. We could still feel the vomit and ammonia smell of the sea in our nostrils, and see the emptiness of water unrelieved by anything but cheerless birds of the sea, and masses of weeds. But from the new way some of the sleepers snored it could be seen that assurance had partly, if not altogether, returned to them; others, however, tossed and moaned upon their bunks.

I dreamt that my dead brother was standing over my bunk. His face was sadly-wise, and he stroked my shoulder with his bony fingers. I tried to move but could not, watching him with horror and fascination. I awoke clutching desperately at the dream, and gazed hopelessly upon the floor, which was strewn with filth.

After breakfast we were all herded together like sheep. Pale, frightened ghosts that we were, hovering between two worlds: one which had castigated us with rods of steel and had afterwards cast us out, the other, rigid, indifferent, before which we had to cringe and weep, and which would admit us only after it had drained our hearts of all hope.

Our will or our pain did not matter, for we were all very tired; and, like most very tired people, we knew that when we reached the point of exhaustion we would fall asleep while standing up or being led about; and we would do, while sleeping, what we had done while awake.

A gangplank was lowered to the terminus of a ferryboat, which took us to Ellis Island.

Ellis Island was as grey and heartbreaking as a third-class cabin; all the buildings were of grey stone, bitten with greenish mould and overgrown with lichens and moss. Some windows were barred with twisted pigiron, others framed heavy nontransparent glass interwoven with fine wire. Through the bars we watched the seaweed float leisurely up the bay.

The doctors who examined us were as cruel as the power which had set them to this task; they pawed over us gingerly, obscenely, with the conviction in their eyes that we were no longer capable of either shame or pain.

Then, with our bundles in our hands, we were questioned in turn by many clerks sitting on very high stools. These clerks all wore black alpaca coats with shiny buttons, and tall starched collars. The desks on which they wrote were also tall and inclined at a curious angle, like the wooden stands on which Jews rest their prayer books in the synagogue; all of them even smiled the same sour way into their sheets as they in turn wrote mother's answers to their questions.

On the other side of the partition was father; he, too, was being questioned, and the answers of both were compared.

Suddenly something stopped; the machinery of procedure jumped out of gear and could not go on. Mother grew panicky; she looked as if she had lied. The clerk stuttered in his anger, because the unusualness of the situation threw him back on his rusty brain; he perspired heavily. He tried to be helpful in an official way, his confusion arousing his sympathy and bringing his humanity to the surface. But it was clear that he did not know how. There was the brutal statement:

"Your husband says he has four children, madam, and you have only three. How do you explain that, madam? What are we to think of it, madam?"

Mother stammered; her lips grew white. Tears streamed from her eyes, and she began to explain things to the clerk in a halting manner.

The clerk looked frightened. He bent his head lower, as her increased sobbing made mother's explanation harder to grasp; his stool swayed dangerously, and he held on to his desk with his thin nervous fingers. A pained smile appeared upon his face; and whether he suddenly understood or did not care to listen any longer to this story which affected him in a painful manner, he said we could go. We all ran after mother like newly hatched chicks.

And father, on the other side of the partition, what did *he* think of at that moment? How did *he* feel?

As soon as he saw us he cried out: "Bessie — my children!"

His face was lined with weariness and his eyes were red. There were two distinct grooves running down his cheeks from his eyes where his tears had fallen. He looked very helpless and broken.

He embraced each of us passionately and protectively. At that moment I had a feeling of love, drawn forth by compassion, for my father. But when he drew me to him, my head and legs bent back like a runner's, and my muscles grew taut as a string. He must have felt my resistance, because he did not try to force his affection upon me.

He was happy then and did not question mother about the dead boy; this raised him greatly in my esteem. And he was the same as he had always been, because when he was happy he was ridiculous, like an old man in love. He took some woolen caps from his pockets and fitted them on the heads of my two sisters and myself; the caps were warm and had red tassels at the top, like the Turkish fez, but because we felt that they were comical we were very uncomfortable in them. And again a moment of tragedy, the sometimes ridiculous but inevitable tragedy which enveloped the life of this man, my father:

He had brought four caps along with him, but had not found the time in which to hide the spare cap somewhere; when mother saw it, she grew hysterical, and father gazed at her helplessly and with twitching lips. He wanted to utter her name, but his thin cruel lips would not obey and the words vibrated in his throat, making a curious sound.

We took the ferry to Bowling Green, then the Elevated, and all the way to our new home people gazed at us as if we had descended from another planet; we wanted to remove our caps, but father pleaded with us in such a way that it was not possible to disobey him.

When we descended the stairs of the Elevated, father walked briskly ahead of us, as was his habit, and the cap intended for the dead boy stuck out of one of his pockets. We ran after him, as if fearful of being abandoned. The snow crunched beneath our feet, and the jagged cinders on the sidewalk punctured the thin soles of our shoes. All the time I kept my eyes on the cap which stuck out of father's pocket, thinking of my dead brother.

A postman, his mailbag hanging from his shoulder, passed us on a bicycle as we came to Brook Avenue, the tires of his machine squealing as they collided with the hard snow.

We entered our new home slowly and with shyness, as if into the house of a stranger. The flat was dark and airless, and for the first few minutes we huddled against the walls in fright. The furniture was old and hastily arranged, and a lot of rubbish was piled on the kitchen floor.

As soon as we passed the threshold, father began to sob helplessly.

Then he put the spare woolen cap on the table, and lit the little gas stove; it hissed suddenly, and slowly the frost began to dissolve on the window panes. We devoured the food he put before us with bulging, greedy, envious eyes, thinking that perhaps this was only a dream and the next meal was far away.

Afterwards he gave us all new clothes. He folded the suit he had prepared for the dead boy and put it away carefully into a drawer, as if he expected him to appear at the door one day and claim it.

Evening came, and a great stillness descended over our lives. We had been tired a long time, and now our tiredness was beginning to thaw; and as we swayed drunkenly in our seats, shadows of madness and grief began to invade the house.

We sat up and listened; our nerves were tense, and the eyelids fluttered like wounded birds over our eyes.

The unclaimed white woolen cap with the red tassel lay on the table and, for some reason, the eyes of all were turned towards it; in the darkness of the room it stood out like a single star on a foggy night. The rust in our blood was heavy and poisonous, sharpening our grief; and at that moment we became aware of the return of the dead boy into our shattered lives.

He, too, had come to America.

## William Saroyan

......................................................................................................

# Resurrection of a Life

FROM *Story*

EVERYTHING BEGINS with inhale and exhale, and never ends, moment after moment, yourself inhaling, and exhaling, seeing, hearing, smelling, touching, tasting, moving, sleeping, waking, day after day and year after year, until it is now, this moment, the moment of your being, the last moment, which is saddest and most glorious. It is because we remember, and I remember myself having lived among dead moments, now deathless because of my remembrance, among people now dead, having been a part of the flux which is now only a remembrance, of myself and this earth, a street I was crossing and the people I saw walking in the opposite direction, automobiles going away from me. Saxons, Dorts, Maxwells, and the street cars and trains, the horses and wagons, and myself, a small boy, crossing a street, alive somehow, going somewhere.

First he sold newspapers. It was because he wanted to do something, he himself, standing in the city, shouting about what was happening in the world. He used to shout so loud, and he used to need to shout so much, that he would forget he was supposed to be selling papers; he would get the idea that he was only supposed to shout, to make people understand what was going on. He used to go through the city like an alley cat, prowling all over the place, into saloons, upstairs into whore houses, into gambling joints, to see: their faces, the faces of those who were alive with him on the earth, and the expressions of their faces, and their forms, the faces of old whores, and the way they talked, and the smell of all the ugly places, and the drabness of all the old and rotting buildings, all of it, of his time and his life, a part of him. He prowled through the city, seeing and smelling, talking, shouting about the big news, inhaling and exhaling, blood moving to the rhythm of the sea, coming and going, to the shore of self and back again to selflessness, inhale and newness, exhale and new death, and the boy in the city, walking through it like an alley cat, shouting headlines.

It was all ugly, but his being there was splendid and not an ugliness. His hands would be black with the filth of the city and his face would be black with it, but it was splendid, himself alive and walking, of the events of the earth, from day to day, new headlines every day, new things happening.

In the summer it would be very hot and his body would thirst for the sweet fluids of melons, and he would long for the shade of thick leaves and the coolness of a quiet stream, but always he would be in the city, shouting. It was his place and he was the guy, and he wanted the city to be the way it was, if that was the way. He would figure it out somehow. He used to stare at the rich people sitting at tables in hightone restaurants eating dishes of ice cream, electric fans making breezes for them, and he used to watch them ignoring the city, not going out to it and being of it, and it used to make him mad. Pigs, he used to say, having everything you want, having everything. What do you know of this place? What do you know of me, seeing this place with a clean eye, any of you? And he used to go, in the summer, to the Crystal Bar, and there he would study the fat man who slept in a chair all summer, a mountain of somebody, a man with a face and substance that lived, who slept all day every summer day, dreaming what? This fat man, three hundred pounds? What did he dream, sitting in the saloon, in the corner, not playing poker or pinochle like the other men, only sleeping and sometimes brushing the flies from his fat face? What was there for him to dream, anyway, with a body like that, and what was hidden beneath the fat of that body, what grace or gracelessness? He used to go into the saloon and spit on the floor like the men did and secretly watch the fat man sleeping, trying to figure it out. Him alive, too? he used to ask. That great big sleeping thing alive? Like myself?

In the winter he wouldn't see the fat man. It would be only in the summer. The fat man was like the hot sun, very near everything, of everything, sleeping, flies on his big nose. In the winter it would be cold and there would be much rain. The rain would fall over him and his clothes would be wet, but he would never get out of the rain, and he would go on prowling around in the city, looking for whatever it was that was there and that nobody else was trying to see, and he would go in and out of all the ugly places to see how it was with the faces of the people when it rained, how the rain changed the expressions of their faces. His body would be wet with the rain, but he would go from one place to another, shouting headlines, telling the city about the things that were going on in the world.

I was this boy and he is dead now, but he will be prowling through the city when my body no longer makes a shadow upon the pavement, and if it is not this boy it will be another, myself again, another boy alive on earth, seeking the essential truth of the scene, seeking the static and precise beneath that which is in motion and which is imprecise.

The theatre stood in the city like another universe, and he entered its darkness, seeking there in the falsity of pictures of man in motion the truth of his own city, and of himself, and the truth of all living. He saw their eyes: *While London Sleeps.* He saw the thin emaciated hand of theft twitching toward crime: *Jean Valjean.* In the darkness the false universe unfolded itself before him and he saw the phantoms of man going and coming, making quiet horrifying shadows: *The Cabinet of Dr. Caligari.* He saw the endless sea, smashing against rocks, birds flying, the great prairie and herds of horses, New York and greater mobs of men, monstrous trains, rolling ships, men marching to war, and a line of infantry charging another line of infantry: *The Birth of a Nation.* And sitting in the secrecy of the theatre he entered the houses of the rich, saw them, the male and the female, the high ceilings, the huge marble pillars, the fancy furniture, great bathrooms, tables loaded with food, rich people laughing and eating and drinking, and then secrecy again and a male seeking a female, and himself watching carefully to understand, one pursuing and the other fleeing, and he felt the lust of man mounting in him, desire for the loveliest of them, the universal lady of the firm white shoulders and the thick round thighs, desire for her, he himself, ten years old, in the darkness.

He is dead and deathless, staring at the magnification of the kiss, straining at the mad embrace of male and female, walking alone from the theatre, insane with the passion to live. And at school he could not bear them. Their shallowness was too much. Don't try to teach me. That was his attitude. Teach the idiots. Don't try to tell me anything. I am getting it direct, straight from the pit, the ugliness with the loveliness. Two times two is many million people all over the earth, lonely and shivering, groaning one at a time, trying to figure it out. Don't try to teach me. I'll figure it out for myself.

Daniel Boone? he said. Don't tell me. I knew him. Walking through Kentucky. He killed a bear. Lincoln? A big fellow walking alone, looking at things as if he pitied them, a face like the face of man. The whole countryside full of dead men, men he loved, and he himself alive. Don't ask me to memorize his speech. I know all about it, the way he stood, the way the words came from his being.

He used to get up before daybreak and walk to The San Joaquin Baking Company. It was good, the smell of freshly baked bread, and it was good to see the machine wrapping the loaves in wax paper. *Chicken bread,* he used to say, and the important man in the fine suit of clothes used to smile at him. The important man used to say, What kind of chickens you got at your house, kid? And the man would smile nicely so that there would be no insult, and he would never have to tell the man that he himself and his brother and sisters were eating the chicken bread. He would just stand by the bin, not saying anything, not asking for the best loaves, and the important man would understand, and he would pick out the best of the loaves and drop them into the sack the boy held open. If the man happened to drop a bad loaf into the sack the boy would say nothing, and a moment later the man would pick out the bad loaf and throw it back into the bin. Those chickens, he would say, they might not like that loaf. And the boy would say nothing. He would just smile. It was good bread, not too stale and sometimes very fresh, sometimes still warm, only it was bread that had fallen from the wrapping machine and couldn't be sold to rich people. It was made of the same dough, in the same ovens, only after the loaves fell they were called chicken bread and a whole sack full cost only a quarter. The important man never insulted. Maybe he himself had known hunger once, maybe as a boy he had known how it felt to be hungry for bread. He was very funny, always asking about the chickens. He knew there were no chickens, and he always picked out the best loaves.

Bread to eat, so that he could move through the city and shout. Bread to make him solid, to nourish his anger, to fill his substance with vigor that shouted at the earth. Bread to carry him to death and back again to life, inhaling, exhaling, keeping the inward flame alive. Chicken bread, he used to say, not feeling ashamed. We eat it. Sure, sure. It isn't good enough for the rich. There are many at our house. We eat every bit of it, all the crumbs. We do not mind a little dirt on the crust. We put all of it inside. A sack of chicken bread. We know we're poor. When the wind comes up our house shakes, but we don't tremble. We can eat the bread that isn't good enough for the rich. Throw in the loaves. It is too good for chickens. It is our life. Sure we eat it. We're not ashamed. We're living on the money we earn selling newspapers. The roof of our house leaks and we catch the water in pans, but we are all there, all of us alive, and the floor of our house sags when we walk over it, and it is full of crickets and spiders, but we are in the house, living there. We eat this bread that isn't good enough for the rich, this bread that you call chicken bread.

Walking, this boy vanished, and now it is myself, another, no longer the boy, and the moment is now this moment, of my remembrance. The fig tree he loved: of all graceful things it was the most graceful, and in the winter it stood leafless, dancing, sculptural whiteness dancing. In the spring the new leaves appeared on the fig tree and the hard green figs. The sun came closer and closer and the heat increased, and he climbed the tree, eating the soft fat figs, the flowering of the lovely white woman, his lips kissing.

But always he returned to the city, back again to the place of man, the street, the structure, the door and window, the hall, the roof and floor, back again to the corners of dark secrecy, where they were dribbling out their lives, back again to the movement of mobs, to beds and chairs and stoves, away from the tree, away from the meadow and the brook. The tree was of the other earth, the older and lovelier earth, solid and quiet and of godly grace, of earth and water and sky, and of the time that was before, ancient places, quietly in the sun, Rome and Athens and Cairo, the white fig tree dancing. He talked to the tree, his mouth clenched, pulling himself over its smooth sensuous limbs, to be of you, he said, to be of your time, to be there, in the old world, and to be here as well, to eat your fruit, to feel your strength, to move with you as you dance, myself, alone in the world, with you only, my tree, that in myself which is of thee.

Dead, dead, the tree and the boy, and yet everlastingly alive, the white tree moving slowly in dance, and the boy talking to it in unspoken, unspeakable language: you, loveliness of the earth, the street waits for me, the moment of my time calls me back, and there he was suddenly, running through the streets, shouting that ten thousand huns had been destroyed. Huns? he asked. What do you mean, huns? They are men, aren't they? And he saw the people of the city smiling and talking with pleasure about the good news. He himself appreciated the goodness of the news because it helped him sell his papers, but after the shouting was over and he was himself again, he used to think of ten thousand men smashed from life to violent death, one man at a time, each man himself as he, the boy, was himself, bleeding, screaming, weeping, remembering life as dying men remember it, wanting it, gasping for breath, to go on inhaling and exhaling, living and dying, but always living somehow, stunned, horrified, ten thousand faces suddenly amazed at the monstrousness of the war, the beastliness of man, who could be so godly.

There were no words with which to articulate his rage. All that he could do was shout: but even now I cannot see the war as historians see it. Succeeding moments have carried the germ of myself to this face and form, the one of this moment, now, my being in this small room, alone, as always, remembering the boy, resurrecting him, and I cannot see the war as historians see it. Those clever fellows study all the facts and they see the war as a large thing, one of the biggest events in the legend of man, something general, involving multitudes. I see it as a large thing too, only I break it into small units of one man at a time, and I see it as a large and monstrous thing for each man involved. I see the war as death in one form or another for men dressed as soldiers, and all the men who survived the war, including myself, I see as men who died with their brothers, dressed as soldiers.

There is no such thing as a soldier. I see death as a private event, the destruction of the universe in the brain and in the senses of one man, and I cannot see any man's death as a contributing factor in the success or failure of a military campaign. The boy had to shout what had happened. Whatever happened, he had to shout it, making the city know. *Ten thousand huns killed, ten thousand,* one at a time, one, two, three, four, inestimably many, ten thousand, alive, and then dead, killed, shot, mangled, ten thousand huns, ten thousand men. I blame the historians for the distortion. I remember the coming of the gas mask to the face of man, the proper grimace of horror for the nightmare we were performing, artfully expressing the monstrousness of the inward face of man, the most pertinent truth that emerged from the whole affair. To the boy who is dead this war was the international epilepsy in the body and soul of man which brought about the systematic destruction of one man at a time until millions of men were destroyed.

There he is suddenly in the street, running, and it is 1917, shouting the most recent crime of man, extra, extra, ten thousand huns killed, himself alive, inhaling, exhaling, *ten thousand, ten thousand,* all the ugly buildings solid, all the streets solid, the city unmoved by the crime, *ten thousand,* windows opening, doors opening, and the people of the city smiling about it, good, good, ten thousand, ten thousand of them killed, good, good. Johnny, get your gun, and another trainload of boys in uniforms, going away, torn from home, from the roots of life, their tragic smiling, and the broken hearts, all things in the world broken. And the fat man, sleeping in a corner of the Crystal Bar, what of him?

Sleeping there, somehow alive in spite of the lewd death in him, but never budging. Pig, he said, ten thousand huns killed, ten thousand men with solid bodies mangled to death. Does it mean nothing to you? Does it not disturb your fat dream? Boys with loves, men with wives and children. What have you, sleeping? They are all dead, all of them dead. Do you think you are alive? Do you dream you are alive? The fly on your nose is more alive than you.

Sunday would come, *O day of rest and gladness, O day of joy and light, O balm of care and sadness, Most beautiful, most bright,* and he would put on his best shirt and his best trousers, and he would try to comb his hair down, to be neat and clean, meeting God, and he would go to the small church and sit in the shadow of religion: in the beginning, the boy David felling the giant Goliath, beautiful Rebecca, mad Saul, Daniel among lions, Jesus talking quietly to the men, and in the boat shouting at them because they feared, angry at them because they had fear, calm yourselves, boys, calm yourselves, let the storm rage, let the boat sink, do you fear going to God? Ah that was lovely, that love of death was lovely, Jesus loving it: calm yourselves, boys, God damn you, calm yourselves, why are you afraid? *Still, still with thee, when purple morning breaketh, abide, abide, with me, fast falls the eventide,* ah lovely. He sat in the basement of the church, among his fellows, singing at the top of his voice. I do not believe, he said. I cannot believe. There cannot be a God. *Saviour, breathe an evening blessing, sun of my soul, begin, my tongue, some heavenly theme, begin, my tongue, begin, begin.* Lovely, lovely, but I cannot believe. The poor and the rich, those who deserve life and those who deserve death, and the ugliness everywhere. Where is God? Big ships sinking at sea, submarines, men in the water, cannon booming, machine guns, men dying, ten thousand, where? But our singing, *Joy to the world, the Lord is come. Let earth receive her King. Silent Night, holy night. What grace, O Lord, my dear redeemer. Ride on, ride on, in majesty. Angels, roll the rock away; death, yield up thy mighty prey.*

No, he could not believe. He had seen for himself. It was there, in the city, all the godlessness, the eyes of the whores, the men at cards, the sleeping fat man, and the mad headlines, it was all there, unbelief, ungodliness, everywhere, all the world forgetting. How could he be-lieve? But the music, so good and clean, so much of the best in man: *lift up, lift up your voices now. Lo, he comes with clouds descending once for favored sinners slain. Arise, my soul, arise, shake off thy guilty fears, O for a thousand tongues to sing. Like a river glorious, holy Bible, book divine, precious treasure, thou art mine.* And spat, right on the floor of the

Crystal Bar. And into Collette's Rooms, over The Rex Drug Store, the men buttoning their clothes, ten thousand huns killed, madam. *Break thou the bread of life, dear Lord, to me, as thou didst break the loaves, beside the sea.* And spat, on the floor, watching the fat man snoring. Another ship sunk. The Marne. Ypres. Russia. Poland. Spat. *Art thou weary, art thou languid, art thou sore distressed?* Zeppelin over Paris. The fat man sleeping. *Haste, traveler, haste, the night comes on.* Spat. *The storm is gathering in the west.* Cannon. Hutt! two three, four! Hutt! two three, four, how many men marching, how many? Onward, onward, unChristian soldiers. *I was a wandering sheep.* Spat. *I did not love my home.* Your deal, Jim. Spat. *Take me, O my father, take me.* Collette, I adore you, ugly whore. Spat. *This holy bread, this holy wine. My God, is an hour so sweet?* Submarine plunging. Spat. *Take my life and let it be consecrated, Lord, to thee.* Spat.

He sat in the basement of the little church, deep in the shadow of faith, and of no faith: I cannot believe, it is too monstrous: where is the God of whom they speak, where? *Your harps, ye trembling saints, down from the willows take.* Where? Cannon. *Lead, oh lead, lead kindly light, amid the encircling gloom.* Spat. *Jesus, Saviour, pilot me.* Airplane: spat: smash. *Guide me, O thou great Jehovah. Bread of heaven, bread of heaven, feed me till I want no more.* The universal lady of the dark theatre: thy lips, beloved, thy shoulders and thighs, thy sea-surging blood. The tree, black figs in sunlight. Spat. *Rock of ages, cleft for me, let me hide myself in thee.* Spat. *Let the water and the blood, from thy riven side which flowed, be of sin the double cure.* Lady your arm, your arm: spat. The mountain of flesh sleeping through the summer. Ten thousand huns killed.

Sunday would come, turning him from the outward world to the inward, to the secrecy of the past, endless as the future, back to Jesus, to God; *when the weary, seeking rest, to thy goodness flee;* back to the earliest quiet: *He leadeth me, O blessed thought.* But he did not believe. He could not believe. Jesus was a remarkable fellow: you couldn't figure him out. He had a sort of pious love of death. An heroic fellow. And as for God. Well, he could not believe.

But the songs he loved and he sang them with all his might: *hold thou my hand, O blessed nothingness, I walk with thee. Awake, my soul, stretch every nerve, and press with vigor on. Work, for the night is coming, work, for the day is done.* Spat. Right on the floor of the Crystal Bar. It is Sunday again: *O blessed nothingness, we worship thee.* Spat. And suddenly the sleeping fat man sneezes. Hallelujah. Amen. Spat. *Sleep on, beloved sleep, and take thy rest.* (Pig, he said.) *Lay down thy head upon thy Saviour's breast.* We love thee well, but Jesus loves thee best. Jesus loves thee. For the Bible tells you so. Amen. The fat man sneezes. He could not believe and he could not disbelieve. Sense? There was none. But glory. There was an abundance of it. Everywhere. Madly everywhere. Those crazy birds vomiting song. Those vast trees, solid and quiet. And clouds. And sun. And night. And day. *It is not death to die,* he sang: *to leave this weary road, to be at home with God.* God? The same. Nothingness. Nowhere. Everywhere. The crazy glory, everywhere: Madam Collette's Rooms, all modern conveniences, including beds. Spat. *I know not, Oh I know not, what joys await us there.* Where? Heaven? No. Madam Collette's: In the church, the house of God, with such thoughts: the boy singing, remembering the city's lust.

Boom: Sunday morning: and the war still booming: after the singing he would go to the newspaper office and get his SPECIAL SUNDAY EXTRAS and run through the city with them, his hair combed for God, and he would shout the news: amen, *I gave my life for Jesus.* Oh yeah? Ten thousand huns killed, and I am the guy, inhaling, exhaling, running through the town, I, myself, seeing, hearing, touching, shouting, smelling, singing, wanting, I, the guy, the latest of the whole lot, alive by the grace of God: ten thousand, two times ten million, by the grace of God dead, by His grace smashed, amen, extra, extra: five cents a copy, extra, ten thousand killed.

I was this boy who is now lost and buried in the succeeding forms of myself, and I am now of this last moment, of this small room, and the night hush, time going, time coming, and gone, and gone, and again coming, and myself here, breathing, this last moment, inhale, exhale, the boy dead and alive. All that I have learned is that we breathe, from moment to moment, now, always now, and then we remember, and we see the boy moving through a city that has become lost, among people who have become dead, alive among dead moments, crossing a street, the scene thus, or standing by the bread bin in the bakery, a sack of chicken bread please so that we can live and shout about it, and it begins nowhere and it ends nowhere, and all that I know is that we are somehow alive, all of us in the light, making shadows, the sun overhead, space all around us, inhaling, exhaling, the face and form of man everywhere, pleasure and pain, sanity and madness, over and over again, war and no war, and peace and no peace, the earth solid and unaware of us, unaware of our cities, our dreams, unaware of this love I have for life, the love that was the boy's, unaware of all things, my going, my coming, the earth everlastingly itself, not of me, everlastingly

precise, and the sea sullen with movement like my breathing, waves
pounding the shore of myself, coming and going, and all that I know
is that I am alive and glad to be, glad to be of this ugliness and this
glory, somehow glad that I can remember, somehow remember the boy
climbing the fig tree, unpraying but religious with joy, somehow of the
earth, of the time of earth, somehow everlastingly of life, nothingness,
blessed or unblessed, somehow deathless like myself, timeless, glad,
insanely glad to be here, and so it is true, there is no death, somehow
there is no death, and can never be.

1938

*Robert Penn Warren*

....................................................................................................................

# Christmas Gift

FROM *The Virginia Quarterly Review*

THE BIG WHITE FLAKES sank down from the sagging sky. A wet grey light hung over everything; and the flakes looked grey against it, then turned white as they sank toward the dark earth. The roofs of the few houses along the road looked sogged and black. The man who sat in the wagon that moved slowly up the road wore an old quilt wrapped around his shoulders and a corduroy cap pulled down over his eyes. His ears stuck out from under the cap, thin as paper and lined with purplish veins. Before him, vanishing, the flakes touched the backs of the mules, which steamed and were black like wet iron.

When the man spoke to the boy on the seat beside him, the ends of his mustache twitched the amber drops that clung to it. "You kin git off at the store," he said.

The boy nodded his head, which looked tight and small under the rusty-felt man's hat he wore.

The hoofs of the mules cracked the skim ice in the ruts, and pale yellow mud oozed up around the fetlocks. The wagon wheels turned laboriously, crackling the ice with a sound like paper.

The man pulled on the reins, and the mules stopped, their heads hanging under the sparse downward drift of flakes. "Whoa," he said, after the mules had already stopped. He pointed his thumb toward the frame building set beside the road. "You kin git off here, son," he said. "Most like they kin tell you here."

The boy climbed over the side of the wagon, set his foot on the hub, and jumped. His feet sank in the half-frozen, viscous mud. Turning, he took a step toward the building, then stopped. "Much obliged," he said, and started on. For a moment the man peered after him from small

red-rimmed eyes. He jerked the reins. "Giddap," he said; and the mules
lay against the traces, their hoofs crackling the skim ice.

The boy mounted the steps to the sloping boards of the porch, and
put his sharp grey claw-like fingers on the latch-bar. Very quietly, he
pushed the door inward a little space, slipped his body through the
opening, and closed the door, letting the latch back down without a
sound. He looked down the shadowy corridor of the store between the
shelves of cans and boxes and the clothing hung on racks against the
other wall. At the end of the corridor some men sat, their bodies in
huddled outline against the red glow of a stove.

With hesitant steps, the boy approached them, stopping just behind
the circle. A big man, whose belly popped the broad leather belt he
wore, let his chair come forward to rest on the floor, and surveyed him.
"What kin I do for you today, buddy?" he said.

The tight skin of the boy's face puckered greyly toward the lips, and
his Adam's apple twitched up his throat. The big man kept on looking at
the boy, who stood dumbly beyond the circle, the over-size mackinaw
hanging to his knees, and shook his head at the big man.

"You wanter git warmed up?" the big man said.

The boy shook his head again.

"Naw, sir," he managed.

"You look cold," the big man said. "You come round here." He
motioned to the open space in front of the stove.

Eyes fixed in question on the big man's face, the boy obeyed the
gesture. He came round, carefully stepping over a man's out-thrust leg.
He stood inside the circle, about six feet from the stove, and spread his
hands out to it.

"Git up closter," the big man said. "Git yore bottom up to hit."

The boy moved forward, and turned his back to the stove, his hands
behind him working weakly toward the warmth. The men kept looking
at him. Steam from the mackinaw rose up against the stove, with the
sick smell of hot, wet wool.

"Now ain't that better?" the big man demanded.

The boy nodded at him.

"Who are you, pardner?" one of the men said.

The boy turned toward him. He was a short stocky man, bald and
swarthy, and he sat with his booted legs bunched under him like an
animal ready to spring.

"I know who he is. I've seen him," another man said. "He's one of
Milt Lancaster's kids."

Another man beyond the stove leaned forward, bucking his chair nearer to the boy. "Now ain't that nice," he said. "Pleased ter meet you. So you're one of Milt's little bastards."

The bald, swarthy man glared at him. "Shut up!" he ordered abruptly.

The other man leaned elaborately back and studied the ceiling, softly whistling between his teeth.

"In doing yore Satiday trading?" the bald swarthy one said.

The boy shook his head. Then he looked at the big man. "I wanter git the docter."

"That's what he's for," the big man admitted, and blinked at the stove.

"Yore folks sick?" the bald, swarthy man said.

"My sister," the boy said, "she's gonna have a baby."

The man who was whistling stopped. "Yore little sister, buddy?" He addressed the ceiling in mock solicitude, and shook his head. "Them Lancasters allus did calf young."

"Hit's my big sister," the boy said to the bald man. "She come up here last summer. She ain't nuthing but my sister on my ma's side."

"Well, well," said the man who was looking at the ceiling. He let his chair thump down on the front legs and spoke to no one in particular. "So they's gonna be another little bastard out to Milt's place."

The bald swarthy man stared glumly across at the speaker. "Bill Stover," he commented with no feeling, "you gonna make me stomp hell outer you fore sun."

The boy glanced quickly from one to the other. The bald swarthy man stared across the space, his legs bunched under him. The other man grinned, and winked sidewise.

"I oughter do hit now," the bald swarthy one said as if to himself.

The other stopped grinning.

"If you want the doc," the big man said, "you go up the road four houses on the right-hand side. It ain't no piece. That's where Doc Small lives. They's a office in his front yard right smack on the road, but you go up to the house, that's where he is."

"Hit's a chicken office," one of the men said. "That's where the doc keeps his chickens now going on twenty years."

"You ain't gonna miss hit," the big man said.

The boy came out of the circle and stopped before the big man. He looked up with a quick, furtive motion of the head. "Much obliged," he said. He pulled his mackinaw about him, taking up the slack in the garment, and moved down the corridor toward the door.

"Wait a minute," the big man called after him. He got up ponderously to his feet, hitched his belt up on his belly, and went forward to the single glass showcase. The men watched him, craning their necks, all except the bald swarthy one, who crouched and stared at the red bulge of the stove.

The big man reached into the glass showcase and took out a half dozen sticks of red-striped candy. He thrust them at the boy, who, looking suspiciously at the objects, shook his head.

"Take 'em," the man ordered.

The boy kept his hands in the pockets of the mackinaw. "I ain't got nuthin' ter pay fer it with," he said.

"Here, take 'em, buddy," the man said.

The boy reached out his hand uneasily, all the while studying the man's face, which was without expression. The fingers, scaled grey by cold like a bird's claw, closed on the candy, jerked back, clutching the sticks. The hand holding the candy slipped into the loose mackinaw pocket.

"Beat it," the big man said, "afore they beat hell outer you at home."

The boy slipped out the door, quick and quiet as a cat.

The big man came back to the stove and sank morosely into his chair. He tilted it back and put his arms behind his head, on which the thin brown hair was slickly parted.

"You sick, Al?" one of the men said to him.

He did not answer.

"You must be sick, giving something away just off-hand like that."

Bill Stover again leaned forward, wet his lips, and winked at the man who spoke. He himself seemed about to speak. Then he saw the face of the bald swarthy man, whose dark eyes burned with a kind of indolent savagery.

"You go straight to hell," the big man was wearily saying.

The snow had almost stopped. It was getting colder now. The flakes were smaller now, drawing downward breathlessly like bits of white lint. They clung to the soaked grass by the road and lay on the frozen mud. The boy's feet cracked the skim ice on the mud, then, in withdrawal, made a sucking sound.

Two hundred yards up the road he came to the place. Jutting on the road, the one-room frame building stood beside a big cedar. A tin sign, obscured by rust and weather, was nailed to the door, carrying the words: *Doctor A. P. Small, Office.* The boy turned up the path by the cedar, whose black boughs swooped down toward the bare ground. The house was set far back from the road, half hidden by trellises to which leafless horny vine clutched and curled. The windows of the house gave blankly, without reflection, on the yard where grass stuck stiffly up from dirty ice-curdled pools at the roots. The door had a glass pane in it; behind the glass a lace curtain hung like a great coarse cobweb.

He tapped the paintless wood of the door.

It was a woman who, at last, opened the door.

"What do you want, boy?" she said.

"I wanter git the docter," he said.

She said, "Clean your feet and come in," and abruptly turned down the low hall. He scraped his shoes, stooped to wipe them with his fingers, and then, wringing the mud from his hands, wiped them on the mackinaw. He followed her, with quick secret glances from one side to the other. She was standing before a door, her thin arm pointing inward. "You come in here," she ordered. He stood back from the hearth while the woman thrust her hands nervously at the blaze. She was a little woman, and while she warmed her hands, she kept looking over her shoulder at him with a wry bird-like asperity. "What's the matter?" she said.

"My sister's gonna have a baby," he said.

"Who are you, boy?"

"Sill Lancaster's my name, mam," he said, looking at her little hands that approached and jerked from the bright blaze.

"Oh," she said. She turned fully at him, inspected him sharply from head to foot. "You ought to take off your hat when you come in the house, boy," she said.

He took the big hat off his head, and standing before her, held it tight in both hands.

She nodded at him; said, "Wait a minute"; and was gone out the door.

With a dubious, inquiring step, as on suspected ice, he went across the straw matting toward the hearth, and put his back to the fire. He looked at all the objects in the room, covertly spying on them as though they had a life of their own: the gilt iron bed covered by a lace counterpane, the unpainted rocking chairs with colored pillows on the seats that were pulled up to the hearth, the table on which stood a basket full of socks rolled up in neat balls. The fire spat and sputtered in mild sibilance, eating at the chunks of sawn wood on the hearth. And the clock, its face supported by plump cupids of painted china, ticked with a small busy sound. The boy laid his hat on the yellow cushion of one of the chairs and put his hands to the fire. Against the plump little cushion, its color so bright, the hat was big and dirty. With hands still stretched out, the boy regarded it. It was soggy black with wet flecks of mud clinging to it; at the creases it was worn through. The boy took it quickly off the chair.

With that neat industrious sound the clock kept on ticking.

"Hello, son," the man in the door said.

The man was buttoning up a brown overcoat that dropped to his ankles. Beneath the coat his small booted feet stuck out. The woman slipped in past him and came to the fire, put her hands toward the blaze again, jerked them back, all the while looking at the boy. The man pulled a black fur cap on his head and turned down the ear-flaps. "Les go," he said.

The woman went up to him, touching his breast with a quick indecisive motion as when she spread her hands to the fire.

"Don't wait up for me," he said.

He put his face down, a sharp expressionless face that seemed inconsequential under the big fur cap; and the woman kissed his cheek. Her kiss made a neat, dry sound, like a click.

"Les go," he said.

He went into the hall, the boy following to the door of the room, where the woman stood aside to let him pass. He paused an instant at the threshold. "Much obliged," he said to her, and slipped down the hall after the man like a shadow.

A horse and buggy, the curtains up, stood beyond the cedar at the corner of the office. The powdery flakes of snow drifted cautiously downward, were lost in the dark branches of the tree, on the road where the horse stood, head down in patience.

"You get in," the man said, and went around to the driver's side. The boy climbed into the buggy, slipping under the curtain. The man got in and bent to fasten the curtain flap on his side. "You fix 'em over there," he said, and picked up the reins. The boy fumbled with the metal catch, the man, reins in hand, watching him. "Don't you know nothing, son?" he said.

"I ain't never fixed one afore," the boy said.

The man thrust the reins into the boy's hands, leaned across his knees to latch the curtain, straightened up, and took the reins as though lifting them from a peg. "You pull that rug off the seat back of you," he said, "and give it here."

The boy obeyed, unfolding the rug. The man took an end, jabbed it under his thigh and wrapped it around the outside leg. "Now fix yourself up over there," he ordered. He shook out the reins through the slit in the curtain.

The horse swung into the road, the front wheel groaning and scraping with the short turn, the buggy jerking sidewise over the ruts. The buggy straightened out, and drew more easily. The hoofs crunched and sloshed, the wheels turning.

"That's right, ain't it," the doctor said, "we go outer the settlement this a-way?"

"Yes, sir," the boy said.

"I thought I recollected it so."

They drew past the store. A man went down the steps and started to walk up the road, walking with a plunging, unsteady stride, plowing the mud. His high shoulders hunched and swayed forward.

"John Graber." The doctor jerked his mittened thumb toward the man. "He better be gitting on home, his woman sick like she is." He shook his head, the sharp features without expression. "A mighty sick woman. Kidneys," he said.

"Yes, sir," the boy said.

"Graber'll be cooking his own supper fore long."

They passed the last house, a small grey house set in the open field. Yellow gullies ran across the field, bald plateaus of snow-smeared sod between gully and gully. A mule stood close to the barbed-wire fence which separated the field from the road, and the fine flakes sank in the field and the gullies. From the chimney of the house a line of smoke stood up very still amidst the descending flakes.

"Graber's house," the doctor said.

The boy sat up straight and peered through the isinglass panels at the house and the smoke and the gutted field.

"Do I turn off up the creek?" the doctor asked.

"Yes, sir."

They crossed the wood bridge, where the timbers creaked and rattled loosely with the turning wheels. Beneath it the swollen water plunged between limestone rocks, sucking the yellow foam. The flakes touched the spewing foam, the water plunging with a hollow constant sound.

"What's your pappy doing now?" the doctor said.

"My pappy's croppin' on a place fer Mr. Porsum, but hit ain't no good."

"Uh-huh," the man grunted. He looked through the isinglass in front. They had turned off the main road up the road by the creek. On one side, the limestone stuck out from the bluff side, thin grey icicles hanging from the grey stone among the shriveled fern fronds. The creek, below the dead growth of the gorge on the other side, made its hollow sound.

"Hit ain't worth nuthin'. Cain't even grow sassafras on hit."

"Uh-huh," the man said.

"We be leaving this year. We ain't gonna have no truck no more with Mr. Porsum that ole son-of-a-bitch. He ain't done nuthin' like he said. He ain't . . ."

"That's what your pappy says," the man said.

"My pappy says he's a goddam sheep-snitching son-a-bitch."

The man stared through the isinglass pane, his sharp nose and chin sticking out in front, his head wobbling with the motion of the buggy. Then he opened his mouth: "I reckon Jim Porsum's got something to say on his side."

The boy took a stolen glance at the man's face, then relapsed to the motion of the buggy. Out of the red mess of the road, limestone poked, grey and slick like wet bone, streaked with red mud. The wheels surmounted the stone, jolting down beyond on the brittle mud. On the bluff side the cedars hung. Their thick roots thrust from the rotten crevices of stone, the roots black with moss, garnished with ice; their tops cut off the light.

The man reached the reins over to the boy. "Hold 'em," he said.

The boy drew his hands from under the rug and held the reins. He grasped them very tight with both hands, the knuckles chapped and tight, and peered through the isinglass panel at the horse; the head of the horse, under the cedars, bobbed up and down.

Clamping his mittens between his knees, the man rolled a cigarette. His breath, as he licked the paper, came frostily out from his mouth in a thin parody of smoke. He lighted the cigarette; then, as he reached for the reins, he found the boy observing him, observing the twisted paper that hung from his lips. He did not put the tobacco sack in his pocket, but, after a moment of hesitation, held it toward the boy. "All right," he said, "go on and take it."

The boy shook his head, watching the sack.

"Aw hell," the man said, and dropped the sack on the boy's lap.

The boy took the sack without assurance, adjusted the paper, poured tobacco into it. Biting the string with his teeth, big square teeth irregularly set in the tight mouth, he pulled the sack together, and dropped it. Then he lifted the paper to his lips; the tip of his tongue darted out between his lips, strangely quick from the stolid, pinched face, and licked the edge of the paper. With that delicacy of motion, with the sharp grey fingers bunched like claws together to hold the bit of paper to his mouth, the boy, crouching there in the dim interior, looked at that instant like a small coon intently feeding.

He took a deep drag of the smoke, the end of the cigarette shriveling with the sucking coal, and his thin chest expanded under the cloth of the mackinaw.

Balancing the sack in his mittened hand, the doctor regarded the process. The smoke drifted colorless from the boy's nostrils, which were red and flattened. "You ought not to do it," the doctor said, "and you just a kid like you are."

"I'm ten," the boy said.

"It's gonna stunt your growth all right."

"Hit never stunted my pappy's growth none, and he's been a-smokin' ever since he was eight. He's big. Ain't you never seen him?"

The doctor looked at the lips which puckered greyly to the twist of paper, the pale eyes set close together under the man-size hat. The two cigarettes, the man's and the boy's, glowed indecisively in the shadow. "I've seen him all right," the man said at length.

"He's a plenty strong son-a-bitch," the boy said.

The man pushed his cigarette through a crack in the curtain, and sank back. His torso, swathed in the heavy overcoat, rolled and jerked to the impact of rut or stone like some lifeless object in uneasy water. Down the gorge, like the sound of wind driving through woods, the creek maintained its hollow constant plunging. "I didn't know Milt Lancaster had any girl big enough to be having babies yet," the man said.

"He ain't. Not I knows anything about."

"You said your sister, didn't you?"

"She's my sister on my maw's side. That's what she says and that's what my maw says."

The live cigarette, burned almost to the very end, hung at the corner of the boy's lips, glowing fitfully and faintly with his speech. It hung there, untouched by his hands, which were thrust under the rug. He no longer drew the smoke in; it seemed to seep in without conscious effort on his part, drifting from his nostrils thinly with his breath.

"She just come up here last summer," the boy said. "I never knowed nuthin' 'bout her afore that. Maw was glad ter see her, I reckin. At first, I reckin."

"Uh-huh," the man said absently, his sharp features fixed forward apparently without attention.

"But pappy warn't, he just raised holy hell fer sartin. She just worked round the house and never said nuthin' ter nobody. 'Cept ter me and the kids. Then pappy got so he didn't pay her no mind ter speak of."

The cigarette burned close to the lip, the paper untwisting so that bits of red ash slipped from it and fell toward the rug. The boy withdrew one hand from beneath the rug, and with thumb and forefinger pinched together, removed the cigarette. The paper had stuck to the flesh of the lip; he jerked it free, licking the place with that strange darting motion of the tongue tip. The tongue was pink and damp against the dry grey flesh of the lips. "Then she up and got sick and she's gonna have a baby," he said.

"So that's why she's up here," the man said.

The boy shook his head. "I dunno," he said. "She just come."

In the gloom of the buggy, their bodies, one long and lax against the back of the seat, the other short and upright, jerked and swayed.

The road climbed a little. The bluff wall lost its steepness, falling to heaps of detritus among boulders. No cedars showed here, only stalks of weeds and the wiry strands of vine showing on the broken surface. Then the road went down again, swinging away from the creek. There was no further sound of the water.

At the foot of the slight grade the bottom spread out: bare corn fields with stubble and shocks that disintegrated to the ground, rail fences lapped by the leafless undergrowth. Away to the left a log house stood black under bare black trees. From it the somnolent smoke ascended, twined white and grey against the grey sky. The snow had stopped.

Beyond the bottoms, the knobs looked cold and smoky. From them, and from the defiles, fingers of mist, white to their blackness, crooked downward toward the bare land. The horizon rim, fading, sustained a smoky wreath that faded upward to the space without sun.

They drew to the lane that led to the log house.

"You go on past here," the boy said. "Hit's up them knobs."

The boy, almost surreptitiously, took a stick of candy from his pocket, broke off half, and stuck it between his lips. He looked at the man's sharp, expressionless profile. Then he held out the piece to him. Without a word the man took it and stuck it between his lips, sucking it.

They moved forward between the empty fields.

1939

*Richard Wright*

........................................................................................................................

# Bright and Morning Star

FROM *New Masses*


I

SHE STOOD with her black face some six inches from the moist win-dow-pane and wondered when on earth would it ever stop raining. It might keep up like this all week, she thought. She heard rain droning upon the roof, and high up in the wet sky her eyes followed the silent rush of a bright shaft of yellow that swung from the airplane beacon in far-off Memphis. Momently she could see it cutting through the rainy dark; it would hover a second like a gleaming sword above her head, then vanish. She sighed, troubling, *Johnny-Boys been trampin in this slop all day wid no decent shoes on his feet.* . . . Through the window she could see the rich black earth sprawling outside in the night. There was more rain than the clay could soak up; pools stood everywhere. She yawned and mumbled: "Rains good n bad. It kin make seeds bus up thu the groun, er it kin bog things down lika watah-soaked coffin." Her hands were folded loosely over her stomach and the hot air of the kitchen traced a filmy veil of sweat on her forehead. From the cookstove came the soft singing of burning wood and now and then a throaty bubble rose from a pot of simmering greens.

"Shucks, Johnny-Boy coulda let somebody else do all tha runnin in the rain. Theres others bettah fixed fer it than he is. But, naw! Johnny-Boy ain the one t trust nobody t do nothin. Hes gotta do it *all* his-sef. . . ."

She glanced at a pile of damp clothes in a zinc tub. *Waal, Ah bettah git to work.* She turned, lifted a smoothing iron with a thick pad of cloth, touched a spit-wet finger to it with a quick, jerking motion: *smiiitz!* Yeah; its hot! Stooping, she took a blue work-shirt from the tub and shook it out. With a deft twist of her shoulder she caught the iron in her right hand; the fingers of her left hand took a piece of wax from a tin box and a frying sizzle came as she smeared the bottom. She was thinking of nothing now; her hands followed a life-long ritual of toil. Spreading a sleeve, she ran the hot iron to and fro until the wet cloth became stiff. She was deep in the midst of her work when a song rose out of the far off days of her childhood and broke through half-parted lips:

> Hes the Lily of the Valley, the Bright n Mawnin Star
> Hes the Fairest of Ten Thousan t mah soul . . .

A gust of wind dashed rain against the window. Johnny-Boy oughta c mon home n eat his suppah. Aw Lawd! Itd be fine ef Sug could eat wid us tonight! Itd be like ol times! Mabbe aftah all it wont be long fo he'll be back. Tha lettah Ah got from im las week said *Don give up hope.* . . . Yeah; we gotta live in hope. Then both of her sons, Sug and Johnny-Boy, would be back with her.

With an involuntary nervous gesture, she stopped and stood still, listening. But the only sound was the lulling fall of rain. Shucks, ain no usa me ackin this way, she thought. Ever time they gits ready to hol them meetings Ah gits jumpity. Ah been a lil scared ever since Sug went t jail. She heard the clock ticking and looked. Johnny-Boys a *hour* late! He sho mus be havin a time doin all tha trampin, trampin thu the mud. . . . But her fear was a quiet one; it was more like an intense brooding than a fear; it was a sort of hugging of hated facts so closely that she could feel their grain, like letting cold water run over her hand from a faucet on a winter morning.

She ironed again, faster now, as if the more she engaged her body in work the less she would think. But how could she forget Johnny-Boy out there on those wet fields rounding up white and black Communists for a meeting tomorrow? And that was just what Sug had been doing when the sheriff had caught him, beat him, and tried to make him tell who and where his comrades were. Po Sug! They sho musta beat tha boy something awful! But, thank Gawd, he didnt talk! He ain no weaklin' Sug ain! Hes been lion-hearted all his life long.

That had happened a year ago. And now each time those meetings came around the old terror surged back. While shoving the iron a cluster of toiling days returned; days of washing and ironing to feed Johnny-Boy and Sug so they could do party work; days of carrying a hundred pounds of white folks' clothes upon her head across fields sometimes wet and sometimes dry. But in those days a hundred pounds was nothing to carry carefully balanced upon her head while stepping by instinct over the corn and cotton rows. The only time it had seemed heavy was when she had heard of Sug's arrest. She had been coming home one morning with a bundle upon her head, her hands swinging idly by her sides, walking slowly with her eyes in front of her, when Bob, Johnny-Boy's pal, had called from across the fields and had come and told her that the sheriff had got Sug. That morning the bundle had become heavier than she could ever remember.

And with each passing week now, though she spoke of it to no one, things were becoming heavier. The tubs of water and the smoothing iron and the bundle of clothes were becoming harder to lift, her with her back aching so, and her work was taking longer, all because Sug was gone and she didn't know just when Johnny-Boy would be taken too. To ease the ache of anxiety that was swelling her heart, she hummed, then sang softly:

> He walks wid me, He talks wid me
> He tells me Ahm His own. . . .

Guiltily, she stopped and smiled. Looks like Ah jus cant seem t fergit them ol songs, no mattah how hard Ah tries. . . . She had learned them when she was a little girl living and working on a farm. Every Monday morning from the corn and cotton fields the slow strains had floated from her mother's lips, lonely and haunting; and later, as the years had filled with gall, she had learned their deep meaning. Long hours of scrubbing floors for a few cents a day had taught her who Jesus was, what a great boon it was to cling to Him, to be like Him and suffer without a mumbling word. She had poured the yearning of her life into the songs, feeling buoyed with a faith beyond this world. The figure of the Man nailed in agony to the Cross, His burial in a cold grave, His transfigured Resurrection, His being breath and clay, God and Man — all had focused her feelings upon an imagery which had swept her life into a wondrous vision.

But as she had grown older, a cold white mountain, the white folks and their laws, had swum into her vision and shattered her songs and their spell of peace. To her that white mountain was temptation, something to lure her from her Lord, a part of the world God had made in order that she might endure it and come through all the stronger, just as Christ had risen with greater glory from the tomb. The days crowded with trouble had enhanced her faith and she had grown to love hardship with a bitter pride; she had obeyed the laws of the white folks with a soft smile of secret knowing.

After her mother had been snatched up to heaven in a chariot of fire, the years had brought her a rough workingman and two black babies, Sug and Johnny-Boy, all three of whom she had wrapped in the charm and magic of her vision. Then she was tested by no less than God; her man died, a trial which she bore with the strength shed by the grace of her vision; finally even the memory of her man faded into the vision itself, leaving her with two black boys growing tall, slowly into manhood.

Then one day grief had come to her heart when Johnny-Boy and Sug had walked forth demanding their lives. She had sought to fill their eyes with her vision, but they would have none of it. And she had wept when they began to boast of the strength shed by a new and terrible vision.

But she had loved them, even as she loved them now; bleeding, her heart had followed them. She could have done no less, being an old woman in a strange world. And day by day her sons had ripped from her startled eyes her old vision; and image by image had given her a new one, different, but great and strong enough to fling her into the light of another grace. The wrongs and sufferings of black men had taken the place of Him nailed to the Cross; the meager beginnings of the party had become another Resurrection; and the hate of those who would destroy her new faith had quickened in her a hunger to feel how deeply her strength went.

"Lawd, Johnny-Boy," she would sometimes say, "Ah jus wan them white folks t try t make me tell *who* is *in* the party n who *ain!* Ah jus wan em t try, n Ahll show em something they never thought a black woman could have!"

But sometimes like tonight, while lost in the forgetfulness of work, the past and the present would become mixed in her; while toiling under a strange star for a new freedom the old songs would slip from her lips with their beguiling sweetness.

The iron was getting cold. She put more wood into the fire, stood again at the window and watched the yellow blade of light cut through the wet darkness. Johnny-Boy ain here yit. . . . Then, before she was aware of it, she was still, listening for sounds. Under the drone of rain she heard the slosh of feet in mud. Tha ain Johnny-Boy. She knew his long, heavy footsteps in a million. She heard feet come on the porch.

Some woman. . . . She heard bare knuckles knock three times, then once. Thas some of them comrades! She unbarred the door, cracked it a few inches, and flinched from the cold rush of damp wind.

"Whos tha?"

"Its me!"

"Who?"

"Me, Reva!"

She flung the door open.

"Lawd, chile, c mon in!"

She stepped to one side and a thin, blonde-haired white girl ran through the door; as she slid the bolt she heard the girl gasping and shaking her wet clothes. Somethings wrong! Reva wouldna walked a mile t mah house in all this slop fer nothin! Tha gals stuck onto Johnny-Boy; ah wondah ef anything happened t im?

"Git on inter the kitchen, Reva, where its warm."

"Lawd, Ah sho is wet!"

"How yuh reckon yuhd be, in all tha rain?"

"Johnny-Boy ain here *yit?*" asked Reva.

"Naw! N ain no usa yuh worryin bout im. Jus yuh git them shoes off! Yuh wanna ketch you deatha col?" She stood looking absently. Yeah; its something bout the party er Johnny-Boy thas gone wrong. Lawd, Ah wondah ef her pa knows how she feels bout Johnny-Boy? "Honey, yuh hadnt oughta come out in sloppy weather like this."

"Ah had t come, An Sue."

She led Reva to the kitchen.

"Git them shoes off n git close t the stove so yuh'll git dry!"

"An Sue, ah got something to tell yuh . . ."

The words made her hold her breath. Ah bet its something bout Johnny-Boy!

"Whut, honey?"

"The sheriff wuz by our house tonight. He come see pa."

"Yeah?"

"He done got word from somewheres bout tha meetin tomorrow."

"Is it Johnny-Boy, Reva?"

"Aw, naw, An Sue! Ah ain hearda word bout im. Ain yuh seem im tonight?"

"He ain come home t eat yit."

"Where kin he be?"

"Lawd knows, chile."

"Somebodys gotta tell them comrades tha meetings off," said Reva.

"The sheriffs got men watchin our house. Ah had t slip out t git here widout em followin me."

"Reva?"

"Hunh?"

"Ahma ol woman n Ah wans yuh t tell me the truth."

"What, An Sue?"

"Yuh ain tryin t fool me, is yuh?"

"*Fool* yuh?"

"Bout Johnny-Boy?"

"Lawd, naw, An Sue!"

"Ef theres anything wrong jus tell me, chile. Ah kin stan it."

She stood by the ironing board, her hands as usual folded loosely over her stomach, watching Reva pull off her water-clogged shoes. She was feeling that Johnny-Boy was already lost to her; she was feeling the pain that would come when she knew it for certain; and she was feeling that she would have to be brave and bear it. She was like a person caught in a swift current of water and knew where the water was sweeping her and did not want to go on but had to go on to the end.

"It ain nothin bout Johnny-Boy, An Sue," said Reva. "But we gotta do something er we'll all git inter trouble."

"How the sheriff know bout tha meetin?"

"Thas whut pa wans t know."

"Somebody done turned Judas."

"Sho looks like it."

"Ah bet it wuz some of them new ones," she said.

"Its hard t tell," said Reva.

"Lissen, Reva, yuh oughta stay here n git dry, but yuh bettah git back n tell yo pa Johnny-Boy ain here n Ah don know when hes gonna show up. *Some*bodys gotta tell them comrades t stay erway from yo pa's house."

She stood with her back to the window, looking at Reva's wide, blue eyes. Po critter! Gotta go back thu all tha slop! Though she felt sorry for Reva, not once did she think that it would not have to be done. Being a woman, Reva was not suspect; she would have to go. It was just as natural for Reva to go back through the cold rain as it was for her to iron night and day or for Sug to be in jail. Right now, Johnny-Boy was out there on those dark fields trying to get home. Lawd, don let em git im tonight! In spite of herself her feelings became torn. She loved her son and, loving him, she loved what he was trying to do. Johnny-Boy was happiest when he was working for the party, and her love for him was for his happiness. She frowned, trying hard to fit something together in her feelings: for her to try to stop Johnny-Boy was to admit that all the toil of years meant nothing; and to let him go meant that sometime or other he would be caught, like Sug. In facing it this way she felt a little stunned, as though she had come suddenly upon a blank wall in the dark. But outside in the rain were people, white and black, whom she had known all her life. Those people depended upon Johnny-Boy, loved him and looked to him as a man and leader. Yeah; hes gotta keep on; he cant stop now. . . . She looked at Reva; she was crying and pulling her shoes back on with reluctant fingers.

"Whut yuh carryin on tha way fer, chile?"

"Yuh done los Sug, now yuh sendin Johnny-Boy . . ."

"Ah got t, honey."

She was glad she could say that. Reva believed in black folks and not for anything in the world would she falter before her. In Reva's trust and acceptance of her she had found her first feelings of humanity; Reva's love was her refuge from shame and degradation. If in the early days of her life the white mountain had driven her back from the earth, then in her last days Reva's love was drawing her toward it, like the beacon that swung through the night outside. She heard Reva sobbing.

"Hush, honey!"

"Mah brothers in jail too! Ma cries ever day . . ."

"Ah know, honey."

She helped Reva with her coat; her fingers felt the scant flesh of the girl's shoulders. She don git ernuff t eat, she thought. She slipped her arms around Reva's waist and held her close for a moment.

"Now, yuh stop tha cryin."

"A-a-ah c-c-cant hep it. . . ."

"Everythingll be awright; Johnny-Boyll be back."

"Yuh think so?"

"Sho, chile. Cos he will."

Neither of them spoke again until they stood in the doorway. Outside they could hear water washing through the ruts of the street.

"Be sho n send Johnny-Boy t tell the folks t stay erway from pas house," said Reva.

"Ahll tell im. Don yuh worry."

"Good-bye!"

"Good-bye!"

Leaning against the door jamb, she shook her head slowly and watched Reva vanish through the falling rain.

II

She was back at her board, ironing, when she heard feet sucking in the mud of the back yard; feet she knew from long years of listening were Johnny-Boy's. But tonight with all the rain and fear his coming was like a leaving, was almost more than she could bear. Tears welled to her eyes and she blinked them away. She felt that he was coming so that she could give him up; to see him now was to say good-bye. But it was a good-bye she knew she could never say; they were not that way toward each other. All day long they could sit in the same room and not speak; she was his mother and he was her son; most of the time a nod or a grunt would carry all the meaning that she wanted to say to him, or he to her.

She did not even turn her head when she heard him come stomping into the kitchen. She heard him pull up a chair, sit, sigh, and draw off his muddy shoes; they fell to the floor with heavy thuds. Soon the kitchen was full of the scent of his drying socks and his burning pipe. Tha boys hongry! She paused and looked at him over her shoulder; he was puffing at his pipe with his head tilted back and his feet propped up on the edge of the stove; his eyelids drooped and his wet clothes steamed from the heat of the fire. Lawd, tha boy gits mo like his pa ever day he lives, she mused, her lips breaking in a faint smile. Hols tha pipe in his mouth jus like his pa usta hol his. Wondah how they woulda got erlong ef his pa hada lived? They oughta liked each other, they so mucha like. She wished there could have been other children besides Sug, so Johnny-Boy would not have to be so much alone. A man needs a woman by his side. . . . She thought of Reva; she liked Reva; the brightest glow her heart had ever known was when she had learned that Reva loved Johnny-Boy. But beyond Reva were cold white faces. Ef theys caught it means *death*. . . . She jerked around when she heard Johnny-Boy's pipe clatter to the floor. She saw him pick it up, smile sheepishly at her, and wag his head.

"Gawd, Ahm sleepy," he mumbled.

She got a pillow from her room and gave it to him.

"Here," she said.

"Hunh," he said, putting the pillow between his head and the back of the chair.

They were silent again. Yes, she would have to tell him to go back out into the cold rain and slop; maybe to get caught; maybe for the last time; she didn't know. But she would let him eat and get dry before telling him that the sheriff knew of the meeting to be held at Lem's tomorrow. And she would make him take a big dose of soda before he went out; soda always helped to stave off a cold. She looked at the clock. It was eleven. Theres time yit. Spreading a newspaper on the apron of the stove, she placed a heaping plate of greens upon it, a knife, a fork, a cup of coffee, a slab of cornbread, and a dish of peach cobbler.

"Yo suppahs ready," she said.

"Yeah," he said.

He did not move. She ironed again. Presently, she heard him eating. When she could no longer hear his knife tinkling against the edge of the plate, she knew he was through. It was almost twelve now. She would let him rest a little while longer before she told him. Till one er'clock, mabbe. Hes so tired. . . . She finished her ironing, put away the board, and stacked the clothes in her dresser drawer. She poured herself a cup of coffee, drew up a chair, sat, and drank.

"Yuh almos dry," she said, not looking around.

"Yeah," he said, turning sharply to her.

The tone of voice in which she had spoken let him know that more was coming. She drained her cup and waited a moment longer.

"Reva wuz here."

"Yeah?"

"She lef bout a hour ergo."

"Whut she say?"

"She said ol man Lem hada visit from the sheriff today."

"Bout the meetin?"

"Yeah."

She saw him stare at the coals glowing red through the crevices of the stove and run his fingers nervously through his hair. She knew he was wondering how the sheriff had found out. In the silence he would ask a wordless question and in the silence she would answer wordlessly. Johnny-Boys too trustin, she thought. Hes tryin t make the party big n hes takin in folks fastern he kin git t know em. You cant trust ever white man yuh meet. . . .

"Yuh know, Johnny-Boy, yuh been takin in a lotta them white folks lately . . ."

"Aw, ma!"

"But, Johnny-Boy . . ."

"Please, don talk t me bout tha now, ma."

"Yuh ain t ol t lissen n learn, son," she said.

"Ah know whut yuh gonna say, ma. N yuh wrong. Yuh cant judge folks jus by how yuh feel bout em n by how long yuh done knowed em. Ef we start tha we wouldnt have *no*body in the party. When folks pledge they word t be with us, then we gotta take em in. Wes too weak t be choosy."

He rose abruptly, rammed his hands into his pockets, and stood facing the window; she looked at his back in a long silence. She knew his faith; it was deep. He had always said that black men could not fight the rich bosses alone; a man could not fight with every hand against him. But he believes so hard hes blind, she thought. At odd times they had had these arguments before; always she would be pitting her feelings against the hard necessity of his thinking, and always she would lose. She shook her head. Po Johnny-Boy; he don know . . .

"But ain nona our folks tol, Johnny-Boy," she said.

"How yuh know?" he asked. His voice came low and with a tinge of anger. He still faced the window and now and then the yellow blade of light flicked across the sharp outline of his black face.

"Cause Ah know em," she said.

"*Any*body mighta tol," he said.

"It wuznt none *our* folks," she said again.

She saw his hand sweep in a swift arc of disgust.

"*Our* folks! Ma, who in Gawds name is *our* folks?"

"The folks we wuz born n raised wid, son. The folks we *know!*"

"We cant make the party grow tha way, ma."

"It mighta been Booker," she said.

"Yuh don know."

". . . er Blattberg . . ."

"Fer Chrissakes!"

". . . er any of the fo-five others whut joined las week."

"Ma, yuh jus don wan me t go out tonight," he said.

"Yo ol ma wans yuh t be careful, son."

"Ma, when yuh start doubtin folks in the party, then there ain no end."

"Son, Ah knows ever black man n woman in this parta the county," she said, standing too. "Ah watched em grow up; Ah even heped birth n nurse some of em; Ah knows em *all* from way back. There ain none of em tha *coulda* tol! The folks Ah know jus don open they dos n ast death t walk in! Son, it wuz some of them white folks! Yuh jus mark mah word!"

"Why is it gotta be *white* folks?" he asked. "Ef they tol, then theys jus Judases, thas all."

"Son, look at whuts befo yuh."

He shook his head and sighed.

"Ma, Ah done tol yuh a hundred times Ah cant see white n Ah cant see black," he said. "Ah sees rich men n Ah sees po men."

She picked up his dirty dishes and piled them in a pan. Out of the corners of her eyes she saw him sit and pull on his wet shoes. Hes goin! When she put the last dish away he was standing fully dressed, warming his hands over the stove. Just a few mo minutes now n he'll be gone, like Sug, mabbe. Her throat swelled. This black mans fight takes *everthing*! Looks like Gawd puts us in this worl jus t beat us down!

"Keep this, ma," he said.

She saw a crumpled wad of money in his outstretched fingers.

"Naw; yuh keep it. Yuh might need it."

"It ain mine, ma. It berlongs t the party."

"But, Johnny-Boy, yuh might hafta go erway!"

"Ah kin make out."

"Don fergit yosef too much, son."

"Ef Ah don come back theyll need it."

He was looking at her face and she was looking at the money.

"Yuh keep tha," she said slowly. "Ahll give em the money."

"From where?"

"Ah got some."

"Where yuh git it from?"

She sighed.

"Ah been savin a dollah a week fer Sug ever since hes been in jail."

"Lawd, ma!"

She saw the look of puzzled love and wonder in his eyes. Clumsily, he put the money back into his pocket.

"Ahm gone," he said.

"Here; drink this glass of soda watah."

She watched him drink, then put the glass away.

"Waal," he said.

"Take the stuff outta yo pockets!"

She lifted the lid of the stove and he dumped all the papers from his pocket into the hole. She followed him to the door and made him turn round.

"Lawd, yuh tryin to maka revolution n yuh cant even keep yo coat buttoned." Her nimble fingers fastened his collar high around his throat. "There!"

He pulled the brim of his hat low over his eyes. She opened the door and with the suddenness of the cold gust of wind that struck her face, he was gone. She watched the black fields and the rain take him, her eyes burning. When the last faint footstep could no longer be heard, she closed the door, went to her bed, lay down, and pulled the cover over her while fully dressed. Her feelings coursed with the rhythm of the rain: Hes gone! Lawd, Ah *know* hes gone! Her blood felt cold.

### III

She was floating in a gray void somewhere between sleeping and dreaming and then suddenly she was wide awake, hearing and feeling in the same instant the thunder of the door crashing in and a cold wind filling the room. It was pitch black and she stared, resting on her elbows, her mouth open, not breathing, her ears full of the sound of tramping feet and booming voices. She knew at once: They lookin fer im! Then, filled with her will, she was on her feet, rigid, waiting, listening.

"The lamps burnin!"

"Yuh see her?"

"Naw!"

"Look in the kitchen!"

"Gee, this place smells like niggers!"

"Say, somebodys here er been here!"

"Yeah; theres fire in the stove!"

"Mabbe hes been here n gone?"

"Boy, look at these jars of jam!"

"Niggers make good jam!"

"Git some bread!"

"Heres some cornbread!"

"Say, lemme git some!"

"Take it easy! Theres plenty here!"

"Ahma take some of this stuff home!"

"Look, heres a pota greens!"

"N some hot cawffee!"

"Say, yuh guys! C mon! Cut it out! We didnt come here fer a feas!"

She walked slowly down the hall. They lookin fer im, but they ain got im yit! She stopped in the doorway, her gnarled, black hands as always folded over her stomach, but tight now, so tightly the veins bulged. The kitchen was crowded with white men in glistening raincoats. Though the lamp burned, their flashlights still glowed in red fists. Across her floor she saw the muddy tracks of their boots.

"Yuh white folks git outta mah house!"

There was quick silence; every face turned toward her. She saw a sudden movement, but did not know what it meant until something hot and wet slammed her squarely in the face. She gasped, but did not move. Calmly, she wiped the warm, greasy liquor of greens from her eyes with her left hand. One of the white men had thrown a handful of greens out of the pot at her.

"How they taste, ol bitch?"

"Ah ast yuh t git outta mah house!"

She saw the sheriff detach himself from the crowd and walk toward her.

"Now, Anty . . ."

"White man, don yuh *Anty* me!"

"Yuh ain got the right sperit!"

"Sperit hell! Yuh git these men outta mah house!"

"Yuh ack like yuh don like it!"

"Naw, Ah don like it, n yuh knows dam waal Ah don!"

"Whut yuh gonna do about it?"

"Ahm tellin yuh t git outta mah house!"

"Gittin sassy?"

"Ef tellin yuh t git outta mah house is sass, then Ahm sassy!"

Her words came in a tense whisper; but beyond, back of them, she was watching, thinking, and judging the men.

"Listen, Anty," the sheriff's voice came soft and low. "Ahm here t hep yuh. How come yuh wanna ack this way?"

"Yuh ain never heped yo *own* sef since yuh been born," she flared. "How kin the likes of yuh hep me?"

One of the white men came forward and stood directly in front of her.

"Lissen, nigger woman, yuh talkin t *white* men!"

"Ah don care who Ahm talkin t!"

"Yuhll wish some day yuh did!"

"Not t the likes of yuh!"

"Yuh need somebody t teach yuh how t be a good nigger!"

"*Yuh* cant teach it t me!"

"Yuh gonna change yo tune."

"Not longs mah bloods warm!"

"Don git smart now!"

"Yuh git outta mah house!"

"Spose we don go?" the sheriff asked.

They were crowded around her. She had not moved since she had taken her place in the doorway. She was thinking only of Johnny-Boy as she stood there giving and taking words; and she knew that they, too, were thinking of Johnny-Boy. She knew they wanted him, and her heart was daring them to take him from her.

"Spose we don go?" the sheriff asked again.

"Twenty of yuh runnin over one ol woman! Now, ain yuh white men glad yuh so brave?"

The sheriff grabbed her arm.

"C mon now! Yuh done did ernuff sass fer one night. Wheres tha nigger son of yos?"

"Don yuh wished yuh knowed?"

"Yuh wanna git slapped?"

"Ah ain never seen one of yo kind tha wuznt too low fer . . ."

The sheriff slapped her straight across her face with his open palm. She fell back against a wall and sank to her knees.

"Is tha whut white men do t nigger women?"

She rose slowly and stood again, not even touching the place that ached from his blow, her hands folded over her stomach.

"Ah ain never seen one of yo kind tha wuznt too low fer . . ."

He slapped her again; she reeled backward several feet and fell on her side.

"Is tha whut we too low t do?"

She stood before him again, dry-eyed, as though she had not been struck. Her lips were numb and her chin was wet with blood.

"Aw, let her go! Its the nigger we wan!" said one.

"Wheres that nigger son of yos?" the sheriff asked.

"Find im," she said.

"By Gawd, ef we hafta find im we'll kill im!"

"He wont be the only nigger yuh ever killed," she said.

She was consumed with a bitter pride. There was nothing on this earth, she felt then, that they could not do to her but that she could take. She stood on a narrow plot of ground from which she would die before she was pushed. And then it was, while standing there feeling warm blood seeping down her throat, that she gave up Johnny-Boy, gave him up to the white folks. She gave him up because they had come tramping into her heart demanding him, thinking they could get him by beating her, thinking they could scare her into making her tell where he was. She gave him up because she wanted them to know that they could not get what they wanted by bluffing and killing.

"Wheres this meetin gonna be?" the sheriff asked.

"Don yuh wish yuh knowed?"

"Ain there gonna be a meetin?"

"How come yuh astin me?"

"There *is* gonna be a meetin', said the sheriff.

"Is it?"

"Ah gotta great mind t choke it outta yuh!"

"Yuh so smart," she said.

"We ain playin wid yuh!"

"Did Ah say yuh wuz?"

"Tha nigger son of yos is erroun here somewheres n we aim t find im," said the sheriff. "Ef yuh tell us where he is n ef he talks, mabbe he'll git off easy. But ef we hafta find im, we'll kill im! Ef we hafta find im, then yuh git a sheet t put over im in the mawnin, see? Git yuh a sheet, cause hes gonna be dead!"

"He wont be the only nigger yuh ever killed," she said again.

The sheriff walked past her. The others followed. Yuh didnt git whut yuh wanted! she thought exultingly. N yuh ain gonna *never* git it! Hotly something ached in her to make them feel the intensity of her pride and freedom; her heart groped to turn the bitter hours of her life into words of a kind that would make them feel that she had taken all they had done to her in her stride and could still take more. Her faith surged so strongly in her she was all but blinded. She walked behind them to the door, knotting and twisting her fingers. She saw them step to the muddy ground. Each whirl of the yellow beacon revealed glimpses of slanting rain. Her lips moved, then she shouted:

"Yuh didn't git whut yuh wanted! N yuh ain gonna nevah git it!"

The sheriff stopped and turned; his voice came low and hard.

"Now, by Gawd, thas ernuff outta yuh!"

"Ah know when Ah done said ernuff!"

"Aw, naw, yuh don!" he said. "Yuh don know when yuh done said ernuff, but Ahma teach yuh ternight!"

He was up the steps and across the porch with one bound. She backed into the hall, her eyes full on his face.

"Tell me when yuh gonna stop talkin!" he said, swinging his fist.

The blow caught her high on the cheek; her eyes went blank; she fell flat on her face. She felt the hard heel of his wet shoes coming into her temple and stomach.

"Lemme hear yuh talk some mo!"

She wanted to, but could not; pain numbed and choked her. She lay

still and somewhere out of the gray void of unconsciousness she heard
someone say: *Aw fer chrissakes leave her erlone its the nigger we wan.* . . .


IV

She never knew how long she had lain huddled in the dark hallway. Her
first returning feeling was of a nameless fear crowding the inside of her,
then a deep pain spreading from her temple downward over her body.
Her ears were filled with the drone of rain and she shuddered from the
cold wind blowing through the door. She opened her eyes and at first
saw nothing. As if she were imagining it, she knew she was half-lying
and half-sitting in a corner against a wall. With difficulty she twisted her
neck, and what she saw made her hold her breath — a vast white blur
was suspended directly above her. For a moment she could not tell if her
fear was from the blur or if the blur was from her fear. Gradually the
blur resolved itself into a huge white face that slowly filled her vision.
She was stone still, conscious really of the effort to breathe, feeling
somehow that she existed only by the mercy of that white face. She had
seen it before; its fear had gripped her many times; it had for her the
fear of all the white faces she had ever seen in her life. *Sue* . . . As from
a great distance, she heard her name being called. She was regaining
consciousness now, but the fear was coming with her. She looked into
the face of a white man, wanting to scream out for him to go; yet
accepting his presence because she felt she had to. Though some remote
part of her mind was active, her limbs were powerless. It was as if an
invisible knife had split her in two, leaving one half of her lying there
helpless, while the other half shrank in dread from a forgotten but
familiar enemy. *Sue its me Sue its me* . . . Then all at once the voice came
clearly.

"Sue, its me! Its Booker!"

And she heard an answering voice speaking inside of her, Yeah, its
Booker . . . The one whut jus joined . . . She roused herself, struggling
for full consciousness; and as she did so she transferred to the person of
Booker the nameless fear she felt. It seemed that Booker towered above
her as a challenge to her right to exist upon the earth.

"Yuh awright?"

She did not answer; she started violently to her feet and fell.

"Sue, yuh hurt!"

"Yeah," she breathed.

"Where they hit yuh?"

"Its mah head," she whispered.

She was speaking even though she did not want to; the fear that had hold of her compelled her.

"They beat yuh?"

"Yeah."

"Them bastards! Them Gawddam bastards!"

She heard him saying it over and over; then she felt herself being lifted.

"Naw!" she gasped.

"Ahma take yuh t the kitchen!"

"Put me down!"

"But yuh cant stay here like this!"

She shrank in his arms and pushed her hands against his body; when she was in the kitchen she freed herself, sank into a chair, and held tightly to its back. She looked wonderingly at Booker; there was nothing about him that should frighten her so; but even that did not ease her tension. She saw him go to the water bucket, wet his handkerchief, wring it, and offer it to her. Distrustfully, she stared at the damp cloth.

"Here; put this on yo fohead . . ."

"Naw!"

"C mon; itll make yuh feel bettah!"

She hesitated in confusion; what right had she to be afraid when someone was acting as kindly as this toward her? Reluctantly, she leaned forward and pressed the damp cloth to her head. It helped. With each passing minute she was catching hold of herself, yet wondering why she felt as she did.

"Whut happened?"

"Ah don know."

"Yuh feel bettah?"

"Yeah."

"Who all wuz here?"

"Ah don know," she said again.

"Yo head still hurt?"

"Yeah."

"Gee, Ahm sorry."

"Ahm awright," she sighed and buried her face in her hands.

She felt him touch her shoulder.

"Sue, Ah got some bad news fer yuh . . ."

She knew; she stiffened and grew cold. It had happened; she stared dry-eyed with compressed lips.

"Its mah Johnny-Boy," she said.

"Yeah; Ahm awful sorry t hafta tell yuh this way. But Ah thought yuh oughta know . . ."

Her tension eased and a vacant place opened up inside of her. A voice whispered, Jesus, hep me!

"W-w-where is he?"

"They got im out t Foleys Woods tryin t make im tell who the others is."

"He ain gonna tell," she said. "They just as waal kill im, cause he ain gonna nevah tell."

"Ah hope he don," said Booker. "But he didn't hava chance t tell the others. They grabbed im jus as he got t the woods."

Then all the horror of it flashed upon her; she saw flung out over the rainy countryside an array of shacks where white and black comrades were sleeping; in the morning they would be rising and going to Lem's; then they would be caught. And that meant terror, prison, and death. The comrades would have to be told; she would have to tell them; she could not entrust Johnny-Boy's work to another, and especially not to Booker as long as she felt toward him as she did. Gripping the bottom of the chair with both hands, she tried to rise; the room blurred and she swayed. She found herself resting in Booker's arms.

"Lemme go!"

"Sue, yuh too weak t walk!"

"Ah gotta tell em!" she said.

"Set down, Sue! Yuh hurt; yuh sick!"

When seated she looked at him helplessly.

"Sue, lissen! Johnny-Boys caught. Ahm here. Yuh tell me who they is n Ahll tell em."

She stared at the floor and did not answer. Yes; she was too weak to go. There was no way for her to tramp all those miles through the rain tonight. But should she tell Booker? If only she had somebody like Reva to talk to. She did not want to decide alone; she must make no mistake about this. She felt Booker's fingers pressing on her arm and it was as though the white mountain was pushing her to the edge of a sheer height; she again exclaimed inwardly, Jesus, hep me! Booker's white face was at her side, waiting. Would she be doing right to tell him? Suppose she did not tell and then the comrades were caught? She could not ever forgive herself for doing a thing like that. But maybe she was wrong; maybe her fear was what Johnny-Boy had always called "jus foolishness." She remembered his saying, Ma we cant make the party ef we start doubtin everbody. . . .

"Tell me who they is, Sue, n Ahll tell em. Ah just joined n Ah don know who they is."

"Ah don know who they is," she said.

"Yuh *gotta* tell me who they is, Sue!"

"Ah tol yuh Ah don know!"

"Yuh *do* know! C mon! Set up n talk!"

"Naw!"

"Yuh wan em all t git *killed?*"

She shook her head and swallowed. Lawd, Ah don blieve in this man!

"Lissen, Ahll call the names n yuh tell me which ones is in the party n which ones ain, see?"

"Naw!"

"Please, Sue!"

"Ah don know," she said.

"Sue, yuh ain doin right by em. Johnny-Boy wouldnt wan yuh t be this way. Hes out there holdin up his end. Les hol up ours. . . ."

"Lawd, Ah don know. . . ."

"Is yuh scareda me cause Ahm *white?* Johnny-Boy ain like tha. Don let all the work we done go fer nothin."

She gave up and bowed her head in her hands.

"Is it Johnson? Tell me, Sue?"

"Yeah," she whispered in horror; a mounting horror of feeling herself being undone.

"Is it Green?"

"Yeah."

"Murphy?"

"Lawd, Ah don know!"

"Yuh gotta tell me, Sue!"

"Mistah Booker, please leave me erlone. . . ."

"Is it Murphy?"

She answered yes to the names of Johnny-Boy's comrades; she answered until he asked her no more. Then she thought, How he know the sheriffs men is watchin Lems house? She stood up and held onto her chair, feeling something sure and firm within her.

"How yuh know bout Lem?"

"Why . . . How Ah know?"

"Whut yuh doin here this tima night? How yuh know the sheriff got Johnny-Boy?"

"Sue, don yuh blieve in me?"

She did not, but she could not answer. She stared at him until her lips hung open; she was searching deep within herself for certainty.

"You meet Reva?" she asked.

"Reva?"

"Yeah; Lems gal?"

"Oh, yeah. Sho, Ah met Reva."

"She tell yuh?"

She asked the question more of herself than of him; she longed to believe.

"Yeah," he said softly. "Ah reckon Ah oughta be goin t tell em now."

"Who?" she asked. "Tell *who?*"

The muscles of her body were stiff as she waited for his answer; she felt as though life depended upon it.

"The comrades," he said.

"Yeah," she sighed.

She did not know when he left; she was not looking or listening. She just suddenly saw the room empty, and from her the thing that had made her fearful was gone.


v

For a space of time that seemed to her as long as she had been upon the earth, she sat huddled over the cold stove. One minute she would say to herself, They both gone now; Johnny-Boy n Sug . . . Mabbe Ahll never see em ergin. Then a surge of guilt would blot out her longing. "Lawd, Ah shouldna tol!" she mumbled. "But no man kin be so lowdown as t do a thing like tha . . ." Several times she had an impulse to try to tell the comrades herself; she was feeling a little better now. But what good would that do? She had told Booker the names. He just couldn't be a Judas t po folks like us . . . He *couldnt!*

"An Sue!"

Thas Reva! Her heart leaped with an anxious gladness. She rose without answering and limped down the dark hallway. Through the open door, against the background of rain, she saw Reva's face lit now and then to whiteness by the whirling beams of the beacon. She was about to call, but a thought checked her. Jesus, hep me! Ah gotta tell her bout Johnny-Boy . . . Lawd, Ah cant!

"An Sue, yuh there?"

"C mon in, chile!"

She caught Reva and held her close for a moment without speaking.

"Lawd, Ahm sho glad yuh here," she said at last.

"Ah thought something had happened t yuh," said Reva, pulling away. "Ah saw the do open . . . Pa tol me to come back n stay wid yuh tonight . . ." Reva paused and stared. "W-w-whuts the mattah?"

She was so full of having Reva with her that she did not understand what the question meant.

"Hunh?"

"Yo neck . . ."

"Aw, it ain nothin, chile. C mon in the kitchen."

"But theres blood on yo neck!"

"The sheriff wuz here . . ."

"Them fools! Whut they wanna bother yuh fer? Ah could kill em! So hep me Gawd, Ah could!"

"It ain nothin," she said.

She was wondering how to tell Reva about Johnny-Boy and Booker. Ahll wait a lil while longer, she thought. Now that Reva was here, her fear did not seem as awful as before.

"C mon, lemme fix yo head, An Sue. Yuh hurt."

They went to the kitchen. She sat silent while Reva dressed her scalp. She was feeling better now; in just a little while she would tell Reva. She felt the girl's finger pressing gently upon her head.

"Tha hurt?"

"A lil, chile."

"Yuh po thing."

"It ain nothin."

"Did Johnny-Boy come?"

She hesitated.

"Yeah."

"He done gone t tell the others?"

Reva's voice sounded so clear and confident that it mocked her. Lawd, Ah cant tell this chile . . .

"Yuh tol im, didnt yuh, An Sue?"

"Y-y-yeah . . ."

"Gee! Thas good! Ah tol pa he didn't hafta worry ef Johnny-Boy got the news. Mabbe thingsll come out awright."

"Ah hope . . ."

She could not go on; she had gone as far as she could; for the first time that night she began to cry.

"Hush, An Sue! Yuh awways been brave. Itll be awright!"

"Ain nothin awright, chile. The worls just too much fer us, Ah reckon."

"Ef yuh cry that way itll make me cry."

She forced herself to stop. Naw; Ah cant carry on this way in fronta Reva . . . Right now she had a deep need for Reva to believe in her. She watched the girl get pine-knots from behind the stove, rekindle the fire, and put on the coffee pot.

"Yuh wan some cawffee?" Reva asked.

"Naw, honey."

"Aw, c mon, An Sue."

"Jusa lil, honey."

"Thas the way t be. Oh, say, Ah fergot," said Reva, measuring out spoonfuls of coffee. "Pa tol me t tell yuh t watch out fer tha Booker man. Hes a stool."

She showed not one sign of outward movement or expression, but as the words fell from Reva's lips she went limp inside.

"Pa tol me soon as Ah got back home. He got word from town . . ."

She stopped listening. She felt as though she had been slapped to the extreme outer edge of life, into a cold darkness. She knew now what she had felt when she had looked up out of her fog of pain and had seen Booker. It was the image of all the white folks, and the fear that went with them, that she had seen and felt during her lifetime. And again, for the second time that night, something she had felt had come true. All she could say to herself was, Ah didnt like im! Gawd knows, Ah didnt! Ah tol Johnny-Boy it wuz some of them white folks . . .

"Here; drink yo cawffee . . ."

She took the cup; her fingers trembled, and the steaming liquid spilt onto her dress and leg.

"Ahm sorry, An Sue!"

Her leg was scalded, but the pain did not bother her.

"Its awright," she said.

"Wait; lemme put something on tha burn!"

"It don hurt."

"Yuh worried bout something."

"Naw, honey."

"Lemme fix yuh so mo cawffee."

"Ah don wan nothin now, Reva."

"Waal, buck up, Don be tha way . . ."

They were silent. She heard Reva drinking. No; she would not tell Reva; Reva was all she had left. But she had to do something, some way, somehow. She was undone too much as it was; and to tell Reva about Booker or Johnny-Boy was more than she was equal to; it would be too coldly shameful. She wanted to be alone and fight this thing out with herself.

"Go t bed, honey. Yuh tired."

"Naw; Ahm awright, An Sue."

She heard the bottom of Reva's empty cup clank against the top of the stove. Ah *got* t make her go t bed! Yes; Booker would tell the names of the comrades to the sheriff. If she could only stop him some way! That was the answer, the point, the star that grew bright in the morning of new hope. Soon, maybe half an hour from now, Booker would reach Foley's Woods. Hes boun t go the long way, cause he don know no short cut, she thought. Ah could wade the creek n beat im there. . . . But what would she do after that?

"Reva, honey, go t bed. Ahm awright. Yuh need res."

"Ah ain sleepy, An Sue."

"Ah knows whuts bes fer yuh, chile. Yuh tired n wet."

"Ah wanna stay up wid yuh."

She forced a smile and said:

"Ah don think they gonna hurt Johnny-Boy . . ."

"Fer *real*, An Sue?"

"Sho, honey."

"But Ah wanna wait up wid yuh."

"Thas mah job, honey. Thas what a mas fer, t wait up fer her chullun."

"Good night, An Sue."

"Good night, honey."

She watched Reva pull up and leave the kitchen; presently she heard the shucks in the mattress whispering, and she knew that Reva had gone to bed. She was alone. Through the cracks of the stove she saw the fire dying to grey ashes; the room was growing cold again. The yellow beacon continued to flit past the window and the rain still drummed. Yes; she was alone; she had done this awful thing alone; she must find some way out, alone. Like touching a festering sore, she put a finger upon that moment when she had shouted her defiance to the sheriff, when she had shouted to feel her strength. She had lost Sug to save others; she had let Johnny-Boy go to save others; and then in a moment of weakness that came from too much strength she had lost all. If she had not shouted to the sheriff, she would have been strong enough to have resisted Booker; she would have been able to tell the comrades herself. Something tightened in her as she remembered and understood the fit of fear she had felt on coming to herself in the dark hallway. A part of her life she thought she had done away with forever had had hold of her then. She had thought the soft, warm past was over; she had thought that it did not mean much when now she sang: "Hes the Lily of the Valley, the Bright n Mawnin Star." . . . The days when she had sung that song were the days when she had not hoped for anything on this earth, the days when the cold mountain had driven her into the arms of Jesus. She had thought that Sug and Johnny-Boy had taught her to forget Him, to fix her hope upon the fight of black men for freedom. Through the gradual years she had believed and worked with them, had felt strength shed from the grace of their terrible vision. That grace had been upon her when she had let the sheriff slap her down; it had been upon her when she had risen time and again from the floor and faced him. But she had trapped herself with her own hunger; to water the long dry thirst of her faith her pride had made a bargain which her flesh could not keep. Her having told the names of Johnny-Boy's comrades was but an incident in a deeper horror. She stood up and looked at the floor while call and counter-call, loyalty and counter-loyalty struggled in her soul. Mired she was between two abandoned worlds, living, dying without the strength of the grace that either gave. The clearer she felt it the fuller did something well up from the depths of her for release; the more urgent did she feel the need to fling into her black sky another star, another hope, one more terrible vision to give her the strength to live and act. Softly and restlessly she walked about the kitchen, feeling herself naked against night, the rain, the world; and shamed whenever the thought of Reva's love crossed her mind. She lifted her empty hands and looked at her writhing fingers. Lawd, whut kin Ah do now? She could still wade the creek and get to Foley's Woods before Booker. And then what? How could she manage to see Johnny-Boy or Booker? Again she heard the sheriff's threatening voice: Git yuh a sheet, cause hes gonna be dead! The sheet! Thas it, the sheet! Her whole being leaped with will; the long years of her life bent toward a moment of focus, a point. Ah kin go wid mah sheet! Ahll be doin whut he said! Lawd Gawd in Heaven, Ahma go lika nigger woman wid mah windin sheet t git mah dead son! But then what? She stood straight and smiled grimly; she had in her heart the whole meaning of her life; her entire personality was poised on the brink of a total act. Ah know! Ah know! She thought of Johnny-Boy's gun in the dresser drawer. Ahll hide the gun in the sheet n go aftah Johnny-Boy's body. . . . She tiptoed to her room, eased out the dresser drawer, and got a sheet. Reva was sleeping; the darkness was filled with her quiet breathing. She groped in the drawer and found the gun. She wound the gun in the sheet and held them both under her apron. Then she stole to the bedside and watched Reva. Lawd, hep her! But mabbee shes bettah off. This had t happen sometimes . . . She n Johnny-Boy couldna been together in this here South . . . N An couldnt tell her bout Booker. Itll come out awright n she wont nevah know. Reva's trust would never be shaken. She caught her breath as the shucks in the mattress rustled dryly; then all was quiet and she breathed easily again. She tiptoed to the door, down the hall, and stood on the porch. Above her the yellow beacon whirled through the rain. She went over muddy ground, mounted a slope, stopped and looked back at her house. The lamp glowed in her window, and the yellow beacon that swung every few seconds seemed to feed it with light. She turned and started across the fields, holding the gun and sheet tightly, thinking, Po Reva . . . Po critter . . . Shes fas ersleep . . .

VI

For the most part she walked with her eyes half shut, her lips tightly compressed, leaning her body against the wind and the slanting rain, feeling the pistol in the sheet sagging cold and heavy in her fingers. Already she was getting wet; it seemed that her feet found every puddle of water that stood between the corn rows.

She came to the edge of the creek and paused, wondering at what point was it low. Taking the sheet from under her apron, she wrapped the gun in it so that her finger could be upon the trigger. Ahll cross here, she thought. At first she did not feel the water; her feet were already wet. But the water grew cold as it came up to her knees; she gasped when it reached her waist. Lawd, this creeks high! When she had passed the middle, she knew that she was out of danger. She came out of the water, climbed a grassy hill, walked on, turned a bend and saw the lights of autos gleaming ahead. Yeah; theys still there! She hurried with her head down. Wondah did Ah beat im here? Lawd, Ah hope so! A vivid image of Booker's white face hovered a moment before her eyes and a driving will surged up in her so hard and strong that it vanished. She was among the autos now. From nearby came the hoarse voices of the men.

"Hey, yuh!"

She stopped, nervously clutching the sheet. Two white men with shotguns came toward her.

"Whut in hell yuh doin out here?"

She did not answer.

"Didnt yuh hear somebody speak t yuh?"

"Ahm comin aftah mah son," she said humbly.

"Yo *son?*"

"Yessuh."

"Whut yo son doin out here?"

"The sheriffs got im."

"Holy Scott! Jim, its the niggers ma!"

"Whut yuh got there?" asked one.

"A sheet."

"A *sheet?*"

"Yessuh."

"Fer whut?"

"The sheriff tol me t bring a sheet t git his body."

"Waal, waal . . ."

"Now, ain tha something?"

The white men looked at each other.

"These niggers sho love one ernother," said one.

"N tha ain no lie," said the other.

"Take me t the sheriff," she begged.

"Yuh ain givin us *orders*, is yuh?"

"Nawsuh."

"We'll take yuh when wes good n ready."

"Yessuh."

"So yuh wan his body?"

"Yessuh."

"Waal, he ain dead yit."

"They gonna kill im," she said.

"Ef he talks they wont."

"He ain gonna talk," she said.

"How yuh know?"

"Cause he ain."

"We got ways of makin niggers talk."

"Yuh ain got no way fer im."

"Yuh thinka lot of tha black Red, don yuh?"

"Hes mah son."

"Why don yuh teach im some sense?"

"Hes mah son," she said again.

"Lissen, ol nigger woman, yuh stan there wid yo hair white. Yuh got bettah sense than t blieve tha niggers kin make a revolution . . ."

"A black republic," said the other one, laughing.

"Take me t the sheriff," she begged.

"Yuh his ma," said one. "Yuh kin make im talk n tell whos in this thing wid im."

"He ain gonna talk," she said.

"Don yuh wan im t live?"

She did not answer.

"C mon, les take her t Bradley."

They grabbed her arms and she clutched hard at the sheet and gun; they led her toward the crowd in the woods. Her feelings were simple; Booker would not tell; she was there with the gun to see to that. The louder became the voices of the men the deeper became her feeling of wanting to right the mistake she had made; of wanting to fight her way back to solid ground. She would stall for time until Booker showed up. Oh, ef theyll only lemme git close t Johnny-Boy! As they led her near the crowd she saw white faces turning and looking at her and heard a rising clamor of voices.

"Whos tha?"

"A nigger woman!"

"Whut she doin out here?"

"This is his ma!" called one of the men.

"Whut she wans?"

"She brought a sheet t cover his body!"

"He ain dead yit!"

"They tryin t make im talk!"

"But he will be dead soon ef he don open up!"

"Say, look! The niggers ma brought a sheet t cover up his body!"

"Now, ain tha sweet?"

"Mabbe she wans t hol a prayer meetin!"

"Did she git a preacher?"

"Say, go git Bradley!"

"O.K.!"

The crowd grew quiet. They looked at her curiously; she felt their cold eyes trying to detect some weakness in her. Humbly, she stood with the sheet covering the gun. She had already accepted all that they could do to her.

The sheriff came.

"So yuh brought yo sheet, hunh?"

"Yessuh," she whispered.

"Looks like them slaps we gave yuh learned yuh some sense, didnt they?"

She did not answer.

"Yuh don need tha sheet. Yo son ain dead yit," he said, reaching.

She backed away, her eyes wide.

"Naw!"

"Now, lissen, Anty!" he said. "There ain no use in yuh ackin a fool! Go in there n tell tha nigger son of yos t tell us whos in this wid im, see? Ah promise we wont kill im ef he talks. We'll let im git outta town."

"There ain nothin Ah kin tell im," she said.

"Yuh wan us t kill im?"

She did not answer. She saw someone lean toward the sheriff and whisper.

"Bring her erlong," the sheriff said.

They led her to a muddy clearing. The rain streamed down through the ghostly glare of the flashlights. As the men formed a semi-circle she saw Johnny-Boy lying in a trough of mud. He was tied with rope; he lay hunched, one side of his face resting in a pool of black water. His eyes were staring questioningly at her.

"Speak t im," said the sheriff.

If she could only tell him why she was there! But that was impossible; she was close to what she wanted and she stared straight before her with compressed lips.

"Say, nigger!" called the sheriff, kicking Johnny-Boy. "Here's yo ma!"

Johnny-Boy did not move or speak. The sheriff faced her again.

"Lissen, Anty," he said. "Yuh got mo say wid im than anybody. Tell im t talk n hava chance. Whut he wanna pertect the other niggers n white folks fer?"

She slid her finger about the trigger of the gun and looked stonily at the mud.

"Go t him," said the sheriff.

She did not move. Her heart was crying out to answer the amazed question in Johnny-Boy's eyes. But there was no way now.

"Waal, yuhre astin fer it. By Gawd, we gotta way to *make* yuh talk t im," he said, turning away. "Say, Tim, git one of them logs n turn tha nigger upsidedown n put his legs on it!"

A murmur of assent ran through the crowd. She bit her lips; she knew what that meant.

"Yuh wan yo nigger son crippled?" she heard the sheriff ask.

She did not answer. She saw them roll the log up; they lifted Johnny-Boy and laid him on his face and stomach, then they pulled his legs over the log. His knee-caps rested on the sheer top of the log's back, the toes of his shoes pointing groundward. So absorbed was she in watching that she felt that it was she that was being lifted and made ready for torture.

"Git a crowbar!" said the sheriff.

A tall, lank man got a crowbar from a near-by auto and stood over the log. His jaws worked slowly on a wad of tobacco.

"Now, its up t yuh, Anty," the sheriff said. "Tell the man whut t do!"

She looked into the rain. The sheriff turned.

"Mabbe she think wes playin. Ef she don say nothin, then break em at the knee-caps!"

"O.K., Sheriff!"

She stood waiting for Booker. Her legs felt weak; she wondered if she would be able to wait much longer. Over and over she said to herself, Ef he came now Ahd kill em both!

"She ain sayin nothin, Sheriff!"

"Waal, Gawddammit, let im have it!"

The crowbar came down and Johnny-Boy's body lunged in the mud and water. There was a scream. She swayed, holding tight to the gun and sheet.

"Hol im! Git the other leg!"

The crowbar fell again. There was another scream.

"Yuh break em?" asked the sheriff.

The tall man lifted Johnny-Boy's legs and let them drop limply again, dropping rearward from the knee-caps. Johnny-Boy's body lay still. His head had rolled to one side and she could not see his face.

"Jus lika broke sparrow wing," said the man, laughing softly.

Then Johnny-Boy's face turned to her; he screamed.

"Go way, ma! Go way!"

It was the first time she had heard his voice since she had come out to the woods; she all but lost control of herself. She started violently forward, but the sheriff's arm checked her.

"Aw, naw! Yuh had yo chance!" He turned to Johnny-Boy. "She kin go ef yuh talk."

"Mistah, he ain gonna talk," she said.

"Go way, ma!" said Johnny-Boy.

"Shoot im! Don make im suffah so," she begged.

"He'll either talk or he'll never hear yuh ergin," the sheriff said. "Theres other things we kin do t im."

She said nothing.

"Whut yuh come here fer, ma?" Johnny-Boy sobbed.

"Ahm gonna split his eardrums," the sheriff said. "Ef yuh got anything t say t im yuh bettah say it *now!*"

She closed her eyes. She heard the sheriff's feet sucking in mud. Ah could save im! She opened her eyes; there were shouts of eagerness from the crowd as it pushed in closer.

"Bus em, Sheriff!"

"Fix im so he cant hear!"

"He knows how t do it, too!"

"He busted a Jew boy tha way once!"

She saw the sheriff stoop over Johnny-Boy, place his flat palm over one ear and strike his fist against it with all his might. He placed his palm over the other ear and struck again. Johnny-Boy moaned; his head rolling from side to side, his eyes showing white amazement in a world without sound.

"Yuh wouldn't talk t im when yuh had the chance," said the sheriff. "Try n talk now."

She felt warm tears on her cheeks. She longed to shoot Johnny-Boy and let him go. But if she did that they would take the gun from her, and Booker would tell who the others were. Lawd, hep me! The men were talking loudly now, as though the main business was over. It seemed ages that she stood there watching Johnny-Boy roll and whimper in his world of silence.

"Say, Sheriff, heres somebody lookin fer yuh!"

"Who is it?"

"Ah don know!"

"Bring em in!"

She stiffened and looked around wildly, holding the gun tight. Is tha Booker? Then she held still, feeling that her excitement might betray her. Mabbe Ah kin shoot em both! Mabbe Ah kin shoot twice! The sheriff stood in front of her, waiting. The crowd parted and she saw Booker hurrying forward.

"Ah know em all, Sheriff!" he called.

He came full into the muddy clearing where Johnny-Boy lay.

"Yuh mean yuh got the names?"

"Sho! The ol nigger . . ."

She saw his lips hang open and silent when he saw her. She stepped forward and raised the sheet.

"Whut . . ."

She fired, once; then, without pausing, she turned, hearing them yell. She aimed at Johnny-Boy, but they had their arms around her, bearing her to the ground, clawing at the sheet in her hand. She glimpsed Booker lying sprawled in the mud, on his face, his hands stretched out before him; then a cluster of yelling men blotted him out. She lay without struggling, looking upward through the rain at the white faces above her. And she was suddenly at peace; they were not a white mountain now; they were not pushing her any longer to the edge of life. Its awright . . .

"She shot Booker!"

"She hada gun in the sheet!"

"She shot him right thu the head!"

"Whut she shoot im fer?"

"Kill the bitch!"

"Ah *thought* something wuz wrong bout her!"

"Ah wuz fer givin it t her from the firs!"

"Thas whut yuh git fer treatin a nigger nice!"

"Say, Bookers dead!"

She stopped looking into the white faces, stopped listening. She waited, giving up her life before they took it from her; she had done what she wanted. Ef only Johnny-Boy . . . She looked at him; he lay looking at her with tired eyes. Ef she could only tell im!

"Whut yuh kill im fer, hunh?"

It was the sheriff's voice; she did not answer.

"Mabbe she wuz shootin at yuh, Sheriff?"

"Whut yuh kill im fer?"

She felt the sheriff's foot come into her side; she closed her eyes.

"Yuh black bitch!"

"Let her have it!"

"Yuh reckon she foun out bout Booker?"

"She mighta."

"Jesus Christ, whut yuh dummies *waitin* on!"

"Yeah; kill her!"

"Kill em *both!*"

"Let her know her nigger sons dead firs!"

She turned her head toward Johnny-Boy; he lay looking puzzled in a world beyond the reach of voices. At leas he cant hear, she thought.

"C mon, let im have it!"

She listened to hear what Johnny-Boy could not. They came, two of them, one right behind the other; so close together that they sounded like one shot. She did not look at Johnny-Boy now; she looked at the white faces of the men, hard and wet in the glare of the flashlights.

"Yuh hear tha, nigger woman?"

"Did tha surprise im? Hes in hell now wonderin whut hit im!"

"C mon! Give it t her, Sheriff!"

"Lemme shoot her, Sheriff! It wuz mah pal she shot!"

"Awright, Pete! Thas fair ernuff!"

She gave up as much of her life as she could before they took it from her. But the sound of the shot and the streak of fire that tore its way through her chest forced her to live again, intensely. She had not moved, save for the slight jarring impact of the bullet. She felt the heat of her own blood warming her cold, wet back. She yearned suddenly to talk. "Yuh didnt git whut yuh wanted! N yuh ain gonna nevah git it! Yuh didnt kill me; Ah come here by mahsef . . ." She felt rain falling into her wide-open, dimming eyes and heard faint voices. Her lips moved soundlessly. *Yuh didnt git yuh didnt yuh didnt* . . . Focused and pointed she was, buried in the depths of her star, swallowed in its peace and strength; and not feeling her flesh growing cold, cold as the rain that fell from the invisible sky upon the doomed living and the dead that never dies.

1940

*Eudora Welty*

# The Hitch-Hikers

FROM *The Southern Review*

TOM HARRIS, a thirty-year-old salesman traveling in office supplies, got out of Thurston a little after noon and saw people in Flat Top and Baxter, but went on toward Memphis. It was a base, and he was thinking he would like to do something that night.

Toward evening, on a long straight stretch of road, he slowed down for some hitch-hikers. One of them stood still by the side of the pavement, with his foot stuck out like an old root, but the other was playing a yellow guitar which caught the late sun.

Harris would get sleepy driving. On the road he did some things rather out of a dream. To him the recurring sight of hitch-hikers waiting against the sky gave him the flash of a sensation he had learned to experience when he was a child: standing still with nothing around him, feeling tall, and having the world come all at once into its round shape underfoot and rush and turn through space and make his stand very precarious, and lonely.

He and the two hitch-hikers spoke to one another almost formally.

Resuming his speed, Harris moved over a little in the seat. The man with the guitar wanted to ride with it between his legs. Harris reached over and turned on the radio.

"Well, music," said the man with the guitar.

"I forget about it," remarked Harris.

"Well, we been there a whole day in that one spot," said the man with the guitar, beginning to grin. "Seen the sun go clear over. Course, part of the time we laid down and taken our ease."

They rode without talking, while the sun went down in red clouds and the radio program changed a few times. Harris switched on his lights. Once the man with the guitar started to sing "The One Rose that's Left in My Heart," which came over the air played by the Aloha Boys. Then, rather shyly, he stopped in the middle of it, but made a streak on the radio dial with his blackly calloused fingertip.

"I appreciate them big 'lectric gittars all right," he said.

"Where are you going?"

"Looks like north."

"So it is," said Harris. "Smoke?"

"Well, rarely," replied the man with the guitar.

At the unexpected use of the word, Harris's cheek twitched, and he handed over his pack of cigarettes. All three lighted up. The silent man held his cigarette in front of him like a piece of money, between his thumb and forefinger, most of the time. Harris realized he wasn't smoking but was watching it burn.

"My, gittin' night agin," said the man with the guitar, in a voice that could assume any surprise.

"Anything to eat?" asked Harris.

The man gave a pluck to a guitar string, and glanced at him.

"Dewberries," said the other man. It was his only remark, and it was made in a slow, pondering voice.

"Some nice little rabbit come skinnin' by," said the man with the guitar, nudging Harris with a slight punch in his side, "but it run off the way it come."

The other man was so bogged in inarticulate anger that Harris could imagine him running after the rabbit. He smiled, but did not look around.

"Now to look out for a place to sleep — is that it?" he remarked doggedly.

A pluck of the strings again, and the man yawned.

There was a town coming up, lighted over a little piece of bluff.

"Clearwater?" Harris yawned too.

"I bet you ain't got no idea where all I've slep'," the man said, turning around in his seat and speaking directly to Harris, with laughter in his face that in the light of a roadsign appeared strangely teasing.

"I could eat a hamburger," said Harris, swinging out of the road under the sign in some automatic gesture of evasion, and turning to a girl in red pants who had leaped onto the running board.

"Three and three beers?" she asked, smiling, with her head poked in the window. "Hi," she said to Harris.

"How are you," said Harris. "That's right."

"My," said the man with the guitar. "Red sailorboy pants." Harris listened for the guitar-note but it did not come. "But not purty," he said.

The screen door of the joint whined and a man's voice called, "Come on in, boys, we got girls."

"Tell them to come out here!" the man with the guitar shouted back in the same breath, and then went into deep silence, as if afraid he had gone too far.

Harris cut off the radio and they listened to the nickelodeon which was playing inside the joint and turning the window blue, red and green in turn.

"Hi," said the car-hop again as she came out with the tray. "Looks like rain."

They ate the hamburgers rapidly, without talking. A girl came and looked out of the window, leaning on her hand. One couple was dancing inside. There was a waltz.

"Same songs ever'where," said the man with the guitar, softly.

Nearly every time the man spoke, Harris's cheek twitched. He was easily amused. Also, he recognized easily any sort of attempt to confide, and then its certain and hasty retreat. The more the man said, the further he was drawn into a willingness to listen. I'll hear him play his guitar yet, he thought. It had got to be a pattern in his days and nights, it was almost automatic, his listening, like the way his hand went to his pocket for money.

"That'n's most the same as a ballat," said the man, licking mustard off his finger. "My ma, she was the one for ballats. Little in the waist as a dirt dauber but her voice carried. Had her a whole lot of tunes. Long ago dead an' gone. Pa'd come home drunk as a wheelbarrow and she'd go sit on the front step facin' the road an' sing ever'thing she knowed. Dead an' gone an' the house burned down." He gulped at his beer. His foot was patting.

"This," said Harris, touching one of the keys on the guitar. "Couldn't you make some money with your guitar?"

Of course it was by the guitar that he had known at once they were not mere hitch-hikers, they were tramps. They were full-blown, abandoned to this. Both of them were — but when he touched it he knew obscurely that it was the yellow guitar, that bold and gay burden in the tramp's arms, that had caused him to stop his car and pick them up.

The man hit it flat with the palm of his hand.

"This box? Just play it for myself."

Harris laughed delightedly, but somehow he had a desire to tease him, to make him swear to his freedom.

"You wouldn't stop and play somewhere like this? For a dance? With girls?"

Now the fellow turned and spoke completely as if the other man were not there. "Well but now I got *him*."

"Him?" Harris stared straight ahead.

"He'd gripe. He don't like foolin' 'round. He wants to git on."

The other tramp belched. Harris laid his hand on the horn.

"Bye," said the car-hop, opening a heart-shaped pocket over her heart and dropping the tip courteously within.

"Aw river!" sang out the man with the guitar.

As they pulled out into the highway again, the other man began to lift a beer bottle, and stared beseechingly at the man with the guitar, as if his mouth were full.

"Drive back. Sobby forgot to give her back her bottle," said the man with the guitar. He laughed. "Drive back. We got to give her back her bottle."

"Haven't got time," said Harris rather firmly, speeding down the road into Clearwater, thinking, I was about to take directions from him.

"You looked like you thought he was goin' to hit you with it," said the man with the guitar softly.

Harris stopped the car in front of the hotel on the main street.

"Appreciated it," said the man, taking up his guitar.

"Wait here."

They sat back at once, both striped by a streetlight, both caved in, and giving out an odor of dust, both sighing with obedience.

Harris took his hand off the car door and went up the walk and up the one step into the hotel.

Mr. Gene, the proprietor, a white-haired man with little dark freckles all over his face and hands, looked up and shoved out his arm.

"If you ain't back." He grinned. "Been about a month to the day; I was thinkin' of you."

"Mr. Gene, I ought to go on, but I got two fellows out in the car. O.K., but they've just got nowhere to sleep tonight, and you know that little back porch."

"Why, it's a beautiful night out!" bellowed Mr. Gene, and laughed silently.

"They'd get fleas in your bed," said Harris, showing the back of his hand. "But you know that old porch. It's not so bad, I slept out there once, I forget how."

The proprietor let his laugh out like a flood. Then he sobered abruptly.

"Sure, O.K.," he said. "Wait a minute: Mike's sick. Come here, Mike, it's just old Harris passin' through."

Mike was an ancient collie dog. He rose from a quilt near the door and moved over the square brown rug, stiffly, like a table walking, and shoved himself between the men, swinging his long head from Mr. Gene's hand to Harris's, and bearing down motionless with his jaw in Harris's palm.

"You sick, Mike?" said Harris.

"Dying of old age!" blurted the proprietor, as if in anger.

Harris began to stroke the dog, but the familiarity in his hands slowly changed to slowness and hesitancy. Mike looked up out of his eyes.

"His spirit's gone. You see?" said Mr. Gene pleadingly.

"Say," said a voice at the front door.

"Come in, come in, and see poor old Mike," said Mr. Gene.

"I knew that was your car, Mr. Harris," said the boy. He was nervously trying to tuck a Bing Crosby cretonne shirt into his pants like a real shirt. Then he looked up and said, "They was tryin' to take your car and down the street one of 'em like-to bust the other one's head wide op'm with a bottle. Looks like you would 'a' heard the commotion. Everybody's out there. I said, 'That's Mr. Tom Harris's car, look at the out-of-state license and look at all the stuff he all time carries around with him all bloody."

"He's not dead though," said Harris, kneeling on the seat of his car.

It was the man with the guitar. The little ceiling light had been turned on. With blood streaming from his broken head, he was slumped down upon the guitar, his legs bowed around it, his arms at either side, his whole body limp in the posture of a bareback rider. Harris was aware of the other face not a yard away; the man the guitar player had called Sobby was standing on the curb with two men unnecessarily holding him. He looked more like a bystander than any of the rest, except that he still held the beer bottle in his right hand. Finally somebody took it away from him.

"Looks like if he was fixin' to hit him, *he* would of hit *him* with that gittar," said a voice. "That'd be a real good thing to hit somebody with. Whang!"

"The way I figure this thing out is," said a penetrating voice, as if a woman were explaining it all to her husband, "the men was left to 'emselves. So — that'n yonder wanted to make off with the car — he's the one they pulled out the driver's seat — he's the bad one. So the good one says naw, that ain't right." (Or was it the other way round, Harris thought dreamily.) "So the other one says bam! bam! He let him have it. And so dumb, right where the movie was letting out."

"Hi, Mr. Harris!" yelled somebody across the street. It was the bearded postmaster walking along, waving a letter.

"Who's got my car keys!" shouted Harris. He had without realizing it kicked away the prop, the guitar, and he had stopped the blood with something.

He knew where the two-room hospital in Clearwater was — he had been there another time. With the constable scuttling along after and then hanging onto the side of the car with his glasses held carefully in one hand, talking continuously to him through the window, dragging the man called Sobby along too, handcuffed to him and trotting along by the slowed-down car with its rain-speckled windshield, and with a long line of little boys in flowered shirts surrounding him on bicycles, riding in and out of the headlight beam, and with Mr. Gene still shouting in a sort of plea from the hotel step and Mike beginning to bark a little behind the other dogs, he drove around the bank corner and through a tree-dark street with his wet hand on the automobile horn.

The old doctor came down the walk and joining them in the car slowly took the guitar player by the shoulders.

"I 'spec' he' gonna die though," said a colored child's voice mournfully. "Wonder who goin' to git his box?"

In a room on the second floor of the two-story hotel, Harris bathed and put on clean clothes while Mr. Gene lay on the bed with Mike across his stomach.

"Ruined that Christmas tie you wear," the proprietor was talking in short breaths. "It took it out of Mike, I'm tellin' you." He sighed. "First time he's barked since Bud Milton shot up that Chinese." He bent his head up and took a long swallow of the hotel whiskey, and tears appeared in his warm brown eyes. "Suppose they'd done it on the porch."

The phone rang.

"Well, everybody knows you're here," said Mr. Gene.

"Ruth?" he said into the phone.

But it was for the proprietor.

"That little runt of a feller, he don't know which end is up by now," he said when he had hung up. "The constable. Got a nigger already in the jail, so he's runnin' 'round for a place to put this fella of yours with the bottle, and damned if all he can think of ain't the hotel."

"Hell, is he going to spend the night with me?"

"Well, down the hall. The other fella may die. Only place with a bunch of keys but the bank, he says."

"What time is it?" asked Harris all at once.

"It ain't too late," said Mr. Gene. He opened the door for Mike and followed him slowly out. "I'll see you. I don't guess you're goin' to get away very shortly in the mornin'. I'm real sorry they did it in your car if they was goin' to do it," he added.

"That's all right," said Harris.

The light was out on the landing. He looked toward the old half-open stained-glass window.

"Is that rain?"

"It ain't sawdust," said the proprietor. "It's been rainin' since dark, but you don't ever know a thing like that, it's proverbial." At the desk he held up a brown package. "Here. I sent Babe down the road and got you some Memphis whiskey."

"Thanks," said Harris. "You better have some now."

"That? It'd kill me," said Mr. Gene.

Up the street he phoned Ruth, a woman he knew in town, and found she was at home having a party.

"Tom Harris, the very person!" she cried. "I was wondering what I'd do about Carol, this *child!*"

"What's the matter with her?"

"Oh — such a child. And no date."

Some other people wanted to say hello from the party. He listened a while and said he'd be out.

After a moment he telephoned the hospital and found out nothing new about the guitar player.

"Like I told you," the doctor said, "we don't have the facilities for giving transfusions, and he's been moved plenty enough without you taking him to Memphis."

Walking over to the party, so as not to use his car, making the only sounds in the dark wet street, and only partly aware of the indeterminate shapes of houses set back with a light or two showing inside and the rain falling mist-like through the trees, he almost forgot what town he was in and which house he was bound for.

Ruth, in a long dark dress, leaned against an open door, laughing. From inside he could hear at least two people playing a skating song on the piano.

"He would come like this and get all wet!" she cried over her shoulder into the room. She was leaning back on her hands. "What happened to your little blue car? I hope you brought us a present."

He went in with her and began shaking hands, and set the bottle wrapped in the paper sack on a table.

"He never forgets!" cried Ruth.

"Drinkin'-whiskey!" Everybody was noisy again.

"My name's Carol," said a blonde.

"He stayed away a long time this time," said a girl who was making the introductions.

"So this is the famous 'he' that everybody talks about all the time," pouted a girl in a white dress, whom everybody was calling "Mrs. Pettibone."

I wish they'd call me "you" when I've got here, he thought tiredly.

"My dear, he's a legend," said Ruth firmly, and led Harris off to the kitchen by the hand.

"So much has happened, and so little," she said, and told him while he poured fresh drinks. He was fairly sure she had not heard about the assault in his car.

"Has this party been going on since afternoon?" he asked.

"Oh, yes." Suddenly she said, "Where did you get that sun-burn?"

"Well, I had to go to the coast last week," he said.

"What did you do?"

"Same old thing," he said. He had started to tell her about something funny in Bay St. Louis, where an eloping couple had flagged him down in the residential section and threatened to break up if he would not carry them to the next town. Then he remembered how Ruth looked when he mentioned other places he had stopped on trips.

The phone rang and rang, and he caught himself jumping, especially when nobody went to answer it.

"I thought you'd quit drinking," she said, picking up the bottle.

"Oh, I start and quit," he said, taking it back and pouring his drink.

She came over and stood near him while he set the glasses on the tray. Was she at all curious about him? he wondered. For a moment, when they were simply close together, her lips parted and she stared off at nothing, her jealousy left her free, the rainy wind from off the back porch stirred her hair.

As if under some illusion, he set down the tray and told her about the two hitch-hikers.

Her eyes flashed. "What a stupid thing for them to do!" she said furiously, picking up the tray when he reached for it. "So messy!"

It was as though he had made a previous engagement with them. Everybody was meeting them at the kitchen door.

"So!" cried one of the men, Jackson. "He tries to put one over on us. Somebody just called up, Ruth, about the murder in Tom's car!"

"Did he die?" cried Harris.

"Sly devil," said the girl in the white dress, looking at him sideways, like part of the Beatrice Lillie imitation she had already given.

"I knew all about it!" cried Ruth, her cheeks flaming. "He told me all about it. It practically ruined his car. Didn't it!"

"Wouldn't he get into something crazy like that!"

"It's because he's sweet," said the girl named Carol, speaking in a hollow voice from her highball glass.

"Who phoned?" asked Harris.

"Old Mrs. Daggett, that old lady about a million years old that's always calling up. She was there. This is the way she talks."

Harris phoned the hospital and the guitar player was still the same.

"This is so exciting, tell us all," said a fat boy in a polo shirt.

"Oh, he wouldn't, he never talks. I'll tell you," said Ruth. "We can sit in the kitchen. Carol, you can cook eggs."

So the incident became a story. Harris got very tired of it.

"It's marvelous the way he always gets in with somebody and then something happens," said Ruth, her eyes confidently on him.

"Oh he's so sweet," said Carol, and went out and sat on the stairs.

"Of course he is," said Ruth. "Maybe you'll still be here, tomorrow, then," she said to Harris, taking his arm. "Will you be detained, maybe?"

"If he dies," said Harris.

He told them all good-bye.

"Aw river," said the girl in the white dress. "Isn't that what the little man said?"

"Yes," said Harris, the rain falling on him, and refused to spend the night or to ride back to the hotel.

In the antlered lobby, Mr. Gene bent over asleep under a lamp by the desk phone. His freckles seemed to come out darker when he was asleep.

Harris woke him up. "Get to bed," he said. "What was the idea? Anything happened?"

"I just wanted to tell you that little buzzard's up in 210. Locked and double-locked, handcuffed to the bed, but I wanted to tell you."

"Oh. Much obliged."

"All a gentleman could do," said Mr. Gene. He was drunk. "Warn you what's sleepin' under the roof with you."

"Thanks," said Harris. "It's two o'clock. Look."

"Poor Mike can't sleep," said Mr. Gene. "Because it hurts him to breathe. Did the other fella poop out?"

"Still unconscious," said Harris. He took the bunch of keys which the proprietor was handing him.

"Lock me in too," Mr. Gene explained. "I want you to lock up, and lock me in."

In the next moment Harris saw his hand tremble, and he took hold of it.

"A murderer!" whispered Mr. Gene. All his freckles stood out. "With not a word to say. You wonder I love old Mike?"

"Not a murderer yet," said Harris, starting to grin.

When he passed 210 and heard no sound, he remembered what old Sobby had said standing handcuffed in front of the hospital, with nobody listening to him. "I was jist tired of him always uppin' and makin' a noise about ever'thing."

In his room, Harris lay down on the bed without undressing or turning out the light. He was too tired to sleep. Half blinded by the unshaded bulb he stared at the bare plaster walls and the equally white surface of the mirror above the empty dresser. Presently he got up and turned on the ceiling fan, to create some motion and sound in the room. It was a defective fan which clicked with each revolution, on and on. He lay perfectly still beneath it with his clothes on, unconsciously breathing in a rhythm related to the beat of the fan.

He shut his eyes suddenly. When they were closed, in the red blackness he felt all patience leave him. It was like the beginning of desire. He remembered the girl dropping money into her heart-shaped pocket, and remembered a disturbing possessiveness, which meant nothing, Ruth leaning on her hands. He knew he would not be held by any of it. It was for relief, almost, that his thoughts turned to pity, to wonder about the two tramps, their conflict, the sudden brutality when his back was turned — how would it turn out? It was in this suspense that it was more acceptable to him to feel the helplessness of his life.

He could forgive nothing in this evening. But it was too like other evenings, this town was too like other towns, for him to move out of this lying undressed on the bed, even into comfort or despair. Even the rain — there was often rain, there was often a party, and there had been other violence not of his doing — other fights, not quite so pointless, but fights in his car; fights, unheralded confessions, sudden lovemaking — none of any of this his, not his to keep, but belonging to the people of these towns he passed through, coming out of their rooted pasts, out of their remaining in one place, coming out of their time. He himself had no time. He was free: helpless. He wished he knew how the guitar player was, if he was still unconscious, if he felt pain.

He sat up on the bed and then got up and walked to the window.

"Tom!" said a voice outside in the dark.

Automatically he answered and listened. It was a girl. He could not see her, but she must have been standing on the little plot of grass that ran around the side of the hotel. Wet feet, pneumonia, he thought. And he was so tired he thought of a girl from the wrong town. There was something indistinct she said, her voice lowered and breathless, as though she were hurrying toward the door, and he started down.

He let her into the lobby, and she ran as far as the middle of the room as though from impetus. It was Carol, from the party.

"You're wet," he said. He touched her.

"Always raining." She looked up at him, stepping back. "How are you?"

"O.K., fine," he said.

"I didn't know very well," she said nervously. "I knew the light would be you. I hope I didn't wake up anybody."

Was old Sobby asleep? he wondered.

"Would you like a drink? Or do you want to go to the All-Nite and get a coffee," he said.

"It's open," she said, making a gesture with her hand. "The All-Nite is open, I just passed it."

They went out into the mist, and she put his coat on with silent protest, in the dark street not drunken but womanly.

"You didn't remember me at the party," she said, and did not look up when he made his exclamation. "They say you never forget anybody, so I found out they were wrong about that anyway."

"They're often wrong," he said. And then hurriedly, "When was it?"

"I used to stay at the Manning Hotel on the coast every summer with my aunt, I wasn't grown. Just dances and all, but you had just started to travel then, it was on your trips, and you — you talked at intermission."

He laughed shortly, but she added:

"You talked about yourself."

They walked past the tall wet church and their steps echoed.

"Oh it wasn't so long ago — five years," she said. Under a magnolia tree she put out her hand and stopped him, looking up at him with her child's face. "But when I saw you again tonight I wanted to know how you are."

He said nothing and she went on.

"You used to play the piano."

They passed under a streetlight and she glanced up as if to look for the little tic in his cheek.

"Out on the big porch where they danced," she said, walking on. "Lanterns. . . ."

"I'd forgotten that, is one thing sure," he said. "Maybe you've got the wrong man."

"You'd put your hands down on the keyboard like you'd say, 'Now this is how it really is!'" she cried, and turned her head away. "I guess I was crazy about you though."

"Crazy about me then?" He struck a match and held a cigarette between his teeth.

"No — yes, and now too!" she cried sharply, as if driven to deny him.

They came to the little depot where a restless switch-engine was hissing, and crossed the black street. The past and present joined like this, he thought, it never happens often to me, it probably won't happen again. He took her arm and led her through the dirty screen-door of the All-Nite.

He ordered at the counter while she sat down by the wall-table and wiped her face all over with her handkerchief. He carried the coffees over to the table himself, smiling at her from a little distance. They sat under a calendar with some pictures of giant trees being cut down.

They said little. A fly bothered her. When the coffee was all gone he put her into the taxi that always waited in front of the depot.

Before he shut the taxi door, he said, frowning, "I appreciate it. . . . You're sweet."

Now she had torn her handkerchief. She held it up and began to cry. "What's sweet about me?" she asked him.

"To come out, like this — in the rain — to be here — " he shut the door, partly from weariness.

She was holding her breath. "I hope your friend doesn't die," she said. "I hope he gets well."

But when he woke up the next morning and phoned the hospital, the guitar player was dead. He had been dead while Harris was sitting in the All-Nite.

"It *was* a murderer," said Mr. Gene, pulling Mike's ears.

The man called Sobby said he would confess. He began to turn his head about a little and almost smiled at all the men standing around him. After one look at him, Mr. Gene, who had come with Harris, went out and slammed the door behind him.

Sobby had found little in the night, asleep or awake, to say about it. "Hell, yes, I done it," he said. "Didn't ever'body see me, or was they blind?"

They asked him about the man he had killed.

"Name Sanford," he said, standing still with his foot out, as if he were trying to recall something particular and minute. "But he didn't have nothing and he didn't have no folks. No more'n me. Him and me, we took up together two weeks back." He looked up at their faces, as if for support. "He was uppity though. He bragged. He carried around a guitar."

Harris, fresh from the barbershop, was standing in the filling station where his car was being polished.

A ring of little boys in bright shirt-tails surrounded him and the car, with some colored boys waiting behind them.

"Could they git all the blood off the seat and the steerin'-wheel, Mr. Harris?"

He nodded. They ran away.

"Mr. Harris," said a little colored boy who stayed. "Does you want the box?"

"The what?"

He pointed, to where it lay in the back seat with the sample-cases. "The po' kilt man's gittar."

"No," said Harris, and handed it over.

1943

*Paul Horgan*

# The Peach Stone

FROM *The Yale Review*

AS THEY ALL KNEW, the drive would take them about four hours, all the way to Weed, where *she* came from. They knew the way from travelling it so often, first in the old car, and now in the new one; new to them, that is, for they'd bought it second hand, last year, when they were down in Roswell to celebrate their tenth wedding anniversary. They still thought of themselves as a young couple, and *he* certainly did crazy things now and then, and always laughed her out of it when she was cross at the money going where it did, instead of where it ought to go. But there was so much droll orneriness in him when he did things like that that she couldn't stay mad, hadn't the heart; and the harder up they got, the more she loved him, and the little ranch he'd taken her to in the rolling plains just below the mountains.

This was a day in spring, rather hot, and the mountain was that melting blue that reminded you of something you could touch, like a china bowl. Over the sandy brown of the earth there was coming a green shadow. The air struck cool and deep in their breasts. *He* came from Texas, as a boy, and had lived here in New Mexico ever since. The word *home* always gave *her* a picture of unpainted, mouse-brown wooden houses in a little cluster by the rocky edge of the last mountain-step — the town of Weed, where Jodey Powers met and married her ten years ago.

They were heading back that way today.

Jodey was driving, squinting at the light. It never seemed so bright as now, before noon, as they went up the valley. He had a rangy look at the wheel of the light blue Chevvie — a bony man, but still fuzzed over with some look of a cub about him, perhaps the way he moved his limbs, a slight appealing clumsiness, that drew on thoughtless strength.

On a rough road, he flopped and swayed at the wheel as if he were on a bony horse that galloped a little sidewise. His skin was red-brown from the sun. He had pale blue eyes, edged with dark lashes. *She* used to say he "turned them on" her, as if they were lights. He was wearing his suit, brown-striped, and a fresh blue shirt, too big at the neck. But he looked well dressed. But he would have looked that way naked, too, for he communicated his physical essence through any covering. It was what spoke out from him to anyone who encountered him. Until Cleotha married him, it had given him a time, all right, he used to reflect.

Next to him in the front seat of the sedan was Buddy, their nine-year-old boy, who turned his head to stare at them both, his father and mother.

She was in back.

On the seat beside her was a wooden box, sandpapered, but not painted. Over it lay a baby's coverlet of pale yellow flannel with cross-stitched flowers down the middle in a band of bright colors. The mother didn't touch the box except when the car lurched or the tires danced over corrugated places in the gravel highway. Then she steadied it, and kept it from creeping on the seat cushions. In the box was coffined the body of their dead child, a two-year-old girl. They were on their way to Weed to bury it there.

In the other corner of the back seat sat Miss Latcher, the teacher. They rode in silence, and Miss Latcher breathed deeply of the spring day, as they all did, and she kept summoning to her aid the fruits of her learning. She felt this was a time to be intelligent, and not to give way to feelings.

The child was burned to death yesterday, playing behind the adobe chickenhouse at the edge of the arroyo out back, where the fence always caught the tumbleweeds. Yesterday, in a twist of wind, a few sparks from the kitchen chimney fell in the dry tumbleweeds and set them ablaze. Jodey had always meant to clear the weeds out; never seemed to get to it; told Cleotha he'd get to it next Saturday morning, before going down to Roswell; but Saturdays went by, and the wind and the sand drove the weeds into a barrier at the fence, and they would look at it every day without noticing, so habitual had the sight become. And so for many a spring morning, the little girl had played out there, behind the gray stucco house, whose adobe bricks showed through in one or two places.

The car had something loose; they believed it was the left rear fender; it chattered and wrangled over the gravel road.

Last night Cleotha stopped her weeping.

Today something happened; it came over her as they started out of
the ranch lane, which curved up towards the highway. She looked as if
she were trying to make the car go by leaning forward; or trying to see
something beyond the edge of Jodey's head and past the windshield.

Of course, she had sight in her eyes; she could not refuse to look at
the world. As the car drove up the valley that morning, she saw in two
ways — one, as she remembered the familiar sights of this region where
she lived; the other, as if for the first time she were really seeing, and not
simply looking. Her heart began to beat faster as they drove. It seemed
to knock at her breast as if to come forth and hurry ahead of her along
the sunlighted lanes of the life after today. She remembered thinking
that her head might be a little giddy, what with the sorrow in her eyes so
bright and slowly shining. But it didn't matter what did it. Ready never
to look at anyone or anything again, she kept still; and through the
window, which had a meandering crack in it like a river on a map, all
that she looked upon seemed dear to her. . . .

Jodey could only drive. He watched the road as if he expected it to
rise up and smite them all over into the canyon, where the trees twinkled and flashed with bright drops of light on their new varnished
leaves. Jodey watched the road and said to himself that if it thought it
could turn him over or make him scrape the rocks along the near side of
the hill they were going around, if it thought for one minute that he was
not master of this car, this road, this journey, why, it was just crazy. The
wheels spraying the gravel across the surface of the road travelled on
outward from his legs; his muscles were tight and felt tired as if he were
running instead of riding. He tried to *think,* but he could not; that is,
nothing came about that he would speak to her of, and he believed that
she sat there, leaning forward, waiting for him to say something to her.

But this he could not do, and he speeded up a little, and his jaw made
hard knots where he bit on his own rage; and he saw a lump of something coming in the road, and it aroused a positive passion in him. He
aimed directly for it, and charged it fast, and hit it. The car shuddered
and skidded, jolting them. Miss Latcher took a sharp breath inward,
and put out her hand to touch someone, but did not reach anyone.
Jodey looked for a second into the rear-view mirror above him, expecting something; but his wife was looking out of the window beside
her, and if he could believe his eyes, she was smiling, holding her mouth
with her fingers pinched up in a little claw.

The blood came up from under his shirt, he turned dark, and a sting
came across his eyes.

He couldn't explain why he had done a thing like that to her, as if it were she he was enraged with, instead of himself.

He wanted to stop the car and get out and go around to the back door on the other side, and open it, and take her hands, bring her out to stand before him in the road, and hang his arms around her until she would be locked upon him. This made a picture that he indulged like a dream, while the car ran on, and he made no change, but drove as before. . . .

The little boy, Buddy, regarded their faces, again, and again, as if to see in their eyes what had happened to them.

He felt the separateness of the three.

He was frightened by their appearance of indifference to each other. His father had a hot and drowsy look, as if he had just come out of bed. There was something in his father's face which made it impossible for Buddy to say anything. He turned around and looked at his mother, but she was gazing out the window, and did not see him; and until she should see him, he had no way of speaking to her, if not with his words, then with his eyes, but if she should happen to look at him, why, he would wait to see what she looked *like*, and if she *did*, why, then he would smile at her, because he loved her, but he would have to know first if she was still his mother, and if everything was all right, and things weren't blown to smithereens — *bla-a-a-sh! wh-o-o-m!* — the way the dynamite did when the highway came past their ranch house, and the men worked out there for months, and whole hillsides came down at a time. All summer long, that was, always something to see. The world, the family, he, between his father and mother, was safe.

He silently begged her to face towards him. There was no security until she should do so.

"Mumma?"

But he said it to himself, and she did not hear him this time, and it seemed intelligent to him to turn around, make a game of it (the way things often were worked out), and face the front, watch the road, delay as long as he possibly could bear to, and *then* turn around again, and *this* time, why, she would probably be looking at him all the time, and it would *be:* it would simply *be.*

So he obediently watched the road, the white gravel ribbon passing under their wheels as steadily as time.

He was a sturdy little boy, and there was a silver nap of child's dust on his face, over his plum-red cheeks. He smelled something like a raw potato that has just been pared. The sun crowned him with a ring of light on his dark hair. . . .

What Cleotha was afraid to do was break the spell by saying anything or looking at any of them. This was *vision*, it was all she could think; never had anything looked so in all her life; everything made her heart lift, when she had believed this morning, after the night, that it would never lift again. There wasn't anything to compare her grief to. She couldn't think of anything to answer the death of her tiny child with. In her first hours of hardly believing what had happened, she had felt her own flesh and tried to imagine how it would have been if she could have borne the fire instead of the child. But all she got out of that was a longing avowal to herself of how gladly she would have borne it. Jodey had lain beside her, and she clung to his hand until she heard how he breathed off to sleep. Then she had let him go, and had wept at what seemed faithless in him. She had wanted his mind beside her then. It seemed to her that the last degree of her grief was the compassion she had had to bestow upon him while he slept.

But she had found this resource within her, and from that time on, her weeping had stopped.

It was like a wedding of pride and duty within her. There was nothing she could not find within herself, if she had to, now, she believed.

And so this morning, getting on towards noon, as they rode up the valley, climbing all the way, until they would find the road to turn off on, which would take them higher and higher before they dropped down towards Weed on the other side, she welcomed the sights of that dusty trip. Even if she had spoken her vision aloud, it would not have made sense to the others.

Look at that orchard of peach trees, she thought. I never saw such color as this year; the trees are like lamps, with the light coming from within. It must be the sunlight shining from the other side, and, of course, the petals are very thin, like the loveliest silk; so any light that shines upon them will pierce right through them and glow on this side. But they are so bright! When I was a girl at home, up to Weed, I remember we had an orchard of peach trees, but the blossoms were always a deeper pink than down here in the valley.

My! I used to catch them up by the handful, and I believed when I was a girl that if I crushed them and tied them in a handkerchief and carried the handkerchief in my bosom, I would come to smell like peach blossoms and have the same high pink in my face, and the girls I knew said that if I took a peach *stone* and held it *long enough* in my hand, it would *sprout;* and I dreamed of this one time, though, of course, I knew it was nonsense; but that was how children thought and talked in those days — we all used to pretend that *nothing* was impossible, if you simply did it hard enough and long enough.

But nobody wanted to hold a peach stone in their hand until it *sprouted,* to find out, and we used to laugh about it, but I think we believed it. I think I believed it.

It seemed to me, in between my *sensible* thoughts, a thing that any woman could probably do. It seemed to me like a parable in the Bible. I could preach you a sermon about it this day.

I believe I see a tree down there in that next orchard which is dead; it has old black sprigs, and it looks twisted by rheumatism. There is one little shoot of leaves up on the top branch, and that is all. No, it is not dead, it is aged, it can no longer put forth blossoms in a swarm like pink butterflies; but there is that one little swarm of green leaves — it is just about the prettiest thing I've seen all day, and I thank God for it, for if there's anything I love, it is to see something growing. . . .

Miss Latcher had on her cloth gloves now, which she had taken from her blue cloth bag a little while back. The little winds that tracked through the moving car sought her out and chilled her nose, and the tips of her ears, and her long fingers, about which she had several times gone to visit various doctors. They had always told her not to worry, if her fingers seemed cold, and her hands moist. It was just a nervous condition, nothing to take very seriously; a good hand lotion might help the sensation, and in any case, some kind of digital exercise was a good thing — did she perhaps play the piano. It always seemed to her that doctors never *paid any attention* to her.

Her first name was Arleen, and she always considered this a very pretty name, prettier than Cleotha; and she believed that there was such a thing as an *Arleen look,* and if you wanted to know what it was, simply look at her. She had a long face, and pale hair; her skin was white, and her eyes were light blue. She was wonderfully clean, and used no cosmetics. She was a girl from "around here," but she had gone away to college, to study for her career, and what she had known as a child was displaced by what she had heard in classrooms. And she had to admit it: people *here* and *away* were not much alike. The men were different. She couldn't imagine marrying a rancher and "sacrificing" everything she had learned in college.

This poor little thing in the other corner of the car, for instance: she seemed dazed by what had happened to her — all she could do evidently was sit and stare out the window. And that man in front, simply driving, without a word. What did they have? What was their life like? They hardly had good clothes to drive to Roswell in, when they had to go to the doctor, or on some social errand.

But I must not think uncharitably, she reflected, and sat in an attitude of sustained sympathy, with her face composed in Arleenish interest and tact. The assumption of a proper aspect of grief and feeling produced the most curious effect within her, and by her attitude of concern she was suddenly reminded of the thing that always made her feel like weeping, though, of course, she never did, but when she stopped and *thought* —

Like that painting at college, in the long hallway leading from the Physical Education lecture hall to the stairway down to the girls' gym: an enormous picture depicting the Agony of the Christian Martyrs, in ancient Rome. There were some days when she simply couldn't look at it; and there were others when she would pause and see those maidens with their tearful faces raised in calm prowess, and in them, she would find herself — they were all Arleens; and after she would leave the picture she would proceed in her imagination to the arena, and there she would know with exquisite sorrow and pain the ordeals of two thousand years ago, instead of those of her own lifetime. She thought of the picture now, and traded its remote sorrows for those of today until she had sincerely forgotten the mother and the father and the little brother of the dead child with whom she was riding up the spring-turning valley, where noon was warming the dust that arose from the gravelled highway. It was white dust, and it settled over them in an enriching film, ever so finely. . . .

Jodey Powers had a fantastic scheme that he used to think about for taking and baling tumbleweed and making a salable fuel out of it. First, you'd compress it — probably down at the cotton compress in Roswell — where a loose bale was wheeled in under the great power-drop, and when the nigger at the handle gave her a yank, down came the weight, and packed the bale into a little thing, and then they let the steam exhaust go, and the press sighed once or twice, and just seemed to *lie* there, while the men ran wires through the gratings of the press and tied them tight. Then up came the weight, and out came the bale.

If he did that to enough bales of tumbleweed, he believed he'd get rich. Burn? It burned like a house afire. It had oil in it, somehow, and the thing to do was get it in shape for use as a fuel. Imagine all the tumbleweed that blew around the State of New Mexico in the fall, and sometimes all winter. In the winter, the weeds were black and brittle. They cracked when they blew against fence posts, and if one lodged there, then another one caught at its thorny lace; and next time it blew, and the sand came trailing, and the tumbleweeds rolled, they'd pile up at the same fence, and build out, locked together against the wires. The wind drew through them, and the sand dropped around them. Soon there was a solid-looking but airy bank of tumbleweeds built right to the top of the fence, in a long windward slope; and the next time the wind blew, and the weeds came, they would roll up the little hill of brittle twigs and leap off the other side of the fence, for all the world like horses taking a jump, and go galloping ahead of the wind across the next pasture on the plains, a black and witchy procession.

If there was an arroyo, they gathered there. They backed up in the miniature canyons of dirt-walled watercourses, which were dry except when it rained hard up in the hills. Out behind the house, the arroyo had filled up with tumbleweeds; and in November, when it blew so hard and so cold, but without bringing any snow, some of the tumbleweeds had climbed out and scattered, and a few had tangled at the back fence, looking like rusted barbed wire. Then there came a few more; all winter the bank grew. Many times he'd planned to get out back there and clear them away, just e-e-ease them off away from the fence posts, so's not to catch the wood up, and then set a match to the whole thing, and in five minutes, have it all cleared off. If he did like one thing, it was a neat place.

How Cleotha laughed at him sometimes when he said that, because she knew that as likely as not he would forget to clear the weeds away. And if he'd said it once he'd said it a thousand times, that he was going to gather up that pile of scrap iron from the front yard, and haul it to Roswell, and sell it — old car parts, and the fenders off a truck that had turned over up on the highway, which he'd salvaged with the aid of the driver.

But the rusting iron was still there, and he had actually come to have a feeling of fondness for it. If someone were to appear one night and silently make off with it, he'd be aroused the next day, and demand to know who had robbed him; for it was dear junk, just through lying around and belonging to him. What was his was part of him, even that heap of fenders that rubbed off on your clothes with a rusty powder, like caterpillar fur.

But even by thinking hard about all such matters, treading upon the fringe of what had happened yesterday, he was unable to make it all seem long ago, and a matter of custom and even of indifference. There was no getting away from it — if anybody was to blame for the terrible moments of yesterday afternoon, when the wind scattered a few sparks from the chimney of the kitchen stove, why he was.

Jodey Powers never claimed to himself or anybody else that he was any *better* man than another. But everything he knew and hoped for, every reassurance his body had had from other people, and the children he had begotten, had been knowledge to him that he was *as good* a man as any.

And of this knowledge he was now bereft.

If he had been alone in his barrenness, he could have solaced himself with heroic stupidities. He could have produced out of himself abominations, with the amplitude of Biblical despair. But he wasn't alone; there they sat; there was Buddy beside him, and Clee in back, even the teacher, Arleen — even to her he owed some return of courage.

All he could do was drive the damned car, and keep *thinking* about it.

He wished he could think of something to say, or else that Clee would.

But they continued in silence, and he believed that it was one of his making. . . .

The reverie of Arleen Latcher made her almost ill, from the sad, sweet experiences she had entered into with those people so long ago. How wonderful it was to have such a rich life, just looking up things! — And the most wonderful thing of all was that even if they were beautiful, and wore semitransparent garments that fell to the ground in graceful folds, the maidens were all pure. It made her eyes swim to think how innocent they went to their death. Could anything be more beautiful, and reassuring, than this? Far, far better. Far better those hungry lions, than the touch of lustful men. Her breath left her for a moment, and she closed her eyes, and what threatened her with real feeling — the presence of the Powers family in the faded blue sedan climbing through the valley sunlight towards the turn-off that led to the mountain road — was gone. Life's breath on her cheek was not so close. Oh, others had suffered. She could suffer.

"All that pass by clap their hands at thee: they hiss and wag their heads at the daughter of Jerusalem — "

This image made her wince, as if she herself had been hissed and wagged at. Everything she knew made it possible for her to see herself as a proud and threatened virgin of Bible times, which were more real to her than many of the years she had lived through. Yet must not Jerusalem have sat in country like this with its sandy hills, the frosty stars that were so bright at night, the simple Mexicans riding their burros as if to the Holy Gates? We often do not see our very selves, she would reflect, gazing ardently at the unreal creature which the name Arleen brought to life in her mind.

On her cheeks there had appeared two islands of color, as if she had a fever. What she strove to save by her anguished retreats into the memories of the last days of the Roman Empire was surely crumbling away from her. She said to herself that she must not give way to it, and that she was just wrought up; the fact was she really *didn't* feel anything — in fact, it was a pity that she *couldn't* take that little Mrs. Powers in her arms, and comfort her, just *let* her go ahead and cry, and see if it wouldn't probably help some. But Miss Latcher was aware that she felt nothing that related to the Powers family and their trouble.

Anxiously she searched her heart again, and wooed back the sacrifice of the tribe of heavenly Arleens marching so certainly towards the lions. But they did not answer her call to mind, and she folded her cloth-gloved hands and pressed them together, and begged of herself that she might think of some way to comfort Mrs. Powers; for if she could do that, it might fill her own empty heart until it became a cup that would run over. . . .

Cleotha knew Buddy wanted her to see him; but though her heart turned towards him, as it always must, no matter what he asked of her, she was this time afraid to do it because if she ever lost the serenity of her sight now she might never recover it this day; and the heaviest trouble was still before her.

So she contented herself with Buddy's look as it reached her from the side of her eye. She glimpsed his head and neck, like a young cat's, the wide bones behind the ears, and the smooth but visible cords of his nape, a sight of him that always made her want to laugh because it was so pathetic. When she caressed him she often fondled those strenuous hollows behind his ears. Heaven only knew, she would think, what went on within the shell of that topknot! She would pray between her words and feelings that those unseen thoughts in the boy's head were ones that would never trouble him. She was often amazed at things in him which she recognized as being like herself; and at those of Buddy's qualities which came from some alien source, she suffered pangs of doubt and fear. He was so young to be a stranger to her!

The car went around the curve that hugged the rocky fall of a hill; and on the other side of it, a green quilt of alfalfa lay sparkling darkly in the light. Beyond that, to the right of the road, the land levelled out, and on a sort of platform of swept earth stood a two-room hut of adobe. It had a few stones cemented against the near corner, to give it strength. Clee had seen it a hundred times — the place where that old man Melendez lived, and where his wife had died a few years ago. He was said to be simple-minded, and claimed he was a hundred years old. In the past, riding by here, she had more or less delicately made a point of looking the other way. It often distressed her to think of such a helpless old man, too feeble to do anything but crawl out when the sun was bright and the wall was warm, and sit there, with his milky gaze resting on the hills he had known since he was born, and had never left. Somebody came to feed him once a day, and see if he was clean enough to keep his health. As long as she could remember, there'd been some kind of dog at the house. The old man had sons and grandsons and great-grandsons — you might say a whole orchard of them, sprung from this one tree that was dying, but that still held a handful of green days in its ancient veins.

Before the car had quite gone by, she had seen him. The sun *was* bright, and the wall must have been warm, warm enough to give his shoulders and back a reflection of the heat which was all he could feel. He sat there on his weathered board bench, his hands on his branch of apple tree that was smooth and shiny from use as a cane. His house door was open, and a deep tunnel of shade lay within the sagged box of the opening. Cleotha leaned forward to see him, as if to look at him were one of her duties today. She saw his jaw moving up and down, not chewing, but just opening and closing. In the wind and flash of the car going by, she could not hear him; but from his closed eyes, and his moving mouth, and the way his head was raised, she wouldn't have been surprised if she had heard him singing. He was singing, some thread of song, and it made her smile to imagine what kind of noise it made, a wisp of voice.

She was perplexed by a feeling of joyful fullness in her breast, at the sight of the very same old witless sire from whom in the past she had turned away her eyes out of delicacy and disgust.

The last thing she saw as they went by was his dog, who came around the corner of the house with a caracole. He was a mongrel puppy, partly hound — a comedian by nature. He came prancing outrageously up to the old man's knees, and invited his response, which he did not get. But as if his master were as great a wag as he, he hurled himself backward, pretending to throw himself recklessly into pieces. Everything on him flopped and was flung by his idiotic energy. It was easy to imagine, watching the puppy-fool, that the sunlight had entered him as it had entered the old man. Cleotha was reached by the hilarity of the hound, and when he tripped over himself and plowed the ground with his flapping jowls, she wanted to laugh out loud.

But they were past the place, and she winked back the merriment in her eyes, and she knew that it was something she could never have told the others about. What it stood for, in her, they would come to know in other ways, as she loved them. . . .

Jodey was glad of one thing. He had telephoned from Hondo last night, and everything was to be ready at Weed. They would rive right up the hill to the family burial ground. They wouldn't have to wait for anything. He was glad, too, that the wind wasn't blowing. It always made his heart sink when the wind rose on the plains and began to change the sky with the color of dust.

Yesterday: it was all he could see, however hard he was *thinking* about everything else.

He'd been on his horse, coming back down the pasture that rose up behind the house across the arroyo, nothing particular in mind — except to make a joke with himself about how far along the peaches would get before the frost killed them all, *snap*, in a single night, like that — when he saw the column of smoke rising from the tumbleweeds by the fence. Now who could've lighted them, he reflected, following the black smoke up on its billows into the sky. There was just enough wind idling across the long front of the hill to bend the smoke and trail it away at an angle, towards the blue.

The hillside, the fire, the wind, the column of smoke.

Oh by God! And the next minute he was tearing down the hill as fast as his horse could take him, and the fire — he could see the flames now — the fire was like a bank of yellow rags blowing violently and torn in the air, rag after rag tearing up from the ground. Cleotha was there, and in a moment, so was he, but they were too late. The baby was unconscious. They took her up and hurried to the house, the back way where the screen door was standing open with its spring trailing on the ground. When they got inside where it seemed so dark and cool, they held the child between them, fearing to lay her down. They called for Buddy, but he was still at school up the road, and would not be home until the orange school bus stopped by their mailbox out front at the highway after four o'clock. The fire poured in cracking tumult through the weeds. In ten minutes there were only little airy lifts of ash off the ground. Everything was black. There were three fence posts still afire; the wires were hot. The child was dead. They let her down on their large bed.

He could remember every word Clee had said to him. They were not many, and they shamed him, in his heart, because he couldn't say a thing. He comforted her, and held her while she wept. But if he had spoken then, or now, riding in the car, all he could have talked about was the image of the blowing rags of yellow fire, and blue, blue, plaster blue behind and above, sky and mountains. But he believed that she knew why he seemed so short with her. He hoped earnestly that she knew. He might just be wrong. She might be blaming him, and keeping so still because it was more proper, now, to *be* still than full of reproaches.

But of the future, he was entirely uncertain; and he drove, and came to the turn-off, and they started winding in back among the sandhills that lifted them towards the rocky slopes of the mountains. Up and up they went; the air was so clear and thin that they felt transported, and across the valleys that dripped between the grand shoulders of the pine-haired slopes, the air looked as if it were blue breath from the trees. . . .

Cleotha was blinded by a dazzling light in the distance, ahead of them, on the road.

It was a ball of diamond-brilliant light.

It danced, and shook, and quivered above the road far, far ahead. It seemed to be travelling between the pine trees on either side of the road, and somewhat above the road, and it was like nothing she had ever seen before. It was the most magic and exquisite thing she had ever seen, and wildly, even hopefully as a child is hopeful when there is a chance and a need for something miraculous to happen, she tried to explain it to herself. It could be a star in daytime, shaking and quivering and travelling ahead of them, as if to lead them. It was their guide. It was shaped like a small cloud, but it was made of shine, and dazzle, and quiver. She held her breath for fear it should vanish, but it did not, and she wondered if the others in the car were smitten with the glory of it as she was.

It was brighter than the sun, whiter; it challenged the daytime, and obscured everything near it by its blaze of flashing and dancing light.

It was almost as if she had approached perfect innocence through her misery, and were enabled to receive portents that might not be visible to anyone else. She closed her eyes for a moment.

But the road curved, and everything travelling on it took the curve too, and the trembling pool of diamond-light ahead lost its liquid splendor, and turned into the tin signs on the back of a huge oil truck which was toiling over the mountain, trailing its links of chain behind.

When Clee looked again, the star above the road was gone. The road and the angle of the sun to the mountain-top and the two cars climbing upward had lost their harmony to produce the miracle. She saw the red oil truck, and simply saw it, and said to herself that the sun might have reflected off the big tin signs on the back of it. But she didn't believe it, for she was not thinking, but rather dreaming; fearful of awakening. . . .

The high climb up this drive always made Miss Latcher's ears pop, and she had discovered once that to swallow often prevented the disagreeable sensation. So she swallowed. Nothing happened to her ears. But she continued to swallow, and feel her ears with her cloth-covered fingers, but what really troubled her now would not be downed, and it came into her mouth as a taste; she felt giddy — that was the altitude, of course — when they got down the other side, she would be all right.

What it was was perfectly clear to her, for that was part of having an education and a trained mind — the processes of thought often went right on once you started them going.

Below the facts of this small family, in the worst trouble it had ever known, lay the fact of envy in Arleen's breast.

It made her head swim to realize this. But she envied them their entanglement with one another, and the dues they paid each other in the humility of the duty they were performing on this ride, to the family burial ground at Weed. Here she sat riding with them, to come along and be of help to them, and she was no help. She was unable to swallow the lump of desire that rose in her throat, for life's uses, even such bitter ones as that of the Powers family today. It had been filling her gradually, all the way over on the trip, this feeling of jealousy and degradation.

Now it choked her, and she knew she had tried too hard to put from her the thing that threatened her, which was the touch of life through anybody else. She said to herself that she must keep control of herself.

But Buddy turned around again, just then, slowly, as if he were a young male cat who just happened to be turning around to see what he could see, and he looked at his mother with his large eyes, so like his father's: pale petal-blue, with drops of light like the centres of cat's eyes, and dark lashes. He had a solemn look, when he saw his mother's face, and he prayed her silently to acknowledge him. If she didn't, why, he was still alone. He would never again feel safe about running off to the highway to watch the scrapers work, or the huge Diesel oil tankers go by, or the cars with strange license plates — of which he had already counted thirty-two different kinds, his collection, as he called it. So if she didn't see him, why, what might he find when he came back home at times like those, when he went off for a little while just to play?

They were climbing down the other side of the ridge now. In a few minutes they would be riding into Weed. The sights as they approached were like images of awakening to Cleotha. Her heart began to hurt when she saw them. She recognized the tall iron smokestack of the sawmill. It showed above the trees down on the slope ahead of them. There was a stone house which had been abandoned even when she was a girl at home here, and its windows and doors standing open always seemed to her to depict a face with an expression of dismay. The car dropped farther down — they were making that last long curve of the road to the left — and now the town stood visible, with the sunlight resting on so many of the unpainted houses and turning their weathered gray to a dark silver. Surely they must be ready for them, these houses; all had been talked over by now. They could all mention that they knew Cleotha as a little girl.

She lifted her head.

There were claims upon her.

Buddy was looking at her soberly, trying to predict to himself how she would *be*. He was ready to echo with his own small face whatever her face would show him.

Miss Latcher was watching the two of them. Her heart was racing in her breast.

The car slowed up. Now Cleotha could not look out the windows at the wandering earthen street, and the places alongside it. They would have to drive right through town, to the hillside on the other side.

"Mumma?" asked the boy softly.

Cleotha winked both her eyes at him, and smiled, and leaned towards him a trifle.

And then he blushed, his eyes swam with happiness, and he smiled back at her, and his face poured forth such radiance that Miss Latcher took one look at him, and with a choke, burst into tears.

She wept into her hands, her gloves were moistened, her square shoulders rose to her ears, and she was overwhelmed by what the mother had been able to do for the boy. She shook her head and made long gasping sobs. Her sense of betrayal was not lessened by the awareness that she was weeping for herself.

Cleotha leaned across to her, and took her hand, and murmured to her. She comforted her, gently.

"Hush, honey, you'll be all right. Don't you cry, now. Don't you think about us. We're almost there, and it'll soon be over. God knows you were mighty sweet to come along and be with us. Hush, now, Arleen, you'll have Buddy crying, too."

But the boy was simply watching the teacher, in whom the person he knew so well every day in school had broken up, leaving an unfamiliar likeness. It was like seeing a reflection in a pond, and then throwing a stone in. The reflection disappeared in ripples of something else.

Arleen could not stop.

The sound of her 'hooping made Jodey furious. He looked into the rear-view mirror and saw his wife patting her and comforting her. Cleotha looked so white and strained that he was frightened, and he said out, without turning around: "Arleen, you cut that out, you shut up, now. I won't have you wearin' down Clee, God damn it, you quit it!"

But this rage, which arose from a sense of justice, made Arleen feel guiltier than ever; and she laid her head against the car window, and her sobs drummed her brow bitterly on the glass.

"Hush," whispered Cleotha, but she could do no more, for they were arriving at the hillside, and the car was coming to a stop. They must awaken from this journey, and come out onto the ground, and begin to toil their way up the yellow hill, where the people were waiting. Over the ground grew yellow grass that was turning to green. It was like velvet, showing dark or light, according to the breeze and the golden afternoon sunlight. It was a generous hill, curving easily and grandly as it rose. Beyond it was only the sky, for the mountains faced it from behind the road. It was called Schoolhouse Hill, and at one time, the whole thing had belonged to Cleotha's father; and before there was any schoolhouse crowning its noble swell of earth, the departed members of his family had been buried halfway up the gentle climb.

Jodey helped her out of the car, and he tried to talk to her with his holding fingers. He felt her trembling, and she shook her head at him. Then she began to walk up there, slowly. He leaned into the car and took the covered box in his arms, and followed her. Miss Latcher was out of the car on her side, hiding from them, her back turned, while she used her handkerchief and positively clenched herself back into control of her thoughts and sobs. When she saw that they weren't waiting for her, she hurried, and in humility, reached for Buddy's hand to hold it for him as they walked. He let her have it, and he marched, watching his father, whose hair was blowing in the wind and sunshine. From behind, Jodey looked like just a kid. . . .

And now for Cleotha, her visions on the journey appeared to have some value, and for a little while longer, when she needed it most, the sense of being in blind communion with life was granted her, at the little graveside where all those kind friends were gathered, on the slow slope up of the hill on the summit of which was the schoolhouse of her girlhood.

It was afternoon, and they were all kneeling towards the upward rise, and Judge Crittenden was reading the prayer book.

Everything left them but a sense of their worship, in the present.

And a boy, a late scholar, is coming down the hill from the school, the sunlight edging him; and his wonder at what the people kneeling there are doing is, to Cleotha, the most memorable thing she is to look upon today; for she has resumed the life of her infant daughter, whom they are burying, and on whose behalf, something rejoices in life anyway, as if to ask the mother whether love itself is not ever-living. And she watches the boy come discreetly down the hill, trying to keep away from them, but large-eyed with a hunger *to know* which claims all acts of life, for him, and for those who will be with him later; and his respectful curiosity about those kneeling mourners, the edge of sunlight along him as he walks away from the sun and down the hill, is of all those things she saw and rejoiced in, the most beautiful; and at that, her breast is full, with the heaviness of a baby at it, and not for grief alone, but for praise.

"I believe, I believe!" her heart cries out in her, as if she were holding the peach stone of her eager girlhood in her woman's hand.

She puts her face into her hands, and weeps, and they all move closer to her. Familiar as it is, the spirit has had a new discovery. . . .

Jodey then felt that she had returned to them all; and he stopped seeing, and just remembered, what happened yesterday; and his love for his wife was confirmed as something he would never be able to measure for himself or prove to her in words.

1944

## Vladimir Nabokov

..........................................................................................................

# "That in Aleppo Once . . ."

FROM *The Atlantic Monthly*

DEAR V. — Among other things, this is to tell you that at last I am here, in the country whither so many sunsets have led. One of the first persons I saw was our good old Gleb Alexandrovich Gekko gloomily crossing Columbus Avenue in quest of the *petit café du coin* which none of us three will ever visit again. He seemed to think that somehow or other you were betraying our national literature, and he gave me your address with a deprecatory shake of his gray head, as if you did not deserve the treat of hearing from me.

I have a story for you. Which reminds me — I mean putting it like this reminds me — of the days when we wrote our first udder-warm bubbling verse, and all things, a rose, a puddle, a lighted window, cried out to us: "I'm a rhyme!" Yes, this is a most useful universe. We play, we die: *ig-rhyme, umi-rhyme.* And the sonorous souls of Russian verbs lend a meaning to the wild gesticulation of trees or to some discarded newspaper sliding and pausing, and shuffling again, with abortive flaps and apterous jerks along an endless windswept embankment. But just now I am not a poet. I come to you like that gushing lady in Chekhov who was dying to be described.

I married, let me see, about a month after you left France, and a few weeks before the gentle Germans roared into Paris. Although I can produce documentary proofs of matrimony, I am positive now that my wife never existed. You may know her name from some other source, but that does not matter: it is the name of an illusion. Therefore, I am able to speak of her with as much detachment as I would of a character in a story (one of your stories, to be precise).

It was love at first touch rather than at first sight, for I had met her several times before without experiencing any special emotions; but one night as I was seeing her home, something quaint she had said made me stoop with a laugh and lightly kiss her on the hair — and of course we all know of that blinding blast which is caused by merely picking up a small doll from the floor of a carefully abandoned house: the soldier involved hears nothing; for him it is but an ecstatic soundless and boundless expansion of what had been during his life a pinpoint of light in the dark center of his being. And really, the reason we think of death in celestial terms is that the visible firmament, especially at night (above our blacked-out Paris with the gaunt arches of its Boulevard Exelmans and the ceaseless Alpine gurgle of desolate latrines), is the most adequate and ever-present symbol of that vast silent explosion.

But I cannot discern her. She remains as nebulous as my best poem — the one you made such gruesome fun of in the *Literaturnye Zapiski*. When I want to imagine her I have to cling mentally to a tiny brown birthmark on her downy forearm, as one concentrates upon a punctuation mark in an illegible sentence. Perhaps, had she used a greater amount of make-up, or used it more constantly, I might have visualized her face today, or at least the delicate transverse furrows of dry, hot rouged lips; but I fail, I fail — although I still feel their elusive touch now and then in the blindman's buff of my senses, in that sobbing sort of dream when she and I clumsily clutch at each other through a heartbreaking mist, and I cannot see the color of her eyes for the blank luster of brimming tears drowning their irises.

She was much younger than I — not as much younger as was Nathalie of the lovely bare shoulders and long earrings in relation to swarthy Pushkin; but still there was a sufficient margin for that kind of retrospective romanticism which finds pleasure in imitating the destiny of a unique genius (down to the jealousy, down to the filth, down to the stab of seeing her almond-shaped eyes turn to her blond Cassio behind her peacock-feathered fan) even if one cannot imitate his verse. She liked mine, though, and would scarcely have yawned as the other was wont to do every time her husband's poem happened to exceed the length of a sonnet. If she has remained a phantom to me, I may have been one to her: I suppose she had been solely attracted by the obscurity of my poetry; then tore a hole through its veil and saw a stranger's unlovable face.

As you know, I had been for some time planning to follow the example of your fortunate flight. She described to me an uncle of hers who lived, she said, in New York: he had taught riding at a Southern college, and had wound up by marrying a wealthy American woman;

they had a little daughter born deaf. She said she had lost their address long ago, but a few days later it miraculously turned up, and we wrote a dramatic letter to which we never received any reply. This did not much matter, as I had already obtained a sound affidavit from Professor Lomchenko of Chicago; but little else had been done in the way of getting the necessary papers when the invasion began, whereas I foresaw that, if we stayed on in Paris, some helpful compatriot of mine would sooner or later point out to the interested party sundry passages in one of my books where I argued that, with all her many black sins, Germany was still bound to remain forever and ever the laughingstock of the world.

So we started upon our disastrous honeymoon. Crushed and jolted amid the apocalyptic exodus, waiting for unscheduled trains that were bound for unknown destinations, walking through the stale stage-setting of abstract towns, living in a permanent twilight of physical exhaustion, we fled; and the farther we fled, the clearer it became that what was driving us on was something more than a booted and buckled fool with his assortment of variously propelled junk — something of which he was a mere symbol, something monstrous and impalpable, a timeless and faceless mass of immemorial horror that still keeps coming at me from behind even here, in the green vacuum of Central Park.

Oh, she bore it gamely enough — with a kind of dazed cheerfulness. Once however, quite suddenly, she started to sob in a sympathetic railway carriage. "The dog," she said, "the dog we left. I cannot forget the poor dog." The honesty of her grief shocked me, as we had never had any dog. "I know," she said, "but I tried to imagine we had actually bought that setter. And just think, he would be now whining behind a locked door." There had never been any talk of buying a setter.

I should also not like to forget a certain stretch of highroad and the sight of a family of refugees (two women, a child) whose old father, or grandfather, had died on the way. The sky was a chaos of black and flesh-colored clouds with an ugly sunburst beyond a hooded hill, and the dead man was lying on his back under a dusty plane tree. With a stick and their hands the women had tried to dig a roadside grave, but the soil was too hard; they had given it up and were sitting side by side, among the anemic poppies, a little apart from the corpse and its upturned beard. But the little boy was still scratching and scraping and tugging until he tumbled a flat stone and forgot the object of his solemn exertions as he crouched on his haunches, his thin, eloquent neck showing all its vertebrae to the headsman, and watched with surprise and delight thousands of minute brown ants seething, zigzagging, dispersing, heading for places of safety in the Gard, and the Aude, and the Drome, and the Var, and the Basses-Pyrénées — we two paused only in Pau.

Spain proved too difficult and we decided to move on to Nice. At a place called Faugères (a ten-minute stop) I squeezed out of the train to buy some food. When a couple of minutes later I came back, the train was gone, and the muddled old man responsible for the atrocious void that faced me (coal dust glittering in the heat between naked indifferent rails, and a lone piece of orange peel) brutally told me that, anyway, I had had no right to get out.

In a better world I could have had my wife located and told what to do (I had both tickets and most of the money); as it was, my nightmare struggle with the telephone proved futile, so I dismissed the whole series of diminutive voices barking at me from afar, sent two or three telegrams which are probably on their way only now, and late in the evening took the next local to Montpellier, farther than which her train would not stumble. Not finding her there, I had to choose between two alternatives: going on because she might have boarded the Marseilles train which I had just missed, or going back because she might have returned to Faugères. I forget now what tangle of reasoning led me to Marseilles and Nice.

Beyond such routine action as forwarding false data to a few unlikely places, the police did nothing to help: one man bellowed at me for being a nuisance; another sidetracked the question by doubting the authenticity of my marriage certificate because it was stamped on what he contended to be the wrong side; a third, a fat *commissaire* with liquid brown eyes, confessed that he wrote poetry in his spare time. I looked up various acquaintances among the numerous Russians domiciled or stranded in Nice. I heard those among them who chanced to have Jewish blood talk of their doomed kinsmen crammed into hell-bound trains; and my own plight, by contrast, acquired a commonplace air of irreality while I sat in some crowded café with the milky blue sea in front of me and a shell-hollow murmur behind telling and retelling the tale of massacre and misery, and the gray paradise beyond the ocean, and the ways and whims of harsh consuls.

A week after my arrival an indolent plain-clothes man called upon me and took me down a crooked and smelly street to a black-stained house with the word "hotel" almost erased by dirt and time; there, he said, my wife had been found. The girl he produced was an absolute stranger, of course, but my friend Holmes kept on trying for some time to make her and me confess we were married, while her taciturn and muscular bedfellow stood by and listened, his bare arms crossed on his striped chest.

When at length I got rid of those people and had wandered back to my neighborhood, I happened to pass by a compact queue waiting at the entrance of a food store, and there, at the very end, was my wife, straining on tiptoe to catch a glimpse of what exactly was being sold. I think the first thing she said to me was that she hoped it was oranges.

Her tale seemed a trifle hazy, but perfectly banal. She had returned to Faugères and gone straight to the Commissariat instead of making inquiries at the station, where I had left a message for her. A party of refugees suggested that she join them; she spent the night in a bicycle shop with no bicycles, on the floor, together with three elderly women who lay, she said, like three logs in a row. Next day she realized that she had not enough money to reach Nice. Eventually she borrowed some from one of the log-women. She got into the wrong train, however, and traveled to a town the name of which she could not remember. She had arrived at Nice two days ago and had found some friends at the Russian church. They had told her I was somewhere around, looking for her, and would surely turn up soon.

Some time later, as I sat on the edge of the only chair in my garret and held her by her slender young hips (she was combing her soft hair and tossing her head back with every stroke), her dim smile changed all at once into an odd quiver and she placed one hand on my shoulder, staring down at me as if I were a reflection in a pool, which she had noticed for the first time.

"I've been lying to you, dear," she said. "*Ya lgunia.* I stayed for several nights in Montpellier with a brute of a man I met on the train. I did not want it at all. He sold hair lotions."

*The time, the place, the torture. Her fan, her gloves, her mask.* I spent that night and many others getting it out of her bit by bit, but not getting it all. I was under the strange delusion that first I must find out every detail, reconstruct every minute, and only then decide whether I could bear it. But the limit of desired knowledge was unattainable, nor could I ever foretell the approximate point after which I might imagine myself satiated, because of course the denominator of every fraction of knowledge was potentially as infinite as the number of intervals between the fractions themselves.

Oh, the first time she had been too tired to mind, and the next had not minded because she was sure I had deserted her; and she apparently considered that such explanations ought to be a kind of consolation prize for me instead of the nonsense and agony they really were. It went on like that for eons, she breaking down every now and then, but soon rallying again, answering my unprintable questions in a breathless whisper or trying with a pitiful smile to wriggle into the semi-security of irrelevant commentaries, and I crushing and crushing the mad molar till my jaw almost burst with pain, a flaming pain which seemed somehow preferable to the dull, humming ache of humble endurance.

And mark, in between the periods of this inquest we were trying to get from reluctant authorities certain papers on the strength of which one might hope to obtain other papers which in their turn would make it lawful to apply for a third kind which would serve as a steppingstone towards a permit enabling the holder to apply for the other papers which might or might not give him the means of discovering how and why it had happened. For even if I could imagine the accursed recurrent scene, I failed to link up its sharp-angled grotesque shadows with the dim limbs of my wife as she shook and rattled and dissolved in my violent grasp.

So nothing remained but to torture each other, to wait for hours on end in the Prefecture, filling forms, conferring with friends who had already probed the innermost viscera of all visas, pleading with secretaries, and filling forms again, with the result that her lusty and versatile traveling salesman became blended in a ghastly mix-up with rat-whiskered snarling officials, rotting bundles of obsolete records, the reek of violet ink, bribes slipped under gangrenous blotting paper, fat flies tickling moist necks with their rapid cold padded feet, new-laid clumsy concave photographs of your six subhuman doubles, the tragic eyes and patient politeness of petitionaries born in Slutzk, Starodub, or Bobruisk, the funnels and pulleys of the Holy Inquisition, the awful smile of the bald man with the glasses, who had been told that his passport could not be found.

I confess that one evening, after a particularly abominable day, I sank down on a stone bench weeping and cursing a mock world where millions of lives were being juggled by the clammy hands of consuls and *commissaires*. I noticed she was crying too, and then I told her that nothing would really have mattered the way it mattered now, had she not gone and done what she did.

"You will think me crazy," she said with a vehemence that, for a second, almost made a real person of her, "but I didn't — I swear that I didn't. Perhaps I live several lives at once. Perhaps I wanted to test you. Perhaps this bench is a dream and we are in Saratov or on some star."

It would be tedious to niggle the different stages through which I passed before accepting finally the first version of her delay. I did not talk to her and was a good deal alone. She would glimmer and fade, and reappear with some trifle she thought I would appreciate — a handful of cherries, three precious cigarettes, or the like — treating me with the unruffled mute sweetness of a nurse that trips from and to a gruff convalescent. I ceased visiting most of our mutual friends because they had lost all interest in my passport affairs and seemed to have turned vaguely inimical. I composed several poems. I drank all the wine I could get. I clasped her one day to my groaning breast, and we went for a week to Caboule and lay on the round pink pebbles of the narrow beach. Strange to say, the happier our new relations seemed, the stronger I felt an undercurrent of poignant sadness, but I kept telling myself that this was an intrinsic feature of all true bliss.

In the meantime, something had shifted in the moving pattern of our fates and at last I emerged from a dark and hot office with a couple of plump *visas de sortie* cupped in my trembling hands. Into these the U.S.A. serum was duly injected, and I dashed to Marseilles and managed to get tickets for the very next boat. I returned and tramped up the stairs. I saw a rose in a glass on the table — the sugar-pink of its obvious beauty, the parasitic air bubbles clinging to its stem. Her two spare dresses were gone, her comb was gone, her checkered coat was gone, and so was the mauve hair-band with a mauve bow that had been her hat. There was no note pinned to the pillow, nothing at all in the room to enlighten me, for of course the rose was merely what French rhymsters call *une cheville*.

I went to the Veretennikovs, who could tell me nothing; to the Hellmans, who refused to say anything; and to the Elaguins, who were not sure whether to tell me or not. Finally, the old lady — and you know what Anna Vladimirovna is like at crucial moments — asked for her rubber-tipped cane, heavily but energetically dislodged her bulk from her favorite armchair, and took me into the garden. There she informed me that, being twice my age, she had the right to say I was a bully and a cad.

You must imagine the scene: the tiny graveled garden with its blue Arabian Nights jar and solitary cypress; the cracked terrace where the old lady's father had dozed with a rug on his knees when he retired from his Novgorod governorship to spend a few last evenings in Nice; the pale-green sky; a whiff of vanilla in the deepening dusk; the crickets emitting their metallic trill pitched at two octaves above middle C; and Anna Vladimirovna, the folds of her cheeks jerkily dangling as she flung at me a motherly but quite undeserved insult.

During several preceding weeks, my dear V., every time she had visited by herself the three or four families we both knew, my ghostly wife had filled the eager ears of all those kind people with an extraordinary story. To wit: that she had madly fallen in love with a young Frenchman who could give her a turreted home and a crested name; that she had implored me for a divorce and I had refused; that, in fact, I had said I would rather shoot her and myself than sail to New York alone; that she had said her father in a similar case had acted like a gentleman; that I had answered I did not give a hoot for her *cocu de père*.

There were loads of other preposterous details of that kind — but they all hung together in such a remarkable fashion that no wonder the old lady made me swear I would not seek to pursue the lovers with a cocked pistol. They had gone, she said, to a chateau in Lozère. I inquired whether she had ever set eyes upon the man. No, but she had been shown his picture. As I was about to leave, Anna Vladimirovna, who had slightly relaxed and had even given me her five fat fingers to kiss, suddenly flared up again, struck the gravel with her cane, and said in her deep strong voice: "But one thing I shall never forgive you — her dog, that poor beast which you hanged with your own hands before leaving Paris."

Whether the gentleman of leisure had changed into a traveling salesman, or whether the metamorphosis had been reversed, or whether again he was neither the one nor the other, but the nondescript Russian who had courted her before our marriage — all this was absolutely unessential. She had gone. That was the end. I should have been a fool had I begun the nightmare business of searching and waiting for her all over again.

On the fourth morning of a long and dismal sea voyage, I met on the deck a solemn but pleasant old doctor with whom I had played chess in

Paris. He asked me whether my wife was very much incommoded by the rough seas. I answered that I had sailed alone; whereupon he looked taken aback and then said he had seen her a couple of days before going on board, namely in Marseilles, walking, rather aimlessly he thought, along the embankment. She said that I would presently join her with bag and tickets.

This is, I gather, the point of the whole story — although if you write it, you had better not make him a doctor, as that kind of thing has been overdone. It was at that moment that I suddenly knew for certain that she had never existed at all. I shall tell you another thing. When I arrived I hastened to satisfy a certain morbid curiosity: I went to the address she had given me once; it proved to be an anonymous gap between two office buildings; I looked for her uncle's name in the directory; it was not there; I made some inquiries, and Gekko, who knows everything, informed me that the man and his horsy wife existed all right, but had moved to San Francisco after their deaf little girl had died.

Viewing the past graphically, I see our mangled romance engulfed in a deep valley of mist between the crags of two matter-of-fact mountains: life had been real before, life will be real from now on, I hope. Not tomorrow, though. Perhaps after tomorrow. You, happy mortal, with your lovely family (how is Inès? how are the twins?) and your diversified work (how are the lichens?), can hardly be expected to puzzle out my misfortune in terms of human communion, but you may clarify things for me through the prism of your art.

*Yet the pity of it.* Curse your art, I am hideously unhappy. She keeps on walking to and fro where the brown nets are spread to dry on the hot stone slabs and the dappled light of the water plays on the side of a moored fishing boat. Somewhere, somehow, I have made some fatal mistake. There are tiny pale bits of broken fish scales glistening here and there in the brown meshes. It may all end in *Aleppo* if I am not careful. Spare me, V.: you would load your dice with an unbearable implication if you took that for a title.

1947

*Jean Stafford*

........................................................................................................

# The Interior Castle

FROM *Partisan Review*

PANSY VANNEMAN, injured in an automobile accident, often woke up
before dawn when the night noises of the hospital still came, in hushed
hurry, through her half-open door. By day, when the nurses talked
audibly with the internes, laughed without inhibition, and took no
pains to soften their footsteps on the resounding composition floors,
the routine of the hospital seemed as bland and commonplace as that of
a bank or a factory. But in the dark hours, the whispering and the
quickly stilled clatter of glasses and basins, the moans of patients whose
morphine was wearing off, the soft squeak of a stretcher as it rolled past
in its way from the emergency ward — these suggested agony and
death. Thus, on the first morning, Pansy had faltered to consciousness
long before daylight and had found herself in a ward from every bed of
which, it seemed to her, came the bewildered protest of someone about
to die. A caged light burned on the floor beside the bed next to hers. Her
neighbor was dying and a priest was administering Extreme Unction.
He was stout and elderly and he suffered from asthma so that the
struggle of his breathing, so close to her, was the basic pattern and all
the other sounds were superimposed upon it. Two middle-aged men in
overcoats knelt on the floor beside the high bed. In a foreign tongue, the
half-gone woman babbled against the hissing and sighing of the Latin
prayers. She played with her rosary as if it were a toy: she tried, and
failed, to put it into her mouth.

Pansy felt horror, but she felt no pity. An hour or so later, when the
white ceiling lights were turned on and everything — faces, counter-
panes, and the hands that groped upon them — was transformed into
a uniform gray sordor, the woman was wheeled away in her bed to die
somewhere else, in privacy. Pansy did not quite take this in, although

she stared for a long time at the new, empty bed that had replaced the other.

The next morning, when she again woke up before the light, this time in a private room, she recalled the woman with such sorrow that she might have been a friend. Simultaneously, she mourned the driver of the taxicab in which she had been injured, for he had died at about noon the day before. She had been told this as she lay on a stretcher in the corridor, waiting to be taken to the x-ray room; an interne, passing by, had paused and smiled down at her and had said, "Your cab-driver is dead. You were lucky."

Six weeks after the accident, she woke one morning just as daylight was showing on the windows as a murky smear. It was a minute or two before she realized why she was so reluctant to be awake, why her uneasiness amounted almost to alarm. Then she remembered that her nose was to be operated on today. She lay straight and motionless under the seersucker counterpane. Her blood-red eyes in her darned face stared through the window and saw a frozen river and leafless elm trees and a grizzled esplanade where dogs danced on the ends of leashes, their bundled-up owners stumbling after them, half blind with sleepiness and cold. Warm as the hospital room was, it did not prevent Pansy from knowing, as keenly as though she were one of the walkers, how very cold it was outside. Each twig of a nearby tree was stark. Cold red brick buildings nudged the low-lying sky which was pale and inert like a punctured sac.

In six weeks, the scene had varied little: there was promise in the skies neither of sun nor of snow; no red sunsets marked these days. The trees could neither die nor leaf out again. Pansy could not remember another season in her life so constant, when the very minutes themselves were suffused with the winter pallor as they dropped from the moon-faced clock in the corridor. Likewise, her room accomplished no alterations from day to day. On the glass-topped bureau stood two potted plants telegraphed by faraway well-wishers. They did not fade, and if a leaf turned brown and fell, it soon was replaced; so did the blossoms renew themselves. The roots, like the skies and like the bare trees, seemed zealously determined to maintain a status quo. The bedside table, covered every day with a clean white towel, though the one removed was always immaculate, was furnished sparsely with a water glass, a bent drinking tube, a sweating pitcher, and a stack of paper handkerchiefs. There were a few letters in the drawer, a hairbrush, a pencil, and some postal cards on which, from time to time, she wrote brief messages to relatives and friends: "Dr. Nash says that my reflexes are shipshape (*sic*) and Dr. Rivers says the frontal fracture has all but healed and that the occipital is coming along nicely. Dr. Nicholas, the nose doctor, promises to operate as soon as Dr. Rivers gives him the go-ahead sign (*sic*)."

The bed itself was never rumpled. Once fretful and now convalescent, Miss Vanneman might have been expected to toss or turn the pillows or to unmoor the counterpane; but hour after hour and day after day she lay at full length and would not even suffer the nurses to raise the head-piece of the adjustable bed. So perfect and stubborn was her body's immobility that it was as if the room and the landscape, mortified by the ice, were extensions of herself. Her resolute quiescence and her disinclination to talk, the one seeming somehow to proceed from the other, resembled, so the nurses said, a final coma. And they observed, in pitying indignation, that she might as *well* be dead for all the interest she took in life. Amongst themselves they scolded her for what they thought a moral weakness: an automobile accident, no matter how serious, was not reason enough for anyone to give up the will to live or to be happy. She had not — to come down bluntly to the facts — had the decency to be grateful that it was the driver of the cab and not she who had died. (And how dreadfully the man had died!) She was twenty-five years old and she came from a distant city. These were really the only facts known about her. Evidently she had not been here long, for she had no visitors, a lack which was at first sadly moving to the nurses but which became to them a source of unreasonable annoyance: had anyone the right to live so one-dimensionally? It was impossible to laugh at her, for she said nothing absurd; her demands could not be complained of because they did not exist; she could not be hated for a sharp tongue nor for a supercilious one; she could not be admired for bravery or for wit or for interest in her fellow creatures. She was believed to be a frightful snob.

Pansy, for her part, took a secret and mischievous pleasure in the bewilderment of her attendants and the more they courted her with offers of magazines, cross-word puzzles, and a radio which she could rent from the hospital, the farther she retired from them into herself and into a world which she had created in her long hours here and which no one could even penetrate nor imagine. Sometimes she did not even answer the nurses' questions; as they rubbed her back with alcohol and steadily discoursed, she was as remote from them as if she were miles away. She did not think that she lived on a higher plane than that of the nurses and the doctors but that she lived on a different one and that at this particular time — this time of exploration and habituation — she had no extra strength to spend on making herself known to them. All she had been before and all the memories she might have brought out to disturb the monotony of, say, the morning bath, and all that the past meant to the future when she would leave the hospital, were of no present consequence to her. Not even in her thoughts did she employ more than a minimum of memory. And when she did remember, it was in flat pictures, rigorously independent of one another: she saw her thin, poetic mother who grew thinner and more poetic in her canvas deck chair at Saranac reading *Lalla Rookh*. She saw herself in an inappropriate pink hat drinking iced tea in a garden so oppressive with the smell of phlox that the tea itself tasted of it. She recalled an afternoon in autumn in Vermont when she had heard three dogs' voices in the north woods and she could tell, by the characteristic minor key struck three times at intervals, like bells from several churches, that they had treed something: the eastern sky was pink and the trees on the horizon looked like some eccentric vascular system meticulously drawn on colored paper.

What Pansy thought of all the time was her own brain. Not only the brain as the seat of consciousness, but the physical organ itself which she envisaged, romantically, now as a jewel, now as a flower, now as a light in a glass, now as an envelope of rosy vellum containing other envelopes, one within the other, diminishing infinitely. It was always pink and always fragile, always deeply interior and invaluable. She believed that she had reached the innermost chamber of knowledge and that perhaps her knowledge was the same as the saint's achievement of pure love. It was only convention, she thought, that made one say "sacred heart" and not "sacred brain."

Often, but never articulately, the color pink troubled her and the picture of herself in the wrong hat hung steadfastly before her mind's eye. None of the other girls had worn hats and since autumn had come early that year, they were dressed in green and rusty brown and dark yellow. Poor Pansy wore a white eyelet frock with a lacing of black ribbon around the square neck. When she came through the arch, overhung with bittersweet, and saw that they had not yet heard her, she almost turned back, but Mr. Oliver was there and she was in love with him. She was in love with him though he was ten years older than she and had never shown any interest in her beyond asking her once, quite fatuously but in an intimate voice, if the yodeling of the little boy who peddled clams did not make her wish to visit Switzerland. Actually, there was more to this question than met the eye, for some days later Pansy learned that Mr. Oliver, who was immensely rich, kept an apartment in Geneva. In the garden that day, he spoke to her only once. He said, "My dear, you look exactly like something out of Katherine Mansfield," and immediately turned and within her hearing asked Beatrice Sherburne to dine with him that night at the Country Club. Afterward, Pansy went down to the sea and threw the beautiful hat onto the full tide and saw it vanish in the wake of a trawler. Thereafter, when she heard the clam boy coming down the road, she locked the door and when the knocking had stopped and her mother called down from her chaise longue, "Who was it, dearie?" she replied, "A salesman."

It was only the fact that the hat had been pink that worried her. The rest of the memory was trivial, for she knew that she could never again love anything as ecstatically as she loved the spirit of Pansy Vanneman, enclosed within her head.

But her study was not without distraction, and she fought two adversaries: pain and Dr. Nicholas. Against Dr. Nicholas, she defended herself valorously and in fear; but pain, the pain, that is, that was independent of his instruments, she sometimes forced upon herself adventurously like a child scaring himself in a graveyard.

Dr. Nicholas greatly admired her crushed and splintered nose which he daily probed and peered at, exclaiming that he had never seen anything like it. His shapely hands ached for their knives; he was impatient with the skull-fracture man's cautious delay. He spoke of "our" nose and said "we" would be a new person when we could breathe again. His own nose, the trademark of his profession, was magnificent. Not even his own brilliant surgery could have improved upon it nor could a first-rate sculptor have duplicated its direct downward line which permitted only the least curvature inward toward the end; nor the delicately rounded lateral declivities; nor the thin-walled, perfectly matched nostrils. Miss Vanneman did not doubt his humaneness nor his talent — he was a celebrated man — but she questioned whether he had imagination. Immediately beyond the prongs of his speculum lay her treasure whose price he, no more than the nurses, could estimate. She believed he could not destroy it, but she feared that he might maim it: might leave a scratch on one of the brilliant facets of the jewel, bruise a petal of the flower, smudge the glass where the light burned, blot the envelopes, and that then she would die or would go mad. While she did not question that in either eventuality her brain would after a time redeem its original impeccability, she did not quite yet wish to enter upon either kind of eternity, for she was not certain that she could carry with her her knowledge as well as its receptacle.

Blunderer that he was, Dr. Nicholas was an honorable enemy, not like the demon, pain, which skulked in a thousand guises within her head, and which often she recklessly willed to attack her and then drove back in terror. After the rout, sweat streamed from her face and soaked the neck of the coarse hospital shirt. To be sure, it came usually of its own accord, running like a wild fire through all the convolutions to fill with flame the small sockets and ravines and then, at last, to withdraw, leaving behind a throbbing and an echo. On these occasions, she was as helpless as a tree in a wind. But at the other times when, by closing her eyes and rolling up the eyeballs in such a way that she fancied she looked directly on the place where her brain was, the pain woke sluggishly and came toward her at a snail's pace. Then, bit by bit, it gained speed. Sometimes it faltered back, subsided altogether, and then it rushed like a tidal wave driven by a hurricane, lashing and roaring until she lifted her hands from the counterpane, crushed her broken teeth into her swollen lip, stared in panic at the soothing walls with her ruby eyes, stretched out her legs until she felt their bones must snap. Each cove, each narrow inlet, every living bay was flooded and the frail brain, a little hat-shaped boat, was washed from its mooring and set adrift. The skull was as vast as the world and the brain was as small as a seashell.

Then came calm weather and the safe journey home. She kept vigil for a while, though, and did not close her eyes, but gazing pacifically at the trees, conceived of the pain as the guardian of her treasure who would not let her see it; that was why she was handled so savagely whenever she turned her eyes inward. Once this watch was interrupted: by chance she looked into the corridor and saw a shaggy mop slink past the door, followed by a senile porter. A pair of ancient eyes, as rheumy as an old dog's, stared uncritically in at her and the toothless mouth formed a brutish word. She was so surprised that she immediately closed her eyes to shut out the shape of the word and the pain dug up the unmapped regions of her head with mattocks, ludicrously huge. It was the familiar pain, but this time, even as she endured it, she observed with detachment that its effect upon her was less than that of its contents, the by-products, for example, of temporal confusion and the bizarre misapplication of the style of one sensation to another. At the moment, for example, although her brain reiterated to her that *it* was being assailed, she was stroking her right wrist with her left hand as though to assuage the ache, long since dispelled, of the sprain in the joint. Some minutes after she had opened her eyes and left off soothing her wrist, she lay rigid experiencing the sequel to the pain, an ideal terror. For, as before on several occasions, she was overwhelmed with the knowledge that the pain had been consummated in the vessel of her mind and for the moment the vessel was unbeautiful: she thought, quailing, of those plastic folds as palpable as the fingers of locked hands containing in their very cells, their fissures, their repulsive hemispheres, the mind, the soul, the inscrutable intelligence.

The porter, then, like the pink hat and like her mother and the hounds' voices, loitered with her.

Dr. Nicholas came at nine o'clock to prepare her for the operation. With him came an entourage of white-frocked acolytes, and one of them wheeled in a wagon on which lay knives and scissors and pincers, cans of swabs and gauze. In the midst of these was a bowl of liquid whose rich purple color made it seem strange like the brew of an alchemist.

"All set?" he asked her, smiling. "A little nervous, what? I don't blame you. I've often said I'd rather lose an arm than have a submucuous resection." Pansy thought for a moment he was going to touch his nose. His approach to her was roundabout. He moved through the yellow light shed by the globe in the ceiling which gave his forehead a liquid gloss; he paused by the bureau and touched a blossom of the cyclamen; he looked out the window and said, to no one and to all, "I couldn't start my car this morning. Came in a cab." Then he came forward. As he came, he removed a speculum from the pocket of his short-sleeved coat and like a cat, inquiring of the nature of a surface with its paws, he put out his hand toward her and drew it back, gently murmuring, "You must not be afraid, my dear. There is no danger, you know. Do you think for a minute I would operate if there were?"

Dr. Nicholas, young, brilliant, and handsome, was an aristocrat, a husband, a father, a clubman, a Christian, a kind counselor, and a trustee of his school alumni association. Like many of the medical profession, even those whose speciality was centered on the organ of the basest sense, he interested himself in the psychology of his patients: in several instances, for example, he had found that severe attacks of sinusitis were coincident with emotional crises. Miss Vanneman more than ordinarily captured his fancy since her skull had been fractured and her behavior throughout had been so extraordinary that he felt he was observing at first hand some of the results of shock, that incommensurable element, which frequently were too subtle to see. There was, for example, the matter of her complete passivity during a lumbar puncture, reports of which were written down in her history and were enlarged upon for him by Dr. Rivers' interne who had been in charge. Except for a tremor in her throat and a deepening of pallor, there were no signs at all that she was aware of what was happening to her. She made no sound, did not close her eyes nor clench her fists. She had had several punctures; her only reaction had been to the very first one, the morning after she had been brought in. When the interne explained to her that he was going to drain off cerebrospinal fluid which was pressing against her brain, she exclaimed, "My God!" but it was not an exclamation of fear. The young man had been unable to name what it was he had heard in her voice; he could only say that it had not been fear as he had observed it in other patients.

He wondered about her. There was no way of guessing whether she had always had a nature of so tolerant and undemanding a complexion. It gave him a melancholy pleasure to think that before her accident she had been high-spirited and loquacious; he was moved to think that perhaps she had been a beauty and that when she had first seen her face in the looking glass she had lost all joy in herself. It was very difficult to tell what the face had been, for it was so bruised and swollen, so hacked-up and lopsided. The black stitches and length of the nose, across the saddle, across the cheekbone, showed that there would be unsightly scars. He had ventured once to give her the name of a plastic surgeon but she had only replied with a vague, refusing smile. He had hoisted a manly shoulder and said, "You're the doctor."

Much as he pondered, coming to no conclusions, about what went on inside that pitiable skull, he was, of course, far more interested in the nose, deranged so badly that it would require his topmost skill to restore its functions to it. He would be obliged not only to make a submucuous resection, a simple run-of-the-mill operation, but to remove the vomer, always a delicate task but further complicated in this case by the proximity of the bone to the frontal fracture line which conceivably was not entirely closed. If it were not and he operated too soon and if a cold germ then found its way into the opening, his patient would be carried off by meningitis in the twinkling of an eye. He wondered if she knew in what potential danger she lay; he desired to assure her that he had brought his craft to its nearest perfection and that she had nothing to fear of him, but feeling that she was perhaps both ignorant and un-imaginative and that such consolation would create a fear rather than dispel one, he held his tongue and came nearer to the bed.

Watching him, Pansy could already feel the prongs of his pliers opening her nostrils for the insertion of his fine probers. The pain he caused her with his instruments was of a different kind from that she felt unaided: it was a naked, clean, and vivid pain which made her faint and ill and made her wish to die. Once she had fainted as he ruthlessly explored and after she was brought around, he continued until he had finished his investigation. The memory of this outrage had afterwards several times made her cry.

This morning she looked at him and listened to him with hatred. Fixing her eyes upon the middle of his high, protuberant brow, she imagined the clutter behind it and she despised its obtuse imperfection, the reason's oblique comprehension of itself. In his bland unawareness, this nobody, this nose-bigot, was about to play with fire and she wished him ill.

He said, "I can't blame you. No, I expect you're not looking for-ward to our little party. But I expect you'll be glad to be able to breathe again."

He stationed his lieutenants. The interne stood opposite him on the left side of the bed. The surgical nurse wheeled the wagon within easy reach of his hands and stood beside it. Another nurse stood at the foot of the bed. A third drew the shades at the windows and attached the blinding light which shone down on the patient hotly, and then she left the room, softly closing the door. Pansy stared at the silver ribbon tied in a great bow round the green crepe paper of one of the flower pots. It made her realize for the first time that one of the days she had lain here had been Christmas, but she had no time to consider this strange and thrilling fact, for Dr. Nicholas was genially explaining his anaesthetic. He would soak packs of gauze in the purple fluid, a cocaine solution, and he would place them then in her nostrils, leaving them there for an hour. He warned her that the packing would be disagreeable (he did not say "painful") but that it would be well worth a few minutes of discom-fort not to be in the least sick after the operation. He asked her if she were ready and when she nodded her head, he adjusted the mirror on his forehead and began.

At the first touch of his speculum, Pansy's fingers mechanically bent to the palms of her hands and she stiffened. He said, "A pack, Miss Kennedy," and Pansy closed her eyes. There was a rush of plunging pain as he drove the sodden gobbet of gauze high up into her nose and something bitter burned in her throat so that she retched. The doctor paused a moment and the surgical nurse wiped her mouth. He returned to her with another pack, pushing it with his bodkin doggedly until it lodged against the first. Stop! Stop! cried all her nerves, wailing along the surface of her skin. The coats that covered them were torn off and they shuddered like naked people screaming, Stop! Stop! But Dr. Nicholas did not hear. Time and again he came back with a fresh pack and did not pause at all until one nostril was finished. She opened her eyes and saw him wipe the sweat off his forehead and saw the dark interne bending over her, fascinated. Miss Kennedy bathed her temples in ice water and Dr. Nicholas said, "There. It won't be much longer. I'll tell them to send you some coffee, though I'm afraid you won't be able to taste it. Ever drink coffee with chicory in it? I have no use for it."

She snatched at his irrelevancy and, though she had never tasted chicory, she said severely, "I love it."

Dr. Nicholas chuckled. "De gustibus. Ready? A pack, Miss Kennedy."

The second nostril was harder to pack since the other side was now distended and the passage was anyhow much narrower, as narrow, he had once remarked, as that in the nose of an infant. In such pain as passed all language and even the farthest fetched analogies, she turned her eyes inward thinking that under the obscuring cloak of the surgeon's pain, she could see her brain without the knowledge of its keeper. But Dr. Nicholas and his aides would give her no peace. They surrounded her with their murmuring and their foot-shuffling and the rustling of their starched uniforms, and her eyelids continually flew back in embarrassment and mistrust. She was claimed entirely by this present, meaningless pain and suddenly and sharply, she forgot what she had meant to do. She was aware of nothing but her ascent to the summit of something; what it was she did not know, whether it was a tower or a peak or Jacob's ladder. Now she was an abstract word, now she was a theorem of geometry, now she was a kite flying, a top spinning, a prism flashing, a kaleidoscope turning.

But none of the others in the room could see inside and when the surgeon was finished, the nurse at the foot of the bed said, "Now you must take a look in the mirror. It's simply too comical." And they all laughed intimately like old, fast friends. She smiled politely and looked at her reflection: over the gruesomely fattened snout, her scarlet eyes stared in fixed reproach upon the upturned lips, gray with bruises. But even in its smile of betrayal, the mouth itself was puzzled: it reminded her that something had been left behind, but she could not recall what it was. She was hollowed out and was as dry as a white bone.

They strapped her ankles to the operating table and put leather nooses round her wrists. Over her head was a mirror with a thousand facets in which she saw a thousand travesties of her face. At her right side was the table, shrouded in white, where lay the glittering blades of the many knives, thrusting out fitful rays of light. All the cloth was frosty; everything was white or silver and as cold as snow. Dr. Nicholas, a tall snowman with silver eyes and silver fingernails, came into the room soundlessly for he walked on layers and layers of snow which deadened his footsteps; behind him came the interne, a smaller snowman, less impressively proportioned. At the foot of the table, a snow figure put her frozen hands upon Pansy's helpless feet. The doctor plucked the packs from the cold, numb nose. His laugh was like a cry on a bitter, still night: "I will show you now," he called across the expanse of snow, "that you can feel nothing." The pincers bit at nothing, snapped at the air and cracked a nerveless icicle. Pansy called back and heard her own voice echo: "I feel nothing."

Here the walls were gray, not tan. Suddenly the face of the nurse at the foot of the table broke apart and Pansy first thought it was in grief. But it was a smile and she said, "Did you enjoy your coffee?" Down the gray corridors of the maze, the words rippled, ran like mice, birds, broken beads: Did you enjoy your coffee? your coffee? your coffee? Similarly once in another room that also had gray walls, the same voice had said, "Shall I give her some whiskey?" She was overcome with gratitude that this young woman (how pretty she was with her white hair and her white face against her china-blue eyes!) had been with her that first night and was with her now.

In the great stillness of the winter, the operation began. The knives carved snow. Pansy was happy. She had been given a hypodermic just before they came to fetch her and she would have gone to sleep had she not enjoyed so much this trickery of Dr. Nicholas' whom now she tenderly loved.

There was a clock in the operating room and from time to time she looked at it. An hour passed. The snowman's face was melting; drops of water hung from his fine nose, but his silver eyes were as bright as ever. Her love was returned, she knew: he loved her nose exactly as she loved his knives. She looked at her face in the domed mirror and saw how the blood had streaked her lily-white cheeks and had stained her shroud. She returned to the private song: Did you enjoy your coffee? your coffee?

At the half-hour, a murmur, anguine and slumbrous, came to her and only when she had repeated the words twice did they engrave their meaning upon her. Dr. Nicholas said, "Stand back now, nurse. I'm at this girl's brain and I don't want my elbow jogged." Instantly Pansy was alive. Her strapped ankles arched angrily; her wrists strained against their bracelets. She jerked her head and she felt the pain flare; she had made the knife slip.

"Be still!" cried the surgeon. "Be quiet, please!"

He had made her remember what it was she had lost when he had rammed his gauze into her nose; she bustled like a housewife to shut the door. She thought, I must hurry before the robbers come. It would be like the time Mother left the cellar door open and the robber came and took, of all things, the terrarium.

Dr. Nicholas was whispering to her. He said, in the voice of a lover, "If you can stand it five minutes more, I can perform the second operation now and you won't have to go through this again. What do you say?"

She did not reply. It took her several seconds to remember why it was her mother had set such store by the terrarium and then it came to her that the bishop's widow had brought her an herb from Palestine to put in it.

The interne said, "You don't want to have your nose packed again, do you?"

The surgical nurse said, "She's a good patient, isn't she, sir?"

"Never had a better," replied Dr. Nicholas. "But don't call me 'sir.' You must be a Canadian to call me 'sir.'"

The nurse at the foot of the bed said, "I'll order some more coffee for you."

"How about it, Miss Vanneman?" said the doctor. "Shall I go ahead?"

She debated. Once she had finally fled the hospital and fled Dr. Nicholas, nothing could compel her to come back. Still, she knew that the time would come when she could no longer live in seclusion, she must go into the world again and must be equipped to live in it; she banally acknowledged that she must be able to breathe. And finally, though the world to which she would return remained unreal, she gave the surgeon her permission.

He had now to penetrate regions that were not anaesthetized and this he told her frankly, but he said that there was no danger at all. He apologized for the slip of the tongue he had made: in point of fact, he had not been near her brain, it was only a figure of speech. He began. The knives ground and carved and curried and scoured the wounds they made; the scissors clipped hard gristle and the scalpels chipped off bone. It was as if a tangle of tiny nerves were being cut dexterously, one by one; the pain writhed spirally and came to her who was a pink bird and sat on the top of a cone. The pain was a pyramid made of a diamond; it was an intense light; it was the hottest fire, the coldest chill, the highest peak, the fastest force, the furthest reach, the newest time. It possessed nothing of her but its one infinitesimal scene: beyond the screen as thin as gossamer, the brain trembled for its life, hearing the knives hunting like wolves outside, sniffing and snapping. Mercy! Mercy! cried the scalped nerves.

At last, miraculously, she turned her eyes inward tranquilly. Dr. Nicholas had said, "The worst is over. I am going to work on the floor of your nose," and at his signal she closed her eyes and this time and this time alone, she saw her brain lying in a shell-pink satin case. It was a pink pearl, no bigger than a needle's eye, but it was so beautiful and so pure that its smallness made no difference. Anyhow, as she watched, it grew. It grew larger and larger until it was an enormous bubble that contained the surgeon and the whole room within its rosy luster. In a long ago summer, she had often been absorbed by the spectacle of flocks of yellow birds that visited a cedar tree and she remembered that everything that summer had been some shade of yellow. One year of childhood, her mother had frequently taken her to have tea with an aged schoolmistress upon whose mantelpiece there was a herd of ivory elephants; that had been the white year. There was a green spring when early in April she had seen a grass snake on a boulder, but the very summer that followed was violet, for vetch took her mother's garden. She saw a swatch of blue tulle lying in a raffia basket on the front porch of Uncle Marion's brown house. Never before had the world been pink, whatever else it had been. Or had it been, one other time? She could not be sure and she did not care. Of one thing she was certain: never had the world enclosed her before and never had the quiet been so smooth.

For only a moment the busybodies left her to her ecstasy and then, impatient and gossiping, they forced their way inside, slashed at her resisting trance with questions and congratulations, with statements of fact and jokes. "Later," she said to them dumbly. "Later on, perhaps. I am busy now." But their voices would not go away. They touched her, too, washing her face with cloths so cold they stung, stroking her wrists with firm, antiseptic fingers. The surgeon, squeezing her arm with avuncular pride, said, "Good girl," as if she were a bright dog that had retrieved a bone. Her silent mind abused him: "You are a thief," it said, "you are a heartless vagabond and you should be put to death." But he was leaving, adjusting his coat with an air of vainglory, and the interne, abject with admiration, followed him from the operating room smiling like a silly boy.

Shortly after they took her back to her room, the weather changed, not for the better. Momentarily the sun emerged from its concealing murk, but in a few minutes the snow came with a wind that promised a blizzard. There was great pain, but since it could not serve her, she rejected it and she lay as if in a hammock in a pause of bitterness. She closed her eyes, shutting herself up within her treasureless head.

1948

*Martha Gellhorn*

# Miami–New York

FROM *The Atlantic Monthly*

THERE WERE FIVE Air Force sergeants and they got in the plane and found seats and began to call to each other across the aisle or over the chair backs, saying, How about it, Joe, I guess this is the way to travel, or saying, Where do they keep the parachutes? or saying, Boy, I've got a pillow, what do you know! They were loud and good-natured for a moment, very young, and young in their new importance of being bomber crews, and they wanted the other people, the civilians, to know that they belonged in a different, fiercer world.

There were a half dozen of the men who seemed always to be going to or coming from Washington, the men with gray suits, hats, hair, skin, and with brown calf brief cases. These have no definite age and curiously similar faces, and are all equally tired and quiet. They always put their hats in the rack above the seat and sit down with their brief cases on their laps. Later they open their brief cases and look at sheets of typed or mimeographed paper, or they go to sleep.

The stewardess was young, with blonde hair hanging to her shoulders. She had a neat body of the right height and weight, and a professionally friendly voice. Fasten your seat belts, please, she said. Would you like some chewing gum? Fasten your seat belt, please, sir. Chewing gum?

A woman who had traveled a great deal in planes, and never trusted them because she understood nothing about them, sat in the double front seat behind the magazine rack. This was the best seat, as she knew, because there was enough room to stretch your legs. Also you could see well from here, if you wanted to see. Now, for a moment she looked out the window and saw that the few palm trees at the far edge of the field were blowing out in heavy plumes against the sky. There was something so wrong about Miami that even a beautiful night, sharp with stars, only seemed a real-estate advertisement. The woman pulled off her earrings and put them carelessly in her coat pocket. She ran her hands through her very short dark upcurling hair, deliberately making herself untidy for the night ahead. She hunched her shoulders to ease the tired stiffness in her neck and slouched down in the chair. She had just leaned her head against the chair back and was thinking of nothing when the man's voice said, Is this place taken? No, she said without looking at him. She moved nearer to the window. Anyhow, she said to herself, only eight or ten hours or whatever it is to New York; even if he snores, he can't snore all the time.

The plane taxied into position, turned, the propellers whirled until in the arc lights of the field they were great silver disks, the motor roared, and the plane started that run down the field that always, no matter how many times you had sat it out, no matter in how many countries, and no matter on how many fields, bad fields, dangerous fields, in whatever weather, always stopped your heart for one moment as you waited to see if this time it would work again; if this time, as all the other times, the enormous machine would rise smoothly into the air where no one really belonged except the birds.

"Made it," the man said softly to himself.

She looked at him then. He had said it as she would have said it, with wonder, with a perpetual amazement that the trick worked.

He turned to her and she could see he wanted to talk. She would only have to say yes, and smile, or say nice take-off, or say, what a lovely night; anything would do. But she was not going to say anything and he was not going to talk to her if she could help it. I have ten hours, she said in her mind to the man, and she said it threateningly, and they are mine and I don't have to talk to anyone and don't try. The man, finding her face closed against him, turned away, pulled a package of cigarettes from his pocket, and made a great distance between them, smoking and looking straight ahead.

She could not ignore him though he did nothing to force her attention. She had seen him without really looking; he was a Navy lieutenant and the braid on his cap, which he still held, was grayish black; his stripes and the active-duty star were tarnished; his uniform looked unpressed, and he had a dark weather-dried sunburn. His hair was a colorless blond, so short that it seemed he must have shaved his head and now the hair was just growing in, a month's growth probably.

With resentment, because she did not want to notice him, she studied him now, not caring if he turned his head and caught her. She looked at him with unfriendly professional eyes, the beady eye of the painter, her husband called it. The man's face, in repose, looked brooding and angry; the whole face was square. His eyebrows lay flat and black above his eyes, his mouth did not curve at all, and his chin seemed to make another straight line. There were three horizontal lines marked one after the other across his face, and blocked in by the hard bones of his jaw. But when he had turned to her, wanting to talk, he had been smiling and his face had been oval then, with all the lines flared gayly upwards. Perhaps the gayety came from his eyes, which were china blue, or was it his mouth, she thought, trying to remember. It was a very interesting face; it belonged to two different men. She wondered where he had picked up this dark, thinking, angry man, who showed on his face now.

Damn, she said to herself, what do I care? Let him have six faces. But it was a fine problem. How could you paint one face and make it at the same time square and oval, gay and longingly friendly, but also shut-in, angry and indifferent.

I wonder what she's sore about, the man thought mildly behind his complicated face. She doesn't look as if she was the type of woman who's sore all the time. Pretty women weren't usually sore all the time. He could place her, in a vague general way, as people of the same nationality can place each other. She had money and she had taste; her clothes were not only expensive and fashionable, which was frequent, they were the right clothes and she wore them without concern. He had not heard her voice but he imagined what it would be; Eastern, he thought, rather English. She would say things like, it's heaven, or he's madly energetic, or what a ghastly bore, saying it all without emphasis. She would be spoiled, as they all were, and at a loose end as they all were too. But her face was better than most. He did not think of women as stupid or not stupid. He simply thought her face was not like everyone's; it was small and pointed and even though she was sore, she could not make her face look dead. It was a lively face and her eyebrows grew in a feather line upwards over very bright, very dark eyes. Her hands were beautiful too, and he noticed, looking at them slantwise and secretly, that the nail varnish was cracking and she had broken or chewed off the nail of her right pointer finger. It was childish and careless to have such nails, and he liked that best about her. Sore as a goat, he thought mildly to himself. Then he forgot her.

He relaxed, behind the angry square of this second face that he had never seen and did not know about. He relaxed and enjoyed himself, thinking of nothing, but simply enjoying being alive and being home or almost home. He had been gone eighteen months, and without ever saying it to himself, because he made no poses, not even practical, realistic poses, he had often doubted that he would get back. Whenever he began almost to think about not ever getting back (and this was different from thinking about dying, there was something like self-pity about not getting back, whereas dying was just a thing that could happen) he would say to himself, grim and mocking, life on a destroyer is a big educational experience; you ought to be grateful.

He had worked briefly in his father's mills before he became an officer on a destroyer, but he did not want to be a businessman again. Or rather he could not remember what it was like, being a man in an office, so he had no interest in it. He did not want anything now except to be happy. He was happy. He rested behind his face and told himself how fine and comfortable the seat was and what a fine time he'd had last night in Miami with Bob Jamison and those two beauties and what a fine time he would have tomorrow and all the other days. Oh boy, he said to himself, and stretched all through his body without moving, and felt the fine time bathing him like soft water and sunlight.

No doubt he has a splendid little wife waiting for him, the woman thought. He is evidently going home and from the looks of him, his face and his clothes, he has been somewhere. He has ribbons sewn to his blue serge chest. Ribbons could mean something or nothing; every man in uniform that she knew had ribbons. They rode nobly and with growing boredom from their homes on the subway down to Church Street and presently they had ribbons. They lived in expensive overcrowdedness in Washington and wandered around the Pentagon building and went to cocktail parties in Georgetown and had ribbons. There were, for instance, those two faintly aging glamour boys, with silver eagles on their shoulders and enough ribbons to trim hats, who had just returned from London. She had always known these two and she was prepared to believe that they knew as much about war as she did, and she was certain that they had never ventured much farther afield than, say, Piccadilly Circus, in case they worked in Grosvenor Square. So what real ribbons were or what they meant, she did not know. However, looking at this man, she thought that his ribbons would mean something. His wife would know about the ribbons at once, if she did not know already, and she would be very proud. Why shouldn't she be, the woman asked herself irritably, what have you got against wives?

Am I not in fact a service wife myself? she thought. Could I not wear a pin with one star on it, a little oblong pin made of enamel if you haven't much money, but you can get it in sapphires, diamonds, and rubies if you feel that way? Have I not just returned from seeing my husband off in Miami? Thomas, she said to herself, is so used to getting what he wants that he believes the emotions will also perform as he wishes. A man is leaving for service overseas; he has forty-eight hours leave; his wife flies to him to say good-bye; they have forty-eight lovely last hours together and the lovely last hours were like being buried alive, though still quite alive so you knew all about it, with a stranger whom you ought to love but there it is, he is a stranger. Fine wife, she told herself, everyone handles this perfectly; all women manage to run their hearts smoothly; patriotism, pride, tenderness, farewell, homesickness. I'm not such a bitch as all that, she thought, defending herself; Thomas is only going to Brazil. I wouldn't mind going to Brazil myself. I should think he'd be enchanted to go to Brazil. As long as you aren't doing your own work, it's far better to be in Brazil than in Miami or Pensacola or the Brooklyn Navy Yard.

Only, if I were a real wife, a good wife, a service wife, I'd have made more of a thing of his going. Why does he want to be fooled, she thought angrily, why does he want to fool himself? Why does he go on about loving me when I am everything he dislikes and distrusts? She could hear Thomas now, and her heart moved with pity despite the anger. I love you more than anything, Kate, you know that; I only want you to be happy. Thomas believed it while he said it, and she felt herself to be cold and hard and ungrateful and somehow hideous, because she did not believe it at all.

She groaned and moved her body as if it were in pain. The man beside her turned, and stared, but he could not see her face. All he saw was the stiff line of her right shoulder, hunched up away from him. The woman was saying to herself, desperately, forget it, forget it. There is nothing to do. It cannot be understood; leave it alone. You cannot know so much about yourself; you cannot know why you thought you loved a man, nor why you think you no longer love him. It is not necessary to know. It's an enormous world, she told herself, with millions of people in it; if you're not even interested in yourself why can't you stop thinking about your own dreary little life? Thomas will be gone months, a year, two years. *Stop thinking about it.*

Suddenly, and without any sort of plan or direction from her brain, she pulled the great square diamond engagement ring and the baguette diamond wedding ring from her left hand, pulling them off brutally as if they would not come unless she forced them, and she thrust the two rings into her coat pocket with her earrings. Then she rubbed her left hand, crushing the bones of the hand together and pulling at the fingers. The man beside her, who had seen all this, said to himself, "Well, for God's sake what goes on here?" She's not sore, he thought, she's nuts. Then he amended that thought; nuts, or in some trouble of her own. He wanted no part of trouble; he did not understand it really. Living had become so simple for him that he understood nothing now except being or staying alive.

The stewardess turned off the overhead lights in the plane and one by one the small reading lights on the walls were turned off and presently the plane was dark. The bright grayish night gleamed in through the windows. Two of the men from Washington snored weakly and one of the Air Force sergeants snored very loudly as if he enjoyed snoring and was going to do as much of it as he wanted. Then the snoring became a part of the plane sounds, and everything was quiet. The woman with the short, upcurling hair slept in a twisted sideways heap. The lieutenant leaned his head quietly against the chair back and stretched out his legs and settled himself without haste to sleep until morning.

In sleep his face was even more square and brooding. He seemed to be dreaming something that made him cold with anger or despair. He was not dreaming; it could not be a dream because it was always the same when he slept. It was as if he went to a certain place to sleep. This place was an enormous darkness; it moved a little but it was not a darkness made up of air or water: it was a solid darkness like being blind. Only the dark something around him had weight and he was under it; he was all alone, lying or floating, at ease, in no pain, pursued by nothing, but simply lying in absolute aloneness in the weight of the dark. He could not see himself, he could only feel himself there. It was terrible because there seemed no way to get out, and yet he did not struggle. He lay there every night and every night he was trapped in it forever, and every morning when he woke he was grateful and astonished though he did not remember why, as he did not remember the place where he had been sleeping.

This sleeping in a complete empty heavy darkness had come on him, gradually, on the ship. He knew nothing about himself and considered himself an ordinary man, quite lucky, doing all right, with nothing on his mind. Nothing had happened to him that had not happened to hundreds of other men. Even talking, in the ward-room, with others of his kind he recognized himself and knew there was nothing special about him. They talked very badly, without thought and without even knowing how to manage their language. It was almost like sign language the way they talked. But surely he felt what they all did.

When the first destroyer was sunk by a bomb, and he jumped over-board (but not nearly so far as he always imagined it would be — it didn't seem any farther than jumping from the high dive at the country club) and swam around and found a raft, he had first been mindless with fury. He did not know what the fury came from: was it because they were hunted and hurled in the sea, was it rage against their own helplessness, was he furious to lose the ship for which he felt now a strong unexpected love, was it fury for himself alone, fury at this outra-geous tampering with life? He was so angry that he could not see or think; he did not remember swimming and he did not know how he had gone to the raft. Then the fear came as he watched the Japa-nese planes, so close above the water, searching them out where they splashed like driven terrified water beetles or hung together like leeches on a log. The fear was as cold as the water and made him weak and nauseated; then it too went. They were picked up very quickly; nothing had happened to him.

There was another time when he stood behind the forward gun crew and seemed to have nothing to do himself. He watched the sailor firing the Oerlikon and saw his body bucking against the crutch-like sup-ports of the gun, and he saw the faint bright stream of the bullets, but the man behind the Oerlikon seemed terribly slow, everything seemed slow, he himself had never had so much time and so little to do. This must have lasted a few seconds, but it was a large quiet piece of time and his mind said clearly: this is crazy, what are we all doing? Then his mind said it much louder: this is crazy. Finally he was not sure he had not shouted it out, because the thought was bursting in his mind. *This is crazy.*

Even that was not very remarkable; most of the other men thought everything was pretty screwy. You had to kill the Japs after they started it all, naturally you couldn't let them get away with it. You had to do it since that was how things were, but it was crazy all the same. If you began to think about it, about yourself and all the men you knew out here in this big god-awful ocean, to hell and gone from anywhere you ever wanted to be, and what you were doing and what everybody was doing everywhere, it was too crazy to think about. Then if you tried to think how it all started and what it was about and what difference it would make afterwards, you went crazy yourself. He had not actually talked this over with anyone but he knew the others felt as he did, Bob Jamison and Truby Bartlett and Joe Parks and the other men he knew well.

They all agreed in a simple easy way: they were the age that was in this war, if they'd been older or younger they wouldn't be, but this was what had happened and this was what they had to do. You made a lot of jokes and longed loudly for tangible things, liquor and a fine room at the Waldorf or the St. Francis, depending on taste, with a handy beauty. You played bridge or poker when you had a chance, for higher stakes than before. Time passed; you were the same man you always were. All you had to do was stay alive if you could.

Yet every night he went to this empty solid darkness and was forever buried in it, without hope or escape or anyone to call to.

The man, who had been asleep, woke suddenly and found his face ten inches from the woman's face. She had turned towards him in her sleep. Her eyes were closed and she looked very pale, tired, and a little ill. Her mouth was wonderfully soft. The man was not quite awake and he looked with surprise at this face he had not expected to see, and thought, she's lonely. He was thinking better than he would have done, had he been awake and protected by a long habit of not noticing and not thinking. She's sick lonely, he thought to himself. Without intending to, he leaned toward those soft lips. There was the face, waiting and needing to be kissed. Then he woke enough to remember where he was, and stopped himself, shocked, and thought, God, if I'd done it, she'd probably have called out and there'd have been a hell of a goings-on. He sighed and turned away from her and let his body relax, and slept again.

The plane skidded a little in the wind; it seemed to be forcing itself powerfully through air as heavy as water. The people in the plane slept or held themselves quietly. The plane began to smell close, smelling of bodies and night and old cigarette smoke.

Suddenly the woman felt a hand on her hair. The hand was not gentle; it pressed down the rumpled curly dark hair and stroked once from the forehead back to the nape of her neck. She woke completely but did not move, being too startled and confused to understand what had happened. The hand now left her hair and with harsh assurance rested on her breast; she could feel it through the thin tweed of her coat. She wondered whether she was dreaming this; it was so unlikely, that she must be dreaming it, and in the dark plane she could not see the hand. She looked over at the man and saw his face, dimly. He was asleep, with that troubled brooding look on his face. The hand was quiet, heavy and certain. The hand held and demanded her. What is he doing, she thought. My God, what is happening here? They certainly come back odd, she thought, with a kind of shaky laugh in her mind.

The hand insisted, and suddenly, to her amazement and to her shame, she knew that she wanted to lie against him, she wanted him to put his arms around her and hold her, with this silent unquestioning ownership. She wanted him to wake and hold her and kiss her. It did not matter who she was or who he was, and the other people in the plane did not matter. They were here together in the night and this incredible thing had happened and she did not want to stop it. She turned to him.

When she moved, the man sighed, still sleeping, and his hand fell from her, rested a moment in her lap, and then slowly dragged back, as if of its own will and apart from the man, and lay flat along his side. She waited, watching him, and presently her eyes woke him. He saw the woman's troubled, sad, somehow questioning face and the soft lips that asked to be kissed. He moved his right arm and pulled her as close to him as he could, but there was something between them though he was too sleepy to notice what it was, and he kissed her. He kissed her as if they had already made love, taking all that went before for granted. Having waked up in other places, and not known exactly what had happened, only knowing there was someone to kiss, he did not feel surprised now. Lovely lips, he thought happily. Then he noticed with real surprise that this thing digging into his side was the arm of the chair and then he knew where he was. The woman had pulled away from him and from his owning arm and his assured possessive mouth.

"I'm Kate Merlin," she whispered idiotically. She sounded panic-stricken.

The man laughed softly. He did not see what anyone's name had to do with it. "I'm John Hanley," he said.

"How do you do?" she said and felt both ridiculous and mad, and suddenly laughed too.

"Let's get rid of this obstruction," he said. The woman was frightened. He took everything so calmly; did he imagine that she always kissed the man sitting next to her on the night plane from Miami? The lieutenant worked at the arm of the chair until he discovered how to get it loose. He laid it on the floor in front of his feet. She was leaning forward and away from him, not knowing what to say in order to explain to him that she really wasn't a woman who could be kissed on planes, in case that happened to be a well-known category of woman.

He said nothing; that was evidently his specialty, she thought. He got everywhere without opening his mouth. His body spoke for him. He collected her, as if she belonged to him and could not have any other idea herself. He brought her close, raised her head so that it was comfortable for him, and kissed her. The harsh and certain hand held her as before.

This is fine, the man thought. It was part of the fine time in Miami and part of the fine time that would follow. He seemed to have a lot of luck — but why not, sometimes you did have luck, and he had felt all along that this leave was going to be wonderful. He had waited for it with such confidence that it could not fail him. Now he would kiss this lovely strange soft woman, and then they would go to sleep. There was nothing else they could do on a plane, which was a pity, but it was foolish to worry about something you couldn't have. Just be very damn grateful, he thought, that it's as fine as it is. You might have been sitting next to the Air Force, he thought with amusement, and what would you have then? She smelled of gardenias and her hair was delicious and like feathers against his cheek. He leaned forward to kiss her again, feeling warm and melted and unhurried and happy.

"How did you know?" the woman said. She seemed to have trouble speaking.

"Know what?"

"That you could kiss me?"

Oh God, he thought, we're going to have to talk about it. Why in hell did she want to talk?

"I didn't know anything," he said. "I didn't plan anything."

"Who are you?" She didn't mean that; she meant, how did it happen?

"Nobody," he said with conviction. "Absolutely nobody. Who are you?"

"I don't know," she said.

"Don't let it worry you," he said. He was beginning to feel impatient of this aimless talk. "Aren't we having a fine time?"

She took in her breath, rigid with distaste. So that was what it was. Just like that; it might have happened with anyone. Come on, baby, give us a kiss, isn't this fun. Oh *Lord*, she thought, what have I got into now? She wanted to say to him, I have never done anything like this in my life, you must not think. She wanted him to appreciate that this was rare and therefore important; it could not have happened any night with any man. It had to be alone of its kind, or she could not accept it.

The man again used silence, which he handled far better than words, and again he simply allowed his body to make what explanations seemed necessary. She felt herself helpless and glad to be helpless. But she could not let him think her only a willing woman; how would she face him in the morning if that was all he understood?

"You see," she began.

He kissed her so that she would not talk and he said, with his lips moving very lightly against hers, "It's all right."

She took that as she needed it, making it mean everything she wanted him to think. She was still amazed but she was full of delight. She felt there had been nothing in her life but talk and reasons, and the talk had been wrong and the reasons proved pointless: here was something that had happened at once, by itself, without a beginning, and it was right because it was like magic.

The man pressed her head against his shoulder, pulled her gently sideways to make her comfortable, leaned his head against the chair back, and prepared to sleep. He felt contented, but if he went on kissing her much longer, since there was nothing further he could do about her now, it might get to be tiresome and thwarted and wearing. It had been good and now it was time to sleep; he was very tired. He kissed the top of her head, remembering her, and said, "Sleep well."

Long ragged gray clouds disordered the sky. The moon was like an illuminated target in a shooting gallery, moving steadily ahead of them. The plane was colder now and one of the Air Force sergeants coughed himself awake, swore, blew his nose, sighed, shifted his position, and went back to sleep. The stewardess wondered whether she ought to make an inspection tour of her passengers and decided they were all right. She was reading a novel about society people in a country house in England, which fascinated her.

The woman lay easily against the lieutenant's shoulder and let her mind float in a smooth warm dream of pleasure. After the months of gnawing unlove, this man sat beside her in a plane in the night, and she no longer needed to dread herself as a creature who loved nothing. She did not love this man but she loved how she felt, she loved this warmth and aliveness and this hope. Now she made plans that were like those faultless daydreams in which one is always beautiful and the heroine and every day is more replete with miracles than the next. He would stay in New York, at her house even, since she was alone. Or would it be better if they went to a hotel so that there would be nothing to remind her of her ordinary life? They would treat New York as if it were a foreign city, Vienna in the spring, she thought. They would find new odd little places to eat, and funny places along Broadway to dance, they would walk in the Park and go to the Aquarium and the Bronx Zoo; they would sight-see and laugh and meet no one they knew and be alone in a strange, wonderful city. Someday he would have to go back where he came from, and she would go back to her work, but they would have this now and it was more than she had ever hoped for or imagined. And she would paint his strange face that was two faces, and he would be fresh and exciting every day and every night, with his silence and his fantastic assurance and his angry and happy look.

The plane circled the field at Washington and seemed to plunge onto the runway. The thump of the wheels striking the cement runway woke the man. He sat up and stared about him.

"Put the chair arm back," the woman whispered. "Good morning." She did not want the stewardess to look at her with a smile or a question. Her hair must be very soft; she would like to touch it, but not now. She looked at him with loving intimate eyes and the man looked at her, quite stupidly, as if he had never seen her before.

"The chair arm," she said again.

The man grinned suddenly and picked up the chair arm and fitted it back into its place. Then he turned to the woman and his face was merry, almost jovial.

"Sleep well?" he said.

"I didn't sleep." She had not imagined his face so gay, as if he were laughing at them both.

"Too bad. Well," he said, "I think I'll go and stretch my legs. Coming?"

"No, thank you," she said, terrified now.

The Air Force sergeants jostled each other getting out of the plane. One of them called to the stewardess, "Don't leave without us, honey." They all laughed and crossed the cement runway, to the airport building, tugging at their clothes, tightening their belts, as if they had just come out of a wrestling match.

The men with brief cases took their hats and coats from the stewardess and thanked her in gray voices for a pleasant journey, and walked away quickly as if they were afraid of being late to their offices.

In the front seat, Kate Merlin sat alone and listened to the stewardess talking with some of the ground crew; their voices were very bright and awake for this hour of the morning. Kate Merlin felt cold and a little sick and dismal, but she would not let herself think about it.

Then he was back beside her and the stewardess was moving down the aisle, like a trained nurse taking temperatures in a hospital ward, to see that they were all properly strapped in for the take-off.

They fastened their seat belts again and then the plane was high in the mauve-gray early morning sky.

"Do I remember you said your name was Kate Merlin?"

"Yes."

"Think of that."

How did he say it? she wondered. How? Complacently?

He was evidently not going to say anything more right now. She looked out the window and her hands were cold. The man was thinking, Well, that's funny. Funny how things happen. He had remembered the night, clearly, while he was walking up and down the cement pavement by the airport building in Washington. It had seemed strange to him, in the morning, but now it seemed less strange. Being an artist, he told himself, they're all a little queer. He had never met an artist before but he was ready to believe that they were not like other people. And being so rich too, he thought, that would make her even queerer. The extremely rich were known to be unlike other people. Her husband, but his name wasn't Merlin, was terrifically rich. He'd read about them: their names, like many other names, seemed to be a sort of tangible asset — like bonds, jewels, or real estate — of the New York columnists. Her husband had inherited millions and owned a famous stable and plane factories or some kind of factories. Thomas Sterling Hamilton, that was his name. It seemed peculiar, her being a successful painter, when her husband was so rich and she didn't need to.

"I've read about you," he remarked.

I have read nothing about you, she thought. What am I supposed to say: you have the advantage of me, sir?

"I even remember one," he said in a pleased voice. "It said something about how your clients, or whatever you call them, were glad to pay thousands for your portraits because you always made them look dangerous. It said that was probably even more flattering than looking beautiful. The women, that is. I wonder where I read it."

It was too awful; it was sickening. It must have been some revolting paragraph in a gossip column. She would surely have been called a society portrait painter and there would be a bit about Thomas and his money.

"What does a painter do during the war?" he asked.

"Paints," she said. Then it seemed too selfish to her and though she was ashamed to be justifying herself to the man, she said quickly, "I don't know how to do anything but paint. I give the money to the Russian Relief or the Chinese Relief or the Red Cross, things like that. It seems the most useful thing I can do, since I'm only trained as a painter." She stopped, horrified at what she had done. What had made her go into a whining explanation, currying favor with this man so he would see what a splendid citizen she really was.

"That's fine." The civilians were all busy as bird dogs for the war, as he knew, and it was very fine of them and all that but it embarrassed him to hear about it. He felt they expected him to be personally grateful and he was not grateful, he did not care what anybody did; he wasn't running this war. Then he thought, This isn't at all like last night. He looked at the woman and saw that she looked even better in the morning. It was amazing how a woman could sit up all night in a plane and look so clean and attractive. He felt his beard rough on his face and his eyes were sticky. She looked delicious and then he remembered how soft she had been in his arms and he wondered what to do about it now.

"I imagined Kate Merlin would be older," he said, thinking aloud.

It was only then that she realized how young he was, twenty-four or perhaps even less. His silence and his assurance and his closed dark second face had made him seem older, or else she had not thought about it at all. She was appalled. What am I becoming, she wondered, am I going to be one of those women without husbands who hunt young men?

"I'm old enough," she said curtly.

He turned and smiled at her. His eyes said, I know about you, don't tell me; I know how you are. It was the man of last night again, the certain one, the one whose body spoke for him. This talent he had when he was silent worked on her like a spell.

He seemed to understand this and very easily he reached his hand over and rested it on the back of her neck, where her hair grew up in soft duck feathers. Her body relaxed under this owning hand. "Yes, I am," she said dreamily, as if he had contradicted her, "I'm thirty-five."

"Are you?" he said. She could feel his hand change. It was quite different. It was a hand that had made a mistake and did not know where it was. It was a hand that would soon move away and become polite.

The man was thinking, thirty-five, well, that *is* old enough. That makes it something else again. And being an artist, he said to himself uneasily. It seemed to him that there was a trick somewhere; he had gotten into something he did not understand. She probably knew more than he did. She had perhaps been playing him along. Perhaps she was thinking he was pretty simple and inexperienced and was amused at how he came up for the bait.

The woman felt that something very bad, very painful, was happening but she could not name it and she held on to her plans of last night because they were happy and they were what she wanted. She said, in a tight voice, and mistrusting the words as she spoke them, "Will you be staying in New York?"

"I don't think so," he said. Speaking gave him a chance to take his hand away and light a cigarette. It might be fun in New York, he thought, meeting all those famous people she would know. He could go with her to El Morocco and the Colony and those places and see her kind of people. She would be something he hadn't had before, thirty-five and a celebrity and all. It might be fun. But he felt uneasy about it; this was not his familiar country. This was not how he saw a fine time, exactly. It was complicated, not safe, you would not know what you were doing. And how about her husband?

"Don't you know?" she said. He did not like that. That sounded like giving orders. That sounded as if she meant to take him over. He was suspicious of her at once.

"No," he said. His face wore the shut-in, indifferent look.

"What might you be doing?" she insisted. Oh stop it, she told herself, for God's sake stop it. What are you doing now; do you want to prove it to yourself?

"I'll be going home first," he said. Give it to her, he thought. He didn't like that bossy, demanding way she suddenly had. "Springfield," he added. She would be thinking now that he was a small-town boy from Massachusetts and that was all right with him.

Then he thought with sudden pleasure of Springfield; he would have a fine time there for a while, a fine time that he understood. He might go on to Boston, where he knew his way around, and have a different but still excellent sort of time. Later, at the end, he would go to New York for a few days but by himself, on his own terms. He did not want to get mixed up. He did not want anything that he could not manage.

He just wanted to have a good easy time with nothing to worry about. She wasn't in his league; he didn't know about married rich, famous women of thirty-five.

The woman felt so cold that she had to hold herself carefully so that she would not shiver. A middle-aged woman, she told herself with horror, hounding a young man. That was what he thought. She had offered herself to him and he had rejected her. He did not want her. She was too old. If only the plane would move faster; if only they would get there so she could hide from him. If only she did not have to sit beside him, sick with the knowledge of what he thought, and sick with shame for herself. She did not know how to protect herself from the shock of this rejection.

The plane flew north along the East River and in the fresh greenish-blue light the city appeared below them. It looked like a great ancient ruin. The towers were vast pillars, planted in the mist, with sharp splintered tops. The squarish skyscrapers were old white temples or giant forts, and there was no life in the jagged quarry of buildings. It was beautiful enough to rock the heart, and suddenly the woman imagined it would look like this, thousands of years from now, enormous and dead.

The man leaned forward to look out the window. "Pretty, isn't it?" he said.

He had really said that and he meant it. That was all he saw. But then it was all right. Whatever he thought of her did not matter; he was too stupid to care about. But she knew this was a lie; nothing had changed. There was the fact and there was no way to escape it; he could have had her and he simply did not want her.

They were the last people off the plane. The other passengers had seemed to block their way on purpose. The woman sent a porter to find a taxi. She would escape from his presence at least, as quickly as she could. When the man saw the taxi stopping before them he said, "Not taking the airline car?"

"No." She did not offer to give him a lift in town. Oh hurry, she thought. The man started to move her bags to the taxi. "Don't bother," she said, "the porter will manage."

He seemed a little puzzled by this flight. "Good luck," he said, shutting the door behind her, "hope I'll see you again some place." It was a thing to say, that was all.

"Good luck to you," she said, and hoped her voice was light and friendly. She did not actually look at him.

"Where to, Miss?" the taxi driver asked. She gave her address and pretended not to see the man saluting good-bye from the curb.

It might have been fun, the man thought, as he watched the taxi turn and head towards the highway. Oh no, hell, he told himself, complications. It was better this way. He began to feel relieved and then he put the whole business out of his mind; he did not want to clutter up his mind with questions or problems and perhaps spoil some of his leave. He thought about Springfield and his face was oval now, smiling. He was in a hurry to get in town and get started. He would not let himself consider the good time ahead in numbered days; he was thinking, now, now, now. He had erased the woman entirely; she was finished and gone.

After the cab passed the gates of the airport, the woman leaned back and took a deep breath to steady herself and to ease the pain in her throat. She covered her eyes with her hand. It's just that I'm so tired, she told herself. This was what she would have to believe. It's nothing to feel desperate about. It's just that I'm so tired, she thought, forcing herself to believe it. It's only because I've been sitting up all night in a plane.

## E. B. White

..................................................................................................................

# The Second Tree from the Corner

FROM *The New Yorker*

"EVER HAVE any bizarre thoughts?" asked the doctor.

Mr. Trexler failed to catch the word. "What kind?" he said.

"Bizarre," repeated the doctor, his voice steady. He watched his patient for any slight change of expression, any wince. It seemed to Trexler that the doctor was not only watching him closely but was creeping slowly toward him, like a lizard toward a bug. Trexler shoved his chair back an inch and gathered himself for a reply. He was about to say "Yes" when he realized that if he said yes the next question would be unanswerable. Bizarre thoughts, bizarre thoughts? Ever have any bizarre thoughts? What kind of thoughts *except* bizarre had he had since the age of two?

Trexler felt the time passing, the necessity for an answer. These psychiatrists were busy men, overloaded, not to be kept waiting. The next patient was probably already perched out there in the waiting room, lonely, worried, shifting around on the sofa, his mind stuffed with bizarre thoughts and amorphous fears. Poor bastard, thought Trexler. Out there all alone in that misshapen antechamber, staring at the filing cabinet and wondering whether to tell the doctor about that day on the Madison Avenue bus.

Let's see, bizarre thoughts. Trexler dodged back along the dreadful corridor of the years to see what he could find. He felt the doctor's eyes upon him and knew that time was running out. Don't be so conscientious, he said to himself. If a bizarre thought is indicated here, just reach into the bag and pick anything at all. A man as well supplied with bizarre thoughts as you are should have no difficulty producing one for the record. Trexler darted into the bag, hung for a moment before one of his thoughts, as a hummingbird pauses in the delphinium. No, he said, not that one. He darted to another (the one about the rhesus monkey), paused, considered. No, he said, not that.

Trexler knew he must hurry. He had already used up pretty nearly four seconds since the question had been put. But it was an impossible situation — just one more lousy, impossible situation such as he was always getting himself into. When, he asked himself, are you going to quit maneuvering yourself into a pocket? He made one more effort. This time he stopped at the asylum, only the bars were lucite — fluted, retractable. Not here, he said. Not this one.

He looked straight at the doctor. "No," he said quietly. "I never have any bizarre thoughts."

The doctor sucked in on his pipe, blew a plume of smoke toward the rows of medical books. Trexler's gaze followed the smoke. He managed to make out one of the titles, "The Genito-Urinary System." A bright wave of fear swept cleanly over him, and he winced under the first pain of kidney stones. He remembered when he was a child, the first time he ever entered a doctor's office, sneaking a look at the titles of the books — and the flush of fear, the shirt wet under the arms, the book on t.b., the sudden knowledge that he was in the advanced stages of consumption, the quick vision of the hemorrhage. Trexler sighed wearily. Forty years, he thought, and I still get thrown by the title of a medical book. Forty years and I still can't stay on life's little bucky horse. No wonder I'm sitting here in this dreary joint at the end of this woebegone afternoon, lying about my bizarre thoughts to a doctor who looks, come to think of it, rather tired.

The session dragged on. After about twenty minutes, the doctor rose and knocked his pipe out. Trexler got up, knocked the ashes out of his brain, and waited. The doctor smiled warmly and stuck out his hand. "There's nothing the matter with you — you're just scared. Want to know how I know you're scared?"

"How?" asked Trexler.

"Look at the chair you've been sitting in! See how it has moved back away from my desk. You kept inching away from me while I asked you questions. That means you're scared."

"Does it?" said Trexler, faking a grin. "Yeah, I suppose it does."

They finished shaking hands. Trexler turned and walked out uncertainly along the passage, then into the waiting room and out past the next patient, a ruddy pin-striped man who was seated on the sofa twirling his hat nervously and staring straight ahead at the files. Poor, frightened guy, thought Trexler, he's probably read in the *Times* that one American male out of every two is going to die of heart disease by twelve o'clock next Thursday. It says that in the paper almost every morning. And he's also probably thinking about that day on the Madison Avenue bus.

A week later, Trexler was back in the patient's chair. And for several weeks thereafter he continued to visit the doctor, always toward the end of the afternoon, when the vapors hung thick above the pool of the mind and darkened the whole region of the East Seventies. He felt no better as time went on, and he found it impossible to work. He discovered that the visits were becoming routine and that although the routine was one to which he certainly did not look forward, at least he could accept it with cool resignation, as once, years ago, he had accepted a long spell with a dentist who had settled down to a steady fooling with a couple of dead teeth. The visits, moreover, were now assuming a pattern recognizable to the patient.

Each session would begin with a résumé of symptoms — dizziness in the streets, the constricting pain in the back of the neck, the apprehensions, the tightness of the scalp, the inability to concentrate, the despondency and the melancholy times, the feeling of pressure and tension, the anger at not being able to work, the anxiety over work not done, the gas on the stomach. Dullest set of neurotic symptoms in the world, Trexler would think, as he obediently trudged back over them for the doctor's benefit. And then, having listened attentively to the recital, the doctor would spring his question: "Have you ever found anything that gives you relief?" And Trexler would answer, "Yes. A drink." And the doctor would nod his head knowingly.

As he became familiar with the pattern Trexler found that he increasingly tended to identify himself with the doctor, transferring himself into the doctor's seat — probably (he thought) some rather slick form of escapism. At any rate, it was nothing new for Trexler to identify himself with other people. Whenever he got into a cab, he instantly became the driver, saw everything from the hackman's angle (and the reaching over with the right hand, the nudging of the flag, the pushing it down, all the way down along the side of the meter), saw everything — traffic, fare, everything — through the eyes of Anthony Rocco, or Isidore Freedman, or Matthew Scott. In a barbershop, Trexler was the barber, his fingers curled around the comb, his hand on the tonic. Perfectly natural, then, that Trexler should soon be occupying the doctor's chair, asking the questions, waiting for the answers. He got quite interested in the doctor, in this way. He liked him, and he found him a not too difficult patient.

It was on the fifth visit, about halfway through, that the doctor turned to Trexler and said, suddenly, "What do you want?" He gave the word "want" special emphasis.

"I d'know," replied Trexler uneasily. "I guess nobody knows the answer to that one."

"Sure they do," replied the doctor.

"Do *you* know what *you* want?" asked Trexler narrowly.

"Certainly," said the doctor. Trexler noticed that at this point the doctor's chair slid slightly backward, away from him. Trexler stifled a small, internal smile. Scared as a rabbit, he said to himself. Look at him scoot!

"What *do* you want?" continued Trexler, pressing his advantage, pressing it hard.

The doctor glided back another inch away from his inquisitor. "I want a wing on the small house I own in Westport. I want more money, and more leisure to do the things I want to do."

Trexler was just about to say, "And what are those things you want to do, Doctor?" when he caught himself. Better not go too far, he mused. Better not lose possession of the ball. And besides, he thought, what the hell goes on here, anyway — me paying fifteen bucks a throw for these séances and then doing the work myself, asking the questions, weighing the answers. So he wants a new wing! There's a fine piece of theatrical gauze for you! A new wing.

Trexler settled down again and resumed the role of patient for the rest of the visit. It ended on a kindly, friendly note. The doctor reassured him that his fears were the cause of his sickness, and that his fears were unsubstantial. They shook hands, smiling.

Trexler walked dizzily through the empty waiting room and the doctor followed along to let him out. It was late; the secretary had shut up shop and gone home. Another day over the dam. "Good-bye," said Trexler. He stepped into the street, turned west toward Madison, and thought of the doctor all alone there, after hours, in that desolate hole — a man who worked longer hours than his secretary. Poor, scared, overworked bastard, thought Trexler. And that new wing!

It was an evening of clearing weather, the Park showing green and desirable in the distance, the last daylight applying a high lacquer to the brick and brownstone walls and giving the street scene a luminous and intoxicating splendor. Trexler meditated, as he walked, on what he wanted. "What do you want?" he heard again. Trexler knew what he wanted, and what, in general, all men wanted; and he was glad, in a way, that it was both inexpressible and unattainable, and that it wasn't a wing. He was satisfied to remember that it was deep, formless, enduring, and impossible of fulfillment, and that it made men sick, and that when you sauntered along Third Avenue and looked through the doorways into the dim saloons, you could sometimes pick out from the unregenerate ranks the ones who had not forgotten, gazing steadily into the bottoms of the glasses on the long chance that they could get another little peek at it. Trexler found himself renewed by the remembrance that what he wanted was at once great and microscopic, and that although it borrowed from the nature of large deeds and of youthful love and of old songs and early intimations, it was not any one of these things, and that it had not been isolated or pinned down, and that a man who attempted to define it in the privacy of a doctor's office would fall flat on his face.

Trexler felt invigorated. Suddenly his sickness seemed health, his dizziness stability. A small tree, rising between him and the light, stood there saturated with the evening, each gilt-edged leaf perfectly drunk with excellence and delicacy. Trexler's spine registered an ever so slight tremor as it picked up this natural disturbance in the lovely scene. "I want the second tree from the corner, just as it stands," he said, answering an imaginary question from an imaginary physician. And he felt a slow pride in realizing that what he wanted none could bestow, and that what he had none could take away. He felt content to be sick, unembarrassed at being afraid; and in the jungle of his fear he glimpsed (as he had so often glimpsed them before) the flashy tail feathers of the bird courage.

Then he thought once again of the doctor, and of his being left there all alone, tired, frightened. (The poor, scared guy, thought Trexler.) Trexler began humming "Moonshine Lullaby," his spirit reacting instantly to the hypodermic of Merman's healthy voice. He crossed Madison, boarded a downtown bus, and rode all the way to Fifty-second Street before he had a thought that could rightly have been called bizarre.

1949

*Elizabeth Bishop*

# The Farmer's Children

FROM *Harper's Bazaar*

ONCE, on a large farm ten miles from the nearest town, lived a hard-working farmer with his wife, their three little girls, and his children by a former marriage, two boys aged eleven and twelve. The first wife had been the daughter of a minister, a plain and simple woman who had named her sons Cato and Emerson; while the stepmother, being romantic and overgenerous, to her own children at least, had given them the names of Lea Leola, Rosina, and Gracie Bell. There was also the usual assortment of horses, cows, and poultry, and a hired man named Judd.

The farm had belonged to the children's father's grandfather, and although pieces of it had been sold from time to time, it was still very large, actually too large. The original farmhouse had been a mile away from the present one, on the "old" road. It had been struck by lightning and burned down ten years before, and Emerson's and Cato's grandparents, who had lived in it, had moved in with their son and his first wife for the year or two they had lived on after the fire. The old home had been long and low, and an enormous willow tree, which had miraculously escaped the fire and still grew, had shaded one corner of the roof. The new home stood beside the macadamized "new" road and was high and boxlike, painted yellow with a roof of glittering tin.

Besides the willow tree, the principal barn at the old home had also escaped the fire and it was still used for storing hay and as a shed in which were kept most of the farm implements. Because farm implements are so valuable, always costing more than the farmer can afford, and because the barn was so far from the house and could easily have been broken into, the hired man slept there every night, in a pile of hay.

Most of these facts later appeared in the newspapers. It also appeared that since Judd had come to be the hired man, three months ago, he and the children's father had formed a habit of taking overnight trips to town. They went on "business," something to do with selling another strip of land, but probably mostly to drink; and while they were away Emerson and Cato would take Judd's place in the old barn and watch over the reaper, the tedder, the hay-rake, the manure-spreader, the harrow, et cetera — all the weird and expensive machinery of jaws and teeth and arms and claws, of direct and reflex actions and odd gestures, apparently so intelligent, but, in this case, so completely helpless because it was still dragged by horses.

It was December and frightfully cold. The full moon was just coming up and the tin roof of the farmhouse and patches of the macadam road caught her light, while the farmyard was still almost in darkness. The children had been put outdoors by their mother, who was in a fit of temper because they got in her way while she was preparing supper. Bundled up in mackinaws, with icy hands, they played at raft and shipwreck. There was a pile of planks in a corner of the yard, with which their father had long been planning to repair some outhouse or other, and on it Lea Leola and Rosina sat stolidly, saved, while Cato, with a clothes-pole, stood up and steered. Still on the sinking ship, a chicken coop across the yard, stood the baby, Gracie Bell, holding out her arms and looking apprehensively around her, just about to cry. But Emerson was swimming to her rescue. He walked slowly, placing his heel against his toes at every step, and swinging both arms round and round like windmills.

"Be brave, Gracie Bell! I'm almost there!" he cried. He gasped loudly. "My strength is almost exhausted, but I'll save you!"

Cato was calling out, over and over, "Now the ship is sinking inch by inch! Now the ship is sinking inch by inch!"

Small and silvery, their voices echoed in the cold countryside. The moon freed herself from the last field and looked evenly across at the imaginary ocean tragedy taking place so far inland. Emerson lifted Gracie Bell in his arms. She clutched him tightly around the neck and burst into loud sobs, but he turned firmly back, treading water with tiny up-and-down steps. Gracie Bell shrieked and he repeated, "I'll save you, Gracie Bell. I'll save you, Gracie Bell," but did not change his pace.

The mother and stepmother suddenly opened the back door.

"Emerson!" she screamed. "Put that child down! Didn't I tell you the next time you made that child cry I'd beat you until you couldn't holler? Didn't I?"

"Oh Ma, we was just . . ."

"What's the matter with you kids, anyway? Fight and scrap, fight and scrap, and yowl, yowl, yowl, from morning to night. And you two boys, you're too big," and so on. The ugly words poured out and the children stood about the yard like stage-struck actors. But as their father said, "her bark was worse than her bite," and in a few minutes, as if silenced by the moon's bland reserve, she stopped and said in a slightly lower voice, "All right, you kids. What are you standing there waiting for? Come inside the house and get your supper."

The kitchen was hot, and the smell of fried potatoes and the warm yellow light of the oil lamp on the table gave an illusion of peacefulness. The two boys sat on one side, the two older girls sat on the other, and Gracie Bell on her mother's lap at the end. The father and Judd had gone to town, one reason why the mother had been unusually bad-tempered all afternoon. They ate in silence, except for the mother's endearments to Gracie Bell, whom she was helping to drink tea and condensed milk out of a white cup. They ate the fried potatoes with pieces of pork in them, slice after slice of white "store" bread and dishes of "preserves," and drank syrupy hot tea and milk. The oilcloth on the table was light molasses-colored, sprinkled with small yellow poppies; it glistened pleasantly, and the "preserves" glowed, dark red blobs surrounded by transparent ruby.

"Tonight's the night for the crumbs," Cato was thinking, and from time to time he managed to slide four slices of bread under the edge of the oilcloth and then up under his sweater. His thoughts sounded loud and ominous to him and he looked cautiously at his sisters to see if they had noticed anything, but their pale, rather flat faces looked blankly back. Anyway, it was the night for crumbs and what else could he possibly do?

The other two times he and Emerson had spent the night in the old barn he had used bits of torn-up newspaper because he hadn't been able to find the white pebbles anywhere. He and his brother had walked home, still half-asleep, in the gray-blue light just before sunrise, and he had been delighted to find the sprinkles of speckled paper here and there all along the way. He had dropped it out of his pocket a little at a time, scarcely daring to look back, and it had worked. But he had longed for the endless full moon of the tale, and the pebbles that would have shone "like silver coins." Emerson knew nothing of his plan — his system, rather — but it had worked without his help and in spite of all discrepancies.

The mother set Gracie Bell down and started to transfer dishes from the table to the sink.

"I suppose you boys forgot you've got to get over to the barn sometime tonight," she said ironically.

Emerson protested a little.

"Now you just put on your things and get started before it gets any later. Maybe sometime your pa will get them doors fixed or maybe he'll get a new barn. Go along, now." She lifted the tea-kettle off the stove.

Cato couldn't find his knitted gloves. He thought they were on the shelf in the corner with the schoolbags. He looked methodically for them everywhere and then at last he became aware of Lea Leola's malicious smile.

"Ma! Lea Leola's got my gloves. She's hid them on me!"

"Lea Leola! Have you got his gloves?" Her mother advanced on her.

"Make her give them to me!"

Lea Leola said, "I ain't even seen his old gloves," and started to weep.

"Now Cato, see what you've done! Shut up, Lea Leola, for God's sake, and you boys hurry up and get out of here. I've had enough trouble for one day."

At the door Emerson said, "It's cold, Ma."

"Well, Judd's got his blankets over there. Go on, go along and shut that door. You're letting the cold in."

Outside it was almost as bright as day. The macadam road looked very gray and rang under their feet, that immediately grew numb with cold. The cold stuck quickly to the little hairs in their nostrils, that felt painfully stuffed with icy straws. But if they tried to warm their noses against the clumsy lapels of their mackinaws, the freezing moisture felt even worse, and they gave it up and merely pointed out their breath to each other as it whitened and then vanished. The moon was behind them. Cato looked over his shoulder and saw how the tin roof of the farmhouse shone, bluish, and how, above it, the stars looked blue, too, blue or yellow, and very small; you could hardly see most of them.

Emerson was talking quietly, enlarging on his favorite theme: how he could obtain a certain bicycle he had seen a while ago in the window of the hardware store in town. He went on and on but Cato didn't pay very much attention, first because he knew quite well already almost every-thing Emerson was saying or could say about the bicycle, and second because he was busy crumbling the four slices of bread which he had worked around into his pants pockets, two slices in each. It seemed to turn into lumps instead of crumbs and it was hard to pull off the little bits with his nails and flick them into the road from time to time under the skirt of his mackinaw.

Emerson made no distinction between honest and dishonest meth-ods of getting the bicycle. Sometimes he would discuss plans for deceiv-ing the owner of the hardware store, who would somehow be maneu-vered into sending it to him by mistake, and sometimes it was to be his reward for a deed of heroism. Sometimes he spoke of a glass-cutter. He had seen his father use one of these fascinating instruments. If he had one he could cut a large hole in the plate glass window of the hardware store in the night. And then he spoke of working next sum-mer as a hired man. He would work for the farmer who had the farm next to theirs; he saw himself performing prodigious feats of haying and milking.

"But Old Man Blackader only pays big boys four dollars a week," said Cato, sensibly, "and he wouldn't pay you that much."

"Well . . ."

Emerson swore and spat toward the side of the road, and they went on while the moon rose steadily higher and higher.

A humming noise ran along the telephone wires over their heads. They thought it might possibly be caused by all the people talking over them at the same time but it didn't actually sound like voices. The glass conductors that bore the wires shone pale green, and the poles were bleached silver by the moonlight, and from each one came a strange roaring, deeper than the hum of the wires. It sounded like a swarm of bees. They put their ears to the deep black cracks. Cato tried to peer into one and almost thought he could see the mass of black and iridescent bees inside.

"But they'd all be frozen — solid," Emerson said.

"No they wouldn't. They sleep all winter."

Emerson wanted to climb a pole. Cato said, "You might get a shock."

He helped him, however, and boosted up his thin haunches in both hands. But Emerson could just barely touch the lowest spike and wasn't strong enough to pull himself up.

At last they came to where their path turned off the road, and went through a cornfield where the stalks still stood, motionless in the cold. Cato dropped quite a few crumbs to mark the turning. On the cornstalks the long, colorless leaves hung in tatters like streamers of old crepe paper, like the remains of booths that had stood along the midway of a county fair. The stalks were higher than their heads, like trees. Double lines of wire, with glinting barbs, were strung along both sides of the wheel tracks.

Emerson and Cato fought all day almost every day, but rarely at night. Now they were arguing amicably about how cold it was.

"It might snow even," Cato said.

"No," said Emerson, "it's too cold to snow."

"But when it gets awful cold it snows," said Cato.

"But when it gets real cold, awful cold like this, it can't snow."

"Why can't it?"

"Because it's too cold. Anyway, there isn't any up there."

They looked. Yes, except for the large white moon, the sky was as empty as could be.

Cato tried not to drop his crumbs in the dry turf between the wagon tracks, where they would not show. In the ruts he could see them a little, small and grayish. Of course there were no birds. But he couldn't seem to think it through — whether his plan was good for anything or not.

Back home in the yellow farmhouse the stepmother was getting ready for bed. She went to find an extra quilt to put over Lea Leola, Rosina, and Gracie Bell, sleeping in one bed in the next room. She spread it out and tucked it in without disturbing them. Then, in spite of the cold, she stood for a moment looking down uneasily at its pattern of large, branching hexagons, blanched, almost colorless, in the moonlight. That had always been such a pretty quilt! Her mother had made it. What was the name of that pattern? What was it it reminded her of? Out from the forms of a lost childish game, from between the pages of a lost schoolbook, the image fell upon her brain: a snowflake.

"Where is that damned old barn?" Emerson asked, and spat again.

It was a relief to get to it and to see the familiar willow tree and to tug at one side of the dragging barn door with hands that had no feeling left in them. At first it seemed dark inside but soon the moon lit it all quite well. At the left were the disused stalls for the cows and horses, the various machines stood down the middle and at the right, and the hay now hung vaguely overhead on each side. But it was too cold to smell the hay.

Where were Judd's blankets? They couldn't find them anywhere. After looking in all the stalls and on the wooden pegs that held the harness, Emerson dropped down on a pile of hay in front of the harrow, by the door.

Cato said, "Maybe it would be better up in the mow." He put his bare hands on a rung of the ladder.

Emerson said, "I'm too cold to climb the ladder," and giggled.

So Cato sat down in the pile of hay on the floor, too, and they started heaping it over their legs and bodies. It felt queer; it had no weight or substance in their hands. It was lighter than feathers and wouldn't seem to settle down over them; it just prickled a little.

Emerson said he was tired and, turning on his side, he swore a few more times, almost cautiously. Cato swore, too, and lay on his back, close to his brother.

The harrow was near his head and its flat, sharp-edged disks gleamed at him coldly. Just beyond it he could make out the hay-rake. Its row of long, curved prongs caught the moonlight too, and from where he lay, almost on a level with them, the prongs made a steely, formal wave that came straight toward him over the floor boards. And around him in darkness and light were all the other machines: the manure-spreader made a huge shadow; the reaper lifted a strong forearm lined with saw teeth, like that of a gigantic grasshopper; and the tedder's sharp little forks were suspended in one of the bright patches, some up, some down, as if it had just that minute stopped a cataleptic kicking.

Up over their heads, between the mows, every crack and hole in the old roof showed, and little flecks, like icy chips of moon, fell on them, on the clutter of implements and on the gray hay. Once in a while one of the shingles would crack, or one of the brittle twigs of the willow tree would snap sharply.

Cato thought with pleasure of the trail of crumbs he had left all the way from the house to here. "And there aren't any birds," he thought almost gleefully. He and Emerson would start home again as they had the previous times, just before sunrise, and he would see the crumbs leading straight back the way they had come, white and steadfast in the early light.

Then he began to think of his father and Judd, off in town. He pictured his father in a bright, electrically lit little restaurant, with blue walls, where it was very hot, eating a plate of dark red kidney beans. He had been there once and that was what he had been given to eat. For a while he thought, with disfavor, of his stepmother and stepsisters, and then his thoughts returned to his father; he loved him dearly.

Emerson muttered something about "that old Judd," and burrowed deeper into the hay. Their teeth were chattering. Cato tried to get his hands between his thighs, to warm them, but the hay got in the way. It felt like hoar-frost. It scratched and then melted against the skin of his numb hands. It gave him the same sensation as when he ate the acid grape jelly his stepmother made each fall and little sticks, little stiff crystal sticks, like ice, would prick and dissolve, also in the dark, against the roof of his mouth.

Through the half-open door the cornstalks in the cornfield stood suspiciously straight and tall. What went on among those leaf-hung stalks? Shouldn't they have been cut down, anyway? There stood the corn and there stood, or squatted, the machines. He turned his head to look at them. All that corn should be reaped. The reaper held out its arm stiffly. The hayrack looked like the set coil of a big trap.

It hurt to move his feet. His feet felt just like a horse's hooves, as if he had horseshoes on them. He touched one and yes, it was true, it felt just like a big horseshoe.

The harnesses were hanging on their pegs above him. Their little bits of metal glittered pale blue and yellow like the little tiny stars. If the harnesses should fall down on him he would have to be a horse and it would be so cold out in the field pulling the heavy harrow. The harnesses were heavy, too; he had tried the collars a few times and they were very heavy. It would take two horses; he would have to wake up Emerson, although Emerson was hard to wake when he got to sleep.

The disks of the harrow looked like the side — those shields hung over the side — of a Viking ship. The harrow was a ship that was going to go up to the moon with the shields all clanging on her sides; he must get up into the seat and steer. That queer seat of perforated iron that looked uncomfortable and yet when one got into it, gave one such a feeling of power and ease. . . .

But how could it be going to the moon when the moon was coming right down on the hill? No, moons; there was a whole row of them. No, those must be the disks of the harrow. No, the moon had split into a sheaf of moons, slipping off each other sideways, off and off and off and off.

He turned to Emerson and called his name, but Emerson only moaned in his sleep. So he fitted his knees into the hollows at the back of his brother's and hugged him tightly around the waist.

At noon the next day their father found them in this position.

The story was in all the newspapers, on the front page of local ones, dwindling as it traveled over the countryside to short paragraphs on middle pages when it got as far as each coast. The farmer grieved wildly for a year; for some reason, one expression he gave to his feelings was to fire Judd.

## J. F. Powers

# Death of a Favorite

FROM *The New Yorker*

I HAD SPENT most of the afternoon mousing — a matter of sport with me and certainly not of diet — in the sunburnt fields that begin at our back door and continue hundreds of miles into the Dakotas. I gradually gave up the idea of hunting, the grasshoppers convincing me that there was no percentage in stealth. Even to doze was difficult, under such conditions, but I must have managed it. At least I was late coming to dinner, and so my introduction to the two missionaries took place at table. They were surprised, as most visitors are, to see me take the chair at Father Malt's right.

Father Malt, breaking off the conversation (if it could be called that), was his usual dear old self. "Fathers," he said, "meet Fritz."

I gave the newcomers the first good look that invariably tells me whether or not a person cares for cats. The mean old buck in charge of the team did not like me, I could see, and would bear watching. The other one obviously did like me, but he did not appear to be long enough from the seminary to matter. I felt that I had broken something less than even here.

"My assistant," said Father Malt, meaning me, and thus unconsciously dealing out our fat friend at the other end of the table. Poor Burner! There was a time when, thinking of him, as I did now, as the enemy, I could have convinced myself I meant something else. But he *is* the enemy, and I was right from the beginning, when it could only have been instinct that told me how much he hated me even while trying (in his fashion!) to be friendly. (I believe his prejudice to be acquired rather than congenital, and very likely, at this stage, confined to me, not to cats as a class — there *is* that in his favor. I intend to be fair about this if it kills me.)

My observations of humanity incline me to believe that one of us — Burner or I — must ultimately prevail over the other. For myself, I should not fear if this were a battle to be won on the solid ground of Father Malt's affections. But the old man grows older, the grave beckons to him ahead, and with Burner pushing him from behind, how long can he last? Which is to say: How long can *I* last? Unfortunately, it is naked power that counts most in any rectory, and as things stand now, I am safe only so long as Father Malt retains it here. Could I — this impossible thought is often with me now — could I effect a reconciliation and alliance with Father Burner? Impossible! Yes, doubtless. But the question better asked is: *How* impossible? (Lord knows I would not inflict this line of reasoning upon myself if I did not hold with the rumors that Father Burner will be the one to succeed to the pastorate.) For I do like it here. It is not at all in my nature to forgive and forget, certainly not as regards Father Burner, but it is in my nature to come to terms (much as nations do) when necessary, and in this solution there need not be a drop of good will. No dog can make that statement, or take the consequences, which I understand are most serious, in the world to come. Shifts and ententes. There is something fatal about the vocation of favorite, but it is the only one that suits me, and, all things considered — to dig I am not able, to bet I am ashamed — the rewards are adequate.

"We go through Chicago all the time," said the boss missionary, who seemed to be returning to a point he had reached when I entered. I knew Father Malt would be off that evening for a convention in Chicago. The missionaries, who would fill in for him and conduct a forty hours' devotion on the side, belonged to an order just getting started in the diocese and were anxious to make a good impression. For the present, at least, as a kind of special introductory offer, they could be had dirt-cheap. Thanks to them, pastors who'd never been able to get away had got a taste of Florida last winter.

"Sometimes we stay over in Chicago," bubbled the young missionary. He was like a rookie ballplayer who hadn't made many road trips.

"We've got a house there," said the first, whose name in religion, as they say, was — so help me — Philbert. Later, Father Burner would get around it by calling him by his surname. Father Malt was the sort who wouldn't see anything funny about "Philbert," but it would be too much to expect him to remember such a name.

"What kind of a house?" asked Father Malt. He held up his hearing aid and waited for clarification.

Father Philbert replied in a shout, "The Order owns a *house* there!"

Father Malt fingered his hearing aid.

Father Burner sought to interpret for Father Philbert. "I think, Father, he wants to know what it's made out of."

"Red brick — it's red brick," bellowed Father Philbert.

"*My* house is red brick," said Father Malt.

"I *noticed* that," said Father Philbert.

Father Malt shoved the hearing aid at him.

"I know it," said Father Philbert, shouting again.

Father Malt nodded and fed me a morsel of fish. Even for a Friday, it wasn't much of a meal. I would not have been sorry to see this housekeeper go.

"All right, all right," said Father Burner to the figure lurking behind the door and waiting for him, always the last one, to finish. "She stands and looks in at you through the crack," he beefed. "Makes you feel like a condemned man." The housekeeper came into the room, and he addressed the young missionary (Burner was a great one for questioning the young): "Ever read any books by this fella Koestler, Father?"

"The Jesuit?" the young one asked.

"Hell, no, he's some kind of a writer. I know the man you mean, though. Spells his name different. Wrote a book — apologetics."

"That's the one. Very — "

"Dull."

"Well . . ."

"This other fella's not bad. He's a writer who's ahead of his time — about fifteen minutes. Good on jails and concentration camps. You'd think he was born in one if you ever read his books." Father Burner regarded the young missionary with absolute indifference. "But you didn't."

"No. Is he a Catholic?" inquired the young one.

"He's an Austrian or something."

"Oh."

The housekeeper removed the plates and passed the dessert around. When she came to Father Burner, he asked her privately, "What is it?"

"Pudding," she said, not whispering, as he would have liked.

"*Bread* pudding?" Now he was threatening her.

"Yes, Father."

Father Burner shuddered and announced to everybody, "No dessert for me." When the housekeeper had retired into the kitchen, he said, "Sometimes I think he got her from a hospital and sometimes, Father, I think she came from one of *your* fine institutions" — this to the young missionary.

Father Philbert, however, was the one to see the joke, and he laughed.

"My God," said Father Burner, growing bolder. "I'll never forget the time I stayed at your house in Louisville. If I hadn't been there for just a day — for the Derby, in fact — I'd have gone to Rome about it. I think I've had better meals here."

At the other end of the table, Father Malt, who could not have heard a word, suddenly blinked and smiled; the missionaries looked to him for some comment, in vain.

"He doesn't hear me," said Father Burner. "Besides, I think he's listening to the news."

"I didn't realize it was a radio too," said the young missionary.

"Oh, hell, yes."

"I think he's pulling your leg," said Father Philbert.

"Well, I thought so," said the young missionary ruefully.

"It's an idea," said Father Burner. Then in earnest to Father Philbert, whom he'd really been working around to all the time — the young one was decidedly not his type — "You the one drivin' that new Olds, Father?"

"It's not mine, Father," said Father Philbert with a meekness that would have been hard to take if he'd meant it. Father Burner understood him perfectly, however, and I thought they were two persons who would get to know each other a lot better.

"Nice job. They say it compares with the Cad in power. What do you call that color — oxford or clerical gray?"

"I really couldn't say, Father. It's my brother's. He's a layman in Minneapolis — St. Stephen's parish. He loaned it to me for this little trip."

Father Burner grinned. He could have been thinking, as I was, that Father Philbert protested too much. "Thought I saw you go by earlier," he said. "What's the matter — didn't you want to come in when you saw the place?"

Father Philbert, who was learning to ignore Father Malt, laughed discreetly. "Couldn't be sure this was it. That house on the *other* side of the church, now —"

Father Burner nodded. "Like that, huh? Belongs to a Mason."

Father Philbert sighed and said, "It would."

"Not at all," said Father Burner. "I like 'em better than K.C.s." If he could get the audience for it, Father Burner enjoyed being broad-minded. Gazing off in the direction of the Mason's big house, he said, "I've played golf with him."

The young missionary looked at Father Burner in horror. Father Philbert merely smiled. Father Burner, toying with a large crumb, propelled it in my direction.

"Did a bell ring?" asked Father Malt.

"His P.A. system," Father Burner explained. "Better tell him," he said to the young missionary. "You're closer. He can't bring me in on those batteries he uses."

"No bell," said the young missionary, lapsing into basic English and gestures.

Father Malt nodded, as though he hadn't really thought so.

"How do you like it?" said Father Burner.

Father Philbert hesitated, and then he said, "Here, you mean?"

"I wouldn't ask you that," said Father Burner, laughing. "Talkin' about that Olds. Like it? Like the Hydromatic?"

"No kiddin', Father. It's not mine," Father Philbert protested.

"All right, all right," said Father Burner, who obviously did not believe him. "Just so you don't bring up your vow of poverty." He looked at Father Philbert's uneaten bread pudding — "Had enough?" — and rose from the table, blessing himself. The other two followed when Father Malt, who was feeding me cheese, waved them away. Father Burner came around to us, bumping my chair — intentionally, I know. He stood behind Father Malt and yelled into his ear. "Any calls for me this aft?" He'd been out somewhere, as usual. I often thought he expected too much to happen in his absence.

"There was something . . ." said Father Malt, straining his memory, which was poor.

"*Yes?*"

"Now I remember — they had the wrong number."

Father Burner, looking annoyed and downhearted, left the room.

"They said they'd call back," said Father Malt, sensing Father Burner's disappointment.

I left Father Malt at the table reading his Office under the orange light of the chandelier. I went to the living room, to my spot in the window from which I could observe Father Burner and the missionaries on the front porch, the young one in the swing with his breviary — the mosquitoes, I judged, were about to join him — and the other two just smoking and standing around, like pool players waiting for a table. I heard Father Philbert say, "Like to take a look at it, Father?"

"Say, that's an idea," said Father Burner.

I saw them go down the front walk to the gray Olds parked at the curb. With Father Burner at the wheel they drove away. In a minute they were back, the car moving uncertainly — this I noted with considerable pleasure until I realized that Father Burner was simply testing the brakes. Then they were gone, and after a bit, when they did not return, I supposed they were out killing poultry on the open road.

That evening, when the ushers dropped in at the rectory, there was not the same air about them as when they came for pinochle. Without fanfare, Mr. Bauman, their leader, who had never worked any but the center aisle, presented Father Malt with a travelling bag. It was nice of him, I thought, when he said, "It's from all of us," for it could not have come from all equally. Mr. Bauman, in hardware, and Mr. Keller, the druggist, were the only ones well off, and must have forked out plenty for such a fine piece of luggage, even after the discount.

Father Malt thanked all six ushers with little nods in which there was no hint of favoritism. "Ha," he kept saying. "You shouldn't done it."

The ushers bobbed and ducked, dodging his flattery, and kept up a mumble to the effect that Father Malt deserved everything they'd ever done for him and more. Mr. Keller came forward to instruct Father Malt in the use of the various clasps and zippers. Inside the bag was another gift, a set of military brushes, which I could see they were afraid he would not discover for himself. But he unsnapped a brush, and, like the veteran crowd-pleaser he was, swiped once or twice at his head with it after spitting into the bristles. The ushers all laughed.

"Pretty snazzy," said the newest usher — the only young blood among them. Mr. Keller had made him a clerk at the store, had pushed through his appointment as alternate usher in the church, and was gradually weaning him away from his motorcycle. With Mr. Keller, the lad formed a block to Mr. Bauman's power, but he was perhaps worse than no ally at all. Most of the older men, though they pretended a willingness to help him meet the problems of an usher, were secretly pleased when he bungled at collection time and skipped a row or over-lapped one.

Mr. Keller produced a box of ten-cent cigars, which, as a *personal* gift from him, came as a bitter surprise to the others. He was not big enough, either, to attribute it to them too. He had anticipated their resentment, however, and now produced a bottle of milk of magnesia. No one could deny the comic effect, for Father Malt had been known to recommend the blue bottle from the confessional.

"Ha!" said Father Malt, and everybody laughed.

"In case you get upset on the trip," said the druggist.

"You know it's the best thing," said Father Malt in all seriousness, and then even he remembered he'd said it too often before. He passed the cigars. The box went from hand to hand, but, except for the druggist's clerk, nobody would have one.

Father Malt, seeing this, wisely renewed his thanks for the bag, insisting upon his indebtedness until it was actually in keeping with the idea the ushers had of their own generosity. Certainly none of them had ever owned a bag like that. Father Malt went to the housekeeper with it and asked her to transfer his clothes from the old bag, already packed, to the new one. When he returned, the ushers were still standing around feeling good about the bag and not so good about the cigars. They'd discuss that later. Father Malt urged them to sit down. He seemed to want them near him as long as possible. They *were* his friends, but I could not blame Father Burner for avoiding them. He was absent now, as he usually managed to be when the ushers called. If he ever succeeded Father Malt, who let them have the run of the place, they would be the first to suffer — after me! As Father Malt was the heart, they were the substance of a parish that remained rural while becoming increasingly suburban. They dressed up occasionally and dropped into St. Paul and Minneapolis, "the Cities," as visiting firemen into Hell, though it would be difficult to imagine any other place as graceless and far-gone as our own hard little highway town — called Sherwood but about as sylvan as a tennis court.

They were regular fellows — not so priestly as their urban colleagues — loud, heavy of foot, wearers of long underwear in wintertime and iron-gray business suits the year round. Their idea of a good time (pilsner beer, cheap cigars smoked with the bands left on, and pinochle) coincided nicely with their understanding of "doing good" (a percentage of every pot went to the parish building fund). Their wives, also active, played cards in the church basement and sold vanilla extract and chances — mostly to each other, it appeared — with all revenue over cost going to what was known as "the missions." This evening I could be grateful that time was not going to permit the usual pinochle game. (In the midst of all their pounding — almost as hard on me as it was on the dining-room table — I often felt they should have played on a meat block.)

The ushers, settling down all over the living room, started to talk about Father Malt's trip to Chicago. The housekeeper brought in a round of beer.

"How long you be gone, Father — three days?" one of them asked.

Father Malt said that he'd be gone about three days.

"Three days! This is Friday. Tomorrow's Saturday. Sunday. Monday." Everything stopped while the youngest usher counted on his fingers. "Back on Tuesday?"

Father Malt nodded.

"Who's takin' over on Sunday?"

Mr. Keller answered for Father Malt. "He's got some missionary fathers in."

"Missionaries!"

The youngest usher then began to repeat himself on one of his two or three topics. "Hey, Father, don't forget to drop in the U.S.O. if it's still there. I was in Chi during the war," he said, but nobody would listen to him.

Mr. Bauman had cornered Father Malt and was trying to tell him where that place was — that place where he'd eaten his meals during the World's Fair; one of the waitresses was from Minnesota. I'd had enough of this — the next thing would be a diagram on the back of an envelope — and I'd heard Father Burner come in earlier. I went upstairs to check on him. For a minute or two I stood outside his room listening. He had Father Philbert with him, and, just as I'd expected, he was talking against Father Malt, leading up to the famous question with which Father Malt, years ago, had received the Sherwood appointment from the Archbishop: "Have dey got dere a goot meat shop?"

Father Philbert laughed, and I could hear him sip from his glass and place it on the floor beside his chair. I entered the room, staying close to the baseboard, in the shadows, curious to know what they were drinking. I maneuvered myself into position to sniff Father Philbert's glass. To my surprise, Scotch. Here was proof that Father Burner considered Father Philbert a friend. At that moment I could not think what it was he expected to get out of a lowly missionary. My mistake, not realizing then how correct and prophetic I'd ben earlier in thinking of them as two of a kind. It seldom happened that Father Burner got out the real Scotch for company, or for himself *in* company. For most guests he had nothing — a safe policy, since a surprising number of temperance cranks passed through the rectory — and for unwelcome guests who would like a drink he kept a bottle of "Scotch-type" whiskey, which was a smooth, smoky blend of furniture polish that came in a fancy bottle, was offensive even when watered, and cheap, though rather hard to get since the end of the war. He had a charming way of plucking the rare bottle from a bureau drawer, as if this were indeed an occasion for him; even so, he would not touch the stuff, presenting himself as a chap of simple tastes, of no taste at all for the things of this world, who would prefer, if anything, the rude wine made from our own grapes — if we'd had any grapes. Quite an act, and one he thoroughly enjoyed, holding his glass of pure water and asking, "How's your drink, Father? Strong enough?"

The housekeeper, appearing at the door, said there's been a change of plans and some of the ushers were driving Father Malt to the train.

"Has he gone yet?" asked Father Burner.

"Not yet, Father."

"Well, tell him goodbye for me."

"Yes, Father."

When she had gone, he said, "I'd tell him myself, but I don't want to run into that bunch."

Father Philbert smiled. "What's he up to in Chicago?"

"They've got one of those pastors' and builders' conventions going on at the Stevens Hotel."

"Is he building?"

"No, but he's a pastor and he'll get a lot of free samples. He won't buy anything."

"Not much has been done around here, huh?" said Father Philbert.

He had fed Father Burner the question he wanted. "He built that fish pond in the back yard — for his minnows. That's the extent of the building program in his time. Of course he's only been here a while."

"How long?"

"Fourteen years," said Father Burner. *He* would be the greatest builder of them all — if he ever got the chance. He lit a cigarette and smiled. "What he's really going to Chicago for is to see a couple of ball games."

Father Philbert did not smile. "Who's playing there now?" he said.

A little irritated at this interest, Father Burner said, "I believe it's the Red Sox — or is it the Reds? Hell, how do I know?"

"Couldn't be the Reds," said Father Philbert. "The boy and I were in

Cincinnati last week and it was the start of a long home stand for them."

"Very likely," said Father Burner.

While the missionary, a Cardinal fan, analyzed the pennant race in the National League, Father Burner sulked. "What's the best train out of Chicago for Washington?" he suddenly inquired.

Father Philbert told him what he could but admitted that his information dated from some years back. "We don't make the run to Washington any more."

"That's right," said Father Burner. "Washington's in the American League."

Father Philbert laughed, turning aside the point that he travelled with the Cardinals. "I thought you didn't know about these things," he said.

"About these things it's impossible to stay ignorant," said Father Burner. "Here, and the last place, and the place before that, and in the seminary — a ball, a bat, and God. I'll be damned, Father, if I'll do as the Romans do."

"What price glory?" inquired Father Philbert, as if he smelt heresy.

"I know," said Father Burner. "And it'll probably cost me the red hat." A brave comment, perhaps, from a man not yet a country pastor, and it showed me where his thoughts were again. He did not disguise his humble ambition by speaking lightly of an impossible one. "Scratch a prelate and you'll find a second baseman," he fumed.

Father Philbert tried to change the subject. "Somebody told me Father Malt's the exorcist for the diocese."

"Used to be." Father Burner's eyes flickered balefully.

"Overdid it, huh?" asked Father Philbert — as if he hadn't heard!

"Some." I expected Father Burner to say more. He could have told some pretty wild stories, the gist of them all that Father Malt, as an exorcist, was perhaps a little quick on the trigger. He had stuck pretty much to livestock, however, which was to his credit in the human view.

"Much scandal?"

"Some."

"Nothing serious, though?"

"No."

"Suppose it depends on what you call serious."

Father Burner did not reply. He had become oddly morose. Perhaps he felt that he was being catered to out of pity, or that Father Philbert, in giving him so many opportunities to talk against Father Malt, was tempting him.

"Who plays the accordion?" inquired Father Philbert, hearing it downstairs.

"He does."

"Go on!"

"Sure."

"How can he hear what he's playing?"

"What's the difference — if he plays an accordion?"

Father Philbert laughed. He removed the cellophane from a cigar, and then he saw me. And at that moment I made no attempt to hide. "There's that damn cat."

"His assistant!" said Father Burner with surprising bitterness. "Coadjutor with right of succession."

Father Philbert balled up the cellophane and tossed it at the wastebasket, missing.

"Get it," he said to me, fatuously.

I ignored him, walking slowly toward the door.

Father Burner made a quick movement with his feet, which were something to behold, but I knew he wouldn't get up, and took my sweet time.

Father Philbert inquired, "Will she catch mice?"

*She!* Since coming to live at the rectory, I've been celibate, it's true, but I daresay I'm as manly as the next one. And Father Burner, who might have done me the favor of putting him straight, said nothing.

"She looks pretty fat to be much of a mouser."

I just stared at the poor man then, as much as to say that I'd think one so interested in catching mice would have heard of a little thing called the mousetrap. After one last dirty look, I left them to themselves — to punish each other with their company.

I strolled down the hall, trying to remember when I'd last had a mouse. Going past the room occupied by the young missionary, I smiled upon his door, which was shut, confident that he was inside hard at prayers.

The next morning, shortly after breakfast, which I took, as usual, in the kitchen, I headed for the cool orchard to which I often repaired on just such a day as this one promised to be. I had no appetite for the sparrows hopping from tree to tree above me, but there seemed no way to convince them of that. Each one, so great is his vanity, thinks himself eminently edible. Peace, peace, they cry, and there is no peace. Finally, tired of their noise, I got up from the matted grass and left, levelling my ears and flailing my tail, in a fake dudgeon that inspired the males to feats of stunt flying and terrorized the young females most delightfully.

I went then to another favorite spot of mine, that bosky strip of green between the church and the brick sidewalk. Here, however, the horseflies found me, and as if that were not enough, visions of stray dogs and children came between me and the kind of sleep I badly needed after an uncommonly restless night.

When afternoon came, I remembered that it was Saturday, and that I could have the rectory to myself. Father Burner and the missionaries would be busy with confessions. By this time the temperature had reached its peak, and though I felt sorry for the young missionary, I must admit the thought of the other two sweltering in the confessionals refreshed me. The rest of the afternoon I must have slept something approaching the sleep of the just.

I suppose it was the sound of dishes that roused me. I rushed into the dining room, not bothering to wash up, and took my customary place at the table. Only then did I consider the empty chair next to me — the utter void. This, I thought, is a foreshadowing of what I must someday face — this, and Father Burner munching away at the other end of the table. And there was the immediate problem: no one to serve me. The young missionary smiled at me, but how can you eat a smile? The other two, looking rather wilted — to their hot boxes I wished them swift return — talked in expiring tones of reserved sins and did not appear to notice me. Our first meal together without Father Malt did not pass without incident, however. It all came about when the young missionary extended a thin sliver of meat to me.

"Hey, don't do that!" said Father Philbert. "You'll never make a mouser out of her that way."

Father Burner, too, regarded the young missionary with disapproval.

"Just this one piece," said the young missionary. The meat was already in my mouth.

"Well, watch it in the future," said Father Philbert. It was the word "future" that worried me. Did it mean that he had arranged to cut off my sustenance in the kitchen too? Did it mean that until Father Malt returned I had to choose between mousing and fasting?

I continued to think along these melancholy lines until the repast, which had never begun for me, ended for them. Then I whisked into the kitchen, where I received the usual bowl of milk. But whether the housekeeper, accustomed as she was to having me eat my main course at table, assumed there had been no change in my life, or was now acting under instructions from these villains, I don't know. I was too sickened by their meanness to have any appetite. When the pastor's away, the curates will play, I thought. On the whole I was feeling pretty glum.

It was our custom to have the main meal at noon on Sundays. I arrived early, before the others, hungrier than I'd been for as long as I could remember, and still I had little or no expectation of food at this table. I was there for one purpose — to assert myself — and possibly, where the young missionary was concerned, to incite sympathy for myself and contempt for my persecutors. By this time I knew that to be the name for them.

They entered the dining room, just the two of them.

"Where's the kid?" asked Father Burner.

"He's not feeling well," said Father Philbert.

I was not surprised. They'd arranged between the two of them to have him say the six- and eleven-o'clock Masses, which meant, of course, that he'd fasted in the interval. I had not thought of him as the hardy type, either.

"I'll have the housekeeper take him some beef broth," said Father Burner. Damned white of you, I was thinking, when he suddenly whirled and swept me off my chair. Then he picked it up and placed it against the wall. Then he went to the lower end of the table, removed his plate and silverware, and brought them to Father Malt's place. Talking and fuming to himself, he sat down in Father Malt's chair. I did not appear very brave, I fear, cowering under mine.

Father Philbert, who had been watching with interest, now greeted the new order with a cheer. "Attaboy, Ernest!"

Father Burner began to justify himself. "More light here," he said, and added, "Cats kill birds," and for some reason he was puffing.

"If they'd just kill mice," said Father Philbert, "they wouldn't be so bad." He had a one-track mind if I ever saw one.

"Wonder how many that black devil's caught in his time?" said Father Burner, airing a common prejudice against cats of my shade (though I do have a white collar). He looked over at me. "Sssss," he said. But I held my ground.

"I'll take a dog any day," said the platitudinous Father Philbert.

"Me, too."

After a bit, during which time they played hard with the roast, Father Philbert said, "How about taking her for a ride in the country?"

"Hell," said Father Burner. "He'd just come back."

"Not if we did it right, she wouldn't."

"Look," said Father Burner. "Some friends of mine dropped a cat off the high bridge in St. Paul. They saw him go under in mid-channel. I'm talking about the Mississippi, understand. Thought they'd never lay eyes on that animal again. That's what they thought. He was back at the house before they were." Father Burner paused — he could see that he was not convincing Father Philbert — and then he tried again. "That's a fact, Father. They might've played a quick round of golf before they got back. Cat didn't even look damp, they said. He's still there. Case a lot like this. Except now they're afraid of *him*."

To Father Burner's displeasure, Father Philbert refused to be awed or even puzzled. He simply inquired: "But did they use a bag? Weights?"

"Millstones," snapped Father Burner. "Don't quibble."

Then they fell to discussing the burial customs of gangsters — poured concrete and the rest — and became so engrossed in the matter that they forgot all about me.

Over against the wall, I was quietly working up the courage to act against them. When I felt sufficiently lionhearted, I leaped up and occupied my chair. Expecting blows and vilification, I encountered only indifference. I saw then how far I'd come down in their estimation. Already the remembrance of things past — the disease of noble politicals in exile — was too strong in me, the hope of restoration unwarrantably faint.

At the end of the meal, returning to me, Father Philbert remarked, "I think I know a better way." Rising, he snatched the crucifix off the wall, passed it to a bewildered Father Burner, and, saying "Nice Kitty," grabbed me behind the ears. "Hold it up to her," said Father Philbert. Father Burner held the crucifix up to me. "See that?" said Father Philbert to my face. I miaowed. "Take that!" said Father Philbert, cuffing me. He pushed my face into the crucifix again. "See that?" he said again, but I knew what to expect next, and when he cuffed me, I went for his hand with my mouth, pinking him nicely on the wrist. Evidently Father Burner had begun to understand and appreciate the proceedings. Although I was in a good position to observe everything, I could not say as much for myself. "Association," said Father Burner with mysterious satisfaction, almost with zest. He poked the crucifix at me. "If he's just smart enough to react properly," he said. "Oh, she's plenty smart," said Father Philbert, sucking his wrist and giving himself, I hoped, hydrophobia. He scuffed off one of his sandals for a paddle. Father

Burner, fingering the crucifix nervously, inquired, "Sure it's all right to go on with this thing?" "It's the intention that counts in these things," said Father Philbert. "Our motive is clear enough." And they went at me again.

After that first taste of the sandal in the dining room, I foolishly believed I would be safe as long as I stayed away from the table; there was something about my presence there, I thought, that brought out the beast in them — which is to say very nearly all that was in them. But they caught me in the upstairs hall the same evening, one brute thundering down upon me, the other sealing off my only avenue of escape. And this beating was worse than the first — preceded as it was by a short delay that I mistook for a reprieve until Father Burner, who had gone downstairs muttering something about "leaving no margin for error," returned with the crucifix from the dining room, although we had them hanging all over the house. The young missionary, coming upon them while they were at me, turned away. "I wash my hands of it," he said. I thought he might have done more.

Out of mind, bruised of body, sick at heart, for two days and nights I held on, I know not how or why — unless I lived in hope of vengeance. I wanted simple justice, a large order in itself, but I would never have settled for that alone. I wanted nothing less than my revenge.

I kept to the neighborhood, but avoided the rectory. I believed, of course, that their only strategy was to drive me away. I derived some little satisfaction from making myself scarce, for it was thus I deceived them into thinking their plan to banish me successful. But this was my single comfort during this hard time, and it was as nothing against their crimes.

I spent the nights in the open fields. I reeled, dizzy with hunger, until I bagged an aged field mouse. It tasted bitter to me, this stale provender, and seemed, as I swallowed it, an ironic concession to the enemy. I vowed I'd starve before I ate another mouse. By way of retribution to myself, I stalked sparrows in the orchard — hating myself for it but persisting all the more when I thought of those bird-lovers, my persecutors, before whom I could stand and say in self-redemption, "You made me what I am now. You thrust the killer's part upon me." Fortunately, I did not flush a single sparrow. Since *my* motive was clear enough, however, I'd had the pleasure of sinning against them and their ideals, the pleasure without the feathers and mess.

On Tuesday, the third day, all caution, I took up my post in the lilac bush beside the garage. Not until Father Malt returned, I knew, would I be safe in daylight. He arrived along about dinnertime, and I must say the very sight of him aroused a sentiment in me akin to human affection. The youngest usher, who must have had the afternoon off to meet him at the station in St. Paul, carried the new bag before him into the rectory. It was for me an act symbolic of the counter-revolution to come. I did not rush out from my hiding place, however. I had suffered too much to play the fool now. Instead I slipped into the kitchen by way of the flap in the screen door, which they had not thought to barricade. I waited under the stove for my moment, like an actor in the wings.

Presently I heard them tramping into the dining room and seating themselves, and Father Malt's voice saying, "I had a long talk with the Archbishop." (I could almost hear Father Burner praying, Did he say anything about *me?*) And then, "Where's Fritz?"

"He hasn't been around lately," said Father Burner cunningly. He would not tell the truth and he would not tell a lie.

"You know, there's something mighty funny about that cat," said Father Philbert. "We think she's possessed."

I was astonished, and would have liked a moment to think it over, but by now I was already entering the room.

"*Possessed!*" said Father Malt. "Aw no!"

"Ah, yes," said Father Burner, going for the meat right away. "And good riddance."

And then I miaowed and they saw me.

"Quick!" said Father Philbert, who made a nice recovery after involuntarily reaching for me and his sandal at the same time. Father Burner ran to the wall for the crucifix, which had been, until now, a mysterious and possibly blasphemous feature of my beatings — the crucifix held up to me by the one not scourging at the moment, as if it were the will behind my punishment. They had schooled me well, for even now, at the sight of the crucifix, an undeniable fear was rising in me. Father Burner handed it to Father Malt.

"Now you'll see," said Father Philbert.

I found now that I could not help myself. What followed was hidden from them — from human eyes. I gave myself over entirely to the fear they'd beaten into me, and in a moment, according to their plan, I was fleeing the crucifix as one truly possessed, out of the dining room and into the kitchen, and from there, blindly, along the house and through the shrubbery, ending in the street, where a powerful gray car ran over me — and where I gave up the old ghost for a new one.

Simultaneously, reborn, redeemed from my previous fear, identical with my former self, so far as they could see, and still in their midst, I padded up to Father Malt — he still sat gripping the crucifix — and jumped into his lap. I heard the young missionary arriving from an errand in Father Philbert's *brother's* car, late for dinner he thought, but just in time to see the stricken look I saw coming into the eyes of my persecutors. This look alone made up for everything I'd suffered at their hands. Purring now, I was rubbing up against the crucifix, myself effecting my utter revenge.

"What have we done?" cried Father Philbert. He was basically an emotional dolt and would have voted then for my canonization.

"I ran over a cat!" said the young missionary excitedly. "I'd swear it was this one. When I looked, there was nothing there!"

"Better go upstairs and rest," growled Father Burner. He sat down — it was good to see him in his proper spot at the low end of the table — as if to wait a long time, or so it seemed to me. I found myself wondering if I could possibly bring about his transfer to another parish — one where they had a devil for a pastor and several assistants, where he would be able to start at the bottom again.

But first things first, I always say, and all in good season, for now Father Malt himself was drawing my chair up to the table, restoring me to my rightful place.

1951

*Tennessee Williams*

...............................................................................

# The Resemblance Between
# a Violin Case and a Coffin

FROM *Flair*

*Inscribed to the memory of Isabel Sevier Williams*

WITH HER ADVANTAGE of more than two years and the earlier maturity of girls, my sister moved before me into that country of mysterious
differences where children grow up. And although we naturally continued to live in the same house, she seemed to have gone on a journey
while she remained in sight. The difference came about more abruptly
than you would think possible, and it was vast, it was like the two sides
of the Sunflower River that ran through the town where we lived. On
one side was a wilderness where giant cypresses seemed to engage in
mute rites of reverence at the edge of the river, and the blurred pallor of
the Dobyne place that used to be a plantation, now vacant and seem-
ingly ravaged by some impalpable violence fiercer than flames, and back
of this dusky curtain, the immense cottonfields that absorbed the whole
visible distance in one sweeping gesture. But on the other side, avenues,
commerce, pavements and homes of people: those two, separated by
only a yellowish, languorous stream that you could throw a rock over.
The rumbling wooden bridge that divided, or joined, those banks was
hardly shorter than the interval in which my sister moved away from
me. Her look was startled, mine was bewildered and hurt. Either there
was no explanation or none was permitted between the one departing
and the one left behind. The earliest beginning of it that I can remember was one day when my sister got up later than usual with an odd
look, not as if she had been crying, although perhaps she had, but as
though she had received some painful or frightening surprise, and I

observed an equally odd difference in the manner toward her of my mother and grandmother. She was escorted to the kitchen table for breakfast as though she were in danger of toppling over on either side, and everything was handed to her as though she could not reach for it. She was addressed in hushed and solicitous voices, almost the way that docile servants speak to an employer. I was baffled and a little disgusted. I received no attention at all, and the one or two glances given me by my sister had a peculiar look of resentment in them. It was as if I had struck her the night before and given her a bloody nose or a black eye, except that she wore no bruise, no visible injury, and there had been no altercation between us in recent days. I spoke to her several times but for some reason she ignored my remarks and when I became irritated and yelled at her, my grandmother suddenly reached over and twisted my ear, which was one of the few times that I can remember when she ever offered me more than the gentlest reproach. It was a Saturday morning, I remember, of a hot yellow day and it was the hour when my sister and I would ordinarily take to the streets on our wheels. But the custom was now disregarded. After breakfast my sister appeared somewhat strengthened but still alarmingly pale and as silent as ever. She was then escorted to the parlor and encouraged to sit down at the piano. She spoke in a low whimpering tone to my grandmother who adjusted the piano stool very carefully and placed a cushion on it and even turned the pages of sheet music for her as if she were incapable of finding the place for herself. She was working on a simple piece called *The Aeolian Harp,* and my grandmother sat beside her while she played, counting out the tempo in a barely audible voice, now and then reaching out to touch the wrists of my sister in order to remind her to keep them arched. Upstairs my mother began to sing to herself which was something she only did when my father had just left on a long trip with his samples and would not be likely to return for quite a while, and my grandfather, up since daybreak, was mumbling a sermon to himself in the study. All was peaceful except my sister's face. I did not know whether to go outside or stay in. I hung around the parlor a little while and finally I said to Grand, "Why can't she practice later?" As if I had made some really brutal remark, my sister jumped up in tears and fled to her upstairs bedroom. What was the matter with her? My grandmother said, "Your sister is not well today." She said it gently and gravely and then she started to follow my sister upstairs, and I was deserted. I was left alone in the very uninteresting parlor. The idea of riding alone on my wheel did not please me for often when I did that, I was set upon by the rougher boys of the town who called me Preacher and took a peculiar delight in asking me obscene questions that would embarrass me to the point of nausea. . . .

In this way was instituted the time of estrangement that I could not understand. From that time on the division between us was ever more clearly established. It seemed that my mother and grandmother were approving and conspiring to increase it. They had never before bothered over the fact that I had depended so much on the companionship of my sister but now they were continually asking me why I did not make friends with other children. I was ashamed to tell them that other children frightened me nor was I willing to admit that my sister's wild imagination and inexhaustible spirits made all other substitute companions seem like the shadows of shades, for now that she had abandoned me, mysteriously and willfully withdrawn her enchanting intimacy, I felt too resentful even to acknowledge secretly, to myself, how much had been lost through what she had taken away. . . .

Sometimes I think she might have fled back into the more familiar country of childhood if she had been allowed to, but the grownup ladies of the house, and even the colored girl, Ozzie, were continually telling her that such and such a thing was not proper for her to do. It was not proper for my sister not to wear stockings or to crouch in the yard at a place where the earth was worn bare to bounce a rubber ball and scoop up starry-pointed bits of black metal called jacks. It was not even proper for me to come into her room without knocking. All of these proprieties struck me as mean and silly and perverse, and the wound of them turned me inward.

My sister had been magically suited to the wild country of childhood but it remained to be seen how she would adapt herself to the uniform and yet more complex world that grown girls enter. I suspect that I have defined that world incorrectly with the word uniform; later, yes, it becomes uniform, it straightens out into an all too regular pattern. But between childhood and adulthood there is a broken terrain which is possibly even wilder than childhood was. The wilderness is interior. The vines and the brambles seem to have been left behind but actually they are thicker and more confusing, although they are not so noticeable from the outside. Those few years of dangerous passage are an ascent into unknown hills. They take the breath sometimes and bewilder the vision. My mother and maternal grandmother came of a calmer blood than my sister and I. They were unable to suspect the hazards that we were faced with, having in us the turbulent blood of our father. Irreconcilables fought for supremacy in us: peace could never be made: at best a smoldering sort of armistice might be reached after many battles. Childhood had held those clashes in abeyance. They were somehow timed to explode at adolescence, silently, shaking the earth where we were standing. My sister now felt those tremors under her feet. It seemed to me that a shadow had fallen on her. Or had it fallen on me, with her light at a distance? Yes, it was as if someone had carried a lamp into another room that I could not enter. I watched her from a distance and under a shadow. And looking back on it now, I see that those two or three years when the fatal dice were still in the tilted box, were the years of her beauty. The long copperish curls which had swung below her shoulders, bobbing almost constantly with excitement, were unexpectedly removed one day, an afternoon of a day soon after the one when she had fled from the piano in reasonless tears. Mother took her downtown. I was not allowed to go with them but told once more to find someone else to play with. And my sister returned without her long copper curls. It was like a formal acknowledgment of the sorrowful differences and division which had haunted the house for some time. I noted as she came in the front door that she had now begun to imitate the walk of grown ladies, the graceful and quick and decorous steps of my mother and that she kept her arms at her sides instead of flung out as if brushing curtains aside as she sprang forward in the abruptly lost days. But there was much more than that. When she entered the parlor, at the fading hour of the afternoon, it was as momentous as if brass horns had sounded, she wore such beauty. Mother came after her looking flushed with excitement, and my grandmother descended the stairs with unusual lightness. They spoke in hushed voices. "Astonishing," said my mother. "She's like Isabel." This was the name of a sister of my father's who was a famed beauty in Knoxville. She was probably the one woman in the world by whom my mother was intimidated, and our occasional summer journeys to Knoxville from the Delta of Mississippi were like priestly tributes to a seat of holiness, for though my mother would certainly never make verbal acknowledgment of my aunt's superiority in matters of taste and definitions of quality, it was nevertheless apparent that she approached Knoxville and my father's younger sister in something very close to fear and trembling. Isabel had a flame, there was no doubt about it, a lambency which, once felt, would not fade from the eyes. It had an awful quality, as though it shone outward while it burned inward. And not long after the time of these recollections she was to die, quite abruptly and irrelevantly, as the result of the removal of an infected wisdom tooth, with her legend entrusted to various bewildered eyes and hearts and memories she had stamped, including mine which have sometimes confused her with very dissimilar ladies. "She is like Isabel," said my mother in a hushed voice. My grandmother did not admit that this was so. She also admired Isabel but thought her too interfering and was unable to separate her altogether from the excessively close blood-connection with my father, who I should say, in passage, was a devilish man, possibly not understood but certainly hard to live with. . . .

What I saw was not Isabel in my sister but a grown stranger whose beauty sharpened my sense of being alone. I saw that it was all over, put away in a box like a doll no longer cared for, the magical intimacy of our childhood together, the soap-bubble afternoons and the games with paper dolls cut out of dress catalogues and the breathless races here and there on our wheels. For the first time, yes, I saw her beauty. I consciously avowed it to myself, although it seems to me that I turned away from it, averted my look from the pride with which she strolled into the parlor and stood by the mantel mirror to be admired. And it was then, about that time, that I began to find life unsatisfactory as an explanation of itself and was forced to adopt the method of the artist of not explaining but putting the blocks together in some other way that seems more significant to him. Which is a rather fancy way of saying I started writing.

My sister also had a separate occupation which was her study of music, at first conducted under my grandmother's instruction but now entrusted to a professional teacher whose name was Miss Aehle, an almost typical spinster, who lived in a small frame house with a porch covered by moonvines and a fence covered by honeysuckle. Her name was pronounced *Ail*-ly. She supported herself and a paralyzed father by giving lessons in violin and piano, neither of which she played very well herself but for which she had great gifts as a teacher. If not great gifts, at least great enthusiasm. She was a true romanticist. She talked so excitedly that she got ahead of herself and looked bewildered and cried out, "What was I saying?" She was one of the innocents of the world, appreciated only by her pupils and a few persons a generation older than herself. Her pupils nearly always came to adore her, she gave them a feeling that playing little pieces on the piano or scratching out little tunes on a fiddle made up for everything that was ostensibly wrong in a world made by God but disarrayed by the devil. She was religious and ecstatic.

She never admitted that any one of her pupils, even the ones who were unmistakably tone-deaf, were deficient in musical talent. And the few who could perform tolerably well she was certain had genius. She had two real star pupils, my sister, on the piano, and a boy named Richard Miles who studied the violin. Her enthusiasm for these two was unbounded. It is true that my sister had a nice touch and that Richard Miles had a pure tone on the fiddle but Miss Aehle dreamed of them in terms of playing duets to great ovations in the world's capital cities.

Richard Miles, I think of him now as a boy, for he was about seventeen, but at that time he seemed a complete adult to me, even immeasurably older than my sister who was fourteen. I resented him fiercely even though I began, almost immediately after learning of his existence, to dream about him as I had formerly dreamed of storybook heroes. His name began to inhabit the rectory. It was almost constantly on the lips of my sister, this strange young lady who had come to live with us. It had a curious lightness, that name, in the way that she spoke it. It did not seem to fall from her lips but to be released from them. The moment spoken, it rose into the air and shimmered and floated and took on gorgeous colors the way that soap bubbles did that we used to blow from the sunny back steps in the summer. Those bubbles lifted and floated and they eventually broke but never until other bubbles had floated beside them. Golden they were, and the name of Richard had a golden sound too. The second name, being Miles, gave a suggestion of distance, so Richard was something both radiant and far away.

My sister's obsession with Richard may have been even more intense than mine. Since mine was copied from hers, it was probably hers that was greater in the beginning. But while mine was of a shy and sorrowful kind, involved with my sense of abandonment, hers at first seemed to be joyous. She had fallen in love. As always, I followed suit. But while love made her brilliant, at first, it made me laggard and dull. It filled me with sad confusion. It tied my tongue or made it stammer and it flashed so unbearably in my eyes that I had to turn them away. These are the intensities that one cannot live with, that he has to outgrow if he wants to survive. But who can help grieving for them? If the blood vessels could hold them, how much better to keep those early loves with us? But if we did, the veins would break and the passion explode into darkness long before the necessary time for it.

I remember one afternoon in fall when my sister and I were walking along a street when Richard Miles appeared suddenly before us from somewhere with a startling cry. I see him bouncing, probably down the steps of Miss Aehle's white cottage, emerging unexpectedly from the vines. Probably Miss Aehle's because he bore his violin case, and I remember thinking how closely it resembled a little coffin, a coffin made for a small child or a doll. About people you knew in your childhood it is rarely possible to remember their appearance except as ugly or beautiful or light or dark. I do not remember if Richard was light in the sense of being blond or if the lightness came from a quality in him deeper than hair or skin. Yes, probably both, for he was one of those people who move in light, provided by practically everything about them. This detail I do remember. He wore a white shirt, and through its cloth could be seen the fair skin of his shoulders. And for the first time prematurely, I was aware of skin as an attraction. A thing that might be desirable to touch. This awareness entered my mind, my senses, like the sudden streak of flame that follows a comet. And my undoing, already started by Richard's mere coming toward us, was now completed. When he turned to me and held his enormous hand out, I did a thing so grotesque that I could never afterward be near him without a blistering sense of shame. Instead of taking the hand I ducked away from him. I made a mumbling sound that could have had very little resemblance to speech and then brushed past their two figures, his and my beaming sister's, and fled into a drugstore just beyond.

That same fall the pupils of Miss Aehle performed in a concert. This concert was held in the parish house of my grandfather's church. And for weeks preceding it the pupils made preparation for the occasion which seemed as important as Christmas. My sister and Richard Miles were to play a duet, she on the piano, of course, and he on the violin. They practiced separately and they practiced together. Separately my sister played the piece very well, but for some reason, more portentous than it had seemed at the time, she had great difficulty in playing to Richard's accompaniment. Suddenly her fingers would turn to thumbs, her wrists would flatten out and become cramped, her whole figure would hunch rigidly toward the piano and her beauty and grace would vanish. It was strange, but Miss Aehle was certain that it would be overcome with repeated practice. And Richard was patient, he was incredibly patient, he seemed to be far more concerned for my sister's sake than his own. Extra hours of practice were necessary. Sometimes when they had left Miss Aehle's, at the arrival of other pupils, they would continue at our house. The afternoons were consequently unsafe. I never knew when the front door might open on Richard's dreadful beauty and his greeting which I could not respond to, could not endure, must fly grotesquely away from. But the house was so arranged that although I hid in my bedroom at these hours of practice, I was still able to watch them at the piano. My bedroom looked out upon the staircase which descended into the parlor where they practiced. The piano was directly within my line of vision. It was in the parlor's lightest corner, with lace-curtained windows on either side of it, the sunlight only fretted by patterns of lace and ferns.

During the final week before the concert — or was it recital they called it? — Richard Miles came over almost invariably at four in the afternoon, which was the last hour of really good sunlight in late October. And always a little before that time I would lower the green blind in my bedroom and with a fantastic stealth, as if a sound would betray a disgusting action, I would open the door two inches, an aperture just enough to enclose the piano corner as by the lateral boundaries of a stage. When I heard them enter the front door, or even before, when I saw their shadows thrown against the oval glass and curtain the door surrounded or heard their voices as they climbed to the porch, I would flatten myself on my belly on the cold floor and remain in that position as long as they stayed, no matter how my knees or elbows ached, and I was so fearful of betraying this watch that I kept over them while they practiced that I hardly dared to breathe.

The transference of my interest to Richard now seemed complete. I would barely notice my sister at the piano, groaned at her repeated blunders only in sympathy for him. When I recall what a little puritan I was in those days, there must have been a shocking ambivalence in my thoughts and sensations as I gazed down upon him through the crack of the door. How on earth did I explain to myself, at that time, the fascination of his physical being without, at the same time, confessing to myself that I was a little monster? Or was that actually before I had begun to associate the sensual with the impure, an error that tortured me during and after pubescence, or did I, and this seems most likely, now, say to myself, "Yes, Tom, you're a monster! But that's how it is and there's nothing to be done about it." This much is certain. Whatever resistance there may have been from the "legion of decency" in my soul was exhausted in the first skirmish, not exterminated but thoroughly trounced, and its subsequent complaints took the form of unseen blushes. Not that there was really anything to be ashamed of in adoring the beauty of Richard. It was surely made for that purpose, the boys of my age to be stirred by such ideals of grace. The sheer white cloth in which I had originally seen his upper body was always worn by it, and now, in those afternoons, because of the position of the piano between two windows that cast their beams at cross angles, the white material became diaphanous with light, the torso shone through it, faintly pink and silver, the nipples on the chest and the armpits a little darker and the diaphragm visibly pulsing as he breathed. It is possible that I have seen more graceful bodies, but I am not sure that I have, and his, I believe, remains a subconscious standard. And looking back upon him now, and upon the devout little mystic of carnality that I was as I crouched on a chill bedroom floor, I think of Camilla Rucellai, that highstrung mystic of Florence who is supposed to have seen Pico della Mirandola entering the streets of that city on a milkwhite horse in a storm of sunlight and flowers and to have fainted at the spectacle of him and murmured as she revived, "*He will pass in the time of lilies!*" meaning that he would die early, since nothing so fair could decline by common degrees in a faded season. The light was certainly there in all its fullness, and even a kind of flowers, at least shadows of them, for there were flowers of lace in the window curtains and actual branches of fern which the light projected across him; no storm of flowers but the shadows of flowers which are perhaps more fitting.

The way that he lifted and handled his violin! First, he would roll up the sleeves of his white shirt and remove his necktie and loosen his collar as though he were making preparations for love. Then there was a metallic snap as he released the lock on the case of the violin. Then the upper lid was pushed back and the sunlight fell on the dazzling interior of the case. It was plush-lined and the plush was emerald. The violin itself was somewhat darker than blood and even more lustrous. To Richard I think it must have seemed more precious. His hands and his arms as he lifted it from the case, they said the word love more sweetly than speech could say it, and oh, what precocious fantasies their grace and tenderness would excite in me. I was a wounded soldier, the youngest of the regiment, and he, Richard, was my young officer, jeopardizing his life to lift me from the field where I had fallen and carry me back to safety in the same cradle of arms that supported his violin now. . . .

I now feel some anxiety that this story will seem to be losing itself like a path that has climbed a hill and then lost itself in an overgrowth of brambles. For I have now told you all but one of the things that stand out very clearly, and yet I have not approached any sort of conclusion.

There is, of course, a conclusion. However indefinite, there always is some point which serves that need of remembrances and stories.

The remaining very clear thing is the evening of the recital in mid-November, but before an account of that, I should tell more of my sister in this troubled state of hers. It might be possible to willfully thrust myself into her mind, her emotions, but I question the wisdom of it: for at that time I was an almost hostile onlooker where she was concerned. Hurt feelings and jealous feelings were too thickly involved in my view of her then. As though she were being punished for a betrayal of our childhood companionship, I felt a gratification tinged with contempt at her difficulties in the duet with Richard. One evening I overheard a telephone call which Mother received from Miss Aehle. Miss Aehle was first perplexed and now genuinely alarmed and totally mystified by the sudden decline of my sister's vaunted aptitude for the piano. She had been singing her praises for months. Now it appeared that my sister was about to disgrace her publicly, for she was not only unable, suddenly, to learn new pieces but was forgetting the old ones. It had been planned, originally, for her to pay several solo numbers at the recital before and leading up to the duet with Richard. The solos now had to be canceled from the program, and Miss Aehle was even fearful that my sister would not be able to perform in the duet. She wondered if my mother could think of some reason why my sister had undergone this very inopportune and painful decline? Was she sleeping badly, how was her appetite, was she very moody? Mother came away from the telephone in a very cross humor with the teacher. She repeated all the complaints and apprehensions and questions to my grandmother who said nothing but pursed her lips and shook her head while she sewed like one of those venerable women who understand and govern the fates of mortals, but she had nothing to offer in the way of a practical solution except to say that perhaps it was a mistake for brilliant children to be pushed into things like this so early. . . .

Richard stayed patient with her most of the time, and there were occasional periods of revival, when she would attack the piano with an explosion of confidence and the melodies would surge beneath her fingers like birds out of cages. Such a resurgence would never last until the end of a piece. There would be a stumble, and then another collapse. Once Richard himself was unstrung. He pushed his violin high into the air like a broom sweeping cobwebs off the ceiling. He strode around the parlor brandishing it like that and uttering groans that were both sincere and comic; when he returned to the piano, where she crouched in dismay, he took hold of her shoulders and gave them a shake. She burst into tears and would have fled upstairs but he caught hold of her by the newelpost of the staircase. He would not let go of her. He detained her with murmurs I couldn't quite hear, and drew her gently back to the piano corner. And then he sat down on the piano stool with his great hands gripping each side of her narrow waist while she sobbed with her face averted and her fingers knotting together. And while I watched them from my cave of darkness, my body learned the fierceness and fire of the will of life to transcend the single body, and so to continue to follow life's curve and time's. . . .

The evening of the recital my sister complained at supper that her hands were stiff, and she kept rubbing them together and even held them over the spout of the teapot to warm them with the steam. She looked very pretty, I remember, when she was dressed. Her color was higher than I had ever seen it, but there were tiny beads of sweat at her temples and she ordered me angrily out of her room when I appeared in the doorway before she was ready to pass the family's inspection. She wore silver slippers and a very grownup-looking dress that was the greenish sea-color of her eyes. It had the low waist that was fashionable at that time and there were silver beads on it in loops and fringes. Her bedroom was steaming from the adjoining bath. She opened the window. Grandmother slammed it down, declaring that she would catch cold. "Oh, leave me alone," she answered. The muscles in her throat were curiously prominent as she stared in the glass. "Stop powdering," said my grandmother, "you're caking your face with powder." "Well, it's my face," she retorted. And then came near to flying into a tantrum at some small critical comment offered by Mother. "I have no talent," she said, "I have no talent for music! Why do I have to do it, why do you make me, why was I forced into this?" Even my grandmother finally gave up and retired from the room. But when it came time to leave for the parish house, my sister came downstairs looking fairly collected and said not another word as we made our departure. Once in the automobile she whispered something about her hair being mussed. She kept her stiff hands knotted in her lap. We drove first to Miss Aehle's and found her in a state of hysteria because Richard had fallen off a bicycle that afternoon and skinned his fingers. She was sure it would hinder his playing. But when we arrived at the parish house Richard was already there as calm as a duckpond, playing delicately with the mute on the strings and no apparent disability. We left them, teacher and performers, in the cloakroom and went to take our seats in the auditorium which was beginning to fill, and I remember noticing a half-erased inscription on a blackboard which had something to do with a Sunday school lesson.

No, it did not go off well. They played without sheet music, and my sister made all the mistakes she had made in practicing and several new ones. She could not seem to remember the composition beyond the first few pages; it was a fairly long one, and those pages she repeated twice, possibly even three times. But Richard was heroic. He seemed to anticipate every wrong note that she struck and to bring down his bow on the strings with an extra strength to cover and rectify it. When she began to lose control altogether, I saw him edging up closer to her position, so that his radiant figure shielded her partly from view, and I saw him, at a crucial moment, when it seemed that the duet might collapse altogether, raise his bow high in the air, at the same time catching his breath in a sort of "Hah!" a sound I heard much later from bullfighters daring a charge, and lower it to the strings in a masterful sweep that took the lead from my sister and plunged them into the passage that she had forgotten in her panic. . . . For a bar or two I think she stopped playing, sat there motionless, stunned. And then, finally, when he turned his back to the audience and murmured something to her, she started again. She started playing again but Richard played so brilliantly and so richly that the piano was barely noticeable underneath him. And so they got through it, and when it was finished they received an ovation. My sister started to rush for the cloakroom. But Richard seized her wrist and held her back. Then something odd happened. Instead of bowing she suddenly turned and pressed her forehead against him, pressed it against the lapel of his blue serge suit. He blushed and bowed and touched her waist with his fingers, gently, his eyes glancing down. . . .

We drove home in silence, almost. There was a conspiracy to ignore that anything unfortunate had happened. My sister said nothing. She sat with her hands knotted in her lap exactly as she had been before the recital, and when I looked at her I noticed that her shoulders were too narrow and her mouth a little too wide for real beauty, and that her recent habit of hunching made her seem a little bit like an old lady being imitated by a child.

At that point Richard Miles faded out of our lives for my sister refused to continue to study music, and not long afterward my father received an advancement, an office job as a minor executive in a Northern shoe company, and we moved from the South. No, I am not putting all of these things in their exact chronological order, I may as well confess it, but if I did I would violate my honor as a teller of stories. . . .

As for Richard, the truth is exactly congruous to the poem. A year or so later we learned, in that Northern city to which we had moved, that he had died of pneumonia. And then I remembered the case of his violin, and how it resembled so much a little black coffin made for a child or a doll. . . .

## John Cheever

·······································································································································

# The Country Husband

FROM *The New Yorker*

TO BEGIN at the beginning, the airplane from Minneapolis in which
Francis Weed was travelling East ran into heavy weather. The sky had
been a hazy blue, with the clouds below the plane lying so close together
that nothing could be seen of the earth. Then mist began to form
outside the windows, and they flew into a white cloud of such density
that it reflected the exhaust fires. The color of the cloud darkened to
gray, and the plane began to rock. Francis had been in heavy weather
before, but he had never been shaken up so much. The man in the seat
beside him pulled a flask out of his pocket and took a drink. Francis
smiled at his neighbor, but the man looked away; he wasn't sharing his
painkiller with anyone. The plane had begun to drop and flounder
wildly. A child was crying. The air in the cabin was overheated and stale,
and Francis' left foot went to sleep. He read a little from a paper book
that he had bought at the airport, but the violence of the storm divided
his attention. It was black outside the ports. The exhaust fires blazed
and shed sparks in the dark, and, inside, the shaded lights, the stuffiness,
and the window curtains gave the cabin an atmosphere of intense and
misplaced domesticity. Then the lights flickered and went out. "You
know what I've always wanted to do?" the man beside Francis said
suddenly. "I've always wanted to buy a farm in New Hampshire and
raise beef cattle." The stewardess announced that they were going to
make an emergency landing. All but the child saw in their minds the
spreading wings of the Angel of Death. The pilot could be heard singing
faintly, "I've got sixpence, jolly, jolly sixpence. I've got sixpence to last
me all my life . . ." There was no other sound.

The loud groaning of the hydraulic valves swallowed up the pilot's
song, and there was a shrieking high in the air, like automobile brakes,

and the plane hit flat on its belly in a cornfield and shook them so violently that an old man up forward howled, "Me kidneys! Me kidneys!" The stewardess flung open the door, and someone opened an emergency door at the back, letting in the sweet noise of their continuing mortality — the idle splash and smell of a heavy rain. Anxious for their lives, they filed out of the doors and scattered over the cornfield in all directions, praying that the thread would hold. It did. Nothing happened. When it was clear that the plane would not burn or explode, the crew and the stewardess gathered the passengers together and led them to the shelter of a barn. They were not far from Philadelphia, and in a little while a string of taxis took them into the city. "It's just like the Marne," someone said, but there was surprisingly little relaxation of that suspiciousness with which many Americans regard their fellow travellers.

In Philadelphia, Francis Weed got a train to New York. At the end of that journey, he crossed the city and caught, just as it was about to pull out, the commuting train that he took five nights a week to his home in Shady Hill.

He sat with Trace Bearden. "You know, I was in that plane that just crashed outside Philadelphia," he said. "We came down in a field . . ." He had travelled faster than the newspapers or the rain, and the weather in New York was sunny and mild. It was a day in late September, as fragrant and shapely as an apple. Trace listened to the story, but how could he get excited? Francis had no powers that would let him re-create a brush with death — particularly in the atmosphere of a commuting train, journeying through a sunny countryside where already, in the slum gardens, there were signs of harvest. Trace picked up his newspaper, and Francis was left alone with his thoughts. He said good night to Trace on the platform at Shady Hill and drove in his second-hand Volkswagen up to the Blenhollow neighborhood, where he lived.

The Weeds' Dutch Colonial house was larger than it appeared to be from the driveway. The living room was spacious and divided like Gaul into three parts. Around an ell to the left as one entered from the vestibule was the long table, laid for six, with candles and a bowl of fruit in the center. The sounds and smells that came from the open kitchen door were appetizing, for Julia Weed was a good cook. The largest part of the living room centered around a fireplace. On the right were some bookshelves and a piano. The room was polished and tranquil, and from the windows that opened to the west there was some late-summer sunlight, brilliant and as clear as water. Nothing here was neglected;

nothing had not been burnished. It was not the kind of household where, after prying open a stuck cigarette box, you would find an old shirt button and a tarnished nickel. The hearth was swept, the roses on the piano were reflected in the polish of the broad top, and there was an album of Schubert waltzes on the rack. Louisa Weed, a pretty girl of nine, was looking out the western windows. Her younger brother Henry was standing beside her. Her still younger brother, Toby, was studying the figures of some tonsured monks drinking beer on the polished brass of the wood box. Francis, taking off his hat and putting down his paper, was not consciously pleased with the scene; he was not that reflective. It was his element, his creation, and he returned to it with that sense of lightness and strength with which any creature returns to its home. "Hi, everybody," he said. "The plane from Minneapolis . . ."

Nine times out of ten, Francis would be greeted with affection, but tonight the children are absorbed in their own antagonisms. Francis has not finished his sentence about the plane crash before Henry plants a kick in Louisa's behind. Louisa swings around, saying "*Damn* you!" Francis makes the mistake of scolding Louisa for bad language before he punishes Henry. Now Louisa turns on her father and accuses him of favoritism. Henry is always right; she is persecuted and lonely; her lot is hopeless. Francis turns to his son, but the boy has justification for the kick — she hit him first; she hit him on the ear, which is dangerous. Louisa agrees with this passionately. She hit him on the ear, and she *meant* to hit him on the ear, because he messed up her china collection. Henry says that this is a lie. Little Toby turns away from the wood box to throw in some evidence for Louisa. Henry claps his hand over little Toby's mouth. Francis separates the two boys but accidentally pushes Toby into the wood box. Toby begins to cry. Louisa is already crying. Just then, Julia Weed comes into that part of the room where the table is laid. She is a pretty, intelligent woman, and the white in her hair is premature. She does not seem to notice the fracas. "Hello, darling," she says serenely to Francis. "Wash your hands, everyone. Dinner is ready." She strikes a match and lights the six candles in this vale of tears.

This simple announcement, like the war cries of the Scottish chieftains, only refreshes the ferocity of the combatants. Louisa gives Henry a blow on the shoulder. Henry, although he seldom cries, has pitched nine innings and is tired. He bursts into tears. Little Toby discovers a splinter in his hand and begins to howl. Francis says loudly that he has been in a plane crash and that he is tired. Julia appears again, from the kitchen, and, still ignoring the chaos, asks Francis to go upstairs and tell

Helen that everything is ready. Francis is happy to go; it is like getting back to headquarters company. He is planning to tell his oldest daughter about the airplane crash, but Helen is lying on her bed reading a *True Romance* magazine, and the first thing Francis does is to take the magazine from her hand and remind Helen that he has forbidden her to buy it. She did not buy it, Helen replies. It was given to her by her best friend, Bessie Black. Everybody reads *True Romance*. Bessie Black's father reads *True Romance*. There isn't a girl in Helen's class who doesn't read *True Romance*. Francis expresses his detestation of the magazine and then tells her that dinner is ready — although from the sounds downstairs it doesn't seem so. Helen follows him down the stairs. Julia has seated herself in the candlelight and spread a napkin over her lap. Neither Louisa nor Henry has come to the table. Little Toby is still howling, lying face down on the floor. Francis speaks to him gently: "Daddy was in a plane crash this afternoon, Toby. Don't you want to hear about it?" Toby goes on crying. "If you don't come to the table now, Toby," Francis says, "I'll have to send you to bed without any supper." The little boy rises, gives him a cutting look, flies up the stairs to his bedroom, and slams the door. "Oh dear," Julia says, and starts to go after him. Francis says that she will spoil him. Julia says that Toby is ten pounds underweight and has to be encouraged to eat. Winter is coming, and he will spend the cold months in bed unless he has his dinner. Julia goes upstairs. Francis sits down at the table with Helen. Helen is suffering from the dismal feeling of having read too intently on a fine day, and she gives her father and the room a jaded look. She doesn't understand about the plane crash, because there wasn't a drop of rain in Shady Hill.

Julia returns with Toby, and they all sit down and are served. "Do I have to look at that big, fat slob?" Henry says, of Louisa. Everybody but Toby enters into this skirmish, and it rages up and down the table for five minutes. Toward the end, Henry puts his napkin over his head and, trying to eat that way, spills spinach all over his shirt. Francis asks Julia if the children couldn't have their dinner earlier. Julia's guns are loaded for this. She can't cook two dinners and lay two tables. She paints with lightning strokes that panorama of drudgery in which her youth, her beauty, and her wit have been lost. Francis says that he must be understood; he was nearly killed in an airplane crash, and he doesn't like to come home every night to a battlefield. Now Julia is deeply committed. Her voice trembles. He doesn't come home every night to a battlefield. The accusation is stupid and mean. Everything was tranquil until he arrived. She stops speaking, puts down her knife and fork, and looks into her plate as if it is a gulf. She begins to cry. "Poor Mummy!" Toby says, and when Julia gets up from the table, drying her tears with a napkin, Toby goes to her side. "Poor Mummy," he says. "Poor Mummy!" And they climb the stairs together. The other children drift away from the battlefield, and Francis goes into the back garden for a cigarette and some air.

It was a pleasant garden, with walks and flower beds and places to sit. The sunset had nearly burned out, but there was still plenty of light. Put into a thoughtful mood by the crash and the battle, Francis listened to the evening sounds of Shady Hill. "Varmits! Rascals!" old Mr. Nixon shouted to the squirrels in his bird-feeding station. "Avaunt and quit my sight!" A door slammed. Someone was playing tennis on the Babcocks' court; someone was cutting grass. Then Donald Goslin, who lived at the corner, began to play the "Moonlight Sonata." He did this nearly every night. He threw the tempo out the window and played it *rubato* from beginning to end, like an outpouring of tearful petulance, lonesome-ness, and self-pity — of everything it was Beethoven's greatness not to know. The music rang up and down the street beneath the trees like an appeal for love, for tenderness, aimed at some lonely housemaid — some fresh-faced, homesick girl from Galway, looking at old snapshots in her third-floor room. "Here, Jupiter, here, Jupiter," Francis called to the Mercers' retriever. Jupiter crashed through the tomato vines with the remains of a felt hat in his mouth.

Jupiter was an anomaly. His retrieving instincts and his high spirits were out of place in Shady Hill. He was as black as coal, with a long, alert, intelligent, rakehell face. His eyes gleamed with mischief, and he held his head high. It was the fierce, heavily collared dog's head that appears in heraldry, in tapestry, and that used to appear on umbrella handles and walking sticks. Jupiter went where he pleased, ransacking wastebaskets, clotheslines, garbage pails, and shoe bags. He broke up garden parties and tennis matches, and got mixed up in the proces-sional at Christ's Church on Sunday, barking at the men in red dresses. He crashed through old Mr. Nixon's rose garden two or three times a day, cutting a wide swath through the Condesa de Sastagos, and as soon as Donald Goslin lighted his barbecue fire on Thursday nights, Jupiter would get the scent. Nothing the Goslins did could drive him away. Sticks and stones and rude commands only moved him to the edge of the terrace, where he remained, with his gallant and heraldic muzzle, waiting for Donald Goslin to turn his back and reach for the salt. Then he would spring onto the terrace, lift the steak lightly off the fire, and run away with the Goslins' dinner. Jupiter's days were numbered. The Wrightsons' German gardener or the Farquarsons' cook would soon poison him. Even old Mr. Nixon might put some arsenic in the garbage that Jupiter loved. "Here, Jupiter, Jupiter!" Francis called, but the dog pranced off, shaking the hat in his white teeth. Looking in at the windows of his house, Francis saw that Julia had come down and was blowing out the candles.

Julia and Francis Weed went out a great deal. Julia was well liked and gregarious, and her love of parties sprang from a most natural dread of chaos and loneliness. She went through her morning mail with real anxiety, looking for invitations, and she usually found some, but she was insatiable, and if she had gone out seven nights a week, it would not have cured her of a reflective look — the look of someone who hears distant music — for she would always suppose that there was a more brilliant party somewhere else. Francis limited her to two week-night parties, putting a flexible interpretation on Friday, and rode through the weekend like a dory in a gale. The day after the airplane crash, the Weeds were to have dinner with the Farquarsons.

Francis got home late from town, and Julia got the sitter while he dressed, and then hurried him out of the house. The party was small and pleasant, and Francis settled down to enjoy himself. A new maid passed the drinks. Her hair was dark, and her face was round and pale and seemed familiar to Francis. He had not developed his memory as a sentimental faculty. Wood smoke, lilac, and other such perfumes did not stir him, and his memory was something like his appendix — a vestigial repository. It was not his limitation at all to be unable to escape the past; it was perhaps his limitation that he had escaped it so successfully. He might have seen the maid at other parties, he might have seen her taking a walk on Sunday afternoons, but in either case he would not be searching his memory now. Her face was, in a wonderful way, a moon face — Norman or Irish — but it was not beautiful enough to account for his feeling that he had seen her before, in circumstances that he ought to be able to remember. He asked Nellie Farquarson who she was. Nellie said that the maid had come through an agency, and that her home was Trénon, in Normandy — a small place with a church and a restaurant that Nellie had once visited. While Nellie talked on about her travels abroad, Francis realized where he had seen the woman before. It had been at the end of the war. He had left a replacement depot with some other men and taken a three-day pass in Trénon. On their second day, they had walked out to a crossroads to see the public chastisement of a young woman who had lived with the German commandant during the Occupation.

It was a cool morning in the fall. The sky was overcast, and poured down onto the dirt crossroads a very discouraging light. They were on high land and could see how like one another the shapes of the clouds and the hills were as they stretched off toward the sea. The prisoner arrived sitting on a three-legged stool in a farm cart. She stood by the cart while the mayor read the accusation and the sentence. Her head was bent and her face was set in that empty half smile behind which the whipped soul is suspended. When the mayor was finished, she undid her hair and let it fall across her back. A little man with a gray mustache cut off her hair with shears and dropped it on the ground. Then, with a bowl of soapy water and a straight razor, he shaved her skull clean. A woman approached and began to undo the fastenings of her clothes, but the prisoner pushed her aside and undressed herself. When she pulled her chemise over her head and threw it on the ground, she was naked. The women jeered; the men were still. There was no change in the falseness or the plaintiveness of the prisoner's smile. The cold wind made her white skin rough and hardened the nipples of her breasts. The jeering ended gradually, put down by the recognition of their common humanity. One woman spat on her, but some inviolable grandeur in her nakedness lasted through her ordeal. When the crowd was quiet, she turned — she had begun to cry — and, with nothing on but a pair of worn black shoes and stockings, walked down the dirt road alone away from the village. The round white face had aged a little, but there was no question but that the maid who passed his cocktails and later served Francis his dinner was the woman who had been punished at the crossroads.

The war seemed now so distant and that world where the cost of partisanship had been death or torture so long ago. Francis had lost track of the men who had been with him in Vésey. He could not count on Julia's discretion. He could not tell anyone. And if he had told the story now, at the dinner table, it would have been a social as well as a human error. The people in the Farquarsons' living room seemed united in their tacit claim that there had been no past, no war — that there was no danger or trouble in the world. In the recorded history of human arrangements, this extraordinary meeting would have fallen into place, but the atmosphere of Shady Hill made the memory unseemly and impolite. The prisoner withdrew after passing the coffee, but the encounter left Francis feeling languid; it had opened his memory and his senses, and left them dilated. He and Julia drove home when the party ended, and Julia went into the house. Francis stayed in the car to take the sitter home.

Expecting to see Mrs. Henlein, the old lady who usually stayed with the children, he was surprised when a young girl opened the door and came out onto the lighted stoop. She stayed in the light to count her textbooks. She was frowning and beautiful. Now, the world is full of beautiful young girls, but Francis saw here the difference between beauty and perfection. All those endearing flaws, moles, birthmarks, and healed wounds were missing, and he experienced in his consciousness that moment when music breaks glass, and felt a pang of recognition as strange, deep, and wonderful as anything in his life. It hung from her frown, from an impalpable darkness in her face — a look that impressed him as a direct appeal for love. When she had counted her books, she came down the steps and opened the car door. In the light, he saw that her cheeks were wet. She got in and shut the door.

"You're new," Francis said.

"Yes. Mrs. Henlein is sick. I'm Anne Murchison."

"Did the children give you any trouble?"

"Oh, no, no." She turned and smiled at him unhappily in the dim dashboard light. Her light hair caught on the collar of her jacket, and she shook her head to set it loose.

"You've been crying."

"Yes."

"I hope it was nothing that happened in our house."

"No, no, it was nothing that happened in your house." Her voice was bleak. "It's no secret. Everybody in the village knows. Daddy's an alcoholic, and he just called me from some saloon and gave me a piece of his mind. He thinks I'm immoral. He called just before Mrs. Weed came back."

"I'm sorry."

"Oh, *Lord!*" She gasped and began to cry. She turned toward Francis, and he took her in his arms and let her cry on his shoulder. She shook in his embrace, and this movement accentuated his sense of the fineness of her flesh and bone. The layers of their clothing felt thin, and when her shuddering began to diminish, it was so much like a paroxysm of love that Francis lost his head and pulled her roughly against him. She drew away. "I live on Belleview Avenue," she said. "You go down Lansing Street to the railroad bridge."

"All right." He started the car.

"You turn left at that traffic light. . . . Now you turn right here and go straight on toward the tracks."

The road Francis took brought him out of his own neighborhood, across the tracks, and toward the river, to a street where the near-poor lived, in houses whose peaked gables and trimmings of wooden lace conveyed the purest feelings of pride and romance, although the houses themselves could not have offered much privacy or comfort, they were all so small. The street was dark, and, stirred by the grace and beauty of the troubled girl, he seemed, in turning in to it, to have come into the deepest part of some submerged memory. In the distance, he saw a porch light burning. It was the only one, and she said that the house with the light was where she lived. When he stopped the car, he could see beyond the porch light into a dimly-lighted hallway with an old-fashioned clothes tree. "Well, here we are," he said, conscious that a young man would have said something different.

She did not move her hands from the books, where they were folded, and she turned and faced him. There were tears of lust in his eyes. Determinedly — not sadly — he opened the door on his side and walked around to open hers. He took her free hand, letting his fingers in between hers, climbed at her side the two concrete steps, and went up a narrow walk through a front garden where dahlias, marigolds, and roses — things that had withstood the light frosts — still bloomed, and made a bittersweet smell in the night air. At the steps, she freed her hand and then turned and kissed him swiftly. Then she crossed the porch and shut the door. The porch light went out, then the light in the hall. A second later, a light went on upstairs at the side of the house, shining into a tree that was still covered with leaves. It took her only a few minutes to undress and get into bed, and then the house was dark.

Julia was asleep when Francis got home. He opened a second window and got into bed to shut his eyes on that night, but as soon as they were shut — as soon as he had dropped off to sleep — the girl entered his mind, moving with perfect freedom through its shut doors and filling chamber after chamber with her light, her perfume, and the music of her voice. He was crossing the Atlantic with her on the old *Mauretania* and, later, living with her in Paris. When he woke from this dream, he got up and smoked a cigarette at the open window. Getting back into bed, he cast around in his mind for something he desired to do that would injure no one, and he thought of skiing. Up through the dimness in his mind rose the image of a mountain deep in snow. It was late in the day. Wherever his eyes looked, he saw broad and heartening things.

Over his shoulder, there was a snow-filled valley, rising into wooded hills where the trees dimmed the whiteness like a sparse coat of hair. The cold deadened all sound but the loud, iron clanking of the lift machinery. The light on the trails was blue, and it was harder than it had been a minute or two earlier to pick the turns, harder to judge — now that the snow was all deep blue — the crust, the ice, the bare spots, and the deep piles of dry powder. Down the mountain he swung, matching his speed against the contours of a slope that had been formed in the first ice age, seeking with ardor some simplicity of feeling and circumstance. Night fell then, and he drank a Martini with some old friend in a dirty country bar.

In the morning, Francis' snow-covered mountain was gone, and he was left with his vivid memories of Paris and the *Mauretania*. He had been bitten gravely. He washed his body, shaved his jaws, drank his coffee, and missed the seven-thirty-one. The train pulled out just as he brought his car to the station, and the longing he felt for the coaches as they drew stubbornly away from him reminded him of the humors of love. He waited for eight-two, on what was now an empty platform. It was a clear morning; the morning seemed thrown like a gleaming bridge of light over his mixed affairs. His spirits were feverish and high. The image of the girl seemed to put him into a relationship to the world that was mysterious and enthralling. Cars were beginning to fill up the parking lot, and he noticed that those that had driven down from the high land above Shady Hill were white with hoarfrost. This first clear sign of autumn thrilled him. An express train — a night train from Buffalo or Albany — came down the tracks between the platforms, and he saw that the roofs of the foremost cars were covered with a skin of ice. Struck by the miraculous physicalness of everything, he smiled at the passengers in the dining car, who could be seen eating eggs and wiping their mouths with napkins as they travelled. The sleeping-car compartments, with their soiled bed linen, trailed through the fresh morning like a string of rooming-house windows. Then he saw an extraordinary thing; at one of the bedroom windows sat an unclothed woman of exceptional beauty, combing her golden hair. She passed like an apparition through Shady Hill, combing and combing her hair, and Francis followed her with his eyes until she was out of sight. Then old Mrs. Wrightson joined him on the platform and began to talk.

"Well, I guess you must be surprised to see me here the third morning in a row," she said, "but because of my window curtains I'm becoming a regular commuter. The curtains I bought on Monday I returned on

Tuesday, and the curtains I bought Tuesday I'm returning today. On Monday, I got exactly what I wanted — it's a wool tapestry with roses and birds — but when I got them home, I found they were the wrong length. Well, I exchanged them yesterday, and when I got them home, I found they were still the wrong length. Now I'm praying to high Heaven that the decorator will have them in the right length, because you know my house, you *know* my living-room windows, and you can imagine what a problem they present. I don't know what to do with them."

"I know what to do with them," Francis said.

"What?"

"Paint them black on the inside, and shut up."

There was a gasp from Mrs. Wrightson, and Francis looked down at her to be sure that she knew he meant to be rude. She turned and walked away from him, so damaged in spirit that she limped. A wonderful feeling enveloped him, as if light were being shaken about him, and he thought again of Venus combing and combing her hair as she drifted through the Bronx. The realization of how many years had passed since he had enjoyed being deliberately impolite sobered him. Among his friends and neighbors, there were brilliant and gifted people — he saw that — but many of them, also, were bores and fools, and he had made the mistake of listening to them all with equal attention. He had confused a lack of discrimination with Christian love, and the confusion seemed general and destructive. He was grateful to the girl for this bracing sensation of independence. Birds were singing — cardinals and the last of the robins. The sky shone like enamel. Even the smell of ink from his morning paper honed his appetite for life, and the world that was spread out around him was plainly a paradise.

If Francis had believed in some hierarchy of love — in spirits armed with hunting bows, in the capriciousness of Venus and Eros — or even in magical potions, philtres, and stews, in scapulae and quarters of the moon, it might have explained his susceptibility and his feverish high spirits. The autumnal loves of middle age are well publicized, and he guessed that he was face to face with one of these, but there was not a trace of autumn in what he felt. He wanted to sport in the green woods, scratch where he itched, and drink from the same cup.

His secretary, Miss Rainey, was late that morning — she went to a psychiatrist three mornings a week — and when she came in, Francis wondered what advice a psychiatrist would have for him. But the girl promised to bring back into his life something like the sound of music. The realization that this music might lead him straight to a trial for statutory rape at the county courthouse collapsed his happiness. The photograph of his four children laughing into the camera on the beach at Gay Head reproached him. On the letterhead of his firm there was a drawing of the Laocoön, and the figure of the priest and his sons in the coils of the snake appeared to him to have the deepest meaning.

He had lunch with Pinky Trabert, who told him a couple of dirty stories. At a conversational level, the mores of his friends were robust and elastic, but he knew that the moral card house would come down on them all — on Julia and the children — if he got caught taking advantage of a baby-sitter. Looking back over the recent history of Shady Hill for some precedent, he found there was none. There was no turpitude; there had not been a divorce since he lived there; there had not even been a breath of scandal. Things seemed arranged with more propriety even than in the Kingdom of Heaven. After leaving Pinky, Francis went to a jeweller's and bought the girl a bracelet. How happy this clandestine purchase made him, how stuffy and comical the jeweller's clerks seemed, how sweet the women who passed at his back smelled! On Fifth Avenue, passing Atlas with his shoulders bent under the weight of the world, Francis thought of the strenuousness of containing his physicalness within the patterns he had chosen.

He did not know when he would see the girl next. He had the bracelet in his inside pocket when he got home. Opening the door of his house, he found her in the hall. Her back was to him, and she turned when she heard the door close. Her smile was open and loving. Her perfection stunned him like a fine day — a day after a thunderstorm. He seized her and covered her lips with his, and she struggled but she did not have to struggle for long, because just then little Gertrude Flannery appeared from somewhere and said, "Oh, Mr. Weed . . ."

Gertrude was a stray. She had been born with a taste for exploration, and she did not have it in her to center her life with her affectionate parents. People who did not know the Flannerys concluded from Gertrude's behavior that she was the child of a bitterly divided family, where drunken quarrels were the rule. This was not true. The fact that Gertrude's clothing was ragged and thin was her own triumph over her mother's struggle to dress her warmly and neatly. Garrulous, skinny, and unwashed, she drifted from house to house around the Blenhollow neighborhood, forming and breaking alliances based on an attachment to babies, animals, children her own age, adolescents, and sometimes adults. Opening your front door in the morning, you would find Gertrude sitting on your stoop. Going into the bathroom to shave, you would find Gertrude using the toilet. Looking into your son's crib, you would find it empty, and, looking further, you would find that Gertrude had pushed him in his baby carriage into the next village. She was helpful, pervasive, honest, hungry, and loyal. She never went home of her own choice. When the time to go arrived, she was indifferent to all its signs. "Go home, Gertrude," people could be heard saying in one house or another, night after night. "Go home, Gertrude." "It's time for you to go home now, Gertrude." "You had better go home and get your supper, Gertrude." "I told you to go home twenty minutes ago, Gertrude." "Your mother will be worrying about you, Gertrude." "Go home, Gertrude, go home."

There are times when the lines around the human eye seem like shelves of eroded stone and when the staring eye itself strikes us with such a wilderness of animal feeling that we are at a loss. The look Francis gave the little girl was ugly and queer, and it frightened her. He reached into his pocket — his hands were shaking — and he took out a quarter. "Go home, Gertrude, go home, and don't tell anyone. Gertrude. Don't —" He choked and ran into the living room as Julia called down to him from upstairs to hurry and dress.

The thought that he would drive Anne Murchison home later that night ran like a golden thread through the events of the party that Francis and Julia went to, and he laughed uproariously at dull jokes, dried a tear when Mabel Mercer told him about the death of her kitten, and stretched, yawned, sighed, and grunted like any other man with a rendezvous in the back of his mind. The bracelet was in his pocket. As he sat talking, the smell of grass was in his nose, and he was wondering where he would park the car. Nobody lived in the old Parker mansion, and the driveway was used as a lovers' lane. Townsend Street was a dead end, and he could park there, beyond the last house. The old lane that used to connect Elm Street to the riverbanks was overgrown, but he had walked there with his children, and he could drive his car deep enough into the brushwoods to be concealed.

The Weeds were the last to leave the party, and their host and hostess spoke of their own married happiness while they all four stood in the hallway saying good night. "She's my girl," their host said, squeezing his wife. "She's my blue sky. After sixteen years, I still bite her shoulders. She makes me feel like Hannibal crossing the Alps."

The Weeds drove home in silence. Francis brought the car up the driveway and sat still, with the motor running. "You can put the car in the garage," Julia said as she got out. "I told the Murchison girl she could leave at eleven. Someone drove her home." She shut the door, and Francis sat in the dark. He would be spared nothing then, it seemed, that a fool was not spared: ravening lewdness, jealousy, this hurt to his feelings that put tears in his eyes, even scorn — for he could see clearly the image he now presented, his arms spread over the steering wheel and his head buried in them for love.

Francis had been a dedicated Boy Scout when he was young, and, remembering the precepts of his youth, he left his office early the next afternoon and played some round-robin squash, but, with his body toned up by exercise and a shower, he realized that he might better have stayed at his desk. It was a frosty night when he got home. The air smelled sharply of change. When he stepped into the house, he sensed an unusual stir. The children were in their best clothes, and when Julia came down, she was wearing a lavender dress and her diamond sunburst. She explained the stir: Mr. Hubber was coming at seven to take their photograph for the Christmas card. She had put out Francis' blue suit and a tie with some color in it, because the picture was going to be in color this year. Julia was lighthearted at the thought of being photographed for Christmas. It was the kind of ceremony she enjoyed.

Francis went upstairs to change his clothes. He was tired from the day's work and tired with longing, and sitting on the edge of the bed had the effect of deepening his weariness. He thought of Anne Murchison, and the physical need to express himself, instead of being restrained by the pink lamps of Julia's dressing table, engulfed him. He went to Julia's desk, took a piece of writing paper, and began to write on it. "Dear Anne, I love you, I love you, I love you . . ." No one would see the letter, and he used no restraint. He used phrases like "heavenly bliss," and "love nest." He salivated, sighed, and trembled. When Julia called him to come down, the abyss between his fantasy and the practical world opened so wide that he felt it affect the muscles of his heart.

Julia and the children were on the stoop, and the photographer and his assistant had set up a double battery of floodlights to show the family and the architectural beauty of the entrance to their house. People who had come home on a late train slowed their cars to see the Weeds being photographed for their Christmas card. A few waved and called to the family. It took half an hour of smiling and wetting their lips before Mr. Hubber was satisfied. The heat of the lights made an unfresh smell in the frosty air, and when they were turned off, they lingered on the retina of Francis' eyes.

Later that night, while Francis and Julia were drinking their coffee in the living room, the doorbell rang. Julia answered the door and let in Clayton Thomas. He had come to pay her for some theatre tickets that she had given his mother some time ago, and that Helen Thomas had scrupulously insisted on paying for, though Julia had asked her not to. Julia invited him in to have a cup of coffee. "I won't have any coffee," Clayton said, "but I will come in for a minute." He followed her into the living room, said good evening to Francis, and sat awkwardly in a chair.

Clayton's father had been killed in the war, and the young man's fatherlessness surrounded him like an element. This may have been conspicuous in Shady Hill because the Thomases were the only family that lacked a piece; all the other marriages were intact and productive. Clayton was in his second or third year of college, and he and his mother lived alone in a large house, which she hoped to sell. Clayton had once made some trouble. Years ago, he had stolen some money and run away; he had got to California before they caught up with him. He was tall and homely, wore horn-rimmed glasses, and spoke in a deep voice.

"When do you go back to college, Clayton?" Francis asked.

"I'm not going back," Clayton said. "Mother doesn't have the money, and there's no sense in all this pretense. I'm going to get a job, and if we sell the house, we'll take an apartment in New York."

"Won't you miss Shady Hill?" Julia asked.

"No," Clayton said. "I don't like it."

"Why not?" Francis asked.

"Well, there's a lot here I don't approve of," Clayton said gravely. "Things like the club dances. Last Saturday night, I looked in toward the end and saw Mr. Granner trying to put Mrs. Minot into the trophy case. They were both drunk. I disapprove of so much drinking."

"It was Saturday night," Francis said.

"And all the dovecotes are phony," Clayton said. "And the way people clutter up their lives. I've thought about it a lot, and what seems to me to be really wrong with Shady Hill is that it doesn't have any future. So much energy is spent in perpetuating the place — in keeping out undesirables, and so forth — that the only idea of the future anyone has is just more and more commuting trains and more parties. I don't think that's healthy. I think people ought to be able to dream big dreams about the future. I think people ought to be able to dream great dreams."

"It's too bad you couldn't continue with college," Julia said.

"I wanted to go to divinity school," Clayton said.

"What's your church?" Francis asked.

"Unitarian, Theosophist, Transcendentalist, Humanist," Clayton said.

"Wasn't Emerson a transcendentalist?" Julia asked.

"I mean the English transcendentalists," Clayton said. "All the American transcendentalists were goops."

"What kind of a job do you expect to get?" Francis asked.

"Well, I'd like to work for a publisher," Clayton said, "but everyone tells me there's nothing doing. But it's the kind of thing I'm interested in. I'm writing a long verse play about good and evil. Uncle Charlie might get me into a bank, and that would be good for me. I need the discipline. I have a long way to go in forming my character. I have some terrible habits. I talk too much. I think I ought to take vows of silence. I ought to try not to speak for a week, and discipline myself. I've thought of making a retreat at one of the Episcopalian monasteries, but I don't like Trinitarianism."

"Do you have any girl friends?" Francis asked.

"I'm engaged to be married," Clayton said. "Of course, I'm not old enough or rich enough to have my engagement observed or respected or anything, but I bought a simulated emerald for Anne Murchison with the money I made cutting lawns this summer. We're going to be married as soon as she finishes school."

Francis recoiled at the mention of the girl's name. Then a dingy light seemed to emanate from his spirit, showing everything — Julia, the boy, the chairs — in their true colorlessness. It was like a bitter turn of the weather.

"We're going to have a large family," Clayton said. "Her father's a terrible rummy, and I've had my hard times, and we want to have lots of children. Oh, she's wonderful, Mr. and Mrs. Weed, and we have so much in common. We like all the same things. We sent out the same Christmas card last year without planning it, and we both have an allergy to tomatoes, and our eyebrows grow together in the middle. Well, good night."

Julia went to the door with him. When she returned, Francis said that Clayton was lazy, irresponsible, affected, and smelly. Julia said that Francis seemed to be getting intolerant; the Thomas boy was young and should be given a chance. Julia had noticed other cases where Francis had been short-tempered. "Mrs. Wrightson has asked everyone in Shady Hill to her anniversary party but us," she said.

"I'm sorry, Julia."

"Do you know why they didn't ask us?"

"Why?"

"Because you insulted Mrs. Wrightson."

"Then you know about it?"

"June Masterson told me. She was standing behind you."

Julia walked in front of the sofa with a small step that expressed, Francis knew, a feeling of anger.

"I did insult Mrs. Wrightson, Julia, and I meant to. I've never liked her parties, and I'm glad she's dropped us."

"What about Helen?"

"How does Helen come into this?"

"Mrs. Wrightson's the one who decides who goes to the assemblies."

"You mean she can keep Helen from going to the dances?"

"Yes."

"I hadn't thought of that."

"Oh, I know you hadn't thought of it," Julia cried, thrusting hilt-deep into this chink of his armor. "And it makes me furious to see this kind of stupid thoughtlessness wreck everyone's happiness."

"I don't think I've wrecked anyone's happiness."

"Mrs. Wrightson runs Shady Hill and has run it for the last forty years. I don't know what makes you think that in a community like this you can indulge every impulse you have to be insulting, vulgar, and offensive."

"I have very good manners," Francis said, trying to give the evening a turn toward the light.

"Damn you, Francis Weed!" Julia cried, and the spit of her words struck him in the face. "I've worked hard for the social position we enjoy in this place, and I won't stand by and see you wreck it. You must have understood when you settled here that you couldn't expect to live like a bear in a cave."

"I've got to express my likes and dislikes."

"You can conceal your dislikes. You don't have to meet everything head-on, like a child. Unless you're anxious to be a social leper. It's no accident that we get asked out a great deal. It's no accident that Helen has so many friends. How would you like to spend your Saturday nights at the movies? How would you like to spend your Sundays raking up dead leaves? How would you like it if your daughter spent the assembly nights sitting at her window, listening to the music from the club? How would you like it —" He did something then that was, after all, not so unaccountable, since her words seemed to raise up between them a wall so deadening that he gagged: He struck her full in the face. She staggered and then, a moment later, seemed composed. She went up the stairs to their room. She didn't slam the door. When Francis followed, a few minutes later, he found her packing a suitcase.

"Julia, I'm very sorry."

"It doesn't matter," she said. She was crying.

"Where do you think you're going?"

"I don't know. I just looked at a timetable. There's an eleven-sixteen into New York. I'll take that."

"You can't go, Julia."

"I can't stay. I know that."

"I'm sorry about Mrs. Wrightson, Julia, and I'm —"

"It doesn't matter about Mrs. Wrightson. That isn't the trouble."

"What is the trouble?"

"You don't love me."

"I do love you, Julia."

"No, you don't."

"Julia, I do love you, and I would like to be as we were — sweet and bawdy and dark — but now there are so many people."

"You hate me."

"I don't hate you, Julia."

"You have no idea of how much you hate me. I think it's subconscious. You don't realize the cruel things you've done."

"What cruel things, Julia?"

"The cruel acts your subconscious drives you to in order to express your hatred of me."

"What, Julia?"

"I've never complained."

"Tell me."

"You don't know what you're doing."

"Tell me."

"Your clothes."

"What do you mean?"

"I mean the way you leave your dirty clothes around in order to express your subconscious hatred of me."

"I don't understand."

"I mean your dirty socks and your dirty pajamas and your dirty underwear and your dirty shirts!" She rose from kneeling by the suitcase and faced him, her eyes blazing and her voice ringing with emotion. "I'm talking about the fact that you've never learned to hang up anything. You just leave your clothes all over the floor where they drop, in order to humiliate me. You do it on purpose!" She fell on the bed, sobbing.

"Julia, darling!" he said, but when she felt his hand on her shoulder she got up.

"Leave me alone," she said. "I have to go." She brushed past him to the closet and came back with a dress. "I'm not taking any of the things you've given me," she said. "I'm leaving my pearls and the fur jacket."

"Oh, Julia!" Her figure, so helpless in its self-deceptions, bent over the suitcase made him nearly sick with pity. She did not understand how desolate her life would be without him. She didn't understand the hours that working women have to keep. She didn't understand that most of her friendships existed within the framework of their marriage, and that without this she would find herself alone. She didn't understand about travel, about hotels, about money. "Julia, I can't let you go! What you don't understand, Julia, is that you've come to be dependent on me."

She tossed her head back and covered her face with her hands. "Did you say that *I* was dependent on *you?*" she asked. "Is that what you said? And who is it that tells you what time to get up in the morning and when to go to bed at night? Who is it that prepares your meals and picks up your dirty closet and invites your friends to dinner? If it weren't for me, your neckties would be greasy and your clothing would be full of moth holes. You were alone when I met you, Francis Weed, and you'll be alone when I leave. When Mother asked you for a list to send out invitations to our wedding, how many names did you have to give her? Fourteen!"

"Cleveland wasn't my home, Julia."

"And how many of your friends came to the church? Two!"

"Cleveland wasn't my home, Julia."

"Since I'm not taking the fur jacket," she said quietly, "you'd better put it back into storage. There's an insurance policy on the pearls that comes due in January. The name of the laundry and the maid's telephone number — all those things are in my desk. I hope you won't drink too much, Francis. I hope that nothing bad will happen to you. If you do get into serious trouble, you can call me."

"Oh my darling, I can't let you go!" Francis said. "I can't let you go, Julia!" He took her in his arms.

"I guess I'd better stay and take care of you for a little while longer," she said.

Riding to work in the morning, Francis saw the girl walk down the aisle of the coach. He was surprised; he hadn't realized that the school she went to was in the city, but she was carrying books, she seemed to be going to school. His surprise delayed his reaction, but then he got up clumsily and stepped into the aisle. Several people had come between them, but he could see her ahead of him, waiting for someone to open the car door, and then, as the train swerved, putting out her hand to support herself as she crossed the platform into the next car. He followed her through that car and halfway through another before calling her name — "Anne! Anne!" — but she didn't turn. He followed her into still another car, and she sat down in an aisle seat. Coming up to her, all his feelings warm and bent in her direction, he put his hand on the back of her seat — even this touch warmed him — and, leaning down to speak to her, he saw that it was not Anne. It was an older woman wearing glasses. He went deliberately into another car, his face red with embarrassment and the much deeper feeling of having his good sense challenged; for if he couldn't tell one person from another, what evidence was there that his life with Julia and the children had as much reality as his dreams of iniquity in Paris or the litter, the grass smell, and the cave-shaped trees in Lovers' Lane.

Late that afternoon, Julia called to remind Francis that they were going out for dinner. A few minutes later, Trace Bearden called. "Look, fellar," Trace said. "I'm calling for Mrs. Thomas. You know? Clayton, that boy of hers, doesn't seem able to get a job, and I wondered if you could help. If you'd call Charlie Bell — I know he's indebted to you — and say a good word for the kid, I think Charlie would —"

"Trace, I hate to say this," Francis said, "but I don't feel that I can do anything for that boy. The kid's worthless. I know it's a harsh thing to say, but it's a fact. Any kindness done for him would backfire in everybody's face. He's just a worthless kid, Trace, and there's nothing to be done about it. Even if we got him a job, he wouldn't be able to keep it for a week. I know that to be a fact. It's an awful thing, Trace, and I know it is, but instead of recommending that kid, I'd feel obliged to warn people against him — people who knew his father and would naturally want to step in and do something. I'd feel obliged to warn them. He's a thief . . ."

The moment this conversation was finished, Miss Rainey came in and stood by his desk. "I'm not going to be able to work for you any more, Mr. Weed," she said. "I can stay until the seventeenth if you need me, but I've been offered a whirlwind of a job, and I'd like to leave as soon as possible."

She went out, leaving him to face alone the wickedness of what he had done to the Thomas boy. His children in their photograph laughed and laughed, glazed with all the bright colors of summer, and he remembered that they had met a bagpiper on the beach that day and he had paid the piper a dollar to play them a battle song of the Black Watch. The girl would be at the house when he got home. He would spend another evening among his kind neighbors, picking and choosing dead-end streets, cart tracks, and the driveways of abandoned houses. There was nothing to mitigate his feeling — nothing that laughter or a game of softball with the children would change — and, thinking back over the plane crash, the Farquarson's new maid, and Anne Murchison's difficulties with her drunken father, he wondered how he could have avoided arriving at just where he was. He was in trouble. He had been lost once in his life, coming back from a trout stream in the north woods, and he had now the same bleak realization that no amount of cheerfulness or hopefulness or valor or perseverance could help him find, in the gathering dark, the path that he'd lost. He smelled the forest. The feeling of bleakness was intolerable, and he saw clearly that he had reached the point where he would have to make a choice.

He could go to a psychiatrist, like Miss Rainey; he could go to church and confess his lusts; he could go to a Danish massage parlor in the West Seventies that had been recommended by a salesman; he could rape the girl or trust that he would somehow be prevented from doing this; or he could get drunk. It was his life, his boat, and, like every other man, he was made to be the father of thousands, and what harm could there be in a tryst that would make them both feel more kindly toward the world? This was the wrong train of thought, and he came back to the first, the psychiatrist. He had the telephone number of Miss Rainey's doctor, and he called and asked for an immediate appointment. He was insistent with the doctor's secretary — it was his manner in business — and when she said that the doctor's schedule was full for the next few weeks, Francis demanded an appointment that day and was told to come at five.

The psychiatrist's office was in a building that was used mostly by doctors and dentists, and the hallways were filled with the candy smell of mouthwash and memories of pain. Francis' character had been formed upon a series of private resolves — resolves about cleanliness, about going off the high diving board or repeating any other feat that challenged his courage, about punctuality, honesty, and virtue. To abdicate the perfect loneliness in which he had made his most vital decisions shattered his concept of character and left him now in a condition that felt like shock. He was stupefied. The scene for his *miserere mei Deus* was, like the waiting room of so many doctors' offices, a crude token gesture toward the sweets of domestic bliss: a place arranged with antiques, coffee tables, potted plants, and etchings of snow-covered bridges and geese in flight, although there were no children, no marriage bed, no stove, even, in this travesty of a house, where no one had ever spent the night and where the curtained windows looked straight onto a dark air shaft. Francis gave his name and address to a secretary and then saw, at the side of the room, a policeman moving toward him. "Hold it, hold it," the policeman said. "Don't move. Keep your hands where they are."

"I think it's all right, officer," the secretary began. "I think it will be —"

"Let's make sure," the policeman said, and he began to slap Francis' clothes, looking for what — pistols, knives, an icepick? Finding nothing, he went off, and the secretary began a nervous apology. "When you called on the telephone, Mr. Weed, you seemed very excited, and one of the doctor's patients has been threatening his life, and we have to be careful. If you want to go in now?" Francis pushed open a door connected to an electrical chime, and in the doctor's lair sat down heavily, blew his nose into a handkerchief, searched in his pockets for cigarettes, for matches, for something, and said hoarsely, with tears in his eyes, "I'm in love, Dr. Herzog."

It is a week or ten days later in Shady Hill. The seven-fourteen has come and gone, and here and there dinner is finished and the dishes are in the dishwashing machine. The village hangs, morally and economically, from a thread; but it hangs by its thread in the evening light. Donald Goslin has begun to worry the "Moonlight Sonata" again. *Marcato ma sempre pianissimo!* He seems to be wringing out a wet bath towel, but the housemaid does not heed him. She is writing a letter to Arthur Godfrey. In the cellar of his house, Francis Weed is building a coffee table. Dr. Herzog recommended woodwork as a therapy, and Francis finds some true consolation in the simple arithmetic involved and in the holy smell of new wood. Francis is happy. Upstairs, little Toby is crying, because he is tired. He puts off his cowboy hat, gloves, and fringed jacket, unbuckles the belt studded with gold and rubies, the silver bullets and holsters, slips off his suspenders, his checked shirt, and Levi's, and sits on the edge of his bed to pull off his high boots. Leaving this equipment in a heap, he goes to the closet and takes his space suit off

a nail. It is a struggle for him to get into the long tights, but he suc-
ceeds. He loops the magic cape over his shoulders and, climbing onto
the footboard of his bed, he spreads his arms and flies the short distance to the floor, landing with a thump that is audible to everyone in
the house but himself.

"Go home, Gertrude, go home," Mrs. Masterson says. "I told you to
go home an hour ago, Gertrude. It's way past your suppertime, and your
mother will be worried. Go home!" A door on the Babcocks' terrace flies
open, and out comes Mrs. Babcock without any clothes on, pursued by
her naked husband. (Their children are away at boarding school, and
their terrace is screened by a hedge.) Over the terrace they go and in at
the kitchen door, as passionate and handsome a nymph and satyr as you
will find on any wall in Venice. Cutting the last of the roses in her
garden, Julia hears old Mr. Nixon shouting at the squirrels in his bird-
feeding station. "Rapscallions! Varmits! Avaunt and quit my sight!" A
miserable cat wanders into the garden, sunk in spiritual and physical
discomfort. Tied to its head is a small straw hat — a doll's hat — and it
is securely buttoned into a doll's dress, from the skirts of which pro-
trudes its long, hairy tail. As it walks, it shakes its feet, as if it had fallen
into water.

"Here, pussy, pussy, pussy!" Julia calls.

"Here, pussy, here, poor pussy!" But the cat gives her a skeptical look
and stumbles away in its skirts. The last to come is Jupiter. He prances
through the tomato vines, holding in his generous mouth the remains
of an evening slipper. Then it is dark; it is a night where kings in golden
suits ride elephants over the mountains.

1957

*Flannery O'Connor*

# Greenleaf

FROM *The Kenyon Review*

MRS. MAY'S BEDROOM window was low and faced on the east, and the bull, silvered in the moonlight, stood under it, his head raised as if he listened — like some patient god come down to woo her — for a stir inside the room. The window was dark and the sound of her breathing too light to be carried outside. Clouds crossing the moon blackened him and in the dark he began to tear at the hedge. Presently they passed and he appeared again in the same spot, chewing steadily, with a hedge-wreath that he had ripped loose for himself caught in the tips of his horns. When the moon drifted into retirement again, there was nothing to mark his place but the sound of steady chewing. Then abruptly a pink glow filled the window. Bars of light slid across him as the venetian blind was slit. He took a step backward and lowered his head as if to show the wreath across his horns.

For almost a minute there was no sound from inside, then as he raised his crowned head again, a woman's voice, guttural as if addressed to a dog, said, "Get away from here, sir!" and in a second muttered, "Some nigger's scrub bull."

The animal pawed the ground and Mrs. May, standing bent forward behind the blind, closed it quickly lest the light make him charge into the shrubbery. For a second she waited, still bent forward, her night-gown hanging loosely from her narrow shoulders. Green rubber curlers sprouted neatly over her forehead and her face beneath them was smooth as concrete with an egg-white paste that drew the wrinkles out while she slept.

She had been conscious in her sleep of a steady rhythmic chewing as if something were eating one wall of the house. She had been aware that whatever it was had been eating as long as she had had the place and had eaten everything from the beginning of her fence line up to the house and now was eating the house and calmly with the same steady rhythm would continue through the house, eating her and the boys, and then on, eating everything but the Greenleafs, on and on, eating everything until nothing was left but the Greenleafs on a little island all their own in the middle of what had been her place. When the munching reached her elbow, she jumped up and found herself, fully awake, standing in the middle of her room. She identified the sound at once: a cow was tearing at the shrubbery under her window. Mr. Greenleaf had left the lane gate open and she didn't doubt that the entire herd was on her lawn. She turned on the dim pink table lamp and then went to the window and slit the blind. The bull, gaunt and long-legged, was standing about four feet from her, chewing calmly like an uncouth country suitor.

For fifteen years, she thought as she squinted at him fiercely, she had been having shiftless people's hogs root up her oats, their mules wallow on her lawn, their scrub bulls breed her cows. If this one was not put up now, he would be over the fence, ruining her herd before morning — and Mr. Greenleaf was soundly sleeping a half mile down the road in the tenant house. There was no way to get him unless she dressed and got in her car and rode down there and woke him up. He would come but his expression, his whole figure, his every pause, would say: "Hit looks to me like one or both of them boys would not make their maw ride out in the middle of the night thisaway. If hit was my boys, they would have got thet bull up theirself."

The bull lowered his head and shook it and the wreath slipped down to the base of his horns where it looked like a menacing prickly crown. She had closed the blind then; in a few seconds she heard him move off heavily.

Mr. Greenleaf would say, "If hit was my boys they would never have allowed their maw to go after hired help in the middle of the night. They would have did it theirself."

Weighing it, she decided not to bother Mr. Greenleaf. She returned to bed thinking that if the Greenleaf boys had risen in the world it was because she had given their father employment when no one else would have him. She had had Mr. Greenleaf fifteen years but no one else would have had him five minutes. Just the way he approached an object was enough to tell anybody with eyes what kind of a worker he was. He walked with a high-shouldered creep and he never appeared to come directly forward. He walked on the perimeter of some invisible circle and if you wanted to look him in the face, you had to move and get in front of him. She had not fired him because she had always doubted she could do better. He was too shiftless to go out and look for another job; he didn't have the initiative to steal, and after she had told him three or four times to do a thing, he did it; but he never told her about a sick cow until it was too late to call the veterinarian, and if her barn had caught on fire he would have called his wife to see the flames before he began to put them out. And of the wife, she didn't even like to think. Beside the wife, Mr. Greenleaf was an aristocrat.

"If hit had been my boys," he would have said, "they would have cut off their right arm before they would have allowed their maw to. . . ."

"If your boys had any pride, Mr. Greenleaf," she would like to say to him some day, "there are many things that they would not *allow* their mother to do."

The next morning as soon as Mr. Greenleaf came to the back door, she told him there was a stray bull on the place and that she wanted him penned up at once.

"Done already been here three days," he said, addressing his right foot which he held forward, turned slightly as if he were trying to look at the sole. He was standing at the bottom of the three back steps while she leaned out the kitchen door, a small woman with pale nearsighted eyes and gray hair that rose on top like the crest of some disturbed bird.

"Three days!" she said in the restrained screech that had become habitual with her.

Mr. Greenleaf, looking into the distance over the near pasture, removed a package of cigarettes from his shirt pocket and let one fall into his hand. He put the package back and stood for a while looking at the cigarette. "I put him in the bull pen but he torn out of there," he said presently. "I didn't see him none after that." He bent over the cigarette and lit it and then turned his head briefly in her direction. The upper part of his face sloped gradually into the lower which was long and narrow, shaped like a rough chalice. He had deep-set fox-colored eyes shadowed under a gray felt hat that he wore slanted forward following the line of his nose. His build was insignificant.

"Mr. Greenleaf," she said, "get that bull up this morning before you do anything else. You know he'll ruin the breeding schedule. Get him up and keep him up and the next time there's a stray bull on this place, tell me at once. Do you understand?"

"Where you want him put at?" Mr. Greenleaf asked.

"I don't care where you put him," she said. "You are supposed to have some sense. Put him where he can't get out. Whose bull is he?"

For a moment Mr. Greenleaf seemed to hesitate between silence and speech. He studied the air to the left of him. "He must be somebody's bull," he said after a while.

"Yes, he must!" she said and shut the door with a precise little slam.

She went into the dining room where the two boys were eating breakfast and sat down on the edge of her chair at the head of the table. She never ate breakfast but she sat with them to see that they had what they wanted. "Honestly!" she said, and began to tell about the bull, aping Mr. Greenleaf saying, "It must be *somebody's* bull."

Wesley continued to read the newspaper folded beside his plate but Scofield interrupted his eating from time to time to look at her and laugh. The two boys never had the same reaction to anything. They were as different, she said, as night and day. The only thing they did have in common was that neither of them cared what happened on the place. Scofield was a business type and Wesley was an intellectual.

Wesley, the younger child, had had rheumatic fever when he was seven and Mrs. May thought that this was what had caused him to be an intellectual. Scofield, who had never had a day's sickness in his life, was an insurance salesman. She would not have minded his selling insurance if he had sold a nicer kind but he sold the kind that only Negroes buy. He was what Negroes call a "policy man." He said there was more money in nigger-insurance than any other kind, and before company, he was very loud about it. He would shout, "Mamma don't like to hear me say it but I'm the best nigger-insurance salesman in this county!"

Scofield was thirty-six and he had a broad pleasant smiling face but he was not married. "Yes," Mrs. May would say, "and if you sold decent insurance, some *nice* girl would be willing to marry you. What nice girl wants to marry a nigger-insurance man? You'll wake up some day and it'll be too late."

And at this Scofield would yodle and say, "Why Mamma, I'm not going to marry until you're dead and gone and then I'm going to marry me some nice fat farm girl that can take over this place!" And once he had added, "Some nice lady like Mrs. Greenleaf." When he had said this, Mrs. May had risen from her chair, her back stiff as a rake handle, and had gone to her room. There she had sat down on the edge of her bed for some time with her small face drawn. Finally she had whispered, "I work and slave, I struggle and sweat to keep this place for them and as soon as I'm dead, they'll marry trash and bring it in here and ruin everything. They'll marry trash and ruin everything I've done," and she had made up her mind at that moment to change her will. The next day she had gone to her lawyer and had had the property entailed so that if they married, they could not leave it to their wives.

The idea that one of them might marry a woman even remotely like Mrs. Greenleaf was enough to make her ill. She had put up with Mr. Greenleaf for fifteen years, but the only way she had endured his wife had been by keeping entirely out of her sight. Mrs. Greenleaf was large and loose. The yard around her house looked like a dump and her five girls were always filthy; even the youngest one dipped snuff. Instead of making a garden or washing their clothes, her preoccupation was what she called "prayer healing."

Every day she cut all the morbid stories out of the newspaper — the accounts of women who had been raped and criminals who had escaped and children who had been burned and of train wrecks and plane crashes and the divorces of movie stars. She took these to the woods and dug a hole and buried them and then she fell on the ground over them and mumbled and groaned for an hour or so, moving her huge arms back and forth under her and out again and finally just lying down flat and, Mrs. May suspected, going to sleep in the dirt.

She had not found out about this until the Greenleafs had been with her a few months. One morning she had been out to inspect a field that she had wanted planted in rye but that had come up in clover because Mr. Greenleaf had used the wrong seeds in the grain drill. She was returning through a wooded path that separated two pastures, muttering to herself and hitting the ground methodically with a long stick she carried in case she saw a snake. "Mr. Greenleaf," she was saying in a low voice, "I cannot afford to pay for your mistakes. I am a poor woman and this place is all I have. I have two boys to educate. I cannot. . . ."

Out of nowhere a guttural agonized voice groaned, "Jesus! Jesus!" In a second it came again with a terrible urgency. "Jesus! Jesus!"

Mrs. May stopped still, one hand lifted to her throat. The sound was so piercing that she felt as if some violent unleashed force had broken out of the ground and was charging toward her. Her second thought was more reasonable: somebody had been hurt on the place and would sue her for everything she had. She had no insurance. She rushed forward and turning a bend in the path, she saw Mrs. Greenleaf sprawled on her hands and knees off the side of the road, her head down.

"Mrs. Greenleaf!" she shrilled, "What's happened!"

Mrs. Greenleaf raised her head. Her face was a patchwork of dirt and tears and her small eyes, the color of two field peas, were red-rimmed and swollen, but her expression was as composed as a bulldog's. She swayed back and forth on her hands and knees and groaned, "Jesus, Jesus."

Mrs. May winced. She thought the word Jesus should be kept inside the church building like other words inside the bedroom. She was a good Christian woman with a large respect for religion, though she did not, of course, believe any of it was true. "What is the matter with you?" she asked sharply.

"You broken my healing," Mrs. Greenleaf said, waving her aside. "I can't talk to you until I finish."

Mrs. May stood, bent forward, her mouth open and her stick raised off the ground as if she were not sure what she wanted to strike with it.

"Oh Jesus, stab me in the heart!" Mrs. Greenleaf shrieked. "Jesus, stab me in the heart!" and she fell back flat in the dirt, a huge human mound, her legs and arms spread out as if she were trying to wrap them around the earth.

Mrs. May felt as furious and helpless as if she had been insulted by a child. "Jesus," she said, drawing herself back, "would be *ashamed* of you. He would tell you to get up from there this instant and go wash your children's clothes!" and she had turned and walked off as fast as she could.

Whenever she thought of how the Greenleaf boys had advanced in the world, she had only to think of Mrs. Greenleaf sprawled obscenely on the ground, and say to herself, "Well, no matter how far they *go*, they *came* from that."

She would like to have been able to put in her will that when she died, Wesley and Scofield were not to continue to employ Mr. Greenleaf. She was capable of handling Mr. Greenleaf; they were not. Mr. Greenleaf had pointed out to her once that her boys didn't know hay from silage. She had pointed out to him that they had other talents, that Scofield was a successful businessman and Wesley a successful intellectual. Mr. Greenleaf did not comment, but he never lost an opportunity of letting her see, by his expression or some simple gesture, that he held the two of them in infinite contempt. As scrub-human as the Greenleafs were, he never hesitated to let her know that in any like circumstance in which his own boys might have been involved, they — O. T. and E. T. Greenleaf — would have acted to better advantage.

The Greenleaf boys were two or three years younger than the May boys. They were twins and you never knew when you spoke to one of them whether you were speaking to O. T. or E. T., and they never had the politeness to enlighten you. They were long-legged and raw-boned and red-skinned, with bright grasping fox-colored eyes like their father's. Mr. Greenleaf's pride in them began with the fact that they were twins. He acted, Mrs. May said, as if this were something smart they had thought of themselves. They were energetic and hard-working and she would admit to anyone that they had come a long way — and that the Second World War was responsible for it.

They had both joined the service and, disguised in their uniforms, they could not be told from other people's children. You could tell, of course, when they opened their mouths but they did that seldom. The smartest thing they had done was to get sent overseas and there to marry French wives. They hadn't married French trash either. They had married nice girls who naturally couldn't tell that they murdered the king's English or that the Greenleafs were who they were.

Wesley's heart condition had not permitted him to serve his country but Scofield had been in the army for two years. He had not cared for it and at the end of his military service, he was only a Private First Class. The Greenleaf boys were both some kind of sergeants, and Mr. Greenleaf, in those days, had never lost an opportunity of referring to them by their rank. They had both managed to get wounded and now they both had pensions. Further, as soon as they were released from the army, they took advantage of all the benefits and went to the school of agriculture at the university — the taxpayers meanwhile supporting their French wives. The two of them were living now about two miles down the highway on a piece of land that the government had helped them to buy and in a brick duplex bungalow that the government had helped to build and pay for. If the war had made anyone, Mrs. May said, it had made the Greenleaf boys. They each had three little children apiece, who spoke Greenleaf English and French, and who, on account of their mothers' backgrounds, would be sent to the convent school and brought up with manners. "And in twenty years," Mrs. May asked Scofield and Wesley, "do you know what those people will be?

"*Society*," she said blackly.

She had spent fifteen years coping with Mr. Greenleaf and, by now, handling him had become second nature with her. His disposition on any particular day was as much a factor in what she could and couldn't do as the weather was, and she had learned to read his face the way real country people read the sunrise and sunset.

She was a country woman only by persuasion. The late Mr. May, a businessman, had bought the place when land was down, and when he died it was all he had to leave her. The boys had not been happy to move to the country to a broken-down farm, but there was nothing else for her to do. She had the timber on the place cut and with the proceeds had set herself up in the dairy business after Mr. Greenleaf had answered her ad. "i seen yor add and i will come have 2 boys," was all his letter said, but he arrived the next day in a pieced-together truck, his wife and five daughters sitting on the floor in the back, himself and the two boys in the cab.

Over the years they had been on her place, Mr. and Mrs. Greenleaf had aged hardly at all. They had no worries, no responsibilities. They lived like the lilies of the field, off the fat that she struggled to put into the land. When she was dead and gone from overwork and worry, the Greenleafs, healthy and thriving, would be just ready to begin draining Scofield and Wesley.

Wesley said the reason Mrs. Greenleaf had not aged was because she released all her emotions in prayer healing. "You ought to start praying, sweetheart," he had said in a voice that, poor boy, he could not help making deliberately nasty.

Scofield only exasperated her beyond endurance but Wesley caused her real anxiety. He was thin and nervous and bald and being an intellectual was a terrible strain on his disposition. She doubted if he would marry until she died but she was certain that then the wrong woman would get him. Nice girls didn't like Scofield but Wesley didn't like nice girls. He didn't like anything. He drove twenty miles every day to the university where he taught and twenty miles back every night, but he said he hated the twenty-mile drive and he hated the second-rate university and he hated the morons who attended it. He hated the country and he hated the life he lived; he hated living with his mother and his idiot brother and he hated hearing about the damn dairy and the damn help and the damn broken machinery. But in spite of all he said, he never made any move to leave. He talked about Paris and Rome but he never went even to Atlanta.

"You'd go to those places and you'd get sick," Mrs. May would say. "Who in Paris is going to see that you get a salt-free diet? And do you think if you married one of those old numbers you take out that *she* would cook a salt-free diet for you? No indeed, she would not!" When she took this line, Wesley would turn himself roughly around in his chair and ignore her. Once when she had kept it up too long, he had snarled, "Well, why don't you do something practical, woman? Why don't you pray for me like Mrs. Greenleaf would?"

"I don't like to hear you boys make jokes about religion," she had said. "If you would go to church, you would meet some nice girls."

But it was impossible to tell them anything. When she looked at the two of them now, sitting on either side of the table, neither one caring the least if a stray bull ruined her herd — which was their herd, their future — when she looked at the two of them, one hunched over a paper and the other teetering back in his chair, grinning at her like an idiot, she wanted to jump up and beat her fist on the table and shout, "You'll find out one of these days, you'll find out what *Reality* is when it's too late!"

"Mamma," Scofield said, "don't you get excited now but I'll tell you whose bull that is." He was looking at her wickedly. He let his chair drop forward and he got up. Then with his shoulders bent and his hands held up to cover his head, he tiptoed to the door. He backed into the hall and pulled the door almost to so that it hid all of him but his face. "You want to know, sugarpie?" he asked.

Mrs. May sat looking at him coldly.

"That's O. T. and E. T.'s bull," he said. "I collected from their nigger yesterday and he told me they were missing it," and he showed her an exaggerated expanse of teeth and disappeared silently.

Wesley looked up and laughed.

Mrs. May turned her head forward again, her expression unaltered. "I am the only *adult* on this place," she said. She leaned across the table and pulled the paper from the side of his plate. "Do you see how it's going to be when I die and you boys have to handle him?" she began. "Do you see why he didn't know whose bull that was? Because it was theirs. Do you see what I have to put up with? Do you see that if I hadn't kept my foot on his neck all these years, you boys might be milking cows every morning at four o'clock?"

Wesley pulled the paper back toward his plate and staring at her full in the face, he murmured, "I wouldn't milk a cow to save your soul from hell."

"I know you wouldn't," she said in a brittle voice. She sat back and began rapidly turning her knife over at the side of her plate. "O. T. and

E. T. are fine boys," she said. "They ought to have been my sons." The thought of this was so horrible that her vision of Wesley was blurred at once by a wall of tears. All she saw was his dark shape, rising quickly from the table. "And you two," she cried, "you two should have belonged to that woman!"

He was heading for the door.

"When I die," she said in a thin voice, "I don't know what's going to become of you."

"You're always yapping about when-you-die," he growled as he rushed out, "but you look pretty healthy to me."

For some time she sat where she was, looking straight ahead through the window across the room into a scene of indistinct grays and greens. She stretched her face and her neck muscles and drew in a long breath but the scene in front of her flowed together anyway into a watery gray mass. "They needn't think I'm going to die anytime soon," she muttered, and some more defiant voice in her added: I'll die when I get good and ready.

She wiped her eyes with the table napkin and got up and went to the window and gazed at the scene in front of her. The cows were grazing on two pale green pastures across the road and behind them, fencing them in, was a black wall of trees with a sharp sawtooth edge that held off the indifferent sky. The pastures were enough to calm her. When she looked out any window in her house, she saw the reflection of her own character. Her city friends said she was the most remarkable woman they knew, to go, practically penniless and with no experience, out to a rundown farm and make a success of it. "Everything is against you," she would say, "the weather is against you and the dirt is against you and the help is against you. They're all in league against you. There's nothing for it but an iron hand!"

"Look at Mamma's iron hand!" Scofield would yell and grab her arm and hold it up so that her delicate blue-veined little hand would dangle from her wrist like the head of a broken lily. The company always laughed.

The sun, moving over the black and white grazing cows, was just a little brighter than the rest of the sky. Looking down, she saw a darker shape that might have been its shadow cast at an angle, moving among them. She uttered a sharp cry and turned and marched out of the house.

Mr. Greenleaf was in the trench silo, filling a wheelbarrow. She stood on the edge and looked down at him. "I told you to get up that bull. Now he's in with the milk herd."

"You can't do two thangs at oncet," Mr. Greenleaf remarked.

"I told you to do that first."

He wheeled the barrow out of the open end of the trench toward the barn and she followed close behind him. "And you needn't think, Mr. Greenleaf," she said, "that I don't know exactly whose bull that is or why you haven't been in any hurry to notify me he was here. I might as well feed O. T. and E. T.'s bull as long as I'm going to have him here ruining my herd."

Mr. Greenleaf paused with the wheelbarrow and looked behind him. "Is that them boys' bull?" he asked in an incredulous tone.

She did not say a word. She merely looked away with her mouth taut.

"They told me their bull was out but I never known that was him," he said.

"I want that bull put up now," she said, "and I'm going to drive over to O. T. and E. T.'s and tell them they'll have to come get him today. I ought to charge for the time he's been here — then it wouldn't happen again."

"They didn't pay but seventy-five dollars for him," Mr. Greenleaf offered.

"I wouldn't have had him as a gift," she said.

"They was just going to beef him," Mr. Greenleaf went on, "but he got loose and run his head into their pickup truck. He don't like cars and trucks. They had a time getting his horn out of the fender and when they finally got him loose, he took off and they was too tired to run after him — but I never known that was him there."

"It wouldn't have paid you to know, Mr. Greenleaf," she said. "But you know now. Get a horse and get him."

In a half hour, from her front window she saw the bull, squirrel-colored, with jutting hips and long light horns, ambling down the dirt road that ran in front of the house. Mr. Greenleaf was behind him on the horse. "That's a Greenleaf bull if I ever saw one," she muttered. She went out on the porch and called, "Put him where he can't get out."

"He likes to bust loose," Mr. Greenleaf said, looking with approval at the bull's rump. "This gentleman is a sport."

"If those boys don't come for him, he's going to be a dead sport," she said. "I'm just warning you."

He heard her but he didn't answer.

"That's the awfullest looking bull I ever saw," she called but he was too far down the road to hear.

It was midmorning when she turned into O. T. and E. T.'s driveway. The house, a new red-brick, low-to-the-ground building that looked like a warehouse with windows, was on top of a treeless hill. The sun was beating down directly on the white roof of it. It was the kind of house that everybody built now and nothing marked it as belonging to Greenleafs except three dogs, part hound and part spitz, that rushed out from behind it as soon as she stopped her car. She reminded herself that you could always tell the class of people by the class of dog, and honked her horn. While she sat waiting for someone to come, she continued to study the house. All the windows were down and she wondered if the government could have air-conditioned the thing. No one came and she honked again. Presently a door opened and several children appeared in it and stood looking at her, making no move to come forward. She recognized this as a true Greenleaf trait — they could hang in a door, looking at you for hours.

"Can't one of you children come here?" she called.

After a minute they all began to move forward, slowly. They had on overalls and were barefooted but they were not as dirty as she might have expected. There were two or three that looked distinctly like Greenleafs; the others not so much so. The smallest child was a girl with untidy black hair. They stopped about six feet from the automobile and stood looking at her.

"You're mighty pretty," Mrs. May said, addressing herself to the smallest girl.

There was no answer. They appeared to share one dispassionate expression between them.

"Where's your mamma?" she asked.

There was no answer to this for some time. Then one of them said something in French. Mrs. May did not speak French.

"Where's your daddy?" she asked.

After a while, one of the boys said, "He ain't hyar neither."

"Ahhhh," Mrs. May said as if something had been proven. "Where's the colored man?"

She waited and decided no one was going to answer. "The cat has six little tongues," she said. "How would you like to come home with me and let me teach you how to talk?" She laughed and her laugh died on the silent air. She felt as if she were on trial for her life, facing a jury of Greenleafs. "I'll go down and see if I can find the colored man," she said.

"You can go if you want to," one of the boys said.

"Well, thank you," she murmured and drove off.

The barn was down the lane from the house. She had not seen it before but Mr. Greenleaf had described it in detail for it had been built according to the latest specifications. It was a milking parlor arrangement where the cows are milked from below. The milk ran in pipes from the machines to the milk house and was never carried in no bucket, Mr. Greenleaf said, by no human hand. "When you gonter get you one?" he had asked.

"Mr. Greenleaf," she had said, "I have to do for myself. I am not assisted hand and foot by the government. It would cost me $20,000 to install a milking parlor. I barely make ends meet as it is."

"My boys done it," Mr. Greenleaf had murmured, and then — "but all boys ain't alike."

"No indeed!" she had said. "I thank God for that!"

"I thank Gawd for everthang," Mr. Greenleaf had drawled.

You might as well, she had thought in the fierce silence that followed; you've never done anything for yourself.

She stopped by the side of the barn and honked but no one appeared. For several minutes she sat in the car, observing the various machines parked around, wondering how many of them were paid for. They had a forage harvester and a rotary hay baler. She had those too. She decided that since no one was here, she would get out and have a look at the milking parlor and see if they kept it clean.

She opened the milking room door and stuck her head in and for the first second she felt as if she were going to lose her breath. The spotless white concrete room was filled with sunlight that came from a row of windows head-high along both walls. The metal stanchions gleamed ferociously and she had to squint to be able to look at all. She drew her head out the room quickly and closed the door and leaned against it, frowning. The light outside was not so bright but she was conscious that the sun was directly on top of her head, like a silver bullet ready to drop into her brain.

A Negro carrying a yellow calf-feed bucket appeared from around the corner of the machine shed and came toward her. He was a light yellow boy dressed in the cast-off army clothes of the Greenleaf twins. He stopped at a respectable distance and set the bucket on the ground.

"Where's Mr. O. T. and Mr. E. T.?" she asked.

"Mist O. T. he in town, Mist E. T. he off yonder in the field," the Negro said, pointing first to the left and then to the right as if he were naming the position of two planets.

"Can you remember a message?" she asked, looking as if she thought this doubtful.

"I'll remember it if I don't forget it," he said with a touch of sullenness.

"Well, I'll write it down then," she said. She got in her car and took a stub of pencil from her pocketbook and began to write on the back of an empty envelope. The Negro came and stood at the window. "I'm Mrs. May," she said as she wrote. "Their bull is on my place and I want him off *today.* You can tell them I'm furious about it."

"That bull lef here Sareday," the Negro said, "and none of us ain't seen him since. We ain't knowed where he was."

"Well, you know now," she said, "and you can tell Mr. O. T. and Mr. E. T. that if they don't come get him today, I'm going to have their daddy shoot him the first thing in the morning. I can't have that bull ruining my herd." She handed him the note.

"If I knows Mist O. T. and Mist E. T.," he said, taking it, "they goin to say you go ahead on and shoot him. He done busted up one of our trucks already and we be glad to see the last of him."

She pulled her head back and gave him a look from slightly blared eyes. "Do they expect me to take my time and my worker to shoot their bull?" she asked. "They don't want him so they just let him loose and expect somebody else to kill him? He's eating my oats and ruining my herd and I'm expected to shoot him too?"

"I speck you is," he said softly. "He done busted up. . . ."

She gave him a very sharp look and said, "Well, I'm not surprised. That's just the way some people are," and after a second she asked, "Which is boss, Mr. O. T. or Mr. E. T.?" She had always suspected that they fought between themselves secretly.

"They never quarls," the boy said. "They like one man in two skins."

"Hmp. I expect you just never heard them quarrel."

"Nor anybody else heard them neither," he said, looking away as if this insolence were addressed to someone else.

"Well," she said, "I haven't put up with their father for fifteen years not to know a few things about Greenleafs."

The Negro looked at her suddenly with a gleam of recognition. "Is you my policy man's mother?" he asked.

"I don't know who your policy man is," she said sharply. "You give them that note and tell them if they don't come for that bull today, they'll be making their father shoot it tomorrow," and she drove off.

She stayed at home all afternoon waiting for the Greenleaf twins to come for the bull. They did not come. I might as well be working for them, she thought furiously. They are simply going to use me to the limit. At the supper table, she went over it again for the boys' benefit because she wanted them to see exactly what O. T. and E. T. would do. "They don't want that bull," she said, " — pass the butter — so they simply turn him loose and let somebody else worry about getting rid of him for them. How do you like that? I'm the victim. I've always been the victim."

"Pass the butter to the victim," Wesley said. He was in a worse humor than usual because he had had a flat tire on the way home from the university.

Scofield handed her the butter and said, "Why Mamma, ain't you ashamed to shoot an old bull that ain't done nothing but give you a little scrub strain in your herd? I declare," he said, "with the mamma I got it's a wonder I turned out to be such a nice boy!"

"You ain't her boy, son," Wesley said.

She eased back in her chair, her fingertips on the edge of the table.

"All I know is," Scofield said, "I done mighty well to be as nice as I am seeing what I come from."

When they teased her they spoke Greenleaf English but Wesley made his own particular tone come through it like a knife edge. "Well lemme tell you one thang, Brother," he said, leaning over the table, "that if you had half a mind you would already know."

"What's that, Brother?" Scofield asked, his broad face grinning into the thin constricted one across from him.

"That is," Wesley said, "that neither you nor me is her boy . . ." but he stopped abruptly as she gave a kind of hoarse wheeze like an old horse lashed unexpectedly. She reared up and ran from the room.

"Oh, for God's sake," Wesley growled. "What did you start her off for?"

"I never started her off," Scofield said. "You started her off."

"Hah."

"She's not as young as she used to be and she can't take it."

"She can only give it out," Wesley said. "I'm the one that takes it."

His brother's pleasant face had changed so that an ugly family resemblance showed between them. "Nobody feels sorry for a lousy bas-

tard like you," he said and grabbed across the table for the other's shirt-
front.

From her room she heard a crash of dishes and she rushed back
through the kitchen into the dining room. The hall door was open and
Scofield was going out of it. Wesley was lying like a large bug on his back
with the edge of the overturned table cutting him across the middle and
broken dishes scattered on top of him. She pulled the table off him and
caught his arm to help him rise but he scrambled up and pushed her off
with a furious charge of energy and flung himself out the door after his
brother.

She would have collapsed but a knock on the back door stiffened her
and she swung around. Across the kitchen and back porch, she could
see Mr. Greenleaf peering eagerly through the screenwire. All her resources returned in full strength as if she had only needed to be challenged by the devil himself to regain them. "I heard a thump," he called,
"and I thought the plastering might have fell on you."

If he had been wanted someone would have had to go on a horse to
find him. She crossed the kitchen and the porch and stood inside the
screen and said, "No, nothing happened but the table turned over. One
of the legs was weak," and without pausing, "the boys didn't come for
the bull so tomorrow you'll have to shoot him."

The sky was crossed with thin red and purple bars and behind them
the sun was moving down slowly as if it were descending a ladder.
Mr. Greenleaf squatted down on the step, his back to her, the top of
his hat on a level with her feet. "Tomorrow I'll drive him home for you,"
he said.

"Oh no, Mr. Greenleaf," she said in a mocking voice, "you drive him
home tomorrow and next week he'll be back here. I know better than
that." Then in a mournful tone, she said, "I'm surprised at O. T. and
E. T. to treat me this way. I thought they'd have more gratitude. Those
boys spent some mighty happy days on this place, didn't they, Mr.
Greenleaf?"

Mr. Greenleaf didn't say anything.

"I think they did," she said. "I think they did. But they've forgotten all
the nice little things I did for them now. If I recall, they wore my boys'
old clothes and played with my boys' old toys and hunted with my boys'
old guns. They swam in my pond and shot my birds and fished in my
stream and I never forgot their birthday and Christmas seemed to roll
around very often if I remember it right. And do they think of any of
those things now?" she asked. "NOOOOO," she said.

For a few seconds she looked at the disappearing sun and Mr. Green-leaf examined the palms of his hands. Presently as if it had just occurred to her, she asked, "Do you know the real reason they didn't come for that bull?"

"Naw I don't," Mr. Greenleaf said in a surly voice.

"They didn't come because I'm a woman," she said. "You can get away with anything when you're dealing with a woman. If there were a man running this place. . . ."

Quick as a snake striking Mr. Greenleaf said, "You got two boys. They know you got two men on the place."

The sun had disappeared behind the tree line. She looked down at the dark crafty face, upturned now, and at the wary eyes, bright under the shadow of the hatbrim. She waited long enough for him to see that she was hurt and then she said, "Some people learn gratitude too late, Mr. Greenleaf, and some never learn it at all," and she turned and left him sitting on the steps.

Half the night in her sleep she heard a sound as if some large stone were grinding a hole on the outside wall of her brain. She was walking on the inside, over a succession of beautiful rolling hills, planting her stick in front of each step. She became aware after a time that the noise was the sun trying to burn through the tree line and she stopped to watch, safe in the knowledge that it couldn't, that it had to sink the way it always did, outside of her property. When she first stopped it was a swollen red ball, but as she stood watching it began to narrow and pale until it looked like a bullet. Then suddenly it burst through the tree line and raced down the hill toward her. She woke up with her hand over her mouth and the same noise, diminished but distinct, in her ear. It was the bull munching under her window. Mr. Greenleaf had let him out.

She got up and made her way to the window in the dark and looked out through the slit blind, but the bull had moved away from the hedge and at first she didn't see him. Then she saw a heavy form some distance away, paused as if observing her. This is the last night I am going to put up with this, she said, and watched until the iron shadow moved away in the darkness.

The next morning she waited until exactly eleven o'clock. Then she got in her car and drove to the barn. Mr. Greenleaf was cleaning milk cans. He had seven of them standing up outside the milk room to get the sun. She had been telling him to do this for two weeks. "All right, Mr. Greenleaf," she said, "go get your gun. We're going to shoot that bull."

"I thought you wanted theseyer cans. . . ."

"Go get your gun, Mr. Greenleaf," she said. Her voice and face were expressionless.

"That gentleman torn out of there last night," he murmured in a tone of regret and bent again to the can he had his arm in.

"Go get your gun, Mr. Greenleaf," she said in the same triumphant toneless voice. "The bull is in the pasture with the dry cows. I saw him from my upstairs window. I'm going to drive you up to the field and you can run him into the empty pasture and shoot him there."

He detached himself from the can slowly. "Ain't nobody ever ast me to shoot my boys' own bull!" he said in a high rasping voice. He moved a rag from his back pocket and began to wipe his hands violently, then his nose.

She turned as if she had not heard this and said, "I'll wait for you in the car. Go get your gun."

She sat in the car and watched him stalk off toward the harness room where he kept a gun. After he had entered the room, there was a crash as if he had kicked something out of his way. Presently he emerged again with the gun, circled behind the car, opened the door violently and threw himself onto the seat beside her. He held the gun between his knees and looked straight ahead. He'd like to shoot me instead of the bull, she thought, and turned her face away so that he could not see her smile.

The morning was dry and clear. She drove through the woods for a quarter of a mile and then out into the open where there were fields on either side of the narrow road. The exhilaration of carrying her point had sharpened her senses. Birds were screaming everywhere, the grass was almost too bright to look at, the sky was an even piercing blue. "Spring is here!" she said gaily. Mr. Greenleaf lifted one muscle somewhere near his mouth as if he found this the most asinine remark ever made. When she stopped at the second pasture gate, he flung himself out of the car door and slammed it behind him. Then he opened the gate and she drove through. He closed it and flung himself back in, silently, and she drove around the rim of the pasture until she spotted the bull, almost in the center of it, grazing peacefully among the cows.

"The gentleman is waiting on you," she said and gave Mr. Greenleaf's furious profile a sly look. "Run him into that next pasture and when you get him in, I'll drive in behind you and shut the gate myself."

He flung himself out again, this time deliberately leaving the car door open so that she had to lean across the seat and close it. She sat smiling as she watched him make his way across the pasture toward the opposite gate. He seemed to throw himself forward at each step and then pull back as if he were calling on some power to witness that he was being forced. "Well," she said aloud as if he were still in the car, "it's your own boys who are making you do this, Mr. Greenleaf." O. T. and E. T. were probably splitting their sides laughing at him now. She could hear their identical nasal voices saying, "Made Daddy shoot our bull for us. Daddy don't know no better than to think that's a fine bull he's shooting. Gonna kill Daddy to shoot that bull!"

"If those boys cared a thing about you, Mr. Greenleaf," she said, "they would have come for that bull. I'm surprised at them."

He was circling around to open the gate first. The bull, dark among the spotted cows, had not moved. He kept his head down, eating constantly. Mr. Greenleaf opened the gate and then began circling back to approach him from the rear. When he was about ten feet behind him, he flapped his arms at his sides. The bull lifted his head indolently and then lowered it again and continued to eat. Mr. Greenleaf stooped again and picked up something and threw it at him with a vicious swing. She decided it was a sharp rock for the bull leapt and then began to gallop until he disappeared over the rim of the hill. Mr. Greenleaf followed at his leisure.

"You needn't think you're going to lose him!" she cried and started the car straight across the pasture. She had to drive slowly over the terraces and when she reached the gate, Mr. Greenleaf and the bull were nowhere in sight. This pasture was smaller than the last, a green arena, encircled almost entirely by woods. She got out and closed the gate and stood looking for some sign of Mr. Greenleaf but he had disappeared completely. She knew at once that his plan was to lose the bull in the woods. Eventually, she would see him emerge somewhere from the circle of trees and come limping toward her and when he finally reached her, he would say, "If you can find that gentleman in them woods, you're better than me."

She was going to say, "Mr. Greenleaf, if I have to walk into those woods with you and stay all afternoon, we are going to find that bull and shoot him. You are going to shoot him if I have to pull the trigger for you." When he saw she meant business, he would return and shoot the bull quickly himself.

She got back into the car and drove to the center of the pasture where he would not have so far to walk to reach her when he came out of the woods. At this moment she could picture him sitting on a stump, marking lines in the ground with a stick. She decided she would wait exactly ten minutes by her watch. Then she would begin to honk. She got out of the car and walked around a little and then sat down on the front bumper to wait and rest. She was very tired and she lay her head back against the hood and closed her eyes. She did not understand why she should be so tired when it was only midmorning. Through her closed eyes, she could feel the sun, red-hot overhead. She opened her eyes slightly but the white light forced her to close them again.

For some time she lay back against the hood, wondering drowsily why she was so tired. With her eyes closed, she didn't think of time as divided into days and nights but into past and future. She decided she was tired because she had been working continuously for fifteen years. She decided she had every right to be tired, and to rest for a few minutes before she began working again. Before any kind of judgment seat, she would be able to say: I've worked, I have not wallowed. At this very instant while she was recalling a lifetime of work, Mr. Greenleaf was loitering in the woods and Mrs. Greenleaf was probably flat on the ground, asleep over her holeful of clippings. The woman had got worse over the years and Mrs. May believed that now she was actually demented. "I'm afraid your wife has let religion warp her," she said once tactfully to Mr. Greenleaf. "Everything in moderation, you know."

"She cured a man oncet that half his gut was eat out with worms," Mr. Greenleaf said, and she had turned away, half-sickened. Poor souls, she thought now, so simple. For a few seconds she dozed.

When she sat up and looked at her watch, more than ten minutes had passed. She had not heard any shot. A new thought occurred to her: suppose Mr. Greenleaf had aroused the bull chunking stones at him and the animal had turned on him and run him up against a tree and gored him? The irony of it deepened: O. T. and E. T. would then get a shyster lawyer and sue her. It would be the fitting end to her fifteen years with the Greenleafs. She thought of it almost with pleasure as if she had hit on the perfect ending for a story she was telling her friends. Then she dropped it, for Mr. Greenleaf had a gun with him and she had insurance.

She decided to honk. She got up and reached inside the car window and gave three sustained honks and two or three shorter ones to let him know she was getting impatient. Then she went back and sat down on the bumper again.

In a few minutes something emerged from the tree line, a black heavy shadow that tossed its head several times and then bounded forward.

After a second she saw it was the bull. He was crossing the pasture toward her at a slow gallop, a gay almost rocking gait as if he were overjoyed to find her again. She looked beyond him to see if Mr. Greenleaf was coming out of the woods too but he was not. "Here he is, Mr. Greenleaf!" she called and looked on the other side of the pasture to see if he could be coming out there but he was not in sight. She looked back and saw that the bull, his head lowered, was racing toward her. She remained perfectly still, not in fright, but in a freezing unbelief. She stared at the violent black streak bounding toward her as if she had no sense of distance, as if she could not decide at once what his intention was, and the bull had buried his head in her lap, like a wild tormented lover, before her expression changed. One of his horns sank until it pierced her heart and the other curved around her side and held her in an unbreakable grip. She continued to stare straight ahead but the entire scene in front of her had changed — the tree line was a dark wound in a world that was nothing but sky — and she had the look of a person whose sight has been suddenly restored but who finds the light unbearable.

Mr. Greenleaf was running toward her from the side with his gun raised and she saw him coming though she was not looking in his direction. She saw him approaching on the outside of some invisible circle, the tree line gaping behind him and nothing under his feet. He shot the bull four times through the eye. She did not hear the shots but she felt the quake in the huge body as it sank, pulling her forward on its head, so that she seemed, when Mr. Greenleaf reached her, to be bent over whispering some last discovery into the animal's ear.

## Lawrence Sargent Hall

·····································································

# The Ledge

FROM *The Hudson Review*

ON CHRISTMAS MORNING before sunup the fisherman embraced his warm wife and left his close bed. She did not want him to go. It was Christmas morning. He was a big, raw man, with too much strength, whose delight in winter was to hunt the sea ducks that flew in to feed by the outer ledges, bare at low tide.

As his bare feet touched the cold floor and the frosty air struck his nude flesh, he might have changed his mind in the dark of this special day. It was a home day, which made it seem natural to think of the outer ledges merely as some place he had shot ducks in the past. But he had promised his son, thirteen, and his nephew, fifteen, who came from inland. That was why he had given them his present of an automatic shotgun each the night before, on Christmas Eve. Rough man though he was known to be, and no spoiler of boys, he kept his promises when he understood what they meant. And to the boys, as to him, home meant where you came for rest after you had had your Christmas fill of action and excitement.

His legs astride, his arms raised, the fisherman stretched as high as he could in the dim privacy of his bedroom. Above the snug murmur of his wife's protest he heard the wind in the pines and knew it was easterly as the boys had hoped and he had surmised the night before. Conditions would be ideal, and when they were, anybody ought to take advantage of them. The birds would be flying. The boys would get a man's sport their first time outside on the ledges.

His son at thirteen, small but steady and experienced, was fierce to grow up in hunting, to graduate from sheltered waters and the blinds along the shores of the inner bay. His nephew at fifteen, an overgrown farm boy, had a farm boy's love of the sea, though he could not swim a stroke and was often sick in choppy weather. That was the reason his father, the fisherman's brother, was a farmer and chose to sleep in on the holiday morning at his brother's house. Many of the ones the farmer had grown up with were regularly seasick and could not swim, but they were unafraid of the water. They could not have dreamed of being anything but fishermen. The fisherman himself could swim like a seal and was never sick, and he would sooner die than be anything else.

He dressed in the cold and dark, and woke the boys gruffly. They tumbled out of bed, their instincts instantly awake while their thoughts still fumbled slumbrously. The fisherman's wife in the adjacent bedroom heard them apparently trying to find their clothes, mumbling sleepily and happily to each other, while her husband went down to the hot kitchen to fry eggs — sunny-side up, she knew, because that was how they all liked them.

Always in winter she hated to have them go outside, the weather was so treacherous and there were so few others out in case of trouble. To the fisherman these were no more than woman's fears, to be taken for granted and laughed off. When they were first married they fought miserably every fall because she was after him constantly to put his boat up until spring. The fishing was all outside in winter, and though prices were high the storms made the rate of attrition high on gear. Nevertheless he did well. So she could do nothing with him.

People thought him a hard man, and gave him the reputation of being all out for himself because he was inclined to brag and be disdainful. If it was true, and his own brother was one of those who strongly felt it was, they lived better than others, and his brother had small right to criticize. There had been times when in her loneliness she had yearned to leave him for another man. But it would have been dangerous. So over the years she had learned to shut her mind to his hard-driving, and take what comfort she might from his unsympathetic competence. Only once or twice, perhaps, had she gone so far as to dwell guiltily on what it would be like to be a widow.

The thought that her boy, possibly because he was small, would not be insensitive like his father, and the rattle of dishes and smell of frying bacon downstairs in the kitchen shut off from the rest of the chilly house, restored the cozy feeling she had had before she was alone in bed. She heard them after a while go out and shut the back door.

Under her window she heard the snow grind dryly beneath their boots, and her husband's sharp, exasperated commands to the boys. She shivered slightly in the envelope of her own warmth. She listened to the noise of her son and nephew talking elatedly. Twice she caught the glimmer of their lights on the white ceiling above the window as they went down the path to the shore. There would be frost on the skiff and freezing suds at the water's edge. She herself used to go gunning when she was younger; now, it seemed to her, anyone going out like that on Christmas morning had to be incurably male. They would none of them think about her until they returned and piled the birds they had shot on top of the sink for her to dress.

Ripping into the quiet predawn cold she heard the hot snarl of the outboard taking them out to the boat. It died as abruptly as it had burst into life. Two or three or four or five minutes later the big engine broke into a warm reassuring roar. He had the best of equipment, and he kept it in the best of condition. She closed her eyes. It would not be too long before the others would be up for Christmas. The summer drone of the exhaust deepened. Then gradually it faded in the wind until it was lost at sea, or she slept.

The engine had started immediately in spite of the temperature. This put the fisherman in a good mood. He was proud of his boat. Together he and the two boys heaved the skiff and outboard onto the stern and secured it athwartships. His son went forward along the deck, iridescent in the ray of the light the nephew shone through the windshield, and cast the mooring pennant loose into darkness. The fisherman swung to starboard, glanced at his compass, and headed seaward down the obscure bay.

There would be just enough visibility by the time they reached the headland to navigate the crooked channel between the islands. It was the only nasty stretch of water. The fisherman had done it often in fog or at night — he always swore he could go anywhere in the bay blindfolded — but there was no sense in taking chances if you didn't have to. From the mouth of the channel he could lay a straight course for Brown Cow Island, anchor the boat out of sight behind it, and from the skiff set their tollers off Devil's Hump three hundred yards to seaward. By then the tide would be clearing the ledge and they could land and be ready to shoot around half-tide.

It was early, it was Christmas, and it was farther out than most hunters cared to go in this season of the closing year, so that he felt sure no one would be taking possession ahead of them. He had shot thousands of ducks there in his day. The Hump was by far the best hunting. Only thing was you had to plan for the right conditions because you didn't have too much time. About four hours was all, and you had to get it before three in the afternoon when the birds left and went out to sea ahead of nightfall.

They had it figured exactly right for today. The ledge would not be going under until after the gunning was over, and they would be home for supper in good season. With a little luck the boys would have a skiff-load of birds to show for their first time outside. Well beyond the legal limit, which was no matter. You took what you could get in this life, or the next man made out and you didn't.

The fisherman had never failed to make out gunning from Devil's Hump. And this trip, he had a hunch, would be above ordinary. The easterly wind would come up just stiff enough, the tide was right, and it was going to storm by tomorrow morning so the birds would be moving. Things were perfect.

The old fierceness was in his bones. Keeping a weather eye to the murk out front and a hand on the wheel, he reached over and cuffed both boys playfully as they stood together close to the heat of the exhaust pipe running up through the center of the house. They poked back at him and shouted above the drumming engine, making bets as they always did on who would shoot the most birds. This trip they had the thrill of new guns, the best money could buy, and a man's hunting ground. The black retriever wagged at them and barked. He was too old and arthritic to be allowed in December water, but he was jaunty anyway at being brought along.

Groping in his pocket for his pipe the fisherman suddenly had his high spirits rocked by the discovery that he had left his tobacco at home. He swore. Anticipation of a day out with nothing to smoke made him incredulous. He searched his clothes, and then he searched them again, unable to believe the tobacco was not somewhere. When the boys inquired what was wrong he spoke angrily to them, blaming them for being in some devious way at fault. They were instantly crestfallen and willing to put back after the tobacco, though they could appreciate what it meant only through his irritation. But he bitterly refused. That would throw everything out of phase. He was a man who did things the way he set out to do.

He clamped his pipe between his teeth, and twice more during the next few minutes he ransacked his clothes in disbelief. He was no stoic. For one relaxed moment he considered putting about and gunning somewhere nearer home. Instead he held his course and sucked the empty pipe, consoling himself with the reflection that at least he had whiskey enough if it got too uncomfortable on the ledge. Peremptorily he made the boys check to make certain the bottle was really in the knapsack with the lunches where he thought he had taken care to put it. When they reassured him he despised his fate a little less.

The fisherman's judgment was as usual accurate. By the time they were abreast of the headland there was sufficient light so that he could wind his way among the reefs without slackening speed. At last he turned his bows toward open ocean, and as the winter dawn filtered upward through long layers of smoky cloud on the eastern rim his spirits rose again with it.

He opened the throttle, steadied on his course, and settled down to the two-hour run. The wind was stronger but seemed less cold coming from the sea. The boys had withdrawn from the fisherman and were talking together while they watched the sky through the windows. The boat churned solidly through a light chop, flinging spray off her flaring bows. Astern the headland thinned rapidly till it lay like a blackened sill on the gray water. No other boats were abroad.

The boys fondled their new guns, sighted along the barrels, worked the mechanisms, compared notes, boasted, and gave each other contradictory advice. The fisherman got their attention once and pointed at the horizon. They peered through the windows and saw what looked like a black scum floating on top of gently agitated water. It wheeled and tilted, rippled, curled, then rose, strung itself out and became a huge raft of ducks escaping over the sea. A good sign.

The boys rushed out and leaned over the washboards in the wind and spray to see the flock curl below the horizon. Then they went and hovered around the hot engine, bewailing their lot. If only they had been already set out and waiting. Maybe these ducks would be crazy enough to return later and be slaughtered. Ducks were known to be foolish.

In due course and right on schedule they anchored at midmorning in the lee of Brown Cow Island. They put the skiff overboard and loaded it with guns, knapsacks, and tollers. The boys showed their eagerness by being clumsy. The fisherman showed his in bad temper and abuse which they silently accepted in the absorbed tolerance of being boys. No doubt they laid it to lack of tobacco.

By outboard they rounded the island and pointed due east in the direction of a ridge of foam which could be seen whitening the surface three hundred yards away. They set the decoys in a broad, straddling vee opening wide into the ocean. The fisherman warned them not to get their hands wet, and when they did he made them carry on with red and painful fingers, in order to teach them. Once the last toller was bobbing among his fellows, brisk and alluring, they got their numbed fingers inside their oilskins and hugged their warm crotches. In the meantime the fisherman had turned the skiff toward the patch of foam where as if by magic, like a black glossy rib of earth, the ledge had broken through the belly of the sea.

Carefully they inhabited their slipper nub of the North American continent, while the unresting Atlantic swelled and swirled as it had for eons round the indomitable edges. They hauled the skiff after them, established themselves as comfortably as they could in a shallow sump on top, lay on their sides a foot or so above the water, and waited, guns in hand.

In time the fisherman took a thermos bottle from the knapsack and they drank steaming coffee, and waited for the nodding decoys to lure in the first flight to the rock. Eventually the boys got hungry and restless. The fisherman let them open the picnic lunch and eat one sandwich apiece, which they both shared with the dog. Having no tobacco the fisherman himself would not eat.

Actually the day was relatively mild, and they were warm enough at present in their woolen clothes and socks underneath oilskins and hip boots. After a while, however, the boys began to feel cramped. Their nerves were agonized by inactivity. The nephew complained and was severely told by the fisherman — who pointed to the dog, crouched unmoving except for his white-rimmed eyes — that part of doing a man's hunting was learning how to wait. But he was beginning to have misgivings of his own. This could be one of those days where all the right conditions masked an incalculable flaw.

If the fisherman had been alone, as he often was, stopping off when the necessary coincidence of tide and time occurred on his way home from hauling trawls, and had plenty of tobacco, he would not have fidgeted. The boys' being nervous made him nervous. He growled at them again. When it came it was likely to come all at once, and then in a few moments be over. He warned them not to slack off, never to slack off, to be always ready. Under his rebuke they kept their tortured peace, though they could not help shifting and twisting until he lost what patience he had left and bullied them into lying still. A duck could see an eyelid twitch. If the dog could go without moving so could they.

"Here it comes!" the fisherman said tersely at last.

The boys quivered with quick relief. The flock came in downwind, quartering slightly, myriad, black, and swift.

"Beautiful —" breathed the fisherman's son.

"All right," said the fisherman, intense and precise. "Aim at singles in the thickest part of the flock. Wait for me to fire and then don't stop shooting till your gun's empty." He rolled up onto his left elbow and spread his legs to brace himself. The flock bore down, arrowy and vibrant, then a hundred yards beyond the decoys it veered off.

"They're going away!" the boys cried, sighting in.

"Not yet!" snapped the fisherman. "They're coming round."

The flock changed shape, folded over itself, and drove into the wind in a tight arc. "Thousands —" the boys hissed through their teeth. All at once a whistling storm of black and white broke over the decoys.

"Now!" the fisherman shouted. "Perfect!" And he opened fire at the flock just as it hung suspended in momentary chaos above the tollers. The three pulled at their triggers and the birds splashed into the water, until the last report went off unheard, the last smoking shell flew unheeded over their shoulders, and the last of the routed flock scattered diminishing, diminishing, diminishing in every direction.

Exultantly the boys dropped their guns, jumped up and scrambled for the skiff.

"I'll handle that skiff!" the fisherman shouted at them. They stopped. Gripping the painter and balancing himself he eased the skiff into the water stern first and held the bow hard against the side of the rock shelf the skiff had rested on. "You stay here," he said to his nephew. "No sense in all three of us going in the boat."

The boy on the reef gazed at the gray water rising and falling hypnotically along the glistening edge. It had dropped about a foot since their arrival. "I want to go with you," he said in a sullen tone, his eyes on the streaming eddies.

"You want to do what I tell you if you want to gun with me," answered the fisherman harshly. The boy couldn't swim, and he wasn't going to have him climbing in and out of the skiff anymore than necessary. Besides he was too big.

The fisherman took his son in the skiff and cruised round and round among the decoys picking up dead birds. Meanwhile the other boy stared unmoving after them from the highest part of the ledge. Before they had quite finished gathering the dead birds, the fisherman cut the outboard and dropped to his knees in the skiff. "Down!" he yelled. "Get down!" About a dozen birds came tolling in. "Shoot — shoot!" his son hollered from the bottom of the boat to the boy on the ledge.

The dog, who had been running back and forth whining, sank to his belly, his muzzle on his forepaws. But the boy on the ledge never stirred. The ducks took late alarm at the skiff, swerved aside and into the air, passing with a whirr no more than fifty feet over the head of the boy, who remained on the ledge like a statue, without his gun, watching the two crouching in the boat.

The fisherman's son climbed onto the ledge and held the painter. The bottom of the skiff was covered with feathery black and white bodies with feet upturned and necks lolling. He was jubilant. "We got twenty-seven!" he told his cousin. "How's that? Nine apiece. Boy —" he added, "what a cool Christmas!"

The fisherman pulled the skiff onto its shelf and all three went and lay down again in anticipation of the next flight. The son, reloading, patted his shotgun affectionately. "I'm going to get me ten next time," he said. Then he asked his cousin, "Whatsamatter — didn't you see the strays?"

"Yeah," the boy said.

"How come you didn't shoot at 'em?"

"Didn't feel like it," replied the boy, still with a trace of sullenness.

"You stupid or something?" The fisherman's son was astounded. "What a highlander!" But the fisherman, though he said nothing, knew that the older boy had had an attack of ledge fever.

"Cripes!" his son kept at it. "I'd at least of tried."

"Shut up," the fisherman finally told him, "and leave him be."

At slack water three more flocks came in, one right after the other, and when it was over, the skiff was half full of clean, dead birds. During the subsequent lull they broke out the lunch and ate it all and finished the hot coffee. For a while the fisherman sucked away on his cold pipe. Then he had himself a swig of whiskey.

The boys passed the time contentedly jabbering about who shot the most — there were ninety-two all told — which of their friends they would show the biggest ones to, how many each could eat at a meal provided they didn't have to eat any vegetables. Now and then they heard sporadic distant gunfire on the mainland, at its nearest point about two miles to the north. Once far off they saw a fishing boat making in the direction of home.

At length the fisherman got a hand inside his oilskins and produced his watch.

"Do we have to go now?" asked his son.

"Not just yet," he replied. "Pretty soon." Everything had been perfect. As good as he had ever had it. Because he was getting tired of the boys' chatter he got up, heavily in his hip boots, and stretched. The tide had turned and was coming in, the sky was more ashen, and the wind had freshened enough so that whitecaps were beginning to blossom. It would be a good hour before they had to leave the ledge and pick up the tollers. However, he guessed they would leave a little early. On account of the rising wind he doubted there would be much more shooting. He stepped carefully along the back of the ledge, to work his kinks out. It was also getting a little colder.

The whiskey had begun to warm him, but he was unprepared for the sudden blaze that flashed upward inside him from belly to head. He was standing looking at the shelf where the skiff was. Only the foolish skiff was not there!

For the second time that day the fisherman felt the deep vacuity of disbelief. He gaped, seeing nothing but the flat shelf of rock. He whirled, started toward the boys, slipped, recovered himself, fetched a complete circle, and stared at the unimaginably empty shelf. Its emptiness made him feel as if everything he had done that day so far, his life so far, he had dreamed. What could have happened? The tide was still nearly a foot below. There had been no sea to speak of. The skiff could hardly have slid off by itself. For the life of him, consciously careful as he in- veterately was, he could not now remember hauling it up the last time. Perhaps in the heat of hunting he had left it to the boy. Perhaps he could not remember which was the last time.

"Christ —" he exclaimed loudly, without realizing it because he was so entranced by the invisible event.

"What's wrong, Dad?" asked his son, getting to his feet.

The fisherman went blind with uncontainable rage. "Get back down there where you belong!" he screamed. He scarcely noticed the boy sink back in amazement. In a frenzy he ran along the ledge thinking the skiff might have been drawn up at another place, though he knew better. There was no other place.

He stumbled, half falling, back to the boys who were gawking at him in consternation, as though he had gone insane. "God damn it!" he yelled savagely, grabbing both of them and yanking them to their knees. "Get on your feet!"

"What's wrong?" his son repeated in a stifled voice.

"Never mind what's wrong," he snarled. "Look for the skiff — it's adrift!" When they peered around he gripped their shoulders, brutally facing them about. "Down-wind —" He slammed his fist against his thigh. "Jesus!" he cried, struck to madness at their stupidity.

At last he sighted the skiff himself, magically bobbing along the grim sea like a toller, a quarter of a mile to leeward on a direct course for home. The impulse to strip himself naked was succeeded instantly by a queer calm. He simply sat down on the ledge and forgot everything except the marvelous mystery.

As his awareness partially returned he glanced toward the boys. They were still observing the skiff speechlessly. Then he was gazing into the clear young eyes of his son.

"Dad," asked the boy steadily, "what do we do now?"

That brought the fisherman upright. "The first thing we have to do," he heard himself saying with infinite tenderness as if he were making love, "is think."

"Could you swim it?" asked his son.

He shook his head and smiled at them. They smiled quickly back, too quickly. "A hundred yards, maybe, in this water. I wish I could," he added. It was the most intimate and pitiful thing he had ever said. He walked in circles round them, trying to break the stall his mind was left in.

He gauged the level of the water. To the eye it was quite stationary, six inches from the shelf at this second. The fisherman did not have to mark it on the side of the rock against the passing of time to prove to his reason that it was rising, always rising. Already it was over the brink of reason, beyond the margins of thought — a senseless measurement. No sense to it.

All his life the fisherman had tried to lick the element of time, by getting up earlier and going to bed later, owning a faster boat, planning more than the day would hold, and tackling just one other job before the deadline fell. If, as on rare occasions he had the grand illusion, he ever really had beaten the game, he would need to call on all his reserves of practice and cunning now.

He sized up the scant but unforgivable three hundred yards to Brown Cow Island. Another hundred yards behind it his boat rode at anchor, where, had he been aboard, he could have cut in a fathometer to plumb the profound and occult seas, or a ship-to-shore radio on which in an interminably short time he would have heard his wife's voice talking to him over the air about homecoming.

"Couldn't we wave something so somebody would see us?" his nephew suggested.

The fisherman spun round. "Load your guns!" he ordered. They loaded as if the air had suddenly gone frantic with birds. "I'll fire once and count to five. Then you fire. Count to five. That way they won't just think it's only somebody gunning ducks. We'll keep doing that."

"We've only got just two and a half boxes left," said his son.

The fisherman nodded, understanding that from beginning to end their situation was purely mathematical, like the ticking of the alarm clock in his silent bedroom. Then he fired. The dog, who had been keeping watch over the decoys, leaped forward and yelped in confusion. They all counted off, fired the first five rounds by threes, and reloaded. The fisherman scanned first the horizon, then the contracting borders of the ledge, which was the sole place the water appeared to be climbing. Soon it would be over the shelf.

They counted off and fired the second five rounds. "We'll hold off a while on the last one," the fisherman told the boys. He sat down and pondered what a trivial thing was a skiff. This one he and the boy had knocked together in a day. Was a gun, manufactured for killing.

His son tallied up the remaining shells, grouping them symmetrically in threes on the rock when the wet box fell apart. "Two short," he announced. They reloaded and laid the guns on their knees.

Behind thickening clouds they could not see the sun going down. The water, coming up, was growing blacker. The fisherman thought he might have told his wife they would be home before dark since it was Christmas day. He realized he had forgotten about its being any particular day. The tide would not be high until two hours after sunset. When they did not get in by nightfall, and could not be raised by radio, she might send somebody to hunt for them right away. He rejected this arithmetic immediately, with a sickening shock, recollecting it was a two-and-a-half-hour run at best. Then it occurred to him that she might send somebody on the mainland who was nearer. She would think he had engine trouble.

He rose and searched the shoreline, barely visible. Then his glance dropped to the toy shoreline at the edges of the reef. The shrinking ledge, so sinister from a boat, grew dearer minute by minute as though the whole wide world he gazed on from horizon to horizon balanced on its contracting rim. He checked the water level and found the shelf awash.

Some of what went through his mind the fisherman told to the boys. They accepted it without comment. If he caught their eyes they looked away to spare him or because they were not yet old enough to face what they saw. Mostly they watched the rising water. The fisherman was unable to initiate a word of encouragement. He wanted one of them to ask him whether somebody would reach them ahead of the tide. He would have found it impossible to say yes. But they did not inquire.

The fisherman was not sure how much, at their age, they were able to imagine. Both of them had seen from the docks drowned bodies put ashore out of boats. Sometimes they grasped things, and sometimes not. He supposed they might be longing for the comfort of their mothers, and was astonished, as much as he was capable of any astonishment except the supreme one, to discover himself wishing he had not left his wife's dark, close, naked bed that morning.

"Is it time to shoot now?" asked his nephew.

"Pretty soon," he said, as if he were putting off making good on a promise. "Not yet."

His own boy cried softly for a brief moment, like a man, his face averted in an effort neither to give or show pain.

"Before school starts," the fisherman said, wonderfully detached, "we'll go to town and I'll buy you boys anything you want."

With great difficulty, in a dull tone as though he did not in the least desire it, his son said after a pause, "I'd like one of those new thirty-horse outboards."

"All right," said the fisherman. And to his nephew, "How about you?"

The nephew shook his head desolately. "I don't want anything," he said.

After another pause the fisherman's son said, "Yes he does, Dad. He wants one too."

"All right —" the fisherman said again, and said no more.

The dog whined in uncertainty and licked the boys' faces where they sat together. Each threw an arm over his back and hugged him. Three strays flew in and sat companionably down among the stiff-necked decoys. The dog crouched, obedient to his training. The boys observed them listlessly. Presently, sensing something untoward, the ducks took off, splashing the wave tops with feet and wingtips, into the dusky waste.

The sea began to make up in the mounting wind, and the wind bore a new and deathly chill. The fisherman, scouring the somber, dwindling shadow of the mainland for a sign, hoped it would not snow. But it did. First a few flakes, then a flurry, then storming past horizontally. The fisherman took one long, bewildered look at Brown Cow Island three hundred yards dead to leeward, and got to his feet.

Then it shut in, as if what was happening on the ledge was too private even for the last wan light of the expiring day.

"Last round," the fisherman said austerely.

The boys rose and shouldered their tacit guns. The fisherman fired into the flying snow. He counted methodically to five. His son fired and counted. His nephew. All three fired and counted. Four rounds.

"You've got one left, Dad," his son said.

The fisherman hesitated another second, then he fired the final shell. Its pathetic report, like the spat of a popgun, whipped away on the wind and was instantly blanketed in falling snow.

Night fell all in a moment to meet the ascending sea. They were now barely able to make one another out through driving snowflakes, dim as ghosts in their yellow oilskins. The fisherman heard a sea break and glanced down where his feet were. They seemed to be wound in a snowy sheet. Gently he took the boys by the shoulders and pushed them in front of him, feeling with his feet along the shallow sump to the place where it triangulated into a sharp crevice at the highest point of the ledge. "Face ahead," he told them. "Put the guns down."

"I'd like to hold mine, Dad," begged his son.

"Put it down," said the fisherman. "The tide won't hurt it. Now brace your feet against both sides and stay there."

They felt the dog, who was pitch black, running up and down in perplexity between their straddled legs. "Dad," said his son, "what about the pooch?"

If he had called the dog by name it would have been too personal. The fisherman would have wept. As it was he had all he could do to keep from laughing. He bent his knees, and when he touched the dog hoisted him under one arm. The dog's belly was soaking wet.

So they waited, marooned in their consciousness, surrounded by a monstrous tidal space which was slowly, slowly closing them out. In this space the periwinkle beneath the fisherman's boots was king. While hovering airborne in his mind he had an inward glimpse of his house as curiously separate, like a June mirage.

Snow, rocks, seas, wind the fisherman had lived by all his life. Now he thought he had never comprehended what they were, and he hated them. Though they had not changed. He was deadly chilled. He set out to ask the boys if they were cold. There was no sense. He thought of the whiskey, and sidled backward, still holding the awkward dog, till he located the bottle under water with his toe. He picked it up squeamishly as though afraid of getting his sleeve wet, worked his way forward and bent over his son. "Drink it," he said, holding the bottle against the boy's ribs. The boy tipped his head back, drank, coughed hotly, then vomited.

"I can't," he told his father wretchedly.

"Try — try —" the fisherman pleaded, as if it meant the difference between life and death.

The boy obediently drank, and again he vomited hotly. He shook his head against his father's chest and passed the bottle forward to his cousin, who drank and vomited also. Passing the bottle back, the boys dropped it in the frigid water between them.

When the waves reached his knees the fisherman set the warm dog loose and said the his son, "Turn around and get up on my shoulders." The boy obeyed. The fisherman opened his oilskin jacket and twisted his hands behind him through his suspenders, clamping the boy's booted ankles with his elbows.

"What about the dog?" the boy asked.

"He'll make his own way all right," the fisherman said. "He can take the cold water." His knees were trembling. Every instinct shrieked for gymnastics. He ground his teeth and braced like a colossus against the sides of the submerged crevice.

The dog, having lived faithfully as though one of them for eleven years, swam a few minutes in and out around the fisherman's legs, not knowing what was happening, and left them without a whimper. He would swim and swim at random by himself, round and round in the blinding night, and when he had swum routinely through the paralyzing water all he could, he would simply, in one incomprehensible moment, drown. Almost the fisherman, waiting out infinity, envied him his pattern.

Freezing seas swept by, flooding inexorably up and up as the earth sank away imperceptibly beneath them. The boy called out once to his cousin. There was no answer. The fisherman, marvelling on a terror without voice, was dumbly glad when the boy did not call again. His own boots were long full of water. With no sensation left in his straddling legs he dared not move them. So long as the seas came sidewise against his hips, and then sidewise against his shoulders, he might balance — no telling how long. The upper half of him was what felt frozen. His legs, disengaged from his nerves and his will, he came to regard quite scientifically. They were the absurd, precarious axis around which reeled and surged universal tumult. The waves would come on and on; he could not visualize how many tossing reinforcements lurked in the night beyond — inexhaustible numbers, and he wept in supernatural fury at each because it was higher, till he transcended hate and took them, swaying like a convert, one by one as they lunged against him and away aimlessly into their own undisputed, wild realm.

From his hips upward the fisherman stretched to his utmost as a man does whose spirit reaches out of dead sleep. The boy's head, none too high, must be at least seven feet above the ledge. Though growing larger every minute, it was a small light life. The fisherman meant to hold it there, if need be, through a thousand tides.

By and by the boy, slumped on the head of his father, asked, "Is it over your boots, Dad?"

"Not yet," the fisherman said. Then through his teeth he added, "If I fall — kick your boots off — swim for it — down-wind — to the island. . . ."

"You . . .?" the boy finally asked.

The fisherman nodded against the boy's belly. "— Won't see each other," he said.

The boy did for the fisherman the greatest thing that can be done. He may have been too young for perfect terror, but he was old enough to know there were things beyond the power of any man. All he could do he did, by trusting his father to do all he could, and asking nothing more.

The fisherman, rocked to his soul by a sea, held his eyes shut upon the interminable night.

"Is it time now?" the boy said.

The fisherman could hardly speak. "Not yet," he said. "Not just yet. . . ."

As the land mass pivoted toward sunlight the day after Christmas, a tiny fleet of small craft converged off shore like iron filings to a magnet. At daybreak they found the skiff floating unscathed off the headland, half full of ducks and snow. The shooting *had* been good, as someone hearing on the nearby mainland the previous afternoon had supposed. Two hours afterward they found the unharmed boat adrift five miles at sea. At high noon they found the fisherman at ebb tide, his right foot jammed cruelly into a glacial crevice of the ledge beside three shotguns, his hands tangled behind him in his suspenders, and under his right elbow a rubber boot with a sock and a live starfish in it. After dragging unlit depths all day for the boys, they towed the fisherman home in his own boat at sundown, and in the frost of evening, mute with discovering purgatory, laid him on his wharf for his wife to see.

She, somehow, standing on the dock as in her frequent dream, gazing at the fisherman pure as crystal on the icy boards, a small rubber boot still frozen under one clenched arm, saw him exaggerated beyond remorse or grief, absolved of his mortality.

1960

*Philip Roth*

...........................................................................................................

# Defender of the Faith

FROM *The New Yorker*


IN MAY OF 1945, only a few weeks after the fighting had ended in
Europe, I was rotated back to the States, where I spent the remainder of
the war with a training company at Camp Crowder, Missouri. Along
with the rest of the Ninth Army, I had been racing across Germany
so swiftly during the late winter and spring that when I boarded the
plane, I couldn't believe its destination lay to the west. My mind might
inform me otherwise, but there was an inertia of the spirit that told me
we were flying to a new front, where we would disembark and continue
our push eastward — eastward until we'd circled the globe, marching
through villages along whose twisting, cobbled streets crowds of the
enemy would watch us take possession of what, up till then, they'd
considered their own. I had changed enough in two years not to mind
the trembling of the old people, the crying of the very young, the uncertainty and fear in the eyes of the once arrogant. I had been fortunate enough to develop an infantryman's heart, which, like his feet, at
first aches and swells but finally grows horny enough for him to travel
the weirdest paths without feeling a thing.

Captain Paul Barrett was my C.O. in Camp Crowder. The day I reported for duty, he came out of his office to shake my hand. He was
short, gruff, and fiery, and — indoors or out — he wore his polished
helmet liner pulled down to his little eyes. In Europe, he had received a
battlefield commission and a serious chest wound, and he'd been returned to the States only a few months before. He spoke easily to me,
and at the evening formation he introduced me to the troops. "Gentlemen," he said, "Sergeant Thurston, as you know, is no longer with this
company. Your new first sergeant is Sergeant Nathan Marx, here. He is a

veteran of the European theater, and consequently will expect to find a company of soldiers here, and not a company of *boys*."

I sat up late in the orderly room that evening, trying halfheartedly to solve the riddle of duty rosters, personnel forms, and morning reports. The Charge of Quarters slept with his mouth open on a mattress on the floor. A trainee stood reading the next day's duty roster, which was posted on the bulletin board just inside the screen door. It was a warm evening, and I could hear radios playing dance music over in the barracks. The trainee, who had been staring at me whenever he thought I wouldn't notice, finally took a step in my direction.

"Hey, Sarge — we having a G.I. party tomorrow night?" he asked. A G.I. party is a barracks cleaning.

"You usually have them on Friday nights?" I asked him.

"Yes," he said, and then he added, mysteriously, "that's the whole thing."

"Then you'll have a G.I. party."

He turned away, and I heard him mumbling. His shoulders were moving, and I wondered if he was crying.

"What's your name, soldier?" I asked.

He turned, not crying at all. Instead, his green-speckled eyes, long and narrow, flashed like fish in the sun. He walked over to me and sat on the edge of my desk. He reached out a hand. "Sheldon," he said.

"Stand on your feet, Sheldon."

Getting off the desk, he said, "Sheldon Grossbart." He smiled at the familiarity into which he'd led me.

"You against cleaning the barracks Friday night, Grossbart?" I said. "Maybe we shouldn't have G.I. parties. Maybe we should get a maid." My tone startled me. I felt I sounded like every top sergeant I had ever known.

"No, Sergeant." He grew serious, but with a seriousness that seemed to be only the stifling of a smile. "It's just — G.I. parties on Friday night, of all nights."

He slipped up onto the corner of the desk again — not quite sitting, but not quite standing, either. He looked at me, with those speckled eyes flashing, and then made a gesture with his hand. It was very slight — no more than a movement back and forth of the wrist — and yet it managed to exclude from our affairs everything else in the orderly room, to make the two of us the center of the world. It seemed, in fact, to exclude everything even about the two of us except our hearts.

"Sergeant Thurston was one thing," he whispered, glancing at the sleeping C.Q., "but we thought that with you here things might be a little different."

"We?"

"The Jewish personnel."

"Why?" I asked, harshly. "What's on your mind?" Whether I was still angry at the "Sheldon" business, or now at something else, I hadn't time to tell, but clearly I was angry.

"We thought you — Marx, you know, like Karl Marx. The Marx Brothers. Those guys are all — M-a-r-x. Isn't that how *you* spell it, Sergeant?"

"M-a-r-x."

"Fishbein said —" He stopped. "What I mean to say, Sergeant —" His face and neck were red, and his mouth moved but no words came out. In a moment, he raised himself to attention, gazing down at me. It was as though he had suddenly decided he could expect no more sympathy from me than from Thurston, the reason being that I was of Thurston's faith, and not his. The young man had managed to confuse himself as to what my faith really was, but I felt no desire to straighten him out. Very simply, I didn't like him.

When I did nothing but return his gaze, he spoke, in an altered tone. "You see, Sergeant," he explained to me, "Friday nights, Jews are supposed to go to services."

"Did Sergeant Thurston tell you you couldn't go to them when there was a G.I. party?"

"No."

"Did he say you had to stay and scrub the floors?"

"No, Sergeant."

"Did the Captain say you had to stay and scrub the floors?"

"That isn't it, Sergeant. It's the other guys in the barracks." He leaned toward me. "They think we're goofing off. But we're not. That's when Jews go to services, Friday night. We have to."

"Then go."

"But the other guys make accusations. They have no right."

"That's not the Army's problem, Grossbart. It's a personal problem you'll have to work out yourself."

"But it's un*fair*."

I got up to leave. "There's nothing I can do about it," I said.

Grossbart stiffened and stood in front of me. "But this is a matter of *religion*, sir."

"Sergeant," I said.

"I mean 'Sergeant,'" he said, almost snarling.

"Look, go see the chaplain. You want to see Captain Barrett, I'll arrange an appointment."

"No, no. I don't want to make trouble, Sergeant. That's the first thing they throw up to you. I just want my rights!"

"Damn it, Grossbart, stop whining. You have your rights. You can stay and scrub floors or you can go to shul —"

The smile swam in again. Spittle gleamed at the corners of his mouth. "You mean church, Sergeant."

"I mean shul, Grossbart!"

I walked past him and went outside. Near me, I heard the scrunching of a guard's boots on gravel. Beyond the lighted windows of the barracks, young men in T shirts and fatigue pants were sitting on their bunks, polishing their rifles. Suddenly there was a light rustling behind me. I turned and saw Grossbart's dark frame fleeing back to the barracks, racing to tell his Jewish friends that they were right — that, like Karl and Harpo, I was one of them.

The next morning, while chatting with Captain Barrett, I recounted the incident of the previous evening. Somehow, in the telling, it must have seemed to the Captain that I was not so much explaining Grossbart's position as defending it. "Marx, I'd fight side by side with a nigger if the fella proved to me he was a man. I pride myself," he said, looking out the window, "that I've got an open mind. Consequently, Sergeant, nobody gets special treatment here, for the good *or* the bad. All a man's got to do is prove himself. A man fires well on the range, I give him a weekend pass. He scores high in P.T., he gets a weekend pass. He *earns* it." He turned from the window and pointed a finger at me. "You're a Jewish fella, am I right, Marx?"

"Yes, sir."

"And I admire you. I admire you because of the ribbons on your chest. I judge a man by what he shows me on the field of battle, Sergeant. It's what he's got *here*," he said, and then, though I expected he would point to his heart, he jerked a thumb toward the buttons straining to hold his blouse across his belly. "Guts," he said.

"O.K., sir. I only wanted to pass on to you how the men felt."

"Mr. Marx, you're going to be old before your time if you worry about how the men feel. Leave that stuff to the chaplain — that's his business, not yours. Let's us train these fellas to shoot straight. If the

Jewish personnel feels the other men are accusing them of goldbricking — well, I just don't know. Seems awful funny that suddenly the Lord is calling so loud in Private Grossman's ear he's just got to run to church."

"Synagogue," I said.

"Synagogue is right, Sergeant. I'll write that down for handy reference. Thank you for stopping by."

That evening, a few minutes before the company gathered outside the orderly room for the chow formation, I called the C.Q., Corporal Robert LaHill, in to see me. LaHill was a dark, burly fellow whose hair curled out of his clothes wherever it could. He had a glaze in his eyes that made one think of caves and dinosaurs. "LaHill," I said, "when you take the formation, remind the men that they're free to attend church services *whenever* they are held, provided they report to the orderly room before they leave the area."

LaHill scratched his wrist, but gave no indication that he'd heard or understood.

"LaHill," I said, "*church.* You remember? Church, priest, Mass, confession."

He curled one lip into a kind of smile; I took it for a signal that for a second he had flickered back up into the human race.

"Jewish personnel who want to attend services this evening are to fall out in front of the orderly room at 1900," I said. Then, as an afterthought, I added, "By order of Captain Barrett."

A little while later, as the day's last light — softer than any I had seen that year — began to drop over Camp Crowder, I heard LaHill's thick, inflectionless voice outside my window: "Give me your ears, troopers. Toppie says for me to tell you that at 1900 hours all Jewish personnel is to fall out in front, here, if they want to attend the Jewish Mass."

At seven o'clock, I looked out the orderly-room window and saw three soldiers in starched khakis standing on the dusty quadrangle. They looked at their watches and fidgeted while they whispered back and forth. It was getting dimmer, and, alone on the otherwise deserted field, they looked tiny. When I opened the door, I heard the noises of the G.I. party coming from the surrounding barracks — bunks being pushed to the walls, faucets pounding water into buckets, brooms whisking at the wooden floors, cleaning the dirt away for Saturday's inspection. Big puffs of cloth moved round and round on the windowpanes. I walked outside, and the moment my foot hit the ground I thought I heard

Grossbart call to the others, "'Ten-*hut!*" Or maybe, when they all three jumped to attention, I imagined I heard the command.

Grossbart stepped forward. "Thank you, sir," he said.

"'Sergeant,' Grossbart," I reminded him. "You call officers 'sir.' I'm not an officer. You've been in the Army three weeks — you know that."

He turned his palms out at his sides to indicate that, in truth, he and I lived beyond convention. "Thank you, anyway," he said.

"Yes," a tall boy behind him said. "Thanks a lot."

And the third boy whispered, "Thank you," but his mouth barely fluttered, so that he did not alter by more than a lip's movement his posture of attention.

"For what?" I asked.

Grossbart snorted happily. "For the announcement. The Corporal's announcement. It helped. It made it —"

"Fancier." The tall boy finished Grossbart's sentence.

Grossbart smiled. "He means formal, sir. Public," he said to me. "Now it won't seem as though we're just taking off — goldbricking because the work has begun."

"It was by order of Captain Barrett," I said.

"Aaah, but you pull a little weight," Grossbart said. "So we thank you." Then he turned to his companions. "Sergeant Marx, I want you to meet Larry Fishbein."

The tall boy stepped forward and extended his hand. I shook it. "You from New York?" he asked.

"Yes."

"Me, too." He had a cadaverous face that collapsed inward from his cheekbone to his jaw, and when he smiled — as he did at the news of our communal attachment — revealed a mouthful of bad teeth. He was blinking his eyes a good deal, as though he were fighting back tears. "What borough?" he asked.

I turned to Grossbart. "It's five after seven. What time are services?"

"Shul," he said, smiling, "is in ten minutes. I want you to meet Mickey Halpern. This is Nathan Marx, our sergeant."

The third boy hopped forward. "Private Michael Halpern." He saluted.

"Salute officers, Halpern," I said. The boy dropped his hand, and, on its way down, in his nervousness, checked to see if his shirt pockets were buttoned.

"Shall I march them over, sir?" Grossbart asked. "Or are you coming along?"

From behind Grossbart, Fishbein piped up. "Afterward, they're having refreshments. A ladies' auxiliary from St. Louis, the rabbi told us
last week."

"The chaplain," Halpern whispered.

"You're welcome to come along," Grossbart said.

To avoid his plea, I looked away, and saw, in the windows of the
barracks, a cloud of faces staring out at the four of us. "Hurry along,
Grossbart," I said.

"O.K., then," he said. He turned to the others. "Double time, *march!*"

They started off, but ten feet away Grossbart spun around and,
running backward, called to me, "Good *shabbus*, sir!" And then the
three of them were swallowed into the alien Missouri dusk.

Even after they had disappeared over the parade ground, whose green
was now a deep blue, I could hear Grossbart singing the double-time
cadence, and as it grew dimmer and dimmer, it suddenly touched a
deep memory — as did the slant of the light — and I was remembering
the shrill sounds of a Bronx playground where, years ago, beside the
Grand Concourse, I had played on long spring evenings such as this. It
was a pleasant memory for a young man so far from peace and home,
and it brought so many recollections with it that I began to grow
exceedingly tender about myself. In fact, I indulged myself in a reverie
so strong that I felt as though a hand were reaching down inside me. It
had to reach so very far to touch me! It had to reach past those days in
the forests of Belgium, and past the dying I'd refused to weep over; past
the nights in German farmhouses whose books we'd burned to warm
us; past endless stretches when I had shut off all softness I might feel for
my fellows, and had managed even to deny myself the posture of a
conqueror — the swagger that I, as a Jew, might well have worn as my
boots whacked against the rubble of Wesel, Münster, and Braunschweig.

But now one night noise, one rumor of home and time past, and
memory plunged down through all I had anesthetized, and came to
what I suddenly remembered was myself. So it was not altogether curious that, in search of more of me, I found myself following Grossbart's
tracks to Chapel No. 3, where the Jewish services were being held.

I took a seat in the last row, which was empty. Two rows in front of
me sat Grossbart, Fishbein, and Halpern, holding little white Dixie cups.
Each row of seats was raised higher than the one in front of it, and I
could see clearly what was going on. Fishbein was pouring the contents
of his cup into Grossbart's, and Grossbart looked mirthful as the liquid
made a purple arc between Fishbein's hand and his. In the glaring

yellow light, I saw the chaplain standing on the platform at the front; he was chanting the first line of the responsive reading. Grossbart's prayer book remained closed on his lap; he was swishing the cup around. Only Halpern responded to the chant by praying. The fingers of his right hand were spread wide across the cover of his open book. His cap was pulled down low onto his brow, which made it round, like a yarmulke. From time to time, Grossbart wet his lips at the cup's edge; Fishbein, his long yellow face a dying light bulb, looked from here to there, craning forward to catch sight of the faces down the row, then of those in front of him, then behind. He saw me, and his eyelids beat a tattoo. His elbows slid into Grossbart's side, his neck inclined toward his friend, he whispered something, and then, when the congregation next responded to the chant, Grossbart's voice was among the others. Fishbein looked into his book now, too; his lips, however, didn't move.

Finally, it was time to drink the wine. The chaplain smiled down at them as Grossbart swigged his in one long gulp, Halpern sipped, meditating, and Fishbein faked devotion with an empty cup. "As I look down amongst the congregation" — the chaplain grinned at the word — "this night, I see many new faces, and I want to welcome you to Friday-night services here at Camp Crowder. I am Major Leo Ben Ezra, your chaplain." Though an American, the chaplain spoke deliberately — syllable by syllable, almost — as though to communicate, above all, with the lip readers in his audience. "I have only a few words to say before we adjourn to the refreshment room, where the kind ladies of the Temple Sinai, St. Louis, Missouri, have a nice setting for you."

Applause and whistling broke out. After another momentary grin, the chaplain raised his hands, palms out, his eyes flicking upward a moment, as if to remind the troops where they were and Who Else might be in attendance. In the sudden silence that followed, I thought I heard Grossbart cackle, "Let the goyim clean the floors!" Were those the words? I wasn't sure, but Fishbein, grinning, nudged Halpern. Halpern looked dumbly at him, then went back to his prayer book, which had been occupying him all through the rabbi's talk. One hand tugged at the black kinky hair that stuck out under his cap. His lips moved.

The rabbi continued. "It is about the food that I want to speak to you for a moment. I know, I know, I know," he intoned, wearily, "how in the mouths of most of you the *trafe* food tastes like ashes. I know how you gag, some of you, and how your parents suffer to think of their children eating foods unclean and offensive to the palate. What can I tell you? I can only say, close your eyes and swallow as best you can. Eat what you must to live, and throw away the rest. I wish I could help more. For those of you who find this impossible, may I ask that you try and try, but then come to see me in private. If your revulsion is so great, we will have to seek aid from those higher up."

A round of chatter rose and subsided. Then everyone sang "Ain Kelohainu"; after all those years, I discovered I still knew the words. Then, suddenly, the service over, Grossbart was upon me. "Higher up? He means the General?"

"Hey, Shelly," Fishbein said, "he means God." He smacked his face and looked at Halpern. "How high can you go!"

"Sh-h-h!" Grossbart said. "What do you think, Sergeant?"

"I don't know," I said. "You better ask the chaplain."

"I'm going to. I'm making an appointment to see him in private. So is Mickey."

Halpern shook his head. "No, no, Sheldon —"

"You have rights, Mickey," Grossbart said. "They can't push us around."

"It's O.K.," said Halpern. "It bothers my mother, not me."

Grossbart looked at me. "Yesterday he threw up. From the hash. It was all ham and God knows what else."

"I have a cold — that was why," Halpern said. He pushed his yarmulke back into a cap.

"What about you, Fishbein?" I asked. "You kosher, too?"

He flushed. "A little. But I'll let it ride. I have a very strong stomach, and I don't eat a lot anyway." I continued to look at him, and he held up his wrist to reinforce what he'd just said; his watch strap was tightened to the last hole, and he pointed that out to me.

"But services are important to you?" I asked him.

He looked at Grossbart. "Sure, sir."

"'Sergeant.'"

"Not so much at home," said Grossbart, stepping between us, "but away from home it gives one a sense of his Jewishness."

"We have to stick together," Fishbein said.

I started to walk toward the door; Halpern stepped back to make way for me.

"That's what happened in Germany," Grossbart was saying, loud enough for me to hear. "They didn't stick together. They let themselves get pushed around."

I turned. "Look, Grossbart. This is the Army, not summer camp."

He smiled. "So?"

Halpern tried to sneak off, but Grossbart held his arm.

"Grossbart, how old are you?" I asked.

"Nineteen."

"And you?" I said to Fishbein.

"The same. The same month, even."

"And what about him?" I pointed to Halpern, who had by now made it safely to the door.

"Eighteen," Grossbart whispered. "But like he can't tie his shoes or brush his teeth himself. I feel sorry for him."

"I feel sorry for all of us, Grossbart," I said, "but jut act like a man. Just don't overdo it."

"Overdo what, sir?"

"The 'sir' business, for one thing. Don't overdo that," I said.

I left him standing there. I passed by Halpern, but he did not look at me. Then I was outside, but, behind, I heard Grossbart call, "Hey, Mickey, my *leben*, come on back. Refreshments!"

"*Leben!*" My grandmother's word for me!

One morning a week later, while I was working at my desk, Captain Barrett shouted for me to come into his office. When I entered, he had his helmet liner squashed down so far on his head that I couldn't even see his eyes. He was on the phone, and when he spoke to me, he cupped one hand over the mouthpiece. "Who the hell is Grossbart?"

"Third platoon, Captain," I said. "A trainee."

"What's all this stink about food? His mother called a goddam congressman about the food." He uncovered the mouthpiece and slid his helmet up until I could see his bottom eyelashes. "Yes, sir," he said into the phone. "Yes, sir. I'm still here, sir. I'm asking Marx, here, right now —"

He covered the mouthpiece again and turned his head back toward me. "Lightfoot Harry's on the phone," he said, between his teeth. "This congressman calls General Lyman, who calls Colonel Sousa, who calls the Major, who calls me. They're just dying to stick this thing on me. Whatsa matter?" He shook the phone at me. "I don't feed the troops? What the hell is this?"

"Sir, Grossbart is strange —" Barrett greeted that with a mockingly indulgent smile. I altered my approach. "Captain, he's a very orthodox Jew, and so he's only allowed to eat certain foods."

"He throws up, the congressman said. Every time he eats something, his mother says, he throws up!"

"He's accustomed to observing the dietary laws, Captain."

"So why's his old lady have to call the White House?"

"Jewish parents, sir — they're apt to be more protective than you expect. I mean, Jews have a very close family life. A boy goes away from home, sometimes the mother is liable to get very upset. Probably the boy mentioned something in a letter, and his mother misinterpreted."

"I'd like to punch him one right in the mouth," the Captain said. "There's a goddam war on, and he wants a silver platter!"

"I don't think the boy's to blame, sir. I'm sure we can straighten it out by just asking him. Jewish parents worry —"

"*All* parents worry, for Christ's sake. But they don't get on their high horse and start pulling strings —"

I interrupted, my voice higher, tighter than before. "The home life, Captain, is very important — but you're right, it may sometimes get out of hand. It's a very wonderful thing, Captain, but because it's so close, this kind of thing . . ."

He didn't listen any longer to my attempt to present both myself and Lightfoot Harry with an explanation for the letter. He turned back to the phone. "Sir?" he said. "Sir — Marx, here, tells me Jews have a tendency to be pushy. He says he thinks we can settle it right here in the company. . . . Yes, sir. . . . I *will* call back, sir, soon as I can." He hung up. "Where are the men, Sergeant?"

"On the range."

With a whack on the top of his helmet, he crushed it down over his eyes again, and charged out of his chair. "We're going for a ride," he said.

The Captain drove, and I sat beside him. It was a hot spring day, and under my newly starched fatigues I felt as though my armpits were melting down onto my sides and chest. The roads were dry, and by the time we reached the firing range, my teeth felt gritty with dust, though my mouth had been shut the whole trip. The Captain slammed the brakes on and told me to get the hell out and find Grossbart.

I found him on his belly, firing wildly at the five-hundred-feet target. Waiting their turns behind him were Halpern and Fishbein. Fishbein, wearing a pair of steel-rimmed G.I. glasses I hadn't seen on him before, had the appearance of an old peddler who would gladly have sold you his rifle and the cartridges that were slung all over him. I stood back by the ammo boxes, waiting for Grossbart to finish spraying the distant targets. Fishbein straggled back to stand near me.

"Hello, Sergeant Marx," he said.

"How are you?" I mumbled.

"Fine, thank you. Sheldon's really a good shot."

"I didn't notice."

"I'm not so good, but I think I'm getting the hang of it now. Sergeant, I don't mean to, you know, ask what I shouldn't —" The boy stopped. He was trying to speak intimately, but the noise of the shooting forced him to shout at me.

"What is it?" I asked. Down the range, I saw Captain Barrett standing up in the jeep, scanning the line for me and Grossbart.

"My parents keep asking and asking where we're going," Fishbein said. "Everybody says the Pacific. I don't care, but my parents — If I could relieve their minds, I think I could concentrate more on my shooting."

"I don't know where, Fishbein. Try to concentrate anyway."

"Sheldon said you might be able to find out."

"I don't know a thing, Fishbein. You just take it easy, and don't let Sheldon —"

"*I'm* taking it easy, Sergeant. It's at home —"

Grossbart had finished on the line, and was dusting his fatigues with one hand. I called to him. "Grossbart, the Captain wants to see you."

He came toward us. His eyes blazed and twinkled. "Hi!"

"Don't point that goddam rifle!" I said.

"I wouldn't shoot you, Sarge." He gave me a smile as wide as a pumpkin, and turned the barrel aside.

"Damn you, Grossbart, this is no joke! Follow me."

I walked ahead of him, and had the awful suspicion that, behind me, Grossbart was *marching*, his rifle on his shoulder, as though he were a one-man detachment. At the jeep, he gave the Captain a rifle salute. "Private Sheldon Grossbart, sir."

"At ease, Grossman." The Captain sat down, slid over into the empty seat, and, crooking a finger, invited Grossbart closer.

"Bart, sir. Sheldon Gross*bart.* It's a common error." Grossbart nodded at me; *I* understood, he indicated. I looked away just as the mess truck pulled up to the range, disgorging a half-dozen K.P.s with rolled-up sleeves. The mess sergeant screamed at them while they set up the chow-line equipment.

"Grossbart, your mama wrote some congressman that we don't feed you right. Do you know that?" the Captain said.

"It was my father, sir. He wrote to Representative Franconi that my religion forbids me to eat certain foods."

"What religion is that, Grossbart?"

"Jewish."

"'Jewish, *sir,*'" I said to Grossbart.

"Excuse me, sir. Jewish, sir."

"What have you been living on?" the Captain said. "You've been in the Army a month already. You don't look to me like you're falling to pieces."

"I eat because I have to, sir. But Sergeant Marx will testify to the fact that I don't eat one mouthful more than I need to in order to survive."

"Is that so, Marx?" Barrett asked.

"I've never seen Grossbart eat, sir," I said.

"But you heard the rabbi," Grossbart said. "He told us what to do, and I listened."

The Captain looked at me. "Well, Marx?"

"I still don't now what he eats and doesn't eat, sir."

Grossbart raised his arms to plead with me, and it looked for a moment as though he were going to hand me his weapon to hold. "But, Sergeant — "

"Look, Grossbart, just answer the Captain's questions," I said sharply.

Barrett smiled at me, and I resented it. "All right, Grossbart," he said. "What is it you want? The little piece of paper? You want out?"

"No, sir. Only to be allowed to live as a Jew. And for the others, too."

"What others?"

"Fishbein, sir, and Halpern."

"They don't like the way we serve, either?"

"Halpern throws up, sir. I've seen it."

"I thought *you* throw up."

"Just once, sir. I didn't know the sausage was sausage."

"We'll give menus, Grossbart. We'll show training films about the food, so you can identify when we're trying to poison you."

Grossbart did not answer. The men had been organized into two long chow lines. At the tail end of one, I spotted Fishbein — or, rather, his glasses spotted me. They winked sunlight back at me. Halpern stood next to him, patting the inside of his collar with a khaki handkerchief. They moved with the line as it began to edge up toward the food. The mess sergeant was still screaming at the K.P.s. For a moment, I was actually terrified by the thought that somehow the mess sergeant was going to become involved in Grossbart's problem.

"Marx," the Captain said, "you're a Jewish fella — am I right?"

I played straight man. "Yes, sir."

"How long you been in the Army? Tell this boy."

"Three years and two months."

"A year in combat, Grossbart. Twelve goddam months in combat all through Europe. I admire this man." The Captain snapped a wrist against my chest. "Do you hear him peeping about the food? Do you? I want an answer, Grossbart. Yes or no."

"No, sir."

"And why not? He's a Jewish fella."

"Some things are more important to some Jews than other things to other Jews."

Barrett blew up. "Look, Grossbart. Marx, here, is a good man — a goddam hero. When you were in high school, Sergeant Marx was killing Germans. Who does more for the Jews — you, by throwing up over a lousy piece of sausage, a piece of first-cut meat, or Marx, by killing those Nazi bastards? If I was a Jew, Grossbart, I'd kiss this man's feet. He's a goddam hero, and *he* eats what we give him. Why do you have to cause trouble is what I want to know! What is it you're buckin' for — a discharge?"

"No, sir."

"I'm talking to a wall! Sergeant, get him out of my way." Barrett swung himself back into the driver's seat. "I'm going to see the chaplain." The engine roared, the jeep spun around in a whirl of dust, and the Captain was headed back to camp.

For a moment, Grossbart and I stood side by side, watching the jeep. Then he looked at me and said, "I don't want to start trouble. That's the first thing they toss up to us."

When he spoke, I saw that his teeth were white and straight, and the sight of them suddenly made me understand that Grossbart actually did have parents — that once upon a time someone had taken little Sheldon to the dentist. He was their son. Despite all the talk about his parents, it was hard to believe in Grossbart as a child, an heir — as related by blood to anyone, mother, father, or, above all, to me. This realization led me to another.

"What does your father do, Grossbart?" I asked as we started to walk back toward the chow line.

"He's a tailor."

"An American?"

"Now, yes. A son in the Army," he said, jokingly.

"And your mother?" I asked.

He winked. "A *ballabusta*. She practically sleeps with a dustcloth in her hand."

"She's also an immigrant?"

"All she talks is Yiddish, still."

"And your father, too?"

"A little English. 'Clean,' 'Press,' 'Take the pants in.' That's the extent of it. But they're good to me."

"Then, Grossbart — " I reached out and stopped him. He turned toward me, and when our eyes met, his seemed to jump back, to shiver in their sockets. "Grossbart — you were the one who wrote that letter, weren't you?"

It took only a second or two for his eyes to flash happy again. "Yes." He walked on, and I kept pace. "It's what my father *would* have written if he had known how. It was his name, though. *He* signed it. He even mailed it. I sent it home. For the New York postmark."

I was astonished, and he saw it. With complete seriousness, he thrust his right arm in front of me. "Blood is blood, Sergeant," he said, pinching the blue vein in his wrist.

"What the hell *are* you trying to do, Grossbart?" I asked. "I've seen you eat. Do you know that? I told the Captain I don't know what you eat, but I've seen you eat like a hound at chow."

"We work hard, Sergeant. We're in training. For a furnace to work, you've got to feed it coal."

"Why did you say in the letter that you threw up all the time?"

"I was really talking about Mickey there. I was talking *for* him. He would never write, Sergeant, though I pleaded with him. He'll waste away to nothing if I don't help. Sergeant, I used my name — my father's name — but it's Mickey, and Fishbein, too, I'm watching out for."

"You're a regular Messiah, aren't you?"

We were at the chow line now.

"That's a good one, Sergeant," he said, smiling. "But who knows? Who can tell? Maybe you're the Messiah — a little bit. What Mickey says is the Messiah is a collective idea. He went to Yeshiva, Mickey, for a wile. He says *together* we're the Messiah. Me a little bit, you a little bit. You should hear that kid talk, Sergeant, when he gets going."

"Me a little bit, you a little bit," I said. "You'd like to believe that, wouldn't you, Grossbart? That would make everything so clean for you."

"It doesn't seem too bad a thing to believe, Sergeant. It only means we should all *give* a little, is all."

I walked off to eat my rations with the other noncoms.

Two days later, a letter addressed to Captain Barrett passed over my desk. It had come through the chain of command — from the office of Congressman Franconi, where it had been received, to General Lyman, to Colonel Sousa, to Major Lamont, now to Captain Barrett. I read it over twice. It was dated May 14, the day Barrett had spoken with Grossbart on the rifle range.

> Dear Congressman:
>
> First let me thank you for your interest in behalf of my son, Private Sheldon Grossbart. Fortunately, I was able to speak with Sheldon on the phone the other night, and I think I've been able to solve our problem. He is, as I mentioned in my last letter, a very religious boy, and it was only with the greatest difficulty that I could persuade him that the religious thing to do — what God Himself would want Sheldon to do — would be to suffer the pangs of religious remorse for the good of his country and all mankind. It took some doing, Congressman, but finally he saw the light. In fact, what he said (and I wrote down the words on a scratch pad so as never to forget), what he said was "I guess you're right, Dad. So many millions of my fellow-Jews gave up their lives to the enemy, the least I can do is live for a while minus a bit of my heritage so as to help end this struggle and regain for all the children of God dignity and humanity." That, Congressman, would make any father proud.
>
> By the way, Sheldon wanted me to know — and to pass on to you — the name of a soldier who helped him reach this decision: SERGEANT NATHAN MARX. Sergeant Marx is a combat veteran who is Sheldon's first sergeant. This man has helped Sheldon over some of the first hurdles he's had to face in the Army, and is in part responsible for Sheldon's changing his mind about the dietary laws. I know Sheldon would appreciate any recognition Marx could receive.
>
> Thank you and good luck. I look forward to seeing your name on the next election ballot.
>
> Respectfully,
> Samuel E. Grossbart

Attached to the Grossbart communiqué was another, addressed to General Marshall Lyman, the post commander, and signed by Representative Charles E. Franconi, of the House of Representatives. The communiqué informed General Lyman that Sergeant Nathan Marx was a credit to the U.S. Army and the Jewish people.

What was Grossbart's motive in recanting? Did he feel he'd gone too far? Was the letter a strategic retreat — a crafty attempt to strengthen what he considered our alliance? Or had he actually changed his mind, via an imaginary dialogue between Grossbart *père* and Grossbart *fils?* I was puzzled, but only for a few days — that is, only until I realized that, whatever his reasons, he had actually decided to disappear from my life; he was going to allow himself to become just another trainee. I saw him at inspection, but he never winked; at chow formations, but he never flashed me a sign. On Sundays, with the other trainees, he would sit around watching the noncoms' softball team, for which I pitched, but not once did he speak an unnecessary word to me. Fishbein and Halpern retreated, too — at Grossbart's command, I was sure. Apparently he had seen that wisdom lay in turning back before he plunged over into the ugliness of privilege undeserved. Our separation allowed me to forgive him our past encounters, and, finally, to admire him for his good sense.

Meanwhile, free of Grossbart, I grew used to my job and my administrative tasks. I stepped on a scale one day, and discovered I had truly become a noncombatant; I had gained seven pounds. I found patience to get past the first three pages of a book. I thought about the future more and more, and wrote letters to girls I'd known before the war. I even got a few answers. I sent away to Columbia for a Law School catalogue. I continued to follow the war in the Pacific, but it was not my war. I thought I could see the end, and sometimes, at night, I dreamed that I was walking on the streets of Manhattan — Broadway, Third Avenue, 116th Street, where I had lived the three years I attended Columbia. I curled myself around these dreams and I began to be happy.

And then, one Saturday, when everybody was away and I was alone in the orderly room reading a month-old copy of the *Sporting News,* Grossbart reappeared.

"You a baseball fan, Sergeant?"

I looked up. "How are you?"

"Fine," Grossbart said. "They're making a soldier out of me."

"How are Fishbein and Halpern?"

"Coming along," he said. "We've got no training this afternoon. They're at the movies."

"How come you're not with them?"

"I wanted to come over and say hello."

He smiled — a shy, regular-guy smile, as though he and I well knew that our friendship drew its sustenance from unexpected visits, remembered birthdays, and borrowed lawnmowers. At first it offended me, and then the feeling was swallowed by the general uneasiness I felt at the thought that everyone on the post was locked away in a dark movie theater and I was here alone with Grossbart. I folded up my paper.

"Sergeant," he said, "I'd like to ask a favor. It is a favor, and I'm making no bones about it."

He stopped, allowing me to refuse him a hearing — which, of course, forced me into a courtesy I did not intend. "Go ahead."

"Well, actually it's two favors."

I said nothing.

"The first one's about these rumors. Everybody says we're going to the Pacific."

"As I told your friend Fishbein, I don't know," I said. "You'll just have to wait to find out. Like everybody else."

"You think there's a chance of any of us going East?"

"Germany?" I said. "Maybe."

"I meant New York."

"I don't think so, Grossbart. Offhand."

"Thanks for the information, Sergeant," he said.

"It's not information, Grossbart. Just what I surmise."

"It certainly would be good to be near home. My parents — you know." He took a step toward the door and then turned back. "Oh, the other thing. May I ask the other?"

"What is it?"

"The other thing is — I've got relatives in St. Louis, and they say they'll give me a whole Passover dinner if I can get down there. God, Sergeant, that'd mean an awful lot to me."

I stood up. "No passes during basic, Grossbart."

"But we're off from now till Monday morning, Sergeant. I could leave the post and no one would even know."

"I'd know. You'd know."

"But that's all. Just the two of us. Last night, I called my aunt, and you should have heard her. 'Come — come,' she said. 'I got gefilte fish, *chrain* — the works!' Just a day, Sergeant. I'd take the blame if anything happened."

"The Captain isn't here to sign a pass."

"You could sign."

"Look, Grossbart —"

"Sergeant, for two months, practically, I've been eating *trafe* till I want to die."

"I thought you'd made up your mind to live with it. To be minus a little bit of heritage."

He pointed a finger at me. "You!" he said. "That wasn't for you to read."

"I read it. So what?"

"That letter was addressed to a congressman."

"Grossbart, don't feed me any baloney. You *wanted* me to read it."

"Why are you persecuting me, Sergeant?"

"Are you kidding!"

"I've run into this before," he said, "but never from my own!"

"Get out of here, Grossbart! Get the hell out of my sight!"

He did not move. "Ashamed, that's what you are," he said. "So you take it out on the rest of us. They say Hitler himself was half a Jew. Hearing you, I wouldn't doubt it."

"What are you trying to do with me, Grossbart?" I asked him. "What are you after? You want me to give you special privileges, to change the food, to find out about your orders, to give you weekend passes."

"You even talk like a goy!" Grossbart shook his fist. "Is this just a weekend pass I'm asking for? Is a Seder sacred, or not?"

Seder! It suddenly occurred to me that Passover had been celebrated weeks before. I said so.

"That's right," he replied. "Who says no? A month ago — and I was in the field eating hash! And now all I ask is a simple favor. A Jewish boy I thought would understand. My aunt's willing to go out of her way — to make a Seder a month later. . . ." He turned to go, mumbling.

"Come back here!" I called. He stopped and looked at me. "Grossbart, why can't you be like the rest? Why do you have to stick out like a sore thumb?"

"Because I'm a Jew, Sergeant. I *am* different. Better, maybe not. But different."

"This is a war, Grossbart. For the time being *be* the same."

"I refuse."

"What?"

"I refuse. I can't stop being me, that's all there is to it." Tears came to his eyes. "It's a hard thing to be a Jew. But now I understand what Mickey says — it's a harder thing to stay one." He raised a hand sadly toward me. "Look at *you*."

"Stop crying!"

"Stop this, stop that, stop the other thing! *You* stop, Sergeant. Stop closing your heart to your own!" And, wiping his face with his sleeve, he ran out the door. "The least we can do for one another — the least . . ."

An hour later, looking out of the window, I saw Grossbart headed across the field. He wore a pair of starched khakis and carried a little leather ditty bag. I went out into the heat of the day. It was quiet; not a soul was in sight except, over by the mess hall, four K.P.s sitting around a pan, sloped forward from their waists, gabbing and peeling potatoes in the sun.

"Grossbart!" I called.

He looked toward me and continued walking.

"Grossbart, get over here!"

He turned and came across the field. Finally, he stood before me.

"Where are you going?" I asked.

"St. Louis. I don't care."

"You'll get caught without a pass."

"So I'll get caught without a pass."

"You'll go to the stockade."

"I'm *in* the stockade." He made an about-face and headed off. I let him go only a step or two. "Come back here," I said, and he followed me into the office, where I typed out a pass and signed the Captain's name, and my own initials after it.

He took the pass and then, a moment later, reached out and grabbed my hand. "Sergeant, you don't know how much this means to me."

"O.K.," I said. "Don't get in any trouble."

"I wish I could show you how much this means to me."

"Don't do me any favors. Don't write any more congressmen for citations."

He smiled. "You're right. I won't. But let me do something."

"Bring me a piece of that gefilte fish. Just get out of here."

"I will!" he said. "With a slice of carrot and a little horse-radish. I won't forget."

"All right. Just show your pass at the gate. And don't tell *anybody*."

"I won't. It's a month late, but a good Yom Tov to you."

"Good Yom Tov, Grossbart," I said.

"You're a good Jew, Sergeant. You like to think you have a hard heart, but underneath you're a fine, decent man. I mean that."

Those last three words touched me more than any words from Grossbart's mouth had the right to. "All right, Grossbart," I said. "Now call me 'sir,' and get the hell out of here."

He ran out the door and was gone. I felt very pleased with myself; it was a great relief to stop fighting Grossbart, and it had cost me nothing. Barrett would never find out, and if he did, I could manage to invent some excuse. For a while, I sat at my desk, comfortable in my decision. Then the screen door flew back and Grossbart burst in again. "Sergeant!" he said. Behind him I saw Fishbein and Halpern, both in starched khakis, both carrying ditty bags like Grossbart's.

"Sergeant, I caught Mickey and Larry coming out of the movies. I almost missed them."

"Grossbart — did I say tell no one?" I said.

"But my aunt said I could bring friends. That I should, in fact."

"*I'm* the Sergeant, Grossbart — not your aunt!"

Grossbart looked at me in disbelief. He pulled Halpern up by his sleeve. "Mickey, tell the Sergeant what this would mean to you."

Halpern looked at me and, shrugging, said, "A lot."

Fishbein stepped forward without prompting. "This would mean a great deal to me and my parents, Sergeant Marx."

"No!" I shouted.

Grossbart was shaking his head. "Sergeant, I could see you denying me, but how you can deny Mickey, a Yeshiva boy — that's beyond me."

"I'm not denying Mickey anything," I said. "You just pushed a little too hard, Grossbart. *You* denied him."

"I'll give him my pass, then," Grossbart said. "I'll give him my aunt's address and a little note. At least let him go."

In a second, he had crammed the pass into Halpern's pants pocket. Halpern looked at me, and so did Fishbein. Grossbart was at the door, pushing it open. "Mickey, bring me a piece of gefilte fish, at least," he said, and then he was outside again.

The three of us looked at one another, and then I said, "Halpern, hand that pass over."

He took it from his pocket and gave it to me. Fishbein had now moved to the doorway, where he lingered. He stood there for a moment with his mouth slightly open, and then he pointed to himself. "And me?" he asked.

His utter ridiculousness exhausted me. I slumped down in my seat and felt pulses knocking at the back of my eyes. "Fishbein," I said, "you understand I'm not trying to deny you anything, don't you? If it was my Army, I'd serve gefilte fish in the mess hall. I'd sell *kugel* in the PX, honest to God."

Halpern smiled.

"You understand, don't you, Halpern?"

"Yes, Sergeant."

"And you, Fishbein? I don't want enemies. I'm just like you — I want to serve my time and go home. I miss the same things you miss."

"Then, Sergeant," Fishbein said, "why don't you come, too?"

"Where?"

"To St. Louis. To Shelly's aunt. We'll have a regular Seder. Play hide-the-matzoh." He gave me a broad, black-toothed smile.

I saw Grossbart again, on the other side of the screen.

"Pst!" He waved a piece of paper. "Mickey, here's the address. Tell her I couldn't get away."

Halpern did not move. He looked at me, and I saw the shrug moving up his arms into his shoulders again. I took the cover off my typewriter and made out passes for him and Fishbein. "Go," I said. "The three of you."

I thought Halpern was going to kiss my hand.

That afternoon, in a bar in Joplin, I drank beer and listened with half an ear to the Cardinal game. I tried to look squarely at what I'd become involved in, and began to wonder if perhaps the struggle with Grossbart wasn't as much my fault as his. What was I that I had to *muster* generous feelings? Who was I to have been feeling so grudging, so tight-hearted? After all, I wasn't being asked to move the world. Had I a right, then, or a reason, to clamp down on Grossbart, when that meant clamping down on Halpern, too? And Fishbein — that ugly, agreeable soul? Out of the many recollections of my childhood that had tumbled over me these past few days I heard my grandmother's voice: "What are you making a *tsimmes?*" It was what she would ask my mother when, say, I had cut myself while doing something I shouldn't have done, and her daughter was busy bawling me out. I needed a hug and a kiss, and my mother would moralize. But my grandmother knew — mercy overrides justice. I should have known it, too. Who was Nathan Marx to be such a penny pincher with kindness? Surely, I thought, the Messiah himself — if He should ever come — won't niggle over nickels and dimes. God willing, he'll hug and kiss.

The next day, while I was playing softball over on the parade ground, I decided to ask Bob Wright, who was noncom in charge of Classification and Assignment, where he thought our trainees would be sent when their cycle ended, in two weeks. I asked casually, between innings, and he said, "They're pushing them all into the Pacific. Shulman cut the orders on your boys the other day."

The news shocked me, as though I were the father of Halpern, Fishbein, and Grossbart.

That night, I was just sliding into sleep when someone tapped on my door. "Who is it?" I asked.

"Sheldon."

He opened the door and came in. For a moment, I felt his presence without being able to see him. "How was it?" I asked.

He popped into sight in the near-darkness before me. "Great, Sergeant." Then he was sitting on the edge of the bed. I sat up.

"How about you?" he asked. "Have a nice weekend?"

"Yes."

"The others went to sleep." He took a deep, paternal breath. We sat silent for a while, and a homey feeling invaded my ugly little cubicle; the door was locked, the cat was out, the children were safely in bed.

"Sergeant, can I tell you something? Personal?"

I did not answer, and he seemed to know why. "Not about me. About Mickey. Sergeant, I never felt for anybody like I feel for him. Last night I heard Mickey in the bed next to me. He was crying so, it could have broken your heart. Real sobs."

"I'm sorry to hear that."

"I had to talk to him to stop him. He held my hand, Sergeant — he wouldn't let it go. He was almost hysterical. He kept saying if he only knew where we were going. Even if he knew it *was* the Pacific, that would be better than nothing. Just to know."

Long ago, someone had taught Grossbart the sad rule that only lies can get the truth. Not that I couldn't believe in the fact of Halpern's crying; his eyes *always* seemed red-rimmed. But, fact or not, it became a lie when Grossbart uttered it. He was entirely strategic. But then — it came with force of indictment — so was I! There are strategies of aggression, but there are strategies of retreat as well. And so, recognizing that I myself had not been without craft and guile, I told him what I knew. "It is the Pacific."

He let out a small gasp, which was not a lie. "I'll tell him. I wish it was otherwise."

"So do I."

He jumped on my words. "You mean you think you could do something? A change, maybe?"

"No, I couldn't do a thing."

"Don't you know anybody over at C. and A.?"

"Grossbart, there's nothing I can do," I said. "If your orders are for the Pacific, then it's the Pacific."

"But Mickey —"

"Mickey, you, me — everybody, Grossbart. There's nothing to be done. Maybe the war'll end before you go. Pray for a miracle."

"But —"

"Good night, Grossbart." I settled back, and was relieved to feel the springs unbend as Grossbart rose to leave. I could see him clearly now; his jaw had dropped, and he looked like a dazed prizefighter. I noticed for the first time a little paper bag in his hand.

"Grossbart." I smiled. "My gift?"

"Oh, yes, Sergeant. Here — from all of us." He handed me the bag. "It's egg roll."

"Egg roll?" I accepted the bag and felt a damp grease spot on the bottom. I opened it, sure that Grossbart was joking.

"We thought you'd probably like it. You know — Chinese egg roll. We thought you'd probably have a taste for —"

"Your aunt served egg roll?"

"She wasn't home."

"Grossbart, she invited you. You told me she invited you and your friends."

"I know," he said. "I just reread the letter. *Next* week."

I got out of bed and walked to the window. "Grossbart," I said. But I was not calling to him.

"What?"

"What are you, Grossbart? Honest to God, what are you?"

I think it was the first I'd asked him a question for which he didn't have an immediate answer.

"How can you do this to people?" I went on.

"Sergeant, the day away did us all a world of good. Fishbein, you should see him, he *loves* Chinese food."

"But the Seder," I said.

"We took second best, Sergeant."

Rage came charging at me. I didn't sidestep. "Grossbart, you're a liar!" I said. "You're a schemer and a crook. You've got no respect for anything. Nothing at all. Not for me, for the truth — not even for poor Halpern! You use us all —"

"Sergeant, Sergeant, I feel for Mickey. Honest to God, I do. I *love* Mickey. I try —"

"You try! You feel!" I lurched toward him and grabbed his shirt front.

I shook him furiously. "Grossbart, get out! Get out and stay the hell away from me. Because if I see you, I'll make your life miserable. *You understand that?*"

"Yes."

I let him free, and when he walked from the room, I wanted to spit on the floor where he had stood. I couldn't stop the fury. It engulfed me, owned me, till it seemed I could only rid myself of it with tears or an act of violence. I snatched from the bed the bag Grossbart had given me and, with all my strength, threw it out the window. And the next morning, as the men policed the area around the barracks, I heard a great cry go up from one of the trainees, who had been anticipating only his morning handful of cigarette butts and candy wrappers. "Egg roll!" he shouted. "Holy Christ, Chinese goddam egg roll!"

A week later, when I read the orders that had come down from C. and A., I couldn't believe my eyes. Every single trainee was to be shipped to Camp Stoneman, California, and from there to the Pacific — every trainee but one. Private Sheldon Grossbart. He was to be sent to Fort Monmouth, New Jersey. I read the mimeographed sheet several times. Dee, Farrell, Fishbein, Fuselli, Fylypowycz, Glinicki, Gromke, Gucwa, Halpern, Hardy, Helebrandt, right down to Anton Zygadlo — all were to be headed West before the month was out. All except Grossbart. He had pulled a string, and I wasn't it.

I lifted the phone and called C. and A.

The voice on the other end said smartly, "Corporal Shulman, sir."

"Let me speak to Sergeant Wright."

"Who is this calling, sir?"

"Sergeant Marx."

And, to my surprise, the voice said, "*Oh!*" Then, "Just a minute, Sergeant."

Shulman's "*Oh!*" stayed with me while I waited for Wright to come to the phone. Why "*Oh!*"? Who was Shulman? And then, so simply, I knew I'd discovered the string that Grossbart had pulled. In fact, I could hear Grossbart the day he'd discovered Shulman in the PX, or in the bowling alley, or maybe even at services. "Glad to meet you. Where you from? Bronx? Me, too. Do you know So-and-So? And So-and-So? Me, too! You work at C. and A.? Really? Hey, how's chances of getting East? Could you do something? Change something? Swindle, cheat, lie? We gotta help each other, you know. If the Jews in Germany . . ."

Bob Wright answered the phone. "How are you, Nate? How's the pitching arm?"

"Good. Bob, I wonder if you could do me a favor." I heard clearly my own words, and they so reminded me of Grossbart that I dropped more easily than I could have imagined into what I had planned. "This may sound crazy, Bob, but I got a kid here on orders to Monmouth who wants them changed. He had a brother killed in Europe, and he's hot to go to the Pacific. Says he'd feel like a coward if he wound up Stateside. I don't know, Bob — can anything be done? Put somebody else in the Monmouth slot?"

"Who?" he asked cagily.

"Anybody. First guy in the alphabet. I don't care. The kid just asked if something could be done."

"What's his name?"

"Grossbart, Sheldon."

Wright didn't answer.

"Yeah," I said. "He's a Jewish kid, so he thought I could help him out. You know."

"I guess I can do something," he finally said. "The Major hasn't been around here for weeks. Temporary duty to the golf course. I'll try, Nate, that's all I can say."

"I'd appreciate it, Bob. See you Sunday." And I hung up, perspiring.

The following day, the corrected orders appeared: Fishbein, Fuselli, Fylypowycz, Glinicki, Gromke, Grossbart, Gucwa, Halpern, Hardy . . . Lucky Private Harley Alton was to go to Fort Monmouth, New Jersey, where, for some reason or other, they wanted an enlisted man with infantry training.

After chow that night, I stopped back at the orderly room to straighten out the guard-duty roster. Grossbart was waiting for me. He spoke first.

"You son of a bitch!"

I sat down at my desk, and while he glared at me, I began to make the necessary alterations in the duty roster.

"What do you have against me?" he cried. "Against my family? Would it kill you for me to be near my father, God knows how many months he has left to him?"

"Why so?"

"His heart," Grossbart said. "He hasn't had enough troubles in a lifetime, you've got to add to them. I curse the day I ever met you, Marx!

Shulman told me what happened over there. There's no limit to your anti-Semitism, is there? The damage you've done here isn't enough. You have to make a special phone call! You really want me dead!"

I made the last few notations in the duty roster and got up to leave. "Good night, Grossbart."

"You owe me an explanation!" He stood in my path.

"Sheldon, you're the one who owes explanations."

He scowled. "To *you?*"

"To me, I think so — yes. Mostly to Fishbein and Halpern."

"That's right, twist things around. I owe nobody nothing, I've done all I could for them. Now I think I've got the right to watch out for myself."

"For each other we have to learn to watch out, Sheldon. You told me yourself."

"You call this watching out for me — what you did?"

"No. For all of us."

I pushed him aside and started for the door. I heard his furious breathing behind me, and it sounded like steam rushing from an engine of terrible strength.

"*You'll* be all right," I said from the door. And, I thought, so would Fishbein and Halpern be all right, even in the Pacific, if only Grossbart continued to see — in the obsequiousness of the one, the soft spirituality of the other — some profit for himself.

I stood outside the orderly room, and I heard Grossbart weeping behind me. Over in the barracks, in the lighted windows, I could see the boys in their T shirts sitting on their bunks talking about their orders, as they'd been doing for the past two days. With a kind of quiet nervousness, they polished shoes, shined belt buckles, squared away underwear, trying as best they could to accept their fate. Behind me, Grossbart swallowed hard, accepting his. And then, resisting with all my will an impulse to turn and seek pardon for my vindictiveness, I accepted my own.

1962

*Stanley Elkin*

......................................................................................................................

# Criers and Kibitzers,
# Kibitzers and Criers

FROM *Perspective*

GREENSPAHN CURSED the steering wheel shoved like the flat, hard edge of someone's hand against his stomach. "God damn lousy cars," he thought. "Forty-five hundred dollars and there's not room to breathe." He thought sourly of the smiling salesman who had sold it to him, calling him Jake all the time he had been in the showroom. "Lousy *podler.*" He slid across the seat, moving carefully as though he carried something fragile, and eased his big body out of the car. Seeing the parking meter he experienced a dark rage. They don't let you live, he thought. "I'll put your nickels in the meter for you, Mr. Greenspahn," he mimicked the Irish cop. Two dollars a week for the lousy grubber. Plus the nickels that were supposed to go into the meter. And they talked about the Jews. Greenspahn saw the cop across the street writing out a ticket. He went around his car, carefully pulling at the handle of each door.

He started toward his store.

"Hey there, Mr. Greenspahn," the cop called.

He turned to look at him. "Yeah?"

"Good morning."

"Yeah. Yeah. Good morning."

The grubber came toward him from across the street. Uniforms, Greenspahn thought, only a fool wears a uniform.

"Fine day, Mr. Greenspahn," the cop said.

Greenspahn nodded grudgingly.

"I was sorry to hear about your trouble, Mr. Greenspahn. Did you get my card?"

"Yeah, I got it. Thanks." He remembered something with flowers on it and rays going up to a pink Heaven. A picture of a cross yet.

"I wanted to come out to the chapel but the brother-in-law was up from Cleveland. I couldn't make it."

"Yeah," Greenspahn said. "Maybe next time."

The cop looked stupidly at him and Greenspahn reached into his pocket.

"No. No. Don't worry about that, Mr. Greenspahn. I'll take care of it for now. Please, Mr. Greenspahn, forget it this time. It's O.K."

Greenspahn felt like giving him the money anyway. Don't mourn for me, *podler*, he thought. Keep your two dollars worth of grief.

The cop turned to go. "Well, Greenspahn, there's nothing anybody can say at times like this, but you know how I feel. You got to go on living, don't you know."

"Sure," Greenspahn said. "That's right, officer." The cop crossed the street and finished writing the ticket. Greenspahn looked after him angrily, watching the gun swinging in the holster at his hip, the sun flashing brightly on the shiny handcuffs. *Podler*, he thought, afraid for his lousy nickels. There'll be an extra parking space sooner than he thinks.

He walked toward his store. He could have parked by his own place but out of habit he left his car in front of a rival grocer's. It was an old and senseless spite. Tomorrow he would change. What difference did it make, one less parking space? Why should he walk?

He felt bloated, heavy. The bowels, he thought. I got to move them soon or I'll bust. He looked at the street vacantly, feeling none of the old excitement. What did he come back for, he wondered suddenly, sadly. He missed Harold. Oh my God. Poor Harold, he thought. I'll never see him again. I'll never see my son again. He was choking, a big pale man beating his fist against his chest in grief. He pulled a handkerchief from his pocket and blew his nose. That was the way it was, he thought. He could go along flat and empty and dull and all of a sudden he could dissolve in a heavy, choking grief. The street was no place for him. His wife was crazy, he thought, swiftly angry. "Be busy. Be busy," she said. What was he, a kid, that because he was making up somebody's lousy order everything would fly out of his mind? The bottom dropped out of his life and he was supposed to go along as though nothing had happened. His wife and the cop, they had the same psychology. Like in the movies after the horse kicks your head in you're supposed to get up and ride him so he can throw you off and finish the job. If he could get a buyer he would sell. That was that.

Mechanically, he looked into the windows he passed. The displays seemed foolish to him now, petty. He resented the wooden wedding cakes, the hollow watches. The manikins were grotesque, giant dolls. Toys, he thought bitterly. Toys. That he used to enjoy the displays himself, had even taken a peculiar pleasure in the complicated tiers of cans, in the amazing pyramids of apples and oranges in his own window, seemed incredible to him. He remembered he had liked to look at the little living rooms in the window of the furniture store, the wax models sitting on the couches offering each other tea. He used to look at the expensive furniture and think, *merchandise.* The word had sounded rich to him, and mysterious. He used to think of camels on a desert, their bellies slung with heavy ropes. On their backs they carried *merchandise.* What did it mean, any of it? Nothing. It meant nothing.

He was conscious of someone watching him.

"Hello, Jake."

It was Margolis from the television shop.

"Hello, Margolis. How are you?"

"Business is terrible. You picked a hell of a time to come back."

A man's son dies and Margolis says business is terrible. Margolis, he thought, jerk, son of a bitch.

"You can't close up a minute. You don't know when somebody might come in. I didn't take coffee since you left," Margolis said.

"You had it tough, Margolis. You should have said something, I would have sent some over."

Margolis smiled helplessly, remembering the death of Greenspahn's son.

"It's O.K., Margolis." He felt his anger tug at him again. It was something he would have to watch, a new thing with him but already familiar, easily released, like something on springs.

"Jake," Margolis whined.

"Not now, Margolis," he said angrily. He had to get away from him. He was like a little kid, Greenspahn thought. His face was puffy, swollen, like a kid about to cry. He looked so meek. He should be holding a hat in his hand. He couldn't stand to look at him. He was afraid Margolis was going to make a speech. He didn't want to hear it. What did he need a speech? His son was in the ground. Under all that earth. Under all that dirt. In a metal box. Airtight, the funeral director told him. Oh my God, *airtight. Vacuum-sealed.* Like a can of coffee. His son was in the ground and on the street the models in the windows had on next season's dresses. He would hit Margolis in his face if he said one word.

Margolis looked at him and nodded sadly, turning his palms out as if to say, "I know. I know." Margolis continued to look at him and Greenspahn thought, He's taking into account, that's what he's doing. He's taking into account the fact that my son has died. He's figuring it in and making apologies for me, making an allowance, like he was making an estimate in his head what to charge a customer.

"I got to go, Margolis," Greenspahn said.

"Sure, me too," Margolis said, relieved. "I'll see you, Jake. The man from R.C.A. is around back with a shipment. What do I need it?"

Greenspahn walked to the end of the block and crossed the street. He looked down the side street and saw the *shul* where that evening he would say prayers for his son.

He came to his store, seeing it with distaste. He looked at the signs, like the balloons in comic strips where they put the words, stuck inside against the glass. The letters big and red like it was the end of the world. The big whitewash numbers on the glass thickly. A billboard, he thought.

He stepped up to the glass door and looked in. Frank, his produce man, stood by the fruit and vegetable bins taking the tissue paper off the oranges. His butcher, Howard, was at the register talking to Shirley, the cashier. Howard saw him through the glass and waved extravagantly. Shirley came to the door and opened it. "Good morning there, Mr. Greenspahn," she said.

"Hey Jake, how are you?" Frank said.

"How's it going, Jake?" Howard said.

"Was Siggie in yet? Did you tell him about the cheese?"

"He ain't yet been in this morning, Jake," Frank said.

"How about the meat? Did you place the order?"

"Sure, Jake," Howard said. "I called the guy Thursday."

"Where are the receipts?" he asked Shirley.

"I'll get them for you, Mr. Greenspahn. You already seen them for the first two weeks you were gone. I'll get last week's."

She handed him a slip of paper. It was four hundred seventy dollars off the last week's low figure. They must have had a picnic, Greenspahn thought. No more though. He looked at them and they watched him with interest. "So," he said. "So."

"Nice to have you back, Mr. Greenspahn," Shirley told him, smiling.

"Yeah," he said, "yeah."

"We got a shipment yesterday, Jake, but the *shvartze* showed up drunk. We couldn't get it all put up," Frank said.

Greenspahn nodded. "The figures are low," he said.

"It's business. Business has been terrible. I figure it's the strike," Frank said.

"In West Virginia the miners are out and you figure that's why my business is bad in this neighborhood?" Greenspahn said.

"There are repercussions," Frank said. "All industries are affected."

"Yeah," Greenspahn said, "yeah. The Pretzel Industry. The Canned Chicken Noodle Soup Industry."

"Well, business has been lousy, Jake," Howard said testily.

"I guess maybe it's so bad, now might be a good time to sell. What do you think?" Greenspahn said.

"Are you really thinking of selling, Jake?" Frank asked.

"You want to buy my place, Frank?"

"You know I don't have that kind of money, Jake," Frank said uneasily.

"Yeah," Greenspahn said, "yeah."

Frank looked at him and Greenspahn waited for him to say something else, but in a moment he turned and went back to the oranges. Some thief, Greenspahn thought. Big shot. I insulted him.

"I got to change," he said to Shirley. "Call me if Siggie comes in."

He went into the toilet off the small room at the back of the store. He reached for the clothes he kept there on a hook on the back of the door and saw, hanging over his own clothes, a woman's undergarments. A brassière hung by one cup over his trousers. What is it here, a locker room? Does she take baths in the sink? he thought. Fastidiously he tried to remove his own clothes without touching the other garments, but he was clumsy and the underwear, together with his trousers, tumbled in a heap to the floor. They looked, lying there, strangely obscene to him, as though two people, desperately in a hurry, had dropped them quickly and were somewhere near him even now, perhaps behind the very door, making love. He picked up his trousers and changed his clothes. Taking a hanger from a pipe under the sink he hung the clothes he had worn to work and put the hanger on the hook. He stooped to pick up Shirley's underwear. Placing it on the hook his hand rested for a moment on the brassière. He was immediately ashamed and he straightened. He was terribly tired. He put his head through the loop of his apron and tied the apron behind the back of the old blue sweater he wore even in summer. He turned the sink's single tap and rubbed his eyes with water. Bums, he thought. Bums. You put up mirrors to watch the customers so they shouldn't get away with a stick of gum, and in the meanwhile Frank and Howard walk off with the whole store. He sat down to try to move his bowels and the apron hung down from his chest like a barber's sheet. He spread it across his knees. I must look like I'm getting a haircut, he thought irrelevantly. He looked suspiciously at Shirley's underwear. My movie star. He wondered if it was true what Howard told him, that she used to be a 26 girl. Something was going on between her and that Howard. Two bums, he thought. He knew they drank together after work. That was one thing, bad enough, but were they screwing around in the back of the store? Howard had a family. You couldn't trust a young butcher. It was too much for him. Why didn't he just sell and get the hell out? Did he have to look for grief? Was he making a fortune that he had to put up with it? It was crazy. All right, he thought, a man in business, there were things a man in business had to put up with. But this? It was crazy. Everywhere he was beset by thieves and cheats. They kept pushing him, pushing him. What did it mean? Why did they do it? All right, he thought, when Harold was alive was it any different? No, of course not, he knew plenty then too. But it didn't make as much difference. Death is an education, he thought. Now there wasn't any reason to put up with it. What did he need it? On the street, in the store, he saw everything. Everything. It was as if everybody else was made out of glass. Why all of a sudden was he like that?

Why? he thought. Jerk, because they're hurting *you*, that's why.

He stood up and looked absently into the toilet. "Maybe I need a laxative," he said. Troubled, he left the toilet.

In the back room, his "office," he stood by the door to the toilet and looked around. Stacked against one wall he saw four or five cases of soups and canned vegetables. Against the meat locker he had pushed a small table, his desk. He went to it to pick up a pencil. Underneath the telephone was a pad of note paper. Something about it caught his eye and he picked up the pad. On the top sheet was writing, his son's. He used to come down on Saturdays sometimes when they were busy and evidently this was an order he had taken down over the phone. He looked at the familiar writing and thought his heart would break. Harold, Harold, he thought. My God, Harold, you're dead. He touched the sprawling, hastily written letters, the carelessly spelled words and thought absently, He must have been busy. I can hardly read it. He looked at it more closely. "He was in a hurry," he said, starting to sob.

"My God, *he* was in a hurry." He tore the sheet from the pad and folding it, put it into his pocket. In a minute he was able to walk back out into the store.

In the front Shirley was talking to Siggie, the cheese man. Seeing him up there, leaning casually on the counter, Greenspahn felt a quick anger. He walked up the aisle toward him.

Siggie saw him coming. "*Shalom*, Jake," he called.

"I want to talk to you."

"Is it important, Jake, because I'm in some terrific hurry. I still got deliveries."

"What did you leave me?"

"The same, Jake. The same. A couple pounds blue. Some Swiss. Delicious," he said, smacking his lips.

"I been getting complaints, Siggie."

"From the Americans, right? Your average American don't know from cheese. It don't mean nothing." He turned to go.

"Siggie, where you running?"

"Jake, I'll be back tomorrow. You can talk to me about it."

"Now."

He turned reluctantly. "What's the matter?"

"You're leaving old stuff. Who's your wholesaler?"

"Jake, Jake," he said. "We already been over this. I pick up the returns, don't I?"

"That's not the point."

"Have you ever lost a penny account of me?"

"Siggie, who's your wholesaler? Where do you get the stuff?"

"I'm cheaper than the dairy, right? Ain't I cheaper than the dairy? Come on, Jake. What do you want?"

"Siggie, don't be a jerk. Who are you talking to? Don't be a jerk. You leave me cheap, crummy cheese, the dairies are ready to throw it away. I get everybody else's returns. It's old when I get it. Do you think a customer wants a cheese it goes off like a bomb two days after she gets it home? And what about the customers who don't return it? They think I'm gypping them and they don't come back. I don't want the *schlak* stuff. Give me fresh or I'll take from somebody else."

"I couldn't give you fresh for the same price, Jake. You know that."

"The same price."

"Jake," he said amazed.

"The same price. Come on Siggie, don't screw around with me."

"Talk to me tomorrow. We'll work something out." He turned to go.

"Siggie," Greenspahn called after him. "Siggie." He was already out of the store.

Greenspahn clenched his fists. "The bum," he said.

"He's always in a hurry, that guy," Shirley said.

"Yeah, yeah," Greenspahn said. He started to cross to the cheese locker to see what Siggie had left him.

"Say, Mr. Greenspahn," Shirley said. "I don't think I have enough change."

"Where's the *shvartze?* Send him to the bank."

"He ain't come in yet. Shall I run over?"

Greenspahn poked his fingers in the cash drawer. "You got till he comes," he said.

"Well," she said, "if you think so."

"What do we do, a big business in change? I don't see customers stumbling over each other in the aisles."

"I told you, Jake," Howard said, coming up behind him. "It's business. Business is lousy. People ain't eating."

"Here," Greenspahn said, "give me ten dollars. I'll go myself." He turned to Howard. "I seen some stock in the back. Put it up, Howard."

"I should put up the stock?" Howard said.

"You told me yourself, business is lousy. Are you here to keep off the streets or something? What is it?"

"What do you pay the *schvartze* for?"

"He ain't here," Greenspahn said. "When he comes in I'll have him cut up some meat, you'll be even."

He took the money and went out into the street. It was lousy, he thought. You had to be able to trust them or you could go crazy. Any retailer had the same problem, and he winked his eye and figured, all right, so I'll allow a certain percentage for shrinkage. You made it up on the register. But in his place it was ridiculous. They were professionals. Like the mafia or something. What did it pay to aggravate himself, his wife would say. Now he was back he could watch them. Watch them. He couldn't stand even to be in the place. They thought they were getting away with something, the *podlers.*

He went into the bank. He saw the ferns. The marble tables where the depositors made out their slips. The calendars, carefully changed each day. The guard, a gun on his hip and a white carnation in his uniform. The big safe, thicker than a wall, shiny and open in the back behind the sturdy iron gate. The tellers behind their cages, small and quiet, as though they went about barefooted. The bank officers, gray-haired and well dressed, comfortable at their big desks, solidly official behind their engraved nameplates. That was something, he thought. A bank. A bank was something. And no shrinkage.

He gave his ten-dollar bill to a teller to be changed.

"Hello there, Mr. Greenspahn. How are you this morning? We haven't seen you lately," the teller said.

"I haven't been in my place for three weeks," Greenspahn said.

"Say," the teller said, "that's quite a vacation."

"My son passed away."

"I didn't know," the teller said. "I'm very sorry, sir."

He took the rolls the teller handed him and stuffed them into his pocket. "Thank you," he said.

The street was quiet. It looks like a Sunday, he thought. There would be no one in the store. He saw his reflection in a window he passed and realized he had forgotten to take his apron off. It occurred to him that the apron somehow gave him the appearance of being very busy. An apron did that, he thought. Not a business suit so much. Unless there was a briefcase. A briefcase and an apron. They made you look busy. A uniform wouldn't. Soldiers didn't look busy, policemen didn't. A fireman did but he had to have that big hat on. Schmo, he thought, a man your age walking in the street in an apron. He wondered if the vice-presidents at the bank had noticed his apron. He felt the heaviness again.

He was restless, nervous, vaguely disappointed in things.

He passed the big plate window of "The Cookery," the restaurant where he ate his lunch, and the cashier waved at him, gesturing that he should come in. He shook his head. He hesitated. For a moment when he saw her hand go up he thought he might go in. The men would be there, the other business people, drinking cups of coffee, cigarettes smearing the saucers, their sweet rolls cut into small, precise sections. Even without going inside he knew familiarly what it would be like. The criers and the kibitzers. The criers, earnest, complaining with a peculiar vigor about their businesses, their gas mileage, their health; their despair articulate, dependably lamenting their lives, vaguely mourning conditions, their sorrow something they could expect no one to understand. The kibitzers, deaf to grief, winking confidentially at the others, their voices high-pitched in kidding or lowered in conspiracy to tell of triumphs, of men they knew downtown, of tickets fixed, or languishing goods moved suddenly and unexpectedly, of the windfall that was life; their fingers sticky, smeared with the sugar from their rolls.

What did he need them, he thought. Big shots. What did they know about anything? Did they lose sons?

He went back to his place and gave Shirley the change.

"Is the *shvartze* in yet?" he asked.

"No, Mr. Greenspahn."

I'll dock him, he thought. I'll dock him.

He looked around and saw that there were several people in the store. It wasn't busy, but there was more activity than he had expected. Young housewives from the university. Good shoppers, he thought. Good customers. They knew what they could spend and that was it. There was no monkey business about prices. He wished his older customers would take lessons from them. The ones who came in in their fur coats and who thought because they knew him from his old place that entitled them to special privileges. In a supermarket. Privileges. Did A&P give discounts? The National? What did they want from him?

He walked around straightening the shelves. Well, he thought, at least it wasn't totally dead. If they came in like this all day he might make a few pennies. A few pennies, he thought. A few dollars. What difference does it make?

A salesman was talking to him when he saw her. The salesman was trying to tell him something about a new product, some detergent, ten cents off on the box, something, but Greenspahn couldn't take his eyes off her.

"Can I put you down for a few trial cases, Mr. Greenspahn? In Detroit when the stores put it on the shelves . . ."

"No," Greenspahn interrupted him. "Not now. It don't sell. I don't want it."

"But, Mr. Greenspahn, I'm trying to tell you. This is something new. It hasn't been on the market more than three weeks."

"Later, later," Greenspahn said. "Talk to Frank, don't bother me."

He left the salesman and followed the woman up the aisle, stopping when she stopped and turning to the shelves, pretending to adjust them. One egg, he thought. She touches one egg, I'll throw her out.

It was Mrs. Frimkin, the doctor's wife. An old customer and a chiseler. An expert. For a long time she hadn't been in because of a fight they had over a thirty-five-cent delivery charge. He had to watch her. She had a million tricks. Sometimes she would sneak over to the eggs and push her finger through two or three of them. Then she would smear a little egg on the front of her dress and come over to him complaining that he'd ruined her dress, that she'd picked up the eggs "in good faith," thinking they were whole. "In good faith," she said. He'd have to give her the whole box and charge her for a half dozen just to shut her up. An expert.

He went up to her. He was somewhat relieved to see that she wore a good dress. She risked the egg trick only in a housecoat.

"Jake," she said, smiling at him.

He nodded.

"I heard about Harold," she said sadly. "The doctor told me. I almost had a heart attack when I heard." She touched his arm. "Listen," she said. "We don't know. We just don't know. Mrs. Baron, my neighbor from when we lived on Drexel, didn't she fall down dead in the street? Her daughter was getting married in a month. How's your wife?"

Greenspahn shrugged. "Something I can do for you, Mrs. Frimkin?"

"What am I, a stranger? I don't need help. Fix, fix your shelves. I can take what I need."

"Yeah," he said, "yeah. Take." She had another trick. She came into a place, his place, the A&P, it didn't make any difference, and she priced everything. She even took notes. He knew she didn't buy a thing until she was absolutely convinced she couldn't get it a penny cheaper someplace else.

"I only want a few items. Don't worry about me," she said.

"Yeah," Greenspahn said. He could wring her neck, the lousy *podler*.

"How's the fruit?" she asked.

"You mean confidentially?"

"What then?"

"I'll tell you the truth," Greenspahn said. "It's so good I don't like to see it get out of the store."

"Maybe I'll buy a banana then."

"You couldn't go wrong," Greenspahn said.

"You got a nice place, Jake. I always said it."

"So buy something," he said.

"We'll see," she said mysteriously. "We'll see."

They were standing by the canned vegetables and she reached out her hand to lift a can of peas from the shelf. With her palm she made a big thing of wiping the dust from the top of the can and then stared at the price stamped there. "Twenty-seven?" she asked, surprised.

"Yeah," Greenspahn said. "It's too much?"

"Well," she said.

"I'll be damned," he said. "I been in the business twenty-two years and I never did know what to charge for a tin of peas."

She looked at him suspiciously and with a tight smile gently replaced the peas. Greenspahn glared at her and then, seeing Frank walk by, caught at his sleeve, pretending he had business with him. He walked up the aisle holding Frank's elbow, conscious that Mrs. Frimkin was looking after them.

"The lousy *podler*," he whispered.

"Take it easy, Jake," Frank said. "She could be a good customer again. So what if she chisels a little? I was happy to see her come in."

"Yeah," Greenspahn said, "happy." He left Frank and went toward the meat counter. "Any phone orders?" he asked Howard.

"A few, Jake. I can put them up."

"Never mind," Greenspahn said. "Give me." He took the slips Howard handed him. "While it's quiet I'll do them."

He read over the orders quickly and in the back of the store selected four cardboard boxes with great care. He picked the stock from the shelves and fit it neatly into the boxes, taking a kind of pleasure in the diminution of the stacks. Each time he put something into a box he had the feeling that there was that much less to sell. At the thick butcher's block behind the meat counter, bloodstains so deep in the wood they seemed almost a part of its grain, he trimmed fat from a thick roast. Howard, beside him, leaned heavily against the paper roll. Greenspahn was conscious that Howard watched him.

"Bernstein's order?" Howard asked.

"Yeah," Greenspahn said.

"She's giving a party. She told me. Her husband's birthday."

"Happy birthday," Greenspahn said.

"Yeah," Howard said. "Say, Jake, maybe I'll go eat."

Greenspahn trimmed the last piece of fat from the roast before he looked up at him. "So go eat," he said.

"I think so," Howard said. "It's slow today. You know?"

Greenspahn nodded.

"Well, I'll grab some lunch. Maybe it'll pick up in the afternoon."

He took a box and began filling another order. He went to the canned goods in high, narrow, canted towers. That much less to sell, he thought bitterly. It was endless. You could never liquidate. There were no big deals in the grocery business. He thought hopelessly of the hundreds of items in his store, of all the different brands, the different sizes. He was terribly aware of each shopper, conscious of what each put into the shopping cart. It was awful, he thought. He wasn't selling diamonds. He wasn't selling pianos. He sold bread. Milk. Eggs. You had to have volume or you were dead. He was losing money. On his electric, his refrigeration, the signs in his window, his payroll, his specials, his stock. It was the chain stores. They had the parking. They advertised. They gave stamps. Two per cent right out of the profits and it made no difference to them. They had the tie-ins. Fantastic. Their own farms, their own dairies, their own bakeries, their own canneries. Everything. The bastards. He was committing suicide to fight them.

In a little while Shirley came up to him. "Is it all right if I get my lunch now, Mr. Greenspahn?"

What did they ask him? Was he a tyrant? "Yeah, yeah. Go eat. I'll watch the register."

She went out and Greenspahn looking after her thought, Something's going on. First one, then the other. They meet each other. What do they do, hold hands? He fit a carton of eggs carefully into a box. What difference does it make? A slut and a bum.

He stood at the checkout counter and pressing the orange key watched the NO SALE flag shoot up into the window of the register. He counted the money sadly.

Frank was at the bins trimming lettuce. "Jake, you want to go eat I'll watch things," he said.

"Not yet," Greenspahn said.

An old woman came into the store and Greenspahn recognized her. She had been in twice before that morning and both times had bought two tins of the coffee Greenspahn was running on a special. She hadn't bought anything else. Already he had lost twelve cents on her. Greenspahn watched her carefully and saw with a quick rage that she went again to the coffee. She picked up another two tins and came toward the checkout counter. She wore a bright red wig which next to her very white, ancient skin gave her strangely the appearance of a clown. She put the coffee down on the counter and looked up at Greenspahn timidly. Greenspahn made no effort to ring up the coffee. She stood for a moment and then pushed the coffee toward him.

"Sixty-nine cents a pound," she said. "Two pounds is a dollar thirty-eight. Six cents tax is a dollar forty-four."

"Lady," Greenspahn said, "don't you ever eat? Is that all you do is drink coffee?" Greenspahn stared at her.

Her lips began to tremble and her body shook. "A dollar forty-four," she said. "I have it right here."

"This is your sixth can, lady. I lose money on it. Do you know that?"

The woman continued to tremble. It was as though she were very cold.

"What do you do, lady? Sell this stuff door to door? Am I your wholesaler?"

Her body continued to shake and she looked out at him from behind faded eyes as though she were unaware of the terrible movements of her body, as though they had, ultimately, nothing to do with her, that really she existed, hiding, crouched, somewhere behind the eyes. Greenspahn had the impression that, frictionless, her old bald head bobbed beneath the wig. "All right," he said finally, "a dollar forty-four. I hope you have more luck with the item than I had." He took the money from her and watched her as she accepted her package wordlessly and walked out of the store. He shook his head. It was all a pile of crap, he thought. He had a vision of the woman on back porches, standing silently at back doors open on their chains, sadly extending the coffee.

He wanted to get out. Frank could watch the store. If he stole, he stole.

"Frank," he said, "it ain't busy. Watch things. I'll eat."

"Go on, Jake. Go ahead. I'm not hungry, I got a cramp. Go ahead."

"Yeah," Greenspahn said.

He walked toward the restaurant. On his way he had to pass a National and seeing the crowded parking lot he felt his stomach tighten. He paused at the window and pressed his face against the glass and looked in at the full aisles. Through the thick glass he saw women moving silently through the store. He stepped back and read the advertisements on the window. My fruit is cheaper, he thought. My meat's the same, practically the same.

He moved on. Passing the familiar shops he crossed the street and went into The Cookery. Pushing open the heavy glass door he heard the babble of the lunchers, the sound rushing to his ears like the noise of a suddenly unmuted trumpet. Criers and kibitzers, he thought. Kibitzers and criers.

The cashier smiled at him. "We haven't seen you, Mr. G. Somebody told me you were on a diet," she said.

Her too, he thought. A kibitzer that makes change.

He went toward the back. "Hey Jake, how are you?" a man in a booth called. "Sit by us."

He nodded at the men who greeted him and pulling a chair from another table placed it in the aisle facing the booth.

He sat down and leaned forward, pulling the chair's rear legs into the air so that the waitress could get by. Sitting there, in the aisle, he felt peculiarly like a visitor, like one there only temporarily, as though he had rushed up to the table merely to say hello or to tell a joke. He knew what it was. It was the way kibitzers sat. The others, cramped in the booth but despite this giving the appearance of lounging there, their lunches begun or already half eaten, gave him somehow the impression that they had been there all day.

"You missed it, Jake," one of the men said. "We almost got Traub here to reach for a check last Friday. Am I lying, Margolis?"

"He almost did, Jake. He really almost did."

"At the last minute he jumped up and down on his own arm and broke it."

The men at the table laughed and Greenspahn looked at Traub sitting little and helpless between two big men. Traub looked down shame-faced into his Coca-Cola.

"It's O.K., Traub," the first man said. "We know. You got all those daughters getting married and having big weddings at the same time. It's terrible. Traub's only got one son. And do you think he'd have the decency to get married so Traub could one time go to a wedding and just enjoy himself? No, *he's* not *old* enough. But he's old enough to turn around and get himself *bar mitzfah'd*, right Traub? The lousy kid."

Greenspahn looked at the men in the booth and at many-daughtered Traub, who seemed as if he were about to cry. Kibitzers and criers, he thought. Everywhere it was the same. At every table. The two kinds of people like two different sexes that had sought each other out. Sure, Greenspahn thought, would a crier listen to another man's complaints? Could a kibitzer kid a kidder? But it didn't mean anything, he thought. Not the jokes, not the grief. It didn't mean anything. They were like birds making noises in a tree. But try to catch them in a deal. They'd murder you. Every day they came to eat their lunch and make their noises. Like cowboys on television hanging up their gun belts to go to a dance.

But even so, he thought, they were the way they pretended to be. Nothing made any difference to them. Did they lose sons? Not even the money they made made any difference to them finally, Greenspahn thought.

"So I was telling you," Margolis said, "the guy from the Chamber of Commerce came around again today."

"He came to me too," Paul Gold said.

"Did you give?" Margolis asked.

"No, of course not," he said.

"Did he hit you yet, Jake? Throw him out. He wants contributions for decorations. Listen, those guys are on the take from the paper flower people. It's fantastic what they get for organizing the big stores downtown. My cousin on State Street told me about it. I told him, I said, 'Who needs the Chamber of Commerce? Who needs Easter baskets and colored eggs hanging from the lamppost?'"

"Not when the ring trick still works, right, Margolis?" Joe Fisher said.

Margolis looked at his lapel and shrugged lightly. It was the most modest gesture Greenspahn had ever seen him make. The men laughed. The ring trick was Margolis' invention. "A business promotion," he had told Greenspahn. "Better than Green Stamps." He had seen him work it. Margolis would stand at the front of his store and signal to some guy who stopped for a minute to look at the TVs in his window. He would rap on the glass with his ring to catch his attention. He would smile and say something to him, anything. It didn't make any difference, the guy in the street couldn't hear him. When Greenspahn had watched him he had turned to him and winked slyly as if to say, "Watch this. Watch how I get this guy." Then he had looked back at the customer outside and still smiling broadly had said, "Hello, Schmuck. Come on in and I'll sell you something. That's right, Jerk, press your greasy nose against the glass to see who's talking to you. Shade your eyes. That-a-jerk. Come on in and I'll sell you something." Always the guy outside would come into the store to find out what Margolis had been saying to him. "Hello there, sir," Margolis would say, grinning. "I was trying to tell you that the model you were looking at out there is worthless. Way overpriced. If the boss knew I was talking to you like this I'd be canned, but what the hell? We're all working people. Come on back here and look at a real set."

Margolis was right. Who needed the Chamber of Commerce? Not the kibitzers and criers. Not even the Gold boys. Criers. Greenspahn saw the other one at another table. Twins, but they didn't even look like brothers. Not even they needed the paper flowers hanging from the lamppost. Paul Gold shouting to his brother in the back, "Mr. Gold, please show this gentleman something stylish." And they'd go into the act, putting on a thick Yiddish accent for some white-haired old man with a lodge button in his lapel, giving him the business. Greenspahn could almost hear the old man telling the others at the Knights of

Columbus Hall, "I picked this suit up from a couple of Yids on 53rd, real greenhorns. But you've got to hand it to them. Those people really know material."

Business was a kind of game with them, Greenspahn thought. Not even the money made any difference.

"Did I tell you about these two kids who came in to look at rings?" Joe Fisher said. "Sure," he went on, "two kids. Dressed up. The boy's a regular *mensch*. I figure they've been downtown at Peacocks and Fields. I think I recognized the girl from the neighborhood. I say to her boy friend — a nice kid, a college kid, you know, he looks like he ain't been *bar mitzfah'd* yet — 'I got a ring here I won't show you the price. Will you give me your check for three hundred dollars right now? No appraisal? No bringing it to Papa on approval? No nothing?'

"'I'd have to see the ring,' he tells me.

"Get this. I put my finger over the tag on a ring *I* paid eleven hundred for. *A big ring.* You got to wear smoked glasses just to look at it. Paul, I mean it, this is some ring. I'll give you a price for your wife's anniversary. No kidding, this is some ring. Think seriously about it. We could make it up into a beautiful cocktail ring. Anyway, this kid stares like a big dummy, I think he's turned to stone. He's scared. He figures something's wrong a big ring like that for only three hundred bucks. His girl friend is getting edgy, she thinks the kid's going to make a mistake, and she starts shaking her head. Finally he says to me, listen to this, he says, 'I wasn't looking for anything that large. Anyway, it's not a blue stone.' Can you imagine? Don't tell me about shoppers. I get prizes."

"What would you have done if he said he wanted the ring?" Traub asked.

"What are you crazy? He was strictly from wholesale. It was like he had a sign on his suit. Don't you think I can tell a guy who's trying to get a price idea from a real customer?"

"Say, Jake," Margolis said, "ain't that your cashier over there with your butcher?"

Greenspahn looked around. It was Shirley and Howard. He hadn't seen them when he came in. They were sitting across the table from each other — evidently they had not seen him either — and Shirley was leaning forward, her chin on her palms, which she had made into a cup to hold it. She looked, sitting there, like a young girl. It annoyed him. It was ridiculous. He knew they met each other. What did he care? It wasn't his business. But for them to let themselves be seen. He thought of Shirley's brassière hanging in his toilet. It was reckless. They were reckless people. All of them. Howard and Shirley and the men in the restaurant. Reckless people.

"They're pretty thick with each other, ain't they?" Margolis said.

"How should I know?" Greenspahn said.

"What do you run over there at that place of yours, a lonely hearts club?"

"It's not my business. They do their work."

"Some work," Paul Gold said.

"I'd like a job like that," Joe Fisher said.

"Ain't he married?" Paul Gold said.

"I'm not a policeman," Greenspahn said.

"Jake's jealous because he's not getting any," Joe Fisher said.

"Loudmouth," Greenspahn said, "I'm a man in mourning."

The others at the table were silent. "Joe was kidding," Traub, the crier, said.

"Sure, Jake," Joe Fisher said.

"O.K.," Greenspahn said. "O.K."

For the rest of the lunch Greenspahn was conscious of Shirley and Howard. He hoped they would not see him, or if they did that they would make no sign to him. He stopped listening to the stories the men told. He chewed on his hamburger wordlessly. He heard someone mention George Stein and he looked up for a moment. Stein had a grocery in a neighborhood that was changing. He had said that he wanted to get out. He was looking for a setup like Greenspahn's. He could speak to him. Sure, he thought. Why not? What did he need the aggravation? What did he need it? He owned the building the store was in. He could live on the rents. Even Joe Fisher was a tenant of his. He could speak to Stein, he thought, feeling he had made up his mind about something. He waited until Howard and Shirley had finished their lunch and then he left. He went back to his store.

In the afternoon Greenspahn thought he might be able to move his bowels. He went into the toilet off the small room at the back of the store. He sat, looking up at the high ceiling. In the smoky darkness above his head he could just make out the small, square steel ceiling plates. They seemed pitted, soiled, like patches of war-ruined armor. Agh, he thought, the place is a pigpen. The sink bowl was stained darkly, the enamel chipped, long fissures radiating like lines on the map of some wasted country, some evacuated capital. The single faucet dripped steadily. Greenspahn thought sadly of his water bill. On the knob of the faucet he saw again a faded blue *S*. *S* he thought, what the hell does *S* stand for? *H* hot, *C* cold. What the hell kind of faucet is *S?* Old clothes hung on a hook on the back of the door. A man's blue wash pants hung inside out, the zipper split like a peeled banana, the crowded concourse of seams at the crotch like carelessly sewn patches.

He heard Howard in the store, his voice raised exaggeratedly. He strained to listen.

"FORTY-FIVE," he heard Howard say. "FORTY-FIVE, POP." He was talking to the old man. Deaf, he came in each afternoon for a piece of liver for his supper. "I CAN'T GIVE YOU TWO OUNCES. I TOLD YOU. I CAN'T BREAK THE SET." He heard a woman laugh. Shirley? Was Shirley back there with him? What the hell, he thought. It was one thing for them to screw around with each other at lunch. They didn't have to bring it into the store. "TAKE EIGHT OUNCES. INVITE SOMEONE OVER FOR DINNER. TAKE EIGHT OUNCES. YOU'LL HAVE FOR FOUR DAYS. YOU WON'T HAVE TO COME BACK." He was a wise guy, that Howard. What did he want to do, drive the old man crazy? What could you do? The old man liked a small slice of liver. He thought it kept him alive.

He heard footsteps coming toward the back room and voices raised in argument.

"I'm sorry," a woman said. "I don't know how it got there. Honest. Look, I'll pay. I'll pay you for it."

"You bet, lady," Frank's voice said.

"What do you want me to do?" the woman pleaded.

"I'm calling the cops," Frank said.

"For a lousy can of salmon?"

"It's the principle. You're a crook. You're a lousy thief, you know that? I'm calling the cops. We'll see what jail does for you."

"Please," the woman said. "Mister, please. This whole thing is crazy. I never did anything like this before. I haven't got any excuses, but please, please give me a chance." The woman was crying.

"No chances," Frank said. "I'm calling the cops. You ought to be ashamed, lady. A woman dressed nice like you are. What are you, sick or something? I'm calling the cops." He heard Frank lift the receiver.

"Please, please," the woman sobbed. "My husband will kill me. I have a little kid, for Christ's sake."

Frank replaced the phone.

"Ten bucks," he said quietly.

"What's that?"

"Ten bucks and you don't come in here no more."

"I haven't got it," she said.

"All right, lady. The hell with you. I'm calling the cops."

"You bastard," she said.

"Watch your mouth," he said. "Ten bucks."

"I'll write you a check."

"Cash," Frank said.

"O.K. O.K.," she said. "Here."

"Now get out of here, lady." Greenspahn heard the woman's footsteps going away. Frank would be fumbling now with his apron, trying to get the big wallet out of his front pocket. Greenspahn flushed the toilet and waited.

"Jake?" Frank asked, frightened.

"Who was she?"

"Jake, I never saw her before, honest. Just a tramp. She gave me ten bucks. She was just a tramp, Jake."

"I told you before. I don't want trouble," Greenspahn said angrily. He came out of the toilet. "What is this, a game with you?"

"Look, I caught her with the salmon. Would you want me to call the cops for a can of salmon? She's got a kid."

"Yeah, you got a big heart, Frank."

"I would have let you handle it if I'd seen you. I looked for you, Jake."

"You shook her down. I told you before about that."

"Jake, it's ten bucks for the store. I get so damned mad when somebody like that tries to get away with something."

"*Podler*," Greenspahn shouted. "You're through here."

"Jake," Frank said. "She was a tramp." He held the can of salmon in his hand and offered it to Greenspahn as though it were evidence.

Greenspahn pushed his hand aside. "Get out of my store. I don't need you. Get out. I don't want a crook in here."

"Who are you calling names, Jake?"

Greenspahn felt his rage, immense, final. It was on him at once, like an animal that had leaped upon him in the dark. His body shook with it. Frightened, he warned himself uselessly that he must be calm. A *podler* like that, he thought. He wanted to hit him in the face.

"Please, Frank. Get out of here," Greenspahn said.

"Sure," Frank screamed. "Sure, sure," he shouted. Greenspahn, startled, looked at him. He seemed angrier than even himself. Greenspahn thought of the customers. They would hear him. What kind of a place, he thought. What kind of a place? "Sure," Frank yelled, "fire me, go ahead. A regular holy man. A saint! What are you, God? He smells everybody's rottenness but his own. Only when your own son — may he rest — when your own son slips five bucks out of the cash drawer, that you don't see."

Greenspahn could have killed him. "Who says that?"

Frank caught his breath.

"Who says that?" Greenspahn repeated.

"Nothing, Jake. It was nothing. He was going on a date probably. That's all. It didn't mean nothing."

"Who calls him a thief?"

"Nobody. I'm sorry."

"My dead son? You call my dead son a thief?"

"Nobody called anybody a thief. I didn't know what I was saying."

"In the ground. Twenty-three years old and in the ground. Not even a wife, not even a business. Nothing. He had nothing. He wouldn't take. Harold wouldn't take. Don't call him what you are. He should be alive today. You should be dead. You should be in the ground where he is. *Podler. Mumser,*" he shouted. "I saw the lousy receipts, liar," Greenspahn screamed. In a minute Howard was beside him. He had his arm around Greenspahn.

"Calm down, Jake. Come on now, take it easy. What happened back here?" he asked Frank.

Frank shrugged.

"Get him away," Greenspahn pleaded. Howard signaled Frank to get out and led Greenspahn to a chair near the table he used as a desk.

"You all right now, Jake? You O.K. now?"

Greenspahn was sobbing heavily. In a few moments he looked up. "All right," he said. "The customers. Howard, please. The customers."

"O.K., Jake. Just stay back here and wait till you feel better."

Greenspahn nodded. When Howard left him he sat for a few minutes and then went back into the toilet to wash his face. He turned the tap and watched the dirty basin fill with water. It's not even cold, he thought sadly. He plunged his hands into the sink and scooped up warm water which he rubbed into his eyes. He took a handkerchief from his back pocket and unfolding it, patted his face carefully. He was conscious of laughter outside the door. It seemed old, brittle. For a moment he thought of the woman with the coffee. Then he remembered. The porter, he thought. He called his name. "Harold?" He heard footsteps coming up to the door.

"That's right, Mr. Greenspahn," the voice said, still laughing.

Greenspahn opened the door. His porter stood before him in torn clothes. His eyes, red, wet, looked as though they were bleeding. "You sure told that Frank," he said.

"You're late," Greenspahn said. "What do you mean coming in so late?"

"I been to Harold's grave," he said.

"What's that?"

"I been to Mr. Harold's grave," he repeated. "I didn't get to the funeral. I been to his grave cause of my dream."

"Put the stock away," Greenspahn said. "Some more came in this afternoon."

"I will," he said. "I surely will." He was an old man. He had no teeth and his gums lay smooth and very pink in his mouth. He was thin. His clothes hung on him, the sleeves of the jacket rounded, puffed from absent flesh. Through the rents in shirt and trouser Greenspahn could see the grayish skin, hairless, creased, the texture like the pit of a peach. Yet he had a strength Greenspahn could only wonder at and could still lift more stock than Howard or Frank or even Greenspahn himself.

"You'd better start now," Greenspahn said uncomfortably.

Greenspahn stepped to the screen door that opened on the alley.

"I tell you about my dream, Mr. Greenspahn?"

"No dreams. Don't tell me your dreams."

"It was about Mr. Harold. Yes, sir. about him. Your boy that's dead, Mr. Greenspahn."

"I don't want to hear. See if Howard needs anything up front."

"I dreamed it twice. That means it's true. You don't count on a dream less you dream it twice."

"Get away with your crazy stories. I don't pay you to dream."

"That time on Halsted I dreamed the fire. I dreamed that twice."

"Yeah," Greenspahn said, "the fire. Yeah."

"I dreamed that dream twice. Them police wanted to question me. Same names, Mr. Greenspahn, me and your boy we got the same names."

"Yeah. I named him after you."

"I tell you that dream, Mr. Greenspahn? It was a mistake. Frank was supposed to die. Just like you said. Just like I heard you say it just now. And he will. Mr. Harold told me in the dream. Frank, he's going to sicken and die his own self." The porter looked at Greenspahn, the red eyes filling with blood. "If you want it," he said. "That's what I dreamed, and I dreamed about the fire on Halsted the same way. Twice."

"You're crazy. Get away from me."

"That's a true dream. It happened just that very way."

"Get away. Get away," Greenspahn shouted.

"My name's Harold, too."

"You're crazy. Crazy."

The porter went off. He was laughing. What kind of a madhouse? Were they all doing it on purpose? Everything to aggravate him? For a moment he had the impression that that was what it was. A big joke, and everybody was in on it but himself. He was being *kibitzed* to death. Everything. The cop. The receipts. His cheese man. Howard and Shirley. The men in the restaurant. Frank and the woman. The *shvartze*. Everything. He wouldn't let it happen. What was he, crazy or something? He reached into his pocket for his handkerchief but pulled out a piece of paper. It was the order Harold had taken down over the phone and left on the pad. Absently he unfolded it and read it again. Something occurred to him. As soon as he had the idea he knew it was true. The order had never been delivered. His son had forgotten about it. It couldn't be anything else. Otherwise would it have still been on the message pad? Sure, he thought, what else could it be? Even his son. What did he care? What the hell did he care about the business? Greenspahn was ashamed. It was a terrible thought to have about a dead boy. Oh God, he thought. Let him rest. He was a boy, he thought. Twenty-three years old and he was only a boy. No wife. No business. Nothing. Was the five dollars so important? In helpless disgust he could see Harold's sly wink to Frank as he slipped the money out of the register. Five dollars, Harold, *Five dollars*, he thought, as though he were admonishing him. "Why didn't you come to me, Harold?" he sobbed. "Why didn't you come to your father?"

He blew his nose. It's crazy, he thought. Nothing pleases me. Frank called him God. Some God, he thought. I sit weeping in the back of my store. The hell with it. The hell with everything. Clear the shelves, that's what he had to do. Sell the groceries. Get rid of the meats. Watch the money pile up. Sell, sell, he thought. That would be something. Sell everything. He thought of the items listed on the order his son had taken down. Were they delivered? He felt restless. He hoped they were delivered. If they weren't they would have to be sold again. He was very weary. Very tired. He went to the front of the store.

It was almost closing time. Another half hour. He couldn't stay to close up. He had to be in *shul* before sundown. He had to get to the *minion*. They would have to close up for him. For a year. If he couldn't sell the store, for a year he wouldn't be in his own store at sundown. He would have to trust them to close up for him. Trust who? he thought. My Romeo, Howard? Shirley? The crazy *shvartze*? Only Frank could do it. How could he have fired him? He looked for him in the store. He was talking to Shirley at the register. He would go up and talk to him. What difference did it make? He would have had to fire all of them. Eventually he would have to fire everybody who ever came to work for him. He would have to throw out his tenants, even the old ones, and finally whoever rented the store from him. He would have to keep on firing and throwing out as long as anybody was left. What difference would one more make?

"Frank," he said. "I want you to forget what we talked about before."

Frank looked at him suspiciously. "It's all right," Greenspahn reassured him. He led him by the elbow away from Shirley. "Listen," he said, "we were both excited before. I didn't mean it what I said."

Frank continued to look at him. "Sure, Jake," he said finally. "No hard feelings." He extended his hand.

Greenspahn took it reluctantly. "Yeah," he said.

"Frank," he said, "do me a favor and close up the place for me. I got to get to the *shul* for the *minion*."

"I got you, Jake," he said.

Greenspahn went to the back to change his clothes. He washed his face and hands and combed his hair. Carefully he removed his working clothes and put on the suit jacket, shirt and tie he had worn in the morning. He walked back into the store.

He was about to leave when he saw that Mrs. Frimkin had come into the store again. That's all right, he told himself, she can be a good customer. He needed some of the old customers now. They could drive you crazy but when they bought, they bought. He watched as she took a cart from the front and pushed it through the aisles. She put things in the cart as though she were in a hurry. She barely glanced at the prices. That was the way to shop, he thought. It was a pleasure to watch her. She reached into the frozen food locker and took out about a half-dozen packages. From the towers of canned goods on his shelves she seemed to take down only the largest cans. In minutes her shopping cart was overflowing. That's some order, Greenspahn thought. Then he watched as she went to the stacks of bread at the bread counter. She picked up a packaged white bread and first looking around to see if anyone were watching her, bent down quickly over the bread, cradling it to her chest as though it were a football. As she stood Greenspahn saw her brush crumbs from her dress. He saw her put the torn package into her cart with the rest of her purchases.

She came up to the counter where Greenspahn stood and unloaded the cart, pushing the groceries toward Shirley to be checked out. The last item she put on the counter was the wounded bread. Shirley punched the keys quickly. As she reached for the bread, Mrs. Frimkin put out her hand to stop her. "Look," she said, "what are you going to charge me for the bread? It's damaged. Can I have it for ten cents?"

Shirley turned to look at Greenspahn.

"Out," he said. "Get out, you *podler*. I don't want you coming in here any more. You're a thief," he shouted. "A thief." Frank came rushing up.

"Jake, what is it? What is it?"

"Her. That one. A crook. She tore the bread. I seen her."

The woman looked at him defiantly. "I don't have to take that," she said. "I can make plenty of trouble for you. You're a crazy man. I'm not going to be insulted by somebody like you."

"Get out of here," Greenspahn shouted, "before I have you locked up."

The woman backed away from him and when he stepped forward she turned and fled.

"Jake," Frank said, putting his hand on Greenspahn's shoulder. "That was a big order. So she tried to get away with a few pennies. What does it mean? You want me to find her and apologize?"

"Look," Greenspahn said, "she comes in again I want to know about it. I don't care what I'm doing. I want to know about it. She's going to pay me for that bread."

"Jake," Frank said.

"No," he said. "I mean it."

"Jake, it's ten cents."

"*My* ten cents. No more," he said. "I'm going to *shul*."

He waved Frank away and went into the street. Already the sun was going down. He felt urgency. He had to get there before the sun went down.

That night Greenspahn had the dream for the first time.

He was in the synagogue waiting to say the prayers for his son. Around him were the old men, the *minion*, their faces brittle and pale.

He recognized them from his youth. They had been old even then. One man stood by the window and watched the sun. At a signal from him the others would begin. There was always some place in the world where the prayers were being said, he thought, some place where the sun had just come up or just gone down, and he supposed there was always a *minion* to watch it and to mark its progress, the prayers following God's bright bird, going up in sunlight or in darkness, always, everywhere. He knew the men never left the *shul*. It was the way they kept from dying. They didn't even eat, but there was about the room the foul lemony smell of urine. Sure, Greenspahn thought in the dream, stay in the *shul*. That's right. Give the *podlers* a wide berth. All they have to worry about is God. Some worry, Greenspahn thought. The man at the window gave the signal and they all started to mourn for Greenspahn's son, their ancient voices betraying the queer melody of the prayers. The rabbi looked at Greenspahn and Greenspahn, imitating the old men, began to rock back and forth on his heels. He tried to sway faster than they did. I'm younger, he thought. When he was swaying so quickly that he thought he would be sick were he to go any faster, the rabbi smiled at him approvingly. The man at the window shouted that the sun was approaching the danger point in the sky and that Greenspahn had better begin as soon as he was ready.

He looked at the strange thick letters in the prayer book. "Go ahead," the rabbi said, "think of Harold and tell God."

He tried then to think of his son, but he could recall him only as he was when he was a baby standing in his crib. It was unreal, like a photograph. The others knew what he was thinking and frowned. "Go ahead," the rabbi said.

Then he saw him as a boy on a bicycle, as once he had seen him at dusk as he looked from his apartment onto the street, riding the gray sidewalks, slapping his buttocks as though he were on a horse. The others were not satisfied.

He tried to imagine him older but nothing came of it. The rabbi said, "Please, Greenspahn, the sun is almost down. You're wasting time. Faster. Faster."

All right, Greenspahn thought. All right. Only let me think. The others stopped their chanting.

Desperately he thought of the store. He thought of the woman with the coffee, incredibly old, older than the old men who prayed with him, her wig, fatuously red, the head beneath it shaking crazily as though even the weight and painted fire of the thick, bright hair were not enough to warm it.

The rabbi grinned.

He thought of the *shvartze,* imagining him on an old cot, on a damp and sheetless mattress, twisting in a fearful dream. He saw him bent under a huge side of red, raw meat he carried to Howard.

The others were still grinning but the rabbi was beginning to look a little bored. He thought of Howard, seeming to watch him through the *shvartze*'s own red, mad eyes, as Howard chopped at the fresh flesh with his butcher's axe.

He saw the men in the restaurant. The criers, ignorant of hope, the *kibitzers,* ignorant of despair. Each with his pitiful piece broken from the whole of life, confidently extending only half of what there was to give.

He saw the cheats with their ten dollars, and their stolen nickels, and their luncheon lusts, and their torn breads.

All right, Greenspahn thought. He saw Shirley naked but for her brassière. It was evening and the store was closed. She lay with Howard on the butcher's block.

"The boy," the rabbi said impatiently, *"the boy."*

He concentrated for a long moment while all of them stood by silently. Gradually, with difficulty, he began to make something out. It was Harold's face in the coffin, his expression at the very moment of death itself, before the undertakers had had time to tamper with it. He saw it clearly. It was soft, puffy with grief; a sneer curled the lips. It was Harold, twenty-three years old, wifeless, jobless, sacrificing nothing even in the act of death, leaving the world with his life not started.

The rabbi smiled at Greenspahn and turned away as though he now had other business.

"No," Greenspahn called, "wait. Wait."

The rabbi turned and with the others looked at him.

He saw it now. They all saw it. The helpless face, the sly wink, the embarrassed, slow smug smile of guilt that must, volitionless as the palpitation of a nerve, have crossed his face when he had turned, his hand in the register, to see Frank watching him.

1964

*Bernard Malamud*

......................................................................................................

# The German Refugee

FROM *The Saturday Evening Post*

OSKAR GASSNER sits in his cotton-mesh undershirt and summer bath-robe at the window of his stuffy, hot, dark hotel room on West Tenth Street while I cautiously knock. Outside, across the sky, a late-June green twilight fades in darkness. The refugee fumbles for the light and stares at me, hiding despair but not pain.

I was in those days a poor student and would brashly attempt to teach anybody anything for a buck an hour, although I have since learned better. Mostly I gave English lessons to recently arrived refugees. The college sent me; I had acquired a little experience. Already a few of my students were trying their broken English, theirs and mine, in the American marketplace. I was then just twenty, on my way into my senior year in college, a skinny, life-hungry kid, eating himself waiting for the next world war to start. It was a goddamn cheat. Here I was palpitating to get going, and across the ocean Adolf Hitler, in black boots and a square mustache, was tearing up all the flowers. Will I ever forget what went on with Danzig that summer?

Times were still hard from the depression but anyway I made a little living from the poor refugees. They were all over uptown Broadway in 1939. I had four I tutored — Karl Otto Alp, the former film star; Wolfgang Novak, once a brilliant economist; Friedrich Wilhelm Wolff, who had taught medieval history at Heidelberg; and, after that night I met him in his disordered cheap hotel room, Oskar Gassner, the Berlin critic and journalist, at one time on the *Acht Uhr Abendblatt*. They were accomplished men. I had my nerve associating with them, but that's what a world crisis does for people — they get educated.

Oskar was maybe fifty, his thick hair turning gray. He had a big face and heavy hands. His shoulders sagged. His eyes, too, were heavy, a clouded blue; and as he stared at me after I had identified myself, doubt spread in them like underwater currents. It was as if, on seeing me, he had again been defeated. I stayed at the door in silence. In such cases I would rather be elsewhere, but I had to make a living. Finally he opened the door and I entered. Rather he released it and I was in. *"Bitte . . ."* He offered me a seat and didn't know where to sit himself. He would attempt to say something and then stop, as though it could not possibly be said. The room was cluttered with clothing, boxes of books he had managed to get out of Germany and some paintings. Oskar sat on a box and attempted to fan himself with his meaty hand. "Zis heat," he muttered, forcing his mind to the deed. "Impozzible. I do not know such heat." It was bad enough for me but terrible for him. He had difficulty breathing. He tried again to speak, lifted a hand and let it drop like a dead duck. He breathed as though he were fighting a battle; and maybe he won because after ten minutes we sat and slowly talked.

Like most educated Germans Oskar had at one time studied English. Although he was certain he couldn't say a word, he managed sometimes to put together a fairly decent, if rather comical, English sentence. He misplaced consonants, mixed up nouns and verbs and mangled idioms, yet we were able at once to communicate. We conversed mostly in English, with an occasional assist by me in pidgin-German or Yiddish, what he called "Jiddish." He had been to America before — last year for a short visit. He had come a month before *Kristallnacht,* when the Nazis shattered the Jewish store windows and burned all the synagogues, to see if he could find a job for himself; he had no relatives in America, and getting a job would permit him quickly to enter the country. He had been promised something, not in journalism but with the help of a foundation, as a lecturer. Then he had returned to Berlin, and after a frightening delay of six months was permitted to emigrate. He had sold whatever he could, managed to get some paintings, gifts of Bauhaus friends, and some boxes of books out by bribing two Nazi border guards; he had said goodbye to his wife and left the accursed country. He gazed at me with cloudy eyes. "We parted amicably," he said in German. "My wife was gentile. Her mother was an appalling anti-Semite. They returned to live in Stettin." I asked no questions. Gentile is gentile, Germany is Germany.

His new job was in the Institute for Public Studies here in New York. He was to give a lecture a week in the fall term, and during next spring, a course, in English translation, on "The Literature of the Weimar Republic." He had never taught before and was afraid to. He was in that way to be introduced to the public, but the thought of giving the lecture in English just about paralyzed him. He didn't see how he could do it. "How is it pozzible? I cannot say two words. I cannot pronounziate. I will make a fool of myself." His melancholy deepened. Already in the two months since his arrival, and after a round of diminishingly expensive hotel rooms, he had had two English tutors, and I was the third. The others had given him up, he said, because his progress was so poor, and he thought also that he depressed them. He asked me whether I felt I could do something for him, or should he go to a speech specialist — someone, say, who charged five dollars an hour — and beg his assistance? "You could try him," I said, "and then come back to me." In those days I figured what I knew, I knew. At that he managed a smile. Still I wanted him to make up his mind, or it would be no confidence down the line. He said, after a while, that he would stay with me. If he went to the five-dollar professor it might help his tongue but not his stomach. He would have no money left to eat with. The institute had paid him in advance for the summer, but it was only three hundred dollars and all he had.

He looked at me dully. *"Ich weiss nicht wie ich weiter machen soll."*

I figured it was time to move past the first step. Either we did that quickly or it would be like drilling rock for a long time. "Let's stand at the mirror," I said.

He rose with a sigh and stood there beside me: I thin, elongated, redheaded, praying for success, his and mine; Oskar uneasy, fearful, finding it hard to face either of us in the faded round glass above his dresser.

"Please," I said to him, "could you say 'right'?"

"Ghight," he gargled.

"No. 'Right.' You put your tongue here." I showed him where. As he tensely watched the mirror, I tensely watched him. "The tip of it curls behind the ridge on top, like this."

He placed his tongue where I showed him.

"Please," I said, "now say 'right.'"

Oskar's tongue fluttered, "Rright."

"That's good. Now say 'treasure' — that's harder."

"Tgheasure."

"The tongue goes up in front, not in the back of the mouth. Look."

He tried, his brow wet, eyes straining. "Trreasure."

"That's it."

"A miracle," Oskar murmured.

I said if he had done that he could do the rest.

We went for a bus ride up Fifth Avenue and then walked for a while around Central Park Lake. He had put on his German hat, with its hatband bow at the back, a broad-lapeled wool suit, a necktie twice as wide as the one I was wearing, and walked with a small-footed waddle. The night wasn't bad; it had got a bit cooler. There were a few large stars in the sky and they made me sad.

"Do you sink I will succezz?"

"Why not?" I asked.

Later he bought me a bottle of beer.

To many of these people, articulate as they were, the great loss was the loss of language — that they could no longer say what was in them to say. They could, of course, manage to communicate, but just to communicate was frustrating. As Karl Otto Alp, the ex-film star who became a buyer for Macy's, put it years later, "I felt like a child, or worse, often like a moron. I am left with myself unexpressed. What I knew, indeed, what I am, becomes to me a burden. My tongue hangs useless." The same with Oskar it figures. There was a terrible sense of useless tongue, and I think the reason for his trouble with his other tutors was that to keep from drowning in things unsaid he wanted to swallow the ocean in a gulp: Today he would learn English and tomorrow wow them with an impeccable Fourth of July speech, followed by a successful lecture at the Institute for Public Studies.

We performed our lessons slowly, step by step, everything in its place. After Oskar moved to a two-room apartment in a house on West Eighty-fifth Street, near the Drive, we met three times a week at four-thirty, worked an hour and a half; then, since it was too hot to cook, had supper at the Seventy-second Street automat and conversed on my time. The lessons we divided into three parts: diction exercises and reading aloud, then grammar, because Oskar felt the necessity of it, and composition correction; with conversation, as I said, thrown in at supper. So far as I could see, he was coming along. None of these exercises was giving him as much trouble as they apparently had in the past. He seemed to be learning and his mood lightened. There were moments of elation as he heard this accent flying off. For instance, when "sink" became "think." He stopped calling himself "hopelezz."

Neither of us said much about the lecture he had to give early in October, and I kept my fingers crossed. It was somehow to come out of what we were doing daily, I think I felt, but exactly *how*, I had no idea; and to tell the truth, although I didn't say so to Oskar, the lecture frightened me. That and the ten more to follow during the fall term. Later when I learned that he had been attempting, with the help of the dictionary, to write in English, and had produced "a complete disahster," I suggested maybe he ought to stick to German and we could afterward both try to put it into passable English. I was cheating when I said that, because my German is meager. Anyway the idea was to get Oskar into production and worry about translating later. He sweated, from enervating morning to exhausted night, but no matter what language he tried, though he had been a professional writer for most of his life and knew his subject cold, the lecture refused to move past page one.

It was a sticky, hot July and the heat didn't help at all.

I had met Oskar at the end of June, and by the seventeenth of July we were no longer doing lessons. They had foundered on the "impozzible" lecture. He had worked on it each day in frenzy and growing despair. After writing more than a hundred opening pages, he furiously flung his pen against the wall, shouting he could no longer write in that filthy tongue. He cursed the German language. He hated the damned country and the damned people. After that, what was bad became worse. When he gave up attempting to write the lecture, he stopped making progress in English. He seemed to forget what he already knew. His tongue thickened and the accent returned in all its fruitiness. The little he had to say was in handcuffed and tortured English. The only German I heard him speak was in a whisper to himself. I doubt he knew he was talking it. That ended our formal work together, though I did drop in every other day or so to sit with him. For hours he sat motionless in a large green velours armchair, hot enough to broil in, and through the tall windows stared at the colorless sky above Eighty-fifth Street, with a wet depressed eye.

Then once he said to me, "If I do not this legture prepare, I will take my life."

"Let's begin again, Oskar," I said. "You dictate and I'll write. The ideas count, not the spelling."

He didn't answer so I stopped talking.

He had plunged into an involved melancholy. We sat for hours, often in profound silence. This was alarming to me, though I had already had some experience with such depression. Wolfgang Novak, the economist, though English came more easily to him, was another. His problems arose mainly, I think, from physical illness. And he felt a greater sense of the lost country than Oskar. Sometimes in the early evening I persuaded Oskar to come with me for a short walk on the Drive. The tail end of sunsets over the Palisades seemed to appeal to him. At least he looked. He would put on full regalia — hat, suit coat, tie, no matter how hot — and we went slowly down the stairs, I wondering whether he would ever make it to the bottom. He seemed to me always suspended between two floors.

We walked slowly uptown, stopping to sit on a bench and watch night rise above the Hudson. When we returned to his room, if I sensed he had loosened up a bit, we listened to music on the radio; but if I tried to sneak in a news broadcast, he said to me, "Please I can not more stand of world misery." I shut off the radio. He was right, it was a time of no good news. I squeezed my brain. What could I tell him? Was it good news to be alive? Who could argue the point? Sometimes I read aloud to him — I remember he liked the first part of *Life on the Mississippi.* We still went to the Automat once or twice a week; he perhaps out of habit, because he didn't feel like going anywhere, and I to get him out of his room. Oskar ate little, he toyed with a spoon. His dull eyes looked as though they had been squirted with a dark dye.

Once after a momentary cooling rainstorm we sat on newspapers on a wet bench overlooking the river, and Oskar at last began to talk. In tormented English he conveyed his intense and everlasting hatred of the Nazis for destroying his career, uprooting his life after half a century and flinging him like a piece of bleeding meat to hawks. He cursed them thickly, the German nation, as an inhuman, conscienceless, merciless people. "They are pigs mazquerading as peacogs," he said. "I feel certain that my wife, in her heart, was a Jew hater." It was a terrible bitterness, an eloquence almost without vocabulary. He became silent again. I hoped to hear more about his wife but decided not to ask.

Afterwards, in the dark Oskar confessed that he had attempted suicide during his first week in America. He was living, at the end of May, in a small hotel, and had filled himself with barbiturates one night, but his phone had fallen off the table and the hotel operator had sent up the elevator boy, who found him unconscious and called the police. He was revived in the hospital.

"I did not mean to do it," he said. "It was a mistage."

"Don't ever think of it again," I said. "It's total defeat."

"I don't," he said wearily, "because it is so arduouz to come back to life."

"Please, for any reason whatever."

Later, when we were walking, he surprised me by saying, "Maybe we ought to try now the legture onze more."

We trudged back to the house and he sat at his hot desk, I trying to read as he slowly began to reconstruct the first page of his lecture. He wrote, of course, in German.

He got nowhere. We were back to nothing, to sitting in silence in the heat. Sometimes after a few minutes I had to take off before his mood overcame mine. One afternoon I came unwillingly up the stairs — there were times I felt momentary surges of irritation with him — and was frightened to find Oskar's door ajar. When I knocked, no one answered. As I stood there, chilled down the spine, I realized I was thinking about the possibility of his attempting suicide again. "Oskar?" I went into the apartment, looked into both rooms and the bathroom, but he wasn't there. I thought he might have drifted out to get something from a store, and took the opportunity to look quickly around. There was nothing startling in the medicine chest, no pills but aspirin, no iodine. Thinking, for some reason, of a gun, I searched his desk drawer. In it I found a thin-paper airmail letter from Germany. Even if I had wanted to, I couldn't have read the handwriting, but as I held the thin paper in my hand I did make out one sentence: *"Ich bin dir siebenundzwanzig Jahre treu gewesen."* Twenty-seven years is a long time, I thought. There was no gun in the drawer. I shut it and stopped looking. It had occurred to me that if you want to kill yourself, all you need is a straight pin. When Oskar returned he said he had been sitting in the public library, unable to read.

Now we are once more enacting the changeless scene, curtain rising on two speechless characters in a furnished apartment, I in a straight-back chair, Oskar in the velours armchair that smothered rather than supported him, his flesh gray, the big gray face, unfocused, sagging. I reached over to switch on the radio, but he looked at me in a way that begged no. I then got up to leave, but Oskar, clearing his throat, thickly asked me to stay. I stayed, thinking, was there more to this than I could see into? His problems, God knows, were real enough, but could there be something more than a refugee's displacement, alienation, financial insecurity, being in a strange land without friends or a speak-able tongue? My speculation was the old one: Not all drown in this ocean, why does he? After a while I shaped the thought and asked him was there something below the surface, invisible? I was full of this thing from college, and wondered if there mightn't be some unknown quantity in his depression that a psychiatrist maybe might help him with, enough to get him started on his lecture.

He meditated on this, and after a few minutes haltingly said he had been psychoanalyzed in Vienna as a young man. "Just the jusual *drek*," he said, "fears and fantazies that afterwaards no longer bothered me."

"They don't now?"

"Not."

"You've written many articles and lectures before," I said. "What I can't understand, though I know how hard the situation is, is why you can never get past page one."

He half lifted his hand. "It is a paralyzis of my will. The whole legture is clear in my mind, but the minute I write down a single word — or in English or in German — I have a terrible fear I will not be able to write the negst. As though someone has thrown a stone at a window and the whole house — the whole idea — zmashes. This repeats until I am dezperate."

He said the fear grew as he worked that he would die before he completed the lecture, or if not that, that he would write it so disgracefully he would wish for death. The fear immobilized him.

"I have lozt faith. I do not — not longer possezz my former value of myself. In my life there has been too much illusion."

I tried to believe what I was saying: "Have confidence, the feeling will pass."

"Confidenze I have not. For this, and alzo whatever elze I have lozt, I thank the Nazis."

It was by then mid-August and things were growing steadily worse wherever one looked. The Poles were mobilizing for war. Oskar hardly moved. I was full of worries though I pretended calm weather.

He sat in his massive armchair with sick eyes, breathing like a wounded animal.

"Who can write about Walt Whitman in such terrible times?"

"Why don't you change the subject?"

"It mages no differenze what is the subject. It is all uzelezz."

I came every day to see him, neglecting my other students and therefore my livelihood. I had a panicky feeling that if things went on as they were going, they would end in Oskar's suicide; and I felt a frenzied desire to prevent that. What's more, I was sometimes afraid I was myself becoming melancholy, a new talent, call it, of taking less pleasure in my little pleasures. And the heat continued, oppressive, relentless. We thought of escape into the country, but neither of us had the money.

One day I bought Oskar a secondhand fan — wondering why we hadn't thought of that before — and he sat in the breeze for hours each day until after a week, shortly after the Soviet-Nazi nonaggression pact was signed, the motor gave out. He could not sleep at night and sat at his desk with a wet towel on his head, still attempting to write his lecture. He wrote reams on a treadmill; it came out nothing. When he did sleep, out of exhaustion, he had fantastic frightening dreams of the Nazis inflicting tortures on him, sometimes forcing him to look upon the corpses of those they had slain. In one dream he told me about, he had gone back to Germany to visit his wife. She wasn't home and he had been directed to a cemetery. There, though the tombstone read another name, her blood seeped out of the earth above her shallow grave. He groaned at the memory of the dream.

Afterwards, he told me something about her. They had met as students, lived together, and were married at twenty-three. It wasn't a very happy marriage. She had turned into a sickly woman, physically unable to have children. "Something was wrong with her interior strugture."

Though I asked no questions, Oskar said, "I offered her to come with me here but she refused this."

"For what reason?"

"She did not think I wished her to come."

"Did you?" I asked.

"Not," he said.

He explained he had lived with her for almost twenty-seven years under difficult circumstances. She had been ambivalent about their Jewish friends and his relatives, though outwardly she seemed not a prejudiced person. But her mother was always a violent anti-Semite.

"I have nothing to blame myself," Oskar said.

He took to his bed. I took to the New York Public Library. I read some of the German poets he was trying to write about, in English translation. Then I read *Leaves of Grass* and wrote down what I thought one or two of them had got from Whitman. One day toward the end of August I brought Oskar what I had written. It was in good part guessing, but my idea wasn't to write the lecture for him. He lay on his back, motionless, and listened utterly sadly to what I had written. Then he said, no, it wasn't the love of death they had got from Whitman — that ran through German poetry — but it was most of all his feeling for *Brudermensch*, his humanity.

"But this does not grow long on German earth," he said, "and is soon deztroyed."

I said I was sorry I had got it wrong, but he thanked me anyway.

I left defeated, and as I was going down the stairs, heard someone sobbing. I will quit this, I thought. It has gotten to be too much for me. I can't drown with him.

I stayed home the next day, tasting a new kind of private misery too old for somebody my age, but that same night Oskar called me on the phone, blessing me wildly for having read those notes to him. He had got up to write me a letter to say what I had missed, and it ended by his having written half the lecture. He had slept all day and tonight intended to finish it up.

"I thank you," he said, "for much, alzo including your faith in me."

"Thank God," I said, not telling him I had just about lost it.

Oskar completed his lecture — wrote and rewrote it — during the first week in September. The Nazis had invaded Poland, and though we were greatly troubled, there was some sense of release; maybe the brave Poles would beat them. It took another week to translate the lecture, but here we had the assistance of Friedrich Wilhelm Wolff, the historian, a gentle, erudite man, who liked translating and promised his help with future lectures. We then had about two weeks to work on Oskar's delivery. The weather had changed, and so, slowly, had he. He had awakened from defeat, battered, after a wearying battle. He had lost close to twenty pounds. His complexion was still gray; when I looked at his face I expected to see scars, but it had lost its flabby unfocused quality. His blue eyes had returned to life and he walked with quick steps, as though to pick up a few for all the steps he hadn't taken during those long, hot days he had lain torpid in his room.

We went back to our former routine, meeting three late afternoons a week for diction, grammar and the other exercises. I taught him the phonetic alphabet and transcribed long lists of words he was mispronouncing. He worked many hours trying to fit each sound into place, holding half a matchstick between his teeth to keep his jaws apart as he exercised his tongue. All this can be a dreadfully boring business unless you think you have a future. Looking at him I realized what's meant when somebody is called "another man."

The lecture, which I now knew by heart, went off well. The director of the institute had invited a number of prominent people. Oskar was the first refugee they had employed, and there was a move to make the public cognizant of what was then a new ingredient in American life. Two reporters had come with a lady photographer. The auditorium was crowded. I sat in the last row, promising to put up my hand if he couldn't be heard, but it wasn't necessary. Oskar, in a blue suit, his hair cut, was of course nervous, but you couldn't see it unless you studied him. When he stepped up to the lectern, spread out his manuscript and spoke his first English sentence in public, my heart hesitated; only he and I, of all the people there, had any idea of the anguish he had been through. His enunciation wasn't at all bad — a few *s*'s for *th*'s, and he once said "bag" for "back," but otherwise he did all right. He read poetry well — in both languages — and though Walt Whitman, in his mouth, sounded a little as though he had come to the shores of Long Island as a German immigrant, still the poetry read as poetry:

> And I know that the spirit of God is the brother of my own,
> And that all the men ever born are also my brothers, and the women
>     my sisters and lovers,
> And that a kelson of creation is love . . .

Oskar read it as though he believed it. Warsaw had fallen but the verses were somehow protective. I sat back, conscious of two things: how easy it is to hide the deepest wounds; and the pride I felt in the job I had done.

Two days later I came up the stairs into Oskar's apartment to find a crowd there. The refugee, his face beet red, lips bluish, a trace of froth in the corners of his mouth, lay on the floor in his limp pajamas, two firemen on their knees, working over him with an inhalator. The windows were open and the air stank of gas.

A policeman asked me who I was and I could only answer, "No, oh no."

I said no, but it was unchangeably yes. He had taken his life — gas — I hadn't even thought of the stove in the kitchen.

"Why?" I asked myself. "Why did he do it?" Maybe it was the fate of Poland on top of everything else, but the only answer anyone could come up with was Oskar's scribbled note that he was not well, and that he left Martin Goldberg all his possessions. I am Martin Goldberg.

I was sick for a week, had no desire either to inherit or investigate, but I thought I ought to look through his things before the court impounded them, so I spent a morning sitting in the depths of Oskar's velours armchair, trying to read his correspondence. I had found in the top drawer of his desk a thin packet of letters from his wife and an airmail letter of recent date from his anti-Semitic mother-in-law.

She writes, in a tight script it takes me hours to decipher, that her daughter, after Oskar abandons her, against her own mother's fervent pleas and anguish, is converted to Judaism by a vengeful rabbi. One night the Brown Shirts appear, and though the mother wildly waves her bronze crucifix in their faces, they drag Frau Gassner, together with the other Jews, out of the apartment house, and transport them in lorries to a small border town in conquered Poland. There, it is rumored, she is shot in the head and topples into an open tank ditch, with the naked Jewish men, their wives and children, some Polish soldiers and a handful of gypsies.

*Joyce Carol Oates*

# Where Are You Going, Where Have You Been?

FROM *Epoch*

*To Bob Dylan*

HER NAME WAS Connie. She was fifteen and she had a quick nervous giggling habit of craning her neck to glance into mirrors, or checking other people's faces to make sure her own was all right. Her mother, who noticed everything and knew everything and who hadn't much reason any longer to look at her own face, always scolded Connie about it. "Stop gawking at yourself, who are you? You think you're so pretty?" she would say. Connie would raise her eyebrows at these familiar complaints and look right through her mother, into a shadowy vision of herself as she was right at that moment: she knew she was pretty and that was everything. Her mother had been pretty once too, if you could believe those old snapshots in the album, but now her looks were gone and that was why she was always after Connie.

"Why don't you keep your room clean like your sister? How've you got your hair fixed — what the hell stinks? Hair spray? You don't see your sister using that junk."

Her sister June was twenty-four and still lived at home. She was a secretary in the high school Connie attended, and if that wasn't bad enough — with her in the same building — she was so plain and chunky and steady that Connie had to hear her praised all the time by her mother and her mother's sisters. June did this, June did that, she saved money and helped clean the house and cooked and Connie couldn't do a thing, her mind was all filled with trashy daydreams. Their father was away at work most of the time and when he came home he wanted supper and he read the newspaper at supper and after supper he went to bed. He didn't bother talking much to them, but around his bent head Connie's mother kept picking at her until Connie wished her mother were dead and she herself were dead and it were all over. "She makes me want to throw up sometimes," she complained to her friends. She had a high, breathless, amused voice which made everything she said sound a little forced, whether it was sincere or not.

There was one good thing: June went places with girlfriends of hers, girls who were just as plain and steady as she, and so when Connie wanted to do that her mother had no objections. The father of Connie's best girlfriend drove the girls the three miles to town and left them off at a shopping plaza, so that they could talk through the stores or go to a movie, and when he came to pick them up again at eleven he never bothered to ask what they had done.

They must have been familiar sights, walking around that shopping plaza in their shorts and flat ballerina slippers that always scuffed the sidewalk, with charm bracelets jingling on their thin wrists; they would lean together to whisper and laugh secretly if someone passed by who amused or interested them. Connie had long dark blond hair that drew anyone's eye to it, and she wore part of it pulled up on her head and puffed out and the rest of it she let fall down her back. She wore a pullover jersey blouse that looked one way when she was at home and another way when she was away from home. Everything about her had two sides to it, one for home and one for anywhere that was not home: her walk that could be childlike and bobbing, or languid enough to make anyone think she was hearing music in her head, her mouth which was pale and smirking most of the time, but bright and pink on these evenings out, her laugh which was cynical and drawling at home — "Ha, ha, very funny" — but high-pitched and nervous anywhere else, like the jingling of the charms on her bracelet.

Sometimes they did go shopping or to a movie, but sometimes they went across the highway, ducking fast across the busy road, to a drive-in restaurant where older kids hung out. The restaurant was shaped like a big bottle, though squatter than a real bottle, and on its cap was a revolving figure of a grinning boy who held a hamburger aloft. One night in midsummer they ran across, breathless with daring, and right away someone leaned out a car window and invited them over, but it was just a boy from high school they didn't like. It made them feel good to be able to ignore him. They went up through the maze of parked and cruising cars to the bright-lit, fly-infested restaurant, their faces pleased and expectant as if they were entering a sacred building that loomed out of the night to give them what haven and what blessing they yearned for. They sat at the counter and crossed their legs at the ankles, their thin shoulders rigid with excitement, and listened to the music that made everything so good: the music was always in the background like music at a church service, it was something to depend upon.

A boy named Eddie came in to talk with them. He sat backward on his stool, turning himself jerkily around in semicircles and then stopping and turning again, and after a while he asked Connie if she would like something to eat. She said she did and so she tapped her friend's arm on her way out — her friend pulled her face up into a brave droll look — and Connie said she would meet her at eleven, across the way. "I just hate to leave her like that," Connie said earnestly, but the boy said that she wouldn't be alone for long. So they went out to his car and on the way Connie couldn't help but let her eyes wander over the windshields and faces all around her, her face gleaming with a joy that had nothing to do with Eddie or even this place; it might have been the music. She drew her shoulders up and sucked in her breath with the pure pleasure of being alive, and just at that moment she happened to glance at a face just a few feet from hers. It was a boy with shaggy black hair, in a convertible jalopy painted gold. He stared at her and then his lips widened into a grin. Connie slit her eyes at him and turned away, but she couldn't help glancing back and there he was still watching her. He wagged a finger and laughed and said, "Gonna get you, baby," and Connie turned away again without Eddie noticing anything.

She spent three hours with him, at the restaurant where they ate hamburgers and drank Cokes in wax cups that were always sweating, and then down an alley a mile or so away, and when he left her off at five to eleven only the movie house was still open at the plaza. Her girlfriend was there, talking with a boy. When Connie came up the two girls smiled at each other and Connie said, "How was the movie?" and the girl said, "*You* should know." They rode off with the girl's father, sleepy and pleased, and Connie couldn't help but look at the darkened shopping plaza with its big empty parking lot and its signs that were faded and ghostly now, and over at the drive-in restaurant where cars were still circling tirelessly. She couldn't hear the music at this distance.

Next morning June asked her how the movie was and Connie said, "So-so."

She and that girl and occasionally another girl went out several times a week that way, and the rest of the time Connie spent around the house — it was summer vacation — getting in her mother's way and thinking, dreaming, about the boys she met. But all the boys fell back and dissolved into a single face that was not even a face, but an idea, a feeling, mixed up with the urgent insistent pounding of the music and the humid night air of July. Connie's mother kept dragging her back to the daylight by finding things for her to do or saying, suddenly, "What's this about the Pettinger girl?"

And Connie would say nervously, "Oh, her. That dope." She always drew thick clear lines between herself and such girls, and her mother was simple and kindly enough to believe her. Her mother was so simple, Connie thought, that it was maybe cruel to fool her so much. Her mother went scuffling around the house in old bedroom slippers and complained over the telephone to one sister about the other, then the other called up and the two of them complained about the third one. If June's name was mentioned her mother's tone was approving, and if Connie's name was mentioned it was disapproving. This did not really mean she disliked Connie and actually Connie thought that her mother preferred her to June because she was prettier, but the two of them kept up a pretense of exasperation, a sense that they were tugging and struggling over something of little value to either of them. Sometimes, over coffee, they were almost friends, but something would come up — some vexation that was like a fly buzzing suddenly around their heads — and their faces went hard with contempt.

One Sunday Connie got up at eleven — none of them bothered with church — and washed her hair so that it could dry all day long, in the sun. Her parents and sister were going to a barbecue at an aunt's house and Connie said no, she wasn't interested, rolling her eyes to let her mother know just what she thought of it. "Stay home alone then," her mother said sharply. Connie sat out back in a lawn chair and watched them drive away, her father quiet and bald, hunched around so that he could back the car out, her mother with a look that was still angry and not at all softened through the windshield, and in the back seat poor old June all dressed up as if she didn't know what a barbecue was, with all the running yelling kids and the flies. Connie sat with her eyes closed in the sun, dreaming and dazed with the warmth about her as if this were a kind of love, the caresses of love, and her mind slipped over onto thoughts of the boy she had been with the night before and how nice he had been, how sweet it always was, not the way someone like June would suppose but sweet, gentle, the way it was in movies and promised in songs; and when she opened her eyes she hardly knew where she was, the back yard ran off into weeds and a fence-line of trees and behind it the sky was perfectly blue and still. The asbestos "ranch house" that was now three years old startled her — it looked small. She shook her head as if to get awake.

It was too hot. She went inside the house and turned on the radio to drown out the quiet. She sat on the edge of her bed, barefoot, and listened for an hour and a half to a program called XYZ Sunday Jamboree, record after record of hard, fast, shrieking songs she sang along with, interspersed by exclamations from "Bobby King": "An' look here you girls at Napoleon's — Son and Charley want you to pay real close attention to this song coming up!"

And Connie paid close attention herself, bathed in a glow of slow-pulsed joy that seemed to rise mysteriously out of the music itself and lay languidly about the airless little room, breathed in and breathed out with each gentle rise and fall of her chest.

After a while she heard a car coming up the drive. She sat up at once, startled, because it couldn't be her father so soon. The gravel kept crunching all the way in from the road — the driveway was long — and Connie ran to the window. It was a car she didn't know. It was an open jalopy, painted a bright gold that caught the sunlight opaquely. Her heart began to pound and her fingers snatched at her hair, checking it, and she whispered "Christ. Christ," wondering how bad she looked. The car came to a stop at the side door and the horn sounded four short taps as if this were a signal Connie knew.

She went into the kitchen and approached the door slowly, then hung out the screen door, her bare toes curling down off the step. There were two boys in the car and now she recognized the driver: he had shaggy, shabby black hair that looked crazy as a wig and he was grinning at her.

"I ain't late, am I?" he said.

"Who the hell do you think you are?" Connie said.

"Toldja I'd be out, didn't I?"

"I don't even know who you are."

She spoke sullenly, careful to show no interest or pleasure, and he spoke in a fast bright monotone. Connie looked past him to the other boy, taking her time. He had fair brown hair, with a lock that fell onto his forehead. His sideburns gave him a fierce, embarrassed look, but so far he hadn't even bothered to glance at her. Both boys wore sunglasses. The driver's glasses were metallic and mirrored everything in miniature.

"You wanta come for a ride?" he said.

Connie smirked and let her hair fall loose over one shoulder.

"Don'tcha like my car? New paint job," he said. "Hey."

"What?"

"You're cute."

She pretended to fidget, chasing flies away from the door.

"Don'tcha believe me, or what?" he said.

"Look, I don't even know who you are," Connie said in disgust.

"Hey, Ellie's got a radio, see. Mine's broke down." He lifted his friend's arm and showed her the little transistor the boy was holding, and now Connie began to hear the music. It was the same program that was playing inside the house.

"Bobby King?" she said.

"I listen to him all the time. I think he's great."

"He's kind of great," Connie said reluctantly.

"Listen, that guy's *great*. He knows where the action is."

Connie blushed a little, because the glasses made it impossible for her to see just what this boy was looking at. She couldn't decide if she liked him or if he was just a jerk, and so she dawdled in the doorway and wouldn't come down or go back inside. She said, "What's all that stuff painted on your car?"

"Can'tcha read it?" He opened the door very carefully, as if he was afraid it might fall off. He slid out just as carefully, planting his feet firmly on the ground, the tiny metallic world in his glasses slowing down like gelatine hardening and in the midst of it Connie's bright green blouse. "This here is my name, to begin with," he said. ARNOLD FRIEND was written in tarlike black letters on the side, with a drawing of a round grinning face that reminded Connie of a pumpkin, except it wore sunglasses. "I wanta introduce myself, I'm Arnold Friend and that's my real name and I'm gonna be your friend, honey, and inside the car's Ellie Oscar, he's kinda shy." Ellie brought his transistor radio up to his shoulder and balanced it there. "Now these numbers are a secret code, honey," Arnold Friend explained. He read off the numbers 33, 19, 17 and raised his eyebrows at her to see what she thought of that, but she didn't think much of it. The left rear fender had been smashed and around it was written, on the gleaming gold background: DONE BY CRAZY WOMAN DRIVER. Connie had to laugh at that. Arnold Friend was pleased at her laughter and looked up at her. "Around the other side's a lot more — you wanta come and see them."

"No."

"Why not?"

"Why should I?"

"Don'tcha wanta see what's on the car? Don'tcha wanta go for a ride?"

"I don't know."

"Why not?"

"I've got things to do."

"Like what?"

"Things."

He laughed as if she had said something funny. He slapped his thighs. He was standing in a strange way, leaning back against the car as if he were balancing himself. He wasn't tall, only an inch or so taller than she would be if she came down to him. Connie liked the way he was dressed, which was the way all of them dressed: tight faded jeans stuffed into black, scuffed boots, a belt that pulled his waist in and showed how tan he was, and a white pullover shirt that was a little soiled and showed the hard small muscles of his arms and shoulders. He looked as if he probably did hard work, lifting and carrying things. Even his neck looked muscular. And his face was a familiar face, somehow: the jaw and chin and cheeks slightly darkened, because he hadn't shaved for a day or two, and the nose long and hawklike, sniffing as if she were a treat he was going to gobble up and it was all a joke.

"Connie, you ain't telling the truth. This is your day set aside for a ride with me and you know it," he said, still laughing. The way he straightened and recovered from his fit of laughing showed that it had been all fake.

"How do you know what my name is?" she said suspiciously.

"It's Connie."

"Maybe and maybe not."

"I know my Connie," he said, wagging his finger. Now she remembered him even better, back at the restaurant, and her cheeks warmed at the thought of how she sucked in her breath just at the moment she passed him — how she must have looked to him. And he had remembered her. "Ellie and I come out here especially for you," he said. "Ellie can sit in back. How about it?"

"Where?"

"Where what?"

"Where're we going?"

He looked at her. He took off the sunglasses and she saw how pale the skin around his eyes was, like holes that were not in shadow but instead in light. His eyes were like chips of broken glass that catch the light in an

amiable way. He smiled. It was as if the idea of going for a ride somewhere, to some place, was a new idea to him.

"Just for a ride, Connie sweetheart."

"I never said my name was Connie," she said.

"But I know what it is. I know your name and all about you, lots of
things," Arnold Friend said. He had not moved yet but stood still leaning back against the side of his jalopy. "I took a special interest in you,
such a pretty girl, and found out all about you like I know your parents and sister are gone somewheres and I know where and how long
they're going to be gone, and I know who you were with last night, and
your best girlfriend's name is Betty. Right?"

He spoke in a simple lilting voice, exactly as if he were reciting the
words to a song. His smile assured her that everything was fine. In the
car Ellie turned up the volume on his radio and did not bother to look
around at them.

"Ellie can sit in the back seat," Arnold Friend said. He indicated his
friend with a casual jerk of his chin, as if Ellie did not count and she
should not bother with him.

"How'd you find out all that stuff?" Connie said.

"Listen: Betty Schultz and Tony Fitch and Jimmy Pettinger and
Nancy Pettinger," he said, in a chant. "Raymond Stanley and Bob Hut-
ter —"

"Do you know all those kids?"

"I know everybody."

"Look, you're kidding. You're not from around here."

"Sure."

"But — how come we never saw you before?"

"Sure you saw me before," he said. He looked down at his boots, as if
he were a little offended. "You just don't remember."

"I guess I'd remember you," Connie said.

"Yeah?" He looked up at this, beaming. He was pleased. He began to
mark time with the music from Ellie's radio, tapping his fists lightly
together. Connie looked away from his smile to the car, which was
painted so bright it almost hurt her eyes to look at it. She looked at that
name, ARNOLD FRIEND. And up at the front fender was an expression
that was familiar — MAN THE FLYING SAUCERS. It was an expression
kids had used the year before, but didn't use this year. She looked at it
for a while as if the words meant something to her that she did not yet
know.

"What're you thinking about? Huh?" Arnold Friend demanded. "Not worried about your hair blowing around in the car, are you?"

"No."

"Think I maybe can't drive good?"

"How do I know?"

"You're a hard girl to handle. How come?" he said. "Don't you know I'm your friend? Didn't you see me put my sign in the air when you walked by?"

"What sign?"

"My sign." And he drew an X in the air, leaning out toward her. They were maybe ten feet apart. After his hand fell back to his side the X was still in the air, almost visible. Connie let the screen door close and stood perfectly still inside it, listening to the music from her radio and the boy's blend together. She stared at Arnold Friend. He stood there so stiffly relaxed, pretending to be relaxed, with one hand idly on the door handle as if he were keeping himself up that way and had no intention of ever moving again. She recognized most things about him, the tight jeans that showed his thighs and buttocks and the greasy leather boots and the tight shirt, and even that slippery friendly smile of his, that sleepy dreamy smile that all the boys used to get across ideas they didn't want to put into words. She recognized all this and also the singsong way he talked, slightly mocking, kidding, but serious and a little melancholy, and she recognized the way he tapped one fist against the other in homage to the perpetual music behind him. But all these things did not come together.

She said suddenly, "Hey, how old are you?"

His smile faded. She could see then that he wasn't a kid, he was much older — thirty, maybe more. At this knowledge her heart began to pound faster.

"That's a crazy thing to ask. Can'tcha see I'm your own age?"

"Like hell you are."

"Or maybe a coupla years older, I'm eighteen."

"Eighteen?" she said doubtfully.

He grinned to reassure her and lines appeared at the corners of his mouth. His teeth were big and white. He grinned so broadly his eyes became slits and she saw how thick the lashes were, thick and black as if painted with a black tarlike material. Then he seemed to become embarrassed, abruptly, and looked over his shoulder at Ellie. "*Him*, he's crazy," he said. "Ain't he a riot, he's a nut, a real character." Ellie was still listening to the music. His sunglasses told nothing about what he was thinking. He wore a bright orange shirt unbuttoned halfway to show his chest, which was a pale, bluish chest and not muscular like Arnold Friend's. His shirt collar was turned up all around and the very tips of the collar pointed out past his chin as if they were protecting him. He was pressing the transistor radio up against his ear and sat there in a kind of daze, right in the sun.

"He's kinda strange," Connie said.

"Hey, she says you're kinda strange! Kinda strange!" Arnold Friend cried. He pounded on the car to get Ellie's attention. Ellie turned for the first time and Connie saw with shock that he wasn't a kid either — he had a fair, hairless face, cheeks reddened slightly as if the veins grew too close to the surface of his skin, the face of a forty-year-old baby. Connie felt a wave of dizziness rise in her at this sight and she stared at him as if waiting for something to change the shock of the moment, make it all right again. Ellie's lips kept shaping words, mumbling along with the words blasting in his ear.

"Maybe you two better go away," Connie said faintly.

"What? How come?" Arnold Friend cried. "We come out here to take you for a ride. It's Sunday." He had the voice of the man on the radio now. It was the same voice, Connie thought. "Don'tcha know it's Sunday all day and honey, no matter who you were with last night today you're with Arnold Friend and don't you forget it! — Maybe you better step out here," he said, and this last was in a different voice. It was a little flatter, as if the heat was finally getting to him.

"No. I got things to do."

"Hey."

"You two better leave."

"We ain't leaving until you come with us."

"Like hell I am —"

"Connie, don't fool around with me. I mean, I mean, don't fool *around*," he said, shaking his head. He laughed incredulously. He placed his sunglasses on top of his head, carefully, as if he were indeed wearing a wig, and brought the stems down behind his ears. Connie stared at him, another wave of dizziness and fear rising in her so that for a moment he wasn't even in focus but was just a blur, standing there against his gold car, and she had the idea that he had driven up the driveway all right but had come from nowhere before that and belonged nowhere and that everything about him and even about the music that was so familiar to her was only half real.

"If my father comes and sees you —"

"He ain't coming. He's at a barbecue."

"How do you know that?"

"Aunt Tillie's. Right now they're — uh — they're drinking. Sitting around," he said vaguely, squinting as if he were staring all the way to town and over to Aunt Tillie's back yard. Then the vision seemed to get clear and he nodded energetically. "Yeah. Sitting around. There's your sister in a blue dress, huh? And high heels, the poor sad bitch — nothing like you, sweetheart! And your mother's helping some fat woman with the corn, they're cleaning the corn — husking the corn —"

"What fat woman?" Connie cried.

"How do I know what fat woman, I don't know every goddam fat woman in the world!" Arnold Friend laughed.

"Oh, that's Mrs. Hornby . . . Who invited her?" Connie said. She felt a little light-headed. Her breath was coming quickly.

"She's too fat. I don't like them fat. I like them the way you are, honey," he said, smiling sleepily at her. They stared at each other for a while, through the screen door. He said softly, "Now what you're going to do is this: you're going to come out that door. You're going to sit up front with me and Ellie's going to sit in the back, the hell with Ellie, right? This isn't Ellie's date. You're my date. I'm your lover, honey."

"What? You're crazy —"

"Yes, I'm your lover. You don't know what that is but you will," he said. "I know that too. I know all about you. But look: it's real nice and you couldn't ask for nobody better than me, or more polite. I always keep my word. I'll tell you how it is, I'm always nice at first, the first time. I'll hold you so tight you won't think you have to try to get away or pretend anything because you'll know you can't. And I'll come inside you where it's all secret and you'll give in to me and you'll love me —"

"Shut up! You're crazy!" Connie said. She backed away from the door. She put her hands against her ears as if she'd heard something terrible, something not meant for her. "People don't talk like that, you're crazy," she muttered. Her heart was almost too big now for her chest and its pumping made sweat break out all over her. She looked out to see Arnold Friend pause and then take a step toward the porch lurching. He almost fell. But, like a clever drunken man, he managed to catch his balance. He wobbled in his high boots and grabbed hold of one of the porch posts.

"Honey?" he said. "You still listening?"

"Get the hell out of here!"

"Be nice, honey. Listen."

"I'm going to call the police —"

He wobbled again and out of the side of his mouth came a fast spat curse, an aside not meant for her to hear. But even this "Christ!" sounded forced. Then he began to smile again. She watched this smile come, awkward as if he were smiling from inside a mask. His whole face was a mask, she thought wildly, tanned down onto his throat but then running out as if he had plastered makeup on his face but had forgotten about his throat.

"Honey — ? Listen, here's how it is. I always tell the truth and I promise you this: I ain't coming in that house after you."

"You better not! I'm going to call the police if you — if you don't —"

"Honey," he said, talking right through her voice, "honey, I'm not coming in there but you are coming out here. You know why?"

She was panting. The kitchen looked like a place she had never seen before, some room she had run inside but which wasn't good enough, wasn't going to help her. The kitchen window had never had a curtain, after three years, and there were dishes in the sink for her to do — probably — and if you ran your hand across the table you'd probably feel something sticky there.

"You listening, honey? Hey?"

"— going to call the police —"

"Soon as you touch the phone I don't need to keep my promise and can come inside. You won't want that."

She rushed forward and tried to lock the door. Her fingers were shaking. "But why lock it," Arnold Friend said gently, talking right into her face. "It's just a screen door. It's just nothing." One of his boots was at a strange angle, as if his foot wasn't in it. It pointed out to the left, bent at the ankle. "I mean, anybody can break through a screen door and glass and wood and iron or anything else if he needs to, anybody at all and specially Arnold Friend. If the place got lit up with a fire honey you'd come runnin' out into my arms, right into my arms an' safe at home — like you knew I was your lover and'd stopped fooling around. I don't mind a nice shy girl but I don't like no fooling around." Part of those words were spoken with a slight rhythmic lilt, and Connie somehow recognized them — the echo of a song from last year, about a girl rushing into her boyfriend's arms and coming home again —

Connie stood barefoot on the linoleum floor, staring at him. "What do you want?" she whispered.

"I want you," he said.

"What?"

"Seen you that night and thought, that's the one, yes sir. I never needed to look any more."

"But my father's coming back. He's coming to get me. I had to wash my hair first —" She spoke in a dry, rapid voice, hardly raising it for him to hear.

"No, your Daddy is not coming and yes, you had to wash your hair and you washed it for me. It's nice and shining and all for me, I thank you, sweetheart," he said, with a mock bow, but again he almost lost his balance. He had to bend and adjust his boots. Evidently his feet did not go all the way down; the boots must have been stuffed with something so that he would seem taller. Connie stared out at him and behind him Ellie in the car, who seemed to be looking off toward Connie's right, into nothing. This Ellie said, pulling the words out of the air one after another as if he were just discovering them, "You want me to pull out the phone?"

"Shut your mouth and keep it shut," Arnold Friend said, his face red from bending over or maybe from embarrassment because Connie had seen his boots. "This ain't none of your business."

"What — what are you doing? What do you want?" Connie said. "If I call the police they'll get you, they'll arrest you —"

"Promise was not to come in unless you touch that phone, and I'll keep that promise," he said. He resumed his erect position and tried to force his shoulders back. He sounded like a hero in a movie, declaring something important. He spoke too loudly and it was as if he were speaking to someone behind Connie. "I ain't made plans for coming in that house where I don't belong but just for you to come out to me, the way you should. Don't you know who I am?"

"You're crazy," she whispered. She backed away from the door but did not want to go into another part of the house, as if this would give him permission to come through the door. "What do you . . . You're crazy, you . . ."

"Huh? What're you saying, honey?"

Her eyes darted everywhere in the kitchen. She could not remember what it was, this room.

"This is how it is, honey: you come out and we'll drive away, have a nice ride. But if you don't come out we're gonna wait till your people come home and then they're all going to get it."

"You want that telephone pulled out?" Ellie said. He held the radio away from his ear and grimaced, as if without the radio the air was too much for him.

"I toldja shut up, Ellie," Arnold Friend said, "you're deaf, get a hearing aid, right? Fix yourself up. This little girl's no trouble and's gonna be nice to me, so Ellie keep to yourself, this ain't your date — right? Don't hem in on me. Don't hog. Don't crush. Don't bird dog. Don't trail me," he said in a rapid meaningless voice, as if he were running through all the expressions he'd learned but was no longer sure which one of them was in style, then rushing on to new ones, making them up with his eyes closed, "Don't crawl under my fence, don't squeeze in my chipmunk hole, don't sniff my glue, suck my popsicle, keep your own greasy fingers on yourself!" He shaded his eyes and peered in at Connie, who was backed against the kitchen table. "Don't mind him honey he's just a creep. He's a dope. Right? I'm the boy for you and like I said you come out here nice like a lady and give me your hand, and nobody else gets hurt, I mean, your nice old bald-headed daddy and your mummy and your sister in her high heels. Because listen: why bring them in this?"

"Leave me alone," Connie whispered.

"Hey, you know that old woman down the road, the one with the chickens and stuff — you know her?"

"She's dead!"

"Dead? What? You know her?" Arnold Friend said.

"She's dead — "

"Don't you like her?"

"She's dead — she's — she isn't here any more —"

"But don't you like her, I mean, you got something against her? Some grudge or something?" Then his voice dipped as if he were conscious of a rudeness. He touched the sunglasses perched on top of his head as if to make sure they were still there. "Now you be a good girl."

"What are you going to do?"

"Just two things, or maybe three," Arnold Friend said. "But I promise it won't last long and you'll like me the way you get to like people you're close to. You will. It's all over for you here, so come on out. You don't want your people in any trouble, do you?"

She turned and bumped against a chair or something, hurting her leg, but she ran into the back room and picked up the telephone. Something roared in her ear, a tiny roaring, and she was so sick with fear that she could do nothing but listen to it — the telephone was clammy and very heavy and her fingers groped down to the dial but were too weak to touch it. She began to scream into the phone, into the roaring. She cried out, she cried for her mother, she felt her breath start jerking back and forth in her lungs as if it were something Arnold Friend were stabbing her with again and again with no tenderness. A noisy sorrowful wailing rose all about her and she was locked inside it the way she was locked inside this house.

After a while she could hear again. She was sitting on the floor with her wet back against the wall.

Arnold Friend was saying from the door, "That's a good girl. Put the phone back."

She kicked the phone away from her.

"No, honey. Pick it up. Put it back right."

She picked it up and put it back. The dial tone stopped.

"That's a good girl. Now you come outside."

She was hollow with what had been fear, but what was now just an emptiness. All that screaming had blasted it out of her. She sat, one leg cramped under her, and deep inside her brain was something like a pinpoint of light that kept going and would not let her relax. She thought, I'm not going to see my mother again. She thought, I'm not going to sleep in my bed again. Her bright green blouse was all wet.

Arnold Friend said, in a gentle-loud voice that was like a stage voice, "The place where you came from ain't there any more, and where you had in mind to go is canceled out. This place you are now — inside your daddy's house — is nothing but a cardboard box I can knock down any time. You know that and always did know it. You hear me?"

She thought, I have got to think. I have to know what to do.

"We'll go out to a nice field, out in the country here where it smells so nice and it's sunny," Arnold Friend said. "I'll have my arms tight around you so you won't need to try to get away and I'll show you what love is like, what it does. The hell with this house! It looks solid all right," he said. He ran a fingernail down the screen and the noise did not make Connie shiver, as it would have the day before. "Now put your hand on your heart, honey. Feel that? That feels solid too but we know better, be nice to me, be sweet like you can because what else is there for a girl like you but to be sweet and pretty and give in? — and get away before her people come back?"

She felt her pounding heart. Her hand seemed to enclose it. She thought for the first time in her life that it was nothing that was hers, that belonged to her, but just a pounding, living thing inside this body that wasn't really hers either.

"You don't want them to get hurt," Arnold Friend went on. "Now get up, honey. Get up all by yourself."

She stood.

"Now turn this way. That's right. Come over here to me — Ellie, put that away, didn't I tell you? You dope. You miserable creepy dope," Arnold Friend said. His words were not angry but only part of an incantation. The incantation was kindly. "Now come out through the kitchen to me honey and let's see a smile, try it, you're a brave sweet little girl and now they're eating corn and hot dogs cooked to bursting over an outdoor fire, and they don't know one thing about you and never did and honey you're better than them because not a one of them would have done this for you."

Connie felt the linoleum under her feet; it was cool. She brushed her hair back out of her eyes. Arnold Friend let go of the post tentatively and opened his arms for her, his elbows pointing in toward each other and his wrists limp, to show that this was an embarrassed embrace and a little mocking, he didn't want to make her self-conscious.

She put out her hand against the screen. She watched herself push the door slowly open as if she were safe back somewhere in the other doorway, watching this body and this head of long hair moving out into the sunlight where Arnold Friend waited.

"My sweet little blue-eyed girl," he said, in a half-sung sigh that had nothing to do with her brown eyes but was taken up just the same by the vast sunlit reaches of the land behind him and on all sides of him, so much land that Connie had never seen before and did not recognize except to know that she was going to it.

1968

*Mary Ladd Gavell*

# The Rotifer

FROM *Psychiatry*

THOUGH I SIT hunched studiously over my microscope, I am gazing dreamily past it and out the open window, at the lazy afternoon campus. But the lab instructor, a graduate student who stutters a little and dreams of the day when he will be an assistant professor, comes hovering down the row of tables, and I return to my microscope. I do not plan to become a biologist. Two sciences are required, and I regard with detachment the sophomores' frogs' legs and sheep's livers, each with a name tag attached, which float in the barrel of formaldehyde in the corner. It gives off a technical, advanced, arcane smell, but it does not stir me. Next year I shall be off to another lab and another science and shall putter about with Bunsen burners or magnetic fields.

It is late in the fall, although it is still warm here in Texas, and the faint sounds of football practice drift in through the open window. We forty freshmen in this room have, since our arrival at the state university from the sleepy cactusy towns and the raw cities and the piny woods and the plains, been learning of the protozoa, the one-celled creatures who simply divide when they want to become two, and are not always sure whether they are plants or animals. The lab instructor has hovered over us yearningly, wanting us to get a *good* view of the amoeba, to really *appreciate* the spyrogyra.

But today, as he gives each of us a glass slide with a drop of pond water on it, he tells us that we are leaving the protozoa and beginning the long evolutionary climb. Today we shall see the rotifers, who belong to the metazoa. We too, at the other end of the microscope, are metazoa; the rotifer, like us, has a brain, a nervous system, and a stomach.

I am fairly good, by this time, at adjusting my microscope. I know that those long, waving fronds are reflections of my own eyelashes, and

I recognize algae when I see it, greenish leafy stuff rather like the broccoli on a dormitory dinner plate. Soon I find the rotifers — furiously alive, almost transparent little animals, churning powerfully along in their native ocean.

Watching, I am a witness to a crisis in the life of a rotifer. He is entangled in a snarl of algae, and he can't get loose. His transparent little body chugs this way and that, but the fence of algae seems impenetrable. He turns, wriggles, oscillates, but he is caught. *Rest a moment, I whisper to him, lie still and catch your breath and then give a good heave to the left.* But he is in a wild panic, beyond any reasonable course of action. It seems to me that his movements are slowing down, as if he is becoming exhausted.

Maybe I can help him. Perhaps I can put my finger on the edge of the glass slide and tip it ever so slightly, tilt it just enough so that the water will wash him over the barrier. Cautiously, gently, I touch the slide.

But the result is a violent revolution in the whole rotifer universe! My rotifer and his algae prison wash recklessly out of sight, and whole other worlds of rotifers and algae and amoebae and miscellaneous creatures of the deep reel by, spinning on the waves of a cataclysm. My rotifer is gone, lost to me. Huge and clumsy, more gargantuan than any Gulliver, I am separated from him forever by my monstrous size, and there is no way I can get through from my dimension to his.

The bell rings; lab is over. I take my slide out from under my microscope; there on it is the merest drop of water, and I look at it uncertainly. I start to wipe it off, to put the slide away, but I hesitate and look at it again. The lab instructor, seeing me still standing there, hurries over. "Did you get a *good* conception of the ciliary movement?" he asks me anxiously.

"I guess so," I answer, and I polish the slide until it is dry and shiny and put it away.

Like that earnest young man, the lab instructor, I became, for a little while a few years later, an intellectual sharecropper, as we called young graduate students who had various ill-defined and ill-paid functions around the university. During this period I was for some reason handed the job of going through the papers of the Benton family, which a descendant, looking for something suitable to do with them, had turned over to the university. The Bentons had been a moderately prominent family who had moved from the East to Tennessee in the 1790's, and then, thirty or so years later, to the Southwest. They were notable for having been respectable, prosperous, God-fearing and right-doing lawyers and landowners, and they were also notable for having saved most of the papers that came into their hands. All these qualities had culminated in Josiah Benton, who had been State Treasurer in the 1840's and had saved every paper he got his hands on.

So for weeks and weeks, I sat in a corner of the archives library and turned through fragile and yellowed papers, making out the dim and faded handwriting of Benton love letters, lists of Benton expenditures for curtain material and camisoles, reports and complaints to various Bentons from their tenants, letters to traveling Benton husbands from Benton wives, bills of sale for Benton slaves, political gossip from Benton cronies and domestic gossip from Benton relatives, diaries begun and never finished, and a few state papers filched by Josiah, like many another bureaucrat after him, from the official files.

It was impossible not to become interested in the Bentons. I sat down with those boxes of ancient gossip and circumstance more eagerly than I asked a friend, what's new? Lydia May Benton feuded with her sister-in-law Sally, and the mysterious trouble about Jonathan Bentley, it turned out, was that he *drank*. Aunt Millie Benton's letters to her traveling husband began and ended with protestations of devotion and obedience, but in between she told him what to do and when to do it. But if Josiah's wife Lizzie had ever had an opinion, it went unrecorded; when she was mentioned at all, it was to say how dear, sweet, good, and ailing poor Lizzie was. Josiah emerged like a rock; he was honest, he was rigid, he was determined, and he carried through what he began. But it was his son, little Robert Josiah Benton, who interested me most.

There was little said about Robert Josiah before 1832, when at ten he was sent away to a school in Massachusetts. There had, of course, been a few references to him earlier. When he was born, Josiah, whose first two children had been girls, wrote proudly to his brother, "My Lizzie was delivered of a fine eight-pound boy this morning. I shall make of him, God willing, a Scholar and a Gentleman." Later on, in one of the few letters that Lizzie seemed to have received, her sister, who had recently been to visit them, exclaimed over what a "Beautiful and Clever child your Robert Josiah is." And once, when Robert Josiah must have been about eight, Josiah's list of expenditures included, "To roan horse for my Son."

Robert Josiah was sent to Massachusetts to be made into a scholar and a gentleman, as Josiah had probably written the headmaster of the school. "According to your instructions," the headmaster replied, "your son will be given a thorough grounding in Mathematics and Latin, with somewhat subordinate attention given to French and to those Sports which befit a Gentleman. You will receive Quarterly Reports from me as to the progress of your Son, and the Rules of our School require that each Scholar shall write his Father fortnightly so that you shall be well inform'd concerning his Welfare. I personally supervise the writing of these letters, ascertaining that they contain no misleading statements, as the inexperience and frivolity of Youth might give them a tendency to do, so that you shall at all times have a True and Correct account."

Robert Josiah went away to school at the end of the summer, and in the fall and winter months the fortnightly letters appeared, painfully neat, carefully spelled, stiff little letters, beginning, "My Dear and Respected Father" — Lizzie was not addressed, although somewhere in the letter Robert Josiah would say, "Give my Dear Love to my Mother." The letters always ended "Your obedient Son." He would report that he was well and that he was studying hard in order to gain the full benefits of the advantages that his father was so generously providing for him, that he was treated with the utmost consideration by the professors and by the headmaster, and that he hoped the headmaster's reports of him would be found to be satisfactory. Once he said that he found Latin very difficult, but he hastened to add, "Do not believe, Dear Father, that I question on this account your Wisdom in desiring me to study it or that I shall Neglect it." Sometimes he apologized for the shortness of a letter by saying, "I am allow'd only one Candle and it is almost finished."

At Christmas he went so far as to say, "I miss my Dear Mother and you Very much, and my Sisters also, but I shall try to overcome it and to Devote my Attention more fully to my Studies." Often he would inquire about his horse, whose name was Jupiter, and about Nero, his dog. "Does Timothy take good care of Jupiter and of Nero?" he would ask.

And so the letters continued — stiff, polite, adult little notes. But sometimes a barely wistful, faintly childish sound crept into them; once in a while it became perfectly clear that Robert Josiah wanted to come home. In January he failed to write, and instead the headmaster wrote that Robert Josiah was ill with a mild attack of the "Grippe," but felt confident that he would soon be fully recovered. And apparently he was, for two weeks later his letters resumed. But now he wrote once, "I wish I could see my Dear Mother."

Then a letter appeared from John Benton, an older cousin of Robert

Josiah's, who was attending Harvard College, and who had had an occasion, on returning to college from a short vacation, to stop by Robert Josiah's school.

"My Dear Uncle," he wrote, "I trust that you will forgive the extreme liberty which I am taking in addressing you regarding my recent visit with your Son Robert Josiah. Your Son looks very thin, as a result of his recent bout with the Grippe, and I think perhaps he is studying too hard. I have no doubt that the Headmaster of the School is an extremely Fine and Conscientious Scholar and that his School is an excellent one, but his regime is most Rigorous, and while some boys no doubt profit greatly from this, I think it may be too severe at this stage for Robert Josiah, who is perhaps of delicate constitution and of course of still tender years. I beg to assure you that the attitude of Robert Josiah is one of loving obedience to your wishes, and I trust that you will forgive, my Dear Uncle, this intrusion of mine into your Family Affairs, since I am confident of your Excellent Judgment in all matters. Your respectful Nephew, John Benton."

Well, it was a good thing that somebody had looked in on little Robert Josiah to see how he really was, but the question was, would anyone as determined as Josiah listen?

Apparently not. The weeks passed, and the stiff little letters kept coming from Robert Josiah. But they were more openly homesick now, and once or twice he wandered curiously from the subject as he was writing. Probably John's letter had merely rubbed Josiah the wrong way; he was, after all, only a young upstart of a nephew. Somebody else would have to try to make Josiah understand that Robert Josiah needed to come home — and there was no relying on Lizzie, poor, pale, ailing little thing, probably worried sick but unable to have an opinion about anything. But somebody had to do something! Josiah was not mean; he was just rigid, opinionated, and ambitious; he could be made to understand. Frantically I searched in my mind for the right tack to take with Josiah, the best way to put it to him.

But then something happened — maybe a student going out of the library banged a door — and past and present whirled around me in waves and washed me up at a library table, well into the second half of the twentieth century, with yellow old papers stacked around me. It had all happened in 1832; they were all dead and gone. There was nothing I could do for little Robert Josiah; I could hold in my hand the letters that he had written, and read the words he had put down there, but I was far,

far away, separated from him by more than a century. There was nothing I could tell his father; there was no way I could get through from my dimension to his.

Rather halfheartedly I looked for the rest of the letters. There were just two or three more from little Robert Josiah, and then they stopped. There was nothing more. There were accounts, bills, business letters, and, later on, more personal letters to Josiah, but there was nothing mentioning Robert Josiah. I read through thirty or forty more years of Benton papers, but I never saw another word about a son of Josiah Benton's.

My cousin Leah and I grew up in different parts of the country and never knew each other well. When she came to live in the city where I now worked, we felt an obligation to be friendly, but the friendliness was a trifle forced, weighted down by our families' expectations that we would have a great deal to say to each other and the inescapable fact that we did not. We rang each other up from time to time to chat and exchange family news, and since she was new to the city I introduced her to my friends. But she was six years younger than I, and the people I knew seemed jaded to her. They were not really jaded at all, but then almost anybody seemed a little battered beside Leah.

Leah's father, my uncle, was old when she was born. His first wife had died, leaving four sons already grown, and eventually he married again, a gentle girl who gave him one daughter and died shortly afterward. People wondered how that stern, hard old man was going to manage with a little girl, but he managed very well. A tender fatherliness flowered in him which his sons had never known. He and Leah were always together; they rode horseback over his farms together, and supervised the haying together, and went shopping for her clothes together, the old man looking as out of place as possible, but calm in the conviction that here, as everywhere else in the world, all you had to do was make it plain what was wanted and be able to pay for it. My uncle was a rich man — not a private-yacht kind of rich, but a Midwest-farming kind of rich, a turn-out-the-lights-when-you're-finished-with-them and don't-dip-into-your-principal kind of rich. When Leah got into her teens and began to be beautiful, he sent her to the best girls' school he could get her into, because he figured their reputation might not mean much, but it was all he had to go on. But first he asked them what they had to teach her that she could earn her living by.

She became a commercial artist, and eventually she came to the city and got a job. The best word I can think of to describe her when I first encountered her, twenty-one, all grown-up and on her own, is dazzling. She was radiant; she twinkled and glittered and dazzled like a diamond, yet her strange, pure, golden-brown eyes looked out at the world with the simplicity and delight of a child.

She saw the best in everyone. She met a notorious misogynist and thought him *so* sweet and shy; and she was introduced to a celebrated old lecher and reported that he was so *good* all through that he reminded her a lot of her Daddy. She made me nervous. But she was sharing an apartment with two former schoolmates, and the three of them — all as lovely and charming and gay as if they had been turned out by some heavenly production line, giggling and putting up each other's hair and wearing each other's clothes, living off peanut butter sandwiches and chewing over their combined worldly wisdom like so many puppies with a shoe — presented themselves in an invincible girls'-dormitory armor to the world. And I was, after all, young myself and in no mood to worry, in love with the city, with my job in an international organization, and, as I recall it, with the Third Executive Assistant of the British Delegation.

Then she called me up one night to say that she was engaged and was going to be married right away. He was a junior associate in the well-known law firm of Judd, Parker, and Avery, and his credentials of age, height, education, and background seemed to be impeccable. I felt that she emphasized his suitability a trifle for my benefit; she put me in the older-relative category. Her father was not too well; he had recently had an operation, and she was planning to go home to see him, and so they had decided to be married here the following Sunday and to go home together. On Saturday night her roommates were throwing a little party for them at the apartment, and would I come and meet Dick then? I said I'd love to, and I wished her all the happiness in the world.

That was Monday night, and I had such a busy week that I didn't have much time to think about Leah. A series of international meetings kept me working late every night. On Wednesday I didn't get away until almost midnight, and I was exhausted when I finally caught a cab. I sank back and wiggled out of my high-heeled shoes in the dark. The cab driver had a girl friend with him in the front seat; I suppose it's lonely work, cruising the night streets. She leaned against his shoulder, and when he stopped at a red light, he rested his head companionably against her; he said something monosyllabic, and she laughed. I thought wisely, looking at the backs of their heads, that they were too comfortable in their closeness to be a young dating pair, but were old lovers, or married. When we got to my address he turned on the light for a moment to make change. I saw that he was good-looking and probably in his late twenties, and that she was about the same age, pretty, with a mop of blond hair, and in blue jeans.

I must pause here to explain that I am a recognizer of people. I am a sort of Paganini, or Escoffier, of recognizing. People who say, "I remember faces but I just can't remember names," are amateurs; I remember thousands of faces for which I have never known a name. The streets swarm with them: People who once did my hair or sold me shoes, stood next to me in elevators, in ticket lines, or at fires, gave me a new blouse in exchange for one that didn't fit, or four words at a cocktail party in exchange for four of mine. I remember them all; but they cut me dead.

The first time I ever set forth on the streets of Paris, I was with a friend, a woman who occupied a high position in the international organization for which I worked, and who had, as it happened, been mainly responsible for the firing from that organization, a year or so before, of a Frenchman named Charpentier, the reason being general quarrelsomeness, I think. No doubt his side of the story was different; I never knew all the ins and outs of it. He returned to the French civil service, from whence he had come, but not before delivering some fairly painful parting shots.

My friend and I stopped from the boat train out into the spring morning sunshine of Paris, bent on none but pleasant errands, and at once I recognized M. Charpentier on the street. I was used to domestic recognizing; at home I damped down the recognizing smile on my face as automatically as I glanced at the traffic lights; but I lost my head at such a stunning foreign success and cried out, "Monsieur Charpentier!" He stopped, we stopped, and the shock turned both their faces to concrete. He gave a short, savage jerk of a bow, and her teeth met like gears as she ground out a greeting between them. It had been the dearest wish of both their hearts never to see each other again. As the hostess, so to speak, in the situation, I babbled something like, "How nice once more to see you again, and how beautiful is your city!" speaking pidgin English, although his own was perfect. He looked at me with a mixture of loathing and bewilderment. We had known each other only slightly a year or more before, and he did not recognize me. My friend and I proceeded on our way, but a shadow had settled over the day. She was rather silent, and I smiled, whenever I caught her eye, Uriah Heepishly. Paris has never been the magic city to me that it is to some.

On Saturday night I went to my cousin's apartment and met her fiancé. He was a good-looking young man in his late twenties, with a conservative tie, a direct eye, and a firm handshake. He greeted me with a special, cousinly warmth, and his manner toward Leah was a charming mixture of serious protectiveness and teasing adoration. And of course he didn't recognize me; there was not the faintest cloud in his clear young gaze. My cousin was radiant; she flitted among the guests like a sprite. "Tell me, Mary," she whispered when she alighted near me for a moment, "what do you think of him? Isn't he *wonderful? Isn't* he?"

"He's very handsome and very charming," I said.

"Oh, I'm *so* glad you like him," she cried, and she gave me a hug. "You and Dad are the people I want to like him — I don't care about anybody else!" And she was off.

Well, I suppose that more than one struggling young professional man has driven a cab at nights to make a little extra. And surely many a young man has an auld luve to be off wi' before he be on wi' the new — and if the timetable's a bit crowded, it's not a hanging offense. I'm as broad-minded as the next, and yet — and yet — this was my little cousin Leah, my beautiful, shining little cousin, with whom I had not a blessed thing in common, who thought all the world loved her as well as her Daddy did. I looked at the young man again, and I imagined that his neatly cut face was clearly sinister and that his every word and gesture was plainly false. Was he really a lawyer with Judd, Parker, and Avery? It would be possible to find out; I could, in fact, simply call them up and ask, on some pretext or other. But it was Saturday night, and the wedding was Sunday, and on Monday I wouldn't want to know.

Or I could, then and there, look him right in the sincere blue eye and tell him that I had seen him driving a cab last Wednesday night with a blond young woman under circumstances suggestive of considerable intimacy, and what, as a promising young lawyer on the eve of marriage to my cousin, did he have to say about it? But how in the name of heaven could I say that? It was melodramatic. It was a line to be delivered by an outraged father, back to the fireplace, or perhaps by a worldly, erect old aunt in her parlor, shooting a severe glance past her teacup. I simply couldn't manage it; I was only a cousin, about his own age and considerably less self-assured than he looked, spectacles slipping woefully down my nose, licensed in neither duenna nor private eye, nervous of making a fool of myself and showing it, in the crush of a large party in a small apartment, where it took a shout to be heard at all, and elbows jostled into conversations from all sides. And, after all, what if I were mistaken? I may be a Paganini, I may be an Escoffier, but the possibility had to be granted, and it would not make a very auspicious beginning for us all. And anyway, it was too late. The chapel was reserved, the wedding dress hung on its satin hanger in the closet, and the organist was instructed to play "I Love You Truly."

When I left that night, I suddenly at the door, without intending to at all, threw my arms around Leah and held her tight. There she was, my little cousin, my equal, my contemporary, within the circle of my arms; but I was separated from her forever by all the complexities of what I did not know and could not do. Our lives carried us on in our own dimensions, like people passing on different escalators, headlong to meet whatever harm or good was to come our way. And so I left her awkwardly, and I smiled jerkily at the bridegroom, who gave me a cousinly peck on the cheek, and we all said something about seeing each other the next day.

I had dinner with them a couple of months later, after they had returned to the city. They seemed very happy, and the stars shone in Leah's eyes as brightly as ever. I couldn't say I liked him; but there was, as I looked him over, this time more quietly and leisurely, something reassuring about his very ordinariness. He simply didn't have the stuff in him to be a Bluebeard or a Landru. He was a bright enough, nice enough young man, who, I surmised, thought his ways to be a little more winning, and other people a little more simple, than they were, and whose eye was firmly fixed on the main chance. But that was the worst I could think of him, and I was glad I hadn't tried to confront him with my silly cab-riding story; it wouldn't have done anyone any good, and perhaps it was all a mistake, anyway. They left the city shortly afterward; Leah called to tell me that an opportunity had opened up for Dick out in the Midwest, and he was leaving Judd, Parker, and Avery. She was glad because she would be nearer her father.

They were divorced about a year later, very shortly after her father died, and my cousin is back in the city, with a job doing fashion-ad illustrations. I assumed she was working just to keep herself busy, but a newsy old aunt of mine who was through town recently tells me that's not so. Leah will be a rich woman, one day, but at present she has to make her living, for her father, just before he died, changed his will so as to tie up the money very securely for a good while to come. I don't know why the divorce, of course — mental cruelty, or something, I suppose; it's nothing I can ask Leah about unless she wants to talk about it. Dick immediately got married again, to a cheap, fuzzy-headed little blonde, as my aunt puts it. Leah's still a handsome woman, but the dazzle is gone, and she looks tired around the eyes. But so do I; so, in time, does everybody.

## James Alan McPherson

......................................................................................................................................

# Gold Coast

FROM *The Atlantic Monthly*

THAT SPRING, when I had a great deal of potential and no money at all, I took a job as a janitor. That was when I was still very young and spent money very freely, and when, almost every night, I drifted off to sleep lulled by sweet anticipation of that time when my potential would suddenly be realized and there would be capsule biographies of my life on dust jackets of many books, all proclaiming: ". . . He knew life on many levels. From shoeshine boy, free-lance waiter, 3rd cook, janitor, he rose to . . ." I had never been a janitor before, and I did not really have to be one, and that is why I did it. But now, much later, I think it might have been because it is possible to be a janitor without becoming one, and at parties or at mixers, when asked what it was I did for a living, it was pretty good to hook my thumbs in my vest pockets and say comfortably: "Why, I am an apprentice janitor." The hippies would think it degenerate and really dig me and people in Philosophy and Law and Business would feel uncomfortable trying to make me feel better about my station while wondering how the hell I had managed to crash the party.

"What's an apprentice janitor?" they would ask.

"I haven't got my card yet," I would reply. "Right now I'm just taking lessons. There's lots of complicated stuff you have to learn before you get your own card and your own building."

"What kind of stuff?"

"Human nature, for one thing. *Race* nature, for another."

"Why race?"

"Because," I would say in a low voice, looking around lest someone else should overhear, "you have to be able to spot Jews and Negroes who are passing."

"That's terrible," would surely be said then with a hint of indignation.

"It's an art," I would add masterfully.

After a good pause I would invariably be asked: "But you're a Negro yourself, how can you keep your own people out?"

At which point I would look terribly disappointed and say: "*I* don't keep them out. But if they get in it's my job to make their stay just as miserable as possible. Things are changing."

Now the speaker would just look at me in disbelief.

"It's Janitorial Objectivity," I would say to finish the thing as the speaker began to edge away. "Don't hate me," I would call after him to considerable embarrassment. "Somebody has to do it."

It was an old building near Harvard Square. Conrad Aiken had once lived there, and in the days of the Gold Coast, before Harvard built its great houses, it had been a very fine haven for the rich; but that was a world ago, and this building was one of the few monuments of that era which had survived. The lobby had a high ceiling with thick redwood beams, and it was replete with marble floor, fancy ironwork, and an old-fashioned house telephone which no longer worked. Each apartment had a small fireplace, and even the large bathtubs and chain toilets, when I was having my touch of nature, made me wonder what prominent personage of the past had worn away all the newness. And, being there, I felt a certain affinity toward the rich.

It was a funny building, because the people who lived there made it old. Conveniently placed as it was between the Houses and Harvard Yard, I expected to find it occupied by a company of hippies, hopeful working girls, and assorted graduate students. Instead, there was a majority of old maids, dowagers, asexual middle-aged men, homosexual young men, a few married couples, and a teacher. No one was shacking up there, and walking through the quiet halls in the early evening, I sometimes had the urge to knock on a door and expose myself just to hear someone breathe hard for once.

It was a Cambridge spring: down by the Charles happy students were making love while sad-eyed middle-aged men watched them from the bridge. It was a time of activity: Law students were busy sublimating, Business School people were making records of the money they would make, the Harvard Houses were clearing out, and in the Square bearded pot-pushers were setting up their restaurant tables in anticipation of the Summer School faithfuls. There was a change of season in the air, and to comply with its urgings, James Sullivan, the old superintendent, passed his three beaten garbage cans on to me with the charge that I should take up his daily rounds of the six floors, and with unflinching humility, gather whatever scraps the old-maid tenants had refused to husband.

I then became very rich, with my own apartment, a sensitive girl, a stereo, two speakers, one tattered chair, one fork, a job, and the urge to acquire. Having all this and youth besides made me pity Sullivan: he had been in that building thirty years and had its whole history recorded in the little folds of his mind, as his own life was recorded in the wrinkles of his face. All he had to show for his time there was a berserk dog, a wife almost as mad as the dog, three cats, bursitis, acute myopia, and a drinking problem. He was well over seventy and could hardly walk, and his weekly check of twenty-two dollars from the company that managed the building would not support anything. So, out of compromise, he was retired to superintendent of my labor.

My first day as janitor, while I skillfully lugged my three overflowing cans of garbage out of the building, he sat on his bench in the lobby, faded and old and smoking, in patched, loose blue pants. He watched me. He was a chain smoker, and I noticed right away that he very carefully dropped all of the ashes and butts on the floor and crushed them under his feet until there was a yellow and gray smear. Then he laboriously pushed the mess under the bench with his shoe, all the while eyeing me like a cat in silence as I hauled the many cans of muck out to the big disposal unit next to the building. When I had finished, he gave me two old plates to help stock my kitchen and his first piece of advice.

"Sit down, for Chrissake, and take a load off your feet," he told me.

I sat on the red bench next to him and accepted the wilted cigarette he offered me from the crushed package he kept in his sweater pocket.

"Now, I'll tell you something to help you get along in the building," he said.

I listened attentively.

"If any of these sons of bitches ever ask you to do something extra, be sure to charge them for it."

I assured him that I absolutely would.

"If they can afford to live here, they can afford to pay. The bastards."

"Undoubtedly," I assured him again.

"And another thing," he added. "Don't let any of these girls shove any cat shit under your nose. That ain't your job. You tell them to put it in a bag and take it out themselves."

I reminded him that I knew very well my station in life and that I was not about to haul cat shit or anything of that nature. He looked at me through his thick-lensed glasses for a long time. He looked like a cat himself. "That's right," he said at last. "And if they still try to sneak it in the trash be sure to make the bastards pay. They can afford it." He crushed his seventh butt on the floor and scattered the mess some more while he lit up another. "I never hauled out no cat shit in the thirty years I been here, and you don't do it either."

"I'm going up to wash my hands," I said.

"Remember," he called after me, "don't take no shit from any of them."

I protested once more that, upon my life, I would never, never do it, not even for the prettiest girl in the building. Going up in the elevator, I felt comfortably resolved that I would never do it. There were no pretty girls in the building.

I never found out what he had done before he came there, but I do know that being a janitor in that building was as high as he ever got in life. He had watched two generations of the rich pass the building on their way to the Yard, and he had seen many governors ride white horses into that same Yard to send sons and daughters of the rich out into life to produce, to acquire, to procreate, and to send back sons and daughters so that the cycle would continue. He had watched the cycle from when he had been able to haul the cans out for himself, and now he could not, and he was bitter.

He was Irish, of course, and he took pride in Irish accomplishments when he could have none of his own. He had known Frank O'Connor when that writer had been at Harvard. He told me on many occasions how O'Connor had stopped to talk every day on his way to the Yard. He had also known James Michael Curley, and his most colorful memory of the man was a long-ago day when he and James Curley sat in a Boston bar and one of Curley's runners had come in and said: "Hey, Jim, Sol Bernstein the Jew wants to see you." And Curley, in his deep, memorial voice, had said to James Sullivan: "Let us go forth and meet this Israelite Prince." These were his memories, and I would obediently put aside my garbage cans and laugh with him over the hundred or so colorful, insignificant little details which made up a whole lifetime of living in the basement of Harvard. And although they were of little value to me then, I knew that they were the reflections of a lifetime and the happiest moments he would ever have, being sold to me cheap, as youthful time is cheap, for as little time and interest as I wanted to spend. It was a buyer's market.

In those days I believed myself gifted with a boundless perception and attacked my daily garbage route with a gusto superenforced by the happy knowledge that behind each of the fifty or so doors in our building lived a story which could, if I chose to grace it with the magic of my pen, become immortal. I watched my tenants fanatically, noting their perversions, their visitors, and their eating habits. So intense was my search for material that I had to restrain myself from going through their refuse scrap by scrap; but at the topmost layers of muck, without too much hand soiling in the process, I set my perception to work. By late June, however, I had discovered only enough to put together a skimpy, rather naive Henry Miller novel, the most colorful discoveries being:

1. The lady in #24 was an alumnus of Paducah College
2. The couple in #55 made love at least 500 times a week, and the wife had not yet discovered the pill
3. The old lady in #36 was still having monthly inconvenience
4. The two fatsos in #56 consumed nightly an extraordinary amount of chili
5. The fat man in #54 had two dogs that were married to each other, but he was not married to anyone at all
6. The middle-aged single man in #63 threw out an awful lot of flowers

Disturbed by the snail's progress I was making, I confessed my futility to James one day as he sat on his bench chain-smoking and smearing butts on my newly waxed lobby floor. "So you want to know about the tenants?" he said, his cat's eyes flickering over me.

I nodded.

"Well, the first thing to notice is how many Jews there are."

"I haven't noticed any Jews," I said.

He eyed me in amazement.

"Well, a few," I said quickly to prevent my treasured perception from being dulled any further.

"A few, hell," he said. "There's more Jews here than anybody."

"How can you tell?"

He gave me that undecided look again. "Where do you think all that garbage comes from?" He nodded feebly toward my bulging cans. I looked just in time to prevent a stray noodle from slipping over the brim. "That's right," he continued. "Jews are the biggest eaters in the world. They eat the best too."

I confessed then that I was of the chicken-soup generation and believed that Jews ate only enough to muster strength for their daily trips to the bank.

"Not so!" he replied emphatically. "You never heard the expression: 'Let's get to the restaurant before the Jews get there'?"

I shook my head sadly.

"You don't know that in certain restaurants they take the free onions and pickles off the tables when they see Jews coming?"

I held my head down in shame over the bounteous heap.

He trudged over to my can and began to turn back the leaves of noodles and crumpled tissues from #47 with his hand. After a few seconds of digging, he unmucked an empty pâté can. "Look at that," he said triumphantly. "Gourmet stuff, no less."

"That's from #44," I said.

"What else?" he said, all-knowingly. "In 1946 a Swedish girl moved in up there and took a Jewish girl for her roommate. Then the Swedish girl moved out and there's been a Jewish Dynasty up there ever since."

I recalled that #44 was occupied by a couple that threw out a good number of S. S. Pierce cans, Chivas Regal bottles, assorted broken records, and back issues of *Evergreen* and the *Realist*.

"You're right," I said.

"Of course," he replied, as if there were never any doubt. "I can spot them anywhere, even when they think they're passing." He leaned closer and said in a you-and-me voice: "But don't ever say anything bad about them in public. The Anti-Defamation League will get you."

Just then his wife screamed for him from the second floor, and the dog joined her and beat against the door. He got into the elevator painfully and said: "Don't ever talk about them in public. You don't know who they are, and that Defamation League will take everything you got."

Sullivan did not really dislike Jews. He was just bitter toward anyone better off than himself. He lived with his wife on the second floor, and his apartment was very dirty because both of them were sick and old, and neither could move very well. His wife swept dirt out into the hall, and two hours after I had mopped and waxed their section of the floor, there was sure to be a layer of dirt, grease, and crushed-scattered tobacco from their door to the end of the hall. There was a smell of dogs and cats and age and death about their door, and I did not ever want to have to go in there for any reason because I feared something about it I cannot name.

Mrs. Sullivan, I found out, was from South Africa. She loved animals much more than people, and there was a great deal of pain in her face. She kept little cans of meat posted at strategic points about the building, and I often came across her in the early morning or late at night throwing scraps out of the second-floor window to stray cats. Once, when James was about to throttle a stray mouse in their apartment, she had screamed at him to give the mouse a sporting chance. Whenever she attempted to walk she had to balance herself against a wall or a rail, and she hated the building because it confined her. She also hated James and most of the tenants. On the other hand, she loved the "Johnny Carson Show," she loved to sit outside on the front steps (because she could go no further unassisted), and she loved to talk to anyone who would stop to listen. She never spoke coherently except when she was cursing James, and then she had a vocabulary like a drunken sailor. She had great, shrill lungs, and her screams, accompanied by the rabid barks of the dog, could be heard all over the building. She was never really clean, her teeth were bad, and the first most pathetic thing in the world was to see her sitting on the steps in the morning watching the world pass, in a stained smock and a fresh summer blue hat she kept just to wear downstairs, with no place in the world to go. James told me, on the many occasions of her screaming, that she was mentally disturbed and could not help herself. The admirable thing about him was that he never lost his temper with her, no matter how rough her curses became and no matter who heard them. And the second most pathetic thing in the world was to see them slowly making their way in Harvard Square, he supporting her, through the hurrying crowds of miniskirted summer girls, J-Pressed Ivy Leaguers, beatniks, and bused Japanese tourists, decked in cameras, who would take pictures of every inch of Harvard Square except them. Once a hippie had brushed past them and called back over his shoulder: "Don't break any track records, Mr. and Mrs. Speedy Molasses."

Also on the second floor lived Miss O'Hara, a spinster who hated Sullivan as only an old maid can hate an old man. Across from her lived a very nice, gentle celibate named Murphy, who had once served with Montgomery in North Africa and who was now spending the rest of his life cleaning his little apartment and gossiping with Miss O'Hara. It was an Irish floor.

I never found out just why Miss O'Hara hated the Sullivans with such a passion. Perhaps it was because they were so unkempt and she was so superciliously clean. Perhaps it was because Miss O'Hara had a great deal of Irish pride, and they were stereotyped Irish. Perhaps it was because she merely had no reason to like them. She was a fanatic about cleanliness and put out her little bit of garbage wrapped very neatly in yesterday's *Christian Science Monitor* and tied in a bow with a fresh piece of string. Collecting all those little neat packages, I would wonder where she got the string and imagined her at night breaking meat market locks with a hairpin and hobbling off with yards and yards of white cord concealed under the gray sweater she always wore. I could even imagine her back in her little apartment chuckling and rolling the cord into a great white ball by candlelight. Then she would stash it away in her bread box. Miss O'Hara kept her door slightly open until late at night, and I suspected that she heard everything that went on in the building. I had the feeling that I should never dare to make love with gusto for fear that she would overhear and write down all my happy-time phrases, to be maliciously recounted to me if she were ever provoked.

She had been in the building longer than Sullivan, and I suppose that her greatest ambition in life was to outlive him and then attend his wake with a knitting ball and needle. She had been trying to get him fired for twenty-five years or so, and did not know when to quit. On summer nights when I painfully mopped the second floor, she would offer me root beer, apples, or cupcakes while trying to pump me for evidence against him.

"He's just a filthy old man, Robert," she would declare in a little-old-lady whisper. "And don't think you have to clean up those dirty old butts of his. Just report him to the Company."

"Oh, I don't mind," I would tell her, gulping the root beer as fast as possible.

"Well, they're both a couple of lushes, if you ask me. They haven't been sober a day in twenty-five years."

"Well, she's sick too, you know."

"Ha!" She would throw up her hands in disgust. "She's only sick when he doesn't give her the booze."

I fought to keep down a burp. "How long have *you* been here?"

She motioned for me to step out of the hall and into her dark apartment. "Don't tell him" — she nodded toward Sullivan's door — "but I've been here thirty-four years." She waited for me to be taken aback. Then she added: "And it was a better building before those two lushes came."

She then offered me an apple, asked five times if the dog's barking bothered me, forced me to take a fudge brownie, said that the cats had wet the floor again last night, got me to dust the top of a large chest too high for her to reach, had me pick up the minute specks of dust which fell from my dustcloth, pressed another root beer on me, and then showed me her family album. As an afterthought, she had me take down a big old picture of her great-grandfather, also too high for her to reach, so that I could dust that too. Then together we picked up the dust from it which might have fallen to the floor. "He's really a filthy old man, Robert," she said in closing, "and don't be afraid to report him to the Property Manager anytime you want."

I assured her that I would do it at the slightest provocation from Sullivan, finally accepted an apple but refused the money she offered, and escaped back to my mopping. Even then she watched me, smiling, from her half-opened door.

"Why does Miss O'Hara hate you?" I asked James once.

He lifted his cigaretted hand and let the long ash fall elegantly to the floor. "That old bitch has been an albatross around my neck ever since I got here," he said. "Don't trust her, Robert. It was her kind that sat around singing hymns and watching them burn saints in this state."

In those days I had forgotten that I was first of all a black and I had a very lovely girl who was not first of all a black. It is quite possible that my ancestors rowed her ancestors across on the *Mayflower*, and she was very rich in that alone. We were both very young and optimistic then, and she believed with me in my potential and liked me partly because of it; and I was happy because she belonged to me and not to the race, which made her special. It made me special too because I did not have to wear a beard or hate or be especially hip or ultra Ivy Leagueish. I did not have to smoke pot or supply her with it, or be for any cause at all except myself. I only had to be myself, which pleased me; and I only had to produce, which pleased both of us. Like many of the artistically inclined rich, she wanted to own in someone else what she could not own in herself. But this I did not mind, and I forgave her for it because she forgave me moods and the constant smell of garbage and a great deal of latent hostility. She only minded James Sullivan, and all the valuable time I was wasting listening to him rattle on and on. His conversations, she thought, were useless, repetitious, and promised nothing of value to me. She was accustomed to the old-rich, whose conversations meandered around a leitmotiv of how well off they were and how much they would leave behind very soon. She was not at all cold, but she had been taught how to tolerate the old-poor and perhaps toss them a greeting in passing. But nothing more.

Sullivan did not like her when I first introduced them because he saw that she was not a beatnik and could not be dismissed. It is in the nature of things that liberal people will tolerate two interracial beatniks more than they will an intelligent, serious-minded mixed couple. The former liaison is easy to dismiss as the dregs of both races, deserving of each other and the contempt of both races; but the latter poses a threat because there is no immediacy of overpowering sensuality or "you-pick-my-fleas-I'll-pick-yours" apparent on the surface of things, and people, even the most publicly liberal, cannot dismiss it so easily.

"That girl is Irish, isn't she?" he had asked one day in my apartment soon after I had introduced them.

"No," I said definitely.

"What's her name?"

"Judy Smith," I said, which was not her name at all.

"Well, I can spot it," he said. "She's got Irish blood all right."

"Everybody's got a little Irish blood," I told him.

He looked at me cattily and craftily from behind his thick lenses. "Well, she's from a good family, I suppose."

"I suppose," I said.

He paused to let some ashes fall to the rug. "They say the Colonel's Lady and Nelly O'Grady are sisters under the skin." Then he added: "Rudyard Kipling."

"That's true," I said with equal innuendo, "that's why you have to maintain a distinction by marrying the Colonel's Lady."

An understanding passed between us then, and we never spoke more on the subject.

Almost every night the cats wet the second floor while Meg Sullivan watched the "Johnny Carson Show" and the dog howled and clawed the door. During commercials Meg would curse James to get out and stop dropping ashes on the floor or to take the dog out or something else, totally unintelligible to those of us on the fourth, fifth, and sixth floors. Even after the Carson show she would still curse him to get out, until finally he would go down to the basement and put away a bottle or two of wine. There was a steady stench of cat functions in the basement, and with all the grease and dirt, discarded trunks, beer bottles, chairs, old tools, and the filthy sofa on which he sometimes slept, seeing him there made me want to cry. He drank the cheapest sherry, the wino kind, straight from the bottle: and on many nights that summer at 2:00 A.M. my phone would ring me out of bed.

"Rob? Jimmy Sullivan here. What are you doing?"

There was nothing suitable to say.

"Come on down to the basement for a drink."

"I have to be at work at 8:30," I would protest.

"Can't you have just one drink?" he would say pathetically.

I would carry down my own glass so that I would not have to drink out of the bottle. Looking at him on the sofa, I could not be mad because now I had many records for my stereo, a story that was going well, a girl who believed in me and who belonged to me and not to the race, a new set of dishes, and a tomorrow morning with younger people.

"I don't want to burden you unduly," he would always preface.

I would force myself not to look at my watch and say: "Of course not."

"My Meg is not in the best health, you know," he would say, handing the bottle to me.

"She's just old."

"The doctors say she should be in an institution."

"That's no place to be."

"I'm a sick man myself, Rob. I can't take much more. She's crazy."

"Anybody who loves animals can't be crazy."

He took another long draw from the bottle. "I won't live another year. I'll be dead in a year."

"You don't know that."

He looked at me closely, without his glasses, so that I could see the desperation in his eyes. "I just hope Meg goes before I do. I don't want them to put her in an institution after I'm gone."

At 2:00 A.M., with the cat stench in my nose and a glass of bad sherry standing still in my hand because I refuse in my mind to touch it, and all my dreams of greatness are above him and the basement and the building itself, I did not know what to say. The only way I could keep

from hating myself was to start him talking about the AMA or the
Medicare program or beatniks. He was pure hell on all three. To him,
the Medical Profession was "morally bankrupt," Medicare was a great
farce which deprived oldsters like himself of their "rainy-day dollars,"
and beatniks were "dropouts from the human race." He could rage on
and on in perfect phrases about all three of his major dislikes, and I
had the feeling that because the sentences were so well constructed and
well turned, he might have memorized them from something he had
read. But then he was extremely well read, and it did not matter if he
had borrowed a phrase or two from someone else. The ideas were still
his own.

It would be 3:00 A.M. before I knew it, and then 3:30, and still he
would go on. He hated politicians in general and liked to recount, at
these times, his private catalog of political observations. By the time he
got around to Civil Rights it would be 4:00 A.M., and I could not feel
responsible for him at that hour. I would begin to yawn, and at first he
would just ignore it. Then I would start to edge toward the door, and he
would see that he could hold me no longer, not even by declaring that
he wanted to be an honorary Negro because he loved the race so much.

"I hope I haven't burdened you unduly," he would say again.

"Of course not," I would say, because it was over then, and I could
leave him and the smell of the cats there, and sometimes I would go out
in the cool night and walk around the Yard and be thankful that I was
only an assistant janitor, and a transient one at that. Walking in the early
dawn and seeing the Summer School fellows sneak out of the girls'
dormitories in the Yard gave me a good feeling, and I thought that
tomorrow night it would be good to make love myself so that I could be
busy when he called.

"Why don't you tell that old man your job doesn't include baby-sit-
ting with him," Jean told me many times when she came over to visit
during the day and found me sleeping.

I would look at her and think to myself about social forces and the
pressures massing and poised, waiting to attack us. It was still July then.
It was hot, and I was working good.

"He's just an old man," I said. "Who else would listen to him."

"You're too soft. As long as you do your work you don't have to be
bothered with him."

"He could be a story if I listened long enough."

"There are too many stories about old people."

"No," I said, thinking about us again, "there are just too many people who have no stories."

Sometimes he would come up and she would be there, but I would let him come in anyway, and he would stand there looking dirty and uncomfortable, offering some invented reason for having intruded. At these times something silent would pass between them, something I cannot name, which would reduce him to exactly what he was: an old man, come out of his basement to intrude where he was not wanted. But all the time this was being communicated, there would be a surface, friendly conversation between them. And after five minutes or so of being unwelcome, he would apologize for having come, drop a few ashes on the rug, and back out the door. Downstairs we could hear his wife screaming.

We endured the aged and August was almost over. Inside the building the cats were still wetting, Meg was still screaming, the dog was getting madder, and Sullivan began to drink during the day. Outside it was hot and lush and green, and the Summer girls were wearing shorter mini-skirts and no panties and the middle-aged men down by the Charles were going wild on their bridge. Everyone was restless for change, for August is the month when undone summer things must be finished or regretted all through the winter.

Being imaginative people, Jean and I played a number of original games. One of them we called "Social Forces," the object of which was to see which side could break us first. We played it with the unknown night riders who screamed obscenities from passing cars. And because that was her side I would look at her expectantly, but she would laugh and say: "No." We played it at parties with unaware blacks who attempted to enchant her with skillful dances and hip vocabularies, believing her to be community property. She would be polite and aloof, and much later, it then being my turn, she would look at me expectantly. And I would force a smile and say: "No." The last round was played while taking her home in a subway car, on a hot August night, when one side of the car was black and tense and hating and the other side was white and of the same mind. There was not enough room on either side for the two of us to sit and we would not separate; so we stood, holding on to a steel post through all the stops, feeling all of the eyes, between the two sides of the car and the two sides of the world. We aged. And getting off finally at the stop which was no longer ours, we looked at each other, again expectantly, and there was nothing left to say.

I began to avoid the old man, would not answer the door when I knew it was he who was knocking, and waited until very late at night, when he could not possibly be awake, to haul the trash down. I hated the building then; and I was really a janitor for the first time. I slept a lot and wrote very little. And I did not give a damn about Medicare, the AMA, the building, Meg, or the crazy dog. I began to consider moving out.

In that same week, Miss O'Hara finally succeeded in badgering Murphy, the celibate Irishman, and a few other tenants into signing a complaint about the dog. No doubt Murphy signed because he was a nice fellow and women like Miss O'Hara had always dominated him. He did not really mind the dog: he did not really mind anything. She called him "Frank Dear," and I had the feeling that when he came to that place, fresh from Montgomery's Campaign, he must have had a will of his own; but she had drained it all away, year by year, so that now he would do anything just to be agreeable.

One day soon after the complaint, the little chubby Property Manager came around to tell Sullivan that the dog had to be taken away. Miss O'Hara told me the good news later, when she finally got around to my door.

"Well, that crazy dog is gone now, Robert. Those two are enough."

"Where is the dog?" I asked.

"I don't know, but Albert Rustin made them get him out. You should have seen the old drunk's face," she said. "That dirty old useless man."

"You should be at peace now," I said.

"Almost," was her reply. "The best thing is to get rid of those two old boozers along with the dog."

I congratulated Miss O'Hara and went out. I knew that the old man would be drinking and would want to talk. But very late that evening he called on the telephone and caught me in.

"Rob?" he said. "James Sullivan here. Would you come down to my apartment like a good fellow? I want to ask you something important."

I had never been in his apartment before and did not want to go then. But I went down anyway.

They had three rooms, all grimy from corner to corner. There was a peculiar odor in that place I did not ever want to smell again, and his wife was dragging herself around the room talking in mumbles. When she saw me come in the door, she said: "I can't clean it up. I just can't.

Look at that window. I can't reach it. I can't keep it clean." She threw up both her hands and held her head down and to the side. "The whole place is dirty, and I can't clean it up."

"What do you want?" I said to Sullivan.

"Sit down." He motioned me to a kitchen chair. "Have you changed that bulb on the fifth floor?"

"It's done."

He was silent for a while, drinking from a bottle of sherry, and he gave me some and a dirty glass. "You're the first person who's been in here in years," he said. "We couldn't have company because of the dog."

Somewhere in my mind was a note that I should never go into his apartment. But the dog had never been the reason. "Well, he's gone now," I said, fingering the dirty glass of sherry.

He began to cry. "They took my dog away," he said. "It was all I had. How can they take a man's dog away from him?"

There was nothing I could say.

"I couldn't do nothing," he continued. After a while he added: "But I know who it was. It was that old bitch O'Hara. Don't ever trust her, Rob. She smiles in your face, but it was her kind that laughed when they burned Joan of Arc in this state."

Seeing him there, crying and making me feel unmanly because I wanted to touch him or say something warm, also made me eager to be far away and running hard.

"Everybody's got problems," I said. "I don't have a girl now."

He brightened immediately, and for a while he looked almost happy in his old cat's eyes. Then he staggered over to my chair and held out his hand. I did not touch it, and he finally pulled it back. "I know how you feel," he said. "I know just how you feel."

"Sure," I said.

"But you're a young man, you have a future. But not me. I'll be dead inside of a year."

Just then his wife dragged herself in to offer me a cigar. They were being hospitable, and I forced myself to drink a little of the sherry.

"They took my dog away today," she mumbled. "That's all I had in the world, my dog."

I looked at the old man. He was drinking from the bottle.

During the first week of September one of the middle-aged men down by the Charles got tired of looking and tried to take a necking girl away from her boyfriend. The police hauled him off to jail, and the girl pulled down her dress tearfully. A few days later another man exposed himself near the same spot. And that same week a dead body was found on the banks of the Charles.

The miniskirted brigade had moved out of the Yard, and it was quiet and green and peaceful there. In our building another Jewish couple moved into #44. They did not eat gourmet stuff, and on occasion, threw out pork-and-beans cans. But I had lost interest in perception. I now had many records for my stereo, loads of S. S. Pierce stuff, and a small bottle of Chivas Regal which I never opened. I was working good again, and I did not miss other things as much; or at least I told myself that.

The old man was coming up steadily now, at least three times a day, and I had resigned myself to it. If I refused to let him in, he would always come back later with a missing bulb on the fifth floor. We had taken to buying cases of beer together, and when he had finished his half, which was very frequently, he would come up to polish off mine. I began to enjoy talking politics, the AMA, Medicare, beatniks, and listening to him recite from books he had read. I discovered that he was very well read in history, philosophy, literature, and law. He was extraordinarily fond of saying: "I am really a cut above being a building superintendent. Circumstances made me what I am." And even though he was drunk and dirty and it was very late at night, I believed him and liked him anyway because having him there was much better than being alone. After he had gone I could sleep, and I was not lonely in sleep; and it did not really matter how late I was at work the next morning because when I thought about it all, I discovered that nothing really matters except not being old and being alive and having potential to dream about, and not being alone.

*Isaac Bashevis Singer*

........................................................................................................

# The Key

FROM *The New Yorker*

AT ABOUT THREE O'CLOCK in the afternoon, Bessie Popkin began to prepare to go down to the street. Going out was connected with many difficulties, especially on a hot summer day: first, forcing her fat body into a corset, squeezing her swollen feet into shoes, and combing her hair, which Bessie dyed at home and which grew wild and was streaked in all colors — yellow, black, gray, red; then making sure that while she was out her neighbors would not break into her apartment and steal linen, clothes, documents, or just disarrange things and make them disappear.

Besides human tormentors, Bessie suffered from demons, imps, Evil Powers. She hid her eyeglasses in the night table and found them in a slipper. She placed her bottle of hair dye in the medicine chest; days later she discovered it under the pillow. Once, she left a pot of borscht in the refrigerator, but the Unseen took it from there and after long searching Bessie came upon it in her clothes closet. On its surface was a thick layer of fat that gave off the smell of rancid tallow.

What she went through, how many tricks were played on her and how much she had to wrangle in order not to perish or fall into insanity, only God knew. She had given up the telephone because racketeers and degenerates called her day and night, trying to get secrets out of her. The Puerto Rican milkman once tried to rape her. The errand boy from the grocery store attempted to burn her belongings with a cigarette. To evict her from the rent-controlled apartment where she had lived for thirty-five years, the company and the superintendent infested her rooms with rats, mice, cockroaches.

Bessie had long ago realized that no means were adequate against those determined to be spiteful — not the metal door, the special lock, her letters to the police, the mayor, the FBI, and even the president in

Washington. But while one breathed one had to eat. It all took time: checking the windows, the gas vents, securing the drawers. Her paper money she kept in volumes of the encyclopedia, in back copies of the *National Geographic,* and in Sam Popkin's old ledgers. Her stocks and bonds Bessie had hidden among the logs in the fireplace, which was never used, as well as under the seats of the easy chairs. Her jewels she had sewn into the mattress. There was a time when Bessie had safe-deposit boxes at the bank, but she long ago convinced herself that the guards there had passkeys.

At about five o'clock, Bessie was ready to go out. She gave a last look at herself in the mirror — small, broad, with a narrow forehead, a flat nose, and eyes slanting and half-closed, like a Chinaman's. Her chin sprouted a little white beard. She wore a faded dress in a flowered print, a misshapen straw hat trimmed with wooden cherries and grapes, and shabby shoes. Before she left, she made a final inspection of the three rooms and the kitchen. Everywhere there were clothes, shoes, and piles of letters that Bessie had not opened. Her husband, Sam Popkin, who had died almost twenty years ago, had liquidated his real-estate business before his death, because he was about to retire to Florida. He left her stocks, bonds, and a number of passbooks from savings banks, as well as some mortgages. To this day, firms wrote to Bessie, sent her reports, checks. The Internal Revenue Service claimed taxes from her. Every few weeks she received announcements from a funeral company that sold plots in an "airy cemetery." In former years, Bessie used to answer letters, deposit her checks, keep track of her income and expenses. Lately she had neglected it all. She even stopped buying the newspaper and reading the financial section.

In the corridor, Bessie tucked cards with signs on them that only she could recognize between the door and the door frame. The keyhole she stuffed with putty. What else could she do — a widow without children, relatives, or friends? There was a time when the neighbors used to open their doors, look out, and laugh at her exaggerated care; others teased her. That had long passed. Bessie spoke to no one. She didn't see well, either. The glasses she had worn for years were of no use. To go to an eye doctor and be fitted for new ones was too much of an effort. Everything was difficult — even entering and leaving the elevator, whose door always closed with a slam.

Bessie seldom went farther than two blocks from her building. The street between Broadway and Riverside Drive became noisier and filthier from day to day. Hordes of urchins ran around half-naked. Dark men with curly hair and wild eyes quarreled in Spanish with little women whose bellies were always swollen in pregnancy. They talked back in rattling voices. Dogs barked, cats meowed. Fires broke out and fire engines, ambulances, and police cars drove up. On Broadway, the old groceries had been replaced by supermarkets, where food must be picked out and put in a wagon and one had to stand in line before the cashier.

God in Heaven, since Sam died, New York, America — perhaps the whole world — was falling apart. All the decent people had left the neighborhood and it was overrun by a mob of thieves, robbers, whores. Three times Bessie's pocketbook had been stolen. When she reported it to the police, they just laughed. Every time one crossed the street, one risked one's life. Bessie took a step and stopped. Someone had advised her to use a cane, but she was far from considering herself an old woman or a cripple. Every few weeks she painted her nails red. At times, when the rheumatism left her in peace, she took clothes she used to wear from the closets, tried them on, and studied herself in the mirror.

Opening the door of the supermarket was impossible. She had to wait till someone held it for her. The supermarket itself was a place that only the Devil could have invented. The lamps burned with a glaring light. People pushing wagons were likely to knock down anyone in their path. The shelves were either too high or too low. The noise was deafening, and the contrast between the heat outside and the freezing temperature inside! It was a miracle that she didn't get pneumonia. More than anything else, Bessie was tortured by indecision. She picked up each item with a trembling hand and read the label. This was not the greed of youth but the uncertainty of age. According to Bessie's figuring, today's shopping should not have taken longer than three-quarters of an hour, but two hours passed and Bessie was still not finished. When she finally brought the wagon to the cashier, it occurred to her that she had forgotten the box of oatmeal. She went back and a woman took her place in line. Later, when she paid, there was new trouble. Bessie had put the bill in the right side of her bag, but it was not there. After long rummaging, she found it in a small change purse on the opposite side. Yes, who could believe that such things were possible? If she told someone, he would think she was ready for the madhouse.

When Bessie went into the supermarket, the day was still bright; now it was drawing to a close. The sun, yellow and golden, was sinking toward the Hudson, to the hazy hills of New Jersey. The buildings on Broadway radiated the heat they had absorbed. From under gratings where the subway trains rumbled, evil-smelling fumes arose. Bessie held the heavy bag of food in one hand, and in the other she grasped her pocketbook tightly. Never had Broadway seemed to her so wild, so dirty. It stank of softened asphalt, gasoline, rotten fruit, the excrement of dogs. On the sidewalk, among torn newspapers and the butts of cigarettes, pigeons hopped about. It was difficult to understand how these creatures avoided being stepped on in the crush of passers-by. From the blazing sky a golden dust was falling. Before a storefront hung with artificial grass, men in sweated shirts poured papaya juice and pineapple juice into themselves with haste, as if trying to extinguish a fire that consumed their insides. Above their heads hung coconuts carved in the shapes of Indians. On a side street, black and white children had opened a hydrant and were splashing naked in the gutter. In the midst of that heat wave, a truck with microphones drove around blaring out shrill songs and deafening blasts about a candidate for political office. From the rear of a truck, a girl with hair that stood up like wires threw out leaflets.

It was all beyond Bessie's strength — crossing the street, waiting for the elevator, and then getting out on the fifth floor before the door slammed. Bessie put the groceries down at the threshold and searched for her keys. She used her nail file to dig the putty out of the keyhole. She put in the key and turned it. But woe, the key broke. Only the handle remained in her hand. Bessie fully grasped the catastrophe. The other people in the building had copies of their keys hanging in the superintendent's apartment, but she trusted no one — some time ago, she had ordered a new combination lock, which she was sure no master key could open. She had a duplicate key somewhere in a drawer, but with her she carried only this one. "Well, this is the end," Bessie said aloud.

There was nobody to turn to for help. The neighbors were her blood enemies. The super only waited for her downfall. Bessie's throat was so constricted that she could not even cry. She looked around, expecting to see the fiend who had delivered this latest blow. Bessie had long since made peace with death, but to die on the steps or in the streets was too harsh. And who knows how long such agony could last? She began to ponder. Was there still open somewhere a store where they fitted keys? Even if there were, what could the locksmith copy from? He would have to come up here with his tools. For that, one needed a mechanic associated with the firm which produced these special locks. If at least she had money with her. But she never carried more than she needed to spend. The cashier in the supermarket had given her back only some twenty-odd cents. "O dear Momma, I don't want to live anymore!" Bessie spoke Yiddish, amazed that she suddenly reverted to that half-forgotten tongue.

After many hesitations, Bessie decided to go back down to the street. Perhaps a hardware store or one of those tiny shops that specialize in keys was still open. She remembered that there used to be such a key stand in the neighborhood. After all, other people's keys must get broken. But what should she do with the food? It was too heavy to carry with her. There was no choice. She would have to leave the bag at the door. "They steal anyhow," Bessie said to herself. Who knows, perhaps the neighbors intentionally manipulated her lock so that she would not be able to enter the apartment while they robbed her or vandalized her belongings.

Before Bessie went down to the street, she put her ear to the door.

She heard nothing except a murmur that never stopped, the cause and origin of which Bessie could not figure out. Sometimes it ticked like a clock; other times it buzzed, or groaned — an entity imprisoned in the walls or the water pipes. In her mind Bessie said goodbye to the food, which should have been in the refrigerator, not standing here in the heat. The butter would melt, the milk would turn sour. "It's a punishment! I am cursed, cursed," Bessie muttered. A neighbor was about to go down in the elevator and Bessie signaled to him to hold the door for her. Perhaps he was one of the thieves. He might try to hold her up, assault her. The elevator went down and the man opened the door for her. She wanted to thank him, but remained silent. Why thank her enemies? These were all sly tricks.

When Bessie stepped out into the street, night had fallen. The gutter was flooded with water. The streetlamps were reflected in the black pool as in a lake. Again there was a fire in the neighborhood. She heard the wailing of a siren, the clang of fire engines. Her shoes were wet. She came out on Broadway, and the heat slapped her like a sheet of tin. She had difficulty seeing in daytime; at night she was almost blind. There was light in the stores, but what they displayed Bessie could not make out. Passers-by bumped into her, and Bessie regretted that she didn't have a cane. Nevertheless, she began to walk along, close to the windows. She passed a drugstore, a bakery, a shop of rugs, a funeral parlor, but nowhere was there a sign of a hardware store. Bessie continued on her way. Her strength was ebbing, but she was determined not to give up. What should a person do when her key was broken off — die? Perhaps apply to the police. There might be some institution that took care of such cases. But where?

There must have been an accident. The sidewalk was crowded with spectators. Police cars and an ambulance blocked the street. Someone sprayed the asphalt with a hose, probably cleaning away the blood. It occurred to Bessie that the eyes of the onlookers gleamed with an uncanny satisfaction. They enjoy other people's misfortunes, she thought. It is their only comfort in this miserable city. No, she wouldn't find anybody to help her.

She had come to a church. A few steps led to the closed door, which was protected by an overhang and darkened by shadows. Bessie was barely able to sit down. Her knees wobbled. Her shoes had begun to pinch in the toes and above the heels. A bone in her corset broke and cut into her flesh. "Well, all the Powers of Evil are upon me tonight." Hunger mixed with nausea gnawed at her. An acid fluid came up to her mouth. "Father in Heaven, it's my end." She remembered the Yiddish proverb "If one lives without a reckoning, one dies without confession." She had even neglected to write her will.

Bessie must have dozed off, because when she opened her eyes there was a late-night stillness, the street half-empty and darkened. Store windows were no longer lit. The heat had evaporated and she felt chilly under her dress. For a moment she thought that her pocketbook had been stolen, but it lay on a step below her, where it had probably slipped. Bessie tried to stretch out her hand for it; her arm was numb. Her head, which rested against the wall, felt as heavy as a stone. Her legs had become wooden. Her ears seemed to be filled with water. She lifted one of her eyelids and saw the moon. It hovered low in the sky over a flat roof, and near it twinkled a greenish star. Bessie gaped. She had almost forgotten that there was a sky, a moon, stars. Years had passed and she never looked up — always down. Her windows were hung with draperies so that the spies across the street could not see her. Well, if there was a sky, perhaps there was also a God, angels, Paradise. Where else did the souls of her parents rest? And where was Sam now? She, Bessie, had abandoned all her duties. She never visited Sam's grave in the cemetery. She didn't even light a candle on the anniversary of his death. She was so steeped in wrangling with the lower powers that she did not remember the higher ones. For the first time in years, Bessie felt the need to recite a prayer. The Almighty would have mercy on her even though she did not deserve it. Father and Mother might intercede for her on high. Some Hebrew words hung on the tip of her tongue, but she could not recall them. Then she remembered. "Hear, O Israel." But what followed? "God forgive me," Bessie said. "I deserve everything that falls on me."

It became even quieter and cooler. Traffic lights changed from red to green, but a car rarely passed. From somewhere a Negro appeared. He staggered. He stopped not far from Bessie and turned his eyes to her. Then he walked on. Bessie knew that her bag was full of important documents, but for the first time she did not care about her property. Sam had left a fortune; it all had gone for naught. She continued to save for her old age as if she were still young. "How old am I?" Bessie asked herself. "What have I accomplished in all these years? Why didn't I go somewhere, enjoy my money, help somebody?" Something in her laughed. "I was possessed, completely not myself. How else can it be explained?" Bessie was astounded. She felt as if she had awakened from a long sleep. The broken key had opened a door in her brain that had shut when Sam died.

The moon had shifted to the other side of the roof — unusually large, red, its face obliterated. It was almost cold now. Bessie shivered. She realized that she could easily get pneumonia, but the fear of death was gone, along with her fear of being homeless. Fresh breezes drifted from the Hudson River. New stars appeared in the sky. A black cat approached from the other side of the street. For a while, it stood on the edge of the sidewalk and its green eyes looked straight at Bessie. Then slowly and cautiously it drew near. For years Bessie had hated all animals — dogs, cats, pigeons, even sparrows. They carried sicknesses. They made everything filthy. Bessie believed that there was a demon in every cat. She especially dreaded an encounter with a black cat, which was always an omen of evil. But now Bessie felt love for this creature that had no home, no possessions, no doors or keys, and lived on God's bounty. Before the cat neared Bessie, it smelled her bag. Then it began to rub its back on her leg, lifting up its tail and meowing. The poor thing is hungry. I wish I could give her something. How can one hate a creature like this, Bessie wondered. O Mother of mine, I was bewitched, bewitched. I'll begin a new life. A treacherous thought ran through her mind: perhaps remarry?

The night did not pass without adventure. Once, Bessie saw a white butterfly in the air. It hovered for a while over a parked car and then took off. Bessie knew it was a soul of a newborn baby, since real butterflies do not fly after dark. Another time, she wakened to see a ball of fire, a kind of lit-up soap bubble, soar from one roof to another and sink behind it. She was aware that what she saw was the spirit of someone who had just died.

Bessie had fallen asleep. She woke up with a start. It was daybreak. From the side of Central Park the sun rose. Bessie could not see it from here, but on Broadway the sky became pink and reddish. On the building to the left, flames kindled in the windows; the panes ran and blinked like the portholes of a ship. A pigeon landed nearby. It hopped on its little red feet and pecked into something that might have been a dirty piece of stale bread or dried mud. Bessie was baffled. How do these birds live? Where do they sleep at night? And how can they survive the rains, the cold, the snow? I will go home, Bessie decided. People will not leave me in the streets.

Getting up was a torment. Her body seemed glued to the step on which she sat. Her back ached and her legs tingled. Nevertheless, she began to walk slowly toward home. She inhaled the moist morning air. It smelled of grass and coffee. She was no longer alone. From the side streets men and women emerged. They were going to work. They bought newspapers at the stand and went down into the subway. They were silent and strangely peaceful, as if they, too, had gone through a night of soul-searching and come out of it cleansed. When do they get up if they are already on their way to work now, Bessie marveled. No, not all in this neighborhood were gangsters and murderers. One young man even nodded good morning to Bessie. She tried to smile at him, realizing she had forgotten that feminine gesture she knew so well in her youth; it was almost the first lesson her mother had taught her.

She reached her building, and outside stood the Irish super, her deadly enemy. He was talking to the garbage collectors. He was a giant of a man, with a short nose, a long upper lip, sunken cheeks, and a pointed chin. His yellow hair covered a bald spot. He gave Bessie a startled look. "What's the matter, Grandma?"

Stuttering, Bessie told him what had happened to her. She showed him the handle of the key she had clutched in her hand all night.

"Mother of God!" he called out.

"What shall I do?" Bessie asked.

"I will open your door."

"But you don't have a passkey."

"We have to be able to open all doors in case of fire."

The super disappeared into his own apartment for a few minutes, then he came out with some tools and a bunch of keys on a large ring. He went up in the elevator with Bessie. The bag of food still stood on the threshold, but it looked depleted. The super busied himself at the lock. He asked, "What are these cards?"

Bessie did not answer.

"Why didn't you come to me and tell me what happened? To be roaming around all night at your age — my God!" As he poked with his tools, a door opened and a little woman in a housecoat and slippers, her hair bleached and done up in curlers, came out. She said, "What happened to you? Every time I opened the door, I saw this bag. I took out your butter and milk and put them in my refrigerator."

Bessie could barely restrain her tears. "O my good people," she said. "I didn't know that . . ."

The super pulled out the other half of Bessie's key. He worked a little longer. He turned a key and the door opened. The cards fell down. He entered the hallway with Bessie and she sensed the musty odor of an apartment that has not been lived in for a long time. The super said, "Next time, if something like this happens call me. That's what I'm here for."

Bessie wanted to give him a tip, but her hands were too weak to open her bag. The neighbor woman brought in the milk and butter. Bessie went into her bedroom and lay down on the bed. There was a pressure on her breast and she felt like vomiting. Something heavy vibrated up from her feet to her chest. Bessie listened to it without alarm, only curious about the whims of the body; the super and the neighbor talked, and Bessie could not make out what they were saying. The same thing had happened to her over thirty years ago when she had been given anesthesia in the hospital before an operation — the doctor and the nurse were talking but their voices seemed to come from far away and in a strange language.

Soon there was silence, and Sam appeared. It was neither day nor night — a strange twilight. In her dream, Bessie knew that Sam was dead but that in some clandestine way he had managed to get away from the grave and visit her. He was feeble and embarrassed. He could not speak. They wandered through a space without a sky, without earth, a tunnel full of debris — the wreckage of a nameless structure — a corridor dark and winding, yet somehow familiar. They came to a region where two mountains met, and the passage between shone like sunset or sunrise. They stood there hesitating and even a little ashamed. It was like that night of their honeymoon when they went to Ellenville in the Catskills and were let by the hotel owner into their bridal suite. She heard the same words he had said to them then, in the same voice and intonation: "You don't need no key here. Just enter — and *mazel tov.*"

## Donald Barthelme

# A City of Churches

FROM *The New Yorker*

"YES," MR. PHILLIPS SAID, "ours is a city of churches all right."

Cecelia nodded, following his pointing hand. Both sides of the street were solidly lined with churches, standing shoulder to shoulder in a variety of architectural styles. The Bethel Baptist stood next to the Holy Messiah Free Baptist, Saint Paul's Episcopal next to Grace Evangelical Covenant. Then came the First Christian Science, the Church of God, All Souls, Our Lady of Victory, the Society of Friends, the Assembly of God, and the Church of the Holy Apostles. The spires and steeples of the traditional buildings were jammed in next to the broad imaginative flights of the "contemporary" designs.

"Everyone here takes a great interest in church matters," Mr. Phillips said.

Will I fit in, Cecelia wondered. She had come to Prester to open a branch office of a car-rental concern.

"I'm not especially religious," she said to Mr. Phillips, who was in the real-estate business.

"Not *now*," he answered. "Not *yet*. But we have many fine young people here. You'll get integrated into the community soon enough. The immediate problem is where are you to live? Most people," he said, "live in the church of their choice. All of our churches have many extra rooms. I have a few belfry apartments that I can show you. What price range were you thinking of?"

They turned a corner and were confronted with more churches. They passed Saint Luke's, the Church of the Epiphany, All Saints Ukrainian Orthodox, Saint Clement's, Fountain Baptist, Union Congregational, Saint Anargyri's, Temple Emanuel, the First Church of Christ

Reformed. The mouths of all the churches were gaping open. Inside, lights could be seen dimly.

"I can go up to a hundred and ten," Cecelia said. "Do you have any buildings here that are *not* churches?"

"None," said Mr. Phillips. "Of course, many of our fine church structures also do double duty as something else." He indicated a handsome Georgian façade. "That one," he said, "houses the United Methodist and the Board of Education. The one next to it, which is the Antioch Pentecostal, has the barbershop."

It was true. A red-and-white striped barber pole was attached inconspicuously to the front of the Antioch Pentecostal.

"Do many people rent cars here?" Cecelia asked. "Or would they, if there was a handy place to rent them?"

"Oh, I don't know," said Mr. Phillips. "Renting a car implies that you want to go somewhere. Most people are pretty content right here. We have a lot of activities. I don't think I'd pick the car-rental business if I was just starting out in Prester. But you'll do fine." He showed her a small, extremely modern building with a severe brick, steel, and glass front. "That's Saint Barnabas. Nice bunch of people over there. Wonderful spaghetti suppers."

Cecelia could see a number of heads looking out of the windows. But when they saw that she was staring at them, the heads disappeared.

"Do you think it's healthy for so many churches to be gathered together in one place?" she asked her guide. "It doesn't seem . . . *balanced*, if you know what I mean."

"We are famous for our churches," Mr. Phillips replied. "They are harmless. Here we are now."

He opened a door and they began climbing many flights of dusty stairs. At the end of the climb they entered a good-sized room, square, with windows on all four sides. There was a bed, a table and two chairs, lamps, a rug. Four very large brass bells hung in the exact center of the room.

"What a view!" Mr. Phillips exclaimed. "Come here and look."

"Do they actually ring these bells?" Cecelia asked.

"Three times a day," Mr. Phillips said, smiling. "Morning, noon, and night. Of course when they're rung you have to be pretty quick at getting out of the way. You get hit in the head by one of these babies and that's all she wrote."

"God Almighty," said Cecelia involuntarily. Then she said, "Nobody lives in the belfry apartments. That's why they're empty."

"You think so?" Mr. Phillips said.

"You can only rent them to new people in town," she said accusingly.

"I wouldn't do that," Mr. Phillips said. "It would go against the spirit of Christian fellowship."

"This town is a little creepy, you know that?"

"That may be, but it's not for you to say, is it? I mean, you're new here. You should walk cautiously, for a while. If you don't want an upper apartment, I have a basement over at Central Presbyterian. You'd have to share it. There are two women in there now."

"I don't want to share," Cecelia said. "I want a place of my own."

"Why?" the real-estate man asked curiously. "For what purpose?"

"Purpose?" asked Cecelia. "There is no particular purpose. I just want —"

"That's not usual here. Most people live with other people. Husbands and wives. Sons with their mothers. People have roommates. That's the usual pattern."

"Still, I prefer a place of my own."

"It's very unusual."

"Do you have any such places? Besides bell towers, I mean?"

"I guess there are a few," Mr. Phillips said, with clear reluctance. "I can show you one or two, I suppose."

He paused for a moment.

"It's just that we have different values, maybe, from some of the surrounding communities," he explained. "We've been written up a lot. We had four minutes on the 'CBS Evening News' one time. Three or four years ago. 'A City of Churches,' it was called."

"Yes, a place of my own is essential," Cecelia said, "if I am to survive here."

"That's kind of a funny attitude to take," Mr. Phillips said. "What denomination are you?"

Cecelia was silent. The truth was, she wasn't anything.

"I said, what denomination are you?" Mr. Phillips repeated.

"I can will my dreams," Cecelia said. "I can dream whatever I want. If I want to dream that I'm having a good time, in Paris or some other city, all I have to do is go to sleep and I will dream that dream. I can dream whatever I want."

"What do you dream, then, mostly?" Mr. Phillips said, looking at her closely.

"Mostly sexual things," she said. She was not afraid of him.

"Prester is not that kind of a town," Mr. Phillips said, looking away.

The doors of the churches were opening, on both sides of the street. Small groups of people came out and stood there, in front of the churches, gazing at Cecelia and Mr. Phillips.

A young man stepped forward and shouted, *"Everyone in this town already has a car! There is no one in this town who doesn't have a car!"*

"Is that true?" Cecelia asked Mr. Phillips.

"Yes," he said. "It's true. No one would rent a car here. Not in a hundred years."

"Then I won't stay," she said. "I'll go somewhere else."

"You must stay," he said. "There is already a car-rental office for you. In Mount Moriah Baptist, on the lobby floor. There is a counter and a telephone and a rack of car keys. And a calendar."

"I won't stay," she said. "Not if there's not any sound business reason for staying."

"We want you," said Mr. Phillips. "We want you standing behind the counter of the car-rental agency, during regular business hours. It will make the town complete."

"I won't," she said. "Not me."

"You must. It's essential."

"I'll dream," she said. "Things you won't like."

"We are discontented," said Mr. Phillips. "Terribly, terribly discontented. Something is wrong."

"I'll dream the Secret," she said. "You'll be sorry."

"We are like other towns, except that we are perfect," he said. "Our discontent can only be held in check by perfection. We need a car-rental girl. Someone must stand behind that counter."

"I'll dream the life you are most afraid of," Cecelia threatened.

"You are ours," he said, gripping her arm. "Our car-rental girl. Be nice. There is nothing you can do."

"Wait and see," Cecelia said.

1975

*Rosellen Brown*

........................................................................................................

# How to Win

FROM *The Massachusetts Review*

ALL THEY NEED at school is permission on a little green card that says *Keep this child at bay. Muffle him, tie his hands, his arms to his ankles, anything at all. Distance, distance. Dose him.* And they gave themselves permission. They never even mentioned a doctor, and their own certified bureaucrat in tweed (does he keep a badge in his pocket like the cops?) drops by the school twice a year for half a day. But I insisted on a doctor. And did and did, had to, because Howard keeps repeating vaguely that he is "within the normal range of boyish activity."

"But I live with it, all day every day."

"It? Live with *it?*"

Well, Howard can be as holy as he likes, I am his mother and I will not say "him." Him is the part I know, Christopher my first child and first son, the boy who was a helpless warm mound once in a blue nightie tied at the bottom to keep his toes in. ("God, Margaret, you are dramatic and sentimental and sloppy. How about being realistic for a change?") "It" is what races around my room at night, a bat, pulling down the curtain cornice, knocking over the lamps, tearing the petals off the flowers and stomping them, real or fake, to a powder.

Watch Christopher take a room some time; that's the word for it, like an army subduing a deserted plain. He stands in the doorway always for one extra split-split second, straining his shoulders down as though he's hitching himself to some machine, getting into harness. He has no hips, and round little six-year-old shoulders that look frail but are made of welded steel that has no give when you grab them. Then what does he see ahead of him? I'm no good at guessing. The room is an animal asleep, trusting the air, its last mistake. (See, I am sympathetic to the animal.) He leaps on it and leaves it disemboweled, then turns his dark eyes to me where I stand — when I stand, usually I'm dervishing around trying to stop the bloodshed — and they ask me Where did it go? What happened? Who killed this thing, it was just breathing, I wanted to *play* with it. Christopher. When you're not here to look at me I have to laugh at your absurd powers. You are incontinent, you leak energy. As for me, I gave birth to someone else's child.

There is a brochure inside the brown bottle that the doctor assigned us, very gay, full-color, busy with children riding their bicycles right through patches of daffodils, sleeping square in the middle of their pillows, doing their homework with a hazy expression to be attributed to concentration, not medication. NON-ADDICTIVE! NO SIGNIFICANT SIDE EFFECTS! Dosage should decrease by or around puberty. Counter-indications epilepsy, heart and circulatory complications, severe myopia and related eye problems. See Journal of Pediatric Medicine, III 136, F'71; Pharmacology Bulletin, v. 798, 18, pp. 19–26, D'72. CAUTION: DO NOT ALLOW CHILDREN ACCESS TO PILLS! SPECIAL FEATURE: U-LOK-IT CAP! REMEMBER, TEACH YOUR CHILD THE ETIQUETTE OF THE MEDICINE CABINET!

I know how he dreams me. I know because I dream his dreams. He runs to hide in me. Battered by the stick of the old dark he comes fast, hiccoughing terror. By the time I am up, holding him, it has hobbled off, it must be, into his memory. I've pulled on a robe, I spread my arms — do they look winged or webbed? — to pull him out of himself, hide him, swear the witch is nowhere near. He doesn't go to his father. But he won't look at my face.

It was you! He looks up at me finally and says nothing but I see him thinking. So: *I* was the witch, with a club behind my bent back. I the hundred-stalked flower with webbed branches. I with the flayed face held in my two hands like a bloody towel. Then how can I help him?

I whisper to him, wordless; just a music. He answers "Mama." It is a faint knocking, through layers of dirt, through flowers.

His sister Jody will dream those dreams, and all the children who will follow her. I suppose she will, like chicken pox every child can expect them: there's a three o'clock in the dark night of children's souls too, let's not be too arrogant taking our prerogatives. But if she does, she'll dream them alone, no accomplices. I won't meet her halfway, give her my own last fillip, myself in shreds.

I've been keeping a sort of log: a day in the life. For no purpose, since my sense of futility runs deeper than any data can testify to. Still it cools me off.

He is playing with Jacqueline. They are in the Rosenbergs' yard. C. is on his way to the sandbox which belongs to Jackie's baby brother, Brian, so I see trouble ahead. I will not interfere. No, *intervene* is the word they use. Interfere is not as objective, it's the mess that parents make, as opposed to the one the doctors make. As he goes down the long narrow yard at a good clip C. pulls up two peonies, knocks over Brian's big blonde blocky wooden horse (for which he has to stop and plant his feet very deliberately, it's that well-balanced, i.e., expensive). Kicks over short picket fence around tulips, finally gets to sandbox, walks up to Jackie whose back is to him and pushes her hard. She falls against fence and goes crying to her mother with a splinter. She doesn't even bother to retaliate, knowing him too well? Then he leans down into the sand. Turns to me again, that innocent face. It is not conniving, or falsely naive, I swear it's not. He isn't that kind of clever. Nor is he a gruff bully boy who likes to fly from trees and conquer turf: he has a small peaked face, a little French, I think, in need of one of those common Gallic caps with the peak on the front; a narrow forehead on which his dark hair lies flat like a salon haircut. Anything but a bully, this helpless child of mine — he has a weird natural elegance that terrifies me, as though it is true, what I feel, that he was intended to be someone else . . . Now he seems to be saying, Well, take all this stuff away if you don't want me to touch it. Get me out of this goddamn museum. Who says I'm not provoked? *That's what you say to each other.*

Why is *he* not glass? He will break us all without so much as chipping.

The worst thing I can think. I am dozing in the sun, Christopher is in kindergarten, Jody is napping, and I am guiltily trying to coax a little color into my late-fall pallor. It's a depressing bleary sun up there. But I sleep a little, waking in fits and snatches when Migdalia next door lets her kid have it and his whine sails across the yards, and when the bus shakes the earth all the way under the gas mains and water pipes to China. The worst thing is crawling through my head like a stream of red ants: What if he and I, Howie and I, had been somewhere else way back that night we smiled and nodded and made Christopher? If the night had been bone-cracking cold? If we were courting some aloneness, back to back? But it was summer, we were married three months, and the bottom sheet was spread like a picnic cloth. If there is an astrologer's clock, that's what we heard announcing to us the time was propitious; but I rehearse the time again. We lived off Riverside Drive that year and the next, I will float a thundercloud across the river from the Palisades and just as Howie turns to me I will have the most extraordinary burst of rain, sludgy and cold, explode through the open windows everywhere and finish us for the evening. The rugs are soaked, our books on the desk are corrugated with dampness, we snap at each other, Howie breaks a beer glass and blames me. We unmake him . . . Another night we will make a different child. Don't the genes shift daily in their milky medium like lottery tickets in their fishbowl? I unmake Christopher's skin and bone: egg in the water, blind; a single sperm thrusts out of its soft side, retreating. Arrow swimming backwards, tail drags the heavy head away from life. All the probability in the universe cheers. He is unjoined. I wake in a clammy sweat. The sun, such as it was, is caught behind the smokestacks at the far end of Pacific Street. I feel dirty, as though I've sinned in my sleep, and there's that fine perpetual silt on my arms and legs and face, the Con Ed sunburn. I go in and start making lunch for Christopher, who will survive me.

Log: He is sitting at the kitchen table trying to string kidney beans on a needle and thread. They do it in kindergarten. I forgot to ask why. Jody wakes upstairs, way at the back of the house with her door closed, and C. says quietly, without looking up from his string, "Ma, she's up." It's like hearing something happening, I don't know, a mile away. He has the instincts of an Indian guide, except when I stand right next to him to talk. Then it blows right by.

And when she's up. He seems to make a very special effort to be gentle with his little sister. I can see him forcibly subdue himself, tuck his hands inside his pockets or push them into the loops of his pants so that he loses no honor in restraint. But every now and then it gets the better of him. He walked by her just a minute ago and did just what he does to anything that's not nailed down or bigger than he is: gave her a casual but precise push. The way the bathmat slips into the tub without protest, the glass bowl gets smashed, its pieces settling with a resigned tinkle. I am, of course, the one who's resigned: I hear them ring against each other before they hit the ground, in the silence that envelops the shove.

This time Jody chose to lie back on the rug — fortunately it wasn't cement, I am grateful for small favors — and watch him. An amazing, endearing thing for a two-year-old. I think she has all the control that was meant for the two of them, and this is fair to neither. Eyes wide open, untearful, Jody the antidote, was thinking something about her brother. She cannot say what.

When his dosage has been up a while he begins to cringe before her. It is unpredictable and unimaginable but true and I bear witness to it here. As I was writing the above he ran in and hid behind my chair. Along came J., who had just righted herself after the attack on her; she was pulling her corn popper, vaguely humming. For C., an imagined assault? Provoked? Real? Wished-for?

Howard, on his way out of the breakfast chaos, bears his briefcase like a shield, holds it in front of him for lack of space while he winds his way around the table in our little alcove, planting firm kisses on our fore- heads. On his way out the door he can be expected to say something cheerful and blind to encourage me through the next unpredictable half hour before I walk Christopher up the block to school. This morning, unlocking the front gate I caught him pondering. "Well, what are other kids like? I mean we've never had any others so how do we know where they fall on the spectrum?"

"We know," I said. "What about Jody?"

"Oh," he said, waving her away like a fly. "I mean boys."

"We also know because we're not knots on logs, some of us, that's how we know. What was it he did to your shaver this morning?"

Smashed it to smithereens is what he did, and left cobweb cracks in the mirror he threw it at.

To which his father shrugged and turned to pull the gate shut fast.

Why did we have Jody? People dare to ask, astonished, though it's none of their business. They mean, and expect us to forgive them, how could we take such a martyr's chance. I tell them that when C. was born I was ready for a large family. You can't be a secretary forever, no matter how many smash titles your boss edits. Nor an administrative assistant, nor an indispensable right hand. I've got my own arms, for which I need all the hands I've got. I like to be boss, thank you, in my own house. It's a routine by now, canned as an Alka-Seltzer ad.

But I'll tell you. For a long time I guarded very tensely against having another baby. C. was hurting me too much, already he was. Howard would rap with his fist on my nightgowned side, demanding admission. For a while I played virgin. I mean, I didn't try, I wasn't playing. He just couldn't make any headway. I've heard it called dys-something; also crossbones, to get right down to what it's like. (Dys-something put me right in there with my son, doesn't it? I'll bet there's some drug, some muscle relaxant that bones you and just lays you out on the knife like a chicken to be stuffed and trussed . . .) Even though it wasn't his fault I'll never forgive Howard for using his fists on me, even as gently and facetiously as he did. Finally I guess he got tired of trying to disarm me one night at a time, of bringing wine to bed or dancing with me obscenely like a kid at a petting party or otherwise trying to distract me while he stole up on me. So that's when he convinced me to have another baby. I guess it seemed easier. "We'll make Christopher our one exceptional child while we surround him with ordinary ones. We'll grow a goddamn garden around him, he'll be outnumbered."

Well — I bought it. We could make this child matter less. It was an old and extravagant solution. Black flowers in his brain, what blight would the next one have, I insisted he *promise* me. He lied, ah, he lied with his hand between my legs, he swore the next would be just as beautiful but timid — "Downright phlegmatic, how's that?" — and would teach Christopher to be human. So I sighed, desperate to believe, and unlocked my thighs, gone rusty and stiff. But I'll tell you, right as he turned out, by luck, to be, I think I never trusted him again, one of my two deceitful boys, because whatever abandon I once had is gone, sure as my waist is gone. I feel it now and Howard is punished for it. Starting right then, making Jody, I have dealt myself out in careful proportions, like an unreliable cook bent only on her batter.

Meanwhile I lose one lamp, half the ivory on the piano keys, and all my sewing patterns to my son in a single day. On the same day I lose my temper, lose it so irretrievably that I am tempted to pop one of Christopher's little red pills myself and go quietly. Who's the most frightening, the skimpy six-year-old flying around on the tail of his bird of prey, or his indispensable right hand mama smashing the canned goods into the closet with a sound generally reserved for the shooting range? All the worse, off his habit for a few days, his eyes clear, his own, he is trying to be sweet, he smiles wanly whenever some catastrophe overtakes him, like an actor with no conviction. But someone else controls his muscles.

He is not riding it now but lives in the beak of something huge and dark that dangles him just out of my reach.

Our brains are all circuitry; not very imaginative, I tend to see it blue and red and yellow like the wires in phones, easier to sort impulses that way. I want to see inside Christopher's head, I stare viciously though I try to do it when he's involved with something else. (He never is, he would feel me a hundred light years behind him.) I vow never to *study* him again, it's futile anyway, his forehead's not a one-way mirror. Promises, always my promises: they are glass. I knew when they shatter — no, when he shatters them, throwing something of value — there will be edges to draw blood, edges everywhere. He says, "What are you *looking* at all the time? Bad Christopher the dragon?" He looks wilted, pathetic, seen-through. But I haven't seen a thing.

"Chrissie." I put my arms around him. He doesn't want to bruise the air he breathes, maybe we're all jumbled in his sight. He doesn't read yet, I know that's why. It's all upside down or somehow mixed together — cubist sight, is there such a thing? He sees my face and the top of my head, say, at the same time. Or everything looms at him, quivering like a fun-house mirror, swollen, then slowly disappears down to a point. He has to subdue it before it overtakes him? How would we ever know? Why, if he saw just what we see — the cool and calm of all the things of the world all sorted out like laundry ("Oh, Margaret, come off it!") why would he look so bewildered most of the time like a terrier being dragged around by his collar, his small face thrust forward into his own perpetual messes?

He comes to me just for a second, pulling on his tan windbreaker, already breathing fast to run away somewhere, and while I hold him tight a minute, therapeutic hug for both of us, he pinches my arm until the purple capillaries dance with pain.

"Let me take him with me when I go to D.C. next week." Howard.

I stare at him. "You've got to be kidding."

"No, why would I kid about it? We'll manage, we can go see some buildings after my conference is out, go to the Smithsonian. He'd love the giant pendulum." His eyes are already there in the cool of the great vaulted room where everything echoes and everything can break. I am fascinated by his casualness. "What would he do all day while you're in your meeting? Friend. My intrepid friend."

"Oh, we'd manage something. He'd keep busy. Paper and pencil . . ."

"*Howie.*" Am I crazy? Is he? Do we live in the same house?

He comes and takes both my hands. There is that slightly conniving look my husband gets that makes me forget, goddamit, why I married him. He is all too reasonable and gentle a man most of the time, but this look is way in the back of his eyes behind a pillar, peeking out. I feel surrounded. "You can't take him." I wrench my hands away.

"Maggie —" and he tries to take them again, bungler, as though they're contested property.

"I forbid it. Insanity. You'll end up crushing him to death to get a little peace! I know."

He smiles with unbearable patience. "I know how to handle my son."

But I walk out of the room, thin-lipped, taking a bowl of fruit to the children who are raging around, both of them, in front of the grade-A educational television that's raging back.

The next week Howie goes to Washington and we all go to the airport to see him off. I don't know what Howard told him but while Jody sleeps Christopher cries noisily in the back of the car and flings himself around so wildly, like a caged bear, that I have to stop the car on the highway shoulder and buckle him into his seat belt. "You will walk home," I threaten, calm because I can see the battle plan. He's got a little of his father in him; that should make me feel better.

He hisses at me and goes on crying, forcing the tears and walloping the back of my seat with his feet the whole way home.

Log: The long long walk to school. A block and a half. Most of the kids in kindergarten with Christopher walk past our house alone, solidly bearing straight west with the bland eight o'clock sun at their backs. They concentrate, they have been told not to cross heavy traffic alone, not to speak to strangers, not to dawdle. All the major wisdom of motherhood pinned to their jackets like a permission slip. Little orders turning into habits and hardening slowly to super-ego: an amber that holds commands forever. Christopher lacks it the way some children are born without a crucial body chemical. Therefore, I walk him to school every day, rain or shine, awake or asleep.

Jody's in her stroller slouching. She'd rather be home. So would I. It's beginning to get chilly out, edgy, and that means the neighborhood's been stripped of summer and fall, as surely as if a man came by one day confiscating color. What little there is, you wouldn't think it could matter. Blame the mayor. The window-boxes are crowded with brown stringy corpses, like tall crabgrass. Our noble pint-sized trees have shrunk back into themselves, they lose five years in winter. Fontaine, always improving his property, has painted his new brick wall *silver* over the weekend — it has a sepulchral gleam in the vague sunlight, twinkling as placidly as a woman who's come in sequins to a business meeting, *believing* in herself. Bless him. Next door to him the Rosenbergs have bought subtle aged wood shutters, they look like some dissected Vermont barn door, and a big rustic barrel that will stand achingly empty all winter, weighted with a hundred pounds of dirt to exhaust the barrel burglars. I wonder what my illusions look like through the front window.

Christopher's off and running. "Not in the street!" I get so tired of my voice, especially because I know he doesn't hear it. "Stay on the curb, Christopher." There's enough damage to be done there. He is swinging on that new couple's gate, straining the hinges, trying to fan up a good wind; then, when I look up from attending to Jody's dropped and splintered Ritz cracker, he's gone — clapping together two garbage can lids across the street. Always under an old lady's window, though with no particular joy — his job, it's there to be done. Jody is left with her stroller braked against a tree for safe keeping while I retrieve him. No one ever told me I'd grow up to be a shepherdess; and bad at it too — undone by a single sheep.

We are somehow at the corner, at least I can demand he hold my hand and drag us across the street where the crossing guard stands and winks at me daily, as dependably as a blinking light. She is a good lady, Mrs. Cortes, from a couple of blocks down in the projects, with many matching daughters, one son, Anibal, on the sixth grade honor roll and another on Riker's Island, a junkie. She is waving cars and people forward in waves, demonstrating "community involvement" to placate the gods who are seeing to Anibal's future, I know it. I recognize something deep behind her lively eyes, sunk there: a certain desperate casualness while the world has its way with her children. Another shepherdess without a chance. I give her my little salute.

By now, my feet heavy with the monotony of this trip, we are on the long school block. The barbed wire of the playground breaks for the entrance halfway down. This street, unlived on, is an unrelenting tangle — no one ever sees the generous souls who bequeath their dead cars to the children, but there are dozens, in various stages of decay; they must make regular deliveries. Christopher's castles; creative playthings, and broken already so he never gets blamed. For some reason he picks the third one. He's already in there, across a moat of broken windshield glass, reaching for the steering wheel. The back seat's burned out, the

better to jump on. All the chrome has been cannibalized by the adults
— everything that twists or lifts off, leaving a carcass of flung bones, its
tin flesh dangling.

"Christopher, you are late and I. Am. Not. Waiting." But he will not
come that way. My son demands the laying-on of hands. Before I can
maneuver my way in, feeling middle-aged and worrying about my skirt,
hiked up over my rear, he is tussling not with one boy but with two.
They fight over nothing — just lock hands and wrestle as a kind of
greeting. "I break the muh-fuh's head," one announces matter-of-factly
— second grader maybe. Christopher doesn't fight for stakes like that,
though. Whoever wants his head can have it, he's fighting to get his
hands on something, keep them warm. I am reaching over the jagged
door, which is split in two and full of rain water. The school bell rings,
that raspy grinding, and the two boys, with a whoop, leap over the
downed windshield and are gone. Christopher is grater-scraped along
one cheek but we have arrived more or less in one piece.

I decide I'd better come in with him and see to it his cheek is washed
off. He is, of course, long gone by the time I park the stroller and
take the baby out. He never bothers to say goodbye. Maybe six-year-olds
don't.

I pull open the heavy door to P.S. 193. It comes reluctantly, like it's in
many parts. These doors are not for children. But then, neither is the
school . . . It's a fairly new building but the 1939 World's Fair architec-
ture has just about caught up with the lobby — those heavy streamlined
effects. A ship, that's what it looks like; a dated ocean liner, or the lobby
of Rockefeller Center, one humble corner of it. What do the kids see, I
wonder? Not grandeur.

There's a big lit-up case to the left that shows off sparse student
pieties, untouchable as seven-layer cakes at the bakery. THIS LAND IS
*Your* LAND, THIS LAND IS *My* LAND. Every figure in the pictures,
brown, black, dead-white (blank), mustard yellow, tulip red and olive
green (who's that?) is connected more or less at the wrist, like uncut
paper dolls (HANDS ACROSS THE SEA). The whole world's afraid to
drop hands, the hell with summit talks, SALT talks, we're on the buddy
system. Well, *they* go up and down the halls irrevocably linked so, their
lips sealed, the key thrown over their endless shoulder, only the teacher
nattering on and on about discipline and respect, wearing heels that
must sound like SS boots, though they are intended merely to mean
business. Christopher tells me only that his teachers are noisy and hurt
his ears; he does not bother to specify how.

And what he sees when he puts his thin shoulder to the door at 8:30 and heaves? He probably catches that glaring unnecessary shine on the floor, an invitation, and takes it. That worried crease between big eyes, his face looks back at him out of deep water. Deeper when he's drugged. So he careens around without ice-skates, knocks against other kids hard, thumps into closed doors, nearly cracks open THIS LAND IS YOUR LAND. He is the wiseacre who dances to hold the door for his class, then when the last dark pigtail is through skips off in the wrong direction, leaps the steps to the gym or the auditorium or whatever lives down there in deserted silence most of the morning, the galley of this ship. I don't blame him, of course I don't, but that isn't the point, is it? I am deprived of these fashionable rebellious points. We only, madam, allow those in control to be out of control. As it were. If you follow. Your son, madam, is not rebelling. He is unable. Is beyond. Is utterly. Is unthinkable. Catch him before we do.

We are certainly late, the lines are all gone, the kids settling into their rooms, their noise dwindling like a cut-back motor. Jody and I just stand for a minute or two tuning in. Her head is heavy on my shoulder. Already there's a steady monitor traffic, the officious kids scurrying to do their teachers' bidding like tailless mice. I was one of them for years and years, God, faceless and obliging: official blackboard eraser (which meant a few cool solitary minutes just before three each day, down in the basement storeroom clapping two erasers together, hard, till they smoked with the day's vanished lessons). I would hardly have stopped my frantic do-gooding to give the time of day (off the clocks that jerked forward with a click every new minute) to the likes of Christopher. I'd have given him a wide berth, I can see myself going the other way if I saw him coming towards me in the narrow hall.

This hall, just like the ones I grew up in except for the "modernistic" shower tile that reaches halfway up, has a muted darkened feeling, an underwater thrum. Even the tile is like the Queens Midtown Tunnel, deserted. I will not be particularly welcome in Christopher's kindergarten room, there is that beleaguered proprietary feeling that any parent is a spy or come to complain. (I, in my own category, have been forbidden to complain, at least tacitly, having been told that my son really needs one whole teacher to himself, if not for his sake, then for the safety of the equipment and "the consumables," of which he is not one.)

Christopher has disappeared into his class which — I see it through the little porthole — is neat and earnest and not so terribly different from a third-grade room, say, with its alphabets and exhortations to patriotism and virtue above eye level. They are allowed to paint in one color at a time. A few, I see, have graduated to two; they must be disciplined, promising children in their securely tied smocks. One spring they will hatch into monitors. Christopher is undoubtedly banned from the painting corner. (Classroom economy? Margaret, your kitchen, your bedroom, your bathroom this morning. Searching for the glass mines hidden between the tiles.) Mrs. Seabury is inspecting hands. The children turn them, patty-cake, and step back when she finishes her scrutiny, which is as grave as a doctor's. Oh Christopher! She has sent him and another little boy to the sink to scrub; to throw water, that is, and stick their fingers in the spout in order to shower the children in the back of the room. I am not going in there to identify myself.

Mrs. Seabury is the kind of teacher who, with all her brown and black kids on one side of the room (this morning in the back, getting showered), talks about discrimination and means big from little, forward from backward, ass from elbow. Now I see she has made Christopher an honorary Black child, or maybe one of your more rambunctious Puerto Ricans. They are all massed back there for the special inattention of the aide, who is one of my least favorite people: she is very young and wears a maxi skirt that the kids keep stepping on when she bends down. (Therefore she bends down as little as possible.) The Future Felons of America and their den mother. I'm caught somewhere between my first flash of anger and then shame at what I suppose, wearily, is arrogance. What am I angry at? That he has attained pariah-hood with them, overcoming his impeccable WASP heritage in a single leap of adrenaline? Jesus. They are the "unruly characters" he's supposed to be afraid of: latchkey babies, battered boys and abused girls, or loved but hungry, scouted by rats while they sleep. Products of this-and-that converging, social, political, economic, each little head impaled on a point of the grid. Christopher? My warm, healthy, nursed and coddled, vitamin-enriched boy, born on Blue Cross, swaddled in his grandparents' gifts from Lord & Taylor? What in the hell is our excuse? My pill-popping baby, so sad, so reduced and taken from himself when he's on, so indescribable, air-borne, when he's off. This week he is off; I am sneaking him a favor.

I see him now flapping around in a sort of ragged circle with the other unimaginables, under the passive eye of that aide. Crows? Buzzards? Not pigeons, anyway. They make their own rowdy music. Then Christopher clenches his whole body, I see it coming, and stops short, slamming half a dozen kids together, solid rear-end collisions. It looks like the New Jersey Turnpike, everybody whiplashed, tumbling down. No reason, no why's, there is never anything to explain. Was the room taking off, spinning him dizzy? Was he fending something off, or trying to catch hold? The others turn to him, shout so loud I can hear them out here where I'm locked, underwater — and they all pile on. Oh, can they pile! It's a sport in itself. Feet and hands and dark faces deepening a shade. The aide gets out of the way, picking her skirt out of the rubble of children at her feet.

One heavy dark boy with no wrists finally breaks through the victor: his foot is on Christopher's neck. The little pale face jerks up stiffly, like an executed man's. I turn away. When I make myself turn back the crowd is unraveling as Mrs. Seabury approaches. Faces all around are taking on that half-stricken, half-delighted "uh-oh" look. I was always good at that, one of the leaders of censure and shock. It felt good.

But Christopher sinks down, quiet. She reaches down roughly and yanks his fresh white collar. Good boy, he doesn't look up at her. But something is broken. The mainspring, the defiant arch of his back that I would recognize, his, mine, I find I am weeping, soundless as everything around me, I feel it suddenly like blood on my cheeks. This teacher, this stranger and her cohorts have him by his pale limp neck. They are teaching him how to lose; or me how to win. My son is down for the count, breathing comfortably, accommodating, only his fingers twitching fiercely at his sides like gill slits puffing, while I stand outside, a baby asleep on my shoulder. I am the traitor, he sees me through my one-way mirror, and he is right. I am the witch. Every day they walk on his neck, I see that now, but he will never tell me about it. I weep but cannot move.

*Alice Adams*

·····································································································

# Roses, Rhododendron

FROM *The New Yorker*

ONE DARK AND RAINY Boston spring of many years ago, I spent all my after-school and evening hours in the living room of our antique-crammed Cedar Street flat, writing down what the Ouija board said to my mother. My father, a spoiled and rowdy Irishman, a sometime engineer, had run off to New Orleans with a girl, and my mother hoped to learn from the board if he would come back. Then, one night in May, during a crashing black thunderstorm (my mother was both afraid and much in awe of such storms), the board told her to move down South, to North Carolina, taking me and all the antiques she had been collecting for years, and to open a store in a small town down there. That is what we did, and shortly thereafter, for the first time in my life, I fell violently and permanently in love: with a house, with a family of three people, and with an area of countryside.

Perhaps too little attention is paid to the necessary preconditions of "falling in love" — I mean the state of mind or place that precedes one's first sight of the loved person (or house or land). In my own case, I remember the dark Boston afternoons as a precondition of love. Later on, for another important time, I recognized boredom in a job. And once the fear of growing old.

In the town that she has chosen, my mother, Margot (she picked out her own name, having been christened Margaret), rented a small house on a pleasant back street. It had a big surrounding screened-in porch, where she put most of the antiques, and she put a discreet sign out in the front yard: "Margot — Antiques." The store was open only in the afternoons. In the mornings and on Sundays, she drove around the countryside in our ancient and spacious Buick, searching for trophies among the area's country stores and farms and barns. (She is nothing if not enterprising; no one else down there had thought of doing that before.)

Although frequently embarrassed by her aggression — she thought nothing of making offers for furniture that was in use in a family's rooms — I often drove with her during those first few weeks. I was excited by the novelty of the landscape. The red clay banks that led up to the thick pine groves, the swollen brown creeks half hidden by flowering tangled vines. Bare, shaded yards from which rose gaunt, narrow houses. Chickens that scattered, barefoot children who stared at our approach.

"Hello there. I'm Mrs. John Kilgore — Margot Kilgore — and I'm interested in buying old furniture. Family portraits. Silver."

Margot a big brassily bleached blonde in a pretty flowered-silk dress and high-heeled patent sandals. A hoarse and friendly voice. Me a scrawny, pale, curious girl, about ten, in a blue linen dress with smocking across the bodice. (Margot has always had a passionate belief in good clothes, no matter what.)

On other days, Margot would say, "I'm going to look over my so-called books. Why don't you go for a walk or something, Jane?"

And I would walk along the sleepy, leafed-over streets, on the unpaved sidewalks, past houses that to me were as inviting and as interesting as unread books, and I would try to imagine what went on inside. The families. Their lives.

The main street, where the stores were, interested me least. Two-story brick buildings — dry-goods stores, with dentists' and lawyers' offices above. There was also a drugstore, with round marble tables and wire-backed chairs, at which wilting ladies sipped at their Cokes (this was to become a favorite haunt of Margot's). I preferred the civic monuments: a pre-Revolutionary Episcopal chapel of yellowish cracked plaster, and several tall white statues to the Civil War dead — all of them quickly overgrown with ivy or Virginia creeper.

These were the early nineteen-forties, and in the next few years the town was to change enormously. Its small textile factories would be given defense contracts (parachute silk); a Navy preflight school would be established at a neighboring university town. But at that moment it was a sleeping village. Untouched.

My walks were not a lonely occupation, but Margot worried that they were, and some curious reasoning led her to believe that a bicycle would help. (Of course, she turned out to be right.) We went to Sears, and she bought me a big new bike — blue, with balloon tires — on which I began to explore the outskirts of town and countryside.

The house I fell in love with was about a mile out of town, on top of a hill. A small stone bank that was all overgrown with tangled roses led up to its yard, and pink and white roses climbed up a trellis to the roof of the front porch — the roof on which, later, Harriet and I used to sit and exchange our stores of erroneous sexual information. Harriet Farr was the daughter of the house. On one side of the house, there was what looked like a newer wing, with a bay window and a long side porch, below which the lawn sloped down to some flowering shrubs. There was a yellow rosebush, rhododendron, a plum tree, and beyond were woods — pines, and oak and cedar trees. The effect was rich and careless, generous and somewhat mysterious. I was deeply stirred.

As I was observing all this, from my halted bike on the dusty white hilltop, a small, plump woman, very erect, came out of the front door and went over to a flower bed below the bay window. She sat down very stiffly. (Emily, who was Harriet's mother, had some terrible, never diagnosed trouble with her back; she generally wore a brace.) She was older than Margot, with very beautiful white hair that was badly cut in that butchered nineteen-thirties way.

From the first, I was fascinated by Emily's obvious dissimilarity to Margot. I think I was also somehow drawn to her contradictions — the shapeless body held up with so much dignity, even while she was sitting in the dirt. The lovely chopped-off hair. (There were greater contradictions, which I learned of later — she was a Virginia Episcopalian who always voted for Norman Thomas, a feminist who always delayed meals for her tardy husband.)

Emily's hair was one of the first things about the Farr family that I mentioned to Margot after we became friends, Harriet and Emily and I, and I began to spend most of my time in that house.

"I don't think she's ever dyed it," I said, with almost conscious lack of tact.

Of course, Margot was defensive. "I wouldn't dye mine if I thought it would be a decent color on its own."

But by that time Margot's life was also improving. Business was fairly good, and she had finally heard from my father, who began to send sizable checks from New Orleans. He had found work with an oil company. She still asked the Ouija board if she would see him again, but her question was less obsessive.

The second time I rode past that house, there was a girl sitting on the front porch, reading a book. She was about my age. She looked up. The next time I saw her there, we both smiled. And the time after that (a Saturday morning in late June) she got up and slowly came out to the road, to where I had stopped, ostensibly to look at the view — the sweep of fields, the white highway, which wound down to the thick greenery bordering the creek, the fields and trees that rose in dim and distant hills.

"I've got a bike exactly like that," Harriet said indifferently, as though to deny the gesture of having come out to meet me.

For years, perhaps beginning then, I used to seek my antithesis in friends. Inexorably following Margot, I was becoming a big blonde, with some of her same troubles. Harriet was cool and dark, with long, gray eyes. A girl about to be beautiful.

"Do you want to come in? We've got some lemon cake that's pretty good."

Inside, the house was cluttered with odd mixtures of furniture. I glimpsed a living room, where there was a shabby sofa next to a pretty, "antique" table. We walked through a dining room that contained a decrepit mahogany table surrounded with delicate fruitwood chairs. (I had a horrifying moment of imagining Margot there, with her accurate eye — making offers in her harsh Yankee voice.) The walls were crowded with portraits and with nineteenth-century oils of bosky landscapes. Books overflowed from rows of shelves along the walls. I would have moved in at once.

We took our lemon cake back to the front porch and ate it there, overlooking that view. I can remember its taste vividly. It was light and tart and sweet, and a beautiful lemon color. With it, we drank cold milk, and then we had seconds and more milk, and we discussed what we liked to read.

We were both at an age to begin reading grownup books, and there was some minor competition between us to see who had read more of them. Harriet won easily, partly because her mother reviewed books for the local paper, and had brought home Steinbeck, Thomas Wolfe, Virginia Woolf, and Elizabeth Bowen. But we also found in common an enthusiasm for certain novels about English children. (Such snobbery!)

"It's the best cake I've ever had!" I told Harriet. I had already adopted something of Margot's emphatic style.

"It's very good," Harriet said judiciously. Then, quite casually, she added, "We could ride our bikes out to Laurel Hill."

We soared dangerously down the winding highway. At the bridge across the creek, we stopped and turned onto a narrow, rutted dirt road that followed the creek through woods as dense and as alien as a jungle would have been — thick pines with low sweeping branches, young leafed-out maples, peeling tall poplars, elms, brambles, green masses of honeysuckle. At times, the road was impassable, and we had to get off our bikes and push them along, over crevices and ruts, through mud or sand. And with all that we kept up our somewhat stilted discussion of literature.

"I love Virginia Woolf!"

"Yes, she's very good. Amazing metaphors."

I thought Harriet was an extraordinary person — more intelligent, more poised, and prettier than any girl of my age I had ever known. I felt that she could become anything at all — a writer, an actress, a foreign correspondent (I went to a lot of movies). And I was not entirely wrong; she eventually became a sometimes-published poet.

We came to a small beach, next to a place where the creek widened and ran over some shallow rapids. On the other side, large gray rocks rose steeply. Among the stones grew isolated, twisted trees, and huge bushes with thick green leaves. The laurel of Laurel Hill. Rhododendron. Harriet and I took off our shoes and waded into the warmish water. The bottom squished under our feet, making us laugh, like the children we were, despite all our literary talk.

Margot was also making friends. Unlike me, she seemed to seek her own likeness, and she found a sort of kinship with a woman named Dolly Murray, a rich widow from Memphis who shared many of Margot's superstitions — fear of thunderstorms, faith in the Ouija board. About ten years older than Margot, Dolly still dyed her hair red; she was a noisy, biased, generous woman. They drank gin and gossiped together, they met for Cokes at the drugstore, and sometimes they drove to a neighboring town to have dinner in a restaurant (in those days, still a daring thing for unescorted ladies to do).

I am sure that the Farrs, outwardly a conventional family, saw me as a neglected child. I was so available for meals and overnight visits. But that is not how I experienced my life — I simply felt free. And an important thing to be said about Margot as a mother is that she never made me feel guilty for doing what I wanted to do. And of how many mothers can that be said?

There must have been a moment of "meeting" Emily, but I have forgotten it. I remember only her gentle presence, a soft voice, and my own sense of love returned. Beautiful white hair, dark deep eyes, and a wide mouth, whose corners turned and moved to express whatever she felt — amusement, interest, boredom, pain. I have never since seen such a vulnerable mouth.

I amused Emily; I almost always made her smile. She must have seen me as something foreign — a violent, enthusiastic Yankee (I used forbidden words, like "God" and "damn"). Very unlike the decorous young Southern girl that she must have been, that Harriet almost was.

She talked to me a lot; Emily explained to me things about the South that otherwise I would not have picked up. "Virginians feel superior to everyone else, you know," she said, in her gentle (Virginian) voice. "Some people in my family were quite shocked when I married a man from North Carolina and came down here to live. And a Presbyterian at that! Of course, that's nowhere near as bad as a Baptist, but only Episcopalians really count." This was all said lightly, but I knew that some part of Emily agreed with the rest of her family.

"How about Catholics?" I asked her, mainly to prolong the conversation. Harriet was at the dentist's, and Emily was sitting at her desk answering letters. I was perched on the sofa near her, and we both faced the sweeping green view. But since my father, Johnny Kilgore, was a lapsed Catholic, it was not an entirely frivolous question. Margot was a sort of Christian Scientist (her own sort).

"We hardly know any Catholics." Emily laughed, and then she sighed. "I do sometimes still miss Virginia. You know, when we drive up there I can actually feel the difference as we cross the state line. I've met a few people from South Carolina," she went on, "and I understand that people down there feel the same way Virginians do." (Clearly, she found this unreasonable.)

"West Virginia? Tennessee?"

"They don't seem Southern at all. Neither do Florida and Texas — not to me."

("Dolly says that Mrs. Farr is a terrible snob," Margot told me, inquiringly.

"In a way." I spoke with a new diffidence that I was trying to acquire from Harriet.

"Oh.")

Once, I told Emily what I had been wanting to say since my first sight of her. I said, "Your hair is so beautiful. Why don't you let it grow?"

She laughed, because she usually laughed at what I said, but at the same time she looked surprised, almost startled. I understood that what I had said was not improper but that she was totally unused to attentions of that sort from anyone, including herself. She didn't think about her hair. In a puzzled way, she said, "Perhaps I will."

Nor did Emily dress like a woman with much regard for herself. She wore practical, seersucker dresses and sensible, low shoes. Because her body had so little shape, no indentations (this must have been at least partly due to the back brace), I was surprised to notice that she had pretty, shapely legs. She wore little or no makeup on her sun-and-wind-weathered face.

And what of Lawrence Farr, the North Carolina Presbyterian for whom Emily had left her people and her state? He was a small, precisely made man, with fine dark features (Harriet looked very like him). A lawyer, but widely read in literature, especially the English nineteenth century. He had a courtly manner, and sometimes a wicked tongue; melancholy eyes, and an odd, sudden, ratchety laugh. He looked ten years younger than Emily; the actual difference was less than two.

"Well," said Margot, settling into a Queen Anne chair — a new antique — on our porch one stifling hot July morning, "I heard some really interesting gossip about your friends."

Margot had met and admired Harriet, and Harriet liked her, too — Margot made Harriet laugh, and she praised Harriet's fine brown hair. But on some instinct (I am not sure whose) the parents had not met. Very likely, Emily, with her Southern social antennae, had somehow sensed that this meeting would be a mistake.

That morning, Harriet and I were going on a picnic in the woods to the steep rocky side of Laurel Hill, but I forced myself to listen, or half listen, to Margot's story.

"Well, it seems that some years ago Lawrence Farr fell absolutely madly in love with a beautiful young girl — in fact, the orphaned daughter of a friend of his. Terribly romantic. Of course, she loved him, too, but he felt so awful and guilty that they never did anything about it."

I did not like this story much; it made me obscurely uncomfortable, and I think that at some point both Margot and I wondered why she was telling it. Was she pointing out imperfections in my chosen other family? But I asked, in Harriet's indifferent voice, "He never kissed her?"

"Well, maybe. I don't know. But of course everyone in town knew all about it, including Emily Farr. And with her back! Poor woman," Margot added somewhat piously but with real feeling, too.

I forgot the story readily at the time. For one thing, there was something unreal about anyone as old as Lawrence Farr "falling in love." But looking back to Emily's face, Emily looking at Lawrence, I can see that pained watchfulness of a woman who has been hurt, and by a man who could always hurt her again.

In those days, what struck me most about the Farrs was their extreme courtesy to each other — something I had not seen before. Never a harsh word. (Of course, I did not know then about couples who cannot afford a single harsh word.)

Possibly because of the element of danger (very slight — the slope was gentle), the roof over the front porch was one of the places Harriet and I liked to sit on warm summer nights when I was invited to stay over. There was a country silence, invaded at intervals by summer country sounds — the strangled croak of tree frogs from down in the glen; the crazy baying of a distant hound. There, in the heavy scent of roses, on the scratchy shingles, Harriet and I talked about sex.

"A girl I know told me that if you do it a lot your hips get very wide."

"My cousin Duncan says it makes boys strong if they do it."

"It hurts women a lot — especially at first. But I knew this girl from Santa Barbara, and she said that out there they say Filipinos can do it without hurting."

"Colored people do it a lot more than whites."

"Of course, they have all those babies. But in Boston so do Catholics!"

We are seized with hysteria. We laugh and laugh, so that Emily hears and calls up to us, "Girls, why haven't you-all gone to bed?" But her voice is warm and amused — she likes having us laughing up there.

And Emily liked my enthusiasm for lemon cake. She teased me about the amounts of it I could eat, and she continued to keep me supplied. She was not herself much of a cook — their maid, a young black girl named Evelyn, did most of the cooking.

Once, but only once, I saw the genteel and opaque surface of that family shattered — saw those three people suddenly in violent opposition to each other, like shards of splintered glass. (But what I have forgotten is the cause — what brought about that terrible explosion?)

The four of us, as so often, were seated at lunch. Emily was at what seemed to be the head of the table. At her right hand was the small silver bell that summoned Evelyn to clear, or to bring a new course. Harriet and I across from each other, Lawrence across from Emily. (There was always a tentativeness about Lawrence's posture. He could have been an honored guest, or a spoiled and favorite child.) We were talking in an easy way. I have a vivid recollection only of words that began to career and gather momentum, to go out of control. Of voices raised. Then Harriet rushes from the room. Emily's face reddens dangerously, the corners of her mouth twitch downward, and Lawrence, in an exquisitely icy voice, begins to lecture me on the virtues of reading Trollope. I am supposed to help him pretend that nothing has happened, but I can hardly hear what he is saying. I am in shock.

That sudden unleashing of violence, that exposed depth of terrible emotions might have suggested to me that the Farrs were not quite as I had imagined them, not the impeccable family in my mind — but it did not. I was simply and terribly — and selfishly — upset, and hugely relieved when it all seemed to have passed over.

During that summer, the Ouija board spoke only gibberish to Margot, or it answered direct questions with repeated evasions:

"Will I ever see Johnny Kilgore again, in this life?"

"Yes no perhaps."

"Honey, that means you've got no further need of the board, not right now. You've got to think everything out with your own heart and instincts," Dolly said.

Margot seemed to take her advice. She resolutely put the board away, and she wrote to Johnny that she wanted a divorce.

I had begun to notice that these days, on these sultry August nights, Margot and Dolly were frequently joined on their small excursions by a man named Larry — a jolly, red-faced man who was in real estate and who reminded me considerably of my father.

I said as much to Margot, and was surprised at her furious reaction. "They could not be more different, they are altogether opposite. Larry is a Southern gentleman. You just don't pay any attention to anyone but those Farrs."

A word about Margot's quite understandable jealousy of the Farrs. Much later in my life, when I was unreasonably upset at the attachment of one of my own daughters to another family (unreasonable because her chosen group were all talented musicians, as she was), a wise friend told me that we all could use more than one set of parents — our relations with the original set are too intense, and need dissipating. But no one, certainly not silly Dolly, was around to comfort Margot with this wisdom.

The summer raced on. ("Not without dust and heat," Lawrence several times remarked, in his private ironic voice.) The roses wilted on the roof and on the banks next to the road. The creek dwindled, and beside it honeysuckle leaves lay limply on the vines. For weeks, there was no rain, and then, one afternoon, there came a dark torrential thunderstorm. Harriet and I sat on the side porch and watched its violent start — the black clouds seeming to rise from the horizon, the cracking, jagged streaks of lightning, the heavy, welcome rain. And, later, the clean smell of leaves and grass and damp earth.

Knowing that Margot would be frightened, I thought of calling her, and then remembered that she would not talk on the phone during storms. And that night she told me, "The phone rang and rang, but I didn't think it was you, somehow."

"No."

"I had the craziest idea that it was Johnny. Be just like him to pick the middle of a storm for a phone call."

"There might not have been a storm in New Orleans."

But it turned out that Margot was right.

The next day, when I rode up to the Farrs' on my bike, Emily was sitting out in the grass where I had first seen her. I went and squatted beside her there. I thought she looked old and sad, and partly to cheer her I said, "You grow the most beautiful flowers I've ever seen."

She sighed, instead of smiling as she usually did. She said, "I seem to have turned into a gardener. When I was a girl, I imagined that I would grow up to be a writer, a novelist, and that I would have at least four children. Instead, I grow flowers and write book reviews."

I was not interested in children. "You never wrote a novel?"

She smiled unhappily. "No. I think I was afraid that I wouldn't come up to Trollope. I married rather young, you know."

And at that moment Lawrence came out of the house, immaculate in white flannels.

He greeted me, and said to Emily, "My dear, I find that I have some rather late appointments, in Hillsboro. You won't wait dinner if I'm a trifle late?"

(Of course she would; she always did.)

"No. Have a good time," she said, and she gave him the anxious look that I had come to recognize as the way she looked at Lawrence.

Soon after that, a lot happened very fast. Margot wrote to Johnny (again) that she wanted a divorce, that she intended to marry Larry. (I wonder if this was ever true.) Johnny telephoned — not once but several times. He told her that she was crazy, that he had a great job with some shipbuilders near San Francisco — a defense contract. He would come to get us, and we would all move out there. Margot agreed. We would make a new life. (Of course, we never knew what happened to the girl.)

I was not as sad about leaving the Farrs and that house, that town, those woods as I was to be later, looking back. I was excited about San Francisco, and I vaguely imagined that someday I would come back and that we would all see each other again. Like parting lovers, Harriet and I promised to write each other every day.

And for quite a while we did write several times a week. I wrote about San Francisco — how beautiful it was: the hills and pastel houses, the sea. How I wished that she could see it. She wrote about school and friends. She described solitary bike rides to places we had been. She told me what she was reading.

In high school, our correspondence became more generalized. Responding perhaps to the adolescent mores of the early nineteen-forties, we wrote about boys and parties; we even competed in making ourselves sound "popular." The truth (my truth) was that I was sometimes popular, often not. I had, in fact, a stormy adolescence. And at that time I developed what was to be a long-lasting habit. As I reviewed a situation in which I had been ill-advised or impulsive, I would reenact the whole scene in my mind with Harriet in my own role — Harriet, cool and controlled, more intelligent, prettier: Even more than I wanted to see her again, I wanted to *be* Harriet.

Johnny and Margot fought a lot and stayed together, and gradually a sort of comradeship developed between them in our small house on Russian Hill.

I went to Stanford, where I halfheartedly studied history. Harriet was at Radcliffe, studying American literature, writing poetry.

We lost touch with each other.

Margot, however, kept up with her old friend Dolly, by means of Christmas cards and Easter notes, and Margot thus heard a remarkable piece of news about Emily Farr. Emily "up and left Lawrence without so much as a by-your-leave," said Dolly, and went to Washington, D.C., to work in the Folger Library. This news made me smile all day. I was so proud of Emily. And I imagined that Lawrence would amuse himself, that they would both be happier apart.

By accident, I married well — that is to say, a man whom I still like and enjoy. Four daughters came at uncalculated intervals, and each is remarkably unlike her sisters. I named one Harriet, although she seems to have my untidy character.

From time to time, over the years, I would see a poem by Harriet Farr, and I always thought it was marvellous, and I meant to write her. But I distrusted my reaction. I had been (I was) so deeply fond of Harriet (Emily, Lawrence, that house and land) and besides, what would I say — "I think your poem is marvellous"? (I have since learned that this is neither an inadequate nor an unwelcome thing to say to writers.) Of course, the true reason for not writing was that there was too much to say.

Dolly wrote to Margot that Lawrence was drinking "all over the place." He was not happier without Emily. Harriet, Dolly said, was travelling a lot. She married several times and had no children. Lawrence developed emphysema, and was in such bad shape that Emily quit her job and came back to take care of him — whether because of feelings of guilt or duty or possibly affection, I didn't know. He died, lingeringly and miserably, and Emily, too, died, a few years later — at least partly from exhaustion, I would imagine.

Then, at last, I did write Harriet, in care of the magazine in which I had last seen a poem of hers. I wrote a clumsy, gusty letter, much too long, about shared pasts, landscapes, the creek. All that. And as soon as I had mailed it I began mentally rewriting, seeking more elegant prose.

When for a long time I didn't hear from Harriet, I felt worse and worse, cumbersome, misplaced — as too often in life I had felt before. It did not occur to me that an infrequently staffed magazine could be at fault.

Months later, her letter came — from Rome, where she was then living. Alone, I gathered. She said that she was writing it at the moment of receiving mine. It was a long, emotional, and very moving letter, out of character for the Harriet that I remembered (or had invented).

She said, in part: "It was really strange, all that time when Lawrence was dying, and God! so long! and as though 'dying' were all that he was doing — Emily, too, although we didn't know that — all that time the picture that moved me most, in my mind, that moved me to tears, was not of Lawrence and Emily but of you and me. On our bikes at the top of the hill outside our house. Going somewhere. And I first thought that that picture simply symbolized something irretrievable, the lost and irrecoverable past, as Lawrence and Emily would be lost. And I'm sure that was partly it.

"But they were so extremely fond of you — in fact, you were a rare area of agreement. They missed you, and they talked about you for years. It's a wonder that I wasn't jealous, and I think I wasn't, only because I felt included in their affection for you. They liked me best with you.

"Another way to say this would be to say that we were all three a little less crazy and isolated with you around, and, God knows, happier."

An amazing letter, I thought. It was enough to make me take a long look at my whole life, and to find some new colors there.

A postscript: I showed Harriet's letter to my husband, and he said, "How odd. She sounds so much like you."

*Harold Brodkey*

# Verona: A Young Woman Speaks

FROM *Esquire*

I KNOW A LOT! I know about happiness! I don't mean the love of God, either: I mean I know the human happiness with the crimes in it.

Even the happiness of childhood.

I think of it now as a cruel, middle-class happiness.

Let me describe one time — one day, one night.

I was quite young, and my parents and I — there were just the three of us — were traveling from Rome to Salzburg, journeying across a quarter of Europe to be in Salzburg for Christmas, for the music and the snow. We went by train because planes were erratic, and my father wanted us to stop in half a dozen Italian towns and see paintings and buy things. It was absurd, but we were all three drunk with this; it was very strange: we woke every morning in a strange hotel, in a strange city. I would be the first one to wake; and I would go to the window and see some tower or palace; and then I would wake my mother and be justified in my sense of wildness and belief and adventure by the way she acted, her sense of romance at being in a city as strange as I had thought it was when I had looked out the window and seen the palace or the tower.

We had to change trains in Verona, a darkish, smallish city at the edge of the Alps. By the time we got there, we'd bought and bought our way up the Italian peninsula: I was dizzy with shopping and new possessions: I hardly knew who I was, I owned so many new things: my reflection in any mirror or shopwindow was resplendently fresh and new, disguised even, glittering, I thought. I was seven or eight years old. It seemed to me we were almost in a movie or in the pages of a book: only the simplest and most light-filled words and images can suggest what I thought we were then. We went around shiningly: we shone everywhere. *Those clothes.* It's easy to buy a child. I had a new dress, knitted, blue and red, expensive as hell, I think; leggings, also red; a red loden-cloth coat with a hood and a knitted cap for under the hood; marvelous lined gloves; fur-lined boots and a fur purse or carryall, and a tartan skirt — and shirts and a scarf, and there was even more: a watch, a bracelet: more and more.

On the trains we had private rooms, and Momma carried games in her purse and things to eat, and Daddy sang carols off-key to me; and sometimes I became so intent on my happiness I would suddenly be in real danger of wetting myself; and Momma, who understood such emergencies, would catch the urgency in my voice and see my twisted face; and she — a large, good-looking woman — would whisk me to a toilet with amazing competence and unstoppability, murmuring to me, "Just hold on for a while," and she would hold my hand while I did it.

So we came to Verona, where it was snowing, and the people had stern, sad faces, beautiful, unlaughing faces. But if they looked at me, those serious faces would lighten, they would smile at me in my splendor. Strangers offered me candy, sometimes with the most excruciating sadness, kneeling or stooping to look directly into my face, into my eyes; and Momma or Papa would judge them, the people, and say in Italian we were late, we had to hurry, or pause, and let the stranger touch me, talk to me, look into my face for a while. I would see myself in the eyes of some strange man or woman; sometimes they stared so gently I would want to touch their eyelashes, stroke those strange, large, glistening eyes. I knew I decorated life. I took my duties with great seriousness. An Italian count in Siena said I had the manners of an English princess — at times — and then he laughed because it was true I would be quite lurid: I ran shouting in his *galleria,* a long room, hung with pictures, and with a frescoed ceiling: and I sat on his lap and wriggled: I was a wicked child, and I liked myself very much; and almost everywhere, almost every day, there was someone new to love me, briefly, while we traveled.

I understood I was special. I understood it *then.*

I knew that what we were doing, everything we did, involved money. I did not know if it involved mind or not, or style. But I knew about money somehow, checks and traveler's checks and the clink of coins. Daddy was a fountain of money: he said it was a spree; he meant for us to be amazed; he had saved money — we weren't really rich but we were to be for this trip. I remember a conservatory in a large house outside Florence and orange trees in tubs; and I ran there too. A servant, a man dressed in black, a very old man, mean-faced — he did not like being a servant anymore after the days of servants were over — and he scowled but he smiled at me, and at my mother, and even once at my father: we were clearly so separate from the griefs and wearinesses and cruelties of the world. We were at play, we were at our joys, and Momma was glad, with a terrible and naive inner gladness, and she relied on Daddy to make it work: oh, she worked too, but she didn't know the secret of such — unreality: is that what I want to say? Of such a game, of such an extraordinary game.

There was a picture in Verona Daddy wanted to see; a painting; I remember the painter because the name Pisanello reminded me I had to go to the bathroom when we were in the museum, which was an old castle, Guelf or Ghibelline, I don't remember which; and I also remember the painting because it showed the hind end of the horse, and I thought that was not nice and rather funny, but Daddy was admiring; and so I said nothing.

He held my hand and told me a story so I wouldn't be bored as we walked from room to room in the museum/castle, and then we went outside into the snow, into the soft light when it snows, light coming through snow; and I was dressed in red and had on boots, and my parents were young and pretty and had on boots too; and we could stay out in the snow if we wanted; and we did. We went to a square, a piazza — the Scaligera, I think; I don't remember — and just as we got there, the snowing began to bellow and then subside, to fall heavily and then sparsely, and then it stopped: and it was very cold, and there were pigeons everywhere in the piazza, on every cornice and roof, and all over the snow on the ground, leaving little tracks as they walked, while the air trembled in its just-after-snow and just-before-snow weight and thickness and grey seriousness of purpose. I had never seen so many pigeons or such a private and haunted place as that piazza, me in my new coat at the far rim of the world, the far rim of who knew what story, the rim of foreign beauty and Daddy's games, the edge, the white border of a season.

I was half mad with pleasure, anyway, and now Daddy brought five or six cones made of newspaper, wrapped, twisted; and they held grains of something like corn, yellow and white kernels of something; and he poured some on my hand and told me to hold my hand out; and then he backed away.

At first there was nothing, but I trusted him and I waited; and then the pigeons came. On heavy wings. Clumsy pigeony bodies. And red, unreal bird's feet. They flew at me, slowing at the last minute; they lit on my arm and fed from my hand. I wanted to flinch, but I didn't. I closed my eyes and held my arm stiffly; and felt them peck and eat — from my hand, these free creatures, these flying things. I liked that moment. I liked my happiness. If I were mistaken about life and pigeons and my own nature, it didn't matter *then*.

The piazza was very silent, with snow; and Daddy poured grains on both my hands and then on the sleeves of my coat and on the shoulders of the coat, and I was entranced with yet more stillness, with this idea of his. The pigeons fluttered heavily in the heavy air, more and more of them, and sat on my arms and on my shoulders; and I looked at Momma and then at my father and then at the birds on me.

Oh, I'm sick of everything as I talk. There is happiness. It always makes me slightly ill. I lose my balance because of it.

The heavy birds, and the strange buildings, and Momma near, and Daddy too: Momma is pleased that I am happy and she is a little jealous; she is jealous of everything Daddy does; she is a woman of enormous spirit; life is hardly big enough for her; she is drenched in wastefulness and prettiness. She knows things. She gets inflexible, though, and foolish at times, and temperamental; but she is a somebody, and she gets away with a lot, and if she is near, you can feel her, you can't escape her, she's that important, that echoing, her spirit is that powerful in the space around her.

If she weren't restrained by Daddy, if she weren't in love with him, there is no knowing what she might do: she does not know. But she manages almost to be gentle because of him; he is incredibly watchful and changeable and he gets tired; he talks and charms people; sometimes, then, Momma and I stand nearby, like moons; we brighten and wane; and after a while, he comes to us, to the moons, the big one, and the little one, and we welcome him, and he is always, to my surprise, he is always surprised, as if he didn't deserve to be loved, as if it were time he was found out.

Daddy is very tall, and Momma is watching us, and Daddy anoints me again and again with the grain. I cannot bear it much longer. I feel joy or amusement or I don't know what; it is all through me, like a nausea — I am ready to scream and laugh, that laughter that comes out like magical, drunken, awful and yet pure spit or vomit or God knows what, that makes me a child mad with laughter. I become brilliant, gleaming, soft: an angel, a great birdchild of laughter.

I am ready to be like that, but I hold myself back.

There are more and more birds near me. They march around my feet and peck at falling and fallen grains. One is on my head. Of those on my arms, some move their wings, fluff those frail, feather-loaded wings, stretch them. I cannot bear it, they are so frail, and I am, at the moment, the kindness of the world that feeds them in the snow.

All at once, I let out a splurt of laughter: I can't stop myself and the birds fly away but not far; they circle around me, above me; some wheel high in the air and drop as they return; they all returned, some in clouds and clusters driftingly, some alone and angry, pecking at others; some with a blind, animal-strutting abruptness. They gripped my coat and fed themselves. It started to snow again.

I was there in my kindness, in that piazza, within reach of my mother and father.

Oh, how will the world continue? Daddy suddenly understood I'd had enough, I was at the end of my strength — Christ, he was alert — and he picked me up, and I went limp, my arm around his neck, and the snow fell. Momma came near and pulled the hood lower and said there were snowflakes in my eyelashes. She knew he had understood, and she wasn't sure she had; she wasn't sure he ever watched her so carefully. She became slightly unhappy, and so she walked like a clumsy boy beside us, but she was so pretty: she had powers, anyway.

We went to a restaurant, and I behaved very well, but I couldn't eat, and then we went to the train and people looked at us, but I couldn't smile; I was too dignified, too sated; some leftover — pleasure, let's call it — made my dignity very deep, I could not stop remembering the pigeons, or that Daddy loved me in a way he did not love Momma; and Daddy was alert, watching the luggage, watching strangers for assassination attempts or whatever; he was on duty; and Momma was pretty and alone and *happy,* defiant in that way.

And then, you see, what she did was wake me in the middle of the night when the train was chugging up a very steep mountainside; and outside the window, visible because our compartment was dark and the sky was clear and there was a full moon, were mountains, a landscape of mountains everywhere, big mountains, huge ones, impossible, all slanted and pointed and white with snow, and absurd, sticking up into an ink-blue sky and down into blue, blue shadows, miraculously deep. I don't know how to say what it was like: they were not like anything I knew: they were high things: and we were up high in the train and we were climbing higher, and it was not at all true, but it was, you see. I put my hands on the window and stared at the wild, slanting, unlikely marvels, whiteness and dizziness and moonlight and shadows cast by moonlight, not real, not familiar, not pigeons, but a clean world.

We sat a long time, Momma and I, and stared, and then Daddy woke up and came and looked too. "It's pretty," he said, but he didn't really understand. Only Momma and I did. She said to him, "When I was a child, I was bored all the time, my love — I thought nothing would ever happen to me — and now these things are happening — and you have happened." I think he was flabbergasted by her love in the middle of the night; he smiled at her, oh, so swiftly that I was jealous, but I stayed quiet, and after a while, in his silence and amazement at her, at us, he began to seem different from us, from Momma and me; and then he fell asleep again; Momma and I didn't; we sat at the window and watched all night, watched the mountains and the moon, the clean world. We watched together.

Momma was the winner.

We were silent, and in silence we spoke of how we loved men and how dangerous men were and how they stole everything from you no matter how much you gave — but we didn't say it aloud.

We looked at mountains until dawn, and then when dawn came, it was too pretty for me — there was pink and blue and gold, in the sky, and on icy places, brilliant pink and gold flashes, and the snow was colored too, and I said, "Oh," and sighed; and each moment was more beautiful than the one before; and I said, "I love you, Momma." Then I fell asleep in her arms.

That was happiness then.

*Saul Bellow*

........................................................................................

# A Silver Dish

FROM *The New Yorker*

WHAT DO YOU DO about death — in this case, the death of an old father? If you're a modern person, sixty years of age, and a man who's been around, like Woody Selbst, what do you do? Take this matter of mourning, and take it against a contemporary background. How, against a contemporary background, do you mourn an octogenarian father, nearly blind, his heart enlarged, his lungs filling with fluid, who creeps, stumbles, gives off the odors, the moldiness or gassiness of old men. I *mean!* As Woody put it, be realistic. Think what times these are. The papers daily give it to you — the Lufthansa pilot in Aden is described by the hostages on his knees, begging the Palestinian terrorists not to execute him, but they shoot him through the head. Later they themselves are killed. And still others shoot others, or shoot themselves. That's what you read in the press, see on the tube, mention at dinner. We know now what goes daily through the whole of the human community, like a global death-peristalsis.

Woody, a businessman in South Chicago, was not an ignorant person. He knew more such phrases than you would expect a tile contractor (offices, lobbies, lavatories) to know. The kind of knowledge he had was not the kind for which you get academic degrees. Although Woody had studied for two years in a seminary, preparing to be a minister. Two years of college during the Depression was more than most high-school graduates could afford. After that, in his own vital, picturesque, original way (Morris, his old man, was also, in his days of nature, vital and picturesque), Woody had read up on many subjects, subscribed to *Science* and other magazines that gave real information, and had taken night courses at De Paul and Northwestern in ecology, criminology, existentialism. Also he had travelled extensively in Japan, Mexico, and

Africa, and there was an African experience that was especially relevant
to mourning. It was this: On a launch near the Murchison Falls in
Uganda, he had seen a buffalo calf seized by a crocodile from the bank
of the White Nile. There were giraffes along the tropical river, and
hippopotamuses, and baboons, and flamingos and other brilliant birds
crossing the bright air in the heat of the morning, when the calf,
stepping into the river to drink, was grabbed by the hoof and dragged
down. The parent buffaloes couldn't figure it out. Under the water the
calf still threshed, fought, churned the mud. Woody, the robust traveller,
took this in as he sailed by, and to him it looked as if the parent cattle
were asking each other dumbly what had happened. He chose to assume
that there was pain in this, he read brute grief into it. On the White Nile,
Woody had the impression that he had gone back to the pre-Adamite
past, and he brought reflections on this impression home to South
Chicago. He brought also a bundle of hashish from Kampala. In this he
took a chance with the customs inspectors, banking perhaps on his
broad build, frank face, high color. He didn't look like a wrongdoer, a
bad guy; he looked like a good guy. But he liked taking chances. Risk was
a wonderful stimulus. He threw down his trenchcoat on the customs
counter. If the inspectors searched the pockets, he was prepared to say
that the coat wasn't his. But he got away with it, and the Thanksgiving
turkey was stuffed with hashish. This was much enjoyed. That was
practically the last feast at which Pop, who also relished risk or defiance,
was present. The hashish Woody had tried to raise in his back yard from
the Africa seeds didn't take. But behind his warehouse, where the Lincoln Continental was parked, he kept a patch of marijuana. There was
no harm at all in Woody but he didn't like being entirely within the law.
It was simply a question of self-respect.

After that Thanksgiving, Pop gradually sank as if he had a slow leak.
This went on for some years. In and out of the hospital, he dwindled,
his mind wandered, he couldn't even concentrate enough to complain,
except in exceptional moments on the Sundays Woody regularly devoted to him. Morris, an amateur who once was taken seriously by
Willie Hoppe, the great pro himself, couldn't execute the simplest billiard shots anymore. He could only conceive shots; he began to theo-
rize about impossible three-cushion combinations. Halina, the Polish
woman with whom Morris had lived for over forty years as man and
wife, was too old herself now to run to the hospital. So Woody had to
do it. There was Woody's mother, too — a Christian convert — needing
care; she was over eighty and frequently hospitalized. Everybody had

diabetes and pleurisy and arthritis and cataracts and cardiac pacemakers. And everybody had lived by the body, but the body was giving out.

There were Woody's two sisters as well, unmarried, in their fifties, very Christian, very straight, still living with Mama in an entirely Christian bungalow. Woody, who took full responsibility for them all, occasionally had to put one of the girls (they had become sick girls) in a mental institution. Nothing severe. The sisters were wonderful women, both of them gorgeous once, but neither of the poor things was playing with a full deck. And all the factions had to be kept separate — Mama, the Christian convert; the fundamentalist sisters; Pop, who read the Yiddish paper as long as he could still see print; Halina, a good Catholic. Woody, the seminary forty years behind him, described himself as an agnostic. Pop had no more religion than you could find in the Yiddish paper, but he made Woody promise to bury him among Jews, and that was where he lay now, in the Hawaiian shirt Woody had bought for him at the tilers' convention in Honolulu. Woody would allow no undertaker's assistant to dress him but came to the parlor and buttoned the stiff into the shirt himself, and the old man went down looking like Ben-Gurion in a simple wooden coffin, sure to rot fast. That was how Woody wanted it all. At the graveside, he had taken off and folded his jacket, rolled up his sleeves on thick freckled biceps, waved back the little tractor standing by, and shovelled the dirt himself. His big face, broad at the bottom, narrowed upward like a Dutch house. And, his small good lower teeth taking hold of the upper lip in his exertion, he performed the final duty of a son. He was very fit, so it must have been emotion, not the shovelling, that made him redden so. After the funeral, he went home with Halina and her son, a decent Polack like his mother, and talented, too — Mitosh played the organ at hockey and basketball games in the Stadium, which took a smart man because it was a rabble-rousing kind of occupation — and they had some drinks and comforted the old girl. Halina was true blue, always one hundred per cent for Morris.

Then for the rest of the week Woody was busy, had jobs to run, office responsibilities, family responsibilities. He lived alone; as did his wife; as did his mistress: everybody in a separate establishment. Since his wife, after fifteen years of separation, had not learned to take care of herself, Woody did her shopping on Fridays, filled her freezer. He had to take her this week to buy shoes. Also, Friday night he always spent with Helen — Helen was his wife de facto. Saturday he did his big weekly shopping. Saturday night he devoted to Mom and his sisters. So he was too busy to attend to his own feelings except, intermittently, to note to himself, "First Thursday in the grave." "First Friday, and fine weather." "First Saturday; he's got to be getting used to it." Under his breath he occasionally said, "Oh, Pop."

But it was Sunday that hit him, when the bells rang all over South Chicago — the Ukrainian, Roman Catholic, Greek, Russian, African-Methodist churches, sounding off one after another. Woody had his offices in his warehouse, and there had built an apartment for himself, very spacious and convenient, in the top story. Because he left every Sunday morning at seven to spend the day with Pop, he had forgotten by how many churches Selbst Tile Company was surrounded. He was still in bed when he heard the bells, and all at once he knew how heartbroken he was. This sudden big heartache in a man of sixty, a practical, physical, healthy-minded, and experienced man, was deeply unpleasant. When he had an unpleasant condition, he believed in taking something for it. So he thought, What shall I take? There were plenty of remedies available. His cellar was stocked with cases of Scotch whiskey, Polish vodka, Armagnac, Moselle, Burgundy. There were also freezers with steaks and with game and with Alaskan king crab. He bought with a broad hand — by the crate and by the dozen. But in the end, when he got out of bed, he took nothing but a cup of coffee. While the kettle was heating, he put on his Japanese judo-style suit and sat down to reflect.

Woody was moved when things were *honest*. Bearing beams were honest, undisguised concrete pillars inside high-rise apartments were honest. It was bad to cover up anything. He hated faking. Stone was honest. Metal was honest. These Sunday bells were very straight. They broke loose, they wagged and rocked, and the vibrations and the banging did something for him — cleansed his insides, purified his blood. A bell was a one-way throat, had only one thing to tell you and simply told it. He listened.

He had had some connections with bells and churches. He was after all something of a Christian. Born a Jew, he was a Jew facially, with a hint of Iroquois or Cherokee, but his mother had been converted more than fifty years ago by her brother-in-law, the Reverend Dr. Kovner. Kovner, a rabbinical student who had left the Hebrew Union College in Cincinnati to become a minister and establish a mission, had given Woody a partly Christian upbringing. Now Pop was on the outs with these fundamentalists. He said that the Jews came to the mission to get coffee, bacon, canned pineapple, day-old bread, and dairy products. And if they had to listen to sermons, that was O.K. — this was the

Depression and you couldn't be too particular — but he knew they sold the bacon.

The Gospels said it plainly: "Salvation is from the Jews."

Backing the Reverend Doctor were wealthy fundamentalists, mainly Swedes, eager to speed up the Second Coming by converting all Jews. The foremost of Kovner's backers was Mrs. Skoglund, who had inherited a large dairy business from her late husband. Woody was under her special protection.

Woody was fourteen years of age when Pop took off with Halina, who worked in his shop, leaving his difficult Christian wife and his converted son and his small daughters. He came to Woody in the back yard one spring day and said, "From now on you're the man of the house." Woody was practicing with a golf club, knocking off the heads of dandelions. Pop came into the yard in his good suit, which was too hot for the weather, and when he took off his fedora the skin of his head was marked with a deep ring and the sweat was sprinkled over his scalp — more drops than hairs. He said, "I'm going to move out." Pop was anxious, but he was set to go — determined. "It's no use. I can't live a life like this." Envisioning the life Pop simply *had* to live, his free life, Woody was able to picture him in the billiard parlor, under the "L" tracks in a crap game, or playing poker at Brown and Koppel's upstairs. "You're going to be the man of the house," said Pop. "It's O.K. I put you all on welfare. I just got back from Wabansia Avenue, from the Relief Station." Hence the suit and the hat. "They're sending out a case-worker." Then he said, "You got to lend me money to buy gasoline — the caddie money you saved."

Understanding that Pop couldn't get away without his help, Woody turned over to him all he had earned at the Sunset Ridge Country Club in Winnetka. Pop felt that the valuable life lesson he was transmitting was worth far more than these dollars, and whenever he was conning his boy a sort of high-priest expression came down over his bent nose, his ruddy face. The children, who got their finest ideas at the movies, called him Richard Dix. Later, when the comic strip came out, they said he was Dick Tracy.

As Woody now saw it, under the tumbling bells, he had bankrolled his own desertion. Ha ha! He found this delightful; and especially Pop's attitude of "That'll teach you to trust your father." For this was a demonstration on behalf of real life and free instincts, against religion and hypocrisy. But mainly it was aimed against being a fool, the disgrace of foolishness. Pop had it in for the Reverend Dr. Kovner, not because he was an apostate (Pop couldn't have cared less), not because the mission was a racket (he admitted that the Reverend Doctor was personally honest), but because Dr. Kovner behaved foolishly, spoke like a fool, and acted like a fiddler. He tossed his hair like a Paganini (this was Woody's addition; Pop had never even heard of Paganini). Proof that he was not a spiritual leader was that he converted Jewish women by stealing their hearts. "He works up all those broads," said Pop. "He doesn't even know it himself, I swear he doesn't know how he gets them."

From the other side, Kovner often warned Woody, "Your father is a dangerous person. Of course, you love him; you should love and forgive him, Voodrow, but you are old enough to understand he is leading a life of wice."

It was all petty stuff: Pop's sinning was on a boy level and therefore made a big impression on a boy. And on Mother. Are wives children, or what? Mother often said, "I hope you put that brute in your prayers. Look what he has done to us. But only pray for him, don't see him." But he saw him all the time. Woodrow was leading a double life, sacred and profane. He accepted Jesus Christ as his personal redeemer. Aunt Rebecca took advantage of this. She made him work. He had to work under Aunt Rebecca. He filled in for the janitor at the mission and settlement house. In winter, he had to feed the coal furnace, and on some nights he slept near the furnace room, on the pool table. He also picked the lock of the storeroom. He took canned pineapple and cut bacon from the flitch with his pocketknife. He crammed himself with uncooked bacon. He had a big frame to fill out.

Only now, sipping Melitta coffee, he asked himself — had he been so hungry? No, he loved being reckless. He was fighting Aunt Rebecca Kovner when he took out his knife and got on a box to reach the bacon. She didn't know, she couldn't prove that Woody, such a frank, strong, positive boy who looked you in the eye, so direct, was a thief also. But he was also a thief. Whenever she looked at him, he knew that she was seeing his father. In the curve of his nose, the movements of his eyes, the thickness of his body, in his healthy face she saw that wicked savage, Morris.

Morris, you see, had been a street boy in Liverpool — Woody's mother and her sister were British by birth. Morris's Polish family, on their way to America, abandoned him in Liverpool because he had an eye infection and they would all have been sent back from Ellis Island. They stopped awhile in England, but his eyes kept running and they ditched him. They slipped away, and he had to make out alone in

Liverpool at the age of twelve. Mother came of better people. Pop, who slept in the cellar of her house, fell in love with her. At sixteen, scabbing during a seamen's strike, he shovelled his way across the Atlantic and jumped ship in Brooklyn. He became an American, and America never knew it. He voted without papers, he drove without a license, he paid no taxes, he cut every corner. Horses, cards, billiards, and women were his lifelong interests, in ascending order. Did he love anyone (he was so busy)? Yes, he loved Halina. He loved his son. To this day, Mother believed that he had loved her most and always wanted to come back. This gave her a chance to act the queen, with her plump wrists and faded Queen Victoria face. "The girls are instructed never to admit him," she said. The Empress of India, speaking.

Bell-battered Woodrow's soul was whirling this Sunday morning, indoors and out, to the past, back to his upper corner of the warehouse, laid out with such originality — the bells coming and going, metal on naked metal, until the bell circle expanded over the whole of steelmaking, oil-refining, power-producing mid-autumn South Chicago, and all its Croatians, Ukrainians, Greeks, Poles, and respectable blacks heading for their churches to hear Mass or to sing hymns.

Woody himself had been a good hymn singer. He still knew the hymns. He had testified, too. He was often sent by Aunt Rebecca to get up and tell a church full of Scandihoovians that he, a Jewish lad, accepted Jesus Christ. For this she paid him fifty cents. She made the disbursement. She was the bookkeeper, fiscal chief, general manager of the mission. The Reverend Doctor didn't know a thing about the operation. What the Doctor supplied was the fervor. He was genuine, a wonderful preacher. And what about Woody himself? He also had fervor. He was drawn to the Reverend Doctor. The Reverend Doctor taught him to lift up his eyes, gave him his higher life. Apart from this higher life, the rest was Chicago — the ways of Chicago, which came so natural that nobody thought to question them. So, for instance, in 1933 (what ancient, ancient times!) at the Century of Progress World's Fair, when Woody was a coolie and pulled a rickshaw, wearing a peaked straw hat and trotting with powerful, thick legs, while the brawny red farmers — his boozing passengers — were laughing their heads off and pestered him for whores, he, although a freshman at the seminary, saw nothing wrong, when girls asked him to steer a little business their way, in making dates and accepting tips from both sides. He necked in Grant Park with a powerful girl who had to go home quickly to nurse her baby. Smelling of milk, she rode beside him on the streetcar to the West Side, squeezing his rickshaw puller's thigh and wetting her blouse. This was the Roosevelt Road car. Then, in the apartment where she lived with her mother, he couldn't remember that there were any husbands around. What he did remember was the strong milk odor. Without inconsistency, next morning he did New Testament Greek: The light shineth in darkness — *to fos en te skotia fainei* — and the darkness comprehended it not.

And all the while he trotted between the shafts on the fairgrounds he had one idea — nothing to do with these horny giants having a big time in the city: that the goal, the project, the purpose was (and he couldn't explain why he thought so; all evidence was against it), God's idea was that this world should be a love-world, that it should eventually recover and be entirely a world of love. He wouldn't have said this to a soul, for he could see himself how stupid it was — personal and stupid. Nevertheless, there it was at the center of his feelings. And at the same time Aunt Rebecca was right when she said to him, strictly private, close to his ear even, "You're a little crook, like your father."

There was some evidence for this, or what stood for evidence to an impatient person like Rebecca. Woody matured quickly — he had to — but how could you expect a boy of seventeen, he wondered, to interpret the viewpoint, the feelings of a middle-aged woman, and one whose breast had been removed? Morris told him that this happened only to neglected women, and was a sign. Morris said that if titties were not fondled and kissed they got cancer in protest. It was a cry of the flesh. And this had seemed true to Woody. When his imagination tried the theory on the Reverend Doctor, it worked out — he couldn't see the Reverend Doctor behaving in that way to Aunt Rebecca's breasts! Morris's theory kept Woody looking from bosoms to husbands and from husbands to bosoms. He still did that. It's an exceptionally smart man who isn't marked forever by the sexual theories he hears from his father, and Woody wasn't all that smart. He knew this himself. Personally, he had gone far out of his way to do right by women in this regard. What nature demanded. He and Pop were common, thick men, but there's nobody too gross to have ideas of delicacy.

The Reverend Doctor preached, Rebecca preached, rich Mrs. Skoglund preached from Evanston, Mother preached. Pop also was on a soapbox. Everyone was doing it. Up and down Division Street, under every lamp, almost, speakers were giving out: anarchists, Socialists, Stalinists, single-taxers, Zionists, Tolstoyans, vegetarians, and fundamentalist Christian preachers — you name it. A beef, a hope, a way of life or salvation, a protest. How was it that the accumulated gripes of all the ages took off so when transplanted to America?

And that fine Swedish immigrant Aase (Osie, they pronounced it), who had been the Skoglunds' cook and married the eldest son to become his rich, religious widow — she supported the Reverend Doctor. In her time she must have been built like a chorus girl. And women seem to have lost the secret of putting up their hair in the high basketry fence of braid she wore. Aase took Woody under her special protection and paid his tuition at the seminary. And Pop said . . . But on this Sunday, at peace as soon as the bells stopped banging, this velvet autumn day when the grass was finest and thickest, silky green: before the first frost, and the blood in your lungs is redder than summer air can make it and smarts with oxygen, as if the iron in your system was hungry for it, and the chill was sticking it to you in every breath — Pop, six feet under, would never feel this blissful sting again. The last of the bells still had the bright air streaming with vibrations.

On weekends, the institutional vacancy of decades came back to the warehouse and crept under the door of Woody's apartment. It felt as empty on Sundays as churches were during the week. Before each business day, before the trucks and the crews got started, Woody jogged five miles in his Adidas suit. Not on this day still reserved for Pop, however. Although it was tempting to go out and run off the grief. Being alone hit Woody hard this morning. He thought, Me and the world; the world and me. Meaning that there always was some activity to interpose, an errand or a visit, a picture to paint (he was a creative amateur), a massage, a meal — a shield between himself and that troublesome solitude which used the world as its reservoir. But Pop! Last Tuesday, Woody had gotten into the hospital bed with Pop because he kept pulling out the intravenous needles. Nurses stuck them back, and then Woody astonished them all by climbing into bed to hold the struggling old guy in his arms. "Easy, Morris, Morris, go easy." But Pop still groped feebly for the pipes.

When the tolling stopped, Woody didn't notice that a great lake of quiet had come over his kingdom, the Selbst Tile Warehouse. What he heard and saw was an old red Chicago streetcar, one of those trams the color of a stockyard steer. Cars of this type went out before Pearl Harbor — clumsy, big-bellied, with tough rattan seats and brass grips for the standing passengers. Those cars used to make four stops to the mile, and ran with a wallowing motion. They stank of carbolic or ozone and throbbed when the air compressors were being charged. The conductor had his knotted signal cord to pull, and the motorman beat the foot gong with his mad heel.

Woody recognized himself on the Western Avenue line and riding through a blizzard with his father, both in sheepskins and with hands and faces raw, the snow blowing in from the rear platform when the doors opened and getting into the longitudinal cleats of the floor. There wasn't warmth enough inside to melt it. And Western Avenue was the longest car line in the world, the boosters said, as if it was a thing to brag about. Twenty-three miles long, made by a draftsman with a T-square, lined with factories, storage buildings, machine shops, used-car lots, trolley barns, gas stations, funeral parlors, six-flats, utility buildings, and junk yards, on and on from the prairies on the south to Evanston on the north. Woodrow and his father were going north to Evanston, to Howard Street, and then some, to see Mrs. Skoglund. At the end of the line they would still have about five blocks to hike. The purpose of the trip? To raise money for Pop. Pop had talked him into this. When they found out, Mother and Aunt Rebecca would be furious, and Woody was afraid, but he couldn't help it.

Morris had come and said, "Son, I'm in trouble. It's bad."

"What's bad, Pop?"

"Halina took money from her husband for me and has to put it back before old Bujak misses it. He could kill her."

"What did she do it for?"

"Son, you know how the bookies collect? They send a goon. They'll break my head open."

"Pop! You know I can't take you to Mrs. Skoglund."

"Why not? You're my kid, aren't you? The old broad wants to adopt you, doesn't she? Shouldn't I get something out of it for my trouble? What am I — outside? And what about Halina? She puts her life on the line, but my own kid says no."

"Oh, Bujak wouldn't hurt her."

"Woody, he'd beat her to death."

Bujak? Uniform in color with his dark-gray work clothes, short in the legs, his whole strength in his tool-and-die-maker's forearms and black fingers; and beat-looking — there was Bujak for you. But, according to Pop, there was big, big violence in Bujak, a regular boiling Bessemer inside his narrow chest. Woody could never see the violence in him. Bujak wanted no trouble. If anything, maybe he was afraid that Morris and Halina would gang up on him and kill him, screaming. But Pop was no desperado murderer. And Halina was a calm, serious woman. Bujak kept his savings in the cellar (banks were going out of business). The worst they did was to take some of his money, intending to put it back. As Woody saw him, Bujak was trying to be sensible. He accepted his sorrow. He set minimum requirements for Halina: cook the meals, clean the house, show respect. But at stealing Bujak might have drawn the line, for money was different, money was vital substance. If they stole his savings he might have had to take action, out of respect for the substance, for himself — self-respect. But you couldn't be sure that Pop hadn't invented the bookie, the goon, the theft — the whole thing. He was capable of it, and you'd be a fool not to suspect him. Morris knew that Mother and Aunt Rebecca had told Mrs. Skoglund how wicked he was. They had painted him for her in poster colors — purple for vice, black for his soul, red for Hell flames: a gambler, smoker, drinker, deserter, screwer of women, and atheist. So Pop was determined to reach her. It was risky for everybody. The Reverend Doctor's operating costs were met by Skoglund Dairies. The widow paid Woody's seminary tuition; she bought dresses for the little sisters.

Woody, now sixty, fleshy and big, like a figure for the victory of American materialism, sunk in his lounge chair, the leather of its arm-rests softer to his fingertips than a woman's skin, was puzzled and, in his depths, disturbed by certain blots within him, blots of light in his brain, a blot combining pain and amusement in his breast (how did *that* get there?). Intense thought puckered the skin between his eyes with a strain bordering on headache. Why had he let Pop have his way? Why did he agree to meet him that day, in the dim rear of the poolroom?

"But what will you tell Mrs. Skoglund?"

"The old broad? Don't worry, there's plenty to tell her, and it's all true. Ain't I trying to save my little laundry-and-cleaning shop? Isn't the bailiff coming for the fixtures next week?" And Pop rehearsed his pitch on the Western Avenue car. He counted on Woody's health and his fresh-ness. Such a straightforward-looking boy was perfect for a con.

Did they still have such winter storms in Chicago as they used to have? Now they somehow seemed less fierce. Blizzards used to come straight down from Ontario, from the Arctic, and drop five feet of snow in an afternoon. Then the rusty green platform cars, with revolving brushes at both ends, came out of the barns to sweep the tracks. Ten or twelve streetcars followed in slow processions, or waited, block after block.

There was a long delay at the gates of Riverview Park, all the amusements covered for the winter, boarded up — the dragon's-back high-rides, the Bobs, the Chute, the Tilt-a-Whirl, all the fun machinery put together by mechanics and electricians, men like Bujak the tool-and-die-maker, good with engines. The blizzard was having it all its own way behind the gates, and you couldn't see far inside; only a few bulbs burned behind the palings. When Woody wiped the vapor from the glass, the wire mesh of the window guards was stuffed solid at eye level with snow. Looking higher, you saw mostly the streaked wind horizontally driving from the north. In the seat ahead, two black coal heavers both in leather Lindbergh flying helmets sat with shovels between their legs, returning from a job. They smelled of sweat, burlap sacking, and coal. Mostly dull with black dust, they also sparkled here and there.

There weren't many riders. People weren't leaving the house. This was a day to sit legs stuck out beside the stove, mummified by both the outdoor and the indoor forces. Only a fellow with an angle, like Pop, would go and buck such weather. A storm like this was out of the compass, and you kept the human scale by having a scheme to raise fifty bucks. Fifty soldiers! Real money in 1933.

"That woman is crazy for you," said Pop.

"She's just a good woman, sweet to all of us."

"Who knows what she's got in mind. You're a husky kid. Not such a kid either."

"She's a religious woman. She really has religion."

"Well, your mother isn't your only parent. She and Rebecca and Kovner aren't going to fill you up with their ideas. I know your mother wants to wipe me out of your life. Unless I take a hand, you won't even understand what life is. Because they don't know — those silly Christers."

"Yes, Pop."

"The girls I can't help. They're too young. I'm sorry about them, but I can't do anything. With you it's different."

He wanted me like himself, an American.

They were stalled in the storm, while the cattle-colored car waited to have the trolley reset in the crazy wind, which boomed, tingled, blasted. At Howard Street they would have to walk straight into it, due north.

"You'll do the talking at first," said Pop.

Woody had the makings of a salesman, a pitchman. He was aware of this when he got to his feet in church to testify before fifty or sixty people. Even though Aunt Rebecca made it worth his while, he moved his own heart when he spoke up about his faith. But occasionally, without notice, his heart went away as he spoke religion and he couldn't find it anywhere. In its absence, sincere behavior got him through. He had to rely for delivery on his face, his voice — on behavior. Then his eyes came closer and closer together. And in this approach of eye to eye he felt the strain of hypocrisy. The twisting of his face threatened to betray him. It took everything he had to keep looking honest. So, since he couldn't bear the cynicism of it, he fell back on mischievousness. Mischief was where Pop came in. Pop passed straight through all those divided fields, gap after gap, and arrived at his side, bent-nosed and broad-faced. In regard to Pop, you thought of neither sincerity nor insincerity. Pop was like the man in the song: he wanted what he wanted when he wanted it. Pop was physical; Pop was digestive, circulatory, sexual. If Pop got serious, he talked to you about washing under the arms or in the crotch or of drying between your toes or of cooking supper, of onions, of draw poker or of a certain horse in the fifth race at Arlington. Pop was elemental. That was why he gave such relief from religion and paradoxes, and things like that. Now Mother *thought* she was spiritual, but Woody knew that she was kidding herself. Oh, yes, in the British accent she never gave up she was always talking to God or about Him — please-God, God-willing, praise-God. But she was a big substantial bread-and-butter, down-to-earth woman, with down-to-earth duties like feeding the girls, protecting, refining, keeping pure the girls. And those two protected doves grew up so overweight, heavy in the hips and thighs, that their poor heads looked long and slim. And mad. Sweet but cuckoo — Paula cheerfully cuckoo, Joanna depressed and having episodes.

"I'll do my best by you, but you have to promise, Pop, not to get me in Dutch with Mrs. Skoglund."

"You worried because I speak bad English? Embarrassed? I have a mockie accent?"

"It's not that. Kovner has a heavy accent, and she doesn't mind."

"Who the hell are those freaks to look down on me? You're practically a man and your dad has a right to expect help from you. He's in a fix. And you bring him to her house because she's big-hearted, and you haven't got anybody else to go to."

"I got you, Pop."

The two coal trimmers stood up at Devon Avenue. One of them wore a woman's coat. Men wore women's clothing in those years, and women men's, when there was no choice. The fur collar was spiky with the wet, and sprinkled with soot. Heavy, they dragged their shovels and got off at the front. The slow car ground on, very slow. It was after four when they reached the end of the line, and somewhere between gray and black, with snow spouting and whirling under the street lamps. In Howard Street, autos were stalled at all angles and abandoned. The sidewalks were blocked. Woody led the way into Evanston, and Pop followed him up the middle of the street in the furrows made earlier by trucks. For four blocks they bucked the wind and then Woody broke through the drifts to the snowbound mansion, where they both had to push the wrought-iron gate because of the drift behind it. Twenty rooms or more in this dignified house and nobody in them but Mrs. Skoglund and her servant Hjordis, also religious.

As Woody and Pop waited, brushing the slush from their sheepskin collars and Pop wiping his big eyebrows with the ends of his scarf, sweating and freezing, the chains began to rattle and Hjordis uncovered the air holes of the glass storm door by turning a wooden bar. Woody called her "monk-faced." You no longer see women like that, who put no female touch on the face. She came plain, as God made her. She said, "Who is it and what do you want?"

"It's Woodrow Selbst. Hjordis? It's Woody."

"You're not expected."

"No, but we're here."

"What do you want?"

"We came to see Mrs. Skoglund."

"What for do you want to see her?"

"Just to tell her we're here."

"I have to tell her what you came for, without calling up first."

"Why don't you say it's Woody with his father, and we wouldn't come in a snowstorm like this if it wasn't important."

The understandable caution of women who live alone. Respectable old-time women, too. There was no such respectability now in those Evanston houses, with their big verandas and deep yards and with a servant like Hjordis, who carried at her belt keys to the pantry and to every closet and every dresser drawer and every padlocked bin in the cellar. And in High Episcopal Christian Science Women's Temperance Evanston no tradespeople rang at the front door. Only invited guests. And here, after a ten-mile grind through the blizzard, came two tramps from the West Side. To this mansion where a Swedish immigrant lady, herself once a cook and now a philanthropic widow, dreamed, snow-bound, while frozen lilac twigs clapped at her storm windows, of a new Jerusalem and a Second Coming and a Resurrection and a Last Judgment. To hasten the Second Coming, and all the rest, you had to reach the hearts of these scheming bums arriving in a snowstorm.

Sure, they let us in.

Then in the heat that swam suddenly up to their mufflered chins Pop and Woody felt the blizzard for what it was; their cheeks were frozen slabs. They stood beat, itching, trickling in the front hall that *was* a hall, with a carved rural post staircase and a big stained-glass window at the top. Picturing Jesus with the Samaritan woman. There was a kind of Gentile closeness to the air. Perhaps when he was with Pop, Woody made more Jewish observations than he would otherwise. Although Pop's most Jewish characteristic was that Yiddish was the only language he could read a paper in. Pop was with Polish Halina, and Mother was with Jesus Christ, and Woody ate uncooked bacon from the flitch. Still now and then he had a Jewish impression.

Mrs. Skoglund was the cleanest of women — her fingernails, her white neck, her ears — and Pop's sexual hints to Woody all went wrong because she was so intensely clean, and made Woody think of a waterfall, large as she was, and grandly built. Her bust was big. Woody's imagination had investigated this. He thought she kept things tied down tight, very tight. But she lifted both arms once to raise a window and there it was, her bust, beside him, the whole unbindable thing. Her hair was like the raffia you had to soak before you could weave with it in a basket class — pale, pale. Pop, as he took his sheepskin off, was in sweaters, no jacket. His darting looks made him seem crooked. Hardest of all for these Selbsts with their bent noses and big, apparently straightforward faces was to look honest. All the signs of dishonesty played over them. Woody had often puzzled about it. Did it go back to the muscles, was it fundamentally a jaw problem — the projecting angles of the jaws? Or was it the angling that went on in the heart? The girls called Pop Dick Tracy, but Dick Tracy was a good guy. Whom could Pop convince? Here, Woody caught a possibility as it flitted by. Precisely because of the way Pop looked, a sensitive person might feel remorse for condemning unfairly or judging unkindly. Just because of a face? Some must have bent over backward. Then he had them. Not Hjordis. She would have put Pop into the street then and there, storm or no storm. Hjordis was religous, but she was wised up, too. She hadn't come over in steerage and worked forty years in Chicago for nothing.

Mrs. Skoglund, Aase (Osie), led the visitors into the front room. This, the biggest room in the house, needed supplementary heating. Because of fifteen-foot ceilings and high windows, Hjordis had kept the parlor stove burning. It was one of those elegant parlor stoves that wore a nickel crown, or mitre, and this mitre, when you moved it aside, automatically raised the hinge of an iron stove lid. That stove lid underneath the crown was all soot and rust, the same as any other stove lid. Into this hole you tipped the scuttle and the anthracite chestnut rattled down. It made a cake or dome of fire visible through the small isinglass frames. It was a pretty room, three-quarters panelled in wood. The stove was plugged into the flue of the marble fireplace, and there were parquet floors and Axminster carpets and cranberry-colored tufted Victorian upholstery, and a kind of Chinese étagère, inside a cabinet, lined with mirrors and containing silver pitchers, trophies won by Skoglund cows, fancy sugar tongs and cut-glass pitchers and goblets. There were Bibles and pictures of Jesus and the Holy Land and that faint Gentile odor, as if things had been rinsed in a weak vinegar solution.

"Mrs. Skoglund, I brought my dad to you. I don't think you ever met him," said Woody.

"Yes, Missus, that's me, Selbst."

Pop stood short but masterful in the sweaters, and his belly sticking out, not soft but hard. He was a man of the hard-bellied type. Nobody intimidated Pop. He never presented himself as a beggar. There wasn't a cringe in him anywhere. He let her see at once by the way he said "Missus" that he was independent and that he knew his way around. He communicated that he was able to handle himself with women. Handsome Mrs. Skoglund, carrying a basket woven out of her own hair, was in her fifties — eight, maybe ten years his senior.

"I asked my son to bring me because I know you do the kid a lot of good. It's natural you should know both of his parents."

"Mrs. Skoglund, my dad is in a tight corner and I don't know anybody else to ask for help."

This was all the preliminary Pop wanted. He took over and told the widow his story about the laundry-and-cleaning business and payments overdue, and explained about the fixtures and the attachment notice, and the bailiff's office and what they were going to do to him; and he said, "I'm a small man trying to make a living."

"You don't support your children," said Mrs. Skoglund.

"That's right," said Hjordis.

"I haven't got it. If I had it, wouldn't I give it? There's bread lines and soup lines all over town. Is it just me? What I have I divvy with. I give the kids. A bad father? You think my son would bring me if I was a bad father into your house? He loves his dad, he trusts his dad, he knows his dad is a good dad. Every time I start a little business going I get wiped out. This one is a good little business, if I could hold on to that little business. Three people work for me, I meet a payroll, and three people will be on the street, too, if I close down. Missus, I can sign a note and pay you in two months. I'm a common man, but I'm a hard worker and a fellow you can trust."

Woody was startled when Pop used the word "trust." It was as if from all four corners a Sousa band blew a blast to warn the entire world. "Crook! This is a crook!" But Mrs. Skoglund, on account of her religious preoccupations, was remote. She heard nothing. Although everybody in this part of the world, unless he was crazy, led a practical life, and you'd have nothing to say to anyone, your neighbors would have nothing to say to you if communications were not of a practical sort, Mrs. Skoglund, with all her money, was unworldly — two-thirds out of this world.

"Give me a chance to show what's in me," said Pop, "and you'll see what I do for my kids."

So Mrs. Skoglund hesitated, and then she said she'd have to go upstairs, she'd have to go to her room and pray on it and ask for guidance — would they sit down and wait. There were two rocking chairs by the stove. Hjordis gave Pop a grim look (a dangerous person) and Woody a blaming one (he brought a dangerous stranger and disrupter to injure two kind Christian ladies). Then she went out with Mrs. Skoglund.

As soon as they left, Pop jumped up from the rocker and said in anger, "What's this with the praying? She has to ask God to lend me fifty bucks?"

Woody said, "It's not you, Pop, it's the way these religious people do."

"No," said Pop. "She'll come back and say that God wouldn't let her."

Woody didn't like that; he thought Pop was being gross and he said, "No, she's sincere. Pop, try to understand; she's emotional, nervous, and sincere, and tries to do right by everybody."

And Pop said, "That servant will talk her out of it. She's a toughie. It's all over her face that we're a couple of chisellers."

"What's the use of us arguing," said Woody. He drew the rocker closer to the stove. His shoes were wet through and would never dry. The blue flames fluttered like a school of fishes in the coal fire. But Pop went over to the Chinese-style cabinet or étagère and tried the handle, and then opened the blade of his penknife and in a second had forced the lock of the curved glass door. He took out a silver dish.

"Pop, what is this?" said Woody.

Pop, cool and level, knew exactly what this was. He relocked the étagère, crossed the carpet, listened. He stuffed the dish under his belt and pushed it down into his trousers. He put the side of his short thick finger to his mouth.

So Woody kept his voice down, but he was all shook up. He went to Pop and took him by the edge of his hand. As he looked into Pop's face, he felt his eyes growing smaller and smaller, as if something were contracting all the skin on his head. They call it hyperventilation when everything feels tight and light and close and dizzy. Hardly breathing, he said, "Put it back, Pop."

Pop said, "It's solid silver; it's worth dough."

"Pop, you said you wouldn't get me in Dutch."

"It's only insurance in case she comes back from praying and tells me no. If she says yes, I'll put it back."

"How?"

"It'll get back. If I don't put it back, you will."

"You picked the lock. I couldn't. I don't know how."

"There's nothing to it."

"We're going to put it back now. Give it here."

"Woody, it's under my fly, inside my underpants, don't make such a noise about nothing."

"Pop, I can't believe this."

"For Cry-99, shut your mouth. If I didn't trust you I wouldn't have let you watch me do it. You don't understand a thing. What's with you?"

"Before they come down, Pop, will you dig that dish out of your long johns."

Pop turned stiff on him. He became absolutely military. He said, "Look, I order you!"

Before he knew it, Woody had jumped his father and begun to wrestle with him. It was outrageous to clutch your own father, to put a heel behind him, to force him to the wall. Pop was taken by surprise and said loudly, "You want Halina killed? Kill her! Go on, you be responsible." He began to resist, angry, and they turned about several times when Woody, with a trick he had learned in a Western movie and used once on the playground, tripped him and they fell to the ground. Woody, who already outweighed the old man by twenty pounds, was on the top. They landed on the floor beside the stove, which stood on a tray of decorated tin to protect the carpet. In this position, pressing Pop's hard belly, Woody recognized that to have wrestled him to the floor counted for nothing. It was impossible to thrust his hand under Pop's belt to recover the dish. And now Pop had turned furious, as a father has every right to be when his son is violent with him, and he freed his hand and hit Woody in the face. He hit him three or four times in mid-face. Then Woody dug his head into Pop's shoulder and held tight only to keep from being struck and began to say in his ear, "Jesus, Pop, for Christ sake remember where you are. Those women will be back!" But Pop brought up his short knee and fought and butted him with his chin and rattled Woody's teeth. Woody thought the old man was about to bite him. And, because he was a seminarian, he thought, "Like an unclean spirit." And held tight. Gradually Pop stopped threshing and struggling. His eyes stuck out and his mouth was open, sullen. Like a stout fish. Woody released him and gave him a hand up. He was then overcome with many many bad feelings of a sort he knew the old man never suffered. Never, never. Pop never had these grovelling emotions. There was his whole superiority. Pop had no such feelings. He was like a horseman from Central Asia, a bandit from China. It was Mother, from Liverpool, who had the refinement, the English manners. It was the preaching Reverend Doctor in his black suit. You have refinements, and all they do is oppress you? The hell with that.

The long door opened and Mrs. Skoglund stepped in, saying, "Did I imagine, or did something shake the house?"

"I was lifting the scuttle to put coal on the fire and it fell out of my hand. I'm sorry I was so clumsy," said Woody.

Pop was too huffy to speak. With his eyes big and sore and the thin hair down over his forehead, you could see by the tightness of his belly how angrily he was fetching his breath, though his mouth was shut.

"I prayed," said Mrs. Skoglund.

"I hope it came out well," said Woody.

"Well, I don't do anything without guidance, but the answer was yes, and I feel right about it now. So if you'll wait I'll go to my office and write a check. I asked Hjordis to bring you a cup of coffee. Coming in such a storm."

And Pop, consistently a terrible little man, as soon as she shut the door said, "A check? Hell with a check. Get me the greenbacks."

"They don't keep money in the house. You can cash it in her bank tomorrow. But if they miss that dish, Pop, they'll stop the check, and then where are you?"

As Pop was reaching below the belt Hjordis brought in the tray. She was very sharp with him. She said, "Is this a place to adjust clothing, Mister? A men's washroom?"

"Well, which way is the toilet, then?" said Pop.

She had served the coffee in the seamiest mugs in the pantry, and she bumped down the tray and led Pop down the corridor, standing guard at the bathroom door so that he shouldn't wander about the house.

Mrs. Skoglund called Woody to her office and after she had given him the folded check said that they should pray together for Morris. So once more he was on his knees, under rows and rows of musty marbled cardboard files, by the glass lamp by the edge of the desk, the shade with flounced edges, like the candy dish. Mrs. Skoglund, in her Scandinavian accent — an emotional contralto — raising her voice to Jesus-uh Christ-uh, as the wind lashed the trees, kicked the side of the house, and drove the snow seething on the windowpanes, to send light-uh, give guidance-uh, put a new heart-uh in Pop's bosom. Woody asked God only to make Pop put the dish back. He kept Mrs. Skoglund on her knees as long as possible. Then he thanked her, shining with candor (as much as he knew how) for her Christian generosity and he said, "I know that Hjordis has a cousin who works at the Evanston Y.M.C.A. Could she please phone him and try to get us a room tonight so that we don't have to fight the blizzard all the way back? We're almost as close to the Y as to the car line. Maybe the cars have even stopped running."

Suspicious Hjordis, coming when Mrs. Skoglund called to her, was burning now. First they barged in, made themselves at home, asked for money, had to have coffee, probably left gonorrhea on the toilet seat. Hjordis, Woody remembered, was a woman who wiped the doorknobs with rubbing alcohol after guests had left. Nevertheless, she telephoned the Y and got them a room with two cots for six bits.

Pop had plenty of time, therefore, to reopen the étagère, lined with reflecting glass or German silver (something exquisitely delicate and tricky), and as soon as the two Selbsts had said thank you and goodbye and were in mid-street again up to the knees in snow, Woody said, "Well, I covered for you. Is that thing back?"

"Of course it is," said Pop.

They fought their way to the small Y building, shut up in wire grille and resembling a police station — about the same dimensions. It was locked, but they made a racket on the grille, and a small black man let them in and shuffled them upstairs to a cement corridor with low doors. It was like the small-mammal house in Lincoln Park. He said there was nothing to eat, so they took off their wet pants, wrapped themselves tightly in the khaki army blankets, and passed out on their cots.

First thing in the morning, they went to the Evanston National Bank and got the fifty dollars. Not without difficulties. The teller went to call Mrs. Skoglund and was absent a long time from the wicket. "Where the hell has he gone," said Pop.

But when the fellow came back he said, "How do you want it?"

Pop said, "Singles." He told Woody, "Bujak stashes it in one-dollar bills."

But by now Woody no longer believed Halina had stolen the old man's money.

Then they went into the street, where the snow-removal crews were at work. The sun shone broad, broad, out of the morning blue, and all Chicago would be releasing itself from the temporary beauty of those vast drifts.

"You shouldn't have jumped me last night, Sonny."

"I know, Pop, but you promised you wouldn't get me in Dutch."

"Well, it's O.K., we can forget it, seeing you stood by me."

Only, Pop had taken the silver dish. Of course he had, and in a few days Mrs. Skoglund and Hjordis knew it, and later in the week they were all waiting for Woody in Kovner's office at the settlement house. The group included the Reverend Dr. Crabbie, head of the seminary, and Woody, who had been flying along, level and smooth, was shot down in flames. He told them he was innocent. Even as he was falling, he warned that they were wronging him. He denied that he or Pop had touched Mrs. Skoglund's property. The missing object — he didn't even know what it was — had probably been misplaced, and they would be very sorry on the day it turned up. After the others were done with him, Dr. Crabbie said until he was able to tell the truth he would be suspended from the seminary, where his work had been unsatisfactory anyway. Aunt Rebecca took him aside and said to him, "You are a little crook, like your father. The door is closed to you here."

To this Pop's comment was "So what, kid?"

"Pop, you shouldn't have done it."

"No? Well, I don't give a care, if you want to know. You can have the dish if you want to go back and square yourself with all those hypocrites."

"I didn't like doing Mrs. Skoglund in the eye, she was so kind to us."

"Kind?"

"Kind."

"Kind has a price tag."

Well, there was no winning such arguments with Pop. But they debated it in various moods and from various elevations and perspectives for forty years and more, as their intimacy changed, developed, matured.

"Why did you do it, Pop? For the money? What did you do with the fifty bucks?" Woody, decades later, asked him that.

"I settled with the bookie, and the rest I put in the business."

"You tried a few more horses."

"I maybe did. But it was a double, Woody. I didn't hurt myself, and at the same time did you a favor."

"It was for me?"

"It was too strange of a life. That life wasn't *you*, Woody. All those women — Kovner was no man, he was an in-between. Suppose they made you a minister? Some Christian minister! First of all, you wouldn't have been able to stand it, and, second, they would throw you out sooner or later."

"Maybe so."

"And you wouldn't have converted the Jews, which was the main thing they wanted."

"And what a time to bother the Jews," Woody said. "At least *I* didn't bug them."

Pop had carried him back to his side of the line, blood of his blood, the same thick body walls, the same coarse grain. Not cut out for a spiritual life. Simply not up to it.

Pop was no worse than Woody, and Woody was no better than Pop. Pop wanted no relation to theory, and yet he was always pointing Woody toward a position — a jolly, hearty, natural, likable, unprincipled position. If Woody had a weakness, it was to be unselfish. This worked to Pop's advantage, but he criticized Woody for it, nevertheless. "You take too much on yourself," Pop was always saying. And it's true that Woody gave Pop his heart because Pop was so selfish. It's usually the selfish people who are loved the most. They do what you deny yourself, and you love them for it. You give them your heart.

Remembering the pawn ticket for the silver dish, Woody startled himself with a laugh so sudden that it made him cough. Pop said to him after his expulsion from the seminary and banishment from the settlement house, "You want in again? Here's the ticket. I hocked that thing. It wasn't so valuable as I thought."

"What did they give?"

"Twelve-fifty was all I could get. But if you want it you'll have to raise the dough yourself, because I haven't got it anymore."

"You must have been sweating in the bank when the teller went to call Mrs. Skoglund about the check."

"I was a little nervous," said Pop. "But I didn't think they could miss the thing so soon."

That theft was part of Pop's war with Mother. With Mother, and Aunt Rebecca, and the Reverend Doctor. Pop took his stand on realism. Mother represented the forces of religion and hypochondria. In four decades, the fighting never stopped. In the course of time, Mother and the girls turned into welfare personalities and lost their individual outlines. Ah, the poor things, they became dependents and cranks. In the meantime, Woody, the sinful man, was their dutiful and loving son and brother. He maintained the bungalow — this took in roofing, pointing, wiring, insulation, air-conditioning — and he paid for heat and light and food, and dressed them all out of Sears, Roebuck and Wieboldt's, and bought them a TV, which they watched as devoutly as they prayed. Paula took courses to learn skills like macramé-making and needlepoint, and sometimes got a little job as recreational worker in a nursing home. But she wasn't steady enough to keep it. Wicked Pop spent most of his life removing stains from people's clothing. He and Halina in the last year ran a Cleanomat in West Rogers Park — a so-so business resembling a laundromat — which gave him leisure for billiards, the horses, rummy and pinochle. Every morning he went behind the partition to check out the filters of the cleaning equipment. He found amusing things that had been thrown into the vats with the clothing — sometimes, when he got lucky, a locket chain or a brooch. And when he had fortified the cleaning fluid, pouring all that blue and pink stuff in from plastic jugs, he read the *Forward* over a second cup of coffee, and went out, leaving Halina in charge. When they needed help with the rent, Woody gave it.

After the new Disney World was opened in Florida, Woody treated all his dependents to a holiday. He sent them down in separate batches, of course. Halina enjoyed this more than anybody else. She couldn't stop talking about the address given by an Abraham Lincoln automaton. "Wonderful, how he stood up and moved his hands, and his mouth. So real! And how beautiful he talked." Of them all, Halina was the soundest, the most human, the most honest. Now that Pop was gone, Woody and Halina's son, Mitosh, the organist at the Stadium, took care of her needs over and above Social Security, splitting expenses. In Pop's opinion, insurance was a racket. He left Halina nothing but some out-of-date equipment.

Woody treated himself, too. Once a year, and sometimes oftener, he left his business to run itself, arranged with the trust department at the bank to take care of his Gang, and went off. He did that in style, imaginatively, expensively. In Japan, he wasted little time on Tokyo. He spent three weeks in Kyoto and stayed at the Tawaraya Inn, dating from the seventeenth century or so. There he slept on the floor, the Japanese way, and bathed in scalding water. He saw the dirtiest strip show on earth, as well as the holy places and the temple gardens. He visited also Istanbul, Jerusalem, Delphi, and went to Burma and Uganda and Kenya on safari, on democratic terms with drivers, Bedouins, bazaar merchants. Open, lavish, familiar, fleshier and fleshier but (he jogged, he lifted weights) still muscular — in his naked person beginning to resemble a Renaissance courtier in full costume — becoming ruddier every year, an outdoor type with freckles on his back and spots across the flaming forehead and the honest nose. In Addis Ababa he took an Ethiopian beauty to his room from the street and washed her, getting into the shower with her to soap her with his broad, kindly hands. In Kenya he taught certain American obscenities to a black woman so that she could shout them out during the act. On the Nile, below Murchison Falls, those fever trees rose huge from the mud, and hippos on the sandbars belched at the passing launch, hostile. One of them danced on his spit of sand, springing from the ground and coming down heavy, on all fours. There, Woody saw the buffalo calf disappear, snatched by the crocodile.

Mother, soon to follow Pop, was being light-headed these days. In company, she spoke of Woody as her boy — "What do you think of my Sonny?" — as though he was ten years old. She was silly with him, her behavior was frivolous, almost flirtatious. She just didn't seem to know the facts. And behind her all the others, like kids at the playground, were waiting their turn to go down the slide; one on each step, and moving toward the top.

Over Woody's residence and place of business there had gathered a pool of silence of the same perimeter as the church bells while they were ringing, and he mourned under it, this melancholy morning of sun and autumn. Doing a life survey, taking a deliberate look at the gross side of his case — of the other side as well, what there was of it. But if this heartache continued, he'd go out and run it off. A three-mile jog — five, if necessary. And you'd think that this jogging was an entirely physical activity, wouldn't you? But there was something else in it. Because, when he was a seminarian, between the shafts of his World's Fair rickshaw, he used to receive, pulling along (capable and stable), his religious experiences while he trotted. Maybe it was all a single experience repeated. He felt truth coming to him from the sun. He received a communication that was also light and warmth. It made him very remote from his horny Wisconsin passengers, those farmers whose whoops and whore-cries he could hardly hear when he was in one of his states. And again out of the flaming of the sun would come to him a secret certainty that the goal set for this earth was that it should be filled with good, saturated with it. After everything preposterous, after dog had eaten dog, after the crocodile death had pulled everyone into his mud. It wouldn't conclude as Mrs. Skoglund, bribing him to round up the Jews and hasten the Second Coming, imagined it but in another way. This was his clumsy intuition. It went no further. Subsequently, he proceeded through life as life seemed to want him to do it.

There remained one thing more this morning, which was explicitly physical, occurring first as a sensation in his arms and against his breast and, from the pressure, passing into him and going into his breast.

It was like this: When he came into the hospital room and saw Pop with the sides of his bed raised, like a crib, and Pop, so very feeble, and writhing, and toothless, like a baby, and the dirt already cast into his face, into the wrinkles — Pop wanted to pluck out the intravenous needles and he was piping his weak death noise. The gauze patches taped over the needles were soiled with dark blood. Then Woody took off his shoes, lowered the side of the bed, and climbed in and held him in his arms to soothe and still him. As if he were Pop's father, he said to him, "Now Pop. Pop." Then it was like the wrestle in Mrs. Skoglund's parlor, when Pop turned angry like an unclean spirit and Woody tried to appease him, and warn him, saying, "Those women will be back!" Beside the coal stove, when Pop hit Woody in the teeth with his head and then became sullen, like a stout fish. But this struggle in the hospital was weak — so weak! In his great pity, Woody held Pop, who was fluttering and shivering. From those people, Pop had told him, you'll never find out what life is, because they don't know what it is. Yes, Pop — well, what is it, Pop? Hard to comprehend that Pop, who was dug in for eighty-three years and had done all he could to stay, should now want nothing but to free himself. How could Woody allow the old man to pull the intravenous needles out? Willful Pop, he wanted what he wanted when he wanted it. But what he wanted at the very last Woody failed to follow, it was such a switch.

After a time, Pop's resistance ended. He subsided and subsided. He rested against his son, his small body curled there. Nurses came and looked. They disapproved, but Woody, who couldn't spare a hand to wave them out, motioned with his head toward the door. Pop, whom Woody thought he had stilled, only had found a better way to get around him. Loss of heat was the way he did it. His heat was leaving him. As can happen with small animals while you hold them in your hand, Woody presently felt him cooling. Then, as Woody did his best to restrain him, and thought he was succeeding, Pop divided himself. And when he was separated from his warmth he slipped into death. And there was his elderly, large, muscular son, still holding and pressing him when there was nothing anymore to press. You could never pin down that self-willed man. When he was ready to make his move, he made it —always on his own terms. And always, always, something up his sleeve. That was how he was.

## John Updike

..................................................................................................................

# Gesturing

FROM *Playboy*

SHE TOLD HIM with a little gesture he had never seen her use before. Joan had called from the station, having lunched, Richard knew, with her lover. It was a Saturday, and his older son had taken his convertible; Joan's Volvo was new and for several minutes refused to go into first gear for him. By the time he had reached the center of town, she had walked down the main street and up the hill to the green. It was September, leafy and warm, yet with a crystal chill on things, an uncanny clarity. Even from a distance they smiled to see each other. She opened the door and seated herself, fastening the safety belt to silence its chastening buzz. Her face was rosy from her walk, her city clothes looked like a costume, she carried a small package or two, token of her "shopping." Richard tried to pull a U-turn on the narrow street, and in the long moment of his halting and groping for reverse gear, she told him. "Darley," she said and, oddly, tentatively, soundlessly, tapped the fingers of one hand into the palm of the other, a gesture between a child's clap of glee and an adult's signal for attention, "I've decided to kick you out. I'm going to ask you to leave town."

Abruptly full, his heart thumped; it was what he wanted. "O.K.," he said carefully. "If you think you can manage." He glanced at her rosy, alert face to see if she meant it; he could not believe she did. A red, white, and blue mail truck that had braked to a stop behind them tapped its horn, more reminder than rebuke; the Maples were known in the town. They had lived here most of their married life.

Richard found reverse, backed up, completed the turn, and they headed home, skimming. The car, so new and stiff, in motion felt high and light, as if it, too, had just been vaporized in her little playful

clap. "Things are stagnant," she explained, "stuck; we're not going anywhere."

"I will not give her up," he interposed.

"Don't tell me, you've told me."

"Nor do I see you giving him up."

"I would if you asked. Are you asking?"

"No. Horrors. He's all I've got."

"Well, then. Go where you want, I think Boston would be most fun
for the kids to visit. And the least boring for you."

"I agree. When do you see this happening?" Her profile, in the side of
his vision, felt brittle, about to break if he said a wrong word, too rough
a word. He was holding his breath, trying to stay up, high and light,
like the car. They went over the bump this side of the bridge; cigarette
smoke jarred loose from Joan's face.

"As soon as you can find a place," she said. "Next week. Is that too
soon?"

"Probably."

"Is this too sad? Do I seem brutal to you?"

"No, you seem wonderful, very gentle and just, as always. It's right.
It's just something I couldn't do myself. How can you possibly live without me?"

In the edge of his vision her face turned; he turned to see, and her
expression was mischievous, brave, flushed. They must have had wine at
lunch. "Easy," Joan said. He knew it was a bluff, a brave gesture; she was
begging for reprieve. But he held silent, he refused to argue. This way, he
had her pride on his side.

The curves of the road poured by, mailboxes, trees, some of which
were already scorched by the turn of the year. He asked, "Is this your
idea, or his?"

"Mine. It came to me on the train. All Andy said was, I seemed to be
feeding you all the time."

Richard had been sleeping, most nights, in the weeks since their
summer of separated vacations, in a borrowed seaside shack two miles
from their home; he tried to sleep there, but each evening, as the nights
grew longer, it seemed easier, and kinder to the children, to eat the
dinner Joan had cooked. He was used to her cooking; indeed, his body,
every cell, was composed of her cooking. Dinner would lead to a post-
dinner drink, while the children (two were off at school, two were still
homebound) plodded through their homework or stared at television,

and drinking would lead to talking, confidences, harsh words, maudlin tears, and an occasional uxorious collapse upward, into bed. She was right; it was not healthy, nor progressive. The twenty years were by when it would have been convenient to love each other.

He found the apartment in Boston on the second day of hunting. The real-estate agent had red hair, a round bottom, and a mask of make-up worn as if to conceal her youth. Richard felt happy and scared, going up and down stairs behind her. Wearier of him than he was of her, she fidgeted the key into the lock, bucked the door open with her shoulder, and made her little openhanded gesture of helpless display.

The floor was neither wall-to-wall shag nor splintered wood, but black-and-white tile, like the floor in a Vermeer; he glanced to the window, saw the skyscraper, and knew this would do. The skyscraper, for years suspended in a famous state of incompletion, was a beautiful disaster, famous because it was a disaster (glass kept falling from it) and disastrous because it was beautiful: the architect had had a vision. He had dreamed of an invisible building, though immense; the glass was meant to reflect the sky and the old low brick skyline of Boston, and to melt into the sky. Instead, the windows of mirroring glass kept falling to the street and were replaced by ugly opacities of black plywood. Yet enough reflecting surface remained to give an impression, through the wavery old window of this sudden apartment, of huge blueness, a vertical cousin to the horizontal huge blueness of the sea that Richard awoke to each morning, in the now bone-deep morning chill of his unheated shack. He said to the redhead, "Fine," and her charcoal eyebrows lifted. His hands trembled as he signed the lease, having written "Sep" in the space for marital status. From a drugstore he phoned the news, not to his wife, whom it would sadden, but to his mistress, equally far away. "Well," he told her in an accusing voice, "I found one. I signed the lease. Incredible. In the middle of all this fine print, there was the one simple sentence, 'There shall be no water beds.'"

"You sound so shaky."

"I feel I've given birth to a black hole."

"Don't do it, if you don't want to." From the way Ruth's voice paused and faded, he imagined she was reaching for a cigarette, or an ashtray, settling herself to a session of lover babying.

"I do want to. She wants me to. We all want me to. Even the children are turned on. Or pretend to be."

She ignored the "pretend." "Describe it to me."

All he could remember was the floor, and the view of the blue disaster with reflected clouds drifting across its face. And the redhead. She had told him where to shop for food, where to do his laundry. He would have laundry?

"It sounds nice," was Ruth's remote response, when he had finished saying what he could. Two people, one of them a sweating black mailman, were waiting to use the phone booth. He hated the city already, its crowding, its hunger.

"What sounds nice about it?" he snapped.

"Are you so upset? Don't do it if you don't want to."

"Stop *saying* that." It was a tedious formality both observed, the pretense that they were free, within each of their marriages, to do as they pleased; guilt avoidance was the game, and Ruth had grown expert at it. Her words often seemed not real words but blank counters, phrases of an etiquette, partitions in a maze. Whereas his wife's words always opened in, transparent with meaning.

"What else can I say," Ruth asked, "except that I love you?" And at its far end, the phone sharply sighed. He could picture the gesture: she had turned her face away from the mouthpiece and forcefully exhaled, in that way she had, expressive of exasperation even when she felt none, of exhaling and simultaneously stubbing out a cigarette smoked not halfway down its length, so it crumpled under her impatient fingers like an insect fighting to live. Her conspicuous unthriftiness pained him. All waste pained him. He wanted abruptly to hang up but saw that, too, as a wasteful, empty gesture, and hung on.

Alone in his apartment, he discovered himself a neat and thrifty housekeeper. When a woman left, he could promptly set about restoring his bachelor order, emptying the ashtrays that, if the visitor had been Ruth, brimmed with long pale bodies prematurely extinguished and, if Joan, with butts so short as to be scarcely more than filters. Neither woman, it somehow pleased him to observe, ever made more than a gesture toward cleaning up — the bed a wreck, the dishes dirty, each of his three ashtrays (one glass, one pottery, and one a tin cookie-jar lid) systematically touched, like the bases in baseball. Emptying them, he would smile, depending, at Ruth's messy morgue or at Joan's nest of filters, discreet as white pebbles in a bowl of narcissi. When he chastised Ruth for stubbing out cigarettes still so long, she pointed out, of course, with her beautiful unblinking assumption of her own primary worth, how much better it was for *her,* for her lungs, to kill the cigarette early; and, of course, she was right, better other-destructive than self-destructive. Ruth was love, she was life, that was why he loved her. Yet Joan's compulsive economy, her discreet death wish, was as dearly familiar to him as her tiny repressed handwriting and the tight curls of her pubic hair, so Richard smiled emptying her ashtrays also. His smile was a gesture without an audience. He, who had originated his act among parents and grandparents, siblings and pets, and who had developed it for a public of schoolmates and teachers, and who had carried it to new refinements before an initially rapt audience of his own children, could not in solitude stop performing. He had engendered a companion of sorts, a single grand spectator — the blue skyscraper. He felt it with him all the time.

Blue, it showed greener than the sky. For a time Richard was puzzled, why the clouds reflected in it drifted in the same direction as the clouds behind it. With an effort of spatial imagination he perceived that a mirror does not reverse our motion, though it does transpose our ears, and gives our mouths a tweak, so that the face even of a loved one looks unfamiliar and ugly when seen in a mirror, the way she — queer thought! — always sees it. He saw that a mirror posed in its midst would not affect the motion of an army; and often half a reflected cloud matched the half of another beyond the building's edge, moving as one, pierced by a jet trail as though by Cupid's arrow. The disaster sat light on the city's heart. At night, it showed as a dim row of little lights, as if a slender ship were sailing the sky, and during a rain or fog, it vanished entirely, while the brick chimney pots and ironstone steeples in Richard's foreground swarthily intensified their substance. He tried to analyze the logic of window replacement, as revealed in the patterns of gap and glass. He detected no logic, just the slow-motion labor of invisible workers, emptying and filling cells of glass with the brainlessness of bees. If he watched for many minutes, he might see, like the condensation of a dewdrop, a blank space go glassy, and reflective, and greenish-blue. Days passed before he realized that, on the old glass near his nose, the wavery panes of his own window, ghostly previous tenants armed with diamonds had scratched initials, names, dates, and, cut deepest and whitest of all, the touching, comical vow, incised in two trisyllabic lines,

*With this ring*
*I thee wed*

What a transparent wealth of previous lives overlay a city's present joy! As he walked the streets, his own happiness surprised him. He had expected to be sad, guilty, bored. Instead, his days were snugly filled with his lists, his quests for food and hardware, his encounters with such problematical wife substitutes as the laundromat, where students pored over Hesse and picked at their chins while their clothes tumbled in eternal circular fall, where young black housewives hummed as they folded white linen. What an unexpected pleasure, walking home in the dark hugging to himself clean clothes hot as fresh bread, past the bow windows of Back Bay glowing like display cases. He felt sober and exhilarated and justified at the hour when, in the suburbs, rumpled from the commute, he would be into his hurried second pre-dinner drink. He liked the bringing home of food, the tautological satisfaction of cooking a meal and then eating it all, as the radio fed Bach or Bechet into his ears and a book gazed open-faced from the reading stand he had bought; he liked the odd orderly game of consuming before food spoiled and drinking before milk soured. He liked the way airplanes roamed the brown night sky, a second, thinner city laid upon this one, and the way police sirens sang, scooping up some disaster not his. It could not last, such happiness. It was an interim, a holiday. But an oddly clean and just one, rectilinear, dignified, though marred by gaps of sudden fear and disorientation. Each hour had to be scheduled, lest he fall through. He moved like a water bug, like a skipping stone, upon the glassy tense surface of his new life. He walked everywhere. Once he walked to the base of the blue skyscraper, his companion and witness. It was hideous. Heavily planked and chicken-wired tunnels, guarded by barking policemen, protected pedestrians from falling glass and the owners of the building, already millions in the hole, from more lawsuits. Trestles and trucks jammed the cacophonous area. The lower floors were solid plywood, of a Stygian black; the building, so lovely in air, had tangled mucky roots. Richard avoided walking that way again.

When Ruth visited, they played a game, of washing — scouring, with a Brillo pad — one white square of the Vermeer floor, so eventually it would all appear clean. The black squares they ignored. Naked, scrubbing, Ruth seemed on her knees a plump little steed, long hair swinging, soft breasts swaying in rhythm to her energetic circular strokes. Behind, her pubic hair, uncurly, made a kind of nether mane. So lovably strange, she rarely was allowed to clean more than one square. Time, so careful and regular for him, sped for them, and vanished. There seemed time even to talk only at the end, her hand on the door. She asked, "Isn't that building amazing, with the sunset in it?"

"I love that building. And it loves me."

"No. It's me who loves you."

"Can't you share?"

"No."

She felt possessive about the apartment; when he told her Joan had been there, too, and, just for "fun," had slept with him, her husband, Ruth wailed into the telephone, "In *our* bed?"

"In *my* bed," he said, with uncharacteristic firmness.

"In your bed," she conceded, her voice husky as a sleepy child's.

When the conversation finally ended, his mistress sufficiently soothed, he had to go lean his vision against his inanimate, giant friend, dimming to mauve on one side, still cerulean on the other, faintly streaked with reflections of high cirrus. It spoke to him, as the gaze of a dumb beast speaks, of beauty and suffering, of a simplicity that must perish, of loss. Evening would soften its shade to slate; night would envelop its sides. Richard's focus shortened and he read, with irritation, for the hundredth time, that impudent, pious marring, that bit of litany, etched bright by the sun's fading fire.

> With this ring
> I thee wed

Ruth, months ago, had removed her wedding ring. Coming here to embark with him upon an overnight trip, she wore on that naked finger, as a reluctant concession to imposture, an inherited diamond ring. In the hotel, Ruth had been distressed to lose her name in the false assumption of his, though he explained it to her as a mere convenience. "But I *like* who I am now," she protested. That was, indeed, her central jewel, infrangible and bright: She liked who she was. They had gone separate ways and, returning before him, she had asked at the hotel desk for the room key by number.

The clerk asked her her name. It was a policy. He would not give the key to a number.

"And what did you tell him your name was?" Richard asked, in this pause of her story.

In her pause and dark-blue stare, he saw re-created her hesitation when challenged by the clerk. Also, she had been, before her marriage, a second-grade teacher, and Richard saw now the manner — prim, fearful, and commanding — with which she must have confronted those roomfuls of children. "I told him Maple."

Richard had smiled. "That sounds right."

Taking Joan out to dinner felt illicit. She suggested it, for "fun," at the end of one of the children's Sundays. He had been two months in Boston, new habits had replaced old, and it was tempting to leave their children, who were bored and found it easier to be bored by television than by their father, this bossy visitor. "Stop telling me you're bored," he had scolded John, the most docile of his children and the one he felt guiltiest about. "Fifteen is *supposed* to be a boring age. When I was fifteen, I lay around reading science fiction. You lie around looking at *Kung Fu*. At least I was learning to read."

"It's good," the child protested, his adolescent voice cracking in fear of being distracted from an especially vivid piece of slow-motion *tai chi*. Richard, when living here, had watched the program with him often enough to know that it was, in a sense, good, that the hero's Oriental passivity, relieved by spurts of mystical violence, was insinuating into the child a system of ethics, just as Richard had taken ideals of behavior from dime movies and comic books — coolness from Bogart, debonair recklessness from Errol Flynn, duality and deceit from Superman.

He dropped to one knee beside the sofa where John, his upper lip fuzzy and his eyebrows manly dark, stoically gazed into the transcendent flickering; Richard's own voice nearly cracked, asking, "Would it be less boring if Dad still lived here?"

"No-*oh*": the answer was instantaneous and impatient, as if the question had been anticipated. Did the boy mean it? His eyes did not for an instant glance sideways, perhaps out of fear of betraying himself, perhaps out of genuine boredom with grownups and their gestures. On television, satisfyingly, gestures killed. Richard rose from his supplicant position, relieved to hear Joan coming down the stairs. She was dressed to go out, in the timeless black dress with the scalloped neckline, and a collar of Mexican silver. At least — a mark, perhaps, of their fascinating maladjustment — he had never bored *her*, nor she, he dreaded to admit, him. He was wary. He must be wary. They had had it. They must have had it.

Yet the cocktails, and the seafood, and the wine, displaced his wariness; he heard himself saying, to the so familiar and so strange face across the table, "She's lovely, and loves me, you know" (he felt embarrassed, like a son suddenly aware that his mother, though politely attentive, is indifferent to the urgency of an athletic contest being described), "but she does spell everything out, and wants everything spelled out to her. It's like being back in the second grade. And the worst thing is, for all this explaining, for all this glorious fucking, she's still not real to me, the way — you are." His voice did break, he had gone too far.

Joan put her left hand, still bearing their wedding ring, flat on the tablecloth in a sensible, level gesture. "She will be," she said. "It's a matter of time."

The old pattern was still the one visible to the world. The waitress, who had taught their children in Sunday school, greeted them as if their marriage were unbroken; they ate in this restaurant three or four times a year, and were on schedule. They had known the contractor who had built it, this mock-antique wing, a dozen years ago, and then left town, bankrupt, disgraced, and oddly cheerful. His memory hovered between the beams. Another couple, older than the Maples — the husband had once worked with Richard on a town committee — came up to their booth beaming, jollying, loving, in that obligatory American way. Did they know? It didn't matter, in this country of temporary arrangements. The Maples jollied back as one, and tumbled loose only when the older couple moved away. Joan gazed after their backs. "I wonder what they have," she asked, "that we didn't?"

"Maybe they had less," Richard said, "so they didn't expect more."

"That's too easy." She was a shade resistant to his veiled compliments; he was grateful. Please resist.

He asked, "How do you think the kids are doing? John seemed withdrawn."

"That's how he is. Stop picking at him."

"I just don't want him to think he has to be your little husband. That house feels huge now."

"You're telling me."

"I'm sorry." He was; he put his hands palms up on the table.

"Isn't it amazing," Joan said, "how a full bottle of wine isn't enough for two people anymore?"

"Should I order another bottle?" He was dismayed, secretly: the waste.

She saw this and said, "No. Just give me half of what's in your glass."

"You can have it all." He poured.

She said, "So your fucking is really glorious?"

He was embarrassed by the remark now and feared it set a distasteful trend. As with Ruth there was an etiquette of adultery, so with Joan some code of separation must be maintained. "It usually is," he told her, "between people who aren't married."

"Is dat right, white man?" A swallow of his wine inside her, Joan began to swell with impending hilarity. She leaned as close as the table would permit. "You must *promise*" — a gesture went with "promise," a protesting little splaying of her hands — "never to tell this to anybody, not even Ruth."

"Maybe you shouldn't tell me. In fact, don't." He understood why she had been laconic up to now; she had been wanting to talk about her lover, holding him warm within her like a baby. She was going to betray him. "Please don't," Richard said.

"Don't be such a prig. You're the only person I can talk to; it doesn't mean a thing."

"That's what you said about our going to bed in my apartment."

"Did she mind?"

"Incredibly."

Joan laughed, and Richard was struck, for the thousandth time, by the perfection of her teeth, even and rounded and white, bared by her lips as if in proof of a perfect skull, an immaculate soul. Her glee whirled her to a kind of heaven as she confided stories about herself and Andy — how he and a motel manageress had quarreled over the lack of towels in a room taken for the afternoon, how he fell asleep for exactly seven minutes each time after making love. Richard had known Andy for years, a slender, swarthy specialist in corporation law, himself divorced, though professionally engaged in the finicking arrangement of giant mergers. A fussy dresser, a churchman, he brought to many occasions an undue dignity and perhaps had been more attracted to Joan's surface glaze, her smooth New England ice, than to the mischievous demons underneath. "My psychiatrist thinks Andy was symbiotic with you, and now that you're gone, I can see him as absurd."

"He's not absurd. He's good, loyal, handsome, prosperous. He tithes. He has a twelve handicap. He loves you."

"He protects you from me, you mean. His buttons! — we have to allow a half hour afterward for him to do up all his buttons. If they made four-piece suits, he'd wear them. And he washes — he washes *everything*, every time."

"Stop," Richard begged. "Stop telling me all this."

But she was giddy amid the spinning mirrors of her betrayals, her face so flushed and tremulous the waitress sympathetically giggled, pouring the Maples their coffee. Joan's face was pink as a peony, her eyes a blue pale as ice, almost transparent. He saw through her words to what she was saying — that these lovers, however we love them, are not us, are not sacred as reality is sacred. We are reality. We have made children. We gave each other our young bodies. We promised to grow old together.

Joan described an incident in her house, once theirs, when the plumber unexpectedly arrived. Richard had to laugh with her; that house's plumbing problems were an old joke, an ongoing saga. "The back-door bell rang, Mr. Kelly stomped right in, you know how the kitchen echoes in the bedroom, we had *had* it." She looked, to see if her meaning was clear. He nodded. Her eyes sparkled. She emphasized, of the knock, "Just at the *very* moment," and, with a gesture akin to the gentle clap in the car a world ago, drew with one fingertip a *v* in the air, as if beginning to write "very." The motion was eager, shy, exquisite, diffident, trusting: he saw all its meanings and knew that she would never stop gesturing within him, never; though a decree come between them, even death, her gestures would endure, cut into glass.

1981

*Cynthia Ozick*

........................................................................................................................

# The Shawl

FROM *The New Yorker*

STELLA, cold, cold, the coldness of hell. How they walked on the roads together, Rosa with Magda curled up between sore breasts, Magda wound up in the shawl. Sometimes Stella carried Magda. But she was jealous of Magda. A thin girl of fourteen, too small, with thin breasts of her own, Stella wanted to be wrapped in a shawl, hidden away, asleep, rocked by the march, a baby, a round infant in arms. Magda took Rosa's nipple, and Rosa never stopped walking, a walking cradle. There was not enough milk; sometimes Magda sucked air; then she screamed. Stella was ravenous. Her knees were tumors on sticks, her elbows chicken bones.

Rosa did not feel hunger; she felt light, not like someone walking but like someone in a faint, in trance, arrested in a fit, someone who is already a floating angel, alert and seeing everything, but in the air, not there, not touching the road. As if teetering on the tips of her fingernails. She looked into Magda's face through a gap in the shawl: a squirrel in a nest, safe, no one could reach her inside the little house of the shawl's windings. The face, very round, a pocket mirror of a face: but it was not Rosa's bleak complexion, dark like cholera, it was another kind of face altogether, eyes blue as air, smooth feathers of hair nearly as yellow as the Star sewn into Rosa's coat. You could think she was one of *their* babies.

Rosa, floating, dreamed of giving Magda away in one of the villages. She could leave the line for a minute and push Magda into the hands of any woman on the side of the road. But if she moved out of line they might shoot. And even if she fled the line for half a second and pushed the shawl-bundle at a stranger, would the woman take it? She might be surprised, or afraid; she might drop the shawl, and Magda would fall out and strike her head and die. The little round head. Such a good child, she gave up screaming, and sucked now only for the taste of the drying nipple itself. The neat grip of the tiny gums. One mite of a tooth tip sticking up in the bottom gum, how shining, an elfin tombstone of white marble gleaming there. Without complaining, Magda relinquished Rosa's teats, first the left, then the right; both were cracked, not a sniff of milk. The duct-crevice extinct, a dead volcano, blind eye, chill hole, so Magda took the corner of the shawl and milked it instead. She sucked and sucked, flooding the threads with wetness. The shawl's good flavor, milk of linen.

It was a magic shawl, it could nourish an infant for three days and three nights. Magda did not die, she stayed alive, although very quiet. A peculiar smell, of cinnamon and almonds, lifted out of her mouth. She held her eyes open every moment, forgetting how to blink or nap, and Rosa and sometimes Stella studied their blueness. On the road they raised one burden of a leg after another and studied Magda's face. "Aryan," Stella said, in a voice grown as thin as a string; and Rosa thought how Stella gazed at Magda like a young cannibal. And the time that Stella said "Aryan," it sounded to Rosa as if Stella had really said "Let us devour her."

But Magda lived to walk. She lived that long, but she did not walk very well, partly because she was only fifteen months old, and partly because the spindles of her legs could not hold up her fat belly. It was fat with air, full and round. Rosa gave almost all her food to Magda, Stella gave nothing; Stella was ravenous, a growing child herself, but not growing much. Stella did not menstruate. Rosa did not menstruate. Rosa was ravenous, but also not; she learned from Magda how to drink the taste of a finger in one's mouth. They were in a place without pity, all pity was annihilated in Rosa, she looked at Stella's bones without pity. She was sure that Stella was waiting for Magda to die so she could put her teeth into the little thighs.

Rosa knew Magda was going to die very soon; she should have been dead already, but she had been buried away deep inside the magic shawl, mistaken there for the shivering mound of Rosa's breasts; Rosa clung to the shawl as if it covered only herself. No one took it away from her. Magda was mute. She never cried. Rosa hid her in the barracks, under the shawl, but she knew that one day someone would inform; or one day someone, not even Stella, would steal Magda to eat her. When

Magda began to walk, Rosa knew that Magda was going to die very soon, something would happen. She was afraid to fall asleep; she slept with the weight of her thigh on Magda's body; she was afraid she would smother Magda under her thigh. The weight of Rosa was becoming less and less; Rosa and Stella were slowly turning into air.

Magda was quiet, but her eyes were horribly alive, like blue tigers. She watched. Sometimes she laughed — it seemed a laugh, but how could it be? Magda had never seen anyone laugh. Still, Magda laughed at her shawl when the wind blew its corners, the bad wind with pieces of black in it, that made Stella's and Rosa's eyes tear. Magda's eyes were always clear and tearless. She watched like a tiger. She guarded her shawl. No one could touch it; only Rosa could touch it. Stella was not allowed. The shawl was Magda's own baby, her pet, her little sister. She tangled herself up in it and sucked on one of the corners when she wanted to be very still.

Then Stella took the shawl away and made Magda die.

Afterward Stella said: "I was cold."

And afterward she was always cold, always. The cold went into her heart: Rosa saw that Stella's heart was cold. Magda flopped onward with her little pencil legs scribbling this way and that, in search of the shawl; the pencils faltered at the barracks opening, where the light began. Rosa saw and pursued. But already Magda was in the square outside the barracks, in the jolly light. It was the roll-call arena. Every morning Rosa had to conceal Magda under the shawl against a wall of the barracks and go out and stand in the arena with Stella and hundreds of others, sometimes for hours, and Magda, deserted, was quiet under the shawl, sucking on her corner. Every day Magda was silent, and so she did not die. Rosa saw that today Magda was going to die, and at the same time a fearful joy ran in Rosa's two palms, her fingers were on fire, she was astonished, febrile: Magda, in the sunlight, swaying on her pencil legs, was howling. Ever since the drying up of Rosa's nipples, ever since Magda's last scream on the road, Magda had been devoid of any syllable; Magda was a mute. Rosa believed that something had gone wrong with her vocal cords, with her windpipe, with the cave of her larynx; Magda was defective, without a voice; perhaps she was deaf; there might be something amiss with her intelligence; Magda was dumb. Even the laugh that came when the ash-stippled wind made a clown out of Magda's shawl was only the air-blown showing of her teeth. Even when the lice, head lice and body lice, crazed her so that she became as wild as one of the big rats that plundered the barracks at daybreak looking for carrion, she rubbed and scratched and kicked and bit and rolled without a whimper. But now Magda's mouth was spilling a long viscous rope of clamor.

"Maaaa —"

It was the first noise Magda had ever sent out from her throat since the drying up of Rosa's nipples.

"Maaaa . . . aaa!"

Again! Magda was wavering in the perilous sunlight of the arena, scribbling on such pitiful little bent shins. Rosa saw. She saw that Magda was grieving for the loss of her shawl, she saw that Magda was going to die. A tide of commands hammered in Rosa's nipples: Fetch, get, bring! But she did not know which to go after first, Magda or the shawl. If she jumped out into the arena to snatch Magda up, the howling would not stop, because Magda would still not have the shawl; but if she ran back into the barracks to find the shawl, and if she found it, and if she came after Magda holding it and shaking it, then she would get Magda back, Magda would put the shawl in her mouth and turn dumb again.

Rosa entered the dark. It was easy to discover the shawl. Stella was heaped under it, asleep in her thin bones. Rosa tore the shawl free and flew — she could fly, she was only air — into the arena. The sunheat murmured of another life, of butterflies in summer. The light was placid, mellow. On the other side of the steel fence, far away, there were green meadows speckled with dandelions and deep-colored violets; beyond them, even farther, innocent tiger lilies, tall, lifting their orange bonnets. In the barracks they spoke of "flowers," of "rain": excrement, thick turd-braids, and the slow stinking maroon waterfall that slunk down from the upper bunks, the stink mixed with a bitter fatty floating smoke that greased Rosa's skin. She stood for an instant at the margin of the arena. Sometimes the electricity inside the fence would seem to hum; even Stella said it was only an imagining, but Rosa heard real sounds in the wire: grainy sad voices. The farther she was from the fence, the more clearly the voices crowded at her. The lamenting voices strummed so convincingly, so passionately, it was impossible to suspect them of being phantoms. The voices told her to hold up the shawl, high; the voices told her to shake it, to whip with it, to unfurl it like a flag. Rosa lifted, shook, whipped, unfurled. Far off, very far, Magda leaned across her air-fed belly, reaching out with the rods of her arms. She was high up, elevated, riding someone's shoulder. But the shoulder that carried Magda was not coming toward Rosa and the shawl, it was drifting away, the speck of Magda was moving more and more into the smoky distance. Above the shoulder a helmet glinted. The light tapped the helmet and sparkled it into a goblet. Below the helmet a black body like a domino and a pair of black boots hurled themselves in the direction of the electrified fence. The electric voices began to chatter wildly. "Maamaa, maaamaaa," they all hummed together. How far Magda was from Rosa now, across the whole square, past a dozen barracks, all the way on the other side! She was no bigger than a moth.

All at once Magda was swimming through the air. The whole of Magda traveled through loftiness. She looked like a butterfly touching a silver vine. And the moment Magda's feathered round head and her pencil legs and balloonish belly and zigzag arms splashed against the fence, the steel voices went mad in their growling, urging Rosa to run and run to the spot where Magda had fallen from her flight against the electrified fence; but of course Rosa did not obey them. She only stood, because if she ran they would shoot, and if she tried to pick up the sticks of Magda's body they would shoot, and if she let the wolf's screech ascending now through the ladder of her skeleton break out, they would shoot; so she took Magda's shawl and filled her own mouth with it, stuffed it in and stuffed it in, until she was swallowing up the wolf's screech and tasting the cinnamon and almond depth of Magda's saliva; and Rosa drank Magda's shawl until it dried.

*Raymond Carver*

........................................................................................................................

# Where I'm Calling From

FROM *The New Yorker*

WE ARE ON the front porch at Frank Martin's drying-out facility. Like the rest of us at Frank Martin's, J.P. is first and foremost a drunk. But he's also a chimney sweep. It's his first time here, and he's scared. I've been here once before. What's to say? I'm back. J.P.'s real name is Joe Penny, but he says I should call him J.P. He's about thirty years old. Younger than I am. Not much younger, but a little. He's telling me how he decided to go into his line of work, and he wants to use his hands when he talks. But his hands tremble. I mean, they won't keep still. "This has never happened to me before," he says. He means the trembling. I tell him I sympathize. I tell him the shakes will idle down. And they will. But it takes time.

We've only been in here a couple of days. We're not out of the woods yet. J.P. has these shakes, and every so often a nerve — maybe it isn't a nerve, but it's something — begins to jerk in my shoulder. Sometimes it's at the side of my neck. When this happens my mouth dries up. It's an effort just to swallow then. I know something's about to happen and I want to head it off. I want to hide from it, that's what I want to do. Just close my eyes and let it pass by, let it take the next man. J.P. can wait a minute.

I saw a seizure yesterday morning. A guy they call Tiny. A big fat guy, an electrician from Santa Rosa. They said he'd been in here for nearly two weeks and that he was over the hump. He was going home in a day or two and would spend New Year's Eve with his wife in front of the TV. On New Year's Eve, Tiny planned to drink hot chocolate and eat cookies. Yesterday morning he seemed just fine when he came down for breakfast. He was letting out with quacking noises, showing some guy how he called ducks right down onto his head. "Blam. Blam," said Tiny, picking off a couple. Tiny's hair was damp and was slicked back along the sides of his head. He'd just come out of the shower. He'd also nicked himself on the chin with his razor. But so what? Just about everybody at Frank Martin's has nicks on his face. It's something that happens. Tiny edged in at the head of the table and began telling about something that had happened on one of his drinking bouts. People at the table laughed and shook their heads as they shovelled up their eggs. Tiny would say something, grin, then look around the table for a sign of recognition. We'd all done things just as bad and crazy, so, sure, that's why we laughed. Tiny had scrambled eggs on his plate, and some biscuits and honey. I was at the table but I wasn't hungry. I had some coffee in front of me. Suddenly Tiny wasn't there anymore. He'd gone over in his chair with a big clatter. He was on his back on the floor with his eyes closed, his heels drumming the linoleum. People hollered for Frank Martin. But he was right there. A couple of guys got down on the floor beside Tiny. One of the guys put his fingers inside Tiny's mouth and tried to hold his tongue. Frank Martin yelled, "Everybody stand back!" Then I noticed that the bunch of us were leaning over Tiny, just looking at him, not able to take our eyes off him. "Give him air!" Frank Martin said. Then he ran into the office and called the ambulance.

Tiny is on board again today. Talk about bouncing back. This morning Frank Martin drove the station wagon to the hospital to get him. Tiny got back too late for his eggs, but he took some coffee into the dining room and sat down at the table anyway. Somebody in the kitchen made toast for him, but Tiny didn't eat it. He just sat with his coffee and looked into his cup. Every now and then he moved his cup back and forth in front of him.

I'd like to ask him if he had any signal just before it happened. I'd like to know if he felt his ticker skip a beat, or else begin to race. Did his eyelid twitch? But I'm not about to say anything. He doesn't look like he's hot to talk about it anyway. But what happened to Tiny is something I won't ever forget. Old Tiny flat on the floor, kicking his heels. So every time this little flitter starts up anywhere, I draw some breath and wait to find myself on my back, looking up, somebody's fingers in my mouth.

In his chair on the front porch, J.P. keeps his hands in his lap. I smoke cigarettes and use an old coal bucket for an ashtray. I listen to J.P. ramble on. It's eleven o'clock in the morning — an hour and a half until lunch.

Neither one of us is hungry. But just the same we look forward to going inside and sitting down at the table. Maybe we'll get hungry.

What's J.P. talking about, anyway? He's saying how when he was twelve years old he fell into a well in the vicinity of the farm he grew up on. It was a dry well, lucky for him. "Or unlucky," he says, looking around him and shaking his head. He says how late that afternoon, after he'd been located, his dad hauled him out with a rope. J.P. had wet his pants down there. He'd suffered all kinds of terror in that well, hollering for help, waiting, and then hollering some more. He hollered himself hoarse before it was over. But he told me that being at the bottom of that well had made a lasting impression. He'd sat there and looked up at the well mouth. Way up at the top he could see a circle of blue sky. Every once in a while a white cloud passed over. A flock of birds flew across, and it seemed to J.P. their wingbeats set up this odd commotion. He heard other things. He heard tiny rustlings above him in the well, which made him wonder if things might fall down into his hair. He was thinking of insects. He heard wind blow over the well mouth, and that sound made an impression on him, too. In short, everything about his life was different for him at the bottom of that well. But nothing fell on him and nothing closed off that little circle of blue. Then his dad came along with the rope, and it wasn't long before J.P. was back in the world he'd always lived in.

"Keep talking, J.P. Then what?" I say.

When he was eighteen or nineteen years old and out of high school and had nothing whatsoever he wanted to do with his life, he went across town one afternoon to visit a friend. This friend lived in a house with a fireplace. J.P. and his friend sat around drinking beer and batting the breeze. They played some records. Then the doorbell rings. The friend goes to the door. This young woman chimney sweep is there with her cleaning things. She's wearing a top hat, the sight of which knocked J.P. for a loop. She tells J.P.'s friend that she has an appointment to clean the fireplace. The friend lets her in and bows. The young woman doesn't pay him any mind. She spreads a blanket on the hearth and lays out her gear. She's wearing these black pants, black shirt, black shoes and socks. Of course by now she's taken her hat off. J.P. says it nearly drove him nuts to look at her. She does the work, she cleans the chimney, while J.P. and his friend play records and drink beer. But they watch her and they watch what she does. Now and then J.P. and his friend look at each other and grin, or else they wink. They raise their eyebrows when the upper half of the young woman disappears into the chimney. She was all-right-looking, too, J.P. said. She was about his age.

When she'd finished her work, she rolled her things up in the blanket. From J.P.'s friend she took a check that had been made out to her by his parents. And then she asks the friend if he wants to kiss her. "It's supposed to bring good luck," she says. That does it for J.P. The friend rolls his eyes. He clowns some more. Then, probably blushing, he kisses her on the cheek. At this minute J.P. made his mind up about something. He put his beer down. He got up from the sofa. He went over to the young woman as she was starting to go out the door.

"Me, too?" J.P. said to her. She swept her eyes over him. J.P. says he could feel his heart knocking. The young woman's name, it turns out, was Roxy.

"Sure," Roxy says. "Why not? I've got some extra kisses." And she kissed him a good one right on the lips and then turned to go.

Like that, quick as a wink, J.P. followed her onto the porch. He held the porch screen door for her. He went down the steps with her and out to the drive, where she'd parked her panel truck. It was something that was out of his hands. Nothing else in the world counted for anything. He knew he'd met somebody who could set his legs atremble. He could feel her kiss still burning on his lips, etc. At that minute J.P. couldn't begin to sort anything out. He was filled with sensations that were carrying him every which way.

He opened the rear door of the panel truck for her. He helped her store her things inside. "Thanks," she told him. Then he blurted it out — that he'd like to see her again. Would she go to a movie with him sometime? He'd realized, too, what he wanted to do with his life. He wanted to do what she did. He wanted to be a chimney sweep. But he didn't tell her that then.

J.P. says she put her hands on her hips and looked him over. Then she found a business card in the front seat of her truck. She gave it to him. She said, "Call this number after ten o'clock tonight. The answering machine will be turned off then. We can talk. I have to go now." She put the top hat on and then took it off. She looked at J.P. once more. She must have liked what she saw, because this time she grinned. He told her there was a smudge near her mouth. Then she got into her truck, tooted the horn, and drove away.

"Then what?" I say. "Don't stop now, J.P." I was interested. But I would have listened if he'd been going on about how one day he'd decided to start pitching horseshoes.

It rained last night. The clouds are banked up against the hills across the valley. J.P. clears his throat and looks at the hills and the clouds. He pulls his chin. Then he goes on with what he was saying.

Roxy starts going out with him on dates. And little by little he talks her into letting him go along on jobs with her. But Roxy's in business with her father and brother and they've got just the right amount of work. They don't need anybody else. Besides, who was this guy J.P.? J.P. what? Watch out, they warned her.

So she and J.P. saw some movies together. They went to a few dances. But mainly the courtship revolved around their cleaning chimneys together. Before you know it, J.P. says, they're talking about tying the knot. And after a while they do it, they get married. J.P.'s new father-in-law takes him in as a full partner. In a year or so, Roxy has a kid. She's quit being a chimney sweep. At any rate, she's quit doing the work. Pretty soon she has another kid. J.P.'s in his mid-twenties by now. He's buying a house. He says he was happy with his life. "I was happy with the way things were going," he says. "I had everything I wanted. I had a wife and kids I loved, and I was doing what I wanted to do with my life." But for some reason — who knows why we do what we do? — his drinking picks up. For a long time he drinks beer and beer only. Any kind of beer — it didn't matter. He says he could drink beer twenty-four hours a day. He'd drink beer at night while he watched TV. Sure, once in a while he drank hard stuff. But that was only if they went out on the town, which was not often, or else when they had company over. Then a time comes, he doesn't know why, when he makes the switch from beer to gin and tonic. And he'd have more gin and tonic after dinner, sitting in front of the TV. There was always a glass of gin and tonic in his hand. He says he actually liked the taste of it. He began stopping off after work for drinks before he went home to have more drinks. Then he began missing some dinners. He just wouldn't show up. Or else he'd show up but he wouldn't want anything to eat. He'd filled up on snacks at the bar. Sometimes he'd walk in the door and for no good reason throw his lunch pail across the living room. When Roxy yelled at him, he'd turn around and go out again. He moved his drinking time up to early afternoon, while he was still supposed to be working. He tells me that he was starting off the morning with a couple of drinks. He'd have a belt of the stuff before he brushed his teeth. Then he'd have his coffee. He'd go to work with a thermos bottle of vodka in his lunch pail.

J.P. quits talking. He just clams up. What's going on? I'm listening. It's helping me relax, for one thing. It's taking me away from my own situation. After a minute, I say, "What the hell? Go on J.P." He's pulling his chin. But pretty soon he starts talking again.

J.P. and Roxy are having some real fights now. I mean *fights*. J.P. says that one time she hit him in the face with her fist and broke his nose. "Look at this," he says. "Right here." He shows me a line across the bridge of his nose. "That's a broken nose." He returned the favor. He dislocated her shoulder for her on that occasion. Another time he split her lip. They beat on each other in front of the kids. Things got out of hand. But he kept on drinking. He couldn't stop. And nothing could make him stop. Not even with Roxy's dad and her brother threatening to beat hell out of him. They told Roxy she should take the kids and clear out. But Roxy said it was her problem. She got herself into it, and she'd solve it.

Now J.P. gets real quiet again. He hunches his shoulders and pulls down in his chair. He watches a car driving down the road between this place and the hills.

I say, "I want to hear the rest of this, J.P. You better keep talking."

"I just don't know," he says. He shrugs.

"It's all right," I say. And I mean it's O.K. for him to tell it. "Go on, J.P."

One way she tried to solve things, J.P. says, was by finding a boyfriend. J.P. would like to know how she found the time with the house and kids.

I looked at him and I'm surprised. He's a grown man. "If you want to do that," I say, "you find the time. You make the time."

J.P. shakes his head. "I guess so," he says.

Anyway, he found out about it — about Roxy's boyfriend — and he went wild. He manages to get Roxy's wedding ring off her finger. And when he does he cuts it into several pieces with a pair of wire cutters. Good solid fun. They'd already gone a couple of rounds on this occasion. On his way to work the next morning he gets arrested on a drunk-driving charge. He loses his driver's license. He can't drive the truck to work anymore. Just as well, he says. He'd already fallen off a roof the week before and broken his thumb. It was just a matter of time until he broke his God-damned neck, he says.

He was here at Frank Martin's to dry out and to figure how to get his life back on track. But he wasn't here against his will, any more than I was. We weren't locked up. We could leave anytime we wanted. But a minimum stay of a week was recommended, and two weeks or a month was, as they put it, "strongly advised."

As I said, this is my second time at Frank Martin's. When I was trying to sign a check to pay in advance for a week's stay, Frank Martin said, "The holidays are always a bad time. Maybe you should think of sticking around a little longer this time? Think in terms of a couple of weeks. Can you do a couple of weeks? Think about it, anyway. You don't have to decide anything right now," he said. He held his thumb on the check and I signed my name. Then I walked my girlfriend to the front door and said goodbye. "Goodbye," she said, and she lurched into the doorjamb and then onto the porch. It's late afternoon. It's raining. I go from the door to the window. I move the curtain and watch her drive away. She's in my car. She's drunk. But I'm drunk, too, and there's nothing I can do. I make it to a big old chair that's close to the radiator, and I sit down. Some guys look up from their TV. Then slowly they shift back to what they were watching. I just sit there. Now and then I look up at something that's happening on the screen.

Later that afternoon the front door banged open and J.P. was brought in between these two big guys — his father-in-law and brother-in-law. I find out afterward. They steered J.P. across the room. The old guy signed him in and gave Frank Martin a check. Then these two guys helped J.P. upstairs. I guess they put him to bed. Pretty soon the old guy and the other guy came downstairs and headed for the front door. They couldn't seem to get out of this place fast enough. It was as if they couldn't wait to wash their hands of all this. I didn't blame them. Hell, no. I don't know how I'd act if I was in their shoes.

A day and a half later J.P. and I meet up on the front porch. We shake hands and comment on the weather. J.P. has a case of the shakes. We sit down and prop our feet on the railing. We lean back in our chairs as if we're just out there taking our ease, as if we might be getting ready to talk about our bird dogs. That's when J.P. gets going with his story.

It's cold out, but not too cold. It's a little overcast. At one point Frank Martin comes outside to finish his cigar. He has on a sweater buttoned up to his Adam's apple. Frank Martin is short and heavyset. He has curly gray hair and a small head. His head is out of proportion with the rest of his body. Frank Martin puts the cigar in his mouth and stands with his arms crossed over his chest. He works that cigar in his mouth and looks across the valley. He stands there like a prizefighter, like somebody who knows the score.

J.P. gets real quiet again. I mean, he's hardly breathing. I toss my cigarette into the coal bucket and look hard at J.P., who scoots farther down in his chair. J.P. pulls up his collar. What the hell's going on, I wonder. Frank Martin uncrosses his arms and takes a puff on the cigar. He lets the smoke carry out of his mouth. Then he raises his chin toward the hills and says, "Jack London used to have a big place on the other side of this valley. Right over there behind that green hill you're looking at. But alcohol killed him. Let that be a lesson. He was a better man than any of us. But he couldn't handle the stuff, either." He looks at what's left of his cigar. It's gone out. He tosses it into the bucket. "You guys want to read something while you're here, read that book of his *The Call of the Wild*. You know the one I'm talking about? We have it inside, if you want to read something. It's about this animal that's half dog and half wolf. They don't write books like that anymore. But we could have helped Jack London, if we'd been here in those days. And if he'd let us. If he'd asked for our help. Hear me? Like we can help you. *If*. *If* you ask for it and *if* you listen. End of sermon. But don't forget. If," he says again. Then he hitches his pants and tugs his sweater down. "I'm going inside," he says. "See you at lunch."

"I feel like a bug when he's around," J.P. says. "He makes me feel like a bug. Something you could step on." J.P. shakes his head. Then he says, "Jack London. What a name! I wish I had me a name like that. Instead of the name I got."

Frank Martin talked about that "if" the first time I was here. My wife brought me up here that time. That's when we were still living together, trying to make things work out. She brought me here and she stayed around for an hour or two, talking to Frank Martin in private. Then she left. The next morning Frank Martin got me aside and said, "We can help you. If you want help and want to listen to what we say." But I didn't know if they could help me or not. Part of me wanted help. But there was another part. All said, it was a very big if.

This time around, six months after my first stay, it was my girlfriend who drove me here. She was driving my car. She drove us through a rainstorm. We drank champagne all the way. We were both drunk when she pulled up in the drive. She intended to drop me off, turn around, and drive home again. She had things to do. One thing she had to do was to go to work the next day. She was a secretary. She had an O.K. job with this electronic-parts firm. She also had this mouthy teen-age son. I wanted her to get a motel room in town, spend the night, and then drive home. I don't know if she got the room or not. I haven't heard from her since she led me up the front steps the other day and walked me into Frank Martin's office and said, "Guess who's here."

But I wasn't mad at her. In the first place she didn't have any idea what she was letting herself in for when she said I could stay with her after my wife asked me to leave. I felt sorry for her. The reason I felt sorry for her was on the day before Christmas her Pap smear came back from the lab, and the news was not cheery. She'd have to go back to the doctor, and real soon. That kind of news was reason enough for both of us to start drinking. So what we did was get ourselves good and drunk. And on Christmas Day we were still drunk. We had to go out to a restaurant to eat, because she didn't feel anything like cooking. The two of us and her mouthy teen-age son opened some presents, and then we went to this steak house near her apartment. I wasn't hungry. I had some soup and a hot roll. I drank a bottle of wine with the soup. She drank some wine, too. Then we started in on Bloody Marys. For the next couple of days I didn't eat anything except cashew nuts. But I drank a lot of bourbon. On the morning of the twenty-eighth I said to her, "Sugar, I think I'd better pack up. I better go back to Frank Martin's. I need to try that place on again. Hey, how about you driving me?"

She tried to explain to her son that she was going to be gone that afternoon and evening, and he'd have to get his own dinner. But right as we were going out the door this God-damned kid screamed at us. He screamed, "You call this love? The hell with you both! I hope you never come back. I hope you kill yourselves!" Imagine this kid!

Before we left town I had her stop at the liquor store, where I bought us three bottles of champagne. Quality stuff — Piper. We stopped someplace else for plastic glasses. Then we picked up a bucket of fried chicken. We set out for Frank Martin's in this rainstorm, drinking champagne and listening to music on the radio. She drove. I looked after the radio and poured champagne. We tried to make a little party out of it. But we were sad, too. There was that fried chicken, but we didn't eat any of it.

I guess she got home O.K. I think I would have heard something if she hadn't made it back. But she hasn't called me, and I haven't called her. Maybe she's had some news about herself by now. Then again, maybe she hasn't heard anything. Maybe it was all a mistake. Maybe it was somebody else's test. But she has my car, and I have things at her house. I know we'll be seeing each other again.

They clang an old farm bell here to signal mealtime. J.P. and I get out of our chairs slowly, like old geezers, and we go inside. It's starting to get too cold on the porch anyway. We can see our breath drifting out from us as we talk.

New Year's Eve morning I try to call my wife. There's no answer. It's O.K. But even if it wasn't O.K., what am I supposed to do? The last time we talked on the phone, a couple of weeks ago, we screamed at each other. I hung a few names on her. "Wet brain!" she said, and put the phone back where it belonged.

But I wanted to talk to her now. Something had to be done about my stuff. I still had things at her house, too.

One of the guys here is a guy who travels. He goes to Europe and the Middle East. That's what he says, anyway. Business, he says. He also says he has his drinking under control and doesn't have any idea why he's here at Frank Martin's. But he doesn't remember getting here. He laughs about it, about his not remembering. "Anyone can have a blackout," he says. "That doesn't prove a thing." He's not a drunk — he tells us this and we listen. "That's a serious charge to make," he says. "That kind of talk can ruin a good man's prospects." He further says that if he'd only stick to whiskey and water, no ice, he'd never get "intoxicated" — his word — and have these blackouts. It's the ice they put into your drink that does it. "Who do you know in Egypt?" he asks me. "I can use a few names over there."

For New Year's Eve dinner Frank Martin serves steak and baked potato. A green salad. My appetite's coming back. I eat the salad. I clean up everything on my plate and I could eat more. I look over at Tiny's plate. Hell, he's hardly touched anything. His steak is just sitting there getting cold. Tiny is not the same old Tiny. The poor bastard had planned to be at home tonight. He'd planned to be in his robe and slippers in front of the TV, holding hands with his wife. Now he's afraid to leave. I can understand. One seizure means you're a candidate for another. Tiny hasn't told any more nutty stories on himself since it happened. He's stayed quiet and kept to himself. Pretty soon I ask him if I can have his steak, and he pushes his plate over to me.

They let us keep the TV on until the New Year has been rung in at Times Square. Some of us are still up, sitting around the TV, watching the crowds on the screen, when Frank Martin comes in to show us his cake. He brings it around and shows it to each of us. I know he didn't make it. It's a God-damned bakery cake. But still it's a cake. It's a big white cake. Across the top of the cake there's writing in pink letters. The writing says "Happy New Year — 1 Day At A Time."

"I don't want any stupid cake," says the guy who goes to Europe and the Middle East. "Where's the champagne?" he says, and laughs.

We all go into the dining room. Frank Martin cuts the cake. I sit next to J.P. J.P. eats two pieces and drinks a Coke. I eat a piece and wrap another piece in a napkin, thinking of later.

J.P. lights a cigarette — his hands are steady now — and he tells me his wife is coming to visit him in the morning. The first day of the New Year.

"That's great," I say. I nod. I lick the frosting off my finger. "That's good news, J.P."

"I'll introduce you," he says.

"I look forward to it," I say.

We say good night. We say Happy New Year. Sleep well. I use a napkin on my fingers. We shake hands.

I go to the pay phone once more, put in a dime, and call my wife collect. But nobody answers this time, either. I think about calling my girlfriend, and I'm dialing her number when I realize I don't want to talk to her. She's probably at home watching the same thing on TV that I've been watching. But maybe she isn't. Maybe she's out. Why shouldn't she be? Anyway, I don't want to talk to her. I hope she's O.K. But if she has something wrong with her I don't want to know about it. Not now. In any case, I won't talk to her tonight.

After breakfast J.P. and I take coffee out to the porch, where we plan to wait for his wife. The sky is clear, but it's cold enough so we're wearing our sweaters and jackets.

"She asked me if she should bring the kids," J.P. says. "I told her she should keep the kids at home. Can you imagine? My God, I don't want my kids up here."

We use the coal bucket for an ashtray. We look across the valley where Jack London used to live. We're drinking more coffee, when this car turns off the road and comes down the drive.

"That's her!" J.P. says. He puts his cup next to his chair. He gets up and goes down the steps to the drive.

I see this woman stop the car and set the brake. I see J.P. open the car door. I watch her get out, and I see them embrace. They hug each other. I look away. Then I look back. J.P. takes the woman's arm and they come up the stairs. This woman has crawled into chimneys. This woman broke a man's nose once. She has had two kids, and much trouble, but she loves this man who has her by the arm. I get up from the chair.

"This is my friend," J.P. says to his wife. "Hey, this is Roxy."

Roxy takes my hand. She's a tall, good-looking woman in a blue knit cap. She has on a coat, a heavy white sweater, and dark slacks. I recall what J.P. told me about the boyfriend and the wire cutters — all that — and I glance at her hands. Right. I don't see any wedding ring. That's in pieces somewhere. Her hands are broad and the fingers have these big knuckles. This is a woman who can make fists if she has to.

"I've heard about you," I say. "J.P. told me how you got acquainted. Something about a chimney, J.P. said."

"Yes, a chimney," she says. Her eyes move away from my face, then return. She nods. She's anxious to be alone with J.P., which I can understand. "There's probably a lot else he didn't tell you," she says. "I bet he didn't tell you everything," she says, and laughs. Then — she can't wait any longer — she slips her arm around J.P.'s waist and kisses him on the cheek. They start to move toward the door. "Nice meeting you," she says over her shoulder. "Hey, did he tell you he's the best sweep in the business?" She lets her hand slide down from J.P.'s waist onto his hip.

"Come on now, Roxy," J.P. says. He has his hand on the doorknob.

"He told me he learned everything he knew from you," I say.

"Well, that much is sure true," she says. She laughs again. But it's as if she's thinking about something else. J.P. turns the doorknob. Roxy lays her hand over his hand. "Joe, can't we go into town for lunch? Can't I take you someplace for lunch?"

J.P. clears his throat. He says, "It hasn't been a week yet." He takes his hand off the doorknob and brings his fingers to his chin. "I think they'd like it, you know, if I didn't leave the place for a little while yet. We can have some coffee inside," he says.

"That's fine," she says. Her eyes light on me once more. "I'm glad Joe's made a friend here. Nice to meet you," she says again.

They start to go inside. I know it's a foolish thing to do, but I do it anyway. "Roxy," I say. And they stop in the doorway and look at me. "I need some luck," I say. "No kidding. I could do with a kiss myself."

J.P. looks down. He's still holding the doorknob, even though the door is open. He turns the doorknob back and forth. He's embarrassed. I'm embarrassed, too. But I keep looking at her. Roxy doesn't know what to make of it. She grins. "I'm not a sweep anymore," she says. "Not for years. Didn't Joe tell you? What the hell. Sure, I'll kiss you. Sure. For luck."

She moves over, she takes me by the shoulders — I'm a big man — and she plants this kiss on my lips. "How's that?" she says.

"That's fine," I say.

"Nothing to it," she says. She's still holding me by the shoulders. She's looking me right in the eyes. "Good luck," she says, and then she lets go of me.

"See you later, pal," J.P. says. He opens the door all the way, and they go inside.

I sit down on the front steps and light a cigarette. I watch what my hand does, then I blow out the match. I've got a case of the shakes. I started out with them this morning. This morning I wanted something to drink. It's depressing, and I didn't say anything about it to J.P. I try to put my mind on something else and for once it works.

I'm thinking about chimney sweeps — all that stuff I heard from J.P. — when for some reason I start to think about the house my wife and I lived in just after we were married. That house didn't have a chimney — hell, no — so I don't know what makes me remember it now. But I remember the house and how we'd only been in there a few weeks when I heard a noise outside one morning and woke up. It was Sunday morning and so early it was still dark in the bedroom. But there was this pale light coming in from the bedroom window. I listened. I could hear something scrape against the side of the house. I jumped out of bed and went to the window.

"My God!" my wife says, sitting up in bed and shaking the hair away from her face. Then she starts to laugh. "It's Mr. Venturini," she says. "The landlord. I forgot to tell you. He said he was coming to paint the house today. Early. Before it gets too hot. I forgot all about it," she says, and laughs some more. "Come on back to bed, honey. It's just the land-lord."

"In a minute," I say.

I push the curtain away from the window. Outside, this old guy in white coveralls is standing next to his ladder. The sun is just starting to break above the mountains. The old guy and I look each other over. It's the landlord, all right — this old guy in coveralls. But his coveralls are too big for him. He needs a shave, too. And he's wearing this baseball cap to cover his bald head. God damn it, I think, if he isn't a weird old hombre, then I've never seen one. And at that minute a wave of happiness comes over me that I'm not him — that I'm me and that I'm inside this bedroom with my wife. He jerks his thumb toward the sun. He pretends to wipe his forehead. He's letting me know he doesn't have all that much time. The old duffer breaks into a grin. It's then I realize I'm naked. I look down at myself. I look at him again and shrug. I'm smiling. What'd he expect?

My wife laughs. "Come *on*," she says. "Get back in this bed. Right now. This minute. Come on back to bed."

I let go of the curtain. But I keep standing there at the window. I can see the landlord nod to himself as if to say, "Go on, sonny, go back to bed. I understand," as if he'd heard my wife calling me. He tugs the bill of his cap. Then he sets about his business. He picks up his bucket. He starts climbing the ladder.

I lean back into the step behind me now and cross one leg over the other. Maybe later this afternoon I'll try calling my wife again. And then I'll call to see what's happening with my girlfriend. But I don't want to get her mouthy son on the line. If I do call, I hope he'll be out somewhere doing whatever he does when he's not hanging around the house. I try to remember if I ever read any Jack London books. I can't remember. But there was a story of his I read in high school. "To Build a Fire" it was called. This guy in the Yukon is freezing. Imagine it — he's actually going to freeze to death if he can't get a fire going. With a fire he can dry his socks and clothing and warm himself. He gets his fire going but then something happens to it. A branchful of snow drops on it. It goes out. Meanwhile, the temperature is falling. Night is coming on.

I bring some change out of my pocket. I'll try my wife first. If she answers, I'll wish her a Happy New Year. But that's it. I won't bring up business. I won't raise my voice. Not even if she starts something. She'll ask me where I'm calling from, and I'll have to tell her. I won't say anything about New Year's resolutions. There's no way to make a joke out of this. After I talk to her, I'll call my girlfriend. Maybe I'll call her first. I'll just have to hope I don't get her son on the line. "Hello, sugar," I'll say when she answers. "It's me."

*Ann Beattie*

......................................................................................................................

# Janus

FROM *The New Yorker*

THE BOWL WAS PERFECT. Perhaps it was not what you'd select if you faced a shelf of bowls, and not the sort of thing that would inevitably attract a lot of attention at a crafts fair, yet it had real presence. It was as predictably admired as a mutt who has no reason to suspect he might be funny. Just such a dog, in fact, was often brought out (and in) along with the bowl.

Andrea was a real estate agent, and when she thought that some prospective buyers might be dog lovers, she would drop off her dog at the same time she placed the bowl in the house that was up for sale. She would put a dish of water in the kitchen for Mondo, take his squeaking plastic frog out of her purse and drop it on the floor. He would pounce delightedly, just as he did every day at home, batting around his favorite toy. The bowl usually sat on a coffee table, though recently she had displayed it on top of a pine blanket chest and on a lacquered table. It was once placed on a cherry table beneath a Bonnard still life, where it held its own.

Everyone who has purchased a house or who has wanted to sell a house must be familiar with some of the tricks used to convince a buyer that the house is quite special: a fire in the fireplace in early evening; jonquils in a pitcher on the kitchen counter, where no one ordinarily has space to put flowers; perhaps the slight aroma of spring, made by a single drop of scent vaporizing from a lamp bulb.

The wonderful thing about the bowl, Andrea thought, was that it was both subtle and noticeable — a paradox of a bowl. Its glaze was the color of cream and seemed to glow no matter what light it was placed in. There were a few bits of color in it — tiny geometric flashes — and some of these were tinged with flecks of silver. They were as mysterious as cells seen under a microscope; it was difficult not to study them, because they shimmered, flashing for a split second, and then resumed their shape. Something about the colors and their random placement suggested motion. People who liked country furniture always commented on the bowl, but then it turned out that people who felt comfortable with Biedermeier loved it just as much. But the bowl was not at all ostentatious, or even so noticeable that anyone would suspect that it had been put in place deliberately. They might notice the height of the ceiling on first entering a room, and only when their eye moved down from that, or away from the refraction of sunlight on a pale wall, would they see the bowl. Then they would go immediately to it and comment. Yet they always faltered when they tried to say something. Perhaps it was because they were in the house for a serious reason, not to notice some object.

Once, Andrea got a call from a woman who had not put in an offer on a house she had shown her. That bowl, she said — would it be possible to find out where the owners had bought that beautiful bowl? Andrea pretended that she did not know what the woman was referring to. A bowl, somewhere in the house? Oh, on a table under the window. Yes, she would ask, of course. She let a couple of days pass, then called back to say that the bowl had been a present and the people did not know where it had been purchased.

When the bowl was not being taken from house to house, it sat on Andrea's coffee table at home. She didn't keep it carefully wrapped (although she transported it that way, in a box); she kept it on the table, because she liked to see it. It was large enough so that it didn't seem fragile, or particularly vulnerable if anyone sideswiped the table or Mondo blundered into it at play. She had asked her husband to please not drop his house key in it. It was meant to be empty.

When her husband first noticed the bowl, he had peered into it and smiled briefly. He always urged her to buy things she liked. In recent years, both of them had acquired many things to make up for all the lean years when they were graduate students, but now that they had been comfortable for quite a while, the pleasure of new possessions dwindled. Her husband had pronounced the bowl "pretty," and he had turned away without picking it up to examine it. He had no more interest in the bowl than she had in his new Leica.

She was sure that the bowl brought her luck. Bids were often put in on houses where she had displayed the bowl. Sometimes the owners, who were always asked to be away or to step outside when the house was being shown, didn't even know that the bowl had been in their house. Once — she could not imagine how — she left it behind, and then she was so afraid that something might have happened to it that she rushed back to the house and sighed with relief when the woman owner opened the door. The bowl, Andrea explained — she had purchased a bowl and set it on the chest for safekeeping while she toured the house with the prospective buyers, and she . . . She felt like rushing past the frowning woman and seizing her bowl. The owner stepped aside, and it was only when Andrea ran to the chest that the lady glanced at her a little strangely. In the few seconds before Andrea picked up the bowl, she realized that the owner must have just seen that it had been perfectly placed, that the sunlight struck the bluer part of it. Her pitcher had been moved to the far side of the chest, and the bowl predominated. All the way home, Andrea wondered how she could have left the bowl behind. It was like leaving a friend at an outing — just walking off. Sometimes there were stories in the paper about families forgetting a child somewhere and driving to the next city. Andrea had only gone a mile down the road before she remembered.

In time, she dreamed of the bowl. Twice, in a waking dream — early in the morning, between sleep and a last nap before rising — she had a clear vision of it. It came into sharp focus and startled her for a moment — the same bowl she looked at every day.

She had a very profitable year selling real estate. Word spread, and she had more clients than she felt comfortable with. She had the foolish thought that if only the bowl were an animate object she could thank it. There were times when she wanted to talk to her husband about the bowl. He was a stockbroker, and sometimes told people that he was fortunate to be married to a woman who had such a fine aesthetic sense and yet could also function in the real world. They were a lot alike, really — they had agreed on that. They were both quiet people — reflective, slow to make value judgments, but almost intractable once they had come to a conclusion. They both liked details, but while ironies attracted her, he was more impatient and dismissive when matters became many sided or unclear. But they both knew this; it was the kind of thing they could talk about when they were alone in the car together, coming home from a party or after a weekend with friends. But she never talked to him about the bowl. When they were at dinner, exchanging their news of the day, or while they lay in bed at night listening to the stereo and murmuring sleepy disconnections, she was often tempted to come right out and say that she thought that the bowl in the living room, the cream-colored bowl, was responsible for her success. But she didn't say it. She couldn't begin to explain it. Sometimes in the morning, she would look at him and feel guilty that she had such a constant secret.

Could it be that she had some deeper connection with the bowl — a relationship of some kind? She corrected her thinking: how could she imagine such a thing, when she was a human being and it was a bowl? It was ridiculous. Just think of how people lived together and loved each other . . . But was that always so clear, always a relationship? She was confused by these thoughts, but they remained in her mind. There was something within her now, something real, that she never talked about.

The bowl was a mystery, even to her. It was frustrating, because her involvement with the bowl contained a steady sense of unrequited good fortune; it would have been easier to respond if some sort of demand were made in return. But that only happened in fairy tales. The bowl was just a bowl. She did not believe that for one second. What she believed was that it was something she loved.

In the past, she had sometimes talked to her husband about a new property she was about to buy or sell — confiding some clever strategy she had devised to persuade owners who seemed ready to sell. Now she stopped doing that, for all her strategies involved the bowl. She became more deliberate with the bowl, and more possessive. She put it in houses only when no one was there, and removed it when she left the house. Instead of just moving a pitcher or a dish, she would remove all the other objects from a table. She had to force herself to handle them carefully, because she didn't really care about them. She just wanted them out of sight.

She wondered how the situation would end. As with a lover, there was no exact scenario of how matters would come to a close. Anxiety became the operative force. It would be irrelevant if the lover rushed into someone else's arms, or wrote her a note and departed to another city. The horror was the possibility of the disappearance. That was what mattered.

She would get up at night and look at the bowl. It never occurred to her that she might break it. She washed and dried it without anxiety, and she moved it often, from coffee table to mahogany corner table or wherever, without fearing an accident. It was clear that she would not be the one who would do anything to the bowl. The bowl was only handled by her, set safely on one surface or another; it was not very likely that anyone would break it. A bowl was a poor conductor of electricity: it would not be hit by lightning. Yet the idea of damage persisted. She did not think beyond that — to what her life would be without the bowl. She only continued to fear that some accident would happen. Why not, in a world where people set plants where they did not belong, so that visitors touring a house would be fooled into thinking that dark corners got sunlight — a world full of tricks?

She had first seen the bowl several years earlier, at a crafts fair she had visited half in secret, with her lover. He had urged her to buy the bowl. She didn't *need* any more things, she told him. But she had been drawn to the bowl, and they had lingered near it. Then she went on to the next booth, and he came up behind her, tapping the rim against her shoulder as she ran her fingers over a wood carving. "You're still insisting that I buy that?" she said. "No," he said. "I bought it for you." He had bought her other things before this — things she liked more, at first — the child's ebony-and-turquoise ring that fitted her little finger; the wooden box, long and thin, beautifully dovetailed, that she used to hold paper clips; the soft gray sweater with a pouch pocket. It was his idea that when he could not be there to hold her hand she could hold her own — clasp her hands inside the lone pocket that stretched across the front. But in time she became more attached to the bowl than to any of his other presents. She tried to talk herself out of it. She owned other things that were more striking or valuable. It wasn't an object whose beauty jumped out at you; a lot of people must have passed it by before the two of them saw it that day.

Her lover had said that she was always too slow to know what she really loved. Why continue with her life the way it was? Why be two-faced, he asked her. He had made the first move toward her. When she would not decide in his favor, would not change her life and come to him, he asked her what made her think she could have it both ways. And then he made the last move and left. It was a decision meant to break her will, to shatter her intransigent ideas about honoring previous commitments.

Time passed. Alone in the living room at night, she often looked at the bowl sitting on the table, still and safe, unilluminated. In its way, it was perfect: the world cut in half, deep and smoothly empty. Near the rim, even in dim light, the eye moved toward one small flash of blue, a vanishing point on the horizon.

1987

*Susan Sontag*

....................................................................................................................

# The Way We Live Now

FROM *The New Yorker*

AT FIRST he was just losing weight, he felt only a little ill, Max said to Ellen, and he didn't call for an appointment with his doctor, according to Greg, because he was managing to keep on working at more or less the same rhythm, but he did stop smoking, Tanya pointed out, which suggests he was frightened, but also that he wanted, even more than he knew, to be healthy, or healthier, or maybe just to gain back a few pounds, said Orson, for he told her, Tanya went on, that he expected to be climbing the walls (isn't that what people say?) and found, to his surprise, that he didn't miss cigarettes at all and reveled in the sensation of his lungs' being ache-free for the first time in years. But did he have a good doctor, Stephen wanted to know, since it would have been crazy not to go for a checkup after the pressure was off and he was back from the conference in Helsinki, even if by then he was feeling better. And he said, to Frank, that he would go, even though he was indeed frightened, as he admitted to Jan, but who wouldn't be frightened now, though, odd as that might seem, he hadn't been worrying until recently, he avowed to Quentin, it was only in the last six months that he had the metallic taste of panic in his mouth, because becoming seriously ill was something that happened to other people, a normal delusion, he observed to Paolo, if one was thirty-eight and had never had a serious illness; he wasn't, as Jan confirmed, a hypochondriac. Of course, it was hard not to worry, everyone was worried, but it wouldn't do to panic, because, as Max pointed out to Quentin, there wasn't anything one could do except wait and hope, wait and start being careful, be careful, and hope. And even if one did prove to be ill, one shouldn't give up, they had new treatments that promised an arrest of the disease's inexorable course, research was progressing. It seemed that everyone was in touch with everyone else several times a week, checking in, I've never spent so many hours at a time on the phone, Stephen said to Kate, and when I'm exhausted after the two or three calls made to me, giving me the latest, instead of switching off the phone to give myself a respite I tap out the number of another friend or acquaintance, to pass on the news. I'm not sure I can afford to think so much about it, Ellen said, and I suspect my own motives, there's something morbid I'm getting used to, getting excited by, this must be like what people felt in London during the Blitz. As far as I know, I'm not at risk, but you never know, said Aileen. This thing is totally unprecedented, said Frank. But don't you think he ought to see a doctor, Stephen insisted. Listen, said Orson, you can't force people to take care of themselves, and what makes you think the worst, he could be just run down, people still do get ordinary illnesses, awful ones, why are you assuming it has to be *that*. But all I want to be sure, said Stephen, is that he understands the options, because most people don't, that's why they won't see a doctor or have the test, they think there's nothing one can do. But is there anything one can do, he said to Tanya (according to Greg), I mean what do I gain if I go to the doctor; if I'm really ill, he's reported to have said, I'll find out soon enough.

And when he was in the hospital, his spirits seemed to lighten, according to Donny. He seemed more cheerful than he had been in the last months, Ursula said, and the bad news seemed to come almost as a relief, according to Ira, as a truly unexpected blow, according to Quentin, but you'd hardly expect him to have said the same thing to all his friends, because his relation to Ira was so different from his relation to Quentin (this according to Quentin, who was proud of their friendship), and perhaps he thought Quentin wouldn't be undone by seeing him weep, but Ira insisted that couldn't be the reason he behaved so differently with each, and that maybe he was feeling less shocked, mobilizing his strength to fight for his life, at the moment he saw Ira but overcome by feelings of hopelessness when Quentin arrived with flowers, because anyway the flowers threw him into a bad mood, as Quentin told Kate, since the hospital room was choked with flowers, you couldn't have crammed another flower into that room, but surely you're exaggerating, Kate said, smiling, everybody likes flowers. Well, who wouldn't exaggerate at a time like this, Quentin said sharply. Don't you think *this* is an exaggeration. Of course I do, said Kate gently, I was only teasing, I mean I didn't mean to tease. I know that, Quentin said, with tears in his eyes, and Kate hugged him and said well, when I go this evening I guess I won't bring flowers, what does he want, and Quentin said, according to Max, what he likes best is chocolate. Is there anything else, asked Kate, I mean like chocolate but not chocolate. Licorice, said Quentin, blowing his nose. And besides that. Aren't *you* exaggerating now, Quentin said, smiling. Right, said Kate, so if I want to bring him a whole raft of stuff, besides chocolate and licorice, what else. Jelly beans, Quentin said.

He didn't want to be alone, according to Paolo, and lots of people came in the first week, and the Jamaican nurse said there were other patients on the floor who would be glad to have the surplus flowers, and people weren't afraid to visit, it wasn't like the old days, as Kate pointed out to Aileen, they're not even segregated in the hospital anymore, as Hilda observed, there's nothing on the door of his room warning visitors of the possibility of contagion, as there was a few years ago; in fact, he's in a double room and, as he told Orson, the old guy on the far side of the curtain (who's clearly on the way out, said Stephen) doesn't even have the disease, so, as Kate went on, you really should go and see him, he'd be happy to see you, he likes having people visit, you aren't not going because you're afraid, are you. Of course not, Aileen said, but I don't know what to say, I think I'll feel awkward, which he's bound to notice, and that will make him feel worse, so I won't be doing him any good, will I. But he won't notice anything, Kate said, patting Aileen's hand, it's not like that, it's not the way you imagine, he's not judging people or wondering about their motives, he's just happy to see his friends. But I never was really a friend of his, Aileen said, you're a friend, he's always liked you, you told me he talks about Nora with you, I know he likes me, he's even attracted to me, but he respects you. But, according to Wesley, the reason Aileen was so stingy with her visits was that she could never have him to herself, there were always others there already and by the time they left still others had arrived, she'd been in love with him for years, and I can understand, said Donny, that Aileen should feel bitter that if there could have been a woman friend he did more than occasionally bed, a woman he really loved, and my God, Victor said, who had known him in those years, he was crazy about Nora, what a heart-rending couple they were, two surly angels, then it couldn't have been she.

And when some of the friends, the ones who came every day, waylaid the doctor in the corridor, Stephen was the one who asked the most informed questions, who'd been keeping up not just with the stories that appeared several times a week in the *Times* (which Greg confessed to have stopped reading, unable to stand it anymore) but with articles in the medical journals published here and in England and France, and who knew socially one of the principal doctors in Paris who was doing some much-publicized research on the disease, but his doctor said little more than that the pneumonia was not life-threatening, the fever was subsiding, of course he was still weak but he was responding well to the antibiotics, that he'd have to complete his stay in the hospital, which entailed a minimum of twenty-one days on the IV, before she could start him on the new drug, for she was optimistic about the possibility of getting him into the protocol; and when Victor said that if he had so much trouble eating (he'd say to everyone when they coaxed him to eat some of the hospital meals, that food didn't taste right, that he had a funny metallic taste in his mouth) it couldn't be good that friends were bringing him all that chocolate, the doctor just smiled and said that in these cases the patient's morale was also an important factor, and if chocolate made him feel better she saw no harm in it, which worried Stephen, as Stephen said later to Donny, because they wanted to believe in the promises and taboos of today's high-tech medicine but here this reassuringly curt and silver-haired specialist in the disease, someone quoted frequently in the papers, was talking like some oldfangled country GP who tells the family that tea with honey or chicken soup may do as much for the patient as penicillin, which might mean, as Max said, that they were just going through the motions of treating him, that they were not sure about what to do, or rather, as Xavier interjected, that they didn't know what the hell they were doing, that the truth, the real truth, as Hilda said, upping the ante, was that they didn't, the doctors, really have any hope.

Oh, no, said Lewis, I can't stand it, wait a minute, I can't believe it, are you sure, I mean are they sure, have they done all the tests, it's getting so when the phone rings I'm scared to answer because I think it will be someone telling me someone else is ill; but did Lewis really not know until yesterday, Robert said testily, I find that hard to believe, everybody is talking about it, it seems impossible that someone wouldn't have called Lewis; and perhaps Lewis did know, was for some reason pretending not to know already, because, Jan recalled, didn't Lewis say something months ago to Greg, and not only to Greg, about his not looking well, losing weight, and being worried about him and wishing

SUSAN SONTAG

he'd see a doctor, so it couldn't come as a total surprise. Well, everybody is worried about everybody now, said Betsy, that seems to be the way we live, the way we live now. And, after all, they were once very close, doesn't Lewis still have the keys to his apartment, you know the way you let someone keep the keys after you've broken up, only a little because you hope the person might just saunter in, drunk or high, late some evening, but mainly because it's wise to have a few sets of keys strewn around town, if you live alone, at the top of a former commercial building that, pretentious as it is, will never acquire a doorman or even a resident superintendent, someone whom you can call on for the keys late one night if you find you've lost yours or have locked yourself out. Who else has keys, Tanya inquired, I was thinking somebody might drop by tomorrow before coming to the hospital and bring some treasures, because the other day, Ira said, he was complaining about how dreary the hospital room was, and how it was like being locked up in a motel room, which got everybody started telling funny stories about motel rooms they'd known, and at Ursula's story, about the Luxury Budget Inn in Schenectady, there was an uproar of laughter around his bed, while he watched them in silence, eyes bright with fever, all the while, as Victor recalled, gobbling that damned chocolate. But, according to Jan, whom Lewis's keys enabled to tour the swank of his bachelor lair with an eye to bringing over some art consolation to brighten up the hospital room, the Byzantine icon wasn't on the wall over his bed, and that was a puzzle until Orson remembered that he'd recounted without seeming upset (this disputed by Greg) that the boy he'd recently gotten rid of had stolen it, along with four of the *maki-e* lacquer boxes, as if these were objects as easy to sell on the street as a TV or a stereo. But he's always been very generous, Kate said quietly, and though he loves beautiful things isn't really attached to them, to things, as Orson said, which is unusual in a collector, as Frank commented, and when Kate shuddered and tears sprang to her eyes and Orson inquired anxiously if he, Orson, had said something wrong, she pointed out that they'd begun talking about him in a retrospective mode, summing up what he was like, what made them fond of him, as if he were finished, completed, already a part of the past.

Perhaps he was getting tired of having so many visitors, said Robert, who was, as Ellen couldn't help mentioning, someone who had come only twice and was probably looking for a reason not to be in regular attendance, but there could be no doubt, according to Ursula, that his spirits had dipped, not that there was any discouraging news from the doctors, and he seemed now to prefer being alone a few hours of the day; and he told Donny that he'd begun keeping a diary for the first time in his life, because he wanted to record the course of his mental reactions to this astonishing turn of events, to do something parallel to what the doctors were doing, who came every morning and conferred at his bedside about his body, and that perhaps it wasn't so important what he wrote in it, which amounted, as he said wryly to Quentin, to little more than the usual banalities about terror and amazement that this was happening to him, to him also, plus the usual remorseful assessments of his past life, his pardonable superficialities, capped by resolves to live better, more deeply, more in touch with his work and his friends, and not to care so passionately about what people thought of him, interspersed with admonitions to himself that in this situation his will to live counted more than anything else and that if he really wanted to live, and trusted life, and liked himself well enough (down, ol' debbil Thanatos!), he *would* live, he would be an exception; but perhaps all this, as Quentin ruminated, talking on the phone to Kate, wasn't the point, the point was that by the very keeping of the diary he was accumulating something to reread one day, slyly staking out his claim to a future time, in which the diary would be an object, a relic, in which he might not actually reread it, because he would want to have put this ordeal behind him, but the diary would be there in the drawer of his stupendous Majorelle desk, and he could already, he did actually say to Quentin one late sunny afternoon, propped up in the hospital bed, with the stain of chocolate framing one corner of a heartbreaking smile, see himself in the penthouse, the October sun streaming through those clear windows instead of this streaked one, and the diary, the pathetic diary, safe inside the drawer.

It doesn't matter about the treatment's side effects, Stephen said (when talking to Max), I don't know why you're so worried about that, every strong treatment has some dangerous side effects, it's inevitable, you mean otherwise the treatment wouldn't be effective, Hilda interjected, and anyway, Stephen went on doggedly, just because there *are* side effects it doesn't mean he has to get them, or all of them, each one, or even some of them. That's just a list of all the possible things that could go wrong, because the doctors have to cover themselves, so they make up a worst-case scenario, but isn't what's happening to him, and to so many other people, Tanya interrupted, a worst-case scenario, a catastro-

phe no one could have imagined, it's too cruel, and isn't everything a
side effect, quipped Ira, even *we* are all side effects, but we're not bad
side effects, Frank said, he likes having his friends around, and we're
helping each other, too; because his illness sticks us all in the same glue,
mused Xavier, and, whatever the jealousies and grievances from the past
that have made us wary and cranky with each other, when something
like this happens (the sky is falling, the sky is falling!) you understand
what's really important. I agree, Chicken Little, he is reported to have
said. But don't you think, Quentin observed to Max, that being as close
to him as we are, making time to drop by the hospital every day, is a way
of our trying to define ourselves more firmly and irrevocably as the well,
those who aren't ill, who aren't going to fall ill, as if what's happened to
him couldn't happen to us, when in fact the chances are that before long
one of us will end up where he is, which is probably what he felt when
he was one of the cohort visiting Zack in the spring (you never knew
Zack, did you?), and, according to Clarice, Zack's widow, he didn't come
very often, he said he hated hospitals, and didn't feel he was doing Zack
any good, that Zack would see on his face how uncomfortable he was.
Oh, he was one of those, Aileen said. A coward. Like me.

And after he was sent home from the hospital, and Quentin had volunteered to move in and was cooking meals and taking telephone messages and keeping the mother in Mississippi informed, well, mainly
keeping her from flying to New York and heaping her grief on her son
and confusing the household routine with her oppressive ministrations,
he was able to work an hour or two in his study, on days he didn't insist
on going out, for a meal or a movie, which tired him. He seemed
optimistic, Kate thought, his appetite was good, and what he said,
Orson reported, was that he agreed when Stephen advised him that the
main thing was to keep in shape, he was a fighter, right, he wouldn't be
who he was if he weren't, and was he ready for the big fight, Stephen
asked rhetorically (as Max told it to Donny), and he said you bet, and
Stephen added it could be a lot worse, you could have gotten the disease
two years ago, but now so many scientists are working on it, the American team and the French team, everyone bucking for that Nobel Prize a
few years down the road, that all you have to do is stay healthy for
another year or two and then there will be good treatment, real treatment. Yes, he said, Stephen said, my timing is good. And Betsy, who had
been climbing on and rolling off macrobiotic diets for a decade, came
up with a Japanese specialist she wanted him to see but thank God,

Donny reported, he'd had the sense to refuse, but he did agree to see Victor's visualization therapist, although what could one possibly visualize, said Hilda, when the point of visualizing disease was to see it as an entity with contours, borders, here rather than there, something limited, something you were the host of, in the sense that you could disinvite the disease, while this was so total; or would be, Max said. But the main thing, said Greg, was to see that he didn't go the macrobiotic route, which might be harmless for plump Betsy but could only be devastating for him, lean as he'd always been, with all the cigarettes and other appetite-suppressing chemicals he'd been welcoming into his body for years; and now was hardly the time, as Stephen pointed out, to be worried about cleaning up his act, and eliminating the chemical additives and other pollutants that we're all blithely or not so blithely feasting on, blithely since we're healthy, healthy as we can be; so far, Ira said. Meat and potatoes is what I'd be happy to see him eating, Ursula said wistfully. And spaghetti and clam sauce, Greg added. And thick cholesterol-rich omelets with smoked mozzarella, suggested Yvonne, who had flown from London for the weekend to see him. Chocolate cake, said Frank. Maybe not chocolate cake, Ursula said, he's already eating so much chocolate.

And when, not right away but still only three weeks later, he was accepted into the protocol for the new drug, which took considerable behind-the-scenes lobbying with the doctors, he talked less about being ill, according to Donny, which seemed like a good sign, Kate felt, a sign that he was not feeling like a victim, feeling not that he *had* a disease but, rather, was living *with* a disease (that was the right cliché, wasn't it?), a more hospitable arrangement, said Jan, a kind of cohabitation which implied that it was something temporary, that it could be terminated, but terminated how, said Hilda, and when you say hospitable, Jan, I hear hospital. And it was encouraging, Stephen insisted, that from the start, at least from the time he was finally persuaded to make the telephone call to his doctor, he was willing to say the name of the disease, pronounce it often and easily, as if it were just another word, like boy or gallery or cigarette or money or deal, as in no big deal, Paolo interjected, because, as Stephen continued, to utter the name is a sign of health, a sign that one has accepted being who one is, mortal, vulnerable, not exempt, not an exception after all, it's a sign that one is willing, truly willing, to fight for one's life. And we must say the name, too, and often, Tanya added, we mustn't lag behind him in honesty, or let him feel that, the effort of honesty having been made, it's something done with and he can go on to other things. One is so much better prepared to help him, Wesley replied. In a way he's fortunate, said Yvonne, who had taken care of a problem at the New York store and was flying back to London this evening, sure, fortunate, said Wesley, no one is shunning him, Yvonne went on, no one's afraid to hug him or kiss him lightly on the mouth, in London we are, as usual, a few years behind you, people I know, people who would seem to be not even remotely at risk, are just terrified, but I'm impressed by how cool and rational you all are; you find us cool, asked Quentin. But I have to say, he's reported to have said, I'm terrified, I find it very hard to read (and you know how he loves to read, said Greg; yes, reading is his television, said Paolo) or to think, but I don't feel hysterical. I feel quite hysterical, Lewis said to Yvonne. But you're able to *do* something for him, that's wonderful, how I wish I could stay longer, Yvonne answered, it's rather beautiful, I can't help thinking, this utopia of friendship you've assembled around him (this pathetic utopia, said Kate), so that the disease, Yvonne concluded, is not, anymore, out there. Yes, don't you think we're more at home here, with him, with the disease, said Tanya, because the imagined disease is so much worse than the reality of him, whom we all love, each in our fashion, having it. I know for me his getting it has quite demystified the disease, said Jan, I don't feel afraid, spooked, as I did before he became ill, when it was only news about remote acquaintances, whom I never saw again after they became ill. But you know you're not going to come down with the disease, Quentin said, to which Ellen replied, on her behalf, that's not the point, and possibly untrue, my gynecologist says that everyone is at risk, everyone who has a sexual life, because sexuality is a chain that links each of us to many others, unknown others, and now the greatest chain of being has become a chain of death as well. It's not the same for you, Quentin insisted, it's not the same for you as it is for me or Lewis or Frank or Paolo or Max, I'm more and more frightened, and I have every reason to be. I don't think about whether I'm at risk or not, said Hilda, I know that I was afraid to know someone with the disease, afraid of what I'd see, what I'd feel, and after the first day I came to the hospital I felt so relieved. I'll never feel that way, that fear, again; he doesn't seem different from me. He's not, Quentin said.

According to Lewis, he talked more often about those who visited more often, which is natural, said Betsy, I think he's even keeping a tally. And among those who came or checked in by phone every day, the inner circle as it were, those who were getting more points, there was still a further competition, which was what was getting on Betsy's nerves, she confessed to Jan; there's always that vulgar jockeying for position around the bedside of the gravely ill, and though we all feel suffused with virtue at our loyalty to him (speak for yourself, said Jan), to the extent that we're carving time out of every day, or almost every day, though some of us are dropping out, as Xavier pointed out, aren't we getting at least as much out of this as he is. Are we, said Jan. We're rivals for a sign from him of special pleasure over a visit, each stretching for the brass ring of his favor, wanting to feel the most wanted, the true nearest and dearest, which is inevitable with someone who doesn't have a spouse and children or an official in-house lover, hierarchies that no one would dare contest, Betsy went on, so we are the family he's founded, without meaning to, without official titles and ranks (we, we, snarled Quentin); and is it so clear, though some of us, Lewis and Quentin and Tanya and Paolo, among others, are ex-lovers and all of us more or less than friends, which one of us he prefers, Victor said (now it's us, raged Quentin), because sometimes I think he looks forward more to seeing Aileen, who has visited only three times, twice at the hospital and once since he's been home, than he does you or me; but, according to Tanya, after being very disappointed that Aileen hadn't come, now he was angry, while, according to Xavier, he was not really hurt but touchingly passive, accepting Aileen's absence as something he somehow deserved. But he's happy to have people around, said Lewis; he says when he doesn't have company he gets very sleepy, he sleeps (according to Quentin), and then perks up when someone arrives, it's important that he not feel ever alone. But, said Victor, there's one person he hasn't heard from, whom he'd probably like to hear from more than most of us; but she didn't just vanish, even right after she broke away from him, and he knows exactly where she lives now, said Kate, he told me he put in a call to her last Christmas Eve, and she said it's nice to hear from you and Merry Christmas, and he was shattered, according to Orson, and furious and disdainful, according to Ellen (what do you expect of her, said Wesley, she was burned out), but Kate wondered if maybe he hadn't phoned Nora in the middle of a sleepless night, what's the time difference, and Quentin said no, I don't think so, I think he wouldn't want her to know.

And when he was feeling even better and had regained the pounds he'd shed right away in the hospital, though the refrigerator started to fill up with organic wheat germ and grapefruit and skimmed milk (he's worried about his cholesterol count, Stephen lamented), and told Quentin he could manage by himself now, and did, he started asking everyone who visited how he looked, and everyone said he looked great, so much better than a few weeks ago, which didn't jibe with what anyone had told him at that time; but then it was getting harder and harder to know how he looked, to answer such a question honestly when among themselves they wanted to be honest, both for honesty's sake and (as Donny thought) to prepare for the worst, because he'd been looking like *this* for so long, at least it seemed so long, that it was as if he'd always been like this, how did he look before, but it was only a few months, and those words, pale and wan looking and fragile, hadn't they always applied? And one Thursday Ellen, meeting Lewis at the door of the building, said, as they rode up together in the elevator, how is he *really?* But you see how he is, Lewis said tartly, he's fine, he's perfectly healthy, and Ellen understood that of course Lewis didn't think he was perfectly healthy but that he wasn't worse, and that was true, but wasn't it, well, almost heartless to talk like that. Seems inoffensive to me, Quentin said, but I know what you mean, I remember once talking to Frank, somebody, after all, who has volunteered to do five hours a week of office work at the Crisis Center (I know, said Ellen), and Frank was going on about this guy, diagnosed almost a year ago, and so much further along, who'd been complaining to Frank on the phone about the indifference of some doctor, and had gotten quite abusive about the doctor, and Frank was saying there was no reason to be so upset, the implication being that *he,* Frank, wouldn't behave so irrationally, and I said, barely able to control my scorn, but Frank, Frank, he has every reason to be upset, he's dying, and Frank said, said according to Quentin, oh, I don't like to think about it that way.

And it was while he was still home, recuperating, getting his weekly treatment, still not able to do much work, he complained, but, according to Quentin, up and about most of the time and turning up at the office several days a week, that bad news came about two remote acquaintances, one in Houston and one in Paris, news that was intercepted by Quentin on the ground that it could only depress him, but Stephen contended that it was wrong to lie to him, it was so important for him to live in the truth; that had been one of his first victories, that he was candid, that he was even willing to crack jokes about the disease, but Ellen said it wasn't good to give him this end-of-the-world feeling, too many people were getting ill, it was becoming such a common destiny that maybe some of the will to fight for his life would be drained out of him if it seemed to be as natural as, well, death. Oh, Hilda said, who didn't know personally either the one in Houston or the one in Paris, but knew *of* the one in Paris, a pianist who specialized in twentieth-century Czech and Polish music, I have his records, he's such a valuable person, and, when Kate glared at her, continued defensively, I know every life is equally sacred, but that *is* a thought, another thought, I mean, all these valuable people who aren't going to have their normal four score as it is now, these people aren't going to be replaced, and it's such a loss to the culture. But this isn't going to go on forever, Wesley said, it can't, they're bound to come up with something (they, they, muttered Stephen), but did you ever think, Greg said, that if some people don't die, I mean even if they can keep them alive (they, they, muttered Kate), they continue to be carriers, and that means, if you have a conscience, that you can never make love, make love fully, as you'd been wont — wantonly, Ira said — to do. But it's better than dying, said Frank. And in all his talk about the future, when he allowed himself to be hopeful, according to Quentin, he never mentioned the prospect that even if he didn't die, if he were so fortunate as to be among the first generation of the disease's survivors, never mentioned, Kate confirmed, that whatever happened it was over, the way he had lived until now, but, according to Ira, he did think about it, the end of bravado, the end of folly, the end of trusting life, the end of taking life for granted, and of treating life as something that, samurai-like, he thought himself ready to throw away lightly, impudently; and Kate recalled, sighing, a brief exchange she'd insisted on having as long as two years ago, huddling on a banquette covered with steel-gray industrial carpet on an upper level of The Prophet and toking up for their next foray onto the dance floor: she'd said hesitantly, for it felt foolish asking a prince of debauchery to, well, take it easy, and she wasn't keen on playing big sister, a role, as Hilda confirmed, he inspired in many women, are you being careful, honey, you know what I mean. And he replied, Kate went on, no, I'm not, listen, I can't, I just can't, sex is too important to me, always has been (he started talking ,like that, according to Victor, after Nora left him), and if I get it, well, I get it. But he wouldn't talk like that now, would he, said Greg; he must feel awfully foolish now, said Betsy, like someone who went on smoking, saying I can't give up cigarettes, but when the bad X-ray is taken even the most besotted nicotine addict can stop on a dime. But sex isn't like cigarettes, is it, said Frank, and, besides, what good does it do to remember that he was reckless, said Lewis angrily, the appalling thing is that you just have to be unlucky once, and wouldn't he feel even worse if he'd stopped three years ago and had come down with it anyway, since one of the most terrifying features of the disease is that you don't know when you contracted it, it could have been ten years ago, because surely this disease has existed for years and years, long before it was recognized; that is, named. Who knows how long (I think a lot about that, said Max) and who knows (I know what you're going to say, Stephen interrupted) how many are going to get it.

I'm feeling fine, he's reported to have said whenever someone asked him how he was, which was almost always the first question anyone asked. Or: I'm feeling better, how are you? But he said other things, too. I'm playing leapfrog with myself, he is reported to have said, according to Victor. And: There must be a way to get something positive out of this situation, he's reported to have said to Kate. How American of him, said Paolo. Well, said Betsy, you know the old American adage: When you've got a lemon, make lemonade. The one thing I'm sure I couldn't take, Jan said he said to her, is becoming disfigured, but Stephen hastened to point out the disease doesn't take that form very often anymore, its profile is mutating, and, in conversation with Ellen, wheeled up words like blood-brain barrier; I never thought there was a barrier *there*, said Jan. But he mustn't know about Max, Ellen said, that would really depress him, please don't tell him, he'll have to know, Quentin said grimly, and he'll be furious not to have been told. But there's time for that, when they take Max off the respirator, said Ellen; but isn't it incredible, Frank said, Max was fine, not feeling ill at all, and then to wake up with a fever of a hundred and five, unable to breathe, but that's the way it often starts, with absolutely no warning, Stephen said, the disease has so many forms. And when, after another week had gone by, he asked Quentin where Max was, he didn't question Quentin's account of a spree in the Bahamas, but then the number of people who visited regularly was thinning out, partly because the old feuds that had been put aside through the first hospitalization and the return home had resurfaced, and the flickering enmity between Lewis and Frank exploded, even though Kate did her best to mediate between them, and also because he himself had done something to loosen the bonds of love that united the friends around him, by seeming to take them all for granted, as if it were perfectly normal for so many people to carve out so much time and attention for him, visit him every few days, talk about him incessantly on the phone with each other; but, according to Paolo, it wasn't that he was less grateful, it was just something he was getting used to, the visits. It had become, with time, a more ordinary kind of situation, a kind of ongoing party, first at the hospital and now since he was home, barely on his feet again, it being clear, said Robert, that I'm on the B list; but Kate said, that's absurd, there's no list; and Victor said, but there is, only it's not he, it's Quentin who's drawing it up. He wants to see us, we're helping him, we have to do it the way he wants, he fell down yesterday on the way to the bathroom, he mustn't be told about Max (but he already knew, according to Donny), it's getting worse.

When I was home, he is reported to have said, I was afraid to sleep, as I was dropping off each night it felt like just that, as if I were falling down a black hole, to sleep felt like giving in to death, I slept every night with the light on; but here, in the hospital, I'm less afraid. And to Quentin he said, one morning, the fear rips through me, it tears me open; and, to Ira, it presses me together, squeezes me toward myself. Fear gives every-thing its hue, its high. I feel so, I don't know how to say it, exalted, he said to Quentin. Calamity is an amazing high, too. Sometimes I feel *so* well, so powerful, it's as if I could jump out of my skin. Am I going crazy, or what? Is it all this attention and coddling I'm getting from everybody, like a child's dream of being loved? Is it the drugs? I know it sounds crazy but sometimes I think this is a *fantastic* experience, he said shyly; but there was also the bad taste in the mouth, the pressure in the head and at the back of the neck, the red, bleeding gums, the painful, if pink-lobed, breathing, and his ivory pallor, color of white chocolate. Among those who wept when told over the phone that he was back in the hospital were Kate and Stephen (who'd been called by Quentin), and Ellen, Victor, Aileen, and Lewis (who were called by Kate), and Xavier and Ursula (who were called by Stephen). Among those who didn't weep were Hilda, who said that she'd just learned that her sev-enty-five-year-old aunt was dying of the disease, which she'd contracted from a transfusion given during her successful double bypass of five years ago, and Frank and Donny and Betsy, but this didn't mean, according to Tanya, that they weren't moved and appalled, and Quentin thought they might not be coming soon to the hospital but would send presents; the room, he was in a private room this time, was filling up with flowers, and plants, and books, and tapes. The high tide of barely suppressed acrimony of the last weeks at home subsided into the routines of hospital visiting, though more than a few resented Quentin's having charge of the visiting book (but it was Quentin who had the idea, Lewis pointed out); now, to insure a steady stream of visitors, preferably no more than two at a time (this, the rule in all hospitals, wasn't enforced here, at least on this floor; whether out of kindness or inefficiency, no one could decide), Quentin had to be called first, to get one's time slot, there was no more casual dropping by. And his mother could no longer be prevented from taking a plane and installing herself in a hotel near the hospital; but he seemed to mind her daily presence less than expected, Quentin said; said Ellen it's we who mind, do you suppose she'll stay long. It was easier to be generous with each other visiting him here in the hospital, as Donny pointed out, than at home, where one minded never being alone with him; coming here, in our twos and twos, there's no doubt about what our role is, how we should be, collective, funny, distracting, undemanding, light, it's important to be light, for in all this dread there is gaiety, too, as the poet said, said Kate. (His eyes, his glittering eyes, said Lewis.) His eyes looked dull, extinguished, Wesley said to Xavier, but Betsy said his face, not just his eyes, looked soulful, warm; whatever is there, said Kate, I've never been so aware of his eyes; and Stephen said, I'm afraid of what my eyes show, the way I watch him, with too much intensity, or a phony kind of casualness, said Victor. And, unlike at home, he was cleanshaven each morning, at whatever hour they visited him; his curly hair was always combed; but he complained that the nurses had changed since he was here the last time, and that he didn't like the change, he wanted everyone to be the same. The room was furnished now with some of his personal effects (odd word for one's things, said Ellen), and Tanya brought drawings and a letter from her nine-year-old dyslexic son, who was writing now, since she'd purchased a computer; and Donny brought champagne and some helium balloons, which were anchored to the foot of his bed; tell me about something that's going on, he said, waking up from a nap to find Donny and Kate at the side of his bed, beaming at him; tell me a story, he said wistfully, said Donny, who couldn't think of anything to say; you're the story, Kate said. And Xavier brought an eighteenth-century Guatemalan wooden statue of Saint Sebastian with upcast eyes and open mouth, and when Tanya said what's that, a tribute to Eros past, Xavier said where I come from Sebastian is venerated as a protector against pestilence. Pestilence symbolized by arrows? Symbolized by arrows. All people remember is the body of a beautiful youth bound to a tree, pierced by arrows (of which he always seems oblivious, Tanya interjected), people forget that the story continues, Xavier continued, that when the Christian women came to bury the martyr they found him still alive and nursed him back to health. And he said, according to Stephen, I didn't know Saint Sebastian didn't die. It's undeniable, isn't it, said Kate on the phone to Stephen, the fascination of the dying. It makes me ashamed. We're learning how to die, said Hilda, I'm not ready to learn, said Aileen; and Lewis, who was coming straight from the other hospital, the hospital where Max was still being kept in ICU, met Tanya getting out of the elevator on the tenth floor, and as they walked together down the shiny corridor past the open doors, averting their eyes from the other patients sunk in their beds, with tubes in their noses, irradiated by the bluish light from the television sets, the thing I can't bear to think about, Tanya said to Lewis, is someone dying with the TV on.

He has that strange, unnerving detachment now, said Ellen, that's what upsets me, even though it makes it easier to be with him. Sometimes he was querulous. I can't stand them coming in here taking my blood every morning, what are they doing with all that blood, he is reported to have said; but where was his anger, Jan wondered. Mostly he was lovely to be with, always saying how are *you*, how are you feeling. He's so sweet now, said Aileen. He's so nice, said Tanya. (Nice, nice, groaned Paolo.) At first he was very ill, but he was rallying, according to Stephen's best information, there was no fear of his not recovering this time, and the doctor spoke of his being discharged from the hospital in another ten days if all went well, and the mother was persuaded to fly back to Mississippi, and Quentin was readying the penthouse for his return. And he was still writing his diary, not showing it to anyone, though Tanya, first to arrive one late-winter morning, and finding him dozing, peeked, and was horrified, according to Greg, not by anything she read but by a progressive change in his handwriting: in the recent pages, it was becoming spidery, less legible, and some lines of script wandered and tilted about the page. I was thinking, Ursula said to Quentin, that the difference between a story and a painting or photograph is that in a story you can write, He's still alive. But in a painting or a photo you can't show "still." You can just show him being alive. He's still alive, Stephen said.

1987

*Tim O'Brien*

......................................................................................................

# The Things They Carried

FROM *Esquire*

FIRST LIEUTENANT Jimmy Cross carried letters from a girl named Martha, a junior at Mount Sebastian College in New Jersey. They were not love letters, but Lieutenant Cross was hoping, so he kept them folded in plastic at the bottom of his rucksack. In the late afternoon, after a day's march, he would dig his foxhole, wash his hands under a canteen, unwrap the letters, hold them with the tips of his fingers, and spend the last hour of light pretending. He would imagine romantic camping trips into the White Mountains in New Hampshire. He would sometimes taste the envelope flaps, knowing her tongue had been there. More than anything, he wanted Martha to love him as he loved her, but the letters were mostly chatty, elusive on the matter of love. She was a virgin, he was almost sure. She was an English major at Mount Sebastian, and she wrote beautifully about her professors and roommates and midterm exams, about her respect for Chaucer and her great affection for Virginia Woolf. She often quoted lines of poetry; she never mentioned the war, except to say, Jimmy, take care of yourself. The letters weighed ten ounces. They were signed "Love, Martha," but Lieutenant Cross understood that "Love" was only a way of signing and did not mean what he sometimes pretended it meant. At dusk, he would carefully return the letters to his rucksack. Slowly, a bit distracted, he would get up and move among his men, checking the perimeter, then at full dark he would return to his hole and watch the night and wonder if Martha was a virgin.

The things they carried were largely determined by necessity. Among the necessities or near necessities were P-38 can openers, pocket knives, heat tabs, wrist watches, dog tags, mosquito repellent, chewing gum, candy, cigarettes, salt tablets, packets of Kool-Aid, lighters, matches, sewing kits, Military Payment Certificates, C rations, and two or three canteens of water. Together, these items weighed between fifteen and twenty pounds, depending upon a man's habits or rate of metabolism. Henry Dobbins, who was a big man, carried extra rations; he was especially fond of canned peaches in heavy syrup over pound cake. Dave Jensen, who practiced field hygiene, carried a toothbrush, dental floss, and several hotel-size bars of soap he'd stolen on R&R in Sydney, Australia. Ted Lavender, who was scared, carried tranquilizers until he was shot in the head outside the village of Than Khe in mid-April. By necessity, and because it was SOP, they all carried steel helmets that weighed five pounds including the liner and camouflage cover. They carried the standard fatigue jackets and trousers. Very few carried underwear. On their feet they carried jungle boots — 2.1 pounds — and Dave Jensen carried three pairs of socks and a can of Dr. Scholl's foot powder as a precaution against trench foot. Until he was shot, Ted Lavender carried six or seven ounces of premium dope, which for him was a necessity. Mitchell Sanders, the RTO, carried condoms. Norman Bowker carried a diary. Rat Kiley carried comic books. Kiowa, a devout Baptist, carried an illustrated New Testament that had been presented to him by his father, who taught Sunday school in Oklahoma City, Oklahoma. As a hedge against bad times, however, Kiowa also carried his grandmother's distrust of the white man, his grandfather's old hunting hatchet. Necessity dictated. Because the land was mined and booby-trapped, it was SOP for each man to carry a steel-centered, nylon-covered flak jacket, which weighed 6.7 pounds, but which on hot days seemed much heavier. Because you could die so quickly, each man carried at least one large compress bandage, usually in the helmet band for easy access. Because the nights were cold, and because the monsoons were wet, each carried a green plastic poncho that could be used as a raincoat or ground sheet or makeshift tent. With its quilted liner, the poncho weighed almost two pounds, but it was worth every ounce. In April, for instance, when Ted Lavender was shot, they used his poncho to wrap him up, then to carry him across the paddy, then to lift him into the chopper that took him away.

They were called legs or grunts.

To carry something was to "hump" it, as when Lieutenant Jimmy Cross humped his love for Martha up the hills and through the swamps. In its intransitive form, "to hump" meant "to walk," or "to march," but it implied burdens far beyond the intransitive.

Almost everyone humped photographs. In his wallet, Lieutenant Cross carried two photographs of Martha. The first was a Kodachrome snapshot signed "Love," though he knew better. She stood against a brick wall. Her eyes were gray and neutral, her lips slightly open as she stared straight-on at the camera. At night, sometimes, Lieutenant Cross wondered who had taken the picture, because he knew she had boyfriends, because he loved her so much, and because he could see the shadow of the picture taker spreading out against the brick wall. The second photograph had been clipped from the 1968 Mount Sebastian yearbook. It was an action shot — women's volleyball — and Martha was bent horizontal to the floor, reaching, the palms of her hands in sharp focus, the tongue taut, the expression frank and competitive. There was no visible sweat. She wore white gym shorts. Her legs, he thought, were almost certainly the legs of a virgin, dry and without hair, the left knee cocked and carrying her entire weight, which was just over one hundred pounds. Lieutenant Cross remembered touching that left knee. A dark theater, he remembered, and the movie was *Bonnie and Clyde*, and Martha wore a tweed skirt, and during the final scene, when he touched her knee, she turned and looked at him in a sad, sober way that made him pull his hand back, but he would always remember the feel of the tweed skirt and the knee beneath it and the sound of the gunfire that killed Bonnie and Clyde, how embarrassing it was, how slow and oppressive. He remembered kissing her good night at the dorm door. Right then, he thought, he should've done something brave. He should've carried her up the stairs to her room and tied her to the bed and touched that left knee all night long. He should've risked it. Whenever he looked at the photographs, he thought of new things he should've done.

What they carried was partly a function of rank, partly of field specialty.

As a first lieutenant and platoon leader, Jimmy Cross carried a compass, maps, code books, binoculars, and a .45-caliber pistol that weighed 2.9 pounds fully loaded. He carried a strobe light and the responsibility for the lives of his men.

As an RTO, Mitchell Sanders carried the PRC-25 radio, a killer, twenty-six pounds with its battery.

As a medic, Rat Kiley carried a canvas satchel filled with morphine and plasma and malaria tablets and surgical tape and comic books and all the things a medic must carry, including M&M's for especially bad wounds, for a total weight of nearly twenty pounds.

As a big man, therefore a machine gunner, Henry Dobbins carried the M-60, which weighed twenty-three pounds unloaded, but which was almost always loaded. In addition, Dobbins carried between ten and fifteen pounds of ammunition draped in belts across his chest and shoulders.

As PFCs or Spec 4s, most of them were common grunts and carried the standard M-16 gas-operated assault rifle. The weapon weighed 7.5 pounds unloaded, 8.2 pounds with its full twenty-round magazine. Depending on numerous factors, such as topography and psychology, the riflemen carried anywhere from twelve to twenty magazines, usually in cloth bandoliers, adding on another 8.4 pounds at minimum, fourteen pounds at maximum. When it was available, they also carried M-16 maintenance gear — rods and steel brushes and swabs and tubes of LSA oil — all of which weighed about a pound. Among the grunts, some carried the M-79 grenade launcher, 5.9 pounds unloaded, a reasonably light weapon except for the ammunition, which was heavy. A single round weighed ten ounces. Their typical load was twenty-five rounds. But Ted Lavender, who was scared, carried thirty-four rounds when he was shot and killed outside Than Khe, and he went down under an exceptional burden, more than twenty pounds of ammunition, plus the flak jacket and helmet and rations and water and toilet paper and tranquilizers and all the rest, plus the unweighed fear. He was dead weight. There was no twitching or flopping. Kiowa, who saw it happen, said it was like watching a rock fall, or a big sandbag or something — just boom, then down — not like the movies where the dead guy rolls around and does fancy spins and goes ass over teakettle — not like that, Kiowa said, the poor bastard just flat-fuck fell. Boom. Down. Nothing else. It was a bright morning in mid-April. Lieutenant Cross felt the pain. He blamed himself. They stripped off Lavender's canteens and ammo, all the heavy things, and Rat Kiley said the obvious, the guy's dead, and Mitchell Sanders used his radio to report one U.S. KIA and to request a chopper. Then they wrapped Lavender in his poncho. They carried him out to a dry paddy, established security, and sat smoking the dead man's dope until the chopper came. Lieutenant Cross kept to himself. He pictured Martha's smooth young face, thinking he loved her more than anything, more than his men, and now Ted Lavender was dead because he loved her so much and could not stop thinking about her. When the dust-off arrived, they carried Lavender aboard. Afterward they burned Than Khe. They marched until dusk, then dug their holes, and that night Kiowa kept explaining how you had to be there, how fast it was, how the poor guy just dropped like so much concrete. Boom-down, he said. Like cement.

In addition to the three standard weapons — the M-60, M-16, and M-79 — they carried whatever presented itself, or whatever seemed appropriate as a means of killing or staying alive. They carried catch-as-catch-can. At various times, in various situations, they carried M-14s and CAR-15s and Swedish Ks and grease guns and captured AK-47s and Chi-Coms and RPGs and Simonov carbines and black-market Uzis and .38-caliber Smith & Wesson handguns and 66 mm LAWs and shotguns and silencers and blackjacks and bayonets and C-4 plastic explosives. Lee Strunk carried a slingshot; a weapon of last resort, he called it. Mitchell Sanders carried brass knuckles. Kiowa carried his grandfather's feathered hatchet. Every third or fourth man carried a Claymore anti-personnel mine — 3.5 pounds with its firing device. They all carried fragmentation grenades — fourteen ounces each. They all carried at least one M-18 colored smoke grenade — twenty-four ounces. Some carried CS or tear-gas grenades. Some carried white-phosphorus grenades. They carried all they could bear, and then some, including a silent awe for the terrible power of the things they carried.

In the first week of April, before Lavender died, Lieutenant Jimmy Cross received a good-luck charm from Martha. It was a simple pebble, an ounce at most. Smooth to the touch, it was a milky-white color with flecks of orange and violet, oval-shaped, like a miniature egg. In the accompanying letter, Martha wrote that she had found the pebble on the Jersey shoreline, precisely where the land touched water at high tide, where things came together but also separated. It was this separate-but-together quality, she wrote, that had inspired her to pick up the pebble and to carry it in her breast pocket for several days, where it seemed weightless, and then to send it through the mail, by air, as a token of her truest feelings for him. Lieutenant Cross found this romantic. But he wondered what her truest feelings were, exactly, and what she meant by separate-but-together. He wondered how the tides and waves had come into play on that afternoon along the Jersey shoreline when Martha saw the pebble and bent down to rescue it from geology. He imagined bare feet. Martha was a poet, with the poet's sensibilities, and her feet would be brown and bare, the toenails unpainted, the eyes chilly and somber like the ocean in March, and though it was painful, he wondered who had been with her that afternoon. He imagined a pair of shadows moving along the strip of sand where things came together but also separated. It was phantom jealousy, he knew, but he couldn't help himself. He loved her so much. On the march, through the hot days of early April, he carried the pebble in his mouth, turning it with his tongue, tasting sea salts and moisture. His mind wandered. He had difficulty keeping his attention on the war. On occasion he would yell at his men to spread out the column, to keep their eyes open, but then he would slip away into daydreams, just pretending, walking barefoot along the Jersey shore, with Martha, carrying nothing. He would feel himself rising. Sun and waves and gentle winds, all love and lightness.

What they carried varied by mission.

When a mission took them to the mountains, they carried mosquito netting, machetes, canvas tarps, and extra bug juice.

If a mission seemed especially hazardous, or if it involved a place they knew to be bad, they carried everything they could. In certain heavily mined AOs, where the land was dense with Toe Poppers and Bouncing Betties, they took turns humping a twenty-eight-pound mine detector. With its headphones and big sensing plate, the equipment was a stress on the lower back and shoulders, awkward to handle, often useless because of the shrapnel in the earth, but they carried it anyway, partly for safety, partly for the illusion of safety.

On ambush, or other night missions, they carried peculiar little odds and ends. Kiowa always took along his New Testament and a pair of moccasins for silence. Dave Jensen carried night-sight vitamins high in carotin. Lee Strunk carried his slingshot; ammo, he claimed, would never be a problem. Rat Kiley carried brandy and M&M's. Until he was shot, Ted Lavender carried the starlight scope, which weighed 6.3 pounds with its aluminum carrying case. Henry Dobbins carried his girlfriend's pantyhose wrapped around his neck as a comforter. They all carried ghosts. When dark came, they would move out single file across the meadows and paddies to their ambush coordinates, where they would quietly set up the Claymores and lie down and spend the night waiting.

Other missions were more complicated and required special equipment. In mid-April, it was their mission to search out and destroy the elaborate tunnel complexes in the Than Khe area south of Chu Lai. To blow the tunnels, they carried one-pound blocks of pentrite high explosives, four blocks to a man, sixty-eight pounds in all. They carried wiring, detonators, and battery-powered clackers. Dave Jensen carried earplugs. Most often, before blowing the tunnels, they were ordered by higher command to search them, which was considered bad news, but by and large they just shrugged and carried out orders. Because he was a big man, Henry Dobbins was excused from tunnel duty. The others would draw numbers. Before Lavender died there were seventeen men in the platoon, and whoever drew the number seventeen would strip off his gear and crawl in head first with a flashlight and Lieutenant Cross's .45-caliber pistol. The rest of them would fan out as security. They would sit down or kneel, not facing the hole, listening to the ground beneath them, imagining cobwebs and ghosts, whatever was down there — the tunnel walls squeezing in — how the flashlight seemed impossibly heavy in the hand and how it was tunnel vision in the very strictest sense, compression in all ways, even time, and how you had to wiggle in — ass and elbows — a swallowed-up feeling — and how you found yourself worrying about odd things — will your flashlight go dead? Do rats carry rabies? If you screamed, how far would the sound carry? Would your buddies hear it? Would they have the courage to drag you out? In some respects, though not many, the waiting was worse than the tunnel itself. Imagination was a killer.

On April 16, when Lee Strunk drew the number seventeen, he laughed and muttered something and went down quickly. The morning was hot and very still. Not good, Kiowa said. He looked at the tunnel opening, then out across a dry paddy toward the village of Than Khe. Nothing moved. No clouds or birds or people. As they waited, the men smoked and drank Kool-Aid, not talking much, feeling sympathy for Lee Strunk but also feeling the luck of the draw. You win some, you lose some, said Mitchell Sanders, and sometimes you settle for a rain check. It was a tired line and no one laughed.

Henry Dobbins ate a tropical chocolate bar. Ted Lavender popped a tranquilizer and went off to pee.

After five minutes, Lieutenant Jimmy Cross moved to the tunnel, leaned down, and examined the darkness. Trouble, he thought — a cave-in maybe. And then suddenly, without willing it, he was thinking about Martha. The stresses and fractures, the quick collapse, the two of them buried alive under all that weight. Dense, crushing love. Kneeling, watching the hole, he tried to concentrate on Lee Strunk and the war, all the dangers, but his love was too much for him, he felt paralyzed, he wanted to sleep inside her lungs and breathe her blood and be smothered. He wanted her to be a virgin and not a virgin, all at once. He wanted to know her. Intimate secrets — why poetry? Why so sad? Why that grayness in her eyes? Why so alone? Not lonely, just alone — riding her bike across campus or sitting off by herself in the cafeteria. Even dancing, she danced alone — and it was the aloneness that filled him with love. He remembered telling her that one evening. How she nodded and looked away. And how, later, when he kissed her, she received the kiss without returning it, her eyes wide open, not afraid, not a virgin's eyes, just flat and uninvolved.

Lieutenant Cross gazed at the tunnel. But he was not there. He was buried with Martha under the white sand at the Jersey shore. They were pressed together, and the pebble in his mouth was her tongue. He was smiling. Vaguely, he was aware of how quiet the day was, the sullen paddies, yet he could not bring himself to worry about matters of security. He was beyond that. He was just a kid at war, in love. He was twenty-two years old. He couldn't help it.

A few moments later Lee Strunk crawled out of the tunnel. He came up grinning, filthy but alive. Lieutenant Cross nodded and closed his eyes while the others clapped Strunk on the back and made jokes about rising from the dead.

Worms, Rat Kiley said. Right out of the grave. Fuckin' zombie.

The men laughed. They all felt great relief.

Spook City, said Mitchell Sanders.

Lee Strunk made a funny ghost sound, a kind of moaning, yet very happy, and right then, when Strunk made that high happy moaning sound, when he went *Ahhooooo,* right then Ted Lavender was shot in the head on his way back from peeing. He lay with his mouth open. The teeth were broken. There was a swollen black bruise under his left eye. The cheekbone was gone. Oh shit, Rat Kiley said, the guy's dead. The guy's dead, he kept saying, which seemed profound — the guy's dead. I mean really.

The things they carried were determined to some extent by superstition. Lieutenant Cross carried his good-luck pebble. Dave Jensen carried a rabbit's foot. Norman Bowker, otherwise a very gentle person, carried a thumb that had been presented to him as a gift by Mitchell Sanders. The thumb was dark brown, rubbery to the touch, and weighed four ounces at most. It had been cut from a VC corpse, a boy of fifteen or sixteen. They'd found him at the bottom of an irrigation ditch, badly burned, flies in his mouth and eyes. The boy wore black shorts and sandals. At the time of his death he had been carrying a pouch of rice, a rifle, and three magazines of ammunition.

You want my opinion, Mitchell Sanders said, there's a definite moral here.

He put his hand on the dead boy's wrist. He was quiet for a time, as if counting a pulse, then he patted the stomach, almost affectionately, and used Kiowa's hunting hatchet to remove the thumb.

Henry Dobbins asked what the moral was.

Moral?

You know. *Moral.*

Sanders wrapped the thumb in toilet paper and handed it across to Norman Bowker. There was no blood. Smiling, he kicked the boy's head, watched the flies scatter, and said, It's like with that old TV show — Paladin. Have gun, will travel.

Henry Dobbins thought about it.

Yeah, well, he finally said. I don't see no moral.

There it *is*, man.

Fuck off.

They carried USO stationery and pencils and pens. They carried Sterno, safety pins, trip flares, signal flares, spools of wire, razor blades, chewing tobacco, liberated joss sticks and statuettes of the smiling Buddha, candles, grease pencils, *The Stars and Stripes*, fingernail clippers, Psy Ops leaflets, bush hats, bolos, and much more. Twice a week, when the resupply choppers came in, they carried hot chow in green Mermite cans and large canvas bags filled with iced beer and soda pop. They carried plastic water containers, each with a two-gallon capacity. Mitchell Sanders carried a set of starched tiger fatigues for special occasions. Henry Dobbins carried Black Flag insecticide. Dave Jensen carried empty sandbags that could be filled at night for added protection. Lee Strunk carried tanning lotion. Some things they carried in common. Taking turns, they carried the big PRC-77 scrambler radio, which weighed thirty pounds with its battery. They shared the weight of memory. They took up what others could no longer bear. Often, they carried each other, the wounded or weak. They carried infections. They carried chess sets, basketballs, Vietnamese-English dictionaries, insignia of rank, Bronze Stars and Purple Hearts, plastic cards imprinted with the Code of Conduct. They carried diseases, among them malaria and dysentery. They carried lice and ringworm and leeches and paddy algae and various rots and molds. They carried the land itself — Vietnam, the place, the soil — a powdery orange-red dust that covered their boots and fatigues and faces. They carried the sky. The whole atmosphere, they carried it, the humidity, the monsoons, the stink of fungus and decay, all of it, they carried gravity. They moved like mules. By daylight they took sniper fire, at night they were mortared, but it was not battle, it was just the endless march, village to village, without purpose, nothing won or lost. They marched for the sake of the march. They plodded along slowly, dumbly, leaning forward against the heat, unthinking, all blood and bone, simple grunts, soldiering with their legs, toiling up the hills and down into the paddies and across the rivers and up again and down, just humping, one step and then the next and then another, but no volition, no will, because it was automatic, it was anatomy, and the war was entirely a matter of posture and carriage, the hump was everything, a kind of inertia, and kind of emptiness, a dullness of desire and intellect and conscience and hope and human sensibility. Their principles were in their feet. Their calculations were biological. They had no sense of strategy or mission. They searched the villages without knowing what to look for, not caring, kicking over jars of rice, frisking children and old men, blowing tunnels, sometimes setting fires and sometimes not, then forming up and moving on to the next village, then other villages, where it would always be the same. They carried their own lives. The pressures were enormous. In the heat of early afternoon, they would remove their helmets and flak jackets, walking bare, which was dangerous but which helped ease the strain. They would often discard things along the route of march. Purely for comfort, they would throw away rations, blow their Claymores and grenades, no matter, because by nightfall the resupply choppers would arrive with more of the same, then a day or two later still more, fresh watermelons and crates of ammunition and sunglasses and woolen sweaters — the resources were stunning — sparklers for the Fourth of July, colored eggs for Easter. It was the great American war chest — the fruits of science, the smokestacks, the canneries, the arsenals at Hartford, the Minnesota forests, the machine shops, the vast fields of corn and wheat — they carried like freight trains; they carried it on their backs and shoulders — and for all the ambiguities of Vietnam, all the mysteries and unknowns, there was at least the single abiding certainty that they would never be at a loss for things to carry.

After the chopper took Lavender away, Lieutenant Jimmy Cross led his men into the village of Than Khe. They burned everything. They shot chickens and dogs, they trashed the village well, they called in artillery and watched the wreckage, then they marched for several hours through the hot afternoon, and then at dusk, while Kiowa explained how Lavender died, Lieutenant Cross found himself trembling.

He tried not to cry. With his entrenching tool, which weighed five pounds, he began digging a hole in the earth.

He felt shame. He hated himself. He had loved Martha more than his men, and as a consequence Lavender was now dead, and this was something he would have to carry like a stone in his stomach for the rest of the war.

All he could do was dig. He used his entrenching tool like an ax, slashing, feeling both love and hate, and then later, when it was full dark, he sat at the bottom of his foxhole and wept. It went on for a long while. In part, he was grieving for Ted Lavender, but mostly it was for Martha, and for himself, because she belonged to another world, which was not quite real, and because she was a junior at Mount Sebastian College in New Jersey, a poet and a virgin and uninvolved, and because he realized she did not love him and never would.

Like cement, Kiowa whispered in the dark. I swear to God — boom-down. Not a word.

I've heard this, said Norman Bowker.

A pisser, you know? Still zipping himself up. Zapped while zipping.

All right, fine. That's enough.

Yeah, but you had to see it, the guy just —

I *heard*, man. Cement. So why not shut the fuck *up?*

Kiowa shook his head sadly and glanced over at the hole where Lieutenant Jimmy Cross sat watching the night. The air was thick and wet. A warm, dense fog had settled over the paddies and there was the stillness that precedes rain.

After a time Kiowa sighed.

One thing for sure, he said. The Lieutenant's in some deep hurt. I mean that crying jag — the way he was carrying on — it wasn't fake or anything, it was real heavy-duty hurt. The man cares.

Sure, Norman Bowker said.

Say what you want, the man does care.

We all got problems.

Not Lavender.

No, I guess not. Bowker said. Do me a favor, though.

Shut up?

That's a smart Indian. Shut up.

Shrugging, Kiowa pulled off his boots. He wanted to say more, just to lighten up his sleep, but instead he opened his New Testament and arranged it beneath his head as a pillow. The fog made things seem hollow and unattached. He tried not to think about Ted Lavender, but then he was thinking how fast it was, no drama, down and dead, and how it was hard to feel anything except surprise. It seemed un-Christian. He wished he could find some great sadness, or even anger, but the emotion wasn't there and he couldn't make it happen. Mostly he felt pleased to be alive. He liked the smell of the New Testament under his cheek, the leather and ink and paper and glue, whatever the chemicals were. He liked hearing the sounds of night. Even his fatigue, it felt fine, the stiff muscles and the prickly awareness of his own body, a floating feeling. He enjoyed not being dead. Lying there, Kiowa admired Lieutenant Jimmy Cross's capacity for grief. He wanted to share the man's pain, he wanted to care as Jimmy Cross cared. And yet when he closed his eyes, all he could think was Boom-down, and all he could feel was the pleasure of having his boots off and the fog curling in around him and the damp soil and the Bible smells and the plush comfort of night.

After a moment Norman Bowker sat up in the dark.

What the hell, he said. You want to talk, *talk*. Tell it to me.

Forget it.

No, man, go on. One thing I hate, it's a silent Indian.

For the most part they carried themselves with poise, a kind of dignity. Now and then, however, there were times of panic, when they squealed or wanted to squeal but couldn't, when they twitched and made moaning sounds and covered their heads and said Dear Jesus and flopped around on the earth and fired their weapons blindly and cringed and sobbed and begged for the noise to stop and went wild and made stupid promises to themselves and to God and to their mothers and fathers, hoping not to die. In different ways, it happened to all of them. Afterward, when the firing ended, they would blink and peek up. They would touch their bodies, feeling shame, then quickly hiding it. They would force themselves to stand. As if in slow motion, frame by frame, the world would take on the old logic — absolute silence, then the wind, then sunlight, then voices. It was the burden of being alive. Awkwardly, the men would reassemble themselves, first in private, then in groups, becoming soldiers again. They would repair the leaks in their eyes. They would check for casualties, call in dust-offs, light cigarettes, try to smile, clear their throats and spit and begin cleaning their weapons. After a time someone would shake his head and say, No lie, I almost shit my pants, and someone else would laugh, which meant it was bad, yes, but the guy had obviously not shit his pants, it wasn't that bad, and in any case nobody would ever do such a thing and then go ahead and talk about it. They would squint into the dense, oppressive sunlight. For a few moments, perhaps, they would fall silent, lighting a joint and tracking its passage from man to man, inhaling, holding in the humiliation. Scary stuff, one of them might say. But then someone else would grin or flick his eyebrows and say, Roger-dodger, almost cut me a new asshole, *almost*.

There were numerous such poses. Some carried themselves with a sort of wistful resignation, others with pride or stiff soldierly discipline or good humor or macho zeal. They were afraid of dying but they were even more afraid to show it.

They found jokes to tell.

They used a hard vocabulary to contain the terrible softness. *Greased*, they'd say. *Offed, lit up, zapped while zipping*. It wasn't cruelty, just stage presence. They were actors and the war came at them in 3-D. When someone died, it wasn't quite dying, because in a curious way it seemed scripted, and because they had their lines mostly memorized, irony mixed with tragedy, and because they called it by other names, as if to encyst and destroy the reality of death itself. They kicked corpses. They cut off thumbs. They talked grunt lingo. They told stories about Ted Lavender's supply of tranquilizers, how the poor guy didn't feel a thing, how incredibly tranquil he was.

There's a moral here, said Mitchell Sanders.

They were waiting for Lavender's chopper, smoking the dead man's dope.

The moral's pretty obvious, Sanders said, and winked. Stay away from drugs. No joke, they'll ruin your day every time.

Cute, said Henry Dobbins.

Mind-blower, get it? Talk about wiggy — nothing left, just blood and brains.

They made themselves laugh.

There it is, they'd say, over and over, as if the repetition itself were an act of poise, a balance between crazy and almost crazy, knowing without going. There it is, which meant be cool, let it ride, because oh yeah, man, you can't change what can't be changed, there it is, there it absolutely and positively and fucking well *is*.

They were tough.

They carried all the emotional baggage of men who might die. Grief, terror, love, longing — these were intangibles, but the intangibles had their own mass and specific gravity, they had tangible weight. They carried shameful memories. They carried the common secret of cowardice barely restrained, the instinct to run or freeze or hide, and in many respects this was the heaviest burden of all, for it could never be put down, it required perfect balance and perfect posture. They carried their reputations. They carried the soldier's greatest fear, which was the fear of blushing. Men killed, and died, because they were embarrassed not to. It was what had brought them to the war in the first place, nothing positive, no dreams of glory or honor, just to avoid the blush of dishonor. They died so as not to die of embarrassment. They crawled into tunnels and walked point and advanced under fire. Each morning, despite the unknowns, they made their legs move. They endured. They kept humping. They did not submit to the obvious alternative, which was simply to close the eyes and fall. So easy, really. Go limp and tumble to the ground and let the muscles unwind and not speak and not budge until your buddies picked you up and lifted you into the chopper that would roar and dip its nose and carry you off to the world. A mere matter of falling, yet no one ever fell. It was not courage, exactly; the object was not valor. Rather, they were too frightened to be cowards.

By and large they carried these things inside, maintaining the masks of composure. They sneered at sick call. They spoke bitterly about guys who had found release by shooting off their own toes or fingers. Pussies, they'd say. Candyasses. It was fierce, mocking talk, with only a trace of envy or awe, but even so, the image played itself out behind their eyes.

They imagined the muzzle against flesh. They imagined the quick, sweet pain, then the evacuation to Japan, then a hospital with warm beds and cute geisha nurses.

They dreamed of freedom birds.

At night, on guard, staring into the dark, they were carried away by jumbo jets. They felt the rush of takeoff. *Gone!* they yelled. And then velocity, wings and engines, a smiling stewardess — but it was more than a plane, it was a real bird, a big sleek silver bird with feathers and talons and high screeching. They were flying. The weights fell off, there was nothing to bear. They laughed and held on tight, feeling the cold slap of wind and altitude, soaring, thinking *It's over, I'm gone!* — they were naked, they were light and free — it was all lightness, bright and fast and buoyant, light as light, a helium buzz in the brain, a giddy bubbling in the lungs as they were taken up over the clouds and the war, beyond duty, beyond gravity and mortification and global entanglements — *Sin loi!* they yelled, *I'm sorry, motherfuckers, but I'm out of it, I'm goofed, I'm on a space cruise, I'm gone!* — and it was a restful, disencumbered sensation, just riding the light waves, sailing that big silver freedom bird over the mountains and oceans, over America, over the farms and great sleeping cities and cemeteries and highways and the golden arches of McDonald's. It was flight, a kind of fleeing, a kind of falling, falling higher and higher, spinning off the edge of the earth and beyond the sun and through the vast, silent vacuum where there were no burdens and where everything weighed exactly nothing. *Gone!* they screamed, *I'm sorry but I'm gone!* And so at night, not quite dreaming, they gave themselves over to lightness, they were carried, they were purely borne.

On the morning after Ted Lavender died, First Lieutenant Jimmy Cross crouched at the bottom of his foxhole and burned Martha's letters. Then he burned the two photographs. There was a steady rain falling, which made it difficult, but he used heat tabs and Sterno to build a small fire, screening it with his body, holding the photographs over the tight blue flame with the tips of his fingers.

He realized it was only a gesture. Stupid, he thought. Sentimental, too, but mostly just stupid.

Lavender was dead. You couldn't burn the blame.

Besides, the letters were in his head. And even now, without photographs, Lieutenant Cross could see Martha playing volleyball in her white gym shorts and yellow T-shirt. He could see her moving in the rain.

When the fire died out, Lieutenant Cross pulled his poncho over his shoulders and ate breakfast from a can.

There was no great mystery, he decided.

In those burned letters Martha had never mentioned the war, except to say, Jimmy, take care of yourself. She wasn't involved. She signed the letters "Love," but it wasn't love, and all the fine lines and technicalities did not matter.

The morning came up wet and blurry. Everything seemed part of everything else, the fog and Martha and the deepening rain.

It was a war, after all.

Half smiling, Lieutenant Jimmy Cross took out his maps. He shook his head hard, as if to clear it, then bent forward and began planning the day's march. In ten minutes, or maybe twenty, he would rouse the men and they would pack up and head west, where the maps showed the country to be green and inviting. They would do what they had always done. The rain might add some weight, but otherwise it would be one more day layered upon all the other days.

He was realistic about it. There was that new hardness in his stomach.

No more fantasies, he told himself.

Henceforth, when he thought about Martha, it would be only to think that she belonged elsewhere. He would shut down the daydreams. This was not Mount Sebastian, it was another world, where there were no pretty poems or midterm exams, a place where men died because of carelessness and gross stupidity. Kiowa was right. Boom-down, and you were dead, never partly dead.

Briefly, in the rain, Lieutenant Cross saw Martha's gray eyes gazing back at him.

He understood.

It was very sad, he thought. The things men carried inside. The things men did or felt they had to do.

He almost nodded at her, but didn't.

Instead he went back to his maps. He was now determined to perform his duties firmly and without negligence. It wouldn't help Lavender, he knew that, but from this point on he would comport himself as a soldier. He would dispose of his good-luck pebble. Swallow it, maybe, or use Lee Strunk's slingshot, or just drop it along the trail. On the march he would impose strict field discipline. He would be careful to send out flank security, to prevent straggling or bunching up, to keep his troops moving at the proper pace and at the proper interval. He would insist on clean weapons. He would confiscate the remainder of Lavender's dope. Later in the day, perhaps, he would call the men together and speak to them plainly. He would accept the blame for what had happened to Ted Lavender. He would be a man about it. He would look them in the eyes, keeping his chin level, and he would issue the new SOPs in a calm, impersonal tone of voice, an officer's voice, leaving no room for argument or discussion. Commencing immediately, he'd tell them, they would no longer abandon equipment along the route of march. They would police up their acts. They would get their shit together, and keep it together, and maintain it neatly and in good working order.

He would not tolerate laxity. He would show strength, distancing himself.

Among the men there would be grumbling, of course, and maybe worse, because their days would seem longer and their loads heavier, but Lieutenant Cross reminded himself that his obligation was not to be loved but to lead. He would dispense with love; it was not now a factor. And if anyone quarreled or complained, he would simply tighten his lips and arrange his shoulders in the correct command posture. He might give a curt little nod. Or he might not. He might just shrug and say Carry on, then they would saddle up and form into a column and move out toward the villages of Than Khe.

1989

*Alice Munro*

......................................................................................................

# Meneseteung

FROM *The New Yorker*

I

Columbine, bloodroot,
And wild bergamot,
Gathering armfuls,
Giddily we go.

OFFERINGS, the book is called. Gold lettering on a dull-blue cover. The author's full name underneath: Almeda Joynt Roth. The local paper, the *Vidette*, referred to her as "our poetess." There seems to be a mixture of respect and contempt, both for her calling and for her sex — or for their predictable conjuncture. In the front of the book is a photograph, with the photographer's name in one corner, and the date: 1865. The book was published later, in 1873.

The poetess has a long face; a rather long nose; full, somber dark eyes, which seem ready to roll down her cheeks like giant tears; a lot of dark hair gathered around her face in droopy rolls and curtains. A streak of gray hair plain to see, although she is, in this picture, only twenty-five. Not a pretty girl but the sort of woman who may age well, who probably won't get fat. She wears a tucked and braid-trimmed dark dress or jacket, with a lacy, floppy arrangement of white material — frills or a bow — filling the deep V at the neck. She also wears a hat, which might be made of velvet, in a dark color to match the dress. It's the un-trimmed, shapeless hat, something like a soft beret, that makes me see artistic intentions, or at least a shy and stubborn eccentricity, in this young woman, whose long neck and forward-inclining head indicate as well that she is tall and slender and somewhat awkward. From the waist up, she looks like a young nobleman of another century. But perhaps it was the fashion.

"In 1854," she writes in the preface to her book, "my father brought us — my mother, my sister Catherine, my brother William, and me — to the wilds of Canada West (as it then was). My father was a harness-maker by trade, but a cultivated man who could quote by heart from the Bible, Shakespeare, and the writings of Edmund Burke. He prospered in this newly opened land and was able to set up a harness and leather-goods store, and after a year to build the comfortable house in which I live (alone) today. I was fourteen years old, the eldest of the children, when we came into this country from Kingston, a town whose hand-some streets I have not seen again but often remember. My sister was eleven and my brother nine. The third summer that we lived here, my brother and sister were taken ill of a prevalent fever and died within a few days of each other. My dear mother did not regain her spirits after this blow to our family. Her health declined, and after another three years she died. I then became housekeeper to my father and was happy to make his home for twelve years, until he died suddenly one morning at his shop.

"From my earliest years I have delighted in verse and I have occupied myself — and sometimes allayed my griefs, which have been no more, I know, than any sojourner on earth must encounter — with many floundering efforts at its composition. My fingers, indeed, were always too clumsy for crochetwork, and those dazzling productions of embroi-dery which one sees often today — the overflowing fruit and flower baskets, the little Dutch boys, the bonneted maidens with their watering cans — have likewise proved to be beyond my skill. So I offer instead, as the product of my leisure hours, these rude posies, these ballads, cou-plets, reflections."

Titles of some of the poems: "Children at Their Games," "The Gypsy Fair," "A Visit to My Family," "Angels in the Snow," "Champlain at the Mouth of the Meneseteung," "The Passing of the Old Forest," and "A Garden Medley." There are some other, shorter poems, about birds and wildflowers and snowstorms. There is some comically intentioned dog-gerel about what people are thinking about as they listen to the sermon in church.

"Children at Their Games": The writer, a child, is playing with her brother and sister — one of those games in which children on different sides try to entice and catch each other. She plays on in the deepening twilight, until she realizes that she is alone, and much older. Still she hears the (ghostly) voices of her brother and sister calling. *Come over, come over, let Meda come over.* (Perhaps Almeda was called Meda in the family, or perhaps she shortened her name to fit the poem.)

"The Gypsy Fair": The Gypsies have an encampment near the town, a "fair," where they sell cloth and trinkets, and the writer as a child is afraid that she may be stolen by them, taken away from her family. Instead, her family has been taken away from her, stolen by Gypsies she can't locate or bargain with.

"A Visit to My Family": A visit to the cemetery, a one-sided conversation.

"Angels in the Snow": The writer once taught her brother and sister to make "angels" by lying down in the snow and moving their arms to create wing shapes. Her brother always jumped up carelessly, leaving an angel with a crippled wing. Will this be made perfect in Heaven, or will he be flying with his own makeshift, in circles?

"Champlain at the Mouth of the Meneseteung": This poem celebrates the popular, untrue belief that the explorer sailed down the eastern shore of Lake Huron and landed at the mouth of the major river.

"The Passing of the Old Forest": A list of all the trees — their names, appearance, and uses — that were cut down in the original forest, with a general description of the bears, wolves, eagles, deer, waterfowl.

"A Garden Medley": Perhaps planned as a companion to the forest poem. Catalogue of plants brought from European countries, with bits of history and legend attached, and final Canadianness resulting from this mixture.

The poems are written in quatrains or couplets. There are a couple of attempts at sonnets, but mostly the rhyme scheme is simple — *abab* or *abcb*. The rhyme used is what was once called "masculine" ("shore"/ "before"), though once in a while it is "feminine" ("quiver"/"river"). Are those terms familiar anymore? No poem is unrhymed.

II

White roses cold as snow
Bloom where those "angels" lie.
Do they but rest below
Or, in God's wonder, fly?

In 1879, Almeda Roth was still living in the house at the corner of Pearl and Dufferin streets, the house her father had built for his family. The

house is there today: the manager of the liquor store lives in it. It's covered with aluminum siding; a closed-in porch has replaced the veranda.
The woodshed, the fence, the gates, the privy, the barn — all these are
gone. A photograph taken in the eighteen-eighties shows them all in
place. The house and fence look a little shabby, in need of paint, but
perhaps that is just because of the bleached-out look of the brownish
photograph. The lace-curtained windows look like white eyes. No big
shade tree is in sight, and, in fact, the tall elms that overshadowed the
town until the nineteen-fifties, as well as the maples that shade it now,
are skinny young trees with rough fences around them to protect them
from the cows. Without the shelter of those trees, there is a great
exposure — back yards, clotheslines, woodpiles, patchy sheds and barns
and privies — all bare, exposed, provisional looking. Few houses would
have anything like a lawn, just a patch of plantains and anthills and
raked dirt. Perhaps petunias growing on top of a stump, in a round box.
Only the main street is graveled; the other streets are dirt roads, muddy
or dusty according to season. Yards must be fenced to keep animals out.
Cows are tethered in vacant lots or pastured in back yards, but sometimes they get loose. Pigs get loose, too, and dogs roam free or nap in a
lordly way on the boardwalks. The town has taken root, it's not going to
vanish, yet it still has some of the look of an encampment. And, like an
encampment, it's busy all the time — full of people, who, within the
town, usually walk wherever they're going; full of animals, which leave
horse buns, cowpats, dog turds, that ladies have to hitch up their skirts
for; full of the noise of building and of drivers shouting at their horses
and of the trains that come in several times a day.

I read about that life in the *Vidette*.

The population is younger than it is now, than it will ever be again.
People past fifty usually don't come to a raw, new place. There are quite
a few people in the cemetery already, but most of them died young, in
accidents or childbirth or epidemics. It's youth that's in evidence in
town. Children — boys — rove through the streets in gangs. School is
compulsory for only four months a year, and there are lots of occasional
jobs that even a child of eight or nine can do — pulling flax, holding
horses, delivering groceries, sweeping the boardwalk in front of stores.
A good deal of time they spend looking for adventures. One day they
follow an old woman, a drunk nicknamed Queen Aggie. They get her
into a wheelbarrow and trundle her all over town, then dump her into a
ditch to sober her up. They also spend a lot of time around the railway

station. They jump on shunting cars and dart between them and dare each other to take chances, which once in a while result in their getting maimed or killed. And they keep an eye out for any strangers coming into town. They follow them, offer to carry their bags, and direct them (for a five-cent piece) to a hotel. Strangers who don't look so prosperous are taunted and tormented. Speculation surrounds all of them — it's like a cloud of flies. Are they coming to town to start up a new business, to persuade people to invest in some scheme, to sell cures or gimmicks, to preach on the street corners? All these things are possible any day of the week. Be on your guard, the *Vidette* tells people. These are times of opportunity and danger. Tramps, confidence men, hucksters, shysters, plain thieves, are traveling the roads, and particularly the railroads. Thefts are announced: money invested and never seen again, a pair of trousers taken from the clothesline, wood from the woodpile, eggs from the henhouse. Such incidents increase in the hot weather.

Hot weather brings accidents, too. More horses run wild then, upsetting buggies. Hands caught in the wringer while doing the washing, a man lopped in two at the sawmill, a leaping boy killed in a fall of lumber at the lumberyard. Nobody sleeps well. Babies wither with summer complaint, and fat people can't catch their breath. Bodies must be buried in a hurry. One day a man goes through the streets ringing a cowbell and calling "Repent! Repent!" It's not a stranger this time, it's a young man who works at the butcher shop. Take him home, wrap him in cold wet cloths, give him some nerve medicine, keep him in bed, pray for his wits. If he doesn't recover, he must go to the asylum.

Almeda Roth's house faces on Dufferin Street, which is a street of considerable respectability. On this street merchants, a mill owner, an operator of salt wells, have their houses. But Pearl Street, which her back windows overlook and her back gate opens onto, is another story. Workmen's houses are adjacent to hers. Small but decent row houses — that is all right. Things deteriorate toward the end of the block, and the next, last one becomes dismal. Nobody but the poorest people, the unrespectable and undeserving poor, would live there at the edge of a boghole (drained since then), called the Pearl Street Swamp. Bushy and luxuriant weeds grow there, makeshift shacks have been put up, there are piles of refuse and debris and crowds of runty children, slops are flung from doorways. The town tries to compel these people to build privies, but they would just as soon go in the bushes. If a gang of boys goes down there in search of adventure, it's likely they'll get more than they bargained for. It is said that even the town constable won't go down Pearl Street on a Saturday night. Almeda Roth has never walked past the row housing. In one of those houses lives the young girl Annie, who helps her with her housecleaning. That young girl herself, being a decent girl, has never walked down to the last block or the swamp. No decent woman ever would.

But that same swamp, lying to the east of Almeda Roth's house, presents a fine sight at dawn. Almeda sleeps at the back of the house. She keeps to the same bedroom she once shared with her sister Catherine — she would not think of moving to the larger front bedroom, where her mother used to lie in bed all day, and which was later the solitary domain of her father. From her window she can see the sun rising, the swamp mist filling with light, the bulky, nearest trees floating against that mist and the trees behind turning transparent. Swamp oaks, soft maples, tamarack, bitternut.

III

Here where the river meets the inland sea,
Spreading her blue skirts from the solemn wood,
I think of birds and beasts and vanished men,
Whose pointed dwellings on these pale sands stood.

One of the strangers who arrived at the railway station a few years ago was Jarvis Poulter, who now occupies the house next to Almeda Roth's — separated from hers by a vacant lot, which he has bought, on Dufferin Street. The house is plainer than the Roth house and has no fruit trees or flowers planted around it. It is understood that this is a natural result of Jarvis Poulter's being a widower and living alone. A man may keep his house decent, but he will never — if he is a proper man — do much to decorate it. Marriage forces him to live with more ornament as well as sentiment, and it protects him, also, from the extremities of his own nature — from a frigid parsimony or a luxuriant sloth, from squalor, and from excessive sleeping, drinking, smoking, or freethinking.

In the interests of economy, it is believed, a certain estimable gentleman of our town persists in fetching water from the public tap and supplementing his fuel supply by picking up the loose coal along the railway track. Does he think to repay the town or the railway company with a supply of free salt?

This is the *Vidette*, full of shy jokes, innuendo, plain accusation, that no newspaper would get away with today. It's Jarvis Poulter they're talking about — though in other passages he is spoken of with great respect, as a civil magistrate, an employer, a churchman. He is close, that's all. An eccentric, to a degree. All of which may be a result of his single condition, his widower's life. Even carrying his water from the town tap and filling his coal pail along the railway track. This is a decent citizen, prosperous: a tall — slightly paunchy? — man in a dark suit with polished boots. A beard? Black hair streaked with gray. A severe and self-possessed air, and a large pale wart among the bushy hairs of one eyebrow? People talk about a young, pretty, beloved wife, dead in childbirth or some horrible accident, like a house fire or a railway disaster. There is no ground for this, but it adds interest. All he has told them is that his wife is dead.

He came to this part of the country looking for oil. The first oil well in the world was sunk in Lambton County, south of here, in the eighteen-fifties. Drilling for oil, Jarvis Poulter discovered salt. He set to work to make the most of that. When he walks home from church with Almeda Roth, he tells her about his salt wells. They are twelve hundred feet deep. Heated water is pumped down into them, and that dissolves the salt. Then the brine is pumped to the surface. It is poured into great evaporator pans over slow, steady fires, so that the water is steamed off and the pure, excellent salt remains. A commodity for which the demand will never fail.

"The salt of the earth," Almeda says.

"Yes," he says, frowning. He may think this disrespectful. She did not intend it so. He speaks of competitors in other towns who are following his lead and trying to hog the market. Fortunately, their wells are not drilled so deep, or their evaporating is not done so efficiently. There is salt everywhere under this land, but it is not so easy to come by as some people think.

Does that not mean, Almeda says, that there was once a great sea?

Very likely, Jarvis Poulter says. Very likely. He goes on to tell her about other enterprises of his — a brickyard, a lime kiln. And he explains to her how this operates, and where the good clay is found. He also owns two farms, whose woodlots supply the fuel for his operations.

Among the couples strolling home from church on a recent, sunny Sabbath morning we noted a certain salty gentleman and literary lady, not perhaps in their first youth but by no means blighted by the frosts of age. May we surmise?

This kind of thing pops up in the *Vidette* all the time.

May they surmise, and is this courting? Almeda Roth has a bit of money, which her father left her, and she has her house. She is not too old to have a couple of children. She is a good enough housekeeper, with the tendency toward fancy iced cakes and decorated tarts which is seen fairly often in old maids. (Honorable mention at the Fall Fair.) There is nothing wrong with her looks, and naturally she is in better shape than most married women of her age, not having been loaded down with work and children. But why was she passed over in her earlier, more marriageable years, in a place that needs women to be partnered and fruitful? She was a rather gloomy girl — that may have been the trouble. The deaths of her brother and sister and then of her mother, who lost her reason, in fact, a year before she died, and lay in her bed talking nonsense — those weighed on her, so she was not lively company. And all that reading and poetry — it seemed more of a drawback, a barrier, an obsession, in the young girl than in the middle-aged woman, who needed something, after all, to fill her time. Anyway, it's five years since her book was published, so perhaps she has got over that. Perhaps it was the proud, bookish father, encouraging her?

Everyone takes it for granted that Almeda Roth is thinking of Jarvis Poulter as a husband and would say yes if he asked her. And she is thinking of him. She doesn't want to get her hopes up too much, she doesn't want to make a fool of herself. She would like a signal. If he attended church on Sunday evenings, there would be a chance, during some months of the year, to walk home after dark. He would carry a lantern. (There is as yet no street lighting in town.) He would swing the lantern to light the way in front of the lady's feet and observe their narrow and delicate shape. He might catch her arm as they step off the boardwalk. But he does not go to church at night.

Nor does he call for her, and walk with her *to* church on Sunday mornings. That would be a declaration. He walks her home, past his gate as far as hers; he lifts his hat then and leaves her. She does not invite him to come in — a woman living alone could never do such a thing. As soon as a man and woman of almost any age are alone together within

four walls, it is assumed that anything may happen. Spontaneous com-
bustion, instant fornication, an attack of passion. Brute instinct, triumph of the senses. What possibilities men and women must see in
each other to infer such dangers. Or, believing in the dangers, how often
they must think about the possibilities.

When they walk side by side she can smell his shaving soap, the
barber's oil, his pipe tobacco, the wool and linen and leather smell of his
manly clothes. The correct, orderly, heavy clothes are like those she used
to brush and starch and iron for her father. She misses that job — her
father's appreciation, his dark, kind authority. Jarvis Poulter's garments,
his smell, his movement, all cause the skin on the side of her body next
to him to tingle hopefully, and a meek shiver raises the hairs on her
arms. Is this to be taken as a sign of love? She thinks of him coming into
her — *their* — bedroom in his long underwear and his hat. She knows
this outfit is ridiculous, but in her mind he does not look so; he has the
solemn effrontery of a figure in a dream. He comes into the room and
lies down on the bed beside her, preparing to take her in his arms.
Surely he removes his hat? She doesn't know, for at this point a fit of
welcome and submission overtakes her, a buried gasp. He would be her
husband.

One thing she has noticed about married women, and that is how
many of them have to go about creating their husbands. They have to
start ascribing preferences, opinions, dictatorial ways. Oh, yes, they say,
my husband is very particular. He won't touch turnips. He won't eat
fried meat. (Or he will only eat fried meat.) He likes me to wear blue
(brown) all the time. He can't stand organ music. He hates to see a
woman go out bareheaded. He would kill me if I took one puff of
tobacco. This way, bewildered, sidelong-looking men are made over,
made into husbands, head of households. Almeda Roth cannot imagine
herself doing that. She wants a man who doesn't have to be made, who
is firm already and determined and mysterious to her. She does not look
for companionship. Men — except for her father — seem to her deprived in some way, incurious. No doubt that is necessary, so that they
will do what they have to do. Would she herself, knowing that there was
salt in the earth, discover how to get it out and sell it? Not likely. She
would be thinking about the ancient sea. That kind of speculation is
what Jarvis Poulter has, quite properly, no time for.

Instead of calling for her and walking her to church, Jarvis Poulter
might make another, more venturesome declaration. He could hire a

horse and take her for a drive out to the country. If he did this, she would be both glad and sorry. Glad to be beside him, driven by him, receiving this attention from him in front of the world. And sorry to have the countryside removed for her — filmed over, in a way, by his talk and preoccupations. The countryside that she has written about in her poems actually takes diligence and determination to see. Some things must be disregarded. Manure piles, of course, and boggy fields full of high, charred stumps, and great heaps of brush waiting for a good day for burning. The meandering creeks have been straightened, turned into ditches with high, muddy banks. Some of the crop fields and pasture fields are fenced with big, clumsy uprooted stumps, others are held in a crude stitchery of rail fences. The trees have all been cleared back to the woodlots. And the woodlots are all second growth. No trees along the roads or lanes or around the farmhouses, except a few that are newly planted, young and weedy looking. Clusters of log barns — the grand barns that are to dominate the countryside for the next hundred years are just beginning to be built — and meanlooking log houses, and every four or five miles a ragged little settlement with a church and school and store and a blacksmith shop. A raw countryside just wrenched from the forest, but swarming with people. Every hundred acres is a farm, every farm has a family, most families have ten or twelve children. (This is the country that will send out wave after wave of settlers — it's already starting to send them — to northern Ontario and the West.) It's true that you can gather wildflowers in spring in the woodlots, but you'd have to walk through herds of horned cows to get to them.

IV

The Gypsies have departed.
Their camping-ground is bare.
Oh, boldly would I bargain now
At the Gypsy Fair.

Almeda suffers a good deal from sleeplessness, and the doctor has given her bromides and nerve medicine. She takes the bromides, but the drops gave her dreams that were too vivid and disturbing, so she has put the bottle by for an emergency. She told the doctor her eyeballs felt dry, like hot glass, and her joints ached. Don't read so much, he said, don't study; get yourself good and tired out with housework, take exercise. He believes that her troubles would clear up if she got married. He believes this in spite of the fact that most of his nerve medicine is prescribed for married women.

So Almeda cleans house and helps clean the church, she lends a hand to friends who are wallpapering or getting ready for a wedding, she bakes one of her famous cakes for the Sunday-school picnic. On a hot Saturday in August she decides to make some grape jelly. Little jars of grape jelly will make fine Christmas presents, or offerings to the sick. But she started late in the day and the jelly is not made by nightfall. In fact, the hot pulp has just been dumped into the cheesecloth bag, to strain out the juice. Almeda drinks some tea and eats a slice of cake with butter (a childish indulgence of hers), and that's all she wants for supper. She washes her hair at the sink and sponges off her body, to be clean for Sunday. She doesn't light a lamp. She lies down on the bed with the window wide open and a sheet just up to her waist, and she does feel wonderfully tired. She can even feel a little breeze.

When she wakes up, the night seems fiery hot and full of threats. She lies sweating on her bed, and she has the impression that the noises she hears are knives and saws and axes — all angry implements chopping and jabbing and boring within her head. But it isn't true. As she comes further awake she recognizes the sounds that she has heard sometimes before — the fracas of a summer Saturday night on Pearl Street. Usually the noise centers on a fight. People are drunk, there is a lot of protest and encouragement concerning the fight, somebody will scream "Murder!" Once, there was a murder. But it didn't happen in a fight. An old man was stabbed to death in his shack, perhaps for a few dollars he kept in the mattress.

She gets out of bed and goes to the window. The night sky is clear, with no moon and with bright stars. Pegasus hangs straight ahead, over the swamp. Her father taught her that constellation — automatically, she counts its stars. Now she can make out distinct voices, individual contributions to the row. Some people, like herself, have evidently been wakened from sleep. "Shut up!" they are yelling. "Shut up that caterwauling or I'm going to come down and tan the arse off yez!"

But nobody shuts up. It's as if there were a ball of fire rolling up Pearl Street, shooting off sparks — only the fire is noise, it's yells and laughter and shrieks and curses, and the sparks are voices that shoot off alone. Two voices gradually distinguish themselves — a rising and falling howling cry and a steady throbbing, low-pitched stream of abuse that contains all those words which Almeda associates with danger and depravity and foul smells and disgusting sights. Someone — the person crying out, "Kill me! Kill me now!" — is being beaten. A woman is being beaten. She keeps crying, "Kill me! Kill me!" and sometimes her mouth seems choked with blood. Yet there is something taunting and triumphant about her cry. There is something theatrical about it. And the people around are calling out, "Stop it! Stop that!" or "Kill her! Kill her!" in a frenzy, as if at the theater or a sporting match or a prizefight. Yes, thinks Almeda, she has noticed that before — it is always partly a charade with these people; there is a clumsy sort of parody, an exaggeration, a missed connection. As if anything they did — even a murder — might be something they didn't quite believe but were powerless to stop.

Now there is the sound of something thrown — a chair, a plank? — and of a woodpile or part of a fence giving way. A lot of newly surprised cries, the sound of running, people getting out of the way, and the commotion has come much closer. Almeda can see a figure in a light dress, bent over and running. That will be the woman. She has got hold of something like a stick of wood or a shingle, and she turns and flings it at the darker figure running after her.

"Ah, go get her!" the voices cry. "Go baste her one!"

Many fall back now; just the two figures come on and grapple, and break loose again, and finally fall down against Almeda's fence. The sound they make becomes very confused — gagging, vomiting, grunting, pounding. Then a long, vibrating, choking sound of pain and self-abasement, self-abandonment, which could come from either or both of them.

Almeda has backed away from the window and sat down on the bed. Is that the sound of murder she has heard? What is to be done, what is she to do? She must light a lantern, she must go downstairs and light a lantern — she must go out into the yard, she must go downstairs. Into the yard. The lantern. She falls over on her bed and pulls the pillow to her face. In a minute. The stairs, the lantern. She sees herself already down there, in the back hall, drawing the bolt of the back door. She falls asleep.

She wakes, startled, in the early light. She thinks there is a big crow sitting on her windowsill, talking in a disapproving but unsurprised way about the events of the night before. "Wake up and move the wheelbarrow!" it says to her, scolding, and she understands that it means something else by "wheelbarrow" — something foul and sorrowful. Then she is awake and sees that there is no such bird. She gets up at once and looks out the window.

Down against her fence there is a pale lump pressed — a body.
*Wheelbarrow.*

She puts a wrapper over her nightdress and goes downstairs. The
front rooms are still shadowy, the blinds down in the kitchen. Something goes *plop, plup,* in a leisurely, censorious way, reminding her of the
conversation of the crow. It's just the grape juice, straining overnight.
She pulls the bolt and goes out the back door. Spiders have draped their
webs over the doorway in the night, and the hollyhocks are drooping,
heavy with dew. By the fence, she parts the sticky hollyhocks and looks
down and she can see.

A woman's body heaped up there, turned on her side with her face
squashed down into the earth. Almeda can't see her face. But there is a
bare breast let loose, brown nipple pulled long like a cow's teat, and a
bare haunch and leg, the haunch bearing a bruise as big as a sunflower.
The unbruised skin is grayish, like a plucked, raw drumstick. Some kind
of nightgown or all-purpose dress she has on. Smelling of vomit. Urine,
drink, vomit.

Barefoot, in her nightgown and flimsy wrapper, Almeda runs away.
She runs around the side of her house between the apple trees and the
veranda; she opens the front gate and flees down Dufferin Street to
Jarvis Poulter's house, which is the nearest to hers. She slaps the flat of
her hand many times against the door.

"There is the body of a woman," she says when Jarvis Poulter appears
at last. He is in his dark trousers, held up with braces, and his shirt is
half unbuttoned, his face unshaven, his hair standing up on his head.
"Mr. Poulter, excuse me. A body of a woman. At my back gate."

He looks at her fiercely. "Is she dead?"

His breath is dank, his face creased, his eyes bloodshot.

"Yes. I think murdered," says Almeda. She can see a little of his
cheerless front hall. His hat on a chair. "In the night I woke up. I heard
a racket down on Pearl Street," she says, struggling to keep her voice
low and sensible. "I could hear this — pair. I could hear a man and a
woman fighting."

He picks up his hat and puts it on his head. He closes and locks the
front door, and puts the key in his pocket. They walk along the boardwalk and she sees that she is in her bare feet. She holds back what she
feels a need to say next — that she is responsible, she could have run
out with a lantern, she could have screamed (but who needed more
screams?), she could have beat the man off. She could have run for help
then, not now.

They turn down Pearl Street, instead of entering the Roth yard. Of course the body is still there. Hunched up, half bare, the same as before.

Jarvis Poulter doesn't hurry or halt. He walks straight over to the body and looks down at it, nudges the leg with the toe of his boot, just as you'd nudge a dog or a sow.

"You," he says, not too loudly but firmly, and nudges again.

Almeda tastes bile at the back of her throat.

"Alive," says Jarvis Poulter, and the woman confirms this. She stirs, she grunts weakly.

Almeda says, "I will get the doctor." If she had touched the woman, if she had forced herself to touch her, she would not have made such a mistake.

"Wait," says Jarvis Poulter. "Wait. Let's see if she can get up."

"Get up, now," he says to the woman. "Come on. Up, now. Up."

Now a startling thing happens. The body heaves itself onto all fours, the head is lifted — the hair all matted with blood and vomit — and the woman begins to bang this head, hard and rhythmically, against Almeda Roth's picket fence. As she bangs her head she finds her voice, and lets out an open-mouthed yowl, full of strength and what sounds like an anguished pleasure.

"Far from dead," says Jarvis Poulter. "And I wouldn't bother the doctor."

"There's blood," says Almeda as the woman turns her smeared face.

"From her nose," he says. "Not fresh." He bends down and catches the horrid hair close to the scalp to stop the head banging.

"You stop that now," he says. "Stop it. Gwan home now. Gwan home, where you belong." The sound coming out of the woman's mouth has stopped. He shakes her head slightly, warning her, before he lets go of her hair. "Gwan home!"

Released, the woman lunges forward, pulls herself to her feet. She can walk. She weaves and stumbles down the street, making intermittent, cautious noises of protest. Jarvis Poulter watches her for a moment to make sure that she's on her way. Then he finds a large burdock leaf, on which he wipes his hand. He says, "There goes your dead body!"

The back gate being locked, they walk around to the front. The front gate stands open. Almeda still feels sick. Her abdomen is bloated; she is hot and dizzy.

"The front door is locked," she says faintly. "I came out by the kitchen." If only he would leave her, she could go straight to the privy. But he follows. He follows her as far as the back door and into the back hall. He speaks to her in a tone of harsh joviality that she has never before heard from him. "No need for alarm," he says. "It's only the consequences of drink. A lady oughtn't to be living alone so close to a bad neighborhood." He takes hold of her arm just above the elbow. She can't open her mouth to speak to him, to say thank you. If she opened her mouth she would retch.

What Jarvis Poulter feels for Almeda Roth at this moment is just what he has not felt during all those circumspect walks and all his own solitary calculations of her probable worth, undoubted respectability, adequate comeliness. He has not been able to imagine her as a wife. Now that is possible. He is sufficiently stirred by her loosened hair — prematurely gray but thick and soft — her flushed face, her light clothing, which nobody but a husband should see. And by her indiscretion, her agitation, her foolishness, her need?

"I will call on you later," he says to her. "I will walk with you to church."

> At the corner of Pearl and Dufferin streets last Sunday morning there was discovered, by a lady resident there, the body of a certain woman of Pearl Street, thought to be dead but only, as it turned out, dead drunk. She was roused from her heavenly — or otherwise — stupor by the firm persuasion of Mr. Poulter, a neighbour and a Civil Magistrate, who had been summoned by the lady resident. Incidents of this sort, unseemly, troublesome, and disgraceful to our town, have of late become all too common.

### V

> I sit at the bottom of sleep,
> As on the floor of the sea.
> And fanciful Citizens of the Deep
> Are graciously greeting me.

As soon as Jarvis Poulter has gone and she has heard her front gate close, Almeda rushes to the privy. Her relief is not complete, however, and she realizes that the pain and fullness in her lower body came from an accumulation of menstrual blood that has not yet started to flow. She closes and locks the back door. Then, remembering Jarvis Poulter's words about church, she writes on a piece of paper, "I am not well, and wish to rest today." She sticks this firmly into the outside frame of the little window in the front door. She locks that door, too. She is trembling, as if from a great shock or danger. But she builds a fire, so that she

can make tea. She boils water, measures the tea leaves, makes a large pot
of tea, whose steam and smell sicken her further. She pours out a cup
while the tea is still quite weak and adds to it several dark drops of nerve
medicine. She sits to drink it without raising the kitchen blind. There, in
the middle of the floor, is the cheesecloth bag hanging on its broom
handle between the two chair backs. The grape pulp and juice has
stained the swollen cloth a dark purple. *Plop, plup* into the basin beneath. She can't sit and look at such a thing. She takes her cup, the
teapot, and the bottle of medicine into the dining room.

She is still sitting there when the horses start to go by on the way to
church, stirring up clouds of dust. The roads will be getting hot as ashes.
She is there when the gate is opened and a man's confident steps sound
on her veranda. Her hearing is so sharp she seems to hear the paper
taken out of the frame and unfolded — she can almost hear him reading it, hear the words in his mind. Then the footsteps go the other way,
down the steps. The gate closes. An image comes to her of tombstones
— it makes her laugh. Tombstones are marching down the street on
their little booted feet, their long bodies inclined forward, their expressions preoccupied and severe. The church bells are ringing.

Then the clock in the hall strikes twelve and an hour has passed.

The house is getting hot. She drinks more tea and adds more medicine. She knows that the medicine is affecting her. It is responsible for
her extraordinary languor, her perfect immobility, her unresisting sur-
render to her surroundings. That is all right. It seems necessary.

Her surroundings — some of her surroundings — in the dining
room are these: walls covered with dark green garlanded wallpaper, lace
curtains and mulberry velvet curtains on the windows, a table with a
crocheted cloth and a bowl of wax fruit, a pinkish-gray carpet with
nosegays of blue and pink roses, a sideboard spread with embroidered
runners and holding various patterned plates and jugs and the silver tea
things. A lot of things to watch. For every one of these patterns, decorations, seems charged with life, ready to move and flow and alter. Or
possibly to explode. Almeda Roth's occupation throughout the day is to
keep an eye on them. Not to prevent their alteration so much as to catch
them at it — to understand it, to be a part of it. So much is going on in
this room that there is no need to leave it. There is not even the thought
of leaving it.

Of course, Almeda in her observations cannot escape words. She may
think she can, but she can't. Soon this glowing and swelling begins to

suggest words — not specific words but a flow of words somewhere, just about ready to make themselves known to her. Poems, even. Yes, again, poems. Or one poem. Isn't that the idea — one very great poem that will contain everything and, oh, that will make all the other poems, the poems she has written, inconsequential, mere trial and error, mere rags? Stars and flowers and birds and trees and angels in the snow and dead children at twilight — that is not the half of it. You have to get in the obscene racket on Pearl Street and the polished toe of Jarvis Poulter's boot and the plucked-chicken haunch with its blue-black flower. Almeda is a long way now from human sympathies or fears or cozy household considerations. She doesn't think about what could be done for that woman or about keeping Jarvis Poulter's dinner warm and hanging his long underwear on the line. The basin of grape juice has overflowed and is running over her kitchen floor, staining the boards of the floor, and the stain will never come out.

She has to think of so many things at once — Champlain and the naked Indians and the salt deep in the earth but as well as the salt the money, the money-making intent brewing forever in heads like Jarvis Poulter's. Also, the brutal storms of winter and the clumsy and benighted deeds on Pearl Street. The changes of climate are often violent, and if you think about it there is no peace even in the stars. All this can be borne only if it is channeled into a poem, and the word "channeled" is appropriate, because the name of the poem will be — it *is* — "The Meneseteung." The name of the poem is the name of the river. No, in fact it is the river, the Meneseteung, that is the poem — with its deep holes and rapids and blissful pools under the summer trees and its grinding blocks of ice thrown up at the end of winter and its desolating spring floods. Almeda looks deep, deep into the river of her mind and into the tablecloth, and she sees the crocheted roses floating. They look bunchy and foolish, her mother's crocheted roses — they don't look much like real flowers. But their effort, their floating independence, their pleasure in their silly selves, does seem to her so admirable. A hopeful sign. *Meneseteung.*

She doesn't leave the room until dusk, when she goes out to the privy again and discovers that she is bleeding, her flow has started. She will have to get a towel, strap it on, bandage herself up. Never before, in health, has she passed a whole day in her nightdress. She doesn't feel any particular anxiety about this. On her way through the kitchen she walks through the pool of grape juice. She knows that she will have to mop it up, but not yet, and she walks upstairs leaving purple footprints and smelling her escaping blood and the sweat of her body that has sat all day in the closed hot room.

No need for alarm.

For she hasn't thought that crocheted roses could float away or that tombstones could hurry down the street. She doesn't mistake that for reality, and neither does she mistake anything else for reality, and that is how she knows that she is sane.

VI

I dream of you by night,
I visit you by day.
Father, Mother,
Sister, Brother,
Have you no word to say?

April 22, 1903. At her residence on Tuesday last, between three and four o'clock in the afternoon, there passed away a lady of talent and refinement whose pen, in days gone by, enriched our local literature with a volume of sensitive, eloquent verse. It is a sad misfortune that in later years the mind of this fine person had become somewhat clouded and her behaviour, in consequence, somewhat rash and unusual. Her attention to decorum and to the care and adornment of her person had suffered, to the degree that she had become, in the eyes of those unmindful of her former pride and daintiness, a familiar eccentric, or even, sadly, a figure of fun. But now all such lapses pass from memory and what is recalled is her excellent published verse, her labours in former days in the Sunday school, her dutiful care of her parents, her noble womanly nature, charitable concerns, and unfailing religious faith. Her last illness was of mercifully short duration. She caught cold, after having become thoroughly wet from a ramble in the Pearl Street bog. (It has been said that some urchins chased her into the water, and such is the boldness and cruelty of some of our youth, and their observed persecution of this lady, that the tale cannot be entirely discounted.) The cold developed into pneumonia, and she died, attended at the last by a former neighbour, Mrs. Bert (Annie) Friels, who witnessed her calm and faithful end.

January, 1904. One of the founders of our community, an early maker and shaker of this town, was abruptly removed from our midst on Monday morning last, whilst attending to his correspondence in the office of his company. Mr. Jarvis Poulter possessed a keen and lively commercial spirit, which was instrumental in the creation of not one but several local enterprises, bringing the benefits of industry, productivity, and employment to our town.

I looked for Almeda Roth in the graveyard. I found the family stone. There was just one name on it — Roth. Then I noticed two flat stones in the ground, a distance of a few feet — six feet? — from the upright stone. One of these said "Papa," the other "Mama." Farther out from these I found two other flat stones, with the names William and Catherine on them. I had to clear away some overgrowing grass and dirt to see the full name of Catherine. No birth or death dates for anybody, nothing about being dearly beloved. It was a private sort of memorializing, not for the world. There were no roses, either — no sign of a rosebush. But perhaps it was taken out. The grounds keeper doesn't like such things, they are a nuisance to the lawnmower, and if there is nobody left to object he will pull them out.

I thought that Almeda must have been buried somewhere else. When this plot was bought — at the time of the two children's deaths — she would still have been expected to marry, and to lie finally beside her husband. They might not have left room for her here. Then I saw that the stones in the ground fanned out from the upright stone. First the two for the parents, then the two for the children, but these were placed in such a way that there was room for a third, to complete the fan. I paced out from "Catherine" the same number of steps that it took to get from "Catherine" to "William," and at this spot I began pulling grass and scrabbling in the dirt with my bare hands. Soon I felt the stone and knew that I was right. I worked away and got the whole stone clear and I read the name "Meda." There it was with the others, staring at the sky.

I made sure I had got to the edge of the stone. That was all the name there was — Meda. So it was true that she was called by that name in the family. Not just in the poem. Or perhaps she chose her name from the poem, to be written on her stone.

I thought that there wasn't anybody alive in the world but me who would know this, who would make the connection. And I would be the last person to do so. But perhaps this isn't so. People are curious. A few people are. They will be driven to find things out, even trivial things. They will put things together, knowing all along that they may be mistaken. You see them going around with notebooks, scraping the dirt off gravestones, reading microfilm, just in the hope of seeing this trickle in time, making a connection, rescuing one thing from the rubbish.

1990

*Lorrie Moore*

........................................................................................................

# You're Ugly, Too

FROM *The New Yorker*

YOU HAD TO GET OUT of them occasionally, those Illinois towns with
the funny names: Paris, Oblong, Normal. Once, when the Dow Jones
dipped two hundred points, a local paper boasted the banner headline
"NORMAL MAN MARRIES OBLONG WOMAN." They knew what was
important. They did! But you had to get out once in a while, even if it
was just across the border to Terre Haute for a movie.

Outside of Paris, in the middle of a large field, was a scatter of brick
buildings, a small liberal-arts college by the improbable name of
Hilldale-Versailles. Zoë Hendricks had been teaching American history
there for three years. She taught "The Revolution and Beyond" to freshmen and sophomores, and every third semester she had the senior
seminar for majors, and although her student evaluations had been
slipping in the last year and a half — *Professor Hendricks is often late for
class and usually arrives with a cup of hot chocolate, which she offers the
class sips of* — generally the department of nine men was pleased to
have her. They felt she added some needed feminine touch to the corridors — that faint trace of Obsession and sweat, the light, fast clicking
of heels. Plus they had had a sex-discrimination suit, and the dean had
said, well, it was time.

The situation was not easy for her, they knew. Once, at the start of last
semester, she had skipped into her lecture hall singing "Getting to Know
You" — all of it. At the request of the dean, the chairman had called her
into his office, but did not ask her for an explanation, not really. He
asked her how she was and then smiled in an avuncular way. She said,
"Fine," and he studied the way she said it, her front teeth catching on
the inside of her lower lip. She was almost pretty, but her face showed
the strain and ambition of always having been close but not quite. There

was too much effort with the eyeliner, and her earrings, worn, no doubt, for the drama her features lacked, were a little frightening, jutting out the sides of her head like antennae.

"I'm going out of my mind," said Zoë to her younger sister, Evan, in Manhattan. *Professor Hendricks seems to know the entire soundtrack to "The King and I." Is this history?* Zoë phoned her every Tuesday.

"You always say that," said Evan, "but then you go on your trips and vacations and then you settle back into things and then you're quiet for a while and then you say you're fine, you're busy, and then after a while you say you're going crazy again, and you start all over." Evan was a part-time food designer for photo shoots. She cooked vegetables in green dye. She propped up beef stew with a bed of marbles and shopped for new kinds of silicone sprays and plastic ice cubes. She thought her life was O.K. She was living with her boyfriend of many years, who was independently wealthy and had an amusing little job in book publishing. They were five years out of college, and they lived in a luxury midtown high rise with a balcony and access to a pool. "It's not the same as having your own pool," Evan was always sighing, as if to let Zoë know that, as with Zoë, there were still things she, Evan, had to do without.

"Illinois. It makes me sarcastic to be here," said Zoë on the phone. She used to insist it was irony, something gently layered and sophisticated, something alien to the Midwest, but her students kept calling it sarcasm, something they felt qualified to recognize, and now she had to agree. It wasn't irony. "What is your perfume?" a student once asked her. "Room freshener," she said. She smiled, but he looked at her, unnerved.

Her students were by and large good midwesterners, spacey with estrogen from large quantities of meat and eggs. They shared their parents' suburban values; their parents had given them things, things, things. They were complacent. They had been purchased. They were armed with a healthy vagueness about anything historical or geographic. They seemed actually to know very little about anything, but they were good-natured about it. "All those states in the East are so tiny and jagged and bunched up," complained one of her undergraduates the week she was lecturing on "The Turning Point of Independence: The Battle at Saratoga." "Professor Hendricks, you're from Delaware originally, right?" the student asked her.

"Maryland," corrected Zoë.

"Aw," he said, waving his hand dismissively. "New England."

Her articles — chapters toward a book called *Hearing the One About: Uses of Humor in the American Presidency* — were generally well received, though they came slowly for her. She liked her pieces to have something from every time of day in them — she didn't trust things written in the morning only — so she reread and rewrote painstakingly. No part of a day — its moods, its light — was allowed to dominate. She hung on to a piece for a year sometimes, revising at all hours, until the entirety of a day had registered there.

The job she'd had before the one at Hilldale-Versailles had been at a small college in New Geneva, Minnesota, Land of the Dying Shopping Mall. Everyone was so blond there that brunettes were often presumed to be from foreign countries. *Just because Professor Hendricks is from Spain doesn't give her the right to be so negative about our country.* There was a general emphasis on cheerfulness. In New Geneva you weren't supposed to be critical or complain. You weren't supposed to notice that the town had overextended and that its shopping malls were raggedy and going under. You were never to say you weren't "fine, thank you — and yourself?" You were supposed to be Heidi. You were supposed to lug goat milk up the hills and not think twice. Heidi did not complain. Heidi did not do things like stand in front of the new IBM photocopier saying, "If this fucking Xerox machine breaks on me one more time, I'm going to slit my wrists."

But now in her second job, in her fourth year of teaching in the Midwest, Zoë was discovering something she never suspected she had: a crusty edge, brittle and pointed. Once she had pampered her students, singing them songs, letting them call her at home even, and ask personal questions, but now she was losing sympathy. They were beginning to seem different. They were beginning to seem demanding and spoiled.

"You act," said one of her senior-seminar students at a scheduled conference, "like your opinion is worth more than everyone else's in the class."

Zoë's eyes widened. "I *am* the teacher," she said. "I do get paid to act like that." She narrowed her gaze at the student, who was wearing a big leather bow in her hair like a cowgirl in a TV ranch show. "I mean, otherwise *everybody* in the class would have little offices and office hours." *Sometimes Professor Hendricks will take up the class's time just talking about movies she's seen.* She stared at the student some more, then added, "I bet you'd like that."

"Maybe I sound whiny to you," said the girl, "but I simply want my history major to mean something."

"Well, there's your problem," said Zoë, and, with a smile, she showed the student to the door. "I like your bow," she said.

Zoë lived for the mail, for the postman — that handsome blue jay — and when she got a real letter with a real full-price stamp from someplace else, she took it to bed with her and read it over and over. She also watched television until all hours and had her set in the bedroom — a bad sign. *Professor Hendricks has said critical things about Fawn Hall, the Catholic religion, and the whole state of Illinois. It is unbelievable.* At Christmastime she gave twenty-dollar tips to the mailman and to Jerry, the only cabbie in town, whom she had gotten to know from all her rides to and from the Terre Haute airport, and who, since he realized such rides were an extravagance, often gave her cut rates.

"I'm flying in to visit you this weekend," announced Zoë.

"I was hoping you would," said Evan. "Charlie and I are having a party for Halloween. It'll be fun."

"I have a costume already. It's a bonehead. It's this thing that looks like a giant bone going through your head."

"Great," said Evan.

"It is, it's great."

"All I have is my moon mask from last year and the year before. I'll probably end up getting married in it."

"Are you and Charlie getting *married*?" Zoë felt slightly alarmed.

"Hmmmmmmnnno, not immediately."

"Don't get married."

"Why?"

"Just not yet. You're too young."

"You're only saying that because you're five years older than I am and *you're* not married."

"*I'm* not married? Oh, my God," said Zoë, "I forgot to get married."

Zoë had been out with three men since she'd come to Hilldale-Versailles. One of them was a man in the municipal bureaucracy who had fixed a parking ticket she'd brought in to protest and then asked her out for coffee. At first, she thought he was amazing — at last, someone who did not want Heidi! But soon she came to realize that all men, deep down, wanted Heidi. Heidi with cleavage. Heidi with outfits. The parking-ticket bureaucrat soon became tired and intermittent. One cool fall day, in his snazzy, impractical convertible, when she asked him what was wrong he said, "You would not be ill served by new clothes, you know." She wore a lot of gray-green corduroy. She had been under the impression that it brought out her eyes, those shy stars. She flicked an ant from her sleeve.

"Did you have to brush that off in the car?" he said, driving. He glanced down at his own pectorals, giving first the left, then the right, a quick survey. He was wearing a tight shirt.

"Excuse me?"

He slowed down at an amber light and frowned. "Couldn't you have picked it up and thrown it outside?"

"The ant? It might have bitten me. I mean, what difference does it make?"

"It might have bitten you! Ha! How ridiculous! Now it's going to lay eggs in my car!"

The second guy was sweeter, lunkier, though not insensitive to certain paintings and songs, but too often, too, things he'd do or say would startle her. Once, in a restaurant, he stole the garnishes off her dinner plate and waited for her to notice. When she didn't, he finally thrust his fist across the table and said, "Look," and when he opened it, there was her parsley sprig and her orange slice crumpled to a wad. Another time, he described to her his recent trip to the Louvre. "And there I was in front of Delacroix's *The Barque of Dante,* and everyone else had wandered off, so I had my own private audience with it, all those agonized shades splayed in every direction, and there's this motion in that painting that starts at the bottom, swirling and building up into the red fabric of Dante's hood, swirling out into the distance, where you see these orange flames — " He was breathless in the telling. She found this touching, and smiled in encouragement. "A painting like that," he said, shaking his head. "It just makes you shit."

"I have to ask you something," said Evan. "I know every woman complains about not meeting men, but really, on my shoots I meet a lot of men. And they're not all gay, either." She paused. "Not anymore."

"What are you asking?"

The third guy was a political-science professor named Murray Peterson, who liked to go out on double dates with colleagues whose wives he was attracted to. Usually, the wives would consent to flirt with him. Under the table sometimes there was footsie, and once there was even kneesie. Zoë and the husband would be left to their food, staring into their water glasses, chewing like goats. "Oh, Murray," said one wife, who had never finished her master's in physical therapy and wore great clothes. "You know, I know everything about you: your birthday, your license-plate number. I have everything memorized. But then that's the kind of mind I have. Once, at a dinner party, I amazed the host by getting up and saying goodbye to every single person there, first *and* last names."

"I knew a dog who could do that," said Zoë with her mouth full. Murray and the wife looked at her with vexed and rebuking expressions, but the husband seemed suddenly twinkling and amused. Zoë swallowed. "It was a talking Lab, and after about ten minutes of listening to the dinner conversation this dog knew everyone's name. You could say, 'Take this knife to Murray Peterson,' and it would."

"Really," said the wife, frowning, and Murray Peterson never called again.

"Are you seeing anyone?" said Evan. "I'm asking for a particular reason. I'm not just being like Mom."

"I'm seeing my house. I'm tending to it when it wets, when it cries, when it throws up." Zoë had bought a mint-green ranch house near campus, though now she was thinking that maybe she shouldn't have. It was hard to live in a house. She kept wandering in and out of the rooms, wondering where she had put things. She went downstairs into the basement for no reason at all except that it amused her to own a basement. It also amused her to own a tree.

Her parents, in Maryland, had been very pleased that one of their children had at last been able to afford real estate, and when she closed on the house they sent her flowers with a congratulations card. Her mother had even UPS'd a box of old decorating magazines saved over the years — photographs of beautiful rooms her mother used to moon over, since there never had been any money to redecorate. It was like getting her mother's pornography, that box, inheriting her drooled-upon fantasies, the endless wish and tease that had been her life. But to her mother it was a rite of passage that pleased her. "Maybe you will get some ideas from these," she had written. And when Zoë looked at the photographs, at the bold and beautiful living rooms, she was filled with longing. Ideas and ideas of longing.

Right now Zoë's house was rather empty. The previous owner had wallpapered around the furniture, leaving strange gaps and silhouettes on the walls, and Zoë hadn't done much about that yet. She had bought furniture, then taken it back, furnishing and unfurnishing, preparing and shedding, like a womb. She had bought several plain pine chests to use as love seats or boot boxes, but they came to look to her more and more like children's coffins, so she returned them. And she had recently bought an Oriental rug for the living room, with Chinese symbols on it she didn't understand. The salesgirl had kept saying she was sure they meant "Peace" and "Eternal Life," but when Zoë got the rug home she worried. What if they didn't mean "Peace" and "Eternal Life"? What if they meant, say, "Bruce Springsteen"? And the more she thought about it, the more she became convinced she had a rug that said "Bruce Springsteen," and so she returned that, too.

She had also bought a little baroque mirror for the front entryway, which, she had been told by Murray Peterson, would keep away evil spirits. The mirror, however, tended to frighten *her*, startling her with an image of a woman she never recognized. Sometimes she looked puffier and plainer than she remembered. Sometimes shifty and dark. Most times she just looked vague. "You look like someone I know," she had been told twice in the last year by strangers in restaurants in Terre Haute. In fact, sometimes she seemed not to have a look of her own, or any look whatsoever, and it began to amuse her that her students and colleagues were able to recognize her at all. How did they know? When she walked into a room, how did she look so that they knew it was she? Like this? Did she look like this? And so she returned the mirror.

"The reason I'm asking is that I know a man I think you should meet," said Evan. "He's fun. He's straight. He's single. That's all I'm going to say."

"I think I'm too old for fun," said Zoë. She had a dark bristly hair in her chin, and she could feel it now with her finger. Perhaps when you had been without the opposite sex for too long, you began to resemble them. In an act of desperate invention, you began to grow your own. "I just want to come, wear my bonehead, visit with Charlie's tropical fish, ask you about your food shoots."

She thought about all the papers on "Our Constitution: How It Affects Us" she was going to have to correct. She thought about how she was going in for ultrasound tests on Friday, because, according to her doctor and her doctor's assistant, she had a large, mysterious growth in her abdomen. Gallbladder, they kept saying. Or ovaries or colon. "You guys practice medicine?" asked Zoë, aloud, after they had left the room. Once, as a girl, she brought her dog to a vet, who had told her, "Well, either your dog has worms or cancer or else it was hit by a car."

She was looking forward to New York.

"Well, whatever. We'll just play it cool. I can't wait to see you, hon. Don't forget your bonehead," said Evan.

"A bonehead you don't forget," said Zoë.

"I suppose," said Evan.

The ultrasound Zoë was keeping a secret, even from Evan. "I feel like I'm dying," Zoë had hinted just once on the phone.

"You're not dying," said Evan, "you're just annoyed."

"Ultrasound," Zoë now said jokingly to the technician who put the cold jelly on her bare stomach. "Does that sound like a really great stereo system or what?"

She had not had anyone make this much fuss over her bare stomach since her boyfriend in graduate school, who had hovered over her whenever she felt ill, waved his arms, pressed his hands upon her navel, and drawled evangelically, "Heal! Heal for thy Baby Jesus' sake!" Zoë would laugh and they would make love, both secretly hoping she would get pregnant. Later they would worry together, and he would sink a cheek to her belly and ask whether she was late, was she late, was she sure, she might be late, and when after two years she had not gotten pregnant they took to quarreling and drifted apart.

"O.K.," said the technician absently.

The monitor was in place, and Zoë's insides came on the screen in all their gray and ribbony hollowness. They were marbled in the finest gradations of black and white, like stone in an old church or a picture of the moon. "Do you suppose," she babbled at the technician, "that the rise in infertility among so many couples in this country is due to completely different species trying to reproduce?" The technician moved the scanner around and took more pictures. On one view in particular, on Zoë's right side, the technician became suddenly alert, the machine he was operating clicking away.

Zoë stared at the screen. "That must be the growth you found there," suggested Zoë.

"I can't tell you anything," said the technician rigidly. "Your doctor will get the radiologist's report this afternoon and will phone you then."

"I'll be out of town," said Zoë.

"I'm sorry," said the technician.

Driving home, Zoë looked in the rearview mirror and decided she looked — well, how would one describe it? A little wan. She thought of the joke about the guy who visits his doctor and the doctor says, "Well, I'm sorry to say, you've got six weeks to live."

"I want a second opinion," says the guy. *You act like your opinion is worth more than everyone else's in the class.*

"You want a second opinion? O.K.," says the doctor. "You're ugly, too." She liked that joke. She thought it was terribly, terribly funny.

She took a cab to the airport. Jerry the cabbie was happy to see her.

"Have fun in New York," he said, getting her bag out of the trunk. He liked her, or at least he always acted as if he did. She called him Jare.

"Thanks, Jare."

"You know, I'll tell you a secret: I've never been to New York. I'll tell you two secrets: I've never been on a plane." And he waved at her sadly as she pushed her way in through the terminal door. "Or an escalator!" he shouted.

The trick to flying safely, Zoë always said, was to never buy a discount ticket and to tell yourself you had nothing to live for anyway, so that when the plane crashed it was no big deal. Then, when it didn't crash, when you succeeded in keeping it aloft with your own worthlessness, all you had to do was stagger off, locate your luggage, and, by the time a cab arrived, come up with a persuasive reason to go on living.

"You're here!" shrieked Evan over the doorbell, before she even opened the door. Then she opened it wide. Zoë set her bags on the hall floor and hugged Evan hard. When she was little, Evan had always been affectionate and devoted. Zoë had always taken care of her — advising, reassuring — until recently, when it seemed Evan had started advising and reassuring *her.* It startled Zoë. She suspected it had something to do with her being alone. It made people uncomfortable.

"How *are* you?"

"I threw up on the plane. Besides that, I'm O.K."

"Can I get you something? Here, let me take your suitcase. Sick on the plane. *Eeeyew.*"

"It was into one of those sickness bags," said Zoë, just in case Evan thought she'd lost it in the aisle. "I was very quiet."

The apartment was spacious and bright, with a view all the way downtown along the East Side. There was a balcony, and sliding glass doors. "I keep forgetting how nice this apartment is. Twenty-first floor, doorman . . ." Zoë could work her whole life and never have an apartment like this. So could Evan. It was Charlie's apartment. He and Evan lived in it like two kids in a dorm, beer cans and clothes strewn around.

Evan put Zoë's bag away from the mess, over by the fish tanks. "I'm so glad you're here," she said. "Now what can I get you?"

Evan made them lunch — soup from a can and saltines.

"I don't know about Charlie," she said after they had finished. "I feel like we've gone all sexless and middle-aged already."

"Hmmm," said Zoë. She leaned back into Evan's sofa and stared out the window at the dark tops of the buildings. It seemed a little unnatural to live up in the sky like this, like birds that out of some wrong-headed derring-do had nested too high. She nodded toward the lighted fish tanks and giggled. "I feel like a bird," she said, "with my own personal supply of fish."

Evan sighed. "He comes home and just sacks out on the sofa, watching fuzzy football. He's wearing the psychic cold cream and curlers, if you know what I mean."

Zoë sat up, readjusted the sofa cushions. "What's fuzzy football?"

"We haven't gotten cable yet. Everything comes in fuzzy. Charlie just watches it that way."

"Hmm, yeah, that's a little depressing," Zoë said. She looked at her hands. "Especially the part about not having cable."

"This is how he gets into bed at night." Evan stood up to demonstrate. "He whips all his clothes off, and when he gets to his underwear he lets it drop to one ankle. Then he kicks up his leg and flips the underwear in the air and catches it. I, of course, watch from the bed. There's nothing else. There's just that."

"Maybe you should just get it over with and get married."

"Really?"

"Yeah. I mean, you guys probably think living together like this is the best of both worlds, but —" Zoë tried to sound like an older sister; an older sister was supposed to be the parent you could never have, the hip, cool mom. "But I've always found that as soon as you think you've got the best of both worlds" — she thought now of herself, alone in her house, of the toad-faced cicadas that flew around like little men at night and landed on her screens, staring; of the size-fourteen shoes she placed at the doorstep, to scare off intruders; of the ridiculous, inflatable blowup doll someone had told her to keep propped up at the breakfast table — "it can suddenly twist and become the worst of both worlds."

"Really?" Evan was beaming. "Oh, Zoë. I have something to tell you. Charlie and I *are* getting married."

"Really." Zoë felt confused.

"I didn't know how to tell you."

"Yeah, I guess the part about fuzzy football misled me a little."

"I was hoping you'd be my maid of honor," said Evan, waiting. "Aren't you happy for me?"

"Yes," said Zoë, and she began to tell Evan a story about an award-winning violinist at Hilldale-Versailles — how the violinist had come home from a competition in Europe and taken up with a local man who made her go to all his summer softball games, made her cheer for him from the stands, with the wives, until she later killed herself. But when Zoë got halfway through, to the part about cheering at the softball games, she stopped.

"What?" said Evan. "So what happened?"

"Actually, nothing," said Zoë lightly. "She just really got into softball. You should have seen her."

Zoë decided to go to a late afternoon movie, leaving Evan to chores she needed to do before the party — "I have to do them alone, really," she'd said, a little tense after the violinist story. Zoë thought about going to an art museum, but women alone in art museums had to look good. They always did. Chic and serious, moving languidly, with a great handbag. Instead, she walked down through Kips Bay, past an earring boutique called Stick It in Your Ear, past a hair salon called Dorian Gray. That was the funny thing about "beauty," thought Zoë. Look it up in the yellow pages and you found a hundred entries, hostile with wit, cutesy with warning. But look up "truth" — Ha! There was nothing at all.

Zoë thought about Evan getting married. Would Evan turn into Peter Pumpkin Eater's wife? Mrs. Eater? At the wedding, would she make Zoë wear some flouncy lavender dress, identical with the other maids'? Zoë hated uniforms, had even in the first grade refused to join Elf Girls because she didn't want to wear the same dress as everyone else. Now she might have to. But maybe she could distinguish it. Hitch it up on one side with a clothespin. Wear surgical gauze at the waist. Clip to her bodice one of those pins that say in loud letters "Shit Happens."

At the movie — *Death by Number* — she bought strands of red licorice to tug and chew. She took a seat off to one side in the theater. She felt strangely self-conscious sitting alone, and hoped for the place to darken fast. When it did, and the coming attractions came on, she reached inside her purse for her glasses. They were in a Baggie. Her Kleenex was also in a Baggie. So were her pen and her aspirin and her mints. Everything was in Baggies. This was what she'd become: *a woman alone at the movies with everything in a Baggie.*

At the Halloween party, there were about two dozen people. There were people with ape heads and large hairy hands. There was someone dressed as a leprechaun. There was someone dressed as a frozen dinner. Some man had brought his two small daughters: a ballerina and a ballerina's sister, also dressed as a ballerina. There was a gaggle of sexy witches — women dressed entirely in black, beautifully made up and jeweled. "I hate those sexy witches. It's not in the spirit of Halloween," said Evan. Evan had abandoned the moon mask and dolled herself up as hausfrau, in curlers and an apron, a decision she now regretted. Charlie, because he liked fish, because he owned fish and collected fish, had decided to go as a fish. He had fins, and eyes on the sides of his head. "Zoë! How are you! I'm sorry I wasn't here when you first arrived!" He spent the rest of his time chatting up the sexy witches.

"Isn't there something I can help you with here?" Zoë asked her sister. "You've been running yourself ragged." She rubbed her sister's arm, gently, as if she wished they were alone.

"Oh, God, not at all," said Evan, arranging stuffed mushrooms on a plate. The timer went off, and she pulled another sheetful out of the oven. "Actually, you know what you can do?"

"What?" Zoë put on her bonehead.

"Meet Earl. He's the guy I had in mind for you. When he gets here, just talk to him a little. He's nice. He's fun. He's going through a divorce."

"I'll try," Zoë groaned. "O.K.? I'll try." She looked at her watch.

When Earl arrived, he was dressed as a naked woman, steel wool glued strategically to a body stocking, and large rubber breasts protruding like hams.

"Zoë, this is Earl," said Evan.

"Good to meet you," said Earl, circling Evan to shake Zoë's hand. He stared at the top of Zoë's head. "Great bone."

Zoë nodded. "Great tits," she said. She looked past him, out the window at the city thrown glittering up against the sky; people were saying the usual things: how it looked like jewels, like bracelets and necklaces unstrung. You could see the clock of the Con Ed building, the orange-and-gold-capped Empire State, the Chrysler like a rocket ship dreamed up in a depression. Far west you could glimpse Astor Plaza, with its flying white roof like a nun's habit. "There's beer out on the balcony, Earl. Can I get you one?" Zoë asked.

"Sure, uh, I'll come along. Hey, Charlie, how's it going?"

Charlie grinned and whistled. People turned to look. "Hey, Earl," someone called from across the room. "Va-va-va-voom."

They squeezed their way past the other guests, past the apes and the sexy witches. The suction of the sliding door gave way in a whoosh, and Zoë and Earl stepped out onto the balcony, a bonehead and a naked woman, the night air roaring and smoky cool. Another couple were out there, too, murmuring privately. They were not wearing costumes. They smiled at Zoë and Earl. "Hi," said Zoë. She found the plastic-foam cooler, dug in and retrieved two beers.

"Thanks," said Earl. His rubber breasts folded inward, dimpled and dented, as he twisted open the bottle.

"Well," sighed Zoë anxiously. She had to learn not to be afraid of a man, the way, in your childhood, you learned not to be afraid of an earthworm or a bug. Often, when she spoke to men at parties, she rushed things in her mind. As the man politely blathered on, she would fall in love, marry, then find herself in a bitter custody battle with him for the kids and hoping for a reconciliation, so that despite all his betrayals she might no longer despise him, and, in the few minutes remaining, learn, perhaps, what his last name was and what he did for a living, though probably there was already too much history between them. She would nod, blush, turn away.

"Evan tells me you're a history professor. Where do you teach?"

"Just over the Indiana border into Illinois."

He looked a little shocked. "I guess Evan didn't tell me that part."

"She didn't?"

"No."

"Well, that's Evan for you. When we were kids we both had speech impediments."

"That can be tough," said Earl. One of his breasts was hidden behind his drinking arm, but the other shone low and pink, full as a strawberry moon.

"Yes, well, it wasn't a total loss. We used to go to what we called peach pearapy. For about ten years of my life, I had to map out every sentence in my mind, way ahead, before I said it. That was the only way I could get a coherent sentence out."

Earl drank from his beer. "How did you do that? I mean, how did you get through?"

"I told a lot of jokes. Jokes you know the lines to already. You can just say them. I love jokes. Jokes and songs."

Earl smiled. He had on lipstick, a deep shade of red, but it was wearing off from the beer. "What's your favorite joke?"

"Uh, my favorite joke is probably — O.K., all right. This guy goes into a doctor's office, and — "

"I think I know this one," interrupted Earl, eagerly. He wanted to tell it himself. "A guy goes into a doctor's office, and the doctor tells him he's got some good news and some bad news — that one, right?"

"I'm not sure," said Zoë. "This might be a different version."

"So the guy says, 'Give me the bad news first,' and the doctor says, 'O.K. You've got three weeks to live.' And the guy cries, 'Three weeks to live! Doctor, what is the good news?' And the doctor says, 'Did you see that secretary out front? I finally fucked her.'"

Zoë frowned.

"That's not the one you were thinking of?"

"No." There was accusation in her voice. "Mine was different."

"Oh," said Earl. He looked away and then back again. "What kind of history do you teach?"

"I teach American, mostly — eighteenth- and nineteenth-century." In graduate school, at bars the pickup line was always, "So what's your century?"

"Occasionally, I teach a special theme course," she added. "Say, 'Humor and Personality in the White House.' That's what my book's on." She thought of something someone once told her about bowerbirds, how they build elaborate structures before mating.

"Your book's on *humor*?"

"Yeah, and, well, when I teach a theme course like that I do all the centuries." *So what's your century?*

"All three of them."

"Pardon?" The breeze glistened her eyes. Traffic revved beneath them. She felt high and puny, like someone lifted into heaven by mistake and then spurned.

"Three. There's only three."

"Well, four, really." She was thinking of Jamestown, and of the Pilgrims coming here with buckles and witch hats to say their prayers.

"I'm a photographer," said Earl. His face was starting to gleam, his rouge smearing in a sunset beneath his eyes.

"Do you like that?"

"Well, actually, I'm starting to feel it's a little dangerous."

"Really?"

"Spending all your time in a dark room with that red light and all those chemicals. There's links with Parkinson's, you know."

"No, I didn't."

"I suppose I should wear rubber gloves, but I don't like to. Unless I'm touching it directly, I don't think of it as real."

"Hmm," said Zoë. Alarm buzzed mildly through her.

"Sometimes, when I have a cut or something, I feel the sting and think, *Shit*. I wash constantly and just hope. I don't like rubber over the skin like that."

"Really."

"I mean, the physical contact. That's what you want, or why bother?"

"I guess," said Zoë. She wished she could think of a joke, something slow and deliberate with the end in sight. She thought of gorillas, how when they had been kept too long alone in cages they would smack each other in the head instead of mating.

"Are you — in a relationship?" Earl suddenly blurted.

"Now? As we speak?"

"Well, I mean, I'm sure you have a relationship to your *work*." A smile, a little one, nestled in his mouth like an egg. She thought of zoos in parks, how when cities were under siege, during world wars, people ate the animals. "But I mean, with a *man*."

"No, I'm not in a relationship with a *man*." She rubbed her chin with her hand and could feel the one bristly hair there. "But my last relationship was with a very sweet man," she said. She made something up. "From Switzerland. He was a botanist — a weed expert. His name was Jerry. I called him Jare. He was so funny. You'd go to the movies with him and all he would notice was the plants. He would never pay attention to the plot. Once, in a jungle movie, he started rattling off all these Latin names, out loud. It was very exciting for him." She paused, caught her breath. "Eventually, he went back to Europe to, uh, study the edelweiss." She looked at Earl. "Are you involved in a relationship? With a *woman?*"

Earl shifted his weight and the creases in his body stocking changed, splintering outward like something broken. His pubic hair slid over to one hip, like a corsage on a saloon girl. "No," he said, clearing his throat. The steel wool in his underarms was inching down toward his biceps. "I've just gotten out of a marriage that was full of bad dialogue like 'You want more *space?* I'll give you more space!' *Clonk*. Your basic Three Stooges."

Zoë looked at him sympathetically. "I suppose it's hard for love to recover after that."

His eyes lit up. He wanted to talk about love. "But I keep thinking love should be like a tree. You look at trees and they've got bumps and scars from tumors, infestations, what have you, but they're still growing. Despite the bumps and bruises, they're — straight."

"Yeah, well," said Zoë, "where I'm from they're all married or gay. Did you see that movie *Death by Number?*"

Earl looked at her, a little lost. She was getting away from him. "No," he said.

One of his breasts had slipped under his arm, tucked there like a baguette. She kept thinking of trees, of parks, of people in wartime eating the zebras. She felt a stabbing pain in her abdomen.

"Want some hors d'oeuvres?" Evan came pushing through the sliding door. She was smiling, though her curlers were coming out, hanging bedraggled at the ends of her hair like Christmas decorations, like food put out for the birds. She thrust forward a plate of stuffed mushrooms.

"Are you asking for donations or giving them away?" said Earl wittily. He liked Evan, and he put his arm around her.

"You know, I'll be right back," said Zoë.

"Oh," said Evan, looking concerned.

"Right back. I promise."

Zoë hurried inside, across the living room into the bedroom, to the adjoining bath. It was empty; most of the guests were using the half-bath near the kitchen. She flicked on the light and closed the door. The pain had stopped, and she didn't really have to go to the bathroom, but she stayed there anyway, resting. In the mirror above the sink, she looked haggard beneath her bonehead, violet-grays showing under the skin like a plucked and pocky bird's. She leaned closer, raising her chin a little to find the bristly hair. It was there, at the end of the jaw, sharp and dark as a wire. She opened the medicine cabinet, pawed through it until she found some tweezers. She lifted her head again and poked at her face with the metal tips, grasping and pinching and missing. Outside the door, she could hear two people talking low. They had come into the bedroom and were discussing something. They were sitting on the bed. One of them giggled in a false way. Zoë stabbed again at her chin, and it started to bleed a little. She pulled the skin tight along the jawbone, gripped the tweezers hard around what she hoped was the hair, and tugged. A tiny square of skin came away, but the hair remained, blood bright at the root of it. Zoë clenched her teeth. "Come on," she whispered. The couple outside in the bedroom were now telling stories, softly, and laughing. There was a bounce and squeak of mattress, and the sound of a chair being moved out of the way. Zoë aimed the tweezers carefully, pinched, then pulled gently, and this time the hair came, too, with a slight twinge of pain, and then a great flood of relief. "Yeah!" breathed Zoë. She grabbed some toilet paper and dabbed at her chin. It came away spotted with blood, and so she tore off some more and pressed hard until it stopped. Then she turned off the light, opened the door, and rejoined the party. "Excuse me," she said to the couple in the bedroom. They were the couple from the balcony, and they looked at her, a bit surprised. They had their arms around each other, and they were eating candy bars.

Earl was still out on the balcony, alone, and Zoë rejoined him there. "Hi," she said.

He turned around and smiled. He had straightened his costume out a bit, though all the secondary sex characteristics seemed slightly doomed, destined to shift and flip and zip around again any moment. "Are you O.K.?" he asked. He had opened another beer and was chugging.

"Oh, yeah. I just had to go to the bathroom." She paused. "Actually, I have been going to a lot of doctors recently."

"What's wrong?" asked Earl.

"Oh, probably nothing. But they're putting me through tests." She sighed. "I've had sonograms. I've had mammograms. Next week I'm going in for a candygram." He looked at her, concerned. "I've had too many gram words," she said.

"Here, I saved you these." He held out a napkin with two stuffed mushroom caps. They were cold and leaving oil marks on the napkin.

"Thanks," said Zoë, and pushed them both in her mouth. "Watch," she said with her mouth full. "With my luck it'll be a gallbladder operation."

Earl made a face. "So your sister's getting married," he said, changing the subject. "Tell me, really, what you think about love."

"*Love?*" Hadn't they done this already? "I don't know." She chewed thoughtfully and swallowed. "All right. I'll tell you what I think about love. Here is a love story. This friend of mine — "

"You've got something on your chin," said Earl, and he reached over to touch it.

"What?" said Zoë, stepping back. She turned her face away and grabbed at her chin. A piece of toilet paper peeled off it, like tape. "It's nothing," she said. "It's just — it's nothing."

Earl stared at her.

"At any rate," she continued, "this friend of mine was this award-winning violinist. She traveled all over Europe and won competitions; she made records, she gave concerts, she got famous. But she had no social life. So one day she threw herself at the feet of this conductor she had a terrible crush on. He picked her up, scolded her gently, and sent her back to her hotel room. After that, she came home from Europe. She went back to her old hometown, stopped playing the violin, and took up with a local boy. This was in Illinois. He took her to some Big Ten bar every night to drink with his buddies from the team. He used to say things like 'Katrina here likes to play the violin,' and then he'd pinch her cheek. When she once suggested that they go home, he said, 'What, you think you're too famous for a place like this? Well, let me tell you something. You may think you're famous, but you're not *famous* famous.' Two famouses. 'No one here's ever heard of you.' Then he went up and bought a round of drinks for everyone but her. She got her coat, went home, and shot a bullet through her head."

Earl was silent.

"That's the end of my love story," said Zoë.

"You're not at all like your sister," said Earl.

"Oh, really," said Zoë. The air had gotten colder, the wind singing minor and thick as a dirge.

"No." He didn't want to talk about love anymore. "You know, you should wear a lot of blue — blue and white — around your face. It would bring out your coloring." He reached an arm out to show her how the blue bracelet he was wearing might look against her skin, but she swatted it away.

"Tell me, Earl. Does the word 'fag' mean anything to you?"

He stepped back, away from her. He shook his head in disbelief. "You know, I just shouldn't try to go out with career women. You're all stricken. A guy can really tell what life has done to you. I do better with women who have part-time jobs."

"Oh, yes?" said Zoë. She had once read an article entitled "Professional Women and the Demographics of Grief." Or, no, it was a poem. *If there were a lake, the moonlight would dance across it in conniptions.* She remembered that line. But perhaps the title was "The Empty House: Aesthetics of Barrenness." Or maybe "Space Gypsies: Girls in Academe." She had forgotten.

Earl turned and leaned on the railing of the balcony. It was getting late. Inside, the party guests were beginning to leave. The sexy witches were already gone. "Live and learn," Earl murmured.

"Live and get dumb," replied Zoë. Beneath them on Lexington there were no cars, just the gold rush of an occasional cab. He leaned hard on his elbows, brooding.

"Look at those few people down there," he said. "They look like bugs. You know how bugs are kept under control? They're sprayed with bug hormones — female bug hormones. The male bugs get so crazy in the presence of this hormone they're screwing everything in sight — trees, rocks, everything but female bugs. Population control. That's what's happening in this country," he said drunkenly. "Hormones sprayed around, and now men are screwing rocks. Rocks!"

In the back, the Magic Marker line on his buttocks spread wide, a sketchy black on pink, like a funnies page. Zoë came up, slow, from behind, and gave him a shove. His arms slipped forward, off the railing, out over the street. Beer spilled out of his bottle, raining twenty stories down to the street.

"Hey, what are you doing!" he said, whipping around. He stood straight and readied, and moved away from the railing, sidestepping Zoë. "What the *hell* are you doing?"

"Just kidding," she said. "I was just kidding." But he gazed at her, appalled and frightened, his Magic Marker buttocks turned away now toward all of downtown, a naked pseudo-woman with a blue bracelet at the wrist, trapped out on a balcony with — with *what?* "Really, I was just kidding!" Zoë shouted. The wind lifted the hair up off her head, skyward in spines behind the bone. If there were a lake, the moonlight would dance across it in conniptions. She smiled at him and wondered how she looked.

1993

*Thom Jones*

........................................................................................

# I Want to Live!

<small>FROM</small> *Harper's Magazine*


<small>SHE WONDERED</small> how many times a week he had to do this. Plenty, no
doubt. At least every day. Maybe twice . . . three times. Maybe, on a big
day, five times. It was the ultimate bad news, and he delivered it dryly,
like Sergeant Joe Friday. He was a young man, but his was a tough
business and he had gone freeze-dried already. Hey, the bad news wasn't
really a surprise! She . . . *knew.* Of course, you always hope for the best.
She heard but she didn't hear.

"What?" she offered timidly. She had hoped . . . for better. Geez! Give
me a break! What was he saying? Breast and uterus? Double trouble!
She *knew* it would be the uterus. There had been the discharge. The
bloating, the cramps. The fatigue. But it was common and easily curable
provided you got it at stage one. Eighty percent cure. But the breast —
that one came out of the blue and that could be really tricky — that was
fifty-fifty. Strip out the lymph nodes down your arm and guaranteed
chemo. God! Chemo. The worst thing in the world. Good-bye hair —
there'd be scarves, wigs, a prosthetic breast, crying your heart out in
"support" groups. Et cetera.

"Mrs. Wilson?" The voice seemed to come out of a can. Now the
truth was revealed and all was out in the open. Yet how — tell me this
— how would it ever be possible to have a life again? The voice from the
can had chilled her. To the core.

"Mrs. Wilson, your last CA 125 hit the ceiling," he said. "I suspect that
this could be an irregular kind of can . . . cer."

Some off-the-wall kind of can . . . cer? A kind of wildfire cancer!
Not the easygoing, 80 percent cure, tortoise, as-slow-as-molasses-in-
January cancer!

January. She looked past the thin oncologist, wire-rimmed glasses, white coat, inscrutable. Outside, snowflakes tumbled from the sky, kissing the pavement — each unique, wonderful, worth an hour of study, a microcosm of the Whole: awe-inspiring, absolutely fascinating, a gift of divinity gratis. Yet how abhorrent they seemed. They were white, but the whole world had lost its color for her now that she'd heard those words. The shine was gone from the world. Had she been Queen of the Universe for a million years and witnessed glory after glory, what would it have mattered now that she had come to this?

She . . . came to . . . went out, came back again . . . went out. There was this . . . wonderful show. Cartoons. It was the best show. This wasn't so bad. True, she had cancer but . . . these wonderful cartoons. Dilaudid. On Dilaudid, well, you live, you die — that's how it is . . . life in the Big City. It happens to everyone. It's part of the plan. Who was she to question the plan?

The only bad part was her throat. Her throat was on fire. "Intubation." The nurse said she'd phone the doctor and maybe he'd authorize more dope.

"Oh, God, please. Anything."

"Okay, let's just fudge a little bit, no one needs to know," the nurse said, twisting a knob on Tube Control Central. Dilaudid. Cartoons. Oh, God, thank God, Dilaudid! Who invented that drug? Write him a letter. Knight him. Award the Nobel Prize to Dilaudid Man. Where was the knob? A handy thing to know. Whew! Whammo! Swirling, throbbing ecstasy! And who was that nurse? Florence Nightingale, Mother Teresa would be proud . . . oh, boy! It wasn't just relief from the surgery; she suddenly realized how much psychic pain she had been carrying and now it was gone with one swoop of a magic wand. The cartoons. Bliss . . .

His voice wasn't in a can, never had been. It was a normal voice, maybe a little high for a man. Not that he was effeminate. The whole problem with him was that he didn't seem real. He wasn't a flesh-and-blood kinda guy. Where was the *empathy?* Why did he get into this field if he couldn't empathize? In this field, empathy should be your stock-in-trade.

"The breast is fine, just a benign lump. We brought a specialist in to get it, and I just reviewed the pathology report. It's nothing to worry about. The other part is not . . . so good. I'm afraid your abdomen . . .

it's spread throughout your abdomen . . . it looks like little Grape-Nuts, actually. It's exceedingly rare and it's . . . it's a rapid form of . . . can . . . cer. We couldn't really take any of it out. I spent most of my time in there untangling adhesions. We're going to have to give you cisplatin . . . if it weren't for the adhesions, we could pump it into your abdomen directly — you wouldn't get so sick that way — but those adhesions are a problem and may cause problems further along." Her room was freezing, but the thin oncologist was beginning to perspire. "It's a shame," he said, looking down at her chart. "You're in such perfect health . . . otherwise."

She knew this was going to happen yet she heard herself say, "Doctor, do you mean . . . I've got to take —"

"Chemo? Yeah. But don't worry about that yet. Let's just let you heal up for a while." He slammed her chart shut and . . . whiz, bang, he was outta there.

Good-bye, see ya.

The guessing game was over and now it was time for the ordeal. She didn't want to hear any more details — he'd said something about a 20 percent five-year survival rate. Might as well bag it. She wasn't a fighter, and she'd seen what chemo had done to her husband, John. This was it. Finis!

She had to laugh. Got giddy. It was like in that song — *Freedom's just another word for nothing left to lose* . . . When you're totally screwed, nothing can get worse, so what's to worry? Of course she could get lucky . . . it would be a thousand-to-one, but maybe . . .

The ovaries and uterus were gone. The root of it all was out. Thank God for that. Those befouled organs were gone. Where? Disposed of. Burned. In a dumpster? Who cares? The source was destroyed. Maybe it wouldn't be so bad. How could it be that bad? After all, the talk about pain from major abdominal surgery was overdone. She was walking with her little cart and tubes by the third day — a daily constitutional through the ward.

Okay, the Dilaudid was permanently off the menu, but morphine sulfate wasn't half bad. No more cartoons but rather a mellow glow. Left, right, left, right. Hup, two, three, four! Even a journey of a thousand miles begins with the first step. On the morphine she was walking a quarter of an inch off the ground and everything was . . . softer, mercifully so. Maybe she could hack it for a thousand miles.

But those people in the hospital rooms, gray and dying, that was her. Could such a thing be possible? To die? Really? Yes, at some point she guessed you did die. But her? Now? So soon? With so little time to get used to the idea?

No, this was all a bad dream! She'd wake up. She'd wake up back in her little girl room on the farm near Battle Lake, Minnesota. There was a Depression, things were a little rough, but big deal. What could beat a sun-kissed morning on Battle Lake and a robin's song? There was an abundance of jays, larks, bluebirds, cardinals, hummingbirds, red-winged blackbirds in those days before acid rain and heavy-metal poisoning, and they came to her yard to eat from the cherry, apple, plum, and pear trees. What they really went for were the mulberries.

Ah, youth! Good looks, a clean complexion, muscle tone, a full head of lustrous hair — her best feature, although her legs were pretty good, too. Strength. Vitality. A happy kid with a bright future. Cheerleader her senior year. Pharmacy scholarship at the college in Fergus Falls. Geez, if her dad hadn't died, she could have been a pharmacist. Her grades were good, but hard-luck stories were the order of the day. It was a Great Depression. She would have to take her chances. Gosh! It had been a great, wide, wonderful world in those days, and no matter what, an adventure lay ahead, something marvelous — a handsome prince and a life happily ever after. Luck was with her. Where had all the time gone? How had all the dreams . . . fallen away? Now she was in the Valley of the Shadow. The morphine sulfate was like a warm and friendly hearth in Gloom City, her one and only consolation.

He was supposed to be a good doctor, one of the best in the field, but he had absolutely no bedside manner. She really began to hate him when he took away the morphine and put her on Tylenol 3. Then it began to sink in that things might presently go downhill in a hurry.

They worked out a routine. If her brother was busy, her daughter drove her up to the clinic and then back down to the office, and the thin oncologist is . . . called away, or he's . . . running behind, or he's . . . *something.* Couldn't they run a business, get their shit together? Why couldn't they anticipate? It was one thing to wait in line at a bank when you're well, but when you've got cancer and you're this cancer patient and you wait an hour, two hours, or they tell you to come back next week . . . come back for something that's worse than anything, the very worst thing in the world! Hard to get up for that. You really had to brace yourself. Cisplatin, God! Metal mouth, restlessness, pacing. Flop on the couch, but that's no good; get up and pace, but you can't handle that, so you flop on the couch again. Get up and pace. Is this really happening to me? *I can't believe this is really happening to me!* How can such a thing be possible?

Then there were the episodes of simultaneous diarrhea and vomiting that sprayed the bathroom from floor to ceiling! Dry heaves and then dry heaves with bile and then dry heaves with blood. You could drink a quart of tequila and then a quart of rum and have some sloe gin too and eat pink birthday cakes and five pounds of licorice, Epsom salts, a pint of kerosene, some Southern Comfort — and you're on a Sunday picnic compared to cisplatin. Only an archfiend could devise a dilemma where to maybe *get well* you first had to poison yourself within a whisker of death, and in fact if you didn't die, you wished that you had.

There were visitors in droves. Flowers. Various intrusions at all hours. Go away. Leave me alone . . . please, God, leave me . . . alone.

*Oh, hi, thanks for coming. Oh, what a lovely — such beautiful flowers . . .*

There were moments when she felt that if she had one more episode of diarrhea, she'd jump out of the window. Five stories. Would that be high enough? Or would you lie there for a time and die slowly? Maybe if you took a header right onto the concrete. Maybe then you wouldn't feel a thing. Cisplatin: she had to pace. But she had to lie down, but she was squirrelly as hell and she couldn't lie down. TV was no good — she had double vision, and it was all just a bunch of stupid shit, anyhow. Soap operas — good grief! What absolute crap. Even her old favorites. You only live once, and to think of all the time she pissed away watching soap operas.

If only she could sleep. God, couldn't they give her Dilaudid? No! Wait! Hold that! Somehow Dilaudid would make it even worse. Ether then. Put her out. Wake me up in five days. Just let me sleep. She *had* to get up to pace. She *had* to lie down. She *had* to vomit. *Oh, hi, thanks for coming. Oh, what a lovely — such beautiful flowers.*

The second treatment made the first treatment seem like a month in the country. The third treatment — oh, damn! The whole scenario had been underplayed. Those movie stars who got it and wrote books about it were stoics, valiant warriors compared to her. She had no idea anything could be so horrible. Starving in Bangladesh? No problem, I'll trade. Here's my MasterCard and the keys to the Buick — I'll pull a rickshaw, anything! Anything but this. HIV-positive? Why just sign right here on the dotted line and you've got a deal! I'll trade with anybody! Anybody.

The thin oncologist with the Bugs Bunny voice said the CA 125 number was still up in the stratosphere. He said it was up to her if she wanted to go on with this. What was holding her up? She didn't know, and her own voice came from a can now. She heard herself say, "Doctor, what would you do . . . if you were me?"

He thought it over for a long time. He pulled off his wire rims and pinched his nose, world-weary. "I'd take the next treatment."

It was the worst by far — square root to infinity. Five days: no sleep, pacing, lying down, pacing. Puke and diarrhea. The phone. She wanted to tear it off the wall. After all these years, couldn't they make a quiet bell? — did they have shit for brains or what? *Oh, hi, well . . . just fine. Just dandy. Coming by on Sunday? With the kids? Well . . . no, I feel great. No. No. No. I'd love to see you . . .*

And then one day the thin-timbre voice delivered good news. "Your CA 125 is almost within normal limits. It's working!"

Hallelujah! Oh my God, let it be so! A miracle. Hurrah!

"It is a miracle," he said. He was almost human, Dr. Kildare, Dr. Ben Casey, Marcus Welby, M.D. — take your pick. "Your CA is down to rock bottom. I think we should do one, possibly two more treatments and then go back inside for a look. If we do too few, we may not kill it all but if we do too much — you see, it's toxic to your healthy cells as well. You can get cardiomyopathy in one session of cisplatin and you can die."

"One more is all I can handle."

"Gotcha, Mrs. Wilson. One more and in for a look."

"I hate to tell you this," he said. Was he making the cartoons go away? "I'll be up front about it, Mrs. Wilson, we've still got a problem. The little Grape-Nuts — fewer than in the beginning, but the remaining cells will be resistant to cisplatin, so our options are running thin. We could try a month of an experimental form of hard chemotherapy right here in the hospital — very, very risky stuff. Or we could resume the cisplatin, not so much aiming for a cure but rather as a holding action. Or we could not do anything at all . . ."

Her voice was flat. She said, "What if I don't do anything?"

"Dead in three months, maybe six."

She said, "Dead how?"

"Lungs, liver, or bowel. Don't worry, Mrs. Wilson, there won't be a lot of pain. I'll see to that." Bingo! He flipped the chart shut and . . . whiz, bang, he was outta there!

She realized that when she got right down to it, she wanted to live, more than anything, on almost any terms, so she took more cisplatin. But the oncologist was right, it couldn't touch those resistant rogue cells; they were like roaches that could live through atomic warfare, grow and thrive. Well then, screw it! At least there wouldn't be pain. What more can you do? She shouldn't have let him open her up again. That had been the worst sort of folly. She'd let him steamroll her with Doctor Knows Best. Air had hit it. No wonder it was a wildfire. A conflagration.

Her friends came by. It was an effort to make small talk. How could they know? How could they *know* what it was like? They loved her, they said, with liquor on their breath. They had to get juiced before they could stand to come by! They came with casseroles and cleaned for her, but she had to sweat out her nights alone. Dark nights of the soul on Tylenol 3 and Xanax. A lot of good that was. But then when she was in her loose, giddy *freedom's just another word for nothing left to lose* mood, about ten days after a treatment, she realized her friends weren't so dumb. They knew that they couldn't really *know.* Bugs Bunny told her there was no point in going on with the cisplatin. He told her she was a very brave lady. He said he was sorry.

A month after she was off that poison, cisplatin, there was a little side benefit. She could see the colors of the earth again and taste food and smell flowers — it was a bittersweet pleasure, to be sure. But her friends took her to Hawaii, where they had this great friend ("You gotta meet him!") and he . . . he made a play for her and brought her flowers every day, expensive roses, et cetera. She had never considered another man since John had died from can . . . cer ten years before. How wonderful to forget it all for a moment here and there. A moment? Qualify that — make that ten, fifteen seconds. How can you forget it? Ever since she got the news she could . . . not . . . forget . . . it.

Now there were stabbing pains, twinges, flutterings — maybe it was normal everyday stuff amplified by the imagination or maybe it was real. How fast would it move, this wildfire brand? Better not to ask.

Suddenly she was horrible again. Those nights alone — killers. Finally one night she broke down and called her daughter. Hated to do it, throw in the towel, but this was the fifteenth round and she didn't have a prayer.

"Oh, hi. I'm just fine" — *blah blah blah* — "but I was thinking maybe I could come down and stay, just a while. I'd like to see Janey and —"

"We'll drive up in the morning."

At least she was with blood. And her darling granddaughter. What a delight. Playing with the little girl, she could forget. It was even better than Hawaii. After a year of sheer hell, in which all of the good stuff added up to less than an hour and four minutes total, there was a way to forget. She helped with the dishes. A little light cleaning. Watched the game shows, worked the *Times* crossword, but the pains grew worse. Goddamn it, it felt like nasty little yellow-tooth rodents or a horde of translucent termites — thousands of them, chewing her guts out! Tylenol 3 couldn't touch it. The new doctor she had been passed to gave her Dilaudid. She was enormously relieved. But what she got was a vial of little pink tablets and after the first dose she realized it wasn't much good in the pill form; you could squeeze by on it but they'd *promised* — no pain! She was losing steam. Grinding down.

They spent a couple of days on the Oregon coast. The son-in-law — somehow it was easy to be with him. He didn't pretend that things were other than they were. He could be a pain in the bun, like everyone, bitching over trivialities, smoking Kool cigarettes, strong ones — jolters! A pack a day easy, although he was considerate enough to go outside and do it. She wanted to tell him, "Fool! Your health is your greatest fortune!" But she was the one who'd let six months pass after that first discharge.

The Oregon coast was lovely, although the surf was too cold for actual swimming. She sat in the hotel whirlpool and watched her granddaughter swim a whole length of the pool all on her own, a kind of dog-paddle thing but not bad for a kid going on seven. They saw a show of shooting stars one night but it was exhausting to keep up a good front and not to be morbid, losing weight big time. After a shower, standing at the mirror, scars zig-zagging all over the joint like the Bride of Frankenstein, it was just awful. She was bald, scrawny, ashen, yet with a bloated belly. She couldn't look. Sometimes she would sink to the floor and just lie there, too sick to even cry, too weak to even get dressed, yet somehow she did get dressed, slapped on that hot, goddamn wig, and showed up for dinner. It was easier to do that if you pretended that it wasn't real, if you pretended it was all on TV.

She felt like a naughty little girl sitting before the table looking at meals her daughter was killing herself to make — old favorites that now tasted like a combination of forty-weight Texaco oil and sawdust. It was a relief to get back to the couch and work crossword puzzles. It was hell imposing on her daughter but she was frightened. Terrified! They were her blood. They *had* to take her. Oh, to come to this!

The son-in-law worked swing shift and he cheered her in the morning when he got up and made coffee. He was full of life. He was real. He was authentic. He even interjected little pockets of hope. Not that he pushed macrobiotics or any of that foolishness, but it was a fact — if you were happy, if you had something to live for, if you loved life, you lived it. It had been a mistake for her to hole up there in the mountains after John died. The Will to Live was more important than doctors and medicines. You had to reinvigorate the Will to Live. The granddaughter was good for that. She just couldn't go the meditation-tape route, imagining microscopic, ravenous, good-guy little sharks eating the bad cancer cells, et cetera. At least the son-in-law didn't suggest that or come on strong with a theology trip. She noticed he read the King James Bible, though.

She couldn't eat. There was a milk-shake diet she choked down. Vanilla, chocolate fudge, strawberry — your choice. Would Madame like a bottle of wine with dinner? Ha, ha, ha.

Dilaudid. It wasn't working, there was serious pain, especially in her chest, dagger thrusts — *Et tu, Brute?* She watched the clock like a hawk and had her pills out and ready every four hours — and that last hour was getting to be murder, a morbid sweat began popping out of her in the last fifteen minutes. One morning she caved in and timidly asked the son-in-law, "Can I take three?"

He said, "Hell, take four. It's a safe drug. If you have bad pain, take four." Her eyes were popping out of her head. "Here, drink it with coffee and it will kick in faster."

He was right. He knew more than the doctor. You just can't do everything by the book. Maybe that had been her trouble all along — she was too compliant, one of those "cancer" personalities. She believed in the rules. She was one of those kind who wanted to leave the world a better place than she found it. She had been a good person, had always done the right thing — this just wasn't right. It wasn't fair. She was so . . . angry!

The next day, over the phone, her son-in-law bullied a prescription of methadone from the cancer doctor. She heard one side of a lengthy heated exchange while the son-in-law made a persuasive case for methadone. He came on like Clarence Darrow or F. Lee Bailey. It was a commanding performance. She'd never heard of anyone giving a doctor hell before. God bless him for not backing down! On methadone tablets a warm orange glow sprung forth and bloomed like a glorious, time-lapse rose in her abdomen and then rolled through her body in orgasmic waves. The sense of relief shattered all fear and doubt though the pain was still there to some extent. It was still there but — so what? And the methadone tablets lasted a very long time — no more of that *every four hours* bullshit.

Purple blotches all over her skin, swollen ankles. Pain in her hips and joints. An ambulance trip to the emergency room. "Oh," they said, "it's nothing . . . vascular purpura. Take aspirin. Who's next?"

Who's next? Why hadn't she taken John's old .38 revolver the very day she heard that voice in the can? Stuck it in the back of her mouth and pulled the trigger? She had no fear of hellfire. She was a decent, moral person but she did not believe. Neither was she the Hamlet type — what lies on the other side? It was probably the same thing that occurred before you were born — zilch. And zilch wasn't that bad. What was wrong with zilch?

One morning she waited overlong for the son-in-law to get up, almost smashed a candy dish to get him out of bed. Was he going to sleep forever? Actually, he got up at his usual time.

"I can't. Get. My breath," she told him.

"You probably have water in your lungs," the son-in-law said. He knew she didn't want to go to the clinic. "We've got some diuretic. They were Boxer's when she had congestive heart failure — dog medicine, but it's the same thing they give humans. Boxer weighed fifty-five pounds. Let me see . . . take four, no, take three. To be cautious. Do you feel like you have to cough?"

"Yes." Kaff, kaff, kaff.

"This might draw the water out of your lungs. It's pretty safe. Try to eat a banana or a potato skin to keep your potassium up. If it doesn't work, we can go over to the clinic."

How would he know something like that? But he was right. It worked like magic. She had to pee like crazy but she could breathe. The panic to end all panics was over. If she could only go . . . number two. Well, the methadone slows you down. "Try some Metamucil," the son-in-law said.

It worked. Kind of, but it sure wasn't anything to write home about.

"I can't breathe. The diuretics aren't working."

The son-in-law said they could tap her lung. It would mean another drive to the clinic, but the procedure was almost painless and provided instantaneous relief. It worked but it was three days of exhaustion after that one.

The waiting room. Why so long? Why couldn't they anticipate? You didn't have to be a genius to know which way the wildfire was spreading. Would the methadone keep that internal orange glow going or would they run out of ammo? Was methadone the ultimate or were there bigger guns? Street heroine? She'd have to put on her wig and go out and score China White.

The little girl began to tune out. Gramma wasn't so much fun anymore; she just lay there and she gave off this smell. There was no more dressing up; it was just the bathrobe. In fact, she felt the best in her old red-and-black tartan pattern, flannel, ratty-ass bathrobe, not the good one. The crosswords — forget it, too depressing. You could live the life of Cleopatra but if it came down to this, what was the point?

The son-in-law understood. Of all the people to come through. It's bad and it gets worse and so on until the worst of all. "I don't know how you can handle this," he'd say. "What does it feel like? Does it feel like a hangover? Worse than a hangover? Not like a hangover? Then what? Like drinking ten pots of boiled coffee? Like that? Really? Jittery! Oh, God, that must be awful. How can you stand it? Is it just like drinking too much coffee or is there some other aspect? Your fingers are numb? Blurred vision? It takes eight years to watch the second hand sweep from twelve to one? Well, if it's like that, how did you handle *five days*? I couldn't — I'd take a bottle of pills, shoot myself. Something. What about the second week? Drained? Washed out? Oh, brother! I had a three-day hangover once — I'd rather die than do that again. I couldn't ride out that hangover again for money. I know I couldn't handle chemo . . ."

One afternoon after he left for work, she found a passage circled in his well-worn copy of Schopenhauer: "In early youth, as we contemplate our coming life, we are like children in a theater before the curtain is raised, sitting there in high spirits and eagerly waiting for the play to begin. It is a blessing that we do not know what is really going to happen." Yeah! She gave up the crosswords and delved into *The World As Will and Idea*. This Schopenhauer was a genius! Why hadn't anyone told her? She was a reader, she had waded through some philosophy in

her time — you just couldn't make any sense out of it. The problem was
the terminology! She was a crossword ace, but words like *eschatology* —
hey! Yet Schopenhauer got right into the heart of all the important
things. The things that really mattered. With Schopenhauer she could
take long excursions from the grim specter of impending death. In
Schopenhauer, particularly in his aphorisms and reflections, she found
an absolute satisfaction, for Schopenhauer spoke the truth and the rest
of the world was disseminating lies!

Her son-in-law helped her with unfinished business: will, mortgage,
insurance, how shall we do this, that, and the other? Cremation, burial
plot, et cetera. He told her the stuff that her daughter couldn't tell her.
He waited for the right moment and then got it all in — for instance, he
told her that her daughter loved her very much but that it was hard for
her to say so. She knew she cringed at this revelation, for it was ditto
with her, and she knew he could see it. Why couldn't she say to her own
daughter three simple words, "I love you?" She just couldn't. Somehow
it wasn't possible. The son-in-law didn't judge her. He had to be under
pressure, too. Was she bringing everyone in the house down? Is that
why he was reading Schopenhauer? No, Schopenhauer was his favorite.
"Someone had to come out and tell it like it is," he would say of the
dour old man with muttonchops whose picture he had pasted on the
refrigerator. From what she picked up from the son-in-law, Schopenhauer wrote his major work by his twenty-sixth birthday — a philosophy that was ignored almost entirely in his lifetime and even now, in
this day and age, it was thought to be more of a work of art than
philosophy in the truest sense. A work of art? Why, it seemed irrefuta-
ble! According to the son-in-law, Schopenhauer spent the majority of
his life in shabby rooms in the old genteel section of Frankfurt, Germany, that he shared with successions of poodles to keep him company
while he read, reflected, and wrote about life at his leisure. He had some
kind of small inheritance, just enough to get by, take in the concerts, do
a little traveling now and then. He was well versed in several languages.
He read virtually everything written from the Greeks on upward, including the Eastern writers, a classical scholar, and had the mind to
chew things over and make something of the puzzle of life. The son-in-
law, eager to discourse, said Freud called Schopenhauer one of the six
greatest men who ever lived. Nietzsche, Thomas Mann, and Richard
Wagner all paid tribute to this genius who had been written off with
one word — pessimist. The son-in-law lamented that his works were
going out of print, becoming increasingly harder to find. He was plan-

ning a trip to Frankfurt, where he hoped to find a little bust of his hero. He had written to officials in Germany making inquiries. They had given him the brushoff. He'd have to fly over himself. And she, too, began to worry that the works of this writer would no longer be available . . . she, who would be worms' meat any day.

Why? Because the *truth* was worthwhile. It was more important than anything, really. She'd had ten years of peaceful retirement, time to think, wonder, contemplate, and had come up with nothing. But new vistas of thought had been opened by the curiously ignored genius with the white muttonchops, whose books were harder and harder to get and whom the world would consider a mere footnote from the nineteenth century — a crank, a guy with an ax to grind, a hypochondriac, a misogynist, an alarmist who slept with pistols under his pillow, a man with many faults. Well, check anyone out and what do you find?

For God's sake, how were you supposed to make any sense out of this crazy-ass shit called life? If only she could simply push a button and never have been born.

The son-in-law took antidepressants and claimed to be a melancholiac, yet he always seemed upbeat, comical, ready with a laugh. He had a sense of the absurd that she had found annoying back in the old days when she liked to pretend that life was a stroll down Primrose Lane. If she wasn't walking down the "sunny side of the street" at least she was "singin' in the rain." Those were the days.

What a fool!

She encouraged the son-in-law to clown and philosophize, and he flourished when she voiced a small dose of appreciation or barked out a laugh. There was more and more pain and discomfort, but she was laughing more too. Schopenhauer: "No rose without a thorn. But many a thorn without a rose." The son-in-law finessed all of the ugly details that were impossible for her. Of all the people to come through!

With her lungs temporarily clear and mineral oil enemas to regulate her, she asked her daughter one last favor. Could they take her home just once more?

They made an occasion of it and drove her up into the mountains for her granddaughter's seventh birthday party. Almost everyone in the picturesque resort town was there, and if they were appalled by her deterioration they did not show it. She couldn't go out on the sun porch, had to semi-recline on the couch, but everyone came in to say hello and all of the bad stuff fell away for . . . an entire afternoon! She was deeply touched by the warm affection of her friends. There were . . .

so many of them. My God! They loved her, truly they did. She could see it. You couldn't bullshit her anymore; she could see deep into the human heart; she knew what people were. What wonderful friends. What a perfect afternoon. It was the last . . . good thing.

When she got back to her daughter's she began to die in earnest. It was in the lungs and the bowel, much as the doctor said it would be. Hell, it was probably in the liver even. She was getting yellow, not just the skin but even the whites of her eyes. There was a week in the hospital, where they tormented her with tests. That wiped out the last of her physical and emotional stamina.

She fouled her bed after a barium lower G.I. practically turned to cement and they had to give her a powerful enema. Diarrhea in the bed. The worst humiliation. "Happens all the time, don't worry," the orderly said.

She was suffocating. She couldn't get the least bit of air. All the main players were in the room. She knew this was it! Just like that. Bingo! There were whispered conferences outside her room. Suddenly the nurses, those heretofore angels of mercy, began acting mechanically. They could look you over and peg you, down to the last five minutes. She could see them give her that *anytime now* look. A minister dropped in. There! That was the tip-off — the fat lady was singing.

When the son-in-law showed up instead of going to work she looked to him with panic. She'd been fighting it back but now . . . he was there, he would know what to do without being asked, and in a moment he was back with a nurse. They cranked up the morphine sulfate, flipped it on full-bore. Still her back hurt like hell. All that morphine and a backache . . . just give it a minute . . . ahhh! Cartoons.

Someone went out to get hamburgers at McDonald's. Her daughter sat next to her holding her hand. She felt sorry for them. They were the ones who were going to have to stay behind and play out their appointed roles. Like Schopenhauer said, the best they would be able to do for themselves was to secure a little room as far away from the fire as possible, for Hell was surely in the here and now, not in the hereafter. Or was it?

She began to nod. She was holding onto a carton of milk. It would spill. Like diarrhea-in-the-bed all over again. Another mess. The daughter tried to take the carton of milk away. She . . . held on defiantly. Forget the Schopenhauer — what a lot of crap that was! She did not want to cross over. She wanted to live! She wanted to live!

The daughter wrenched the milk away. The nurse came back and cranked up the morphine again. They were going for "comfort." Finally the backache . . . the cartoons . . . all of that was gone.

(She was back on the farm in Battle Lake, Minnesota. She was nine years old and she could hear her little red rooster, Mr. Barnes, crowing at first light. Then came her brother's heavy work boots clomping downstairs and the vacuum swoosh as he opened up the storm door, and then his boots crunch-crunching through the frozen snow. Yes, she was back on the farm all right. Her brother was making for the outhouse and presently Barnes would go after him, make a dive-bomb attack. You couldn't discourage Mr. Barnes. She heard her brother curse him and the thwap of the tin feed pan hitting the bird. Mr. Barnes's frontal assaults were predictable. From the sound of it, Fred walloped him good. As far as Mr. Barnes was concerned, it was his barnyard. In a moment she heard the outhouse door slam shut and another tin thwap. That Barnes — he was something. She should have taken a lesson. Puffed out her chest and walked through life — "I want the biggest and the best and the most of whatever you've got!" There were people who pulled it off. You really could do it if you had the attitude.

Her little red rooster was a mean little scoundrel, but he had a soft spot for her in his heart of steel and he looked out for her, cooed for her and her alone. Later, when young men came to see her, they soon arranged to meet her thereafter at the drugstore soda fountain uptown. One confrontation with Barnes, even for experienced farm boys, was one too many. He was some kind of rooster all right, an eccentric. Yeah, she was back on the farm. She . . . could feel her sister shifting awake in the lower bunk. It was time to get up and milk the cows. Her sister always awoke in good humor. Not her. She was cozy under a feather comforter and milking the cows was the last thing she wanted to do. Downstairs she could hear her mother speaking cheerfully to her brother as he came back inside, cursing the damn rooster, threatening to kill it. Her mother laughed it off; she didn't have a mean bone in her body.

She . . . could smell bacon in the pan, the coffee pot was percolating, and her grandmother was up heating milk for her Ovaltine. She hated Ovaltine, particularly when her grandmother overheated the milk — burned it — but she pretended to like it, insisted that she needed it for her bones, and forced it down so she could save up enough labels to get a free decoder ring to get special messages from Captain Cody, that intrepid hero of the airwaves. She really wanted to have that ring, but there was a Great Depression and money was very dear, so she never got the decoder or the secret messages or the degree in pharmacology. Had she been more like that little banty rooster, had she been a real go-getter . . . Well — it was all but over now.)

The main players were assembled in the room. She . . . was nodding in and out but she could hear. There she was, in this apparent stupor, but she was more aware than anyone could know. She heard someone say somebody at McDonald's put "everything" on her hamburger instead of "cheese and ketchup only." They were making an issue out of it. One day, when they were in her shoes, they would learn to ignore this kind of petty stuff, but you couldn't blame them. That was how things were, that's all. Life. That was it. That was what it was. And here she lay . . . dying.

Suddenly she realized that the hard part was all over now. All she had to do was . . . let go. It really wasn't so bad. It wasn't . . . anything special. It just was. She was trying to bring back Barnes one last time — that little memory of him had been fun, why not go out with a little fun? She tried to remember his coloring — orange would be too bright, rust too drab, scarlet too vivid. His head was a combination of green, yellow, and gold, all blended, and his breast and wings a kind of carmine red? No, not carmine. He was just a little red rooster, overly pugnacious, an ingrate. He could have been a beautiful bird if he hadn't gotten into so many fights. He got his comb ripped off by a raccoon he'd caught stealing eggs in the henhouse, a big bull raccoon that Barnes had fought tooth and nail until Fred ran into the henhouse with his .410 and killed the thieving intruder. Those eggs were precious. They were income. Mr. Barnes was a hero that day. She remembered how he used to strut around the barnyard. He always had his eye on all of the hens; they were his main priority, some thirty to forty of them, depending. They were his harem and he was the sheik. Boy, was he ever. She remembered jotting down marks on a pad of paper one day when she was home sick with chicken pox. Each mark represented an act of rooster fornication. In less than a day, Mr. Barnes had committed the sexual act forty-seven times that she could see — and she didn't have the whole lay of the land from her window by any means. Why, he often went out roving and carousing with hens on other farms. There were bitter complaints from the neighbors. Barnes really could stir things up. She had to go out on her bicycle and round him up. Mr. Barnes was a legend in the county. Mr. Barnes thought the whole world belonged to him and beyond that

— the suns, the stars, and the Milky Way — all of it! Did it feel good or was it torment? It must have been a glorious feeling, she decided. Maybe that was what Arthur Schopenhauer was driving at in his theory about the Will to Live. Mr. Barnes was the very personification of it.

Of course it was hard work being a rooster, but Barnes seemed the happiest creature she had ever known. Probably because when you're doing what you really want to do, it isn't work. No matter how dull things got on the farm, she could watch Barnes by the hour. Barnes could even redeem a hot, dog-day afternoon in August. He wasn't afraid of anything or anybody. Did he ever entertain a doubt? Some kind of rooster worry? Never! She tried to conjure up one last picture of him. He was just a little banty, couldn't have weighed three pounds. Maybe Mr. Barnes would be waiting for her on the other side and would greet her there and be her friend again.

She nodded in and out. In and out. The morphine was getting to be too much. Oh, please God. She hoped she wouldn't puke . . . So much left unsaid, undone. Well, that was all part of it. If only she could see Barnes strut his stuff one last time. "Come on, Barnes. Strut your stuff for me." Her brother, Fred, sitting there so sad with his hamburger. After a couple of beers, he could do a pretty good imitation of Mr. Barnes. Could he . . . would he . . . for old time's sake? Her voice was too weak, she couldn't speak. Nowhere near. Not even close. Was she dead already? Fading to black? It was hard to tell. "Don't feel bad, my darling brother. Don't mourn for me. I'm okay" . . . and . . . one last thing — "Sarah, I do love you, darling! Love you! Didn't you know that? Didn't it show? If not, I'm so, so very sorry . . ." But the words wouldn't come — couldn't come. She . . . was so sick. You can get only so sick and then there was all that dope. Love! She should have shown it to her daughter instead of . . . assuming. She should have been more demonstrative, more forthcoming. . . . That's what it was all about. *Love your brother as yourself and love the Lord God almighty with all your heart and mind and soul.* You were sent here to love your brother. Do your best. Be kind to animals, obey the Ten Commandments, stuff like that. Was that it? Huh? Or was that all a lot of horseshit?

She . . . nodded in and out. Back and forth. In and out. She went back and forth. In and out. Back and forth . . . in and out. There wasn't any tunnel or white light or any of that. She just . . . died.

1994

*Alice Elliott Dark*

......................................................................................................

# In the Gloaming

FROM *The New Yorker*

HER SON wanted to talk again, suddenly. During the days, he still brooded, scowling at the swimming pool from the vantage point of his wheelchair, where he sat covered with blankets despite the summer heat. In the evenings, though, Laird became more like his old self — his *old* old self, really. He became sweeter, the way he'd been as a child, before he began to cloak himself with layers of irony and clever remarks. He spoke with an openness that astonished her. No one she knew talked that way — no man, at least. After he was asleep, Janet would run through the conversations in her mind, and realize what it was she wished she had said. She knew she was generally considered sincere, but that had more to do with her being a good listener than with how she expressed herself. She found it hard work to keep up with him, but it was the work she had pined for all her life.

A month earlier, after a particularly long and grueling visit with a friend who'd come up on the train from New York, Laird had declared a new policy: no visitors, no telephone calls. She didn't blame him. People who hadn't seen him for a while were often shocked to tears by his appearance, and, rather than having them cheer him up, he felt obliged to comfort them. She'd overheard bits of some of those conversations. The final one was no worse than the others, but he was fed up. He had said more than once that he wasn't cut out to be the brave one, the one who would inspire everybody to walk away from a visit with him feeling uplifted, shaking their heads in wonder. He had liked being the most handsome and missed it very much; he was not a good victim. When he had had enough he went into a self-imposed retreat, complete with a wall of silence and other ascetic practices that kept him busy for several weeks.

Then he softened. Not only did he want to talk again; he wanted to talk to *her.*

It began the night they ate outside on the terrace for the first time all summer. Afterward, Martin — Laird's father — got up to make a telephone call, but Janet stayed in her wicker chair, resting before clearing the table. It was one of those moments when she felt nostalgic for cigarettes. On nights like this, when the air was completely still, she used to blow her famous smoke rings for the children, dutifully obeying their commands to blow one through another or three in a row, or to make big, ropy circles that expanded as they floated up to the heavens. She did exactly what they wanted, for as long as they wanted, sometimes going through a quarter of a pack before they allowed her to stop. Incredibly, neither Anne nor Laird became smokers. Just the opposite; they nagged at her to quit, and were pleased when she finally did. She wished they had been just a little bit sorry; it was a part of their childhood coming to an end, after all.

Out of habit, she took note of the first lightning bug, the first star. The lawn darkened, and the flowers that had sulked in the heat all day suddenly released their perfumes. She laid her head back on the rim of the chair and closed her eyes. Soon she was following Laird's breathing, and found herself picking up the vital rhythms, breathing along. It was so peaceful, being near him like this. How many mothers spend so much time with their thirty-three-year-old sons? she thought. She had as much of him now as she had had when he was an infant; more, in a way, because she had the memory of the intervening years as well, to round out her thoughts about him. When they sat quietly together she felt as close to him as she ever had. It was still him in there, inside the failing shell. *She still enjoyed him.*

"The gloaming," he said, suddenly.

She nodded dreamily, automatically, then sat up. She turned to him. "What?" Although she had heard.

"I remember when I was little you took me over to the picture window and told me that in Scotland this time of day was called the 'gloaming.'"

Her skin tingled. She cleared her throat, quietly, taking care not to make too much of an event of his talking again. "You thought I said 'gloomy.'"

He gave a smile, then looked at her searchingly. "I always thought it hurt you somehow that the day was over, but you said it was a beautiful time because for a few moments the purple light made the whole world look like the Scottish Highlands on a summer night."

"Yes. As if all the earth were covered with heather."

"I'm sorry I never saw Scotland," he said.

"You're a Scottish lad nonetheless," she said. "At least on my side." She remembered offering to take him to Scotland once, but Laird hadn't been interested. By then, he was in college and already sure of his own destinations, which had diverged so thoroughly from hers. "I'm amazed you remember that conversation. You couldn't have been more than seven."

"I've been remembering a lot lately."

"Have you?"

"Mostly about when I was very small. I suppose it comes from having you take care of me again. Sometimes, when I wake up and see your face, I feel I can remember you looking in on me when I was in my crib. I remember your dresses."

"Oh, no!" She laughed lightly.

"You always had the loveliest expressions," he said.

She was astonished, caught off guard. Then, she had a memory, too — of her leaning over Laird's crib and suddenly having a picture of looking up at her own mother. "I know what you mean," she said.

"You do, don't you?"

He looked at her in a close, intimate way that made her self-conscious. She caught herself swinging her leg nervously, like a pendulum, and stopped.

"Mom," he said. "There are still a few things I need to do. I have to write a will, for one thing."

Her heart went flat. In his presence she had always maintained that he would get well. She wasn't sure she could discuss the other possibility.

"Thank you," he said.

"For what?"

"For not saying that there's plenty of time for that, or some similar sentiment."

"The only reason I didn't say it was to avoid the cliché, not because I don't believe it."

"You believe there is plenty of time?"

She hesitated; he noticed, and leaned forward slightly. "I believe there is time," she said.

"Even if I were healthy, it would be a good idea."

"I suppose."

"I don't want to leave it until it's too late. You wouldn't want me to suddenly leave everything to the nurses, would you?"

She laughed, pleased to hear him joking again. "All right, all right, I'll call the lawyer."

"That would be great." There was a pause. "Is this still your favorite time of day, Mom?"

"Yes, I suppose it is," she said, "although I don't think in terms of favorites anymore."

"Never mind favorites, then. What else do you like?"

"What do you mean?" she asked.

"I mean exactly that."

"I don't know. I care about all the ordinary things. You know what I like."

"Name one thing."

"I feel silly."

"Please?"

"All right. I like my patch of lilies of the valley under the trees over there. Now can we change the subject?"

"Name one more thing."

"Why?"

"I want to get to know you."

"Oh, Laird, there's nothing to know."

"I don't believe that for a minute."

"But it's true. I'm average. The only extraordinary thing about me is my children."

"All right," he said. "Then let's talk about how you feel about me."

"Do you flirt with your nurses like this when I'm not around?"

"I don't dare. They've got me where they want me." He looked at her. "You're changing the subject."

She smoothed her skirt. "I know how you feel about church, but if you need to talk I'm sure the minister would be glad to come over. Or if you would rather have a doctor . . ."

He laughed.

"What?"

"That you still call psychiatrists 'doctors.'"

She shrugged.

"I don't need a professional, Ma." He laced his hands and pulled at them as he struggled for words.

"What can I do?" she asked.

He met her gaze. "You're where I come from. I need to know about you."

That night she lay awake, trying to think of how she could help, of what, aside from her time, she had to offer. She couldn't imagine.

She was anxious the next day when he was sullen again, but the next night, and on each succeeding night, the dusk worked its spell. She set dinner on the table outside, and afterward, when Martin had vanished into the maw of his study, she and Laird began to speak. The air around them seemed to crackle with the energy they were creating in their effort to know and be known. Were other people so close, she wondered. She never had been, not to anybody. Certainly she and Martin had never really connected, not soul to soul, and with her friends, no matter how loyal and reliable, she always had a sense of what she could do that would alienate them. Of course, her friends had the option of cutting her off, and Martin could always ask for a divorce, whereas Laird was a captive audience. Parents and children were all captive audiences to each other; in view of this, it was amazing how little comprehension there was of one another's stories. Everyone stopped paying attention so early on, thinking they had figured it all out. She recognized that she was as guilty of this as anyone. She was still surprised whenever she went over to her daughter's house and saw how neat she was; in her mind, Anne was still a sloppy teenager who threw sweaters into the corner of her closet and candy wrappers under her bed. It still surprised her that Laird wasn't interested in girls. He had been, hadn't he? She remembered lying awake listening for him to come home, hoping that he was smart enough to apply what he knew about the facts of life, to take precautions.

Now she had the chance to let go of these old notions. It wasn't that she liked everything about Laird — there was much that remained foreign to her — but she wanted to know about all of it. As she came to her senses every morning in the moment or two after she awoke, she found herself aching with love and gratitude, as if he were a small, perfect creature again and she could look forward to a day of watching him grow. Quickly, she became greedy for their evenings. She replaced her half-facetious, half-hopeful reading of the horoscope in the daily newspaper with a new habit of tracking the time the sun would set, and drew satisfaction from seeing it come earlier as the summer waned; it meant she didn't have to wait as long. She took to sleeping late, shortening the day even more. It was ridiculous, she knew. She was behaving like a girl with a crush, behaving absurdly. It was a feeling she had thought she'd never have again, and now here it was. She immersed herself in it, living her life for the twilight moment when his eyes would begin to glow, the signal that he was stirring into consciousness. Then her real day would begin.

"Dad ran off quickly," he said one night. She had been wondering when he would mention it.

"He had a phone call to make," she said automatically.

Laird looked directly into her eyes, his expression one of gentle reproach. He was letting her know he had caught her in the central lie of her life, which was that she understood Martin's obsession with his work. She averted her gaze. The truth was that she had never understood. Why couldn't he sit with her for half an hour after dinner, or, if not with her, why not with his dying son?

She turned sharply to look at Laird. The word "dying" had sounded so loudly in her mind that she wondered if she had spoken it, but he showed no reaction. She wished she hadn't even thought it. She tried to stick to good thoughts in his presence. When she couldn't, and he had a bad night afterward, she blamed herself, as her efficient memory dredged up all the books and magazine articles she had read emphasizing the effect of psychological factors on the course of the disease. She didn't entirely believe it, but she felt compelled to give the benefit of the doubt to every theory that might help. It couldn't do any harm to think positively. And if it gave him a few more months . . .

"I don't think Dad can stand to be around me."

"That's not true." It was true.

"Poor Dad. He's always been a hypochondriac — we have that in common. He must hate this."

"He just wants you to get well."

"If that's what he wants, I'm afraid I'm going to disappoint him again. At least this will be the last time I let him down."

He said this merrily, with the old, familiar light darting from his eyes. She allowed herself to be amused. He had always been fond of teasing, and held no subject sacred. As the de facto authority figure in the house — Martin hadn't been home enough to be the real disciplinarian — she had often been forced to reprimand Laird, but, in truth, she shared his sense of humor. She responded to it now by leaning over to cuff him on the arm. It was an automatic response, prompted by a burst of high spirits that took no notice of the circumstances. It was a mistake. Even through the thickness of his terrycloth robe, her knuckles knocked on bone. There was nothing left of him.

"It's his loss," she said, the shock of Laird's thinness making her serious again. It was the furthest she would go in criticizing Martin. She had always felt it her duty to maintain a benign image of him for the children. He had become a character of her invention, with a whole range of postulated emotions whereby he missed them when he was away on a business trip and thought of them every few minutes when he had to work late. Some years earlier, when she was secretly seeing a doctor — a psychiatrist — she had finally admitted to herself that Martin was never going to be the lover she had dreamed of. He was an ambitious, competitive, self-absorbed man who probably should never have got married. It was such a relief to be able to face it that she wanted to share the news with her children, only to discover that they were dependent on the myth. They could hate his work, but they could not bring themselves to believe he had any choice in the matter. She had dropped the subject.

"Thank you, Ma. It's his loss in your case, too."

A throbbing began behind her eyes, angering her. The last thing she wanted to do was cry. There would be plenty of time for that. "It's not all his fault," she said when she had regained some measure of control. "I'm not very good at talking about myself. I was brought up not to."

"So was I," he said.

"Yes, I suppose you were."

"Luckily, I didn't pay any attention." He grinned.

"I hope not," she said, and meant it. "Can I get you anything?"

"A new immune system?"

She rolled her eyes, trying to disguise the way his joke had touched on her prayers. "Very funny. I was thinking more along the lines of an iced tea or an extra blanket."

"I'm fine. I'm getting tired, actually."

Her entire body went on the alert, and she searched his face anxiously for signs of deterioration. Her nerves darted and pricked whenever he wanted anything; her adrenaline rushed. The fight-or-flight response, she supposed. She had often wanted to flee, but had forced herself to stay, to fight with what few weapons she had. She responded to his needs, making sure there was a fresh, clean set of sheets ready when he was tired, food when he was hungry. It was what she could do.

"Shall I get a nurse?" She pushed her chair back from the table.

"O.K.," Laird said weakly. He stretched out his hand to her, and the incipient moonlight illuminated his skin so it shone like alabaster. His face had turned ashy. It was a sight that made her stomach drop. She ran for Maggie, and by the time they returned Laird's eyes were closed, his head lolling to one side. Automatically, Janet looked for a stirring in his chest. There it was: his shoulders expanded; he still breathed. Always, in the second before she saw movement, she became cold and clinical as she braced herself for the possibility of discovering that he was dead.

Maggie had her fingers on his wrist and was counting his pulse against the second hand on her watch, her lips moving. She laid his limp hand back on his lap. "Fast," she pronounced.

"I'm not surprised," Janet said, masking her fear with authority. "We had a long talk."

Maggie frowned. "Now I'll have to wake him up again for his meds."

"Yes, I suppose that's true. I forgot about that."

Janet wheeled him into his makeshift room downstairs and helped Maggie lift him into the rented hospital bed. Although he weighed almost nothing, it was really a job for two; his weight was dead weight. In front of Maggie, she was all brusque efficiency, except for the moment when her fingers strayed to touch Laird's pale cheek and she prayed she hadn't done any harm.

"Who's your favorite author?" he asked one night.

"Oh, there are so many," she said.

"Your real favorite."

She thought. "The truth is there are certain subjects I find attractive more than certain authors. I seem to read in cycles, to fulfill an emotional yearning."

"Such as?"

"Books about people who go off to live in Africa or Australia or the South Seas."

He laughed. "That's fairly self-explanatory. What else?"

"When I really hate life I enjoy books about real murders. 'True crime,' I think they're called now. They're very punishing."

"Is that what's so compelling about them? I could never figure it out. I just know that at certain times I loved the gore, even though I felt absolutely disgusted with myself for being interested in it."

"You need to think about when those times were. That will tell you a lot." She paused. "I don't like reading about sex."

"Big surprise!"

"No, no," she said. "It's not for the reason you think, or not only for that reason. You see me as a prude, I know, but remember, it's part of a mother's job to come across that way. Although perhaps I went a bit far . . ."

He shrugged amiably. "Water under the bridge. But go on about sex."

"I think it should be private. I always feel as though these writers are showing off when they describe a sex scene. They're not really trying to describe sex, but to demonstrate that they're not afraid to write about it. As if they're thumbing their noses at their mothers."

He made a moue.

Janet went on. "You don't think there's an element of that? I *do* question their motives, because I don't think sex can ever actually be portrayed — the sensations and the emotions are . . . beyond language. If you only describe the mechanics, the effect is either clinical or pornographic, and if you try to describe intimacy instead, you wind up with abstractions. The only sex you could describe fairly well is bad sex — and who wants to read about that, for God's sake, when everyone is having bad sex of their own?"

"Mother!" He was laughing helplessly, his arms hanging limply over the sides of his chair.

"I mean it. To me it's like reading about someone using the bathroom."

"Good grief!"

"Now who's the prude?"

"I never said I wasn't," he said. "Maybe we should change the subject."

She looked out across the land. The lights were on in other people's houses, giving the evening the look of early fall. The leaves were different, too, becoming droopy. The grass was dry, even with all the watering and tending from the gardener. The summer was nearly over.

"Maybe we shouldn't," she said. "I've been wondering. Was that side of life satisfying for you?"

"Ma, tell me you're not asking me about my sex life."

She took her napkin and folded it carefully, lining up the edges and running her fingers along the hems. She felt very calm, very pulled together and all of a piece, as if she'd finally got the knack of being a dignified woman. She threaded her fingers and laid her hands in her lap. "I'm asking about your love life," she said. "Did you love, and were you loved in return?"

"Yes."

"I'm glad."

"That was easy," he said.

"Oh, I've gotten very easy, in my old age."

"Does Dad know about this?" His eyes were twinkling wickedly.

"Don't be fresh," she said.

"You started it."

"Then I'm stopping it. Now."

He made a funny face, and then another, until she could no longer keep from smiling. His routine carried her back to memories of his childhood efforts to charm her: watercolors of her favorite vistas (unrecognizable without the captions), bouquets of violets self-consciously flung into her lap, chores performed without prompting. He had always gone too far, then backtracked to regain even footing. She had always allowed herself to be wooed.

Suddenly she realized: Laird had been the love of her life.

One night it rained hard. Janet decided to serve the meal in the kitchen, since Martin was out. They ate in silence; she was freed from the compulsion to keep up the steady stream of chatter that she used to affect when Laird hadn't talked at all; now she knew she could save her words for afterward. He ate nothing but comfort foods lately: mashed potatoes, vanilla ice cream, rice pudding. The days of his strict macrobiotic regime, and all the cooking classes she had taken in order to help him along with it, were past. His body was essentially a thing of the past, too; when he ate, he was feeding what was left of his mind. He seemed to want to recapture the cosseted feeling he'd had when he'd been sick as a child and she would serve him flat ginger ale, and toast soaked in cream, and play endless card games with him, using his blanket-covered legs as a table. In those days, too, there'd been a general sense of giving way to illness: then, he let himself go completely because he knew he would soon be better and active and have a million things expected of him again. Now he let himself go because he had fought long enough.

Finally, he pushed his bowl toward the middle of the table, signaling that he was finished. (His table manners had gone to pieces. Who cared?) She felt a light, jittery excitement, the same jazzy feeling she got when she was in a plane that was picking up speed on the runway. She arranged her fork and knife on the rim of her plate and pulled her chair in closer. "I had an odd dream last night," she said.

His eyes remained dull.

She waited uncertainly, thinking that perhaps she had started to talk too soon. "Would you like something else to eat?"

He shook his head. There was no will in his expression; his refusal was purely physical, a gesture coming from the satiation in his stomach. An animal walking away from its bowl, she thought.

To pass the time, she carried the dishes to the sink, gave them a good hot rinse, and put them in the dishwasher. She carried the ice cream to the counter, pulled a spoon from the drawer and scraped off a mouthful of the thick, creamy residue that stuck to the inside of the lid. She ate it without thinking, so the sudden sweetness caught her by surprise. All the while she kept track of Laird, but every time she thought she noticed signs of his readiness to talk and hurried back to the table, she found his face still blank.

She went to the window. The lawn had become a floodplain and was filled with broad pools; the branches of the evergreens sagged, and the sky was the same uniform grayish yellow it had been since morning. She saw him focus his gaze on the line where the treetops touched the heavens, and she understood. There was no lovely interlude on this rainy night, no heathered dusk. The gray landscape had taken the light out of him.

"I'm sorry," she said aloud, as if it were her fault.

He gave a tiny, helpless shrug.

She hovered for a few moments, hoping, but his face was slack, and she gave up. She felt utterly forsaken, too disappointed and agitated to sit with him and watch the rain. "It's all right," she said. "It's a good night to watch television."

She wheeled him to the den and left him with Maggie, then did not know what to do with herself. She had no contingency plan for this time. It was usually the one period of the day when she did not need the anesthesia of tennis games, bridge lessons, volunteer work, errands. She had not considered the present possibility. For some time, she hadn't given any thought to what Martin would call "the big picture." Her conversations with Laird had lulled her into inventing a parallel big picture of her own. She realized that a part of her had worked out a whole scenario: the summer evenings would blend into fall; then, gradually, the winter would arrive, heralding chats by the fire, Laird resting his feet on the pigskin ottoman in the den while she dutifully knitted her yearly Christmas sweaters for Anne's children.

She had allowed herself to imagine a future. That had been her mistake. This silent, endless evening was her punishment, a reminder of how things really were.

She did not know where to go in her own house, and ended up wandering through the rooms, propelled by a vague, hunted feeling. Several times, she turned around, expecting someone to be there, but, of course, no one ever was. She was quite alone. Eventually, she realized that she was imagining a person in order to give material properties to the source of her wounds. She was inventing a villain. There should be a villain, shouldn't there? There should be an enemy, a devil, an evil force that could be driven out. Her imagination had provided it with aspects of a corporeal presence so she could pretend, for a moment, that there was a real enemy hovering around her, someone she could have the police come and take away. But the enemy was part of Laird, and neither he nor she nor any of the doctors or experts or ministers could separate the two.

She went upstairs and took a shower. She barely paid attention to her own body anymore, and only noticed abstractly that the water was too hot, her skin turning pink. Afterward, she sat on the chaise longue in her bedroom and tried to read. She heard something; she leaned forward and cocked her head toward the sound. Was that Laird's voice? Suddenly she believed that he had begun to talk after all — she believed he was talking to Maggie. She dressed and went downstairs. He was alone in the den, alone with the television. He didn't hear or see her. She watched him take a drink from a cup, his hand shaking badly. It was a plastic cup with a straw poking through the lid, the kind used by small children while they are learning to drink. It was supposed to prevent accidents, but it couldn't stop his hands from trembling. He managed to spill the juice anyway.

Laird had always coveted the decadent pile of cashmere lap blankets she had collected over the years in the duty-free shops of the various British airports. Now he wore one around his shoulders, one over his knees. She remembered similar balmy nights when he would arrive home from soccer practice after dark, a towel slung around his neck.

"I suppose it has to be in the church," he said.

"I think it should," she said, "but it's up to you."

"I guess it's not the most timely moment to make a statement about

my personal disbeliefs. But I'd like you to keep it from being too lugu-
brious. No lilies, for instance."

"God forbid."

"And have some decent music."

"Such as?"

"I had an idea, but now I can't remember."

He pressed his hands to his eyes. His fingers were so transparent that
they looked as if he were holding them over a flashlight.

"Please buy a smashing dress, something mournful yet elegant."

"All right."

"And don't wait until the last minute."

She didn't reply.

Janet gave up on the idea of a rapprochement between Martin and
Laird; she felt freer when she stopped hoping for it. Martin rarely came
home for dinner anymore. Perhaps he was having an affair? It was a
thought she'd never allowed herself to have before, but it didn't threaten
her now. Good for him, she even decided, in her strongest, most mag-
nanimous moments. Good for him if he's actually feeling bad and
trying to do something to make himself feel better.

Anne was brave and chipper during her visits, yet when she walked
back out to her car, she would wrap her arms around her ribs and
shudder. "I don't know how you do it, Mom. Are you really all right?"
she always asked, with genuine concern.

"Anne's become such a hopeless matron," Laird always said, with
fond exasperation, when he and his mother were alone again later.
Once, Janet began to tease him for finally coming to friendly terms with
his sister, but she cut it short when she saw that he was blinking furiously.

They were exactly the children she had hoped to have: a companionable girl, a mischievous boy. It gave her great pleasure to see them
together. She did not try to listen to their conversations but watched
from a distance, usually from the kitchen as she prepared them a snack
reminiscent of their childhood, like watermelon boats or lemonade.
Then she would walk Anne to the car, their similar good shoes clacking
across the gravel. They hugged, pressing each other's arms, and their
brief embraces buoyed them up — forbearance and grace passing back
and forth between them like a piece of shared clothing, designated for
use by whoever needed it most. It was the kind of parting toward which
she had aimed her whole life, a graceful, secure parting at the close of a

peaceful afternoon. After Anne left, Janet always had a tranquil moment or two as she walked back to the house through the humid September air. Everything was so still. Occasionally there were the hums and clicks of a lawnmower or the shrieks of a band of children heading home from school. There were the insects and the birds. It was a straightforward, simple life she had chosen. She had tried never to ask for too much, and to be of use. Simplicity had been her hedge against bad luck. It had worked for so long. For a brief moment, as she stepped lightly up the single slate stair and through the door, her legs still harboring all their former vitality, she could pretend her luck was still holding.

Then she would glance out the window and there would be the heart-catching sight of Laird, who would never again drop by for a casual visit. Her chest would ache and flutter, a cave full of bats.

Perhaps she had asked for too much, after all.

"What did you want to be when you grew up?" Laird asked.

"I was expected to be a wife and mother. I accepted that. I wasn't a rebel."

"There must have been something else."

"No," she said. "Oh, I guess I had all the usual fantasies of the day, of being the next Amelia Earhart or Margaret Mead, but that was all they were — fantasies. I wasn't even close to being brave enough. Can you imagine me flying across the ocean on my own?" She laughed and looked over for his laughter, but he had fallen asleep.

A friend of Laird's had somehow got the mistaken information that Laird had died, so she and Martin received a condolence letter. There was a story about a time a few years back when the friend was with Laird on a bus in New York. They had been sitting behind two older women, waitresses who began to discuss their income taxes, trying to decide how much of their tip income to declare to sound realistic so they wouldn't attract an audit. Each woman offered up bits of folk wisdom on the subject, describing in detail her particular situation. During a lull in the conversation, Laird stood up.

"Excuse me, I couldn't help overhearing," he said, leaning over them. "May I have your names and addresses, please? I work for the IRS."

The entire bus fell silent as everyone watched to see what would happen next. Laird took a small notebook and pen from the inside pocket of his jacket. He faced his captive audience. "I'm part of a new IRS outreach program," he told the group. "For the next ten minutes

I'll be taking confessions. Does anyone have anything he or she wants to tell me?"

Smiles. Soon the whole bus was talking, comparing notes — when they'd first realized he was kidding, and how scared they had been before they caught on. It was difficult to believe these were the same New Yorkers who were supposed to be so gruff and isolated.

"Laird was the most vital, funniest person I ever met," his friend wrote.

Now, in his wheelchair, he faced off against slow-moving flies, waving them away.

"The gloaming," Laird said.

Janet looked up from her knitting, startled. It was midafternoon, and the living room was filled with bright October sun. "Soon," she said.

He furrowed his brow. A little flash of confusion passed through his eyes, and she realized that for him it was already dark.

He tried to straighten his shawl, his hands shaking. She jumped up to help; then, when he pointed to the fireplace, she quickly laid the logs as she wondered what was wrong. Was he dehydrated? She thought she recalled that a dimming of vision was a sign of dehydration. She tried to remember what else she had read or heard, but even as she grasped for information, facts, her instincts kept interrupting with a deeper, more dreadful thought that vibrated through her, rattling her and making her gasp as she often did when remembering her mistakes, things she wished she hadn't said or done, wished she had the chance to do over. She knew what was wrong, and yet she kept turning away from the truth, her mind spinning in every other possible direction as she worked on the fire, only vaguely noticing how wildly she made the sparks fly as she pumped the old bellows.

Her work was mechanical — she had made hundreds of fires — and soon there was nothing left to do. She put the screen up and pushed him close, then leaned over to pull his flannel pajamas down to meet his socks, protecting his bare shins. The sun streamed in around him, making him appear trapped between bars of light. She resumed her knitting, with mechanical hands.

"The gloaming," he said again. It did sound somewhat like "gloomy," because his speech was slurred.

"When all the world is purple," she said, hearing herself sound falsely bright. She wasn't sure whether he wanted her to talk. It was some time since he had talked — not long, really, in other people's lives, perhaps two weeks — but she had gone on with their conversations, gradually expanding into the silence until she was telling him stories and he was listening. Sometimes, when his eyes closed, she trailed off and began to drift. There would be a pause that she didn't always realize she was making, but if it went on too long he would call out "Mom?" with an edge of panic in his voice, as if he were waking from a nightmare. Then she would resume, trying to create a seamless bridge between what she had been thinking and where she had left off.

"It was really your grandfather who gave me my love for the gloaming," she said. "Do you remember him talking about it?" She looked up politely, expectantly, as if Laird might offer her a conversational reply. He seemed to like hearing the sound of her voice, so she went on, her needles clicking. Afterward, she could never remember for sure at what point she had stopped talking and had floated off into a jumble of her own thoughts, afraid to move, afraid to look up, afraid to know at which exact moment she became alone. All she knew was that at a certain point the fire was in danger of dying out entirely, and when she got up to stir the embers she glanced at him in spite of herself and saw that his fingers were making knitting motions over his chest, the way people did as they were dying. She knew that if she went to get the nurse, Laird would be gone by the time she returned, so she went and stood behind him, leaning over to press her face against his, sliding her hands down his busy arms, helping him along with his fretful stitches until he finished this last piece of work.

Later, after the most pressing calls had been made and Laird's body had been taken away, Janet went up to his old room and lay down on one of the twin beds. She had changed the room into a guest room when he went off to college, replacing his things with guest room decor, thoughtful touches such as luggage racks at the foot of each bed, a writing desk stocked with paper and pens, heavy wooden hangers and shoe trees. She made an effort to remember the room as it had been when he was a little boy; she had chosen a train motif, then had to redecorate when Laird decided trains were silly. He had wanted it to look like a jungle, so she had hired an art student to paint a jungle mural on the walls. When he decided *that* was silly, he hadn't bothered her to do anything about it, but had simply marked time until he could move on.

Anne came over, offered to stay, but was relieved to be sent home to her children.

Presently, Martin came in. Janet was watching the trees turn to mere silhouettes against the darkening sky, fighting the urge to pick up a true-crime book, a debased urge. He lay down on the other bed.

"I'm sorry," he said.

"It's so wrong," she said angrily. She hadn't felt angry until that moment; she had saved it up for him. "A child shouldn't die before his parents. A young man shouldn't spend his early thirties wasting away talking to his mother. He should be out in the world. He shouldn't be thinking about me, or what I care about, or my opinions. He shouldn't have had to return my love to me — it was his to squander. Now I have it all back and I don't know what I'm supposed to do with it," she said.

She could hear Martin weeping in the darkness. He sobbed, and her anger veered away.

They were quiet for some time.

"Is there going to be a funeral?" Martin asked finally.

"Yes. We should start making the arrangements."

"I suppose he told you what he wanted."

"In general. He couldn't decide about the music."

She heard Martin roll onto his side, so that he was facing her across the narrow chasm between the beds. He was still in his office clothes. "I remember being very moved by the bagpipes at your father's funeral."

It was an awkward offering, to be sure, awkward and late, and seemed to come from someone on the periphery of her life who knew her only slightly. It didn't matter; it was perfectly right. Her heart rushed toward it.

"I think Laird would have liked that idea very much," she said.

It was the last moment of the gloaming, the last moment of the day her son died. In a breath, it would be night; the moon hovered behind the trees, already rising to claim the sky, and she told herself she might as well get on with it. She sat up and was running her toes across the bare floor, searching for her shoes, when Martin spoke again, in a tone she used to hear on those long-ago nights when he rarely got home until after the children were in bed and he relied on her to fill him in on what they'd done that day. It was the same curious, shy, deferential tone that had always made her feel as though all the frustrations and bore-dom and mistakes and rushes of feeling in her days as a mother did indeed add up to something of importance, and she decided that the next round of telephone calls could wait while she answered the question he asked her: "Please tell me — what else did my boy like?"

1994

*Carolyn Ferrell*

......................................................................................................

# Proper Library

FROM *Ploughshares*

BOYS, MEN, GIRLS, children, mothers, babies. You got to feed them.
You always got to keep them fed. Winter summer. They always have to
feel satisfied. Winter summer. But then you stop and ask: Where is the
food going to come from? Because it's never-ending, never-stopping.
Where? Because your life is spent on feeding them and you never stop
thinking about where the food is going to come from.

Formula, pancakes, syrup, milk, roast turkey with cornbread stuffing,
Popsicles, love, candy, tongue kisses, hugs, kisses behind backs, hands
on faces, warmth, tenderness, Boston cream pie, fucking in the butt. You
got to feed them, and it's always going to be you. Winter summer.

My ma says to me, Let's practice the words this afternoon when you get
home, baby. I nod to her. I don't have to use any words with her to let
her know I will do what she wants. When family people come over and
they see me and Ma in the kitchen like that with the words, they say she
has the same face as the maid in the movies. She does have big brown
hands like careful shovels, and she loves to touch and pat and warm you
up with them. And when she walks, she shuffles. But if anyone is like the
maid in the movies, it is Aunt Estine. She likes to give mouth, 'specially
when I got the kids on my hands. She's sassy. She's got what people call
a bad attitude. She makes sure you hear her heels clicking all the time,
'specially when you are lying in bed before dawn and thinking things
in order, how you got to keep moving, all day long. Click, click. Ain't
nobody up yet? Click. Lazy-ass Negroes, you better not be 'specting me
to cook y'all breakfast when you do get up! Click, click. I'm hungry.
Click. I don't care what time it is, I'm hungry y'all and I'm tired and

depressed and I need someone to talk to. Well, the hell with all y'all. That's my last word. Click, click, click.

My ma pats her hands on my schoolbag, which is red like a girl's, but that's all right. She pats it like it was my head. The books I have in it are: Biology, Woodworking for You, Math 1, The History of Civilization.

I'm supposed to be in Math 4, but the people keep holding me back. I know it's no real fault of mine. I been teaching the kids Math 4 from a book I took out of the Lending Mobile in the schoolyard. The kids can do most of Math 4. They like the way I teach it to them, with real live explanations, not the kind where you are supposed to have everything already in your head and it's just waiting to come out. And the kids don't ask to see if I get every one right. They trust me. They trust my smart. They just like the feel of the numbers and seeing them on a piece of paper: division of decimals, division of fractions. It's these numbers that keep them moving and that will keep them moving when I am gone. At school I just keep failing the City Wide Tests every May and the people don't ask any questions: they just hold me back. Cousin Cee Cee said, If you wasn't so stupid you would realize the fact of them holding you back till you is normal.

The kids are almost as sad as Ma when I get ready to go to school in the morning. They cry and whine and carry on and ask me if they can sit on my lap just one more time before I go, but Ma is determined. She checks the outside of my books to make sure nothing is spilled over them or that none of the kids have torn out any pages. Things got to be in place. There got to be order if you gonna keep on moving, and Ma knows that deep down. This morning I promise to braid Lasheema's hair right quick before I go, and as I'm braiding, she's steady smiling her four-year-old grin at Shawn, who is a boy and therefore has short hair, almost a clean shave, and who can't be braided and who weeps with every strand I grease, spread, and plait.

Ma warns me, Don't let them boys bother you now, Lorrie. Don't let 'em.

I tell her, Ma, I have not let you down in a long time. I know what I got to do for you.

She smiles but I know it is a fake smile, and she says, Lorrie, you are my only son, the only real man I got. I don't want them boys to get you from me.

I tell her because it's the only thing I can tell her, You cooking up something special tonight?

Ma smiles and goes back to fixing pancake mix from her chair in the kitchen. The kids are on their way to forgetting about me 'cause they love pancakes more than anything and that is the only way I'll get out of here today. Sheniqua already has the bottle of Sugar Shack Syrup and Tonya is holding her plate above her nappy lint head.

Tommy, Lula Jean's Navy husband, meets me at the front door as I open it. Normally he cheers me up by testing me on Math 4 and telling me what a hidden genius I am, a still river running deep, he called it one time. He likes to tell me jokes and read stories from the Bible out loud. And he normally kisses my sister Lula Jean right where I and everybody else can see them, like in the kitchen or in the bedroom on the bed, surrounded by at least nine kids and me, all flaming brown heads and eyes. He always says: This is what love should be. And he searches into Lula Jean's face for whole minutes.

I'm leaving for Jane Addams High School and I meet Tommy and he has a lady tucked under his arm and it ain't Lula Jean. Her hair is wet and smells like mouthwash and I hate him in a flash. I never hate anybody, but now I hate him. I know that when I close the door behind me a wave of mouths will knock Tommy and this new lady down but it won't drown them. My sister Anita walks into the room and notices and carries them off into the bathroom, quick and silent. But before that she kisses me on my cheek and pats her hand, a small one of Ma's, on my chest. She whispers, You are my best man, remember that. She slips a letter knife in my jacket pocket. She says, If that boy puts his thing on you, cut it off. I love you, baby. She pushes me out the door.

Layla Jackson who lives in the downtown Projects and who might have AIDS comes running up to me as I walk out our building's door to the bus stop. She is out of breath. I look at her and could imagine a boy watching her chest heave up and down like that and suddenly get romantic feelings, it being so big and all, split like two kickballs bouncing. I turn my eyes to hers, which are crying. Layla Jackson's eyes are red. She has her baby Tee Tee in her arms but it's cold out here and she doesn't have a blanket on him or nothing. I say to her, Layla, honey, you gonna freeze that baby to death.

And I take my jacket off and put it over him, the tiny bundle.

Layla Jackson says, Thanks Lorrie man I got a favor to ask you please don't tell me no please man.

Layla always makes her words into a worry sandwich.

She says, Man, I need me a new baby sitter 'cause I been took Tee Tee over to my mother's but now she don't want him with the others and now I can't do nothing till I get me a sitter.

I tell her, Layla, I'm going back to school now. I can't watch Tee Tee in the morning but if you leave him with me in the cafeteria after fifth period I'll take him on home with me.

She says, That means I got to take this brat to Introduction to Humanities with me. Shit, man. He's gonna cry and I won't pass the test on Spanish Discoverers. Shit, man.

Then Layla Jackson thinks a minute and says, Okay, Lorrie, I'll give Tee to you at lunch in the cafeteria, bet. And I'll be 'round your place 'round six for him or maybe seven, thanks, man.

Then she bends down and kisses Tee Tee on his forehead and he glows with what I know is drinking up an oasis when you are in the desert for so long. And she turns and walks to the downtown subway, waving at me. At the corner she comes running back because she still has my jacket and Tee Tee is waving the letter knife around like a flag. She says that her cousin Rakeem was looking for me and to let me know he would be waiting for me 'round his way. *Yes.* I say to her, See you, Layla, honey.

Before I used to not go to Jane Addams when I was supposed to. I got in the habit of looking for Rakeem, Layla's cousin, underneath the Bruckner Expressway, where the Spanish women sometimes go to buy oranges and watermelons and apples cheap. He was what you would call a magnet, only I didn't know that then. I didn't understand the different flavors of the pie. I saw him one day and I had a feeling like I wanted him to sit on my lap and cradle me. That's when I had to leave school. Rakeem, he didn't stop me. His voice was just as loud as the trucks heading towards Manhattan on the Bruckner above us: This is where your real world begins, man. The women didn't watch us. We stared each other in the eyes. Rakeem taught me how to be afraid of school and of people watching us. He said, Don't go back, and I didn't. A part of me was saying that his ear was more delicious than Math 4. I didn't go to Jane Addams for six months.

On the BX 17 bus I see Tammy Ferguson and her twins and Joe Smalls and that white girl Laura. She is the only white girl in these Bronx projects that I know of. I feel sorry for her. She has blue eyes and red hair and one time when the B-Crew-Girls were going to beat her butt in front of the building, she broke down crying and told them that her real parents were black from the South. She told them she was really a Negro and they all laughed and that story worked the opposite than we all thought. Laura became their friend, like the B-Crew-Girls' mascot. And now she's still their friend. People may laugh when she ain't around but she's got her back covered. She's loyal and is trying to wear her thin flippy hair in cornrows, which in the old days woulda made the B-Crew, both boys and girls, simply fall out. When Laura's around, the B-Crew-Girls love to laugh. She looks in my direction when I get on the bus and says, Faggot.

She says it loud enough for all the grown-up passengers to hear. They don't look at me, they keep their eyes on whatever their eyes are on, but I know their ears are on me. Tammy Ferguson always swears she would never help a white girl, but now she can't pass up this opportunity, so she says, You tight-ass homo, go suck some faggot dick. Tammy's kids are taking turns making handprints on the bus window.

I keep moving. It's the way I learned: keep moving. I go and sit next to Joe Smalls in the back of the bus and he shows me the Math 3 homework he got his baby's mother Tareen to do for him. He claims she is smarter now than when she was in school at Jane Addams in the spring. He laughs.

The bus keeps moving. I keep moving even though I am sitting still. I feel all of the ears on us, on me and Joe and the story of Tareen staying up till 4 a.m. on the multiplication of fractions and then remembering that she had promised Joe some ass earlier but seeing that he was sound asleep snoring anyway, she worked on ahead and got to the percent problems by the time the alarm went off. Ha ha, Joe laughs, I got my girl in deep check. Ha ha.

All ears are on us, but mainly on me. Tammy Ferguson is busy slapping the twins to keep quiet and sit still, but I can feel Laura's eyes like they are a silent machine gun. Faggot faggot suck dick faggot. Now repeat that one hundred times in one minute and that's how I am feeling.

Keep moving. The bus keeps rolling and you always have to keep moving. Like water like air like outer space. I always pick something for my mind. Like today I am remembering the kids and how they will be waiting for me after fifth period and I remember the feel of Lasheema's soft dark hair.

Soft like the dark hair that covers me, not an afro but silky hair, covering me all over. Because I am so cold. Because I am so alone. A mat of thick delicious hair that blankets me in warmth. And therefore safety. And peace. And solitude. And ecstasy. Lasheema and me are ecstatic when we look at ourselves in the mirror. She's only four and I am fourteen. We hold each other smiling.

Keep moving. Then I am already around the corner from school while the bus pulls away with Laura still on it because she has fallen asleep in her seat and nobody has bothered to touch her.

On the corner of Prospect Avenue and East 167th Street where the bus lets me out, I see Rakeem waiting for me. I am not supposed to really know he's there for me and he is not supposed to show it. He is opening a Pixie Stick candy and then he fixes his droopy pants so that they are hanging off the edge of his butt. I can see Christian Dior undies. When I come nearer he throws the Pixie Stick on the ground next to the other garbage and gives me his hand just like any B-Crew-Boy would do when he saw his other crew member. Only we are not B-Crew members, we get run over by the B-Crew.

He says, Yo, man, did you find Layla?

I nod and listen to what he is really saying.

Rakeem says, Do you know that I got into Math 3? Did you hear that shit? Ain't that some good shit?

He smiles and hits me on the back and he lets his hand stay there.

I say, See what I told you before, Rakeem? You really got it in you to move on. You doing all right, man.

He grunts and looks at his sneakers. Last year the B-Crew boys tried to steal them from him but Rakeem screamed at them that he had AIDS from his cousin and they ran away rubbing their hands on the sides of the buildings on the Grand Concourse.

Rakeem says, Man, I don't have nothing in me except my brain that tells me: Nigger, first thing get your ass up in school. Make them know you can do it.

I say, Rakeem, you are smart, man! I wish I had your smart. I would be going places if I did.

He says, And then, Lorrie, I got to get people to like me and to stop seeing me. I just want them to think they like me. So I got to hide *me* for a while. Then you watch, Lorrie, man: *much* people will be on my side!

I say to him, Rakeem, you got Layla and baby Tee Tee and all the teachers on your side. And you got smart. You have it made.

He answers me after he fixes his droopy pants again so that they are hanging off exactly the middle of his ass: Man, they are whack! You know what I would like to do right now, Lorrie? You know what I would like? Shit, I ain't seen you since you went back to school and since I went back. Hell, you know what I would like? But it ain't happening 'cause you think Ima look at my cousin Layla and her bastard and love them and that will be enough. But it will never be enough.

I think about sitting on his lap. I did it before but then I let months go by because it was under the Bruckner Expressway and I believed it could only last a few minutes. It was not like the kind of love when I had the kids because I believed they would last forever.

He walks backwards away and when he gets to the corner, he starts running. No one else is on the street. He shouts, Rocky's Pizza! Ima be behind there, man. We got school fooled. This is the master plan. Ima be there, Lorrie! *Be there.*

I want to tell Rakeem that I have missed him and that I will not be there but he is gone. The kids are enough. The words are important. They are all enough.

The front of Jane Addams is gray-green with windows with gates over all of them. I am on the outside.

The bell rings first period and I am smiling at Mr. D'Angelo and feeling like this won't be a complete waste of a day. The sun has hit the windows of Jane Addams and there is even heat around our books. Mr. D'Angelo notices me but looks away. Brandy Bailey, who doesn't miss a thing, announces so that only us three will hear: Sometimes when a man's been married long he needs to experience a new kind of loving, ain't that what you think, Lorrie?

For that she gets thrown out of the classroom and an extra day of in-school suspension. All ears are now on me and Mr. D'Angelo. I am beyond feeling but I know he isn't. And that makes me happy in a way, like today ain't going to be a complete waste of a day.

He wipes his forehead with an imported handkerchief. He starts out saying, Class, what do we remember about the piston, the stem, and the insects? He gets into his questions and his perspiration stops and in two minutes he is free of me.

And I'm thinking: Why couldn't anything ever happen, why does every day start out one way hopeful but then point to the fact that ain't

nothing ever going to happen? The people here at school call me ugly,
for one. I know I got bug eyes and I know I am not someone who lovely
things ever happen to, but I ask you: Doesn't the heart count? Love is a
pie and I am lucky enough to have almost every flavor in mine. Mr.
D'Angelo turns away from my desk and announces a surprise quiz and
everybody groans and it is a sea of general unhappiness but no one is
more than me, knowing that nothing will ever happen the way I'd like it
to, not this flavor of the pie. And I am thinking: Mr. D'Angelo, do you
know that I would give anything to be like you, what with all your
smarts and words and you know how to make the people here laugh
and they love you. And I would give anything if you would ask me to
sit on your lap and ask me to bite into your ear so that it tingles like
the bell that rips me in and out of your class. I would give anything.
Love is a pie. Didn't you know that? Mr. D'Angelo, I am in silent love in
a loud body.

So don't turn away. *Sweat.*

Mrs. Cabrini pulls me aside and whispers, My dear Lorrie, when are
you ever going to pass this City Wide? You certainly have the brains.
And I know that your intelligence will take you far, will open new
worlds for you. Put your mind to your dreams, my dear boy, and you
will achieve them. You are your own universe, you are your own shooting star.

People 'round my way know me as Lorrie and the name stays. Cousin
Cee Cee says the name fits and she smacks her gum in my face whenever
she mentions that. She also adds that if anyone ever wants to kick my
ass, she'll just stand around and watch because a male with my name
and who likes it just deserves to be watched when whipped.

Ma named me for someone else. My real name is Lawrence Lincoln
Jefferson Adams. It's the name on my school records. It's the name Ma
says I got to put on my application to college when the time comes. She
knows I been failing these City Wide Tests and that's why she wants to
practice words with me every day. She laughs when I get them wrong
but she's afraid I won't learn them on my own, so she asks me to
practice them with her and I do. Not every day, but a whole lot: look
them up and pronounce them. Last Tuesday: Independence. Chagrin.
Symbolism. Nomenclature. Filament. On Wednesday, only: Apocrypha.
Ma says they have to be proper words with proper meanings from a

dictionary. You got to say them right. This is important if you want to reach your destiny, Ma says.

Like for instance the word Library. All my life I been saying that "Liberry." And even though I knew it was a place to read and do your studying, I still couldn't call it right. Do you see what I mean? I'm about doing things, you see, *finally* doing things right.

Cousin Cee Cee always says, What you learning all that shit for? Don't you know it takes more than looking up words to get into a college, even a damn community college? Practicing words like that! Is you a complete asshole?

And her two kids, Byron and Elizabeth, come into the kitchen and ask me to teach them the words too, but Cee Cee says it will hurt their eyes to be doing all that reading and besides they are only eight and nine. When she is not around I give them words with up to ten letters, then they go back to TV with the other kids.

When we have a good word sitting, me and Ma, she smoothes my face with her hands and calls me Lawrence, My Fine Boy. She says, You are on your way to good things. You just got to do things the proper way.

We kiss each other. Her hands are like the maid in the movies. I know I am taken care of.

Zenzile Jones passes me a note in History of Civilization. It's the part where Ptolemy lets everyone know the world is round. Before I open it, I look at her four desks away and I remember the night when I went out for baby diapers and cereal and found her crying in front of a fire hydrant. I let her cry on my shoulder. I told her that her father was a sick man for sucking on her like that.

The note says, Please give me a chance.

Estine Smith, my mother's sister who wants me and the kids to call her by both names, can't get out of her past. Sometimes I try on her clothes when I'm with the kids and we're playing dress-up. My favorite dress is her blue organza without the back. I seen Estine Smith wear this during the daytime and I fell in love with it. I also admired her for wearing a dress with the back out in the day, but it was only a ten-second admiration. Because then she opens her mouth and she is forever in her past. Her favorite time to make us all go back to is when they lynched her husband, David Saul Smith, from a tree in 1986 and called the TV station to come and get a look. She can't let us go one day without reminding us in words. I never want to be like her, ever. Everybody cries when they are in her words because they feel sorry for her, and Estine Smith is not someone but a walking hainted house.

Third period. I start dreaming about the kids while the others are standing in line to use the power saw. I love to dream about the kids. They are the only others who think I am beautiful besides Ma and Anita. They are my favorite flavor of the pie, even if I got others in my mind.

Most of the time there are eight but when my other aunt, Samantha, comes over I got three more. Samantha cries in the kitchen and shows Ma her blue marks and it seems like her crying will go on forever. Me, I want to take the kids' minds away. We go into Ma's room where there is the TV and we sing songs like "Old Gray Mare" and "Bingo Was His Name O" or new ones like "Why You Treat Me So Bad?" and "I Try to Let Go." Or else I teach them Math 4. Or else I turn on the TV so they can watch Bugs or He-Man and so I can get their ironing done.

Me, I love me some kids. I need me some kids.

Joe Smalls talks to me in what I know is a friendly way. The others in Woodworking for You don't know that. They are like the rest of the people who see me and hear the action and latch on.

Joe Smalls says, Lorrie, man, that bitch Tareen got half the percentage problems wrong. Shit. Be glad you don't have to deal with no dumb-ass Tareen bitch. She nearly got my ass a F in Math 3.

I get a sad look on my face, understanding, but it's a fake look because I'm feeling the rest of the ears on us, latching, readying. I pause to heaven. I am thinking I wish Ma had taught me how to pray. But she doesn't believe in God.

Junior Sims says, Why you talking that shit, Joe, man? Lorrie don't ever worry about bitches!

Perry Samson says, No, Lorrie never ever thinks about pussy as a matter of fact. Never ever.

Franklin says, Hey, Lorrie, man, tell me what you think about, then? What can be better than figuring out how you going to get that hole, man? Tell me what?

Mr. Samuels, the teacher, turns off the power saw just when it gets to Barney Moore's turn. He has heard the laughter from underneath the saw's screeching. Everybody gets quiet. His face is like a piece of lumber. Mr. Samuels is never soft. He doesn't fail me even though I don't do any cutting or measuring or shellacking. He wants me the hell out of there.

And after the saw is turned off, Mr. Samuels, for the first time in the world, starts laughing. The absolute first time. And everybody joins in because they are afraid of this and I laugh too because I'm hoping all the ears will go off me.

Mr. Samuels is laughing Haw Haw like he's from the country. Haw Haw. Haw Haw. His face is red. Everyone cools down and is just smiling now.

Then he says, Class, don't mess with the only *girl* we got in here!

Now it's laughter again.

Daniel Fibbs says, Yeah, Mr. Samuels is *on!*

Franklin laughs, No fags allowed, you better take your sissy ass out of here 'less you want me to cut it into four pieces.

Joe Smalls is quiet and looking out the window.

Junior Sims laughs, Come back when you start fucking bitches!

Keep moving, keep moving.

I pick up my red bag and wade towards the door. My instinct is the only thing that's working, and it is leading me back to Biology. But first out the room. Inside me there is really nothing except for Ma's voice: *Don't let them boys.* But inside there is nothing else. My bones and my brain and my heart would just crumble if it wasn't for that swirling wind of nothing in me that keeps me moving and moving.

Perry laughs, I didn't know Mr. Samuels was from the South.

With his eyelashes, Rakeem swept the edges of my face. He let me know they were beautiful to him. His face went in a circle around mine and dipped in my eyes and dipped in my mouth. He traveled me to a quiet place where his hands were the oars and I drifted off to sleep. The thin bars of the shopping cart where I was sitting in made grooves in my back, but it was like they were rows of tender fingers inviting me to stay. The roar of the trucks was a lullaby.

Layla Jackson comes running up to me but it's only fourth period because she wants to try and talk some sense into Tyrone. She hands me little Tee Tee. Tyrone makes like he wants to come over and touch the baby but instead he flattens his back against the wall to listen to Layla. I watch as she oozes him. In a minute they are tongue kissing. Because they are the only two people who will kiss each other. Everyone says that they gave themselves AIDS and now have to kiss each other because there ain't no one else. People walk past them and don't even notice that he has his hand up her shirt, squeezing the kickball.

Tee Tee likes to be in my arms. I like for him to be there.

The ladies were always buying all kinds of fruits and vegetables for their families underneath the Bruckner Expressway. They all talked Spanish and made the sign of the cross and asked God for forgiveness and gossiped.

Rakeem hickeyed my neck. We were underneath the concrete bridge supports and I had my hands on the handle of a broken shopping cart, where I was sitting. Don't go back, Rakeem was telling me, don't go back. And he whispered in my ear. And I thought of all the words I had been practicing, and how I was planning to pass that City Wide. Don't go back, he sang, and he sat me on his lap and he moved me around there. They don't need *you*, he said, and *you* don't need *them*.

But I do, I told him.

This feeling can last forever, he said.

No, it can't, I said, but I wound up leaving school for six months anyway. That shopping cart was my school.

I am thinking: It will never be more. I hold Tee Tee carefully because he is asleep on my shoulder and I go to catch the BX 17 back to my building.

Estine Smith stays in her past and that is where things are like nails. I want to tell her to always wear her blue organza without the back. If you can escape, why don't you all the time? You could dance and fling your arms and maybe even feel love from some direction. You would not perish. *You* could be free.

When I am around and she puts us in her past in her words, she tells me that if I hada twitched my ass down there like I do here, they woulda hung me up just by my black balls.

The last day Rakeem and I were together, I told him I wanted to go back, to school, to everyone. The words, I tried to explain about the words to Rakeem. I could welcome him into my world if he wanted me to. Hey, wasn't there enough room for him and me and the words?

Hell no, he shouted, and all the Spanish women turned around and stared at us. He shouted, You are an ugly-ass bastard who will always be hated big time and I don't care what you do; this is where your world begins and this is where your world will end. Fuck you. You are a pussy, man. Get the hell out of my face.

Ma is waiting for me at the front door, wringing her hands. She says it's good that I am home because there is trouble with Tommy again and I need to watch him and the kids while she goes out to bring Lula Jean home from the movies, which is where she goes when she plans on leaving Tommy. They got four kids here and if Lula Jean leaves, I might have to drop out of school again because she doesn't want to be tied to anything that has Tommy's stamp on it.

I set Tee Tee down next to Tommy on the sofa bed where I usually sleep. Tommy wakes up and says, Hey, man, who you bringing to visit me?

I go into the kitchen to fix him some tea and get the kids' lunch ready. Sheniqua is playing the doctor and trying to fix up Shawn, who always has to have an operation when she is the doctor. They come into the kitchen to hug my legs and then they go back in the living room.

Tommy sips his tea and says, Who was that chick this morning, Lorrie, man?

I say I don't know. I begin to fold his clothes.

Tommy says, Man, you don't know these bitches out here nowadays. You want to show them love, a good time, and a real deep part of yourself and all they do is not appreciate it and try to make your life miserable.

He says, Well, at least I got Lula. Now that's some woman.

And he is asleep. Sheniqua and her brother Willis come in and ask me if I will teach them Math 4 tonight. Aunt Estine rolls into the bedroom and asks me why do I feel the need to take care of this bum, and then she hits her head on the doorframe. She is clicking her heels. She asks, Why do we women feel we always need to teach them? They ain't going to learn the right way. They ain't going to learn shit. That's why we always so alone. Click, click.

The words I will learn before Ma comes home are: Soliloquy, Disenfranchise, Catechism. I know she will be proud. This morning before I left she told me she would make me a turkey dinner with all the trimmings if I learned four new words tonight. I take out my dictionary but then the kids come in and want me to give them a bath and baby Tee Tee has a fever and is throwing up all over the place. I look at the words and suddenly I know I will know them without studying.

And I realize this in the bathroom and then again a few minutes later when Layla Jackson comes in cursing because she got a 60 on the Humanities quiz. She holds Tee but she doesn't touch him. She thinks Tyrone may be going to some group where he is meeting other sick girls and she doesn't want to be alone. She curses and cries, curses and cries. She asks me why things have to be so fucked. Her braids are coming undone and I tell her that I will tighten them up for her. That makes Layla Jackson stop crying. She says, And to top it off, Rakeem is a shit. He promised me he wouldn't say nothing but now that he's back in school he is broadcasting my shit all over the place. And that makes nobody like me. And that makes nobody want to touch me.

I put my arm around Layla. Soon her crying stops and she is thinking about something else.

But me, I know these new words and the old words without looking at them, without the dictionary, without Ma's hands on my head. Lasheema and Tata come in and want their hair to be like Layla's and they bring in the Vaseline and sit around my feet like shoes. Tommy wakes up still in sleep and shouts, Lula, get your ass on in here. Then he falls back to sleep.

Because I know I will always be able to say the words on my own. I can do the words on my own and that is what matters. I have this flavor of the pie and I will always have it. Here in this kitchen I was always safe, learning the words till my eyes hurt. The words are in my heart.

Ma comes in and shoves Lula Jean into a kitchen chair. She says, Kids, make room for your cousin, go in the other room and tell Tommy to get his lame ass out here. Layla, you can get your ass out of here and don't bring it back no more with this child sick out his mind, do your 'ho'ing somewhere out on the street where you belong. Tommy, since when I need to tell you how to treat your wife? You are a stupid heel. Learn how to be a man.

Everybody leaves and Ma changes.

She says, I ain't forgot that special dinner for you, baby. I'm glad you're safe and sound here with me. Let's practice later.

I tell her, Okay, Ma, but I got to go meet Rakeem first.

She looks at me in shock and then out the corner of my eye I can tell she wants me to say no, I'll stay, I won't go to him. Because she knows.

But I'm getting my coat on and Ma has got what will be tears on her face because she can't say no and she can't ask any questions. Keep moving.

And I am thinking of Rocky's Pizza and how I will be when I get there and how I will be when I get home. Because I am coming back home. And I am going to school tomorrow. I know the words, and I can tell them to Rakeem and I can share what I know. Now he may be ready. I want him to say to me in his mind: Please give me a chance. And I know that behind Rocky's Pizza is the only place where I don't have to keep moving. Where there is not just air in me that keeps me from crumbling, but blood and meat and strong bones and feelings. I will be me for a few minutes behind Rocky's Pizza and I don't care if it's just a few minutes. I pat my hair down in the mirror next to the kitchen door. I take Anita's letter knife out my jacket pocket and leave it on the table next to where Tommy is standing telling his wife that she never knew what love was till she met him and why does she have to be like that, talking about leaving him and shit? You keep going that way and you won't ever know how to keep a man, bitch.

1995

*Gish Jen*

# Birthmates

FROM *Ploughshares*

THIS WAS WHAT responsibility meant in a dinosaur industry, toward the end of yet another quarter of bad-to-worse news: You called the travel agent back, and even though there was indeed an economy room in the hotel where the conference was being held, a room overlooking the cooling towers, you asked if there wasn't something still cheaper. And when Marie the new girl came back with something amazingly cheap, you took it — only to discover, as Art Woo was discovering now, that the doors were locked after nine o'clock. The neighborhood had looked not great but not bad, and the building itself, regular enough. Brick, four stories, a rolled-up awning. A bright-lit hotel logo, with a raised-plastic, smiling sun. But there was a kind of crossbar rigged across the inside of the glass door, and that was not at all regular. A two-by-four, it appeared, wrapped in rust-colored carpet. Above this, inside the glass, hung a small gray sign. If the taxi had not left, Art might not have rung the buzzer, as per the instructions.

But the taxi had indeed left, and the longer Art huddled on the stoop in the clumpy December snow, the emptier and more poorly lit the street appeared. His buzz was answered by an enormous black man wearing a neck brace. The shoulder seams of the man's blue waffle-weave jacket were visibly straining; around the brace was tied a necktie, which reached only a third of the way down his chest. All the same, it was neatly fastened together with a hotel-logo tie tack about two inches from the bottom. The tie tack was smiling; the man was not. He held his smooth, round face perfectly expressionless, and he lowered his gaze at every opportunity — not so that it was rude, but so that it was clear he wasn't selling anything to anybody. Regulation tie, thought Art, regulation jacket. He wondered if the man would turn surly soon enough.

For Art had come to few conclusions about life in his thirty-eight years, but this was one of them — that men turned surly when their clothes didn't fit them. This man, though, belied the rule. He was courteous, almost formal in demeanor; and if the lobby seemed not only too small for him, like his jacket, but also too much like a bus station, what with its smoked mirror wall, and its linoleum, and its fake wood, and its vending machines, what did that matter to Art? The sitting area looked as though it was in the process of being cleaned — the sixties Scandinavian chairs and couch and coffee table were pulled every which way, as if by someone hellbent on the dust balls. Still, Art proceeded with his check-in. He was going with his gut here. Here, as in any business situation, he was looking foremost at the personnel; and the man with the neck brace had put him at some ease. It wasn't until after Art had taken his credit card back that he noticed, above the check-out desk, a wooden plaque from a neighborhood association. He squinted at its brass face plate: FEWEST CUSTOMER INJURIES, 1972–73.

What about the years since '73? Had the hotel gotten more dangerous since then, or had other hotels gotten safer? Maybe neither. For all he knew, the neighborhood association had dissolved and was no longer distributing plaques. Art reminded himself that in life, some signs were no signs. It's what he used to tell his ex-wife, Lisa — Lisa who loved to read everything into everything; Lisa who was attuned. She left him on a day when she saw a tree get split by lightning. Of course, that was an extraordinary thing to see. An event of a lifetime. Lisa said the tree had sizzled. He wished he had seen it, too. But what did it mean, except that the tree had been the tallest in the neighborhood, and was no longer? It meant nothing; ditto with the plaque. Art made his decision, which perhaps was not the right decision. Perhaps he should have looked for another hotel.

But it was late — on the way out, his plane had sat on the runway, just sat and sat, as if it were never going to take off — and God only knew what he would have ended up paying if he had relied on a cabbie to simply bring him somewhere else. Forget twice — it could have been three, four times what he would have paid for that room with the view of the cooling towers, easy. At this hour, after all, and that was a conference rate.

So he double-locked his door instead. He checked behind the hollow-core doors of the closet, and under the steel-frame bed, and also in the swirly green shower-stall unit. He checked behind the seascapes, to be sure there weren't any peepholes. That *Psycho* — how he wished he'd never seen that movie. Why hadn't anyone ever told him that movies could come back to haunt you? No one had warned him. The window opened onto a fire escape; not much he could do about that except check the window locks, big help that those were — a sure deterrent for the subset of all burglars that was burglars too skittish to break glass. Which was what percent of intruders, probably? Ten percent? Fifteen? He closed the drapes, then decided he would be more comfortable with the drapes open. He wanted to be able to see what approached, if anything did. He unplugged the handset of his phone from the rest, a calculated risk. On the one hand, he wouldn't be able to call the police if there was an intruder. On the other, he would be armed. He had read somewhere a story about a woman who threw the handset of her phone at an attacker, and killed him. Needless to say, there had been some luck involved in that eventuality. Still, Art thought (a) surely he could throw as hard as that woman, and (b) even without the luck, his throw would most likely be hard enough to at least slow up an intruder. Especially since this was an old handset, the hefty kind that made you feel the seriousness of human communication. In a newer hotel, he probably would have had a new phone, with lots of buttons he would never use but which would make him feel he had many resources at his disposal. In the hotel where the conference was, there were probably buttons for the health club, and for the concierge, and for the three restaurants, and for room service. He tried not to think about this as he went to sleep, clutching the handset.

He did not sleep well.

In the morning he debated whether to take the handset with him into the elevator. Again he wished he hadn't seen so many movies. It was movies that made him think, that made him imagine things like, *What if in the elevator?* Of course, a handset was an awkward thing to hide. It wasn't like a knife, say, that could be whipped out of nowhere. Even a pistol at least fit in a guy's pocket. Whereas a telephone handset did not. All the same, he brought it with him. He tried to carry it casually, as if he were going out for a run and using it for a hand weight, or as if he were in the telephone business.

He strode down the hall. Victims shuffled; that's what everybody said. A lot of mugging had to do with nonverbal cues, which is why Lisa used to walk tall after dark, sending vibes. For this he used to tease her. If she was so worried, she should lift weights and run, the way he did; that, he maintained, was the substantive way of helping oneself. She had agreed. For a while they had met after work at the gym. That was before she dropped a weight on her toe and decided she preferred to sip piña coladas and watch. Naturally, he grunted on. But to what avail? Who could appreciate his pectorals through his suit and overcoat? Pectorals had no deterrent value, that was what he was thinking now. And he was, though not short, not tall. He continued striding. Sending vibes. He was definitely going to eat in the dining room of the hotel where the conference was being held, he decided. What's more, he was going to have a full American breakfast, with bacon and eggs, none of this Continental breakfast bullshit.

In truth, he had always considered the sight of men eating croissants slightly ridiculous, especially at the beginning, when for the first bite they had to maneuver the point of the crescent into their mouths. No matter what a person did, he ended up with an asymmetrical mouthful of pastry, which he then had to relocate with his tongue to a more central location, and this made him look less purposive than he might. Also, croissants were more apt than other breakfast foods to spray little flakes all over one's clean dark suit. Art himself had accordingly never ordered a croissant in any working situation, and he believed that attention to this sort of detail was how it was that he had not lost his job like so many of his colleagues.

This was, in other words, how it was that he was still working in his fitfully dying industry, and was now carrying a telephone handset with him into the elevator. Art braced himself as the elevator doors opened slowly, jerkily, in the low-gear manner of elevator doors in the Third World. He strode in, and was surrounded by, of all things, children. Down in the lobby, too, there were children, and here and there, women he knew to be mothers by their looks of dogged exasperation. A welfare hotel! He laughed out loud. Almost everyone was black, the white children stood out like little missed opportunities of the type that made Art's boss throw his tennis racket across the room. Of course, the racket was always in its padded protective cover and not in much danger of getting injured, though the person in whose vicinity it was aimed sometimes was. Art once suffered what he rather hoped would turn out to be a broken nose, but was only a bone bruise with so little skin discoloration that people had a hard time believing the incident had actually taken place. Yet it had. *Don't talk to me about fault, bottom line it's you Japs who are responsible for this whole fucking mess,* his boss had said — this though what was the matter with minicomputers, really, was personal computers. A wholly American phenomenon. And of course, Art could have sued over this incident if he could have proved that it had happened. Some people, most notably Lisa, thought he certainly ought to have at least quit.

But he didn't sue and he didn't quit. He took his tennis racket on the nose, so to speak, and when the next day his boss apologized for losing control, Art said he understood. And when his boss said that Art shouldn't take what he said personally, in fact he knew Art was not a Jap, but a Chink, plus he had called someone else a lazy wop just that morning, it was just his style, Art said again that he understood. And then Art said that he hoped his boss would remember Art's great understanding come promotion time. Which his boss did, to Art's satisfaction. In Art's view, this was a victory. In Art's view, he had perceived leverage where others would only perceive affront. He had maintained a certain perspective.

But this certain perspective was, in addition to the tree, why Lisa left him. He thought of that now, the children underfoot, his handset in hand. So many children. It was as if he were seeing before him all the children he would never have. He stood a moment, paralyzed; his heart lost its muscle. A child in a red running suit ran by, almost grabbed the handset out of Art's grasp; then another, in a brown jacket with a hood. He looked up to see a group of grade-school boys arrayed about the seating area, watching. Already he had become the object of a dare, apparently — there was so little else in the way of diversion in the lobby — and realizing this, he felt renewed enough to want to laugh again. When a particularly small child swung by in his turn — a child of maybe five or six, small enough to be wearing snowpants — Art almost tossed the handset to him, but thought better of the idea. Who wanted to be charged for a missing phone?

As it was, Art wondered if he shouldn't put the handset back in his room rather than carry it around all day. For what was he going to do at the hotel where the conference was, check it? He imagined himself running into Billy Shore — that was his counterpart at Info-Edge, his competitor in the insurance market. A man with no management ability, and no technical background either. But he could offer customers a personal computer option, which Art could not; and what's more, Billy had been a quarterback in college. This meant he strutted around as though it still mattered that he had connected with his tight end in the final minutes of what Art could not help but think of as the Wilde-Beastie game. And it meant that Billy was sure to ask him, *What are you doing with a phone in your hand? Talking to yourself again?* Making everyone around them laugh.

Billy was that kind of guy. He had come up through sales, and was always cracking a certain type of joke — about drinking, or sex, or how much the wife shopped. Of course, he never used those words. He never called things by their plain names. He always talked in terms of knocking back some brewskis, or running the triple option, or doing some damage. He made assumptions as though it were a basic bodily function: of course his knowledge was the common knowledge. Of course people understood what it was that he was referring to so delicately. *Listen, champ,* he said, putting his arm around you. If he was smug, it was in an affable kind of way. *So what do you think the poor people are doing tonight?* Billy not only spoke what Art called Mainstreamese, he spoke such a pure dialect of it that Art once asked him if he realized that he was a pollster's delight. He spoke the thoughts of thousands, Art told him, he breathed their very words. Naturally, Billy did not respond, except to say, *What's that?* and turn away. He rubbed his torso as he turned, as if ruffling his chest hairs through the long-staple cotton. Primate behavior, Lisa used to call this. It was her belief that neckties evolved in order to check this very motion, uncivilized as it was. She also believed that this was the sort of thing you never saw Asian men do — at least not if they were brought up properly.

Was that true? Art wasn't so sure. Lisa had grown up on the West Coast, she was full of Asian consciousness; whereas all he knew was that no one had so much as smiled politely at his pollster remark. On the other hand, the first time Art was introduced to Billy, and Billy said, *Art Woo, how's that for a nice Pole-ack name,* everyone broke right up in great rolling guffaws. Of course, they laughed the way people laughed at conferences, which was not because something was really funny, but because it was part of being a good guy, and because they didn't want to appear to have missed their cue.

The phone, the phone. If only Art could fit it in his briefcase! But his briefcase was overstuffed; it was always overstuffed; really, it was too bad he had the slim silhouette type, and hard-side besides. Italian. That was Lisa's doing, she thought the fatter kind made him look like a salesman. Not that there was really anything the matter with that, in his view. Billy Shore notwithstanding, sales were important. But she was the liberal arts type, Lisa was, the type who did not like to think about money, but only about her feelings. Money was not money to her, but support, and then a means of support much inferior to hand-holding or other forms of finger play. She did not believe in a modern-day economy, in which everyone played a part in a large and complex whole that introduced efficiencies that at least theoretically raised everyone's standard of living. She believed in expressing herself. Also in taking classes, and in knitting. There was nothing, she believed, like taking a walk in the autumn woods wearing a hand-knit sweater. Of course, she did look beautiful in them, especially the violet ones. That was her color — Asians are winters, she always said — and sometimes she liked to wear the smallest smidgeon of matching violet eyeliner, even though it was, as she put it, less than organic to wear eyeliner on a hike.

Little Snowpants ran at Art again, going for the knees — *a tackle,* thought Art, as he went down; Red Running Suit snatched away the handset and went sprinting off, triumphant. Teamwork! The children chortled together; how could Art not smile a little, even if they had gotten his overcoat dirty? He brushed himself off, ambled over.

"Hey, guys," he said. "That was some move back there."

"Ching chang polly wolly wing wong," said Little Snowpants.

"Now, now, that's no way to talk," said Art.

"Go to hell!" Brown Jacket pulled at the corners of his eyes to make them slanty.

"Listen up," said Art. "I'll make you a deal." Really he only meant to get the handset back, so as to avoid getting charged for it.

But the next thing he knew, something had hit his head with a crack, and he was out.

Lisa had left in a more or less amicable way. She had not called a lawyer, or a mover; she had simply pressed his hands with both of hers and, in her most California voice, said, *Let's be nice.* And then she had asked him if he wouldn't help her move her boxes, at least the heavy ones that really were too much for her. He had helped. He had carried the heavy boxes, and also the less heavy ones. Being a weight lifter, after all. He had sorted books and rolled glasses into pieces of newspaper, feeling all the while like a statistic. A member of the modern age, a story for their friends to rake over, and all because he had not gone with Lisa to her grieving group. Or at least that was the official beginning of the trouble; probably the real beginning had been when Lisa — no, *they* — had trouble getting pregnant. When they decided to, as the saying went, do infertility. Or had he done the deciding, as Lisa later maintained? He had thought it was a joint decision, though it was true that he had done the analysis that led to the joint decision. He had been the one to figure the odds, to do the projections. He had drawn the decision tree, according to whose branches they had nothing to lose by going ahead.

Neither one of them had realized then how much would be involved — the tests, the procedures, the drugs, the ultrasounds. Lisa's arms were black and blue from having her blood drawn every day, and before long he was giving practice shots to an orange, that he might prick her some more. He was telling her to take a breath so that on the exhale he could poke her in the buttocks. This was no longer practice, and neither was it like poking an orange. The first time, he broke out in such a sweat that his vision blurred and he had to blink, with the result that he pulled the needle out slowly and crookedly, occasioning a most unorangelike cry. The second time, he wore a sweatband. Later he jabbed her like nothing; her ovaries swelled to the point where he could feel them through her jeans.

He still had the used syringes — snapped in half and stored, as per their doctor's recommendation, in plastic soda bottles. She had left him those. Bottles of medical waste, to be disposed of responsibly, meaning that he was probably stuck with them, ha-ha, for the rest of his life. A little souvenir of this stage of their marriage, his equivalent of the pile of knit goods she had to show for the ordeal; for through it all, she had knit, as if to gently demonstrate an alternative use of needles. Sweaters, sweaters, but also baby blankets, mostly to give away, only one or two to keep. She couldn't help herself. There was anesthesia, and egg harvesting, and anesthesia and implanting, until she finally did get pregnant, twice, and then a third time she went to four and a half months before they found a problem. On the amnio, it showed up, brittle bone disease — a genetic abnormality such as could happen to anyone.

He steeled himself for another attempt; she grieved. And this was the difference between them, that he saw hope still, some feeble, skeletal hope, where she saw loss. She called the fetus her baby, though it was not a baby, just a baby-to-be, as he tried to say; as even the grieving-group facilitator tried to say. She said he didn't understand, couldn't possibly understand, it was something you understood with your body, and it was not his body but hers that knew the baby, loved the baby, lost the baby. In the grieving class the women agreed. They commiserated. They bonded, subtly affirming their common biology by doing 85 percent of the talking. The room was painted mauve — a feminine color that seemed to support them in their process. At times it seemed that the potted palms were female, too, nodding, nodding, though really their sympathy was just rising air from the heating vents. Other husbands started missing sessions — they never talked, anyway, you hardly noticed their absence — and finally he missed some also. One, maybe two, for real reasons, nothing cooked up. But the truth was, as Lisa sensed, that he thought she had lost perspective. They could try again, after all. What did it help to despair? Look, they knew they could get pregnant and, what's more, sustain the pregnancy. That was progress. But she was like an island in her grief, a retreating island, if there was such a thing, receding to the horizon of their marriage, and then to its vanishing point.

Of course, he had missed her terribly at first; now he missed her still, but more sporadically. At odd moments, for example now, waking up in a strange room with ice on his head. He was lying on an unmade bed just like the bed in his room, except that everywhere around it were heaps of what looked to be blankets and clothes. The only clothes on a hanger were his jacket and overcoat; these hung neatly, side by side, in the otherwise empty closet. There was also an extra table in this room, with a two-burner hot plate, a pan on top of that, and a pile of dishes. A brown cube refrigerator. The drapes were closed; a chair had been pulled up close to him; the bedside light was on. A woman was leaning into its circle, mopping his brow. *Don't you move, now.* She was the shade of black Lisa used to call mochaccino, and she was wearing a blue flowered apron. Kind eyes, and a long face — the kind of face where you could see the muscles of the jaw working alongside the cheekbone. An upper lip like an archery bow, and a graying Afro, shortish. She smelled of smoke. Nothing unusual except that she was so very thin, about the thinnest person he had ever seen, and yet she was cooking something — burning something, it smelled like, though maybe it was just a hair fallen onto the heating element. She stood up to tend the pan. The acrid smell faded. He saw powder on the table. It was white, a plastic bagful. His eyes widened. He sank back, trying to figure out what to do. His head pulsed. Tylenol, he needed, two. Lisa always took one because she was convinced the dosages recommended were based on large male specimens; and though she had never said that she thought he ought to keep it to one also, not being so tall, he was adamant about taking two. Two, two, two. He wanted his drugs, he wanted them now. And his own drugs, that was, not somebody else's.

"Those kids kind of rough," said the woman. "They getting to that age. I told them one of these days somebody gonna get hurt, and sure enough, they knocked you right out. You might as well been hit with a bowling ball. I never saw anything like it. We called the man, but they got other things on their mind besides to come see about trouble here.

Nobody shot, so they went on down to the Dunkin' Donuts. They know they can count on a ruckus there." She winked. "How you feeling? That egg hurt?"

He felt his head. A lump sat right on top of it, incongruous as something left by a glacier. What were those called, those stray boulders you saw perched in hair-raising positions? On cliffs?

"I feel like I died and came back to life head-first," he said.

"I'm going to make you something nice. Make you feel a whole lot better."

"Uh," said Art. "If you don't mind, I'd rather just have a Tylenol. You got any Tylenol? I had some in my briefcase. If I still have my briefcase."

"Your what?"

"My briefcase," said Art again, with a panicky feeling. "Do you know what happened to my briefcase?"

"Oh, it's right by the door. I'll get it, don't move."

And then there it was, his briefcase, its familiar hard-sided, Italian slenderness resting right on his stomach. He clutched it. "Thank you," he whispered.

"You need help with that thing?"

"No," said Art, but when he opened the case, it slid, and everything spilled out — his notes, his files, his papers. All that figuring — how strange his concerns looked here, on this brown shag carpet.

"Here," said the woman, and again — "I'll get it, don't move" — as gently, beautifully, she gathered up all the folders and put them in the case. There was an odd, almost practiced finesse to her movements; the files could have been cards in a card dealer's hands. "I used to be a nurse," she explained, as if reading his mind. "I picked up a few folders in my time. Here's the Tylenol."

"I'll have two."

"Course you will," she said. "Two Tylenol and some hot milk with honey. Hope you don't mind the powdered, we just got moved here, we don't have no supplies. I used to be a nurse, but I don't got no milk and I don't got no Tylenol, my guests got to bring their own. How you like that."

Art laughed as much as he could. "You got honey, though, how's that?"

"I don't know, it got left here by somebody," said the nurse. "Hope there's nothing growing in it."

Art laughed again, then let her help him sit up to take his pills. The nurse — her name was Cindy — plumped his pillows. She adminis-tered his milk. Then she sat — very close to him, it seemed — and chatted amiably about this and that. How she wasn't going to be staying at the hotel for too long, how her kids had had to switch schools, how she wasn't afraid to take in a strange, injured man. After all, she grew up in the projects, she could take care of herself. She showed him her switchblade, which had somebody's initials carved on it, she didn't know whose. She had never used it, she said, somebody gave it to her. And that somebody didn't know whose initials those were, either, she said, at least so far as she knew. Then she lit a cigarette and smoked while he told her first about his conference and then about how he had ended up at the hotel by mistake. He told her the latter with some hesitation, hoping he wasn't offending her. But she wasn't offended. She laughed with a cough, emitting a series of smoke puffs.

"Sure must've been a shock," she said. "Land up in a place like this. This no place for a nice boy like you."

That stung a little. *Boy!* But more than the stinging, he felt something else. "What about you? It's no place for you, either, you and your kids."

"Maybe so," she said. "But that's how the Almighty planned it, right? You folk rise up while we set and watch." She said this with so little rancor, with something so like intimacy, that it almost seemed an invitation of sorts.

But maybe he was kidding himself. Maybe he was assuming things, just like Billy Shore, just like men throughout the ages. Projecting desire where there was none, assigning and imagining, and in juicy detail. Being Asian didn't exempt him from that. *You folk.* Art was late, but it didn't much matter. This conference was being held in conjunction with a much larger conference, the real draw; the idea being that maybe between workshops and on breaks, the conferees would drift down and see what minicomputers could do for them. That mostly meant lunch.

In the meantime, things were totally dead, allowing Art to appreciate just how much the trade show floor had shrunk — down to a fraction of what it had been in previous years, and the booths were not what they had been, either. It used to be that the floor was crammed with the fanciest booths on the market; Art's used to be twenty by twenty. It took days to put together. Now you saw blank spots on the floor where exhibitors didn't even bother to show up, and those weren't even as demoralizing as some of the makeshift jobbies — exhibit booths that looked like high school science fair projects. They might as well have been made out of cardboard and Magic Marker. Art himself had a booth you could buy from an airplane catalog, the kind that rolled up into cordura bags. And people were stingy with brochures now, too. Gone were the twelve-page, four-color affairs; now the pamphlets were four-page, two-color, with extra bold graphics for attempted pizzazz, and not everybody got one, only people who were serious.

Art set up. Then, even though he should have been manning his spot, he drifted from booth to booth, saying hello to people he should have seen at breakfast. They were happy to see him, to talk shop, to pop some grapes off the old grapevine. Really, if he weren't staying in a welfare hotel, he would have felt downright respected. *You folk.* What folk did Cindy mean? Maybe she was just being matter-of-fact, keeping her perspective. Although how could anyone be so matter-of-fact about something so bitter? He wondered this even as he took his imaginative liberties with her. These began with a knock on her door and coursed through some hot times but ended (what a good boy he was) with him rescuing her and her children (he wondered how many there were) from their dead-end life. What was the matter with him, that he could not imagine mating without legal sanction? His libido was not what it should be, clearly, or at least it was not what Billy Shore's was. Art tried to think *game plan,* but in truth he could not even identify what a triple option would be in this case. All he knew was that, assuming, to begin with, that she was willing, he couldn't sleep with a woman like Cindy and then leave her flat. She could *you folk* him, he could never *us folk* her.

He played with some software at a neighboring booth; it appeared interesting enough but kept crashing so he couldn't tell too much. Then he dutifully returned to his own booth, where he was visited by a number of people he knew, people with whom he was friendly enough. The sort of people to whom he might have shown pictures of his children. He considered telling one or two of them about the events of the morning. Not about the invitation that might not have been an invitation, but about finding himself in a welfare hotel and being beaned with his own telephone. Phrases drifted through his head. *Not so bad as you'd think. You'd be surprised how friendly the people are. Unpretentious. Though, of course, no health club.* But in the end the subject simply did not come up and did not come up until he realized that he was keeping it to himself, and that he was committing more resources to this task than he had readily available. He felt invaded — as if he had been infected by a self-replicating bug. Something that was iterating and iterating, growing and growing, crowding out everything else in the CPU.

The secret was intolerable; it was bound to spill out of him sooner or later. He just hoped it wouldn't be sooner.

He just hoped it wouldn't be to Billy Shore, for whom he began to search, so as to be certain to avoid him.

Art had asked about Billy at the various booths, but no one had seen him; his absence was weird. It spooked Art. When finally some real live conferees stopped by to see his wares, he had trouble concentrating; everywhere in the conversation he was missing opportunities, he knew it. And all because his CPU was full of iterating nonsense. Not too long ago, in looking over some database software in which was loaded certain fun facts about people in the industry, Art had looked up Billy, and discovered that he had been born the same day Art was, only four years later. It just figured that Billy would be younger. That was irritating. But Art was happy for the information, too. He had made a note of it, so that when he ran into Billy at this conference, he would remember to kid him about their birthdays. Now, he rehearsed. *Have I got a surprise for you. I always knew you were a Leo. I believe this makes us birthmates.* Anything not to mention the welfare hotel and all that had happened to him there.

In the end, he did not run into Billy at all. In the end, he wondered about Billy all day, only to finally learn that Billy had moved on to a new job in the Valley, with a start-up. In personal computers, naturally. A good move, no matter what kind of beating he took on his house.

"Life is about the long term," said Ernie Ford, the informant. "And let's face it, there is no long term here."

Art agreed as warmly as he could. In one way, he was delighted that his competitor had left — if nothing else, that would mean a certain amount of disarray at Info-Edge. The insurance market was, unfortunately, some 40 percent of his business, and he could use any advantage he could get. Another bonus was that Art was never going to have to see Billy again. Billy his birthmate, with his jokes and his Mainstreamese. Still, Art felt depressed.

"We should all have gotten out before this," he said.

"Truer words were never spoke," said Ernie. Ernie had never been a particular friend of Art's, but somehow, talking about Billy was making him chummier. It was as if Billy were a force even in his absence. "I tell you, I'd have packed my bags by now if it weren't for the wife, the kids — they don't want to leave their friends, you know? Plus the oldest is a junior in high school, we can't afford for him to move now, he's got to stay put and make those nice grades so he can make a nice college. Meaning I've got to stay, if it means pushing McMuffins for Ronald McDonald. But now you . . ."

"Maybe I should go," said Art.

"Definitely, you should go," said Ernie. "What's keeping you?"

"Nothing," said Art. "I'm divorced now. And that's that, right? Sometimes people get undivorced, but you can't exactly count on it."

"Go," said Ernie. "Take my advice. If I hear of anything, I'll send it your way."

"Thanks," said Art.

But of course, he did not expect that Ernie would really turn anything up. It had been a long time since anyone had called him or anybody else he knew of; too many people had gotten stranded, and they were too desperate. Everybody knew it. Also, the survivors were looked upon with suspicion. Anybody who was any good had jumped ship early, that was the conventional wisdom. There was Art, struggling to hold on to his job, only to discover that there were times you didn't want to hold on to your job, times to maneuver for the golden parachute and jump. That was another thing no one had told him, that sometimes it spoke well of you to be fired. Who would have figured that? Sometimes it seemed to Art that he knew nothing at all, that he had dug his own grave and didn't even know to lie down in it, he was still trying to stand up.

A few more warm-blooded conferees at the end of the day — at least they were polite. Then, as he was packing up to go back to the hotel, a mega-surprise. A headhunter approached him, a friend of Ernest's, he said.

"Ernest?" said Art. "Oh, Ernie! Ford! Of course!"

The headhunter was a round, ruddy man with a ring of hair like St. Francis of Assisi, and sure enough, a handful of bread crumbs: A great opportunity, he said. Right now he had to run, but he knew just the guy Art had to meet, a guy who was coming in that evening. For something else, it happened, but he also needed someone like Art. Needed him yesterday, really. Should've been a priority, the guy realized that now, had said so the other day. It might just be a match. Maybe a quick breakfast in the a.m.? Could he call in an hour or so? Art said, *Of course.* And when St. Francis asked his room number, Art hesitated, but then gave the name of the welfare hotel. How would St. Francis know what kind of hotel it was? Art gave the name out confidently, making his manner count. He almost didn't make it to the conference at all, he said. Being so busy. It was only at the last minute that he realized he could do it — things moved around, he found an opening and figured what the hell. But it was too late to book the conference hotel, he explained. That was why he was staying elsewhere.

Success. All day Art's mind had been churning; suddenly it seemed to empty. He might as well have been Billy, born on the same day as Art was, but in another year, under different stars. How much simpler things seemed. He did not labor on two, three, six tasks at once, multi-processing. He knew one thing at a time, and that thing just now was that the day was a victory. And all because he had kept his mouth shut. He had said nothing; he had kept his cool. He walked briskly back to the hotel. He crossed the lobby in a no-nonsense manner. An impervious man. He did not knock on Cindy's door. He was moving on, moving west. There would be a good job there, and a new life. Perhaps he would take up tennis. Perhaps he would own a Jacuzzi. Perhaps he would learn to like all those peculiar foods they ate out there, like jicama, and seaweed. Perhaps he would go macrobiotic.

It wasn't until he got to his room that he remembered that his telephone had no handset.

He sat on his bed. There was a noise at his window, followed, sure enough, by someone's shadow. He wasn't even surprised. Anyway, the fellow wasn't stopping at his room, at least not on this trip. That was luck. *You folk,* Cindy had said, taking back the ice bag. Art could see her perspective; she was right. He was luckier than she, by far. But just now, as the shadow crossed his window again, he thought mostly about how unarmed he was. If he had a telephone, he would probably call Lisa — that was how big a pool seemed to be forming around him, all of a sudden; an ocean, it seemed. Also, he would call the police. But first he would call Lisa, and see how she felt about his possibly moving west. *Quite possibly,* he would say, not wanting to make it sound as though he was calling her for nothing, not wanting to make it sound as though he was awash, at sea, perhaps drowning. He would not want to sound like a haunted man; he would not want to sound as though he was calling from a welfare hotel, years too late, to say, *Yes, that was a baby, it would have been a baby.* For he could not help now but recall the doctor explaining about that child, a boy, who had appeared so mysteriously perfect in the ultrasound. Transparent, he had looked, and gelatinous, all soft head and quick heart; but he would have, in being born, broken every bone in his body.

# Pam Durban

........................................................................................................

# Soon

FROM *The Southern Review*

### 1

MARTHA'S MOTHER, Elizabeth Long Crawford, had been born with a lazy eye, and one morning when she was twelve her father and the doctor sat her down in the dining room at Marlcrest, the Longs' place near Augusta, Georgia, and told her they were going to fix her so that a man would want to marry her someday. Her father held her on his lap while the doctor pressed a handkerchief soaked with chloroform over her nose and mouth, and she went under, dreaming of the beauty she would be. But the doctor's hand slipped, and when Elizabeth came to, she was blind in her right eye. For the rest of her life what she remembered of that morning were the last sights she'd seen through two eyes: the shadows of leaves on the sunny floor, the hair on the backs of her father's hands, the stripe on the doctor's trousers, the handkerchief coming down. Then blindness. The rise and the downfall of hope, one complete revolution of the wheel that turned the world, that's what she'd lived through.

Marlcrest was a hard name to pronounce. The first syllable sprawled, it wouldn't be hurried; the last climbed a height and looked down on the rest of the world the way Martha's mother had done all her life. It had been a hard place to live, too. One hundred acres of level, sandy land on a bluff above the Savannah River, and a house raised high on brick pillars to offer the people of the house a view of the river, a chance at the river breezes. When Elizabeth married Perry Crawford, he agreed to live there, too. *She* wasn't leaving. In the family cemetery on the bluff stood the Long tomb and the graves of the children who'd died at birth, who had fallen or been trampled by horses or killed by cholera or yellow fever during the two hundred years the Longs had lived at Marlcrest.

Before the Civil War, slaves hauled muck up from the river — the *marl* of which the *crest* was made — to spread on the fields. Many died there: smothered in the mud, collapsed in the heat, snakebit, drowned. They were buried in a corner of a distant field that the pine woods had taken back years before Martha was born, though even in Martha's time a person could still find pieces of broken dishes, shells, empty brown medicine bottles under the pine needles, as if the people buried there had been carried out and lowered down by others who believed that the dead could be quieted and fed.

After the botched operation, Martha's mother lived where the wheel had stopped and she'd stepped off. The blind eye that the doctor had closed gave her a proud, divided look, as though half her face slept while the other stayed fiercely alert, on the lookout for the next betrayal. It was how she'd looked at seventy-five — disfigured and ferocious — when she'd summoned Martha and her brother, Perry Jr., to the nursing home in Augusta where they'd put her after a series of small strokes had made it dangerous for her to live alone at Marlcrest any longer. For six months before they'd put her in the home, there'd been trouble after trouble. She'd stopped payment on every check she wrote. The doors of the house, inside and out, had filled up with locks. Every night her calls to her children were packed with complaint. The woman they'd hired to stay with her was a thief, a drunk. Someone was downstairs picking the locks. It was that Herbert Long from up the road. He and his family, descendants of the slaves who'd once lived on the place. For a hundred years they'd bided their time; now they'd come to steal from her.

At the nursing home that day, Martha and Perry Jr. found their mother in her wheelchair in the sun by the window. She was dressed in beige linen, her best earrings, heirloom pearls. Her hair had been freshly restored to a cresting silver wave, and she was draped in Arpège perfume, as she had been in all her finest hours. "Well, don't you look nice, Mother. What's the occasion?" Martha asked, kissing her mother's sweet, powdered cheek.

Some papers their mother had in her purse, that was the occasion. Notarized contracts. Smiling brilliantly, she handed over the documents, one by one, to Martha and Perry Jr. She'd sold Marlcrest — the whole kit and caboodle — to a developer who planned to bulldoze the house, clear the land, build a subdivision there. Plantation Oaks, he'd call it. "Here is a copy of the title deed," she said, passing it to Perry Jr. "As you will see, it is properly signed and notarized." He turned it over, held it up to the light, looking for the error that would void the contract. As for the family records and belongings — the *contents* of the house, she said, leaning toward them from her wheelchair with her hands folded in her lap and high color in her cheeks, savoring (Martha saw) the vengeful triumph of this theft — she'd sold them all to a young man from a southern history museum in Atlanta. *Smack*, she struck the wheelchair's armrest. *Done*. He'd been coming to visit her in the nursing home since Martha and Perry Jr. had put her there — it had been almost exactly one year now. He'd even driven her out to Marlcrest a time or two to pick up something she'd forgotten. The Long family had many possessions of historical interest; already the museum people were calling their belongings the most important collection of southern artifacts ever acquired in Georgia. Fine linen shirts and baby gowns sewn by slave seamstresses. Diaries and ledgers and sharecropper contracts. Tools, portraits. A complete record of plantation life. The young man had been so sweet to her. He had all the time in the world to sit and talk. He never sneaked looks at his watch or found some excuse to jump up and rush off five minutes after he'd sat down.

Not that Martha and Perry Jr. hadn't been expecting it somehow. What has been lived will be handed on. Throughout their childhoods their mother had told them she lived by *high ideals,* which meant that everything had to be right — but since nothing ever was right, she was constantly, deeply, and bitterly disappointed by every person and every circumstance. *Horsy* had been her word for Martha, and in it were catalogued all of Martha's lacks. A long face, big teeth, lank hair, eyes that shone with dark, equine clarity. Yes, and Martha was also too *big*, too meaty. She sweated in the summer heat, and in winter her fingertips stayed cold. Perry Jr. was never more than an adequate student, a lukewarm son. Even her husband, Perry Sr., had failed her. When Martha was sixteen and Perry Jr. eighteen, their father sneaked off early one October morning to go duck hunting alone in the swamp below the old slave burying ground and was struck dead by a heart attack. After dark the sheriff found him up in the duck blind, still seated on his camp stool with his gun across his knees, looking out the little window hole in the sidewall of the blind, as though he were watching the mallards flash and preen in the dark water below.

His death made their mother furious; afterward she widened her search for the thief who'd robbed her. And yet, though Martha and Perry Jr. had both expected that someday their mother would get to their names on her long list of suspects in the crimes against her, neither was prepared for it. Is anyone *prepared* for the actuality of life, which is always more surprising or horrifying or sweet than we could ever have imagined? Not at all. We dream and wish and plan, but something more subtle, more generous and devious, arranges reality for us.

After they'd heard all their mother had to say about what she'd taken from them, after she'd leaned back, satisfied, and looked from one to the other of them with that brilliant and terrible *any questions?* look on her face, Martha had closed her eyes. She saw the bulldozer push the house. It swayed, cracked, fell, carrying beds, tables, chairs, the smell of closets, her grandmother's round hatboxes and furs, the river's wide curve that she could see from her bedroom window in winter when the leaves had fallen and the trees along the banks were bare. Carrying even the slave cemetery, where, in the spring just past, Martha had found weeded ground, plastic lilies in a Mason jar. Propped against a pine tree. In the nursing home that day, Martha felt the world fail and move away from her for the first time; fail and move away the way her mother had taught her it would, not with words exactly, though Elizabeth had certainly given her children enough of those, but with her footsteps walking away from them, her closed face, her fury.

Their mother died within a year of that day. A stroke, of a magnitude even *she* would have approved — maybe — as the cause of death of a person of her stature, knocked her out of her wheelchair in the nursing home dining room one Saturday evening and killed her before the first hand touched her. In her coffin, Martha was startled to discover, her mother looked different than she had in life. The perfect wave of silver hair was intact, as were the long, elegant fingers, and yet, lacking the ferocious hauteur that had been its life, her face looked wasted and starved, as if under the rage a ravenous sadness had been at work. Not even the undertaker's crafted composure, the small rueful smile he'd shaped on her mouth, or the benign glow of the pink light bulbs in the funeral home lamps could soften the face she would wear now into eternity.

2

What do you do with what you've been handed? Martha would not have her children saying *poor Mother* over her coffin. She went back to the life she wanted, a calm and common life, firmly planted. As Martha saw it, her mother's bitterness and rage were exactly as large and violent as her hopes and her longings, and so it was these longings that Martha would uproot in herself. That's why she'd married Raymond Maitland in the first place (against her mother's wishes), a decent man from a decent family, a big, careful, sober man with jug ears who wanted what she wanted. They lived in the country outside Augusta, and Raymond, a salesman, traveled up and down the coast, only he called it the *eastern seaboard*, because he believed the high-minded sound of those words gave him a competitive edge over his coarser peers. His territory stretched from Myrtle Beach, South Carolina, to Jacksonville, Florida, and at one time or another, he sold insurance, encyclopedias, building materials, pharmaceuticals, vending machine snacks, and office supplies. The drawers in their kitchen and den filled up with pencils, ballpoint pens, rulers, rubber jar-lid openers, key chains, thermometers, and spatulas, all printed with the names and slogans of companies he'd represented.

In the spring, summer, and early fall, he drove with the windows rolled down (this was in the fifties, before air conditioners were standard in most cars), his left arm resting on the window ledge, so that his arm was always sunburned when he returned from a sales trip. At home, it was one of their pleasures for him to shower, lie on their bed in his undershorts, and doze, with the fan blowing across him and the radio tuned to the light classics station, while she rubbed Solarcaine on his sunburned arm as gently and patiently as if his skin were her skin, so that he imagined sometimes that the spreading cool relief came from her fingertips, their delicate, swirling touch.

Then one day in late July, the summer he was fifty-eight and Martha had just turned fifty-six, the summer Raymond Jr. finished graduate school at Georgia Tech and their daughter, Louise, had her second baby, Raymond returned from a week-long trip up the coast. He traveled for Tom's Peanut Company then. He threw his car keys onto the kitchen counter and fell into her arms, groaning about the six hundred miles he'd just driven through the *goddamn* heat, and at his age, too. He smelled of fry grease and cigarette smoke overlaid subtly with sweat and metal, the smell of the road. Someday they'd find him dead of a heart attack, slumped over the steering wheel on the shoulder of some sweltering back road in the Pee Dee swamp. A desk job, that's what he wanted now. To keep him closer to home, closer to *her*, that was the ticket. "Take a shower," she said. "Come lie down."

While she rubbed the cream into his arm, she felt the silky slackness of aging flesh under her hands; she saw that his muscles were starting to droop, go ropy. His chest had begun to sag, too. And as she tenderly catalogued the marks of time on her husband's body, she noticed that his left arm was as pale as the rest of him. She looked at the small, pleased, and peaceful smile on his mouth. She sat on the edge of the bed with the fan blowing across them, the Solarcaine squeezed onto her fingers, and a picture rose up to meet her as though his skin had released it, like a smell: a woman in green shorts lounging in a white wicker chair, her big tanned legs crossed, smoking a cigarette and laughing.

She rubbed the Solarcaine into his pale arm. Next day she went through the phone bills for the last six months, found call after call to a number in Little River, South Carolina. The voice that answered when Martha called matched the thick legs, the cigarettes, the indolence of the woman whose image had wormed its way into her mind. That night, when she showed him the phone bills, Raymond put his hands over his face and cried. It was true, he said, it was true, he'd gotten in over his head. He would break off with her, her name was — "Don't you dare speak her name in my house," Martha shouted — if Martha would just be patient and give him time. If she would just forgive him.

Patience she had, and time. Plenty of both, and also the will to forgive. For six months they tried, but it had gone too far with the other woman. The story came out in pieces: the things he'd given her — jewelry and cash, a semester's tuition for her son at the University of South Carolina — the promises he'd made. She was a widow, twenty years younger than Martha. It almost drove Martha crazy. Just when she thought she'd heard the whole story, he'd choke out more until it seemed there was no end to the future he'd planned with this woman.

When Raymond left to go live with his big-legged woman in Little River, Martha told him she wanted two things — no, three, she wanted three things: she wanted the house in Augusta, and she wanted the house in Scaly Mountain. Louise and Raymond Jr. had been in grade school when Raymond and Martha had bought a beat-up old white clapboard house two stories tall and one room wide, roofed with tin, that sat on a foundation of stacked stones in a valley at the foot of Scaly Mountain, North Carolina; they went there every summer and at Thanksgiving, too, if they could manage it. Always, when they got there, Raymond had to be first out of the car. "Let Daddy have his minute," she'd say to the children, holding them back. He'd make a big show of stretching and breathing, as if he couldn't get enough of that air. Then he'd stand with his hands on his hips, his chest thrown out, king of the hill. Next he'd lean his elbows on the car door, push his wide, smiling face through the open window, squeeze her arm and say, "We're fifty-cent millionaires, Martha, sure enough," as if this discovery were new to him every time, meaning it didn't take much to make him feel rich. Meaning that what he had was all of what he wanted. Then he'd kiss her richly on the mouth, and they had arrived.

The last thing she wanted from Raymond was never to hear from him again. She meant it, too, about cutting him out of her life for good. She knew the way to the cold, bare space inside herself where she could live by the absolutes she declared. Goodbye, Raymond. "I thank my mother for the strength she instilled in me," she told Louise during the divorce. "No, really. She's the one who gave me the backbone for this." Finishing cleanly, she meant, cutting the cord.

### 3

Five years after the divorce, Martha announced that she was moving to the house in Scaly Mountain. "My thermostat must be broken, I can't take this heat any longer," she told Louise, who was frantic about her mother's moving so far away, and all alone, too. "What if you fall?" Louise asked. "What if you have a stroke or a heart attack?"

"Friend, come up higher," Martha joked with her friends from the Episcopal church when they asked her if she'd thought through what she was doing. She told others that she was retiring. From what? they demanded to know. From what? From canasta on Monday and bridge on Tuesday (she did not say), from standing in the vestibule before Sunday morning services, alert for a new face. ("Welcome to All Saints'. Are you visiting with us this morning? Would you please fill out this card and drop it in the collection basket? We're glad to have you.") From taping books for the blind and pushing the book cart around the hospital corridors, intruding on the desperately ill, challenging them with her smile to cheer up. From muffins and casseroles and sympathy calls and notes of congratulation or consolation. From rushing to church every time the doors swung open or having to explain her absence to some anxious friend. Goodbye to all that.

She did not speak to anyone of the solitude she craved: to be alone, with new vistas in front of her eyes and unfamiliar, rocky ground below her feet. She did not tell anyone how she wanted to be rid of Raymond, whose cigarette smoke clung to the paneling in the den and lingered in the closets of the Augusta house. The week before she decided to move, she'd come across a moldy package of Tom's cheese crackers way in the back of a kitchen drawer, and she'd known then that this house would always push reminders of Raymond up to the surface, no matter how hard she scrubbed and bleached and aired. He rested more lightly on the mountain house. There she would lift Raymond's few T-shirts out of the bottom drawer of the dresser in their bedroom and tear them into rags; she would take down his coffee mug from a kitchen shelf, tear his meticulous handwritten instructions off the wall between the hot-water heater and furnace and be finished with him for good. Then he would be gone the way her mother was gone. The mother whose grave she still visited dutifully twice a year, carrying a poinsettia at Christmas, a lily at Eastertime, standing with head bowed, her heart empty of any longing to see her mother, of any wish to speak.

But a person can't just do *nothing*, can she? Can't sit all day with her hands folded or a game of solitaire spread out on the kitchen table. Can't not talk to other people without beginning to hear strange echoes in the conversation she's carrying on with herself. So she went to work. She had the pasture behind the house cleared, she put in a pond. She added two rooms and a porch onto the back of the house, and she lengthened the kitchen until the house looked like a white, wooden shirt with outstretched arms. Over the mountain, to Highlands, twice a week she drove her white Dodge Dart to the senior citizens' center for canasta and talk.

Every week she wrote to her children, letters full of questions and advice. "Have Sarah Lynn's teeth shown any signs of straightening?" she asked her daughter. "If not, do *please* take her to the orthodontist." And "Those old linen napkins I gave you are to be used as *tea towels*," she wrote after she'd visited Louise and found the napkins balled up in the rag basket under the kitchen sink. Her daughter's letters were long and chatty, with fabric swatches stapled to them or pictures of the children enclosed. Raymond Jr. wrote his full-speed-ahead notes on "Memo from Raymond Maitland Jr." paper. He was big in Coca-Cola down in Atlanta, she told her friends over the canasta table. Very big, she'd repeat, arching her eyebrows to show that words simply could not map the circumference of his orbit.

Without fail she wrote a weekly letter to her brother, Perry Jr. After his wife died, he'd drifted into mysticism, joined the Rosicrucians. His letters were about the migration of souls, the power of the spirit to transcend time and space, to enter that place where there was no death, no beginning or end, only a current that carried you up and up, endlessly spiraling toward fulfillment, completion, bliss. He wanted to join his wife, he wrote. He could hardly wait for that day.

Martha sat in her bedroom in the mountain house she had made her own — no trace left of her traitor husband or her bitter black wind of a mother, not so much as a photograph of either of them — a plain, tall woman in a sleeveless blouse and a full skirt made of a coarse woven material like burlap. Her braids were crossed and pinned over the top of her head; she wore orthopedic sandals with wool socks and sat with her ankles crossed, her back very straight in a high-backed chair pulled up to a white wooden table. One must be *realistic,* she wrote to her brother, apply the styptic pencil to one's scratches, pour iodine into the deeper wounds, get on with life in *this* world. Reality (she underlined it twice) was a constant and trustworthy companion who, once befriended, never let one down or walked away and loved someone else. A person must not wear himself out with wanting what it is impossible to have. What was finished must be done with and put away. "False hopes are cruel, Perry," she wrote. "We must not exhaust ourselves waiting for what will never happen. I speak from experience when I say this. As you well know, I have suffered indignities at the hands of life, we all have, but the longer I live the surer I become that the consolations of life — if any — must be sought and found in facing life squarely, as it is. The mind must not be allowed to wander where it wants, else it might end up lost in a wilderness of longing and regret. This I believe."

And then, late one September afternoon, when she'd lived in Scaly Mountain for a year, when the pond was full, the meadow fenced, the hay rolled and drying in the field she leased to a neighbor, as she sat on the porch after supper, watching the evening light flood into her valley and spread across the foot of her meadow, something changed in her. She felt it catch and roll over the way tumblers move inside a big lock. Maybe it was the gold light slanting across the fat rolls of hay that invited the change. Maybe it was the chore she'd finished — writing her mother's name and the date of her death in the Long family Bible — or the way she sat with the book open on her lap, watching the ink dry on the page.

Now this was no modest Sunday school Bible with a white pebbled cover and gold-leaf pages, a tiny gold cross dangling from a red-ribbon marker. It was the original family Bible in which the record of Long births, weddings, and deaths had been written since 1825. A serious and heavy book with a tooled leather cover, a lock and key. It smelled of the smoke of many fires, and its registry pages were stained and soft as cloth. When her father had opened it for family devotions, Martha used to imagine thunder rolling off its pages. She had gone to Marlcrest after her mother had sold everything; without hesitation and without guilt, she'd lifted the Bible off the carved wooden stand next to the fireplace in the downstairs parlor, where it had rested throughout her life and her mother's life and her mother's and her mother's lives, and taken it home. For a year, the museum wrote to her about the Bible. They were tentative, respectful letters at first. Later, letters from lawyers began to arrive. She'd ignored them all. Now, looking from her mother's name out to the hay drying in her meadow, she felt herself lifted, carried, and then set down one place closer to the head of the line her mother had vacated.

That's when the idea of the reunion came to her. She would gather what was left of the Long clan around her, here, in this place. The next morning she drove into Highlands and ordered stationery printed up with *Long Family Reunion* embossed across the top. She set the date for the following summer: July 6–9, 1969. All winter she wrote letters and logged in the answers, then sent back diagrams of the house with rooms and beds assigned.

Give Martha time, her brother used to say, and she could plan anything. Perry Jr. had landed with the Allies on D-Day; he always said that Martha could have planned the Normandy landing. She'd certainly planned *this*. Collected promises from twenty-five far-flung Longs, then stood in the parking lot she'd leveled in her meadow and waved them to their designated spaces with a flashlight, like a state trooper at a football game. She carried their suitcases and marched them up to the house and directed them to their rooms.

For the children there were relay races and treasure hunts and nature hikes down the valley with Martha at the head of the column, like the Scout leader she'd been when Louise was growing up, a walking catalogue of the lore of trees, reptiles, and stones. The girls in her troop had nicknamed her Skink, the lizard, for her bright-eyed, darting restlessness. For the grownups there was plenty of food, plenty of talk; the family Bible and photographs traveled from hand to hand. There was the Long family tree, a scroll as big as a blueprint, on which their genealogist had mapped every twig and root. At night there were games and prizes. A prize for the oldest Long, a dim old uncle, ninety-three that summer, who sat patiently wherever he was put until someone came back for him. And for the youngest, a son born in June to Lamar

Long, who'd been promoted that summer to foreman of the weave room at the Bibb Mill in Porterdale, Georgia. A blue baby, they called him, born with a defective valve in his heart. A good baby, all eyes, who lay quietly in his basket studying the faces that followed each other like clouds across his sky.

Bossiest woman in the world, they whispered among themselves. Exactly like her mother, poor soul, some of the other ones said. Even her own brother had butted heads with her in the kitchen over something silly, over cream. One morning he came whistling into the kitchen, intending to skim a dollop of cream for his coffee from the top of one of the bottles of raw milk that Martha had bought from a neighbor. Right behind him came Martha, who plucked the bottle out of his hand before he could shut the refrigerator door. "I am saving this, Perry," she told him, "to go on top of the blackberry pie I shall make for the fare-well dinner."

"Oh, come on, Martha, I only want a teaspoon," he said.

"No, I cannot spare that much." For half an hour it went on this way.

Then Perry tried for the last word. "I want some of that cream, Martha," he said, holding out his cup to her. It trembled in his hand. "Just a smidgen to put in my damn coffee."

"Well, you can't have it, Perry," she said. "I told you, it's for the pie. I need it all." She held the bottle out to show him — not the thick yellow clot in the neck of the bottle, but the cream, the *cream* whipped into high, stiff points and her pie, warm and rich beneath that sweet, smoth-ering layer. Couldn't he see it? She could, and the thought of that cream-to-be made tears stand in her eyes. Then the thought of herself crying over *whipped cream* made her furious. She who'd written to her brother about dignity and the pitfalls of looking too far into future or past for happiness or consolation, who had thrown all the force of her considerable will into living in the world as it *is*. Finally Perry Jr. slammed his coffee cup down onto the kitchen counter and walked out. That night he said to one of the other men, "I had to lock horns with Martha today." And a child who overheard the remark and the laughter that followed pictured two warring moose in a mountain meadow, their enormous racks locked, shoving each other until they fell from exhaus-tion and died. Then the passing seasons, then the bones covered with hide, the bleached antlers still entangled.

On the last day of the reunion, as she'd planned, Martha climbed the rickety wooden stepladder, shooed away helpers, and strung Japanese paper lanterns between the big silver maple beside the road and the cedar nearest the house. At six-fifteen they would eat, followed at seven by speeches, testimonials, recollections, a song or two, and a final word from the genealogist, who'd traced the family back to England and tonight would name for them the place from which the first Longs had set out for the New World hundreds of years before. Exactly at six, Martha struck a small silver bell with a silver fork and waited until its clear note had died away, then invited everyone to line up, which they did, oldest to youngest, as she'd planned. Then they filed past the tables made of sawhorses and planks and covered with white cloths and filled their plates. Chicken and corn and beans — they heaped it on — banana pudding and coconut cake and, of course, Martha's blackberry pie topped with a mountain range of whipped cream.

They'd just settled down to eat when she heard Abel Rankin coming down the road. He was her neighbor, the one who sold her the raw milk out of cans that he carried in the back of his wagon, that wholesome milk from his own cows from which she'd salvaged *all* the cream. When she heard the clink of the cans, the jolting rattle of the wagon, the jingle of Sawdust the mule's bridle and the stumbling crack of his hooves on the rocky road, she dished up a plate — chicken and beans and coconut cake — and walked out to the edge of the yard to wait for him. When Abel Rankin saw her, he reined in the dun-colored mule and said, "Evening" (never quite meeting her eyes), touched the brim of his brown felt hat, and took the plate of food she held up to him. "Eat this, Mr. Rankin," she said.

He ate quickly, hunched over on the wagon seat as though eating were a chore he had to finish before nightfall, while she held Sawdust's bridle, patted his face, felt the bony plank of his nose, his breath on her hands. When the children came running to pat the mule, she took charge. She made them line up and listen to her. "Now, stroke his nose lightly," she said. "You must stroke an animal as lightly as you'd stroke a hummingbird. You want him to remember you?" she asked. "Blow into his nostrils. Gently, gently, like this, you hear me talking to you?"

Those were her mother's teachings, her mother's actual *words*. As soon as they'd left her mouth, she felt her mother walk up and stand behind her, listening, to hear if she'd gotten it right, how to treat an animal. Her mother had always kept a reservoir of tenderness toward animals unpolluted by her general disappointment and bitterness. No animal had ever betrayed her. Oh, no. When Martha was a child, there had always been a pack of half-starved stray dogs skulking around the back steps at Marlcrest, waiting for her mother to feed them. There had always been a shoebox on top of the stove full of baby squirrels rescued from a fallen pine, tenderly wrapped in flannel and bottle-fed into independence.

Her mother had owned a Tennessee walking horse, a flashy bay named Jimbo, whose black mane and tail she'd braided with red ribbons before she rode him in shows. She used to nuzzle, stroke, pat the horse, bury her face in his mane, while Martha hung on the paddock fence, listening to the dark-gold and fluid warmth that filled her mother's voice when she talked to him, waiting for that warm and liquid love to overflow the dam in her mother's heart and pour over her. Waiting, still waiting. And now her mother had come and stood so close that Martha imagined she heard her mother's breath whistling down the bony narrows of her imperial nose. Her mother, who'd traveled this long way to find Martha and withhold her love again, just to remind her daughter, as a good mother should, that her love might still be won if Martha would just be patient and not lose heart, if she would just get it right for once.

Martha held her breath, then shook her head to clear it and turned to see if anyone had noticed her standing there like a fool with her eyes squeezed shut and her fists clenched at her sides, swept away in a fit of hope. Up on the wagon seat, Abel Rankin worked steadily at his supper; the children cooed and stroked Sawdust's nose and laid their cheeks against his whiskery muzzle. Back in the yard, people sat on the green grass and on the porch, enjoying their food. They circled the table and filled their plates a second time, a third; they lifted thick slabs from her beautiful pie. What a ridiculous old woman you are, she thought. Standing there waiting for your dead mother to touch you. But there it was again, percolating up through the layers of years, bubbling out at Martha's feet like a perverse spring. This sly and relentless force that moved through the world, this patient and brutal something that people called hope, which would not be stopped, ever, in its work of knitting and piecing and binding, recovering, reclaiming, making whole. Which formed from the stuff of your present life a future where you would be healed or loved and sent you running forward while it dissolved and remade itself ahead of you, so that you lived always with the feeling, so necessary to survival in this world, that you were not just trudging along but moving *toward* something.

She guessed that if you could just give up hope, your time on earth would be free of longing and its disfigurements. God knows she'd tried.

But you couldn't. Not even her mother had done that, finally. Even after she'd sold Marlcrest out from under them and momentarily righted the wrong of her life by taking from someone else what she felt had been taken from her, she hadn't been satisfied. Instead, she'd begun to pine and grieve over her old poodle.

Rowdy was his name, Martha's only inheritance. She'd taken him to her house when she and Perry Jr. had put their mother in the nursing home. He was thirteen years old then, morose and incontinent, a trembler, a fear-biter. Nothing left of him but gluey old eyes, a curly coat, and bones. On a Saturday morning soon after he came to live with her, he turned over her garbage while she was at the grocery store and ate rancid bacon drippings out of a small Crisco can. She found him on her kitchen floor, greasy and struggling to breathe, and rushed him to the vet's, where he died two hours later, his blood so clogged with fat his old heart just choked on it.

Until her dying day their mother had been greedy for news of Rowdy, details of his diet, the consistency of his stools, and Martha and Perry Jr. had given them to her. They'd even pretended to be passing Rowdy back and forth between them, sharing the wealth. On one visit, Perry Jr. would tell their mother how on cool fall mornings Rowdy had enough spark to chase squirrels around Perry's back yard. On the next visit, Martha would continue the story, say that Rowdy still enjoyed his dog biscuits even though he gummed them now and it took him forever to eat one. He's a little constipated, she would say, but he's fine. "Well, then, you're not feeding him enough roughage," their mother would say. "Feed him apples. I must have told you that a thousand times, don't you listen when I talk to you?" she would say, the old fierceness darkening her good eye. Then she would smile. Toward the end, when she smiled at them, it was her skull that smiled; then the weeping would begin, the longing, the sorrow. "Why don't you bring my little dog to see me?" she would sob. "Soon, Mother," they would promise, patting her hand, smoothing back her hair. "Next time."


4

Now it is August, twenty-five years past the summer of the reunion. Olivia Hudson, one of Martha's grandnieces, is driving through the mountains with her husband and small son when they pass a road that runs up a narrow valley, and she says, "That looks like the road to my great-aunt Martha's house, the one where we had the family reunion, remember my telling you about that?" She had been seven that summer, the blue baby was her brother; in photographs she stands protectively close, her hand always resting near him, on the side of bed or blanket. Now they turn back and head up the valley, and as they drive Olivia studies the landscape, looking for clues. She cannot imagine that the house is still standing, but she hopes that some arrangement of trees and pastures and fences will rebuild it in her mind's eye and set it down on its lost foundation. She hopes for sheets of roofing tin, a standing chimney, steps leading up to an overgrown field. Anything.

Instead, they drive around a curve and she sees the house, the *house* itself, rising out of a jungle of saplings and shaggy cedars. Silver maple saplings, hundreds of them, Olivia sees as they drive closer. The leaves flash and flutter in the breeze. A realtor's sign lies on its side in the grass, near the stump of the big silver maple that has spawned the little trees, the one that threw its wide shade across the front lawn the summer of the reunion. And what Olivia feels as they wade and push toward the house through the thick grass and saplings is an emotion so quick and powerful it takes her by surprise. It is as potent as love *recovered*, the feeling itself, not the memory of the feeling — an urge to laugh out loud and also a dragging sadness, and a longing for no particular person or thing, a longing to *know* what the longing is for.

And Olivia thinks that if the house had been sold, had become someone else's house, unpainted, the screens kicked out, the yard full of junk cars, if a picket fence had been thrown around it, a straw hat with flowers in the band hung on the door, its power to move her would have dissolved into its new life. As it is, its power is original, strong. She feels as if she could look in and find them all at dinner, Martha circling the long table, pouring raw milk into the children's glasses, and the mothers following her, pouring it out, refilling their children's glasses with the store-bought, pasteurized kind.

Of course, what she sees when they've waded through the grass and stepped over the rotten place on the porch and looked in through the cloudy glass of the narrow window beside the door is the front room of an abandoned and neglected house. Bloated chairs, scattered papers, white droppings everywhere, a cardboard box packed with blue bottles. She *has* to get inside.

Down the mountain they find the realtor. Billie is her name. She has diamonds on the wings of her glasses, jewels on her long black T-shirt, ragged black hair and Cherokee-dark eyes, Cherokee cheekbones. She is so heavy and short of breath that Olivia's husband has to boost her up the broken front steps, but when they get inside the house, she turns brisk, businesslike. Martha's children still own the place, but they're so busy they never come here. That's why they've put it up for sale. Someone is about to buy this place and turn it into a bed-and-breakfast inn, take advantage of the business from the new ski slope over at Scaly Mountain. Since Olivia is kin (now that she's been around Olivia for a while, Billie can see the resemblance, yes: "You favor your aunt Martha," she says), wouldn't she be interested in buying it? Of course, Olivia would have to make an offer right away, today in fact. Billie checks her watch. She's expecting an offer any minute from the bed-and-breakfast people.

Books lie scattered on the floor of every room; faded curtains sag from bowed rods; blackberry vines tap against the glass in the kitchen door. "You know, people around here say this place is haunted," Billie calls to Olivia as Olivia starts up the stairs to the second floor. "Your great-aunt Martha died in this house, and they say she came back as a cat to haunt it."

Olivia laughs. "If anyone would haunt a place, it would be Martha," she calls down the stairs, thinking of the grizzled tabby with the shredded ear and stony face that had been sitting on the porch when they'd driven up, that had dissolved like smoke between the foundation stones when they'd stepped out of the car. Thinking of Martha's tenacity. The famous struggle with her brother over the cream. She thinks of Martha fighting battles, righting wrongs, the clean, bleached smell of her clothes. Martha had wanted something out of life that couldn't be found in one lifetime, no doubt about it. Naturally, her spirit would go on poking and probing and quarreling here, striding, big nose first, into a room.

Remembering all that, Olivia comes into the long room under the eaves where the women and girls slept during the reunion. Now it is full of rusty file cabinets and busted-open suitcases and, strangest of all, in a closet, a wedding dress and veil, vacuum packed in a white box under a clear plastic window, without a date to place it in time or a name to connect it with anyone's life. Outside the window that's set so low in the wall she has to stoop to look through it, she sees her husband following their son through the tall grass behind the house, and beyond him, a dip in the overgrown meadow where Martha's pond once lay, that shallow, cold, muddy pond that never cleared except where it ran over the spillway.

Olivia opens a drawer in one of the file cabinets — she has to yank it because of the rust — and flips through crumbling file folders stuffed with brown and brittle papers. Real estate forms, a Rosicrucian newsletter, yellowed stationery with *Long Family Reunion* printed across the top. She thinks of the week she spent in this room, The Henhouse, the men had named it. All that clucking, fussing, preening, a bunch of broody hens. Her father, who loved jokes, had lettered the name on a piece of cardboard, along with a drawing of a plump hen with a big behind and long eyelashes looking coyly over her shoulder, and tacked it onto the door. Olivia had never before been included among the women nor surrounded by so many of them. They slept under starched sheets and thin blankets on old camp beds set in rows. She'd pulled her bed over near the window, next to her mother's bed and the baby's basket. From there she'd watched the moon rise, the constellations wheel up from behind the mountain, the morning light fill the valley. The month before she died, so Olivia has heard, Martha added a sunroom onto the south side of the house. And now this house and all its rooms have been died out of, left and locked away, abandoned, begun again and never finished.

"Your aunt Martha really knew her way around these mountains," Billie calls up from the bottom of the stairs. "One time she went to a neighbor's funeral at the Church of God up the road there and another woman went with her who wasn't from around here either. But that other woman, she dressed up in high heels, a nice navy dress, a mink stole, and a hat. You know those Church of God people are *strict*. They don't allow any fancy show in their churches. They say that when that woman came in dressed in her finery and took a seat, everybody turned and stared until she got up and left their church. But your aunt Martha now, she wore a plain black cardigan sweater over a dark dress. She wore low-heeled shoes. She came in and sat in a back pew, quiet as a mouse. They accepted her just like she was one of their own kind."

Olivia is pleased to hear about Martha's dignity for a change. Billie's story restores height and luster to the foolish and shopworn figure her aunt has become over time, handed down through the family. All over that part of the mountains, Billie says, people had talked about Martha at the funeral as though she'd done something remarkable by going there properly dressed. But when the story got back to Martha, she didn't see what all the fuss was about. It didn't surprise her that she'd done the right thing. Dressing for the funeral that morning, she hadn't given a thought to what she should wear: everyone knows what to wear to a *funeral*. She'd just reached into her closet and pulled out a black dress. Since it was a cool fall morning, she'd added a black sweater. At the last minute she'd even slipped off her wristwatch and left it in a dresser drawer to keep its gold band from offending the eye of any member of that stern congregation. The watch had been a birthday gift from her children one year, and looking at it reminded her of their faces — small and clear and full of light — when they were young and the days ahead seemed numberless.

She'd gone into the crowded, chilly church and sat in the back pew and listened to the congregation sing a hymn. Harsh, unaccompanied, the singing had reminded her of a creekbed in a drought with the sun beating down on dry stones, but that dry creek had carried her anyway, back to the summer of the reunion and the walk she'd taken with her grandchildren to see the orchard. The haunted orchard, the children had called it, where a blight had killed the trees and withered apples had clung to the branches through a whole year of seasons. Standing there with the children, she'd turned to her daughter's oldest boy. "And what do you intend to make of yourself when you grow up, Mr. Albert Redmond?" she'd asked.

He'd look up at her out of pale blue eyes as he pivoted on his heels, inscribing circles in the dirt of the road. He was ten, beginning to fizz. He wore red high-tops, a whistle on a lumpy purple-and-orange lanyard that he'd made at Boy Scout camp earlier that summer. "A fifty-cent millionaire," he'd answered her, grinning.

Hearing Raymond's words in the child's mouth had made her heart pound, her cheeks flush. And just like that, Raymond had joined them. Uninvited, unwelcome, he'd come back with his gosh-and-golly face, his pale traitor's arm, all the things she'd made herself cold and deaf and blind to years ago. "Well, son-of-a-gun," she'd heard him whisper warmly in her ear, insinuating more, "how about them apples?"

"Well, I hope you won't waste too much of your valuable time pursuing that course," she'd said to the boy that day, staring at the orchard, dizzy, suddenly, as though she'd waked up to the earth's circling, the endless motion of return that had brought her here, where it had seemed for a moment that the stubborn and contradictory truths of those trees had merged with the warring truths of her own life: the trees had died, but the fruit would not fall. Hope could cling to nothing, and a shriveled apple was all it took to coax love to come slinking back into this world. Inside the fruit she saw seeds; inside the seeds, more fruit. In this motion she saw the turning shadow that eternity throws across this world and also the current that carries us there. She had not forgotten.

When the hymn was done, the preacher told the story of the narrow gate, the strict accounting, the raked, leveled, and weeded ground of the promised land toward which they traveled in sure and certain hope of the resurrection. And when the service was over, she stood outside the church and greeted those harsh and unblinking souls as if they were kin.

1998

*Annie Proulx*

......................................................................................................

# The Half-Skinned Steer

FROM *The Atlantic Monthly*

IN THE LONG UNFURLING of his life, from tight-wound kid hustler in a wool suit riding the train out of Cheyenne to geriatric limper in this spooled-out year, Mero had kicked down thoughts of the place where he began, a so-called ranch on strange ground at the south hinge of the Big Horns. He'd got himself out of there in 1936, had gone to a war and come back, married and married again (and again), made money in boilers and air-duct cleaning and smart investments, retired, got into local politics and out again without scandal, never circled back to see the old man and Rollo, bankrupt and ruined, because he knew they were.

They called it a ranch and it had been, but one day the old man said cows couldn't be run in such tough country, where they fell off cliffs, disappeared into sinkholes, gave up large numbers of calves to marauding lions; where hay couldn't grow but leafy spurge and Canada thistle throve, and the wind packed enough sand to scour windshields opaque. The old man wangled a job delivering mail, but looked guilty fumbling bills into his neighbors' mailboxes.

Mero and Rollo saw the mail route as a defection from the work of the ranch, work that consequently fell on them. The breeding herd was down to eighty-two, and a cow wasn't worth more than fifteen dollars, but they kept mending fence, whittling ears and scorching hides, hauling cows out of mudholes, and hunting lions in the hope that sooner or later the old man would move to Ten Sleep with his woman and his bottle and they could, as had their grandmother Olive when Jacob Corn disappointed her, pull the place taut. That bird didn't fly, and Mero wound up sixty years later as an octogenarian vegetarian widower pumping an Exercycle in the living room of a colonial house in Woolfoot, Massachusetts.

One of those damp mornings the nail-driving telephone voice of a woman said she was Louise, Tick's wife, and summoned him back to Wyoming. He didn't know who she was, who Tick was, until she said, Tick Corn, your brother Rollo's son, and that Rollo had passed on, killed by a waspy emu, though prostate cancer was waiting its chance. Yes, she said, you bet Rollo still owned the ranch. Half of it anyway. Me and Tick, she said, we been pretty much running it the past ten years.

An emu? Did he hear right?

Yes, she said. Well, of course you didn't know. You heard of Wyoming Down Under?

He had not. And thought, What kind of name is Tick? He recalled the bloated gray insects pulled off the dogs. This tick probably thought he was going to get the whole damn ranch and bloat up on it. He said, What the hell is this about an emu? Were they all crazy out there?

That's what the ranch is called now, she said. Wyoming Down Under. Rollo'd sold the place way back when to the Girl Scouts, but one of the girls was dragged off by a lion, and the GSA sold out to the Banner ranch, next door, which ran cattle on it for a few years and then unloaded it on a rich Australian businessman, who started Wyoming Down Under, but it was too much long-distance work and he'd had bad luck with his manager, a feller from Idaho with a pawnshop rodeo buckle, so he'd looked up Rollo and offered to swap him a half interest if he'd run the place. That was back in 1978. The place had done real well. Course we're not open now, she said. It's winter and there's no tourists. Poor Rollo was helping Tick move the emus to another building when one of them turned on a dime and come right for him with its big razor claws. Emus is bad for claws.

I know, he said. He watched the nature programs on television.

She shouted, as though the telephone lines were down all across the country, Tick got your number off the computer. Rollo always said he was going to get in touch. He wanted you to see how things turned out. He tried to fight it off with his cane, but it laid him open from belly to breakfast.

Maybe, he thought, things hadn't finished turning out. Impatient with this game, he said he would be at the funeral. No point talking about flights and meeting him at the airport, he told her; he didn't fly, a bad experience years ago with hail, the plane had looked like a waffle iron when it landed. He intended to drive. Of course he knew how far it was. Had a damn fine car, Cadillac, always drove Cadillacs, Gislaved tires, interstate highways, excellent driver, never had an accident in his life, knock on wood. Four days; he would be there by Saturday afternoon. He heard the amazement in her voice, knew she was plotting his age, figuring he had to be eighty-three, a year or so older than Rollo, figuring he must be dotting around on a cane too, drooling the tiny days away — she was probably touching her own faded hair. He flexed his muscular arms, bent his knees, thought he could dodge an emu. He would see his brother dropped in a red Wyoming hole. That event could jerk him back; the dazzled rope of lightning against the cloud is not the downward bolt but the compelled upstroke through the heated ether.

He had pulled away at the sudden point when the old man's girlfriend — now he couldn't remember her name — seemed to have jumped the track, Rollo goggling at her bloody bitten fingers, nails chewed to the quick, neck veins like wires, the outer forearms shaded with hairs, and the cigarette glowing, smoke curling up, making her wink her bulging mustang eyes, a teller of tales of hard deeds and mayhem. The old man's hair was falling out, Mero was twenty-three and Rollo twenty, and she played them all like a deck of cards. If you admired horses, you'd go for her with her arched neck and horsy buttocks, so high and haunchy you'd want to clap her on the rear. The wind bellowed around the house, driving crystals of snow through the cracks of the warped log door, and all of them in the kitchen seemed charged with some intensity of purpose. She'd balanced that broad butt on the edge of the dog-food chest, looking at the old man and Rollo, now and then rolling her glossy eyes over at Mero, square teeth nipping a rim of nail, sucking the welling blood, drawing on her cigarette.

The old man drank his Everclear stirred with a peeled willow stick for the bitter taste. The image of him came sharp in Mero's mind as he stood at the hall closet contemplating his hats. Should he take one for the funeral? The old man had had the damnedest curl to his hat brim, a tight roll on the right where his doffing or donning hand gripped it, and a wavering downslope on the left like a shed roof. You could recognize him two miles away. He wore it at the table listening to the woman's stories about Tin Head, steadily emptying his glass until he was nine times nine drunk, his gangstery face loosening, the crushed rodeo nose and scar-crossed eyebrows, the stub ear, dissolving as he drank. Now he must be dead fifty years or more, buried in the mailman sweater.

The girlfriend started a story, Yeah, there was this guy named Tin Head down around Dubois when my dad was a kid. Had a little ranch, some horses, cows, kids, a wife. But there was something funny about him. He had a metal plate in his head from falling down some cement steps.

Plenty of guys has them, Rollo said in a challenging way.

She shook her head. Not like his. His was made out of galvy, and it eat at his brain.

The old man held up the bottle of Everclear, raised his eyebrows at her: Well, darlin'?

She nodded, took the glass from him, and knocked it back in one swallow. Oh, that's not gonna slow *me* down, she said.

Mero expected her to neigh.

So what then, Rollo said, picking at the horse manure under his boot heel. What about Tin Head and his galvanized skull plate?

I heard it this way, she said. She held out the glass for another shot of Everclear, and the old man poured it, and she went on.

Mero had thrashed all that ancient night, dreamed of horse breeding or hoarse breathing, whether the act of sex or bloody, cutthroat gasps he didn't know. The next morning he woke up drenched in stinking sweat, looked at the ceiling, and said aloud, It could go on like this for some time. He meant cows and weather as much as anything, and what might be his chances two or three states over in any direction. In Woolfoot, riding the Exercycle, he thought the truth was somewhat different: he'd wanted a woman of his own, not the old man's leftovers.

What he wanted to know now, tires spanking the tar-filled road cracks and potholes, funeral homburg sliding on the back seat, was if Rollo had got the girlfriend away from the old man, thrown a saddle on her, and ridden off into the sunset.

The interstate, crippled by orange cones, forced traffic into single lanes, broke his expectation of making good time. His Cadillac, boxed between semis with hissing air brakes, showed snuffling huge rear tires in the windshield, framed a looming Peterbilt in the back window. His thoughts clogged as if a comb working through his mind had stuck against a snarl. When the traffic eased and he tried to cover some ground, the highway patrol pulled him over. The cop, a pimpled, mustached specimen with mismatched eyes, asked his name, where he was going. For the minute he couldn't think what he was doing there. The cop's tongue dapped at the scraggy mustache while he scribbled.

Funeral, he said suddenly. Going to my brother's funeral.

Well, you take it easy, gramps, or they'll be doing one for you.

You're a little polecat, aren't you? he said, staring at the ticket, at the pathetic handwriting, but the mustache was a mile gone, peeling through the traffic as Mero had peeled out of the ranch road that long time ago, squinting through the abraded windshield. He might have made a more graceful exit, but urgency had struck him as a blow on the humerus sends a ringing jolt up the arm. He believed it was the horse-haunched woman leaning against the chest and Rollo fixed on her, the old man swilling Everclear and not noticing or, if noticing, not caring, that had worked in him like a key in an ignition. She had long, gray-streaked braids; Rollo could use them for reins.

Yeah, she said, in her low and convincing liar's voice. I'll tell you, on Tin Head's ranch things went wrong. Chickens changed color overnight, calves was born with three legs, his kids was piebald, and his wife always crying for blue dishes. Tin Head never finished nothing he started, quit halfway through a job every time. Even his pants was half buttoned, so his weenie hung out. He was a mess with the galvy plate eating at his brain, and his ranch and his family was a mess. But, she said, they had to eat, didn't they, just like anybody else?

I hope they eat pies better than the ones you make, said Rollo, who didn't like the mouthful of pits that came with the chokecherries.

His interest in women had begun a few days after the old man had said, Take this guy up and show him them Ind'an drawrings, jerking his head at the stranger. Mero had been eleven or twelve at the time, no older. They rode along the creek and put up a pair of mallards who flew downstream and then suddenly reappeared, pursued by a goshawk who struck the drake with a sound like a handclap. The duck tumbled through the trees and into deadfall trash, and the hawk shot away as swiftly as it had come.

They climbed through the stony landscape, limestone beds eroded by wind into fantastic furniture, stale gnawed bread crusts, tumbled bones, stacks of dirty folded blankets, bleached crab claws and dog teeth. He tethered the horses in the shade of a stand of limber pine and led the anthropologist up through the stiff-branched mountain mahogany to the overhang. Above them reared corroded cliffs brilliant with orange lichen, pitted with holes, ridged with ledges darkened by millennia of raptor feces.

The anthropologist moved back and forth scrutinizing the stone gallery of red and black drawings: bison skulls, a line of mountain sheep, warriors carrying lances, a turkey stepping into a snare, a stick man upside-down dead and falling, red-ocher hands, violent figures with rakes on their heads that he said were feather headdresses, a great red bear dancing forward on its hind legs, concentric circles and crosses and latticework. He copied the drawings in his notebook, saying Rubba-dubba a few times.

That's the sun, said the anthropologist, who resembled an unfinished drawing himself, pointing at an archery target, ramming his pencil into the air as though tapping gnats. That's an atlatl, and that's a dragonfly. There we go. You know what this is, and he touched a cloven oval, rubbing the cleft with his dusty fingers. He got down on his hands and knees and pointed out more, a few dozen.

A horseshoe?

A horseshoe! The anthropologist laughed. No, boy, it's a vulva. That's what all of these are. You don't know what this is, do you? You go to school on Monday and look it up in the dictionary.

It's a symbol, he said. You know what a symbol is?

Yes, said Mero, who had seen them clapped together in the high school marching band. The anthropologist laughed and told him he had a great future, gave him a dollar for showing him the place. Listen, kid, the Indians did it just like anybody else, he said.

He had looked the word up in the school dictionary, slammed the book closed in embarrassment, but the image was fixed for him (with the brassy background sound of a military march), blunt ocher tracing on stone, and no fleshly examples ever conquered his belief in the subterranean stony structure of female genitalia, the pubic bone a proof, except for the old man's girlfriend, whom he imagined down on all fours, entered from behind and whinnying like a mare, a thing not of geology but of flesh.

Thursday night, balked by detours and construction, he was on the outskirts of Des Moines. In the cinder-block motel room he set the alarm, but his own stertorous breathing woke him before it rang. He was up at five-fifteen, eyes aflame, peering through the vinyl drapes at his snow-hazed car flashing blue under the motel sign, SLEEP SLEEP. In the bathroom he mixed the packet of instant motel coffee and drank it black, without ersatz sugar or chemical cream. He wanted the caffeine. The roots of his mind felt withered and punky.

A cold morning, light snow slanting down: he unlocked the Cadillac, started it, and curved into the vein of traffic, all semis, double and triple trailers. In the headlights' glare he missed the westbound ramp and got into torn-up muddy streets, swung right and right again, using the motel's SLEEP sign as a landmark, but he was on the wrong side of the interstate, and the sign belonged to a different motel.

Another mudholed lane took him into a traffic circle of commuters sucking coffee from insulated cups, pastries sliding on dashboards. Half around the hoop he spied the interstate entrance ramp, veered for it, collided with a panel truck emblazoned STOP SMOKING! HYPNOSIS THAT WORKS!, was rammed from behind by a stretch limo, the limo in its turn rear-ended by a yawning hydroblast operator in a company pickup.

He saw little of this, pressed into his seat by the airbag, his mouth full of a rubbery, dusty taste, eyeglasses cutting into his nose. His first thought was to blame Iowa and those who lived in it. There were a few round spots of blood on his shirt cuff.

A star-spangled Band-Aid over his nose, he watched his crumpled car, pouring dark fluids onto the highway, towed away behind a wrecker. When the police were through with him, a taxi took him, his suitcase, the homburg funeral hat, in the other direction, to Posse Motors, where lax salesmen drifted like disorbited satellites and where he bought a secondhand Cadillac, black like the wreck but three years older and the upholstery not cream leather but sun-faded velour. He had the good tires from the wreck brought over and mounted. He could do that if he liked, buy cars like packs of cigarettes and smoke them up. He didn't care for the way the Caddy handled out on the highway, throwing itself abruptly aside when he twitched the wheel, and he guessed it might have a bent frame. Damn. He'd buy another for the return trip. He could do what he wanted.

He was half an hour past Kearney, Nebraska, when the full moon rose, an absurd visage balanced in his rearview mirror, above it a curled wig of a cloud, filamented edges like platinum hairs. He felt his swollen nose, palped his chin, tender from the stun of the airbag. Before he slept that night, he swallowed a glass of hot tap water enlivened with whiskey, crawled into the damp bed. He had eaten nothing all day, but his stomach coiled at the thought of road food.

He dreamed that he was in the ranch house but all the furniture had been removed from the rooms and in the yard troops in dirty white uniforms fought. The concussive reports of huge guns were breaking the window glass and forcing the floorboards apart, so that he had to walk on the joists. Below the disintegrating floors he saw galvanized tubs filled with dark, coagulated fluid.

On Saturday morning, with four hundred miles in front of him, he swallowed a few bites of scorched eggs, potatoes painted with canned salsa verde, a cup of yellow coffee, left no tip, got on the road. The food was not what he wanted. His breakfast habit was two glasses of mineral water, six cloves of garlic, a pear. The sky to the west hulked sullen; behind him were smears of tinselly orange shot through with blinding streaks. The thick rim of sun bulged against the horizon.

He crossed the state line, hit Cheyenne for the second time in sixty years. He saw neon, traffic, and concrete, but he knew the place, a railroad town that had been up and down. That other time he had been painfully hungry, had gone into the restaurant in the Union Pacific station although he was not used to restaurants, and had ordered a steak. When the woman brought it and he cut into the meat, the blood spread across the white plate and he couldn't help it, he saw the beast, mouth agape in mute bawling, saw the comic aspects of his revulsion as well, a cattleman gone wrong.

Now he parked in front of a phone booth, locked the car although he stood only seven feet away, and telephoned the number Tick's wife had given him. The ruined car had had a phone. Her voice roared out of the earpiece.

We didn't hear so we wondered if you changed your mind.

No, he said, I'll be there late this afternoon. I'm in Cheyenne now.

The wind's blowing pretty hard. They're saying it could maybe snow. In the mountains. Her voice sounded doubtful.

I'll keep an eye on it, he said.

He was out of town and running north in a few minutes.

The country poured open on each side, reduced the Cadillac to a finger snap. Nothing had changed, not a goddamn thing, the empty pale place and its roaring wind, the distant antelope as tiny as mice, landforms shaped true to the past. He felt himself slip back; the calm of eighty-three years sheeted off him like water, replaced by a young man's scalding anger at a fool world and the fools in it. What a damn hard time it had been to hit the road. You don't know what it was like, he had told his wives, until they said they did know, he'd pounded it into their ears two hundred times, the poor youth on the street holding up a sign asking for work, the job with the furnace man, *yatata yatata ya.* Thirty miles out of Cheyenne he saw the first billboard:

WYOMING DOWN UNDER, Western Fun the Other Way, over a blown-up photograph of kangaroos hopping through the sagebrush and a blond child grinning in a manic imitation of pleasure. A diagonal banner warned, Open May 31.

So what, Rollo had said to the old man's girlfriend, what about that Mr. Tin Head? Looking at her, not just her face but up and down, eyes moving over her like an iron over a shirt and the old man in his mailman's sweater and lopsided hat tasting his Everclear and not noticing or not caring, getting up every now and then to lurch onto the porch and water the weeds. When he left the room, the tension ebbed and they were only ordinary people to whom nothing happened. Rollo looked away from the woman, leaned down to scratch the dog's ears, saying Snarleyow Snapper, and the woman took a dish to the sink and ran water on it, yawning. When the old man came back to his chair, the Everclear like sweet oil in his glass, glances resharpened and inflections of voice again carried complex messages.

Well, well, she said, tossing her braids back, every year Tin Head butchers one of his steers, and that's what they'd eat all winter long, boiled, fried, smoked, fricasseed, burned, and raw. So one time he's out there by the barn, and he hits the steer a good one with the ax, and it drops stun down. He ties up the back legs, hoists it up and sticks it, shoves the tub under to catch the blood. When it's bled out pretty good, he lets it down and starts skinning it, starts with the head, cuts back of the poll down past the eye to the nose, peels the hide back. He don't cut the head off but keeps on skinning, dewclaws to hock, up the inside of the thigh and then to the cod and down the middle of the belly to brisket. Now he's ready to start siding, working that tough old skin off. But siding is hard work (the old man nodded) and he gets the hide off about halfway and starts thinking about dinner. So he leaves the steer half-skinned there on the ground and he goes into the kitchen, but first he cuts out the tongue, which is his favorite dish all cooked up and eat cold with Mrs. Tin Head's mustard in a forget-me-not teacup. Sets it on the ground and goes in to dinner. Dinner is chicken and dumplins, one of them changed-color chickens started out white and ended up blue, yessir, blue as your old daddy's eyes.

She was a total liar. The old man's eyes were murk brown.

Onto the high plains sifted the fine snow, delicately clouding the air, a rare dust, beautiful, he thought, silk gauze, but there was muscle in the wind rocking the heavy car, a great pulsing artery of the jet stream swooping down from the sky to touch the earth. Plumes of smoke rose hundreds of feet into the air, elegant fountains and twisting snow devils, shapes of veiled Arab women and ghost riders dissolving in white fume. The snow snakes writhing across the asphalt straightened into rods. He was driving in a rushing river of cold whiteout foam. He could see nothing; he trod on the brake, the wind buffeting the car, a bitter, hard-flung dust hissing over metal and glass. The car shuddered. And as suddenly as it had risen, the wind dropped and the road was clear; he could see a long, empty mile.

How do you know when there's enough of anything? What trips the lever that snaps up the Stop sign? What electrical currents fizz and crackle in the brain to shape the decision to quit a place? He had listened to her damn story and the dice had rolled. For years he believed he had left without hard reason and suffered for it. But he'd learned from television nature programs that it had been time for him to find his own territory and his own woman. How many women were out there! He had married three of them and sampled plenty.

With the lapping subtlety of an incoming tide the shape of the ranch began to gather in his mind; he could recall sharply the fences he'd made, taut wire and perfect corners, the draws and rock outcrops, the watercourse valley steepening, cliffs like bones with shreds of meat on them rising and rising, and the stream plunging suddenly underground, disappearing into a subterranean darkness of blind fish, shooting out of the mountain ten miles west on a neighbor's place but leaving their ranch some badland red country as dry as a cracker, steep canyons with high caves suited to lions. He and Rollo had shot two early in that winter, close to the overhang with the painted vulvas. There were good caves up there from a lion's point of view.

He traveled against curdled sky. In the last sixty miles the snow began again. He climbed out of Buffalo. Pallid flakes as distant from one another as galaxies flew past, then more, and in ten minutes he was crawling at twenty miles an hour, the windshield wipers thumping like a stick dragged down the stairs.

The light was falling out of the day when he reached the pass, the blunt mountains lost in snow, the greasy hairpin turns ahead. He drove slowly and steadily in a low gear; he had not forgotten how to drive a winter mountain. But the wind was up again, rocking and slapping

the car, blotting out all but whipping snow, and he was sweating with
the anxiety of keeping to the road, dizzy with the altitude. Twelve
more miles, sliding and buffeted, before he reached Ten Sleep, where
streetlights glowed in revolving circles like Van Gogh's sun. There had
not been electricity when he left the place. In those days there were
seventeen black, lightless miles between the town and the ranch, and
now the long arch of years compressed into that distance. His headlights
picked up a sign: 20 MILES TO WYOMING DOWN UNDER. Emus and
bison leered above the letters.

He turned onto the snowy road, marked with a single set of tracks,
faint but still discernible, the heater fan whirring, the radio silent, all
beyond the headlights blurred. Yet everything was as it had been, the
shape of the road achingly familiar, sentinel rocks looming as they had
in his youth. There was an eerie dream quality in seeing the deserted
Farrier place leaning east as it had leaned sixty years ago, and the
Banner ranch gate, where the companionable tracks he had been following turned off, the gate ghostly in the snow but still flying its
wrought-iron flag, unmarked by the injuries of weather, and the taut
five-strand fences and dim shifting forms of cattle. Next would come
the road to their ranch, a left-hand turn just over the crest of a rise. He
was running now on the unmarked road through great darkness.

Winking at Rollo, the girlfriend had said, Yes, she had said, Yes, sir, Tin
Head eats half his dinner and then he has to take a little nap. After a
while he wakes up again and goes outside, stretching his arms and
yawning, says, Guess I'll finish skinning out that steer. But the steer ain't
there. It's gone. Only the tongue, laying on the ground all covered with
dirt and straw, and the tub of blood and the dog licking at it.

It was her voice that drew you in, that low, twangy voice, wouldn't
matter if she was saying the alphabet, what you heard was the rustle of
hay. She could make you smell the smoke from an imagined fire.

How could he not recognize the turnoff to the ranch? It was so clear and
sharp in his mind: the dusty crimp of the corner, the low section where
the snow drifted, the run where willows slapped the side of the truck.
He went a mile, watching for it, but the turn didn't come up; then he
watched for the Bob Kitchen place, two miles beyond, but the distance
unrolled and there was nothing. He made a three-point turn and backtracked. Rollo must have given up the old entrance road, for it wasn't
there. The Kitchen place was gone to fire or wind. If he didn't find the

turn, it was no great loss; back to Ten Sleep and scout a motel. But he hated to quit when he was close enough to spit, hated to retrace black miles on a bad night when he was maybe twenty minutes away from the ranch.

He drove very slowly, following his tracks, and the ranch entrance appeared on the right, although the gate was gone and the sign down. That was why he'd missed it, that and a clump of sagebrush that obscured the gap.

He turned in, feeling a little triumph. But the road under the snow was rough and got rougher, until he was bucking along over boulders and slanted rock and knew wherever he was, it was not right.

He couldn't turn around on the narrow track and began backing gingerly, the window down, craning his stiff neck, staring into the redness cast by the taillights. The car's right rear tire rolled up over a boulder, slid, and sank into a quaggy hole. The tires spun in the snow, but he got no purchase.

I'll sit here, he said aloud. I'll sit here until it's light and then walk down to the Banner place and ask for a cup of coffee. I'll be cold but I won't freeze to death. It played like a joke the way he imagined it, with Bob Banner opening the door and saying, Why, it's Mero, come on in and have some java and a hot biscuit, before he remembered that Bob Banner would have to be 120 years old to fill that role. He was maybe three miles from Banner's gate, and the Banner ranch house was another seven miles beyond the gate. Say a ten-mile hike at altitude in a snowstorm. On the other hand, he had half a tank of gas. He could run the car for a while, turn it off, start it again, all through the night. It was bad luck, but that's all. The trick was patience.

He dozed half an hour in the wind-rocked car, woke shivering and cramped. He wanted to lie down. He thought perhaps he could put a flat rock under the goddamn tire. Never say die, he said, feeling around the passenger-side floor for the flashlight in his emergency bag, and then remembering the wrecked car towed away, the flares and car phone and AAA card and flashlight and matches and candle and power bars and bottle of water still in it, and probably now in the damn tow driver's damn wife's car. He might get a good enough look anyway in the snow-reflected light. He put on his gloves and buttoned his coat, got out and locked the car, sidled around to the rear, bent down. The taillights lit the snow beneath the rear of the car like a fresh bloodstain. There was a cradle-sized depression eaten out by the spinning tire. Two or three flat ones might get him out, or small round ones — he was not going to insist on the perfect stone. The wind tore at him; the snow was certainly drifting up. He began to shuffle on the road, feeling with his feet for rocks he could move, the car's even throbbing promising motion and escape. The wind was sharp and his ears ached. His wool cap was in the damn emergency bag.

My Lord, she continued, Tin Head is just startled to pieces when he don't see that steer. He thinks somebody, some neighbor, don't like him, plenty of them, come and stole it. He looks around for tire marks or footprints but he don't see nothing except old cow tracks. He puts his hand up to his eyes and stares away. Nothing in the north, the south, the east, but way over there in the west, on the side of the mountain, he sees something moving stiff and slow, stumbling along. It looks raw and it's got something bunchy and wet hanging down over its hindquarters. Yeah, it was the steer, never making no sound. And just then it stops and it looks back. And all that distance Tin Head can see the raw meat of the head and the shoulder muscles and the empty mouth without no tongue open wide and its red eyes glaring at him, pure teetotal hate like arrows coming at him, and he knows he is done for and all of his kids and their kids is done for, and that his wife is done for and that every one of her blue dishes has got to break, and the dog that licked the blood is done for, and the house where they lived has to blow away or burn up and every fly or mouse in it.

There was a silence and she added, That's it. And it all went against him too.

That's it? Rollo said in a greedy, hot way.

Yet he knew he was on the ranch, he felt it, and he knew this road too. It was not the main ranch road but some lower entrance he could not quite recollect that cut in below the river. Now he remembered that the main entrance gate was on a side road that branched off well before the Banner place. He found another good stone, another, wondering which track this could be; the map of the ranch in his memory was not as bright now, but scuffed and obliterated as though trodden. The remembered gates collapsed, fences wavered, while the badland features swelled into massive prominence. The cliffs bulged into the sky, lions snarled, the river corkscrewed through a stone hole at a tremendous rate, and boulders cascaded from the heights. Beyond the barbwire something moved.

He grasped the car-door handle. It was locked. Inside, by the dashboard glow, he could see the gleam of the keys in the ignition where he'd left them to keep the car running. The situation was almost comic. He picked up a big two-hand rock, smashed it on the driver's-side window, and slipped his arm in through the hole, into the delicious warmth of the car, a contortionist's reach, twisting behind the steering wheel and down, and had he not kept limber with exercise and nut cutlets and green leafy vegetables he could never have reached the keys. His fingers grazed and then grasped, and he had them. This is how they sort out the men from the boys, he said aloud. As his fingers closed on the keys, he glanced at the passenger door. The lock button stood high. And even had it been locked as well, why had he strained to reach the keys when he had only to lift the lock button on the driver's side? Cursing, he pulled out the rubber floor mats and arranged them over the stones, stumbled around the car once more. He was dizzy, tremendously thirsty and hungry, opened his mouth to snowflakes. He had eaten nothing for two days but the burned eggs that morning. He could eat a dozen burned eggs now.

The snow roared through the broken window. He put the car in reverse and slowly trod the gas. The car lurched and steadied in the track, and once more he was twisting his neck, backing in the red glare, twenty feet, thirty, but slipping and spinning; the snow was too deep. He was backing up an incline that had seemed level on the way in but now showed itself as a remorselessly long hill, studded with rocks and deep in snow. His incoming tracks twisted like rope. He forced out another twenty feet, spinning the tires until they smoked, and then the rear wheels slued sideways off the track and into a two-foot ditch, the engine died, and that was it. He was almost relieved to have reached this point where the celestial fingernails were poised to nip his thread. He dismissed the ten-mile distance to the Banner place: it might not be that far, or maybe they had pulled the ranch closer to the main road. A truck might come by. Shoes slipping, coat buttoned awry, he might find the mythical Grand Hotel in the sagebrush.

On the main road his tire tracks showed as a faint pattern in the pearly apricot light from the risen moon, winking behind roiling clouds of snow. His blurred shadow strengthened whenever the wind eased. Then the violent country showed itself, the cliffs rearing at the moon, the snow rising off the prairie like steam, the white flank of the ranch slashed with fence cuts, the sagebrush glittering, and along the creek black tangles of willow, bunched like dead hair. Cattle were in the field beside the road, their plumed breath catching the moony glow like comic-strip dialogue balloons.

His shoes filled with snow, he walked against the wind, feeling as easy to tear as a man cut from paper. As he walked, he noticed that one from the herd inside the fence was keeping pace with him. He walked more slowly, and the animal lagged. He stopped and turned. It stopped as well, huffing vapor, regarding him, a strip of snow on its back like a linen runner. It tossed its head, and in the howling, wintry light he saw he'd been wrong again, that the half-skinned steer's red eye had been watching for him all this time.

# Biographical Notes

The author of more than one hundred short stories and ten novels, **Alice Adams** (1926– ) lives and writes in San Francisco. Her most recent novels are *Medicine Men, A Southern Exposure,* and *Caroline's Daughters.* She has received numerous awards, including the O. Henry Special Award for Continuing Achievement.

**Sherwood Anderson** (1876–1941) began his writing career in 1913 after serving in the Spanish-American War, working as a copywriter, and managing a paint plant. He initially received critical notice for *Winesburg, Ohio,* the first of several collections of stories. His other works include poetry, criticism, essays, and novels, including *Dark Laughter; Tar, A Midwest Childhood;* and *A Story-Teller's Story.*

Known for his irreverent, innovative fiction, **Donald Barthelme** (1931–1989) wrote a dozen books, including the novels *Sadness, Snow White,* and *The Dead Father.* His story collections include *Come Back, Dr. Caligari; Unspeakable Practices, Unnatural Acts; City Life; Amateurs;* and *Great Days.* He won the National Book Award in 1972 for *The Slightly Irregular Fire Engine,* a book for children, and was nominated for the National Book Award in 1974 for *Guilty Pleasures.*

One of the most distinctive voices of her generation, **Ann Beattie** (1947– ) is the author of several novels, including *Chilly Scenes of Winter, Falling in Place, Love Always, Picturing Will,* and *Another You.* Her story collections include *The Burning House, Distortions, Where You'll Find Me and Other Stories, What Was Mine, Secrets and Surprises,* and, most recently, *Convergences: New and Selected Stories.*

**Saul Bellow** (1915– ) was born in Canada and grew up in Chicago. His works include *The Dangling Man, Henderson the Rain King, Seize the Day,* and *Mosby's Memoirs and Other Stories.* The recipient of many literary awards, he won the National Book Award in 1954 for *The Adventures of Augie March,* in 1965 for

*Herzog,* and in 1971 for *Mr. Sammler's Planet.* In 1976 he was awarded the Pulitzer Prize for *Humboldt's Gift* and the Nobel Prize for Literature.

A celebrated poet, **Elizabeth Bishop** (1911–1979) was also a teacher, translator, and avid traveler. The recipient of many awards for her poetry, she received a Pulitzer Prize in 1955 for *North and South — A Cold Spring.* Her other work includes the travel books *Questions of Travel* and *Brazil;* the collections of poems *Geography III* and *The Complete Poems;* and *The Collected Prose.*

**Harold Brodkey** was born in 1930 in Alton, Illinois. His story collections include *First Love and Other Sorrows, Stories in an Almost Classical Mode, Profane Friendship,* and *Women and Angels. This Wild Darkness: The Story of My Death,* a memoir chronicling his death from AIDS, was published in 1996.

The poet, short story writer, and novelist **Rosellen Brown** (1939– ) is the author most recently of *Cora Fry's Pillow Book,* a book-length poem. Her fiction includes *The Autobiography of My Mother, Tender Mercies, Civil Wars, Before and After, Banquet,* and *Street Games.*

**Raymond Carver** (1938–1988) was an influential writer of short fiction as well as poetry. His collection *Will You Please Be Quiet, Please* was nominated for the National Book Award. Two other collections, *Cathedral* and *Where I'm Calling From: New and Selected Stories,* were nominated for the Pulitzer Prize and the National Book Critics Circle Award.

**Willa Cather** (1876–1947) was born in Virginia and moved to Nebraska with her parents at the age of nine. Among her many novels, the best-known may be *O Pioneers!, My Ántonia,* and *Death Comes for the Archbishop,* though she won the Pulitzer Prize in 1923 for *One of Ours.* Cather also published several collections of stories, poems, and criticism.

One of the century's great short story writers, **John Cheever** (1912–1982) won the O. Henry Memorial Prize twice, in 1956 for "A Country Husband" and in 1964 for "The Embarkment of the Cythers." He also received the National Book Award in 1958 for *The Wapshot Chronicles* and the Pulitzer Prize, the National Book Critics Circle Award, and the American Book Award for *The Stories of John Cheever,* published in 1979. In 1982 he was awarded the National Medal for Literature.

**Grace Stone Coates** (1881–1976) was born in Ruby, Kansas, and attended the University of Chicago. She spent most of her life in Montana, where she was the assistant editor of *The Frontier,* an important western literary journal. Her publications include two works of fiction, *Black Cherries* and *Riding the High Country,* and two books of verse.

**Alice Elliott Dark** (1953– ) is the author of *Naked to the Waist,* a collection of short fiction. Her work has been published in *The New Yorker* and *DoubleTake.* "In the Gloaming" was the subject of two films, one made by Trinity Playhouse and the other by HBO. She has received a grant from the National Endowment for the Arts and lives in Montclair, New Jersey.

**Pam Durban** (1947– ) is the author of a collection of short stories, *All Set*

*About with Fever Trees,* and a novel, *The Laughing Place.* She is the recipient of a Whiting Writer's Award and a fellowship from the National Endowment for the Arts. A professor at Georgia State University in Atlanta, she serves as fiction editor of *Five Points* magazine.

**Stanley Elkin** (1930–1995) was the author of more than a dozen works of fiction, including *Why I Live Where I Live, Mrs. Ted Bliss, Van Gogh's Room at Arles, The MacGuffin, The Magic Kingdom,* and *Criers and Kibitzers, Kibitzers and Criers.* His novel *George Mills* won the National Book Critics Circle Award in 1982, and he was nominated three times for the National Book Award.

A native of Oxford, Mississippi, **William Faulkner** (1897–1962) was a prolific writer of short stories, poetry, and novels. Among the best-known of his books are *Absalom, Absalom!, As I Lay Dying, Sanctuary, Light in August, Intruder in the Dust, Go Down, Moses,* and *The Sound and the Fury.* Faulkner won the Pulitzer Prize in 1954 for *A Fable* and in 1962 for *The Reivers,* and he received the 1949 Nobel Prize for Literature.

**Carolyn Ferrell** (1962– ) is the author of the collection *Don't Erase Me,* which won the Los Angeles Times Book Prize for First Fiction. She has held residencies at the William T. Flannagan Memorial Creative Persons Center, Yaddo, the Blue Mountain Center, the Bread Loaf Writers Conference, and the Imagination Writers Conference at Cleveland State University. She lives in Bronx, New York, with her husband and son and is on the faculty of Sarah Lawrence College.

The first writing of **F. Scott Fitzgerald** (1896–1940) to appear in print was a detective story in his school newspaper when he was thirteen. He was the author of four collections of short stories, including *Tales of the Jazz Age* and *All the Sad Young Men,* and five novels, including *The Beautiful and Damned, This Side of Paradise, The Great Gatsby,* and *Tender Is the Night.*

**Mary Ladd Gavell** (1919–1967) was born in Cuero, Texas, and became the managing editor of *Psychiatry* magazine in 1955. "The Rotifer" is her only published story; it appeared in *Psychiatry* after her death, as a memorial to her.

**Martha Gellhorn** (1908–1998) began her groundbreaking career as a war correspondent for *Collier's* magazine, covering the Spanish civil war. Her fiction includes *The Trouble I've Seen, A Stricken Field, The Heart of Another, Liana,* and *The Wine of Astonishment,* and she also wrote an autobiography, *Travels with Myself and Another.*

**Susan Glaspell** (1882–1948) is best known for her many plays, including *Alison's House,* which won the Pulitzer Prize in 1931. Among her other books are a collection of short stories, a biography, and seven novels. Glaspell was a founder of the Provincetown Players and the Playwright's Theatre.

**Alexander Godin** (1909–?) was born in the Ukraine and came to New York in 1922. He worked as a bottler in a chemical plant while writing the novel *On the Threshold.* Nothing more is known about him.

**Lawrence Sargent Hall** (1915–1993) graduated from Bowdoin College in 1936 and received his Ph.D. from Yale in 1941. "The Ledge" won the O. Henry Memorial Award in 1960, and *Stowaway*, Hall's first novel, won the William Faulkner Award in 1961. In addition to fiction, Hall published several books of criticism.

**Ernest Hemingway** (1899–1961) began his writing career with two collections of stories and went on to publish numerous novels, including *The Sun Also Rises* and *For Whom the Bell Tolls*; several story collections; a memoir; and a play, *The Fifth Column*. In 1953 he won the Pulitzer Prize for *The Old Man and the Sea*, and in 1954 he won the Nobel Prize for Literature.

**Paul Horgan** (1903–1995) was the author of forty-seven books, including seventeen novels, four volumes of short stories, five biographies, several histories, and various other works. He won the Pulitzer Prize in 1955 for *Great River*, a book about the Rio Grande, and in 1976 for *Lamy of Santa Fe*, a biography.

**Gish Jen** (1956– ) is the author of two novels, *Typical American* and *Mona in the Promised Land*. She has received awards from the Bunting Institute at Radcliffe College, the National Endowment for the Arts, and the Guggenheim Foundation. She lives in Massachusetts. Her most recent book is a collection of stories entitled *Who's Irish? and Other Stories*.

**Thom Jones** (1945– ) is the author of three story collections: *The Pugilist at Rest*, a National Book Award finalist; *Cold Snap*; and *Sonny Liston Was a Friend of Mine*. A former Guggenheim fellow, he won the O. Henry Award in 1993. He lives in Olympia, Washington.

**Ring Lardner** (1885–1933) began his literary career in 1905 as a sportswriter and columnist. In addition to numerous story collections, including *How to Write Short Stories* and *The Love Nest*, he published a book of verse, a humorous novel, and a spoof autobiography, *The Story of a Wonder Man*. He also collaborated on two Broadway plays.

**Mary Lerner** published several short stories in national magazines. Nothing more is known about her.

**Bernard Malamud** (1914–1986) began his career writing stories for the *Washington Post* and went on to publish eight novels and four collections of short stories. He received the National Book Award in 1959 for *The Magic Barrel* and the National Book Award and the Pulitzer Prize in 1967 for *The Fixer*.

**James Alan McPherson** (1943– ) is the author of two collections of short stories, *Hue and Cry* and *Elbow Room*, which was awarded the Pulitzer Prize in 1978. He is also well known as an essayist. His most recent publication is *Fathering Daughters: Reflections by Men*, edited with DeWitt Henry.

**Lorrie Moore** (1957– ) is the author of two novels, *Who Will Run the Frog Hospital?* and *Anagrams*, and three collections of stories, *Like Life*, *Self-Help*, and *Birds of America*. She lives in Madison, Wisconsin.

A native of Ontario, **Alice Munro** (1931– ) has twice received Canada's

Governor's General Award and is the author of numerous collections of short stories, including *Who Do You Think You Are?*, *The Moons of Jupiter*, *Dance of the Happy Shades*, *Open Secrets*, *Friend of My Youth*, *The Progress of Love*, *The Beggar Maid: Stories of Flo and Rose*, and, most recently, *The Selected Stories of Alice Munro*.

**Vladimir Nabokov** (1899–1977) wrote more than forty volumes of fiction, criticism, and poetry, including *Invitation to a Beheading*, *The Real Life of Sebastian Knight*, *Lolita*, *Laughter in the Dark*, *Pale Fire*, *Bend Sinister*, *Ada*, and *Speak, Memory*, and translated the work of Pushkin and other Russian authors. He also had a worldwide reputation as a lepidopterist.

**Tim O'Brien** (1946– ) is the author of *Going After Cacciato*, which won the 1979 National Book Award in fiction, and *The Things They Carried*, which received the Chicago Tribune Heartland Award in fiction and was a finalist for both the Pulitzer Prize and the National Book Critics Circle Award. His novel *In the Lake of the Woods* received the James Fenimore Cooper Prize from the Society of American Historians. His other books are *If I Die in a Combat Zone*, *Northern Lights*, *The Nuclear Age*, and, most recently, *Tomcat in Love*.

An acknowledged master of short fiction, **Flannery O'Connor** (1925–1964) published the collections *A Good Man Is Hard to Find* and *Everything That Rises Must Converge* as well as two novels, *Wise Blood* and *The Violent Bear It Away*. "Greenleaf" won the O. Henry Memorial Award in 1957, and *The Collected Short Stories of Flannery O'Connor* won the National Book Award in 1972.

**Joyce Carol Oates** (1938– ) is a prolific writer of fiction, poetry, drama, and criticism. Among her many awards and honors are the National Book Award, the Pushcart Prize, three O. Henry awards, the Rea Award, and the O. Henry, PEN/Malamud, Bobst, and Bram Stoker lifetime achievement awards. Her most recent books are the story collection *Will You Always Love Me?* and the novella *First Love*.

**Cynthia Ozick** (1928– ) is the author of short stories, essays, novels, criticism, and a play. Among her works are *The Messiah of Stockholm*, *Trust*, *Art & Ardor*, *The Pagan Rabbi and Other Stories*, and *Levitation: Five Fictions*. She has won four O. Henry first prizes and the Rea Award for the short story. Her most recent books are *Fame & Folly*, a collection of essays, and *The Puttermesser Papers*, a novel.

**Dorothy Parker** (1893–1967) developed a reputation for caustic wit through her critical reviews for *Vanity Fair* and *The New Yorker* and in such books of verse as *Enough Rope* and *Death and Taxes*. Her short story collections include *Here Lies* and *Laments for the Living*.

**Katherine Anne Porter** (1890–1980) won the Pulitzer Prize and the National Book Award in 1965 for her *Collected Stories*. Her works of fiction include *Flowering Judas; Noon Wine; Pale Horse, Pale Rider;* and the novel *Ship of Fools*. She is also the author of a collection of essays and an account of the Sacco-Vanzetti trial.

**J. F. Powers** (1917– ) has published numerous collections of short stories, including *Prince of Darkness and Other Stories, The Presence of Grace, Look How the Fish Live,* and *Wheat That Springeth Green.* He won the National Book Award in 1963 for his novel *Morte d'Urban.*

**Annie Proulx** (1935– ) lives and works in Wyoming. The author of three novels and a collection of short stories, she is currently working on a second collection of stories. She has received many literary awards, including the Pulitzer Prize, the National Book Award, the Irish Times International Fiction Prize, and the PEN/Faulkner Award. Her books have been translated into several languages.

**Benjamin Rosenblatt** (1880–?) immigrated from Russia to New York with his family at age ten. His first story was published in a Yiddish magazine when he was seventeen; his first English story appeared in *The Outlook.* Rosenblatt attended New York University and worked as an insurance agent in Brooklyn.

**Philip Roth** (1933– ) has written more than twenty books, most recently *I Married a Communist,* published in 1998. He received the National Book Award in 1960 for *Goodbye, Columbus* and in 1995 for *Sabbath's Theater;* the National Book Critics Circle Award in 1991 for *Patrimony;* the PEN/Faulkner Award in 1993 for *Operation Shylock;* and the Pulitzer Prize in 1998 for *American Pastoral.*

**William Saroyan** (1908–1981) was a prolific writer of Armenian background. His many short story collections include *The Daring Young Man on the Flying Trapeze* and *My Name Is Aram.* In addition to novels and memoirs, he wrote several plays, notably *My Heart's in the Highlands* and *The Time of Your Life,* for which he was awarded a Pulitzer Prize in 1940.

The son and grandson of rabbis, **Isaac Bashevis Singer** (1904–1991) was born in Poland and came to America in 1935. Although he originally wrote in Hebrew, he soon adopted Yiddish as his favored language for fiction. His dozens of works available in English include *Gimpel the Fool, The Magician of Lublin, The Family Moskat, Selected Short Stories,* and the posthumously published *Shadows on the Hudson.* Singer won many literary awards, including two National Book Awards, and received the Nobel Prize for Literature in 1978.

**Susan Sontag** (1933– ) is the author of three novels, *The Benefactor, Death Kit,* and *The Volcano Lover;* a collection of short stories, *I, etcetera;* a play, *Alice in Bed;* and numerous essay collections and works of nonfiction, including *Against Interpretation and Other Essays, On Photography* (which won the National Book Critics Circle Award for criticism), *AIDS and Its Metaphors,* and *A Susan Sontag Reader.*

**Jean Stafford** (1915–1979) achieved recognition with her first novel, *Boston Adventure,* but is generally better known for her short stories. A frequent contributor to *The New Yorker, Harper's Bazaar, The Sewanee Review,* and other magazines, she won numerous awards, including the O. Henry Prize for her

1955 story "In the Zoo" and the Pulitzer Prize for fiction in 1970 for her *Collected Stories.*

**Jean Toomer** (1894–1967) studied in New York City and became a prominent member of the Harlem Renaissance. His major work, published in 1923, is the experimental novel *Cane,* a collection of stories, drama, and poetry describing the people and landscape of rural Georgia. Toomer gave up writing later in life.

**John Updike** (1932– ) was born in Shillington, Pennsylvania, and graduated from Harvard College in 1954. After a year at an English art school and a two-year stint as a "Talk of the Town" reporter for *The New Yorker,* he moved to Massachusetts, in 1957, and has lived there ever since. His most recent novel is *Toward the End of Time.* Updike made his first appearance in *The Best American Short Stories* in 1959, and his stories have been represented in these pages in every succeeding decade.

**Robert Penn Warren** (1905–1989) is the only writer ever to receive Pulitzer Prizes in both fiction and poetry. The best-known of his novels, *All the King's Men,* earned him the 1947 Pulitzer Prize for fiction, and both *Promises: Poems 1954–1956* (which also won the National Book Award) and *Now and Then: Poems 1976–1978* won the Pulitzer for poetry, in 1957 and 1979, respectively. In 1986 he was named the first poet laureate of the United States.

A native of Jackson, Mississippi, **Eudora Welty** (1909– ) won the Pulitzer Prize in 1973 for *The Optimist's Daughter* and has received numerous other awards, including the National Medal for Literature and the Presidential Medal of Freedom. Her many works of fiction include *Delta Wedding, The Ponder Heart, Collected Stories,* and *Losing Battles,* and she has also published collections of essays, a book of photographs, a story for children, and a memoir.

**E. B. White** (1899–1985) became a contributing editor and writer for *The New Yorker* in 1926 and is widely acknowledged as the preeminent essayist of the twentieth century, although he also achieved prominence as a humorist, short story writer, and the author of two classic books for children, *Stuart Little* and *Charlotte's Web.* He was awarded a Pulitzer Prize special citation for his work in 1978.

Known for the brilliant dialogue of his plays, **Tennessee Williams** (1911–1983) first published under his pen name in 1939 in *Story* magazine. He was awarded the Pulitzer Prize for drama in 1948 for *A Streetcar Named Desire* and again in 1955 for *Cat on a Hot Tin Roof.* In addition to eleven other full-length plays, he published two collections of short dramas, four collections of stories, a book of poems, and a novel, *The Roman Spring of Mrs. Stone.*

**Richard Wright** (1908–1960) is the author of numerous books about race relations. Of his three novels, the best known is *Native Son.* He also published two autobiographies, *Black Boy* and *American Hunger;* two collections of stories, *Uncle Tom's Children* and *Eight Men;* and two works of nonfiction.